Praise for Malcolm Mackay

'Superb . . . Mackay is a true original, managing to conjure up a gripping new way of portraying city-noir. This, from a writer who has lived his whole life in far-off Stornoway, with only few short visits to the Glasgow he has so vividly created. He's no longer a rising star. He's risen' **Marcel Berlins,** *The Times*

'[Mackay's] Glasgow Trilogy attracted the sort of acclaim normally reserved for far more experienced novelists' *Daily Express*

'Gripping and vivid, with a labyrinthine plot involving double- and triple-crossing . . . Mackay succeeds magnificently' *Guardian*

'Mackay ratchets up the tension like a master, and his ability to create rounded characters makes his book, despite its dark subject matter, a breath of fresh air' *Daily Telegraph*

'Remarkable . . . "tartan noir" will have a new star' *Daily Mail*

'There aren't too many crime novels that take the reader into the mind, such as it is, of a hitman, but Malcolm Mackay's *The Necessary Death of Lewis Winter*, the first volume of a trilogy set in gangland Glasgow, does so with steely assurance . . . a truly exceptional debut' **Paul Bailey,** *Independent*

'Brutal, witty and well-written . . . brilliant' *Sunday Telegraph*

THE NIGHT THE RICH MEN BURNED

Malcolm Mackay was born and grew up in Stornoway, where he still lives. His much-lauded Glasgow-set novels have won the Crime Thriller Book Club Best Read Award and the Deanston Scottish Crime Book of the Year Award, and been shortlisted for the CWA John Creasey New Blood Dagger and the Scottish First Book of the Year Award. *The Night The Rich Men Burned* is Malcolm Mackay's fourth novel.

Follow Malcolm @malcolm_mackay

THE
NIGHT THE
RICH MEN
BURNED

MALCOLM MACKAY

PAN BOOKS

First published 2014 by Mantle

This edition published 2015 by Pan Books
an imprint of Pan Macmillan
20 New Wharf Road, London N1 9RR
Associated companies throughout the world
www.panmacmillan.com

ISBN 978-1-4472-6438-5

1 3 5 7 9 8 6 4 2

A CIP catalogue record for this book is available from the British Library.

Typeset by Ellipsis Digital Limited, Glasgow
Printed and bound by CPI Group (UK) Ltd, Croydon, CR0 4YY

Visit www.panmacmillan.com to read more about all our books
and to buy them. You will also find features, author interviews and
news of any author events, and you can sign up for e-newsletters
so that you're always first to hear about our new releases.

THE
NIGHT THE
RICH MEN
BURNED

CHARACTERS

Oliver Peterkinney – A young man ready to make his way in a world that seems determined to give him few options. He's smart enough to make his own.

Alex Glass – As unemployable as his best friend Oliver, but much more of a dreamer. There are chances out there for tough young men, he's sure of it.

Ella Fowler – They call her a party girl, but it's all about work for Ella. Work a horrible job to pay for what will one day be a good life.

Ronald 'Potty' Cruickshank – Certainly the biggest, and probably the most unpleasant debt collector in the business. People are money, and money is king.

Arnold Peterkinney – Has looked after his grandson Oliver for a few years now, still worried about what direction the boy's life might meander in.

Billy Patterson – Ruthless, efficient and tough. Don't let the rough exterior fool you though, he's more than smart enough to grow his debt collection business in a crowded market.

Marty Jones – Marty is a lot of things. Pimp and debt collector are two of them, and a lot of people find those things ugly. Marty makes money though, and everyone loves that.

Alan Bavidge – There's nobody Patterson trusts more than Bavidge. Tough, yeah, and seemingly without emotion, he does his job as well as anyone in the city.

Jim Holmes – There are plenty of men like Jim. Big, brutal and inexplicably angry, he bounces from one employer to the next, wasting no time in making himself expendable.

Norah Faulkner – It's not easy building a life with a man like Jim Holmes, you have to make yourself at least as tough as he is. So she has.

Gary 'Jazzy' Jefferson – Jazzy provides a public service, lending money to those who couldn't otherwise borrow. Charge creative interest rates and sell the debt on when they can't pay. Easy money.

PC Paul Greig – A cop, and to many, a criminal. He'll take money from criminals, slip them some info now and then, but it's all in the name of crime management, you understand.

Roy Bowles – Decades doing a steady trade in selling weapons to the criminal industry. A good, reliable, solid individual: who could be better to work for?

Jamie Stamford – Alex MacArthur's hard man of choice, therefore a man who doesn't often have to face consequences. But then, you gamble like he does, and consequences will catch you up.

Neil Fraser – A tough guy, sure, but not a smart guy. Doing a few menial jobs for John Young doesn't make you important, he doesn't seem to have realized that yet.

Alex MacArthur – His organization has been running at the top for decades now, but that makes him old, and illness has left him weak. Even he can sense the change coming.

Howard 'Howie' Lawson – A man with connections and no money, looking to get a little by selling guns to the suppliers who desire them most.

Peter Jamieson – Runs one of the biggest organizations in the city, maybe the fastest-growing too. A lot of people, like Marty, are happy to be under his umbrella.

Ray Buller – People think of them as old men, maybe a little feeble, but you don't get to be Alex MacArthur's second in command without being as sharp and dangerous as a razor.

Ronald 'Rolly' Cruickshank – He created the Cruickshank family business, collecting bad debts from weak people, and trained his delightful, beloved nephew to replace him.

Kevin Currie – Controls the counterfeit end of the Jamieson business, and controls it well. A man to be trusted, a man to listen to.

Angus Lafferty – The drug business is a constant battlefield, and Lafferty is the man importing the goods for the Jamieson army.

John Young – Peter Jamieson's right-hand man, has been since the start. Very little gets past him, so you'd better stick to whatever rules he gives you. Not much to ask, is it?

Don Park – He's the brightest star in the MacArthur organization, which, coincidentally, makes him the biggest threat to MacArthur's leadership.

Mark Garvey – A gun seller, not as cautious as some, not as desperate as others. Always on the lookout for a good connection.

Gordon Aird – Mr Typical, when it comes to a debt collector's clients. A man who only knows the value of what goes into his arm and will pay for it any way he can.

Conn Griffiths – Ranks among the best muscle in the city. Like all the best, he's not just brutal, he's smart too. That's where the danger lies, and it's why Patterson hired him.

Mikey Summers – Got a reputation for brutality, and once he got it, the offers flooded in. Chooses to work alongside Conn for Patterson.

John Kilbanne – He used to be a legitimate bookkeeper with ambitions. Might not be legitimate any more, but he's still occasionally ambitious.

Andy Leven – Businesses like Patterson's are built on men like Leven, at the bottom of the ladder, doing the dirty work for him.

Collette Duffy – She hasn't quite switched on to the real world yet. When she does she might just realize borrowing money to pay your previous debt isn't clever financial management.

Liam Duffy – He has a good job working for Chris Argyle, and a sister he constantly needs to keep an eye on. It can be a hard life.

Chris Argyle – Everyone's known for years that Argyle has a growing business as an importer. Always been good at keeping himself off bigger people's target lists.

Willie Caldwell – He was Uncle Rolly's moneyman for years, carried on working for Potty. Not much lately though, poor old sod hasn't been well.

Steven Wales – Potty's full-time moneyman, charged with making sure dirty money comes out of the accounts smelling of roses, or any similarly fragrant cliché.

Ewan Drummond – A pal of Oliver and Alex, a boy with the same problems and the same ambitions. Bigger than them, and maybe a little dumber. Not a great combination, really.

Adam Jones – He's Marty's twin brother, and runs a club that Marty uses for some private parties. Whether Adam knows it or not, he's in his brother's shadow for keeps.

Nate Colgan – In the conversation about hardest men in a hard city, Colgan often tops the list. A man who can scare the beasts out of nightmares.

Russell Conrad – Like many gunmen, he's a hard man to know, harder still to like. If he's looking for you, you have a problem.

Ian Allen – With his cousin Charlie, he runs an efficient drug business that makes an effort to stay out of the city itself. Why pick a big fight when you're winning all the little ones?

Charlie Allen – Yes, he does get fed up of people calling him and Ian brothers, but who really cares? More than cousins, they're a damned profitable business partnership.

Donall 'Spikey' Tokely – Trying to elbow his way into the gun market, but he's mostly selling to the young and inexperienced right now. People like himself.

Robby Draper – He'll sell you a gun if you want one, whoever you are. In desperate times, anyone who'll buy is a good customer.

Stephen 'Gully' Fitzgerald – An old-school hard man, taught the likes of Bavidge and Colgan a lot of lessons they've put into meaningful practice.

PROLOGUE

He ended up unconscious and broken on the floor of a warehouse, penniless and alone. He was two weeks in hospital, unemployable thereafter, but that didn't matter. What mattered was that, for a few weeks beforehand, he had money. Not just a little money, but enough to show off with, and that was the impression that stuck.

It had been a while since they'd seen him. Months, probably. They were heading back from the jobcentre having made a typically fruitless effort at sniffing out employment. They went in, they searched the touchscreen computer near the door, and they left. Two friends, officially unemployed since the day they left school together a year before, both willing to do unofficial work if that was available. They bumped into Ewan Drummond as they walked back up towards Peterkinney's grandfather's flat.

'All right lads,' Drummond said, grinning at them, 'need a lift anywhere?' He was as big and gormless as ever, but the suggestion of transport was new.

'Lift? From you?' Glass asked.

'Yeah, me. Got myself a motor these days. Got to have one in my line of work, you know.' He said it to provoke

1

questions that would allow him to trot out boastful answers.

Glass and Peterkinney looked at each other before they looked at Drummond. There wasn't a lot of work among their circle of friends. The kind of work that let a man like Drummond make enough money to buy a car was unheard of. They could guess what was involved in the work, but they wanted to hear it.

'Yeah, we'll take a lift,' Peterkinney nodded.

They followed Drummond back down to where his car was parked. Turned out to be a very respectable-looking saloon, not some old banger or boy racer's toy.

'Well, yeah, got to keep up appearances you see.'

Glass dropped into the passenger seat, Peterkinney the back. They were in no hurry to get anywhere, but this was too intriguing to pass on.

'Come on then big man,' Glass said with a mischievous smile, 'what's this big job you got?'

'Well, uh, I can't really tell you much. Shouldn't tell you much, I mean. Hush-hush, you know.'

By this point Peterkinney was leaning over from the back seat, crowding Drummond, knowing he couldn't keep quiet for long. Drummond's mouth and brain had always been loosely acquainted, so things he shouldn't say frequently slipped out.

'I mean, I suppose I can tell you a bit, but you got to keep it quiet, right.'

2

'Sure,' they answered together.

'I'm working for Potty Cruickshank. I'm one of his boys.' He said it with such pride, such force, that they both assumed it meant something. Then they thought about it.

'Who?' Glass asked.

'One of his boys? The hell does that mean?' Peterkinney asked warily.

'Nah, nothing like that. He's, like, a debt collector. I go round and pick up money that people owe him. It's all legit. Well, sort of, financial services, that sort of thing. Good money, real good money. You know how much I made last week alone?'

'Isn't that dangerous?' Peterkinney asked.

'Not really, no. Well, now and again, but you got to be tough to make a living these days, guys, that's how it is. How else you going to make good money?' Said with wisdom he presumed but didn't possess. 'So come on, guess what I made last week.' He was desperate to tell them by this point and unwilling to wait for a guess that might be accurate enough to take the wind out of his sails. 'Six-fifty I made last week. Worked four days, couple of hours a day. Six-fifty. I'm telling you, it's the life.'

They didn't say much more to Drummond; just let him rumble on about how much money he was making until he dropped them off. They walked up to the flat Peterkinney shared with his grandfather, a poky little place you would

3

only invite a real friend back to. They went silently into Peterkinney's small bedroom, a cramped room with nothing in the way of luxuries. There was only one subject of conversation.

'Six-fifty a week he's making. Him,' Glass said. 'He's making ten times what we make on Job Seekers'.'

'Come on, it ain't six-fifty a week. It was six-fifty in one week, but that doesn't mean he'll get it every week. And look what he has to do for it. How long you think it's going to be before someone kicks the living shit out of him? His teeth will be down his throat and his money will be up the wall.'

Glass sighed. 'All right, yeah, fine, but look at the money. He's making good money. Even if it's short-term, right, it's still money. And he's got to do some shitty stuff for it, but come on, you think we're going to get a job that pays us that for non-shitty work?'

'I don't think we're going to get a job at all,' Peterkinney sighed, and slumped back on his bed.

A sentence he was tired of uttering. Glass sat on the chair in the room and tilted his head back, thinking about Ewan Drummond. No smarter than either him or Peterkinney, probably less so. No tougher when push came to shove, although he was bigger than them, which helped. He was no better connected than they were, which was to say that he hadn't been connected to the criminal industry at all as far as Glass knew. Must have gotten his foot in the door without realizing where he was stepping. All of which suggested that employment in the business, and six hundred and fifty quid a week, was within their grasp.

Glass didn't say any of this to Peterkinney because he knew what the reaction would be. Peterkinney would pour scorn on it; tell him he needed to get real. Peterkinney was all about getting whatever job he could, no daydreaming attached. That was fine by Glass; how his best friend had always been. A realist. They left school underqualified and stumbled together into a job market that had no room for them or interest in them. So they struggled along together, and were still struggling.

Glass couldn't stop thinking about it, and that was really the point. People like Ewan Drummond were useful both in the work they did and the people they encouraged. None too bright and loaded with cash. He was a walking billboard for employers like Potty Cruickshank. A debt collector like Potty had a high turnover of staff, so that positive PR was worth its weight. Glass saw Drummond and knew he was at least as capable. Six-fifty a week, four days a week, a couple of hours a day. Think about it. The money, the cars, the women, the parties. Him and Peterkinney, lounging around doing fuck-all, waiting for some godawful nine-to-five that would pay them buttons and last six months if they were lucky. No, what Drummond was doing, that was real work.

It wouldn't have mattered if Glass had known. Even if

he'd seen Drummond lying on that warehouse floor two weeks later, it would have made no impact. He would have spent the previous two weeks thinking of nothing but the money Drummond was making, and working out how he and Peterkinney could do the same. Nothing, no matter how grim, was going to change his mind. That was the way to make good money. That was the best option.

'I'll ask the old man if he's heard of anything going,' Peterkinney said quietly. 'We can go back down the job-centre again in a couple of days.' His grandfather was going to have a word with a friend at a packaging factory on their behalf sometime today, although that would lead nowhere as usual. Their names on a list for future reference.

'Yeah,' Glass said. But he wasn't thinking about the job-centre. Wasn't thinking about any sort of work that was going to be advertised. He was thinking of the world Drummond now inhabited. He was thinking of the money. He was think-ing of the life.

PART ONE

1

Start with a kick to the door. He got a crack out of it, and the plain door shuddered in the frame. Didn't open though. Still staring back at them. Try again. Not a boot this time. Give it a shoulder. A short run-up and a collision with the door. A bigger crack and the door caves in, buckled on the hinges and smashed around the lock. Alex Glass stumbles in with it.

'Shit.' A mutter under his breath. Embarrassed by his ungainly entrance. Embarrassment pushed aside by an attempt at professionalism. He's taking the lead here. Older by six months. His accomplice, Oliver Peterkinney, is still only nineteen. Anyway, this is Glass's job. He set it up. He found the target.

They're searching downstairs, through the kitchen, through the living room. It's a small house, which helps. Tidy as well, everything where it should be. No rubbish for some-one to leap out from behind. Flicking lights on and off as they check each room. No attempt at subtlety, not after that entrance. To the bottom of the stairs. If he's here, he's heard them by now. He's had time enough to get a weapon. They didn't plan for that. What if he keeps a weapon by his bed?

Something else to put on the long list of things they didn't plan for.

A light comes on at the top of the stairs. Glass and Peterkinney look at each other. Never been here before. Never been in this situation. If they had to make a split-second decision, they would be too late. A man has emerged at the top of the stairs. Older than these two by ten years. Fatter by three stone. Wearing nothing but his boxer shorts. That makes up their minds for them.

They're looking up the stairs, necks craned. Suddenly feeling confident. The amateurs just got lucky, as all amateurs need to in this business. Peterkinney moves up one step.

'All right, Holmes,' he's saying. Because it is Jim Holmes, the target. He doesn't need clothes to look like his picture. Big and broad, with a thick head of dark hair and a dimpled chin. 'We can sort this out nice and quiet. No need for trouble.' Peterkinney's smart enough to know how dumb that sounds. You smash your way into a guy's house and tell him there's no need for trouble. This isn't how Peterkinney would have played it.

Holmes had his hands in the air, but they're falling now. Who did he think he was going to find at the bottom of the stairs? Maybe the police. Probably the police. Would be about fucking time. He'd raise his hands to them; try to make a good impression. Could have been worse than the police. Could have been a real tough guy. He knows Marty Jones is looking for him. Wants to send a strong message. Marty's big on sending messages. Marty is under the protection of Peter Jamieson. That could get him the use of a man like Nate Colgan. Now there's a man you raise your hands to, no matter how tough you are. But these two? These are just kids. The one coming up the stairs doesn't even look like he's started shaving.

'The fuck are you pair?' Holmes is growling. Going for his best tough-guy voice, which is pretty good by general standards. He's had plenty of practice. Being a tough guy is his job. It's how he makes his living. Marty lends money to people. That money gathers interest at a mathematically improbable rate. Men like Holmes collect the debt. But Holmes got a little tired of handing all that nice money over to a smarmy prick like Marty. Holmes did the hard work, deserved more of the reward. So he started keeping a bigger share for himself. Took Marty an awful long time to work that out, for a guy who figures himself as sharp as a razor. But he was always going to work it out eventually. Marty's no mug.

'We're here for Marty,' Glass is saying. Saying it like it means something.

Peterkinney, three steps up, is looking back at him. Scowling. Shouldn't have said Marty. Should have said Jamieson. That would have carried more weight. Common sense says you exaggerate the power you have behind you.

'*Pft.*' A snort of derision. Not aimed at Marty. Holmes

isn't stupid either; he knows how dangerous Marty can be. A well-connected guy with a big ego and a short temper? Those are always dangerous. 'He sending kids to do his fighting for him now?' There's a smile in his eyes. Marty actually has sent kids. There are other debt collectors he could have sent. Tough guys. They'd have done it too, for the right price, even though they know Holmes. Plenty of general muscle he could have hired for the job. But Marty sent the cheap option. A couple of kids looking to make a good first impression.

'Look, we can sort this out,' Glass is saying from the bottom of the stairs. Still trying to lure him down. Trying to fool a man who does this for a living. Still hoping this can be easy. It was never going to be that easy.

Peterkinney isn't waiting. Holmes won't be won round. Once he has it in his head that they're kids, he's going to treat them that way until they change his mind. Only way to change his mind is to do what they came here to do. And the clock is ticking. You don't think the neighbours heard them smash the door in? You don't think they'll be calling the police right now?

Glass is about to open his mouth to say something else when Peterkinney moves. Jumping two steps at a time, getting to Holmes and making a grab for him. So what if he's older? So what if he's tougher, has a reputation for bad things? He's nearly naked. There are two of them. They came here to send a message for Marty. They can't leave until they've tried and they need to leave soon. So you do something, don't you?

Holmes has seen him coming. Leaning his weight forwards on the balls of his feet. Shoulders down, ready. Peterkinney is two steps from the top and reaching out for a grab. It looks like a wild attempt. A throw of the arms in the general direction of the target. An amateur lunging at a pro. That's what Holmes thinks. It's what he thinks when he throws his weight directly at Peterkinney. He thinks he's going to knock the kid back down the way he came.

That's not what Peterkinney's thinking. He's thrown his arms out there, but he's not watching where he's throwing. He's watching Holmes's feet. Waiting for that reactive lurch forwards. And now it's coming, and Peterkinney's moving his feet, pushing himself backwards against the stair wall with a thud. Watching as Holmes goes sailing past. Holmes's shoulder catches him, but it's glancing, no impact. Holmes is falling onto the stairs, shouting something loud that doesn't involve words. But Holmes has experience of falling over at other people's insistence. This is standard for him. He's managed to push out and wedge himself in the stairs, three steps down from the top.

But that isn't enough to make him safe. Not nearly enough, and Holmes knows it. You can't be on your back in this situation. You're either on your feet or you're out of the fight. You can rely on them being kids, but you can't rely on them being stupid. Before Holmes can struggle to his feet, Peterkinney's got his first kick in.

Knocking Holmes down a couple of steps with the first kick. Holmes shouting, but this fight is over. All Holmes has left is noise. Peterkinney jumping downward, kicking into Holmes with both feet. Peterkinney's landing on his arse, it's jarring but worth it. Holmes is bouncing down the stairs now. Glass had been moving up the stairs to help, now jumping down the last three to get out of the way. A grunting ball of flesh crashing down after him. Holmes has rolled to the bottom. Lying there. Not moving. Groaning, but not moving.

Glass is watching, doing nothing. Standing beside Holmes, looking up at Peterkinney. As far as Glass is concerned, this is over. Peterkinney's quickly down the stairs, standing beside Glass now. Looking down at Holmes. Taking a step back and kicking him hard in his ample guts.

'Try and knock me down the fucking stairs,' Peterkinney's saying. Speaking low, a little spit on his lips. 'That's for Marty. You remember that. That's what happens.' An intensity conjured from a place Glass didn't know his friend possessed.

Glass is pulling at Peterkinney's arm. The job is more than done, time to go. A second person has emerged at the top of the stairs. A thickset woman, glaring down at them. The woman who keeps this house organized and tidy.

'Get out,' she's shouting at them. 'Go on, get out.' She's

starting to march down the stairs towards them. Wrapped up in a thick dressing gown, hair tied back, slippers too big for her making an unsettling slapping noise as she walks. Scowling like she was born that way. Moving towards her partner at the bottom of the stairs. He's groaning on the floor, rolling slightly. Trying to twist into a position that relieves the pain. Trying to turn his back on them, so they can't kick him in the stomach again. Facing the striped wallpaper, hoping this is over. Peterkinney's given him one last kick in the small of the back, he and Glass turning for the door.

The woman's still shouting something, but it's unintelligible and entirely her own business. They're out into the night, across the small front garden with no fence and moving down the street. Trying not to run, but walking fast enough to draw attention. The neighbours will have heard the door being broken. They'll hear the shouting. People will be looking out of windows.

'We should have brought balaclavas,' Glass is saying.

'We should have brought a lot of things.' Peterkinney's thinking of all the things they did wrong in this job. More than he realizes. Their first job. Thrown into it by Marty Jones. Someone with experience, a professional, would have done it differently. They did the best that amateurs could.

'First thing I'm spending money on is a car,' Glass is saying. They're still walking too fast, but they're putting distance between themselves and the house. Looking backwards half the time. Nobody following. But then, nobody would need to. You can see their guilt from a distance.

Peterkinney isn't saying anything. Glass wanted this. He's in charge, so let him do the talking. He's his best mate, and you don't puncture your best mate's balloon. But this has been a shambles. They didn't think about it beforehand. Marty gave Glass the job. Their first chance to make a good impression. They rushed out to do it, knowing the prize that will be waiting for them. Next time will be different. Next time they'll make an effort to plan it. Having a vehicle to get away in will be a good start. Neither of them owns a car. Peterkinney doesn't even have a licence.

They've reached the bottom of the street, round the corner. A little relief. They're out of view of the scene of the crime. Walking faster, almost jogging. Anyone looks out a window and they see two guilty-looking young men running past. The kind of guilty young men you remember. Maybe mention to the police if they knock on your door looking for information.

'We did it though,' Glass is saying. 'We fucking did it.'

'Yeah,' Peterkinney's nodding, and he's smiling despite himself. 'We fucking did.'

2

He's tired. They say you shouldn't drive when you're tired. He's driving, and driving carefully. Got the call twenty minutes ago. Doesn't know why the hell he's bothering. Petty games, and they've lost this round. So what, just win the next one and move on. But Patterson insisted. Get round there, talk to the man. Try to keep him onside. So Alan Bavidge is nearly there. Nearly ready for his conversation with Jim Holmes. Nearly caring about it. But not quite.

He's pulling into the street and already there's a problem. There are people around Holmes's front door. Must be four or five of them, standing on the patch of grass that serves as a front garden. Neighbours, probably. Some of them are still in pyjamas. Nosey bastards. Get a little dignity, for God's sake. Semi-detached houses in batches of two, tightly packed along either side of the street. A mix of former and current council housing, he's guessing. Bavidge is stopping the car at the side of the road. Switching the lights off. None of the neighbours have clocked him yet. He's waiting. Hoping they'll bugger off back home before he goes in. An unknown guy in his late twenties at the scene of the crime will instantly become a suspect.

One of the neighbours has turned round and is staring at the car. A middle-aged man, glaring right at him. Turning and saying something to the group, proud to be breaking news. Now they're all looking at him and murmuring. A broad woman in her mid-thirties pushing her way past them. Norah Faulkner. Holmes's girlfriend. Not the sort of woman you marry. Not if you can help it. A tough one, her. At least as tough as her man. Kind of woman you might have thought would do a better job keeping Holmes out of trouble. Bavidge knows who she is; she doesn't know who he is. With another sigh, he's getting out of the car.

Across the patch of grass and walking towards her. Making a noticeable effort at ignoring the gawkers. Nodding, and hoping she's bright enough to let him speak before she gets abusive.

'Norah? I'm Alan, you were told to expect me.' Speaking as quietly as possible. Trying to keep this between the two of them.

She's nodding now. Still scowling, but nodding. 'Come in.' She's turning and walking back to the door. Stopping suddenly enough that Bavidge almost crashes into the back of her. Turning to her neighbours. 'All right, you had your wee nose about, now piss off.' Some of them are shaking their heads, giving her looks, but not one of them will disobey. She's coarse, and they're all just a little bit scared of her. Sure, they all want her arguing their case when the housing association routinely lets them down on repairs. But even when she's on your side, you're scared of her. They're all turning and walking back to their houses.

Norah's inside, holding the door for Bavidge. Once he's inside, she's trying to push it shut. Isn't working. Won't hold shut, just leans open of its own accord. The top hinge is damaged, Bavidge can see.

'Buggers managed to smash this in the process,' she's saying redundantly.

Bavidge doesn't care about the door. If his boss is serious about Holmes, then Bavidge will send someone round in the morning to put a new door in. He's concerned about what he's not seeing. He's not seeing Holmes. She told his boss, Billy Patterson, that Holmes was unconscious at the bottom of the stairs. There's nothing at the bottom of the stairs. Just a wet patch where Norah's been trying to wipe blood off her plain fitted carpet.

'Through here,' she's saying. She has a more feminine voice than he expected. Especially now that she's calmed down. A broad face on broad shoulders, a hard look about her. No soft edges that Bavidge will ever see. But they're there. She cares about Holmes, and she looks after him. This is a better life than most people in Holmes's profession get to live. She's leading Bavidge into the living room.

Holmes is sitting on the floor, back against the black leather couch. He's tilting his head back, holding something to his nose that used to be white and is now red. He's still in his boxer shorts. He's looking at Bavidge. A glare. They've never met. Bavidge can only hope his reputation goes before him. When it does, it buys him all the respect he needs.

'I'm Alan Bavidge,' he's saying. 'Billy sent me round.'

'Uh-huh,' Holmes is saying. Turning and staring back up at the ceiling, more interested in what's pouring from his nose.

'Who was it?' Bavidge is asking. Not here for polite conversation. Not here to make a new chum. Get this over and get out.

Holmes went to Patterson. Ran to him when Marty Jones found out he was skimming money off his collections. Wanted protection from Billy. Offered himself as an employee in exchange. It was a hell of a job application. I want to work for you because you can protect me from my old boss. By the way, my old boss hates me because I ripped him off. Yeah, that'll get you through the door. But Holmes did get through the door. Not because he offered to work for Patterson. He got through because everyone knows he worked for Marty. He was one of Marty's boys for a few years. Throwing his weight around, trying to make a name for himself. Suddenly he starts working for Patterson, and people think Patterson is taking employees away from Marty. A cheap way of making a rival look vulnerable. So Patterson took him on. Just wasn't able to offer him protection in time.

'Them,' Holmes is mumbling. 'There was two of them.'

'Who?' There's impatience in Bavidge's voice now. Doesn't care if Holmes hears it. Holmes is a thug. The sort of guy who goes round picking fights with drug addicts and hopeless cases. That's the difference between a tough guy like Holmes and a tough guy like Bavidge. The reason Bavidge has a reputation and Holmes doesn't. The standard of person they have to intimidate.

'Kids. I don't know who they were. Kids, working for Marty. Some shitty little bastards he picked up from some-where. I can handle them.'

'Uh-huh,' Bavidge is saying now.

Holmes doesn't want to talk about it. Probably wouldn't have told Patterson at all if it wasn't for Norah. Doesn't want to admit that he got battered by a couple of kids. The big bad bastard, bloodied and beaten. It wounds his pride. A lot of thugs live off their pride because they have nothing else. Proud and stupid. He's a hell of a new employee to have on board. There's a few seconds of silence, before Norah decides to stamp on it.

'Smashed their way in through the front door. The *front* door. Jim challenged them. One of them came up the stairs, got into a fight with him. Threw Jim down the stairs. Top to bottom. Then they started laying into him. Vicious, like animals.'

Holmes is glaring across at her, saying nothing. He

doesn't want her causing trouble. He knows the position he's in. Screwed over one boss, already bothering another. Patterson doesn't need to stand by Holmes. Could just as easy leave him out in the rain. Holmes needs to be useful, and this isn't a good start.

Bavidge is looking round at Norah. Surprised by her disgust at the violence of the kids. She knows what her man does for a living. She's not daft. She must know that Holmes behaves like those very same animals on a near daily basis. The only talent he's known to have. Yet she seems repulsed by them.

'Billy Patterson said he would protect us,' Norah is saying. 'Said we'd be looked after. Well, a fine fucking job he did of that, uh? Where were you?'

'Norah,' Holmes is saying loudly, then groaning and tipping his head back again.

'Well, where were you? Where were you when Jim was bouncing down the stairs? When I was confronted by those kids in my dressing gown? They could have killed us. We could be dead now. What sort of protection is that?'

Bavidge is waiting a second. Let her vent. Let her have her moment, she's not at fault here. Then tell her the truth. 'You will get protection. What you won't get is a fucking baby-sitter. You're not important enough. You're not in enough danger. You got to earn that sort of protection. All your man has done for us so far is wake me up. When he's done something more useful, you'll get more in return from us. Until then, the best we can do is make sure there's punishment. Did either of you see them?'

Holmes knows enough about the business to know that Bavidge is close to Patterson. Not just some muscle, but a senior man. Right-hand man, maybe. You piss off Bavidge and you piss off Patterson. That's the way it works. Tell him what he wants to know.

'I saw them. Couple of kids,' Holmes is saying quietly. 'They didn't even cover their faces. No weapon. Didn't even have a car, Norah reckons.'

Norah's nodding. 'They walked to the bottom of the street. If they had a car, it was round the corner.' She's talking quietly now too. Catching Holmes's mood. Bavidge's authority has subdued them both.

'Couple of first-timers, I reckon,' Holmes is saying. 'One of them was tall, over six feet. Skinny-looking, sort of light-brown, blond hair. Looked about twelve in the face, but he'd be a teenager, early twenties. That's the one that threw me down the stairs. Other one was shorter, darker hair. Never seen either of them before. They weren't working for Marty a week ago, I know that. Probably not in the business. New blood.'

Bavidge is nodding. It's as much of a description as Holmes can give. Seems like he spent most of their visit rolling down the stairs. Should be grateful he can manage this much. Just need to find a couple of kids that have recently started working for Marty. Not impossible, but he does hire and fire a lot. All the kids go to him first. He has the recruitment tool of throwing parties with whores and drugs. It works.

'You going to be okay?' he's asking Holmes.

Holmes is nodding very slowly. 'Don't think anything's broken. Nose is burst. Sore guts. That's where they kicked me. I'll live.'

Bavidge is nodding. He hates these situations. People looking to him for leadership, just because he's close to the boss. He's not a leader. Doesn't want to be, anyway. 'We'll find out who it was. We'll do something about it. Billy will be in touch soon about work. We'll try and sort this out so that Marty isn't a problem any more.'

A grunt from Holmes, nothing from his woman. Bavidge is leaving the house, happy to get out. One of those disgruntled neighbours might have phoned the police the minute they got back in the house. Doubtful. Wouldn't risk the wrath of Norah Faulkner. Just glad to be out of that atmosphere of stupidity and entitlement. Back into the car and driving away.

There's a feeling he gets. Like a weight, pushing him down. Like it's all basically pointless, and it's all going to end badly anyway.

3

Out the front it's all locked up. You wouldn't think a soul was alive in the place. Glass is starting to have his doubts. The Heavenly nightclub. A large front entrance, shabby trying to look grand. Its dim name in lights. Glass and Peterkinney are walking past. They were told to go in a side door by Marty. They were told that side door would be open. Glass is leading the way round the corner and onto a narrow street where the side door is waiting. Hopefully unlocked.

'Hey,' Peterkinney's saying. 'Take off that jumper; we'll put them in the bin there. Come on.'

Glass is staring at him, watching Peterkinney pull his sweater over his head. 'Chuck them? The hell would I chuck this for? Cost me forty quid, this. It's a good top.'

'People saw us. We were wearing these tops. The police will be looking for them. It's what people will remember about us. We need to get rid of them. If we go in there wearing the same clothes we used at the scene of a crime, what's Marty going to say? Us leading the police right to him?'

Glass is nodding. He suspects, wrongly, that Marty wouldn't say a word. Wouldn't much care. He suspects that if it didn't occur to him, it wouldn't occur to Marty. But it's a good point, so he's looking around to make sure no one can see him, and he's taking the top off. Something else to mention to Marty. How they sacrificed decent clothing to do a decent job. That might impress. Might even get them a little more money. Now that is naive.

Peterkinney was wearing a dark-green shirt underneath his top. Glass was wearing a black T-shirt, which is hardly appropriate attire for the company they hope to keep tonight. If Marty has a problem with it he'll just have to find a spare shirt. He was the one who sent them on the job. Promised them an invite to the private party in the club as a reward for a job well done. The job was done and done well. Now the reward.

Once the tops are stuffed into the black wheelie bin on the street, Peterkinney's dropping back. Let Glass lead the way. He's the one that this matters to. He knows Marty, or thinks he does. He's the one with dreams of working for the man. Glass is pushing open the side door, stopping and turning as it opens. Looking at Peterkinney with a smile. They can both hear the music. Not too loud, but a thumping background beat. The welcoming sound of a waiting party.

'You hear that,' Glass is saying. 'That's our reward, man, that's what it was all for.' Giddy excitement in his voice. The reward he's always imagined but never seen.

Glass is walking in. Standing in the corridor as Peterkinney pulls the door shut behind them. Glass is itching to get to the party, but business first. Doesn't matter how good the reward is, business first. Glass is leading the way along the corridor, clapping his hands together. All kinds of adrenalin at work. Peterkinney behind him, sauntering along with hands in pockets. No need to feel giddy when it's not your ambition being realized.

Glass stopping outside the door of the manager's office. Knocking twice. Thinking there's no guarantee that Marty will be in there. He might be on the dance floor like any sensible person. Peterkinney is guessing different. This won't be a party to Marty. This will be work, and work will keep him in the office.

'In.' A loud shout, making itself heard over the music.

Glass opens the door, steps inside. It's a small office. A grotty little place, in fact. It was painted once, but only once. There are scuff marks on the wall, little blobs of Blu-tac that once held up posters. At a glance, Peterkinney can see little holes where something was once screwed into the wall. Probably a shelf that was removed for daring to take up so much space in this dingy little office.

A small desk under a small window, facing the door. Adam Jones is sitting behind the desk, staring back at them. Manager of the club, twin brother of Marty. He lacks Marty's charisma, Marty's ability to spot a good opportunity. Adam ain't dumb, he just ain't Marty. Marty, prone though he is to occasional misguided outbursts of ambition and emotion, is sharp. Not well educated. Not book smart. Just the kind of sharp you have to be to make it in this business. This revenge attack on Holmes would fall into the emotional category.

Marty's sitting on the only other chair in the room, to the right of his brother's desk. There's a relaxed smile on his face that his brother hasn't thought to replicate. Sharp, you see. Pretending that all is well and nothing can ever go wrong. It spreads confidence to these kids. The smile is false. Three girls didn't turn up for the party, which has left him short-staffed. This Holmes thing has the potential to be trouble if Billy Patterson can show off that he's gotten the better of Marty. There's a lot to hide behind that cocky grin.

'Fellows,' Marty's saying, looking to disguise the fact that he can't remember their names. So many young men come and go. You use them; you throw them away when you're done. Bad idea to keep them on too long. Not unless they're specialists. You keep muscle because you need men that have a reputation to do your collecting. Kids like these, doing menial stuff? Nah. Use them once or twice, then chuck them before they get complacent. Bring in the next bunch of enthusiastic young whelps that'll do whatever you demand of them. Gratitude gives you an opportunity to exploit. It can be the difference between profit and loss.

'So how did it go?' The smile on Marty's face suggests he already knows. Both of them have walked back in here without a scratch and the short one's smiling proudly. They could walk in without a scratch if they hadn't bothered doing the job, but there would be no smiles. Not unless they were good actors, and Marty's seen too many of them over the years to be fooled.

'Went well, Marty,' Glass is saying, and wondering if he should call him Mr Jones. But there's two Mr Joneses in the room. Better to differentiate. 'He was at the house, like you said. We had to smash the door to get in, but we got in. Then we delivered the message.' Saying it with an enthusiastic nod. Trying to sound casually tough.

Marty seems pleased, but there's more he needs to know. You hang around with big players like Peter Jamieson and you learn that detail is king. Marty doesn't know that Glass has skimped on the detail because he'd be embarrassed to tell about Holmes being in his boxers. Doesn't seem like a fair fight, when you tell the story that way. Almost makes Holmes sound harmless. Like he was the victim here. Marty doesn't care. Wouldn't care if Holmes was chained upside down to a wall when they got there, naked as the day he was born. He wants to know that the message was properly delivered.

'Tell me what happened. Details, boys, details.' Marty's sitting back in his chair, looking up at them with that plastic grin. His brother looks depressed, but that seems to be a default setting. The look of the spare wheel.

'We had to smash the door in, like I said,' Glass is saying with a nod. 'Searched downstairs but he wasn't there. Then he came to the top of the stairs. Oliver went up the stairs. Holmes threw himself at Oliver, Oliver dodged. Holmes fell over. Oliver kicked him down the stairs. Bounced right down. We gave him a couple of kicks at the bottom. Told him it was from you. Made sure he knew that we were delivering your message, Marty. He knows. He won't forget.'

Marty's nodding. Sounds like it went well. According to the general plan, anyway. They're probably putting some gloss on it, but they're entitled. 'Anyone see you?'

Glass is shrugging. 'Holmes, maybe his wife.'

'Girlfriend,' Marty's interrupting.

'Girlfriend, yeah. Don't think anyone else did. No one else in the house, no one out on the street when we left. We ditched the tops we were wearing as well, so . . .' he's saying, trailing off.

Marty's nodding. All sounds good. Sounds like they took the right precautions. He's assuming they wore balaclavas, because common sense says they did. He's assuming they drove away from the scene, common sense tripping him up and laughing behind his back again. If nobody outside of the Holmes house saw them, they'll be fine. Nobody inside the house is going to get the police involved.

'Sounds like you did well,' Marty's saying. 'Why don't you both go out there and enjoy the party. It's a good one.' A pause, thinking of a little test. Play games with the dumb kids. 'What do you think of the club?' His brother's giving him a dirty look. Adam knows what Marty thinks of the club, and it's not an opinion he would put on a poster.

'It's great Marty, yeah,' Glass is saying quickly. 'Great club, great party, can't wait.'

Marty's nodding, still smiling the patented Marty smile. 'What about you, Silent Bob?' he's asking Peterkinney. 'What do you think of this place?'

Peterkinney, standing slightly behind Glass, is shrugging. 'Club's a bit of a dive,' he's saying. Quietly but casually, knowing he's right and not seeing why anyone would have a problem with his opinion. He's not important enough to care about, not wrong enough to argue with. Not here to suck up to this pair. 'Party should be good though. Location doesn't matter if the party's good.'

Adam Jones is frowning from behind his desk, shaking his head slightly. Who wants to hear that casual insult, even if you've heard it many times before? That's nothing compared to Glass. He's turned right round on the spot and is glaring at Peterkinney. If he gets them thrown out, by God, he won't be responsible. He won't. Peterkinney's this close to blowing it.

The only person not frowning is Marty. He's laughing. 'Brilliant. This place is a shithole. Everyone knows that much. But you're right; the party is the main thing. People don't give a shit about location if the girls are good, the music's loud and the coke is free. Overwhelm the senses, obliterate reality,' he's saying, sounding like he's said that before and is proud of it. There's a pause as Marty looks at the two of them. Judging them both. He fancies himself a good judge of people. One of his many skills. The shorter one at the front, so eager to please. He's the desperate one, trying to get into the business. A head full of dreams and nothing else. The one at the back is different. Yeah, the taller one is the sort of person you might just keep around. He doesn't care if he's a part of it or not. Having a little fun, seeing what happens. Honest, tough, willing to offend. Knocked Holmes down the stairs, then came here and insulted the club. 'What's your name, kid?' Marty's asking.

'Oliver Peterkinney.'

Marty's giving him a look. A what-the-hell-sort-of-name-is-that-for-a-Glaswegian look. He's not saying it though. 'Okay. Good. You two go enjoy the party. When I have another job for either of you, I'll be in touch.'

As soon as they're out in the corridor and the door's shut behind them, Glass is turning on Peterkinney. He's started to talk, but stopped, realizing how loud his voice was. They're moving up the corridor, away from the office. Towards the door that leads out to the main entrance. One left turn from the dance floor. The music's getting louder. They can feel the little thumps in the soles of their feet as they walk towards the door. That's relaxing Glass, but not enough.

'What the hell was that? You want to get us chucked out of here?'

'For what? For telling him what he already knows? They want you to be honest. Surely you know that. How many arse-lickers does a guy like Marty Jones see every day? And I ain't just talking about the hookers he employs.' Saying it with a smile, cutting the anger from the conversation.

Glass is rolling his shoulders. It's a thing he does when he knows he's lost an argument but wants to pretend it's ended inconclusively. It would look like a dismissive shrug, if it wasn't so self-aware.

Out into the corridor at the front door. The doors to the dance floor are shut, just in case someone presses their nose to the glass of the front door and looks in. Big heavy things, Glass leaning against one to push it open. Both of them stepping through and stopping. Must be fifty people in the club. About half of them are men in suits, the other half are all young women. Everyone looks like they're enjoying themselves, but only the women are making an effort. The men are playing, the women are working. Some of the people are on the dance floor. The rest are sitting round large tables on the right-hand side of the room. The VIP area. Glass and Peterkinney look at each other with a smile, and head for the tables.

4

There are a few different kinds of people who end up in the money business. Moneylending, debt collection, that sort of thing. There are people like Marty Jones. Marty does it because he can. It's a way of making money, but it's not the only way he has. He's the consummate opportunist. He found his way into the criminal industry with women. A pimp, not to put too fine a point on it. Since then, he's always been on the lookout for a good opportunity. Raising more money, raising his profile. And he got into money because it was a chance at fast cash. Wouldn't have done it if he didn't have the protection of Peter Jamieson. The boss of one of the biggest criminal organizations in the city. With his protection, Marty's taking his chance to elbow into the collection business.

For Marty it's just another string to the bow. Something he'll do while he can make easy money from it. When the going gets tough, Marty will shrug and walk away. Money's only good for him if it's easy. For someone like Billy Patterson, it's an ambition. He'll tough it out, no matter the threats. Surround himself with people like Alan Bavidge. Go out there and specifically target the debt business. Billy wants to build something that'll last. This isn't just a short-term money-maker; he's in it for the long haul. Focused only on the money business, all day every day.

Then there's the third kind. Not a short-term money-grabber, not an aggressive grower of his business. The kind who've always been around. The lifers. People like Ronald 'Potty' Cruickshank. He's actually only forty-eight, but he looks older. A big unit, fat and broad. Bald on top, and recognizable. Everyone knows Potty. Everyone knew his uncle Rolly. Had the same proper name as Potty, and Potty followed him everywhere. Rolly is still remembered to this day as one of the biggest bastards to walk the streets of Glasgow. A memory he earned.

Rolly set up the debt collection business back in the late sixties. He was lawless. Had no concept of the rule of law. Seemed to genuinely assume that it didn't apply to him. Treated people like seven colours of shit. Except for Potty. He loved his little nephew. The boy was always hanging around the offices. Worshipped his uncle. Learned everything he knows from him, which is the problem.

Potty was working for the family business from the age of fourteen. When big fat Rolly dropped dead of the world's most predictable heart attack, young fat Potty just kept on running the business. Did everything exactly the same way his uncle had. Kept things rolling along. But times have changed. The market isn't the same as it was in the sixties and seventies. More competition, for a start. More awkward police. But there's always a market. There will always be a market for money.

So Potty goes through life looking to hold on to what he's got. Always strictly following the rules his uncle laid down. No lending. You don't give money away; you just go and collect it. Always know your employees. You don't have to like them, don't have to treat them well, but you do have to pay them properly. If they're getting a decent share of the money they see, you won't have a problem with them. And protect your reputation. It's the single most important thing you have. Nothing matters more when persuading a person to hand over money. You lose your reputation, you lose your business.

Protecting reputation isn't just about keeping up the standard of the work you do. It's also about making sure that nobody else grows to challenge you. People will accept your standards are the best if they have little to compare them to. Potty has the biggest debt collection service in the city. Nobody's ever been allowed to get close. Forty-five years of Cruickshank dominance. As soon as he spots a threat, Potty stamps on it with all his considerable weight.

That's why Potty's been thinking about Billy Patterson so much recently. He's aware of Marty. Doesn't care about him at all. Marty won't last. Fly-by-night. He has good protection in Jamieson, but that's not the point. Marty isn't committed to it. Doesn't understand how much hard work it takes to maintain credibility in this brutal part of the business. He'll go back to chasing easier money somewhere else. That's inevitable. Not Patterson. Patterson's a threat.

Potty's on the phone right now. Sitting in the large drawing room of the large house that other people's violence has bought him. Potty, like his uncle, never lifted a finger. You hire dumb muscle for that. You do the organizing. You set up deals with moneylenders who aren't getting their money back. Buy the debt from them, and then collect it in your own way.

'I get that, Gary. I do, I get it,' Potty's saying. He doesn't hide his impatience well. He's always either been indulged or in charge. When he has to deal with defiance, deal with people with a mind of their own . . . Well, it's not easy. It's why his two marriages ended violently. It's why he sees so little of his two teenage kids, both from the first marriage.

'Gary, listen to me.' Said with more force than he realizes. Trying to be persuasive, but wandering off into vicious. 'You sell debts to Billy Patterson at that percentage, and a few months down the road he'll be biting you for it. He'll have to make all that money back somehow. The money you save now, you lose later. You know the business, Gary. You know how it works. Really, Gary, I'm surprised at you. He can't buy those debts at ninety and turn a profit. When he needs that money back, he'll take it from you. Mark my words, Gary.

Six months from now, you'll be lucky to break 50 per cent from him.'

Gary is Gary Jefferson. Everyone calls him Jazzy, but not to his face. Gary, like Potty, has a strict understanding of professional respect. Unlike Potty, Gary Jefferson can see the benefit of Billy Patterson. Potty buys debts at 75 to 80 per cent of their supposed value on a safe debt. It varies, of course. Some debts are less likely to be paid than others. Some can be collected, but will cost more in manpower to recover. But Potty's always been a good buyer. He'll take on the bad debts as well as the good, just to keep his sellers happy.

'I know it's late, Gary. I appreciate that it's late. I can see the time as well as you can. I have a watch on my wrist. What you do not seem to appreciate is just how important this is. This could have a serious effect on your business, Gary. A serious effect on our professional relationship. I don't want that, and I really don't think you do either.'

That was much more of a threat than intended. But it's true. Say what you want, history suggests Potty is right. Doesn't change Gary Jefferson's point of view. He can sell 70 per cent of a debt to Potty or he can sell 90 per cent of a debt to Patterson. People like Marty aren't in this equation. A jack of all trades, lending and collecting. A specialist lender like Jefferson wants a long-term, specialist collector. And he wants the one that will give him the most of his money back.

'That's all good and well, Gary, but you're not looking at the bigger picture.' A pause. 'Yes, I do know it's late. You have already pointed that out, thank you. Fine, I will speak to you tomorrow.' He's pressed the button on the phone to hang up. Pausing with the phone in his hand, bouncing it slowly up and down. Now throwing it across the room. Not with much force, not at anything in particular. It's clattering against the wall and falling to the thick carpet. It'll be fine. It's made that journey before.

Not easy to get up. He's meant to lose weight for years, but there's so much else to do. He's busy. That's his excuse. Too busy to avoid eating badly. Too busy to exercise. Getting up in stages from the low cushioned chair. His second wife furnished the house. She picked what was attractive to her, rather than convenient for him. Potty's walking in a small circle. Doesn't know where to go. Doesn't know what to do next.

Target Patterson. That goes without saying. Doesn't need you to tell him that. But what do you use? How do you get at him? There have been others in the past. People who were brutal and ambitious, same as Patterson. Something's changed. Maybe Patterson is different from the others. More ruthless. Certainly done a good job of surrounding himself exclusively with hard nuts. Hard to remember a collection service run by such a collection of tough guys. No weak links near the top of that business. Or maybe it's Potty that's changed. Second divorce. No kids from that marriage. No relationship in his life like the one he had with his uncle. Nobody looking up to him. Nobody to pass it all on to.

He's growling loudly at himself and walking with what little pace he has. Through to the kitchen. To the fridge. For a bottle this time, as a matter of fact. A beer, and sitting at the large kitchen table. Sitting proudly at the head of a long table that only he ever uses. Tapping the bottle on the top of the table, and thinking. Plan every move. Better to be meticulous and dull than sloppy and dead. Another lesson passed down from Rolly Cruickshank.

There's a grim expression across his face as he makes his way to bed ten minutes later. A bedroom with flowery wallpaper and an oversized bed for his second wife to hide from him in. All the different strategies that have served him well have been considered and discarded. The go-to options that require nothing more than instinct these days. Patterson doesn't have the weak spots needed. He's been allowed to grow for too long. Growing in the shadows, nobody stepping in to slap him down. Well, whose fault's that? There's no worse anger than the one pointing towards you. Now that Potty needs to stamp on Patterson, he can't think of a way. Get help from someone else? Done it before. Use someone who isn't a threat to you. Nobody who could benefit from stabbing you in the back. But who? That's a tough one. Who?

5

The house is in darkness. Bavidge is ringing the doorbell anyway. It takes less than ten seconds for the door to open. Billy Patterson looking back at him. Short, skinny, shaven head. There are a lot of things you think when you first look at Patterson. Clever and ruthless are not necessarily two of them. That's part of his success. He's built a reputation as being relatively harmless. A tough wee fellow, a stereotype of the little hard man with lots of anger and little brains. Nothing the big movers need to worry about. Persuading people not to worry about you is quite a trick to pull.

Nobody would believe he cultivated that image for himself. None of the established collectors could believe that anyone would deliberately play themselves down. It's invariably the other way round. People come into the business, exaggerate their power. It's a way of attracting business. You convince people that you're bigger than they are. Convince them you're big enough to fear. Patterson was too smart for that. Why draw attention to yourself? Why invite rivalry? Let people think you're small and they leave you alone. While they leave you alone, you contact their debt sellers and do some deals. That's Patterson's genius, the ability to grow in shadow.

He's stepping aside to let Bavidge in. Walking through to the back of the house. A dim little lamp on in a spare room at the back of the house. The curtains shut, keeping the little light in. There's a small round table in the middle of the room for card games, a couple of seats around it. This is where Patterson has his business conversations.

'So?' Patterson's asking.

'They kicked the fat guy down the stairs. His girlfriend scared them off. No bloody wonder. Just about scared me off too. Beast of a woman. It was for Marty Jones. They named him. Couple of kids. Just need to find out what suckers he has working for him now. They come and go though, so . . .' All said in the sighing tone of a man who couldn't give a shit.

Patterson's nodding. He knows Bavidge doesn't see a lot of potential in Holmes. There isn't a lot, to be fair. But there's some, and you have to take the little opportunities as well as the big ones. Ten little ones can add up to stronger business than one big one.

'What was his reaction to being kicked down the stairs?'

'Got a little pissy about a lack of protection. Well, the girl-friend did. He didn't want to rock the boat. I don't know, I don't think they'll say anything about it. Never know.'

Patterson's nodding again. Mulling over his next step. He could go down the tit-for-tat route that Bavidge is suggesting. Find out who these kids were and give them a kicking. It's what people would expect him to do. It's what Marty will be expecting. That's probably why he used the kids, because he doesn't care if they get battered senseless. They're not important enough to care about. So it would be no punishment to Marty if they went down that road, just PR for Patterson. And Patterson has never been about PR. Growing in the dark. Never predictable in his responses.

'What do you think we should do next, Alan?' he's asking. A slight smile, because he knows what the reaction is going to be.

Patterson does this all the time. He asks you a question he's already decided the answer to. Sometimes it's to buy himself time to think of a way of explaining it to you. Sometimes it's a test to see if you agree with him or not. With those he doesn't know, it's a test of their judgement. With Bavidge, who he knows so well, it's a game. Let him whine about how he doesn't care and how he'll do whatever Patterson wants him to do. Let him get all that out of his system before they talk about what's actually going to happen. What they've both known for some time was going to happen.

'I think if you go after the kids, this just keeps happening. I think I'm fed up of chasing little arseholes around the city, just to give them a kicking. I'm not kidding, Billy, I'm sick of it. I can find these kids if you want me to. I can kick the shit out of them if you want me to. I can kill them if you really want me to. But where does that put us? Marty Jones still has a queue of spotty-faced, snot-nosed little pricks banging at his door. You'll never scare them away from the life he's offering them. You knock two over, another two spring up. We need to do something decisive. We need to make bigger moves.'

Patterson's leaning back in his chair. The ferocity of the answer has surprised him. It shouldn't; he's known Bavidge has felt this way for a long time. Just didn't expect it to all come pouring out like that. That concern he has about his friend is being washed away though, replaced with contentment. Bavidge sees it too. Sees the pettiness of moving against these kids. They need to do something bigger. Now Patterson's nodding, and smiling. Now he can share the answer he already had to the question he asked.

'You're right about the kids. There's nothing to gain from going after them. Not if we can go after a bigger target.'

'Marty?'

'Maybe not Marty. Not if he still has protection from Jamieson. We're not ready to go up against that. Jamieson would crush us, if he could be bothered. Actually, I don't think Marty's even the right target for us, protection or not. We go after him, after those kids, what difference does it make? Amounts to nothing. As long as we keep chipping away at Marty, he'll get bored and go back to his hookers.'

Bavidge is grimacing. 'How sure are you of that? Everyone thinks he's flaky, but he didn't make money out of his women by being soft. Don't underestimate him, is all I'm saying.'

'I don't,' Patterson's saying. A little quieter. A rare warning has quieted him. 'I don't underestimate that he's tough and smart. And I don't underestimate what Jamieson could do. I just don't see him as the right target.'

'So?'

'So we need to look somewhere else.'

'This is Potty Cruickshank again, isn't it?' Said with another grimace. Not necessarily arguing, but obviously not a cheerleader for the idea either. Potty still seems like too big a target to Bavidge. His history, his strength in this business, doesn't get wiped out quickly. It wouldn't be a battle to defeat him, it would be a war. They'd be smarter growing their business more before they turn their aim towards that sort of competition.

'Yes. Potty Cruickshank. We need to move against him, because he's going to move against us.'

'I've seen no sign of that. His people haven't made any move against us . . .'

'I got a call just before you got here,' Patterson's saying, raising his hand. 'Jazzy Jefferson. Seems like Potty found out about my offer. Someone's been telling stories. Probably someone working for Jazzy. Potty tried to talk him out of it. Did a piss-poor job by the sound of things. Jazzy's still up for the deal, seemed a bit pissed off at Potty, but he needs reassurance. Needs to see we can handle Potty if things get nasty. I told him yeah, course we can. You leave that to me. I'll put Potty in his place.'

Bavidge is leaning back in his chair. He doesn't like the sound of this. This sounds horribly like the start of a war a lot of people won't survive until the end of. The very war Bavidge has been hoping to avoid. The key to their success has been picking their fights carefully. This is throwing caution to the wind. The start of a new era.

'This is the way of it, Alan, we both know that. Can't keep creeping around forever. This stuff with Holmes and Marty. That's baby stuff. We both know that. You can't live off that forever. Eventually you got to step it up. It's either that or stay as we are now. Well, we're going to step it up, because I don't want to stand still. I'm not saying we go after Potty personally. He's still too strong for that. But we weaken him around the edges. Do the sorts of jobs that make Potty vulnerable. If we take him down, we have the whole industry in our pocket. I'm telling you, Alan, we take down a Cruickshank and we're it.'

Bavidge is nodding. Nodding because it's true, and because it is ultimately what he wants. But all he can see ahead are the pitfalls. The risks. The fact that they're woefully untested at this sort of thing. There's a comfort in knowing you're good at what you do. Knowing that you will be successful. They're about to shed that comfort. Take a walk down a dark path where they can't see what lies ahead. It's easy to see that Patterson's excited by that. Not Bavidge. Patterson lives this life because he enjoys it. Bavidge does this job because he's reluctantly good at it.

'Look, Alan, go home, get some sleep. You're working too hard anyway. Forget about Holmes, I'll get someone else to handle him. He's not worth this much of your attention. Sure as shit not worth as much of mine.'

Bavidge is nodding, getting up from the little table. Can't argue with any of that. 'Let me know about Cruickshank. We don't want to hurl ourselves into this until we're ready.'

'Course I will.'

Bavidge is up and walking out of the room. Patterson's sitting back, watching him go. There's a creeping feeling he gets, watching his friend. Only known Bavidge for about three years. In that time he's become the person he trusts the most. An honest man, for this business. Intelligent way beyond his years and experience. And willing to do whatever it takes, no matter how much he hates doing it. But there's something about him. A feeling Patterson always gets when he's in Bavidge's company. The feeling that Bavidge is a man doomed.

6

Oh, it's a party all right. This is what they thought it would be like. What they hoped it would be like. Girls, basically. Let's not pretend they were looking for anything else here. The drugs they can get anywhere. The club is a dive. The music is one long headache with a faint hint of rhythm. Most of the other men at the club are in the industry in some capacity. All of them are more senior than Glass and Peterkinney. None of them are paying the young men any attention at all. Which is fine. Better to be ignored than looked down on, which is the other option.

Glass thinks he recognized a footballer at one of the tables, but he's not sure. Might have been. Only two kinds of celebrities stay in this city: gangsters and footballers. The former always happy to get their claws into the latter. They've ignored that table and sat at a quieter one. More sense than to impose themselves on others. Not really knowing what to do next.

Everyone else seems like they know the rules. Know how all this works. They feel like the only two first-timers. They're not, as it happens, but that's how it feels. Not that it matters. This is exactly what they pictured. Girls everywhere, and willing. Not exactly enthusiastic, but they're doing their jobs. If they want to get paid, they have to keep all the men at the party happy. That now includes Glass and Peterkinney. Being in a world where others exist to satisfy you is intoxicating.

This is where natural ebullience begins to pay off. They took a seat at a table that only had two other men at it. They were both at the other end of the table, on the other side, with two young women. Older guys, don't recognize either of them. Took about four seconds for Glass to start looking for women. He doesn't have a lot of experience with them. Neither of them has much. No experience at all with the kind of experienced women here. But that's what should make it fun. You're in a room full of women whose job it is to say yes.

Took him about five minutes to spot two alone. Went over and talked to them. Talked them back to the table. They're not pretending to be thrilled about being there. That's because they've done these parties before. They know the kind of person you should go for. First off, you want someone very drunk. Someone so drunk you're almost certainly not going to have to do any work that night. As long as you keep them happy, you get paid. There's no guideline on what you have to do to make them happy. Happy is all that matters. A drunk guy can be happy with his clothes on, because he's too drunk to get them off. Glass and Peterkinney are not drunk. They're also young, which is bad.

The inexperienced ones are the worst. They think they can do whatever they please. Live out any gangster fantasy they have. They have less understanding of manners.

The girls have sat next to each other, the more talkative of them sitting next to Glass. Peterkinney now has two bodies between him and the girl he's guessing is supposed to be his. He's the patient type. He'll let Glass spin whatever yarn he's concocted first.

'I mean, okay, we don't have a lot of experience,' Glass is saying to the girl, 'but when you have a start like we've had, that doesn't matter. I mean, look at what we've done.'

'What have you done?'

'Well, I can't tell you that, can I,' Glass is grinning. 'I hardly know you. Yet.'

Peterkinney's wincing. Glass has always been terrible at talking to women. Pretty bad at talking to people generally when the pressure's on. Always comes over a little desperate, very rehearsed. In moments like that, Peterkinney's reminded that his friend just isn't that bright.

'How about we hit the dance floor,' the girl is saying. 'We can get to know each other better there.' A smart way of saying, let's spend time together without you talking.

The yes that comes out of Glass's mouth is so filled with enthusiasm, Peterkinney laughs. Glass is getting up quickly from the table, but it's the girl who's leading the way down to the dance floor. She knows the routine. She knows that Glass doesn't. He's a dumb kid, trying too hard to impress. One of so many kids learning to be a gangster from bad movies. She's left her friend behind with Peterkinney, but neither of them is the talkative type. Or the dancing type, it seems. Sitting there, with two empty chairs between them. Peterkinney occasionally sneaking a glance, hoping the girl will be glancing back. She never is.

Must be the best part of ten minutes now since Glass went dancing. Still down there, putting all sorts of effort into looking cool for his girl. Truth is, most of the men are older than Glass, most of them are either pissed or off their face on something. He may just be the coolest dancer out there. All relative, obviously.

Peterkinney still hasn't spoken to the girl, and it looks like he never will. Another man has just walked past Peterkinney, over to the girl. Standing at the side of her, his back to Peterkinney. It's a big back, that's as much as Peterkinney can decipher. Tall fellow, broad shoulders, short hair. Sort of fellow you don't want to pick a fair fight with. You can guess his occupation from that, presumptuous as that might be.

The big fellow is pulling out the chair that Glass's dance partner was sitting in. He's leaning close to the silent girl and saying something to her. Too quiet to hear over the music. She's looking back at him. Peterkinney's just tall enough to see her face over the slouching man's shoulder. She looks unhappy. A little frightened perhaps. She looks like she doesn't want to be a part of anything the new arrival has brought to the table. She's saying something to him, nodding her head back towards Peterkinney.

Doesn't matter that she's sat there and ignored him since Glass and his girl went dancing. Doesn't matter that she has no more enthusiasm for him than she has for being set on fire. She's obviously scared of this guy. That makes Peterkinney take notice. Maybe not enough notice to help her, mind you. He might only be nineteen, but he's a smart nineteen. The kind that knows how to avoid trouble, by and large. But when the big guy turns round and looks at him with that ugly, beaten face of snorting contempt, it seals the deal. The damsel has herself a potential saviour.

'You're with her?' the big guy's saying.

A slight pause. The big guy is too dumb, drunk, high and dumb a second time round to notice it. It's indecision. The girl recognizes it. There's a pleading look on her face. Yeah, she gets that look now. Where was that ten minutes ago? Anyway, he's helping. Helping because, smart as he is, he can be vicious too. That little streak that needs to be let out once in a while. Like now.

'Yeah, I'm with her.'

Big guy's turn to pause. A nose that's been broken more than once. Lips that have been burst. The puffed and ugly look of a man who can't say no to a good fight. A slow smile spreading across his face. The smile he gets when he's thought of something clever. A smile he doesn't get often.

'So why are there two chairs between you then, huh? Two fucking chairs. What for?'

'Our friends were sitting there,' Peterkinney's saying. His voice is loud, has to be over the music. But it's steady, and his expression is calm. He feels calm, as a matter of fact. Dancing with danger, and he's not nervous. He has the moves to keep up. 'Now they're dancing.'

But the big guy is still grinning. Sitting between the aspiring couple, turning in the chair to leer at Peterkinney. 'I been watching since your mates went down there,' he's saying. Slurring his words and nodding his head down the three steps to the dance floor. 'You ain't said a fucking word since then. Neither of you has.'

'You ever been in the sort of relationship where you don't need to talk all the time? Where you can just be happy to be together?' Peterkinney is asking. There's smugness in the tone, even when shouting. 'Course you haven't, a guy like you. I feel sorry for you.'

The big guy's not going to sit there and take that. You're a big guy, and you work as muscle. The only thing you have is reputation. You let people make fun of you and get away with it, what have you got left then? You're soft muscle, and nobody's going to pay good money for that. So he's standing up and he's glaring at Peterkinney. Ready to make this a fight. His first instinct, every time.

'Come on, get up,' the big guy's shouting. 'Come on.' Shouting so loud people are looking. Loud enough to be more than a regular shout.

Peterkinney's looking up at him. Smiling. Not planning on getting up. He wants to sit where he is, try and force the big guy to back down. But it's not up to Peterkinney.

The big guy is lurching forwards. A big boot crashing into the side of Peterkinney's chair, a hand shoving him on the shoulder. Tipping him and the chair sideways. The big guy stumbling with the effort, but getting what he wanted. Peterkinney sprawled on the floor. It's embarrassing, but it's no more than that. Getting caught out by the big guy. Being face down on the floor, everyone looking. It's a humiliation, not a hurt. Humiliation doesn't keep you down.

Peterkinney's getting to his feet. The big guy is turning to look at the girl, grinning at her. She's stony faced. No change there then. She thinks her rescuer has lost the fight already. Peterkinney's getting to his feet, slowly. Considering his options before he picks the right one. Another new situation. You can handle it any number of ways. Laugh it off. The girl is nothing to him. Why should he take a risk on her behalf? But then it happens again and again. People see you as a guy that can easily be tipped off his chair. A guy that can be pushed around. No, don't want to be one of those. Seen what happens to them. That's not a life Peterkinney's going to accept for himself. Won't get him where he wants to go. You could try and bluff it. Talk the talk, play it out and hope it never turns nasty. Nah, any smart person will know you're a fraud, and it's the smart people you need to impress. You have to take the fight. Accept it, win it.

So now, in the second split second since he stood up, Peterkinney is thinking strategy. How do you win a fight you shouldn't win? This guy's bigger. Tougher. Definitely more experienced. If this is a fair fight, Peterkinney loses. So it can't be a fair fight, obviously. That means a weapon. None to hand. Create one. Only option. Might not be popular in a place like this, but anything's better than being humiliated by this moron.

Peterkinney's turned to face the big guy. Smiling slightly at him. Keeping it smug. Let him think that Peterkinney isn't nervous in the least. He is a little nervous now, but knows he should be more nervous. This could go very wrong, but that's okay, because he's decided it's still the right thing to do. He's standing beside the table, taking a casual glance at it. Picking up a champagne glass. Not his. Someone must have been at the table drinking it before they got there. Holding it casually in his hand for about half a second, then slowly bringing it down against the edge of the table. When it breaks, more of the glass falls away than he expected. Enough left to constitute a weapon. Enough left to intimidate.

The big guy is looking at him. Still grinning, but it's an uncertain effort now. The silent girl's eyes have gone wider. There's noticeably less movement around the club. People are watching. The people nearest them turning first, then the rest turning to see what everyone else is looking at. The key, having smashed the glass, is to not take any more initiative. Make sure people think you're using it only in defence. Otherwise you look like a nutter, and people blame you instead of the big guy.

'Why don't you fuck off,' Big Guy is saying. Still smiling, still uncertain. This moved out of his control real quick. Not used to someone else escalating matters like this. Smashing the glass was his kind of move.

Peterkinney's about to say something when a figure moves between him and the big guy. It's Glass. Pushing out his chest, standing on his tiptoes and still only reaching Big Guy's chin.

'Why don't you fuck off instead,' he's saying. Sounds childish. The little guy trying to be the big hero, but there's more to it. Looking to throw himself in the middle of the fight, sure. Also looking to stop Peterkinney from using that broken glass. Protecting his friend from himself, as much as this big lump.

'You're a pair of fucking idiots,' the big guy is saying, emphasizing *pair*. Already looking for a way out. Trying to make it clear to everyone in earshot that it's two against one.

That a man of his standing shouldn't have to bother with this sort of thing. Trying to make a withdrawal look like a victory.

'They'd have to go some to be as big an idiot as you are, Fraser,' a voice is interrupting.

Peterkinney and Glass turning. Looking at the middle-aged man at the other end of the table. Standing up, watching the conflict. He looks angry. He looks important. That's enough to silence all of them. Balding on top, a middle-aged spread. Short fellow, good suit, takes more care of his hair than he should. Nothing much to look at, frankly. But there's a look on his face that straddles the border between angry and bored. The look of a man who doesn't like his night out being interrupted by those less important. A look that says he's used to people doing just exactly what he tells them. He's telling Fraser to back off.

Fraser, obviously the big guy, is looking at him too. Just staring back. Not saying anything. Leaving it too long. Anything he said now would sound too considered. Taking a step back. Trying to stare down the more important man, but not willing to open his mouth. Now turning and stepping down to the dance floor. Peterkinney and Glass are watching him go, walking along the edge of the floor to the exit.

As soon as he's gone, Peterkinney is turning to Glass. Nodding a thank you, getting a nod back.

'Find a bin for that,' Glass is saying. Sooner the mess is cleared up, sooner everyone chooses to forget about what they saw. If there's no evidence, no consequence, there's no need to let it spoil a good night.

Peterkinney is gathering up the bigger bits of glass he can find. Glass is leading his girl back to the table, exaggerating his gentlemanly performance. Hoping he's scored a few macho points. The silent girl is moving seat, dropping into Glass's seat before he can take it. Making sure she's next to Peterkinney now. He's standing up with the glass in his hands. Smiling at the girl, who's now smiling back. That's a step forwards.

Now he's turning to look at the middle-aged man who stepped in to help. Too late. He's already sitting back down, whispering something to the girl next to him. She looks like a teenager. A pretty teenager. Not one of the bottle-blonde, orange skin brigade. There's a few of them here, but not many. Marty's more discerning than that. He knows his clients look for something better. Something that gives the appearance of being a higher class, even when it's not. The aura of unattainability; nothing sells better. No point interrupting. That wouldn't be any kind of a thank you.

There was a bin over by the doorway. He tipped the broken glass into it. On the way over and the way back, three people patted him on the back. A couple of others gave him a smile and a nod. Men and women. People here to party, and people here to work. Obviously Fraser was not a popular partygoer. Back at the table, sitting in his seat. Someone's tipped it back the right way. On the tabletop there are white lines ready. Silent Girl is passing him a note and smiling. It suits her. The party's starting.

7

Had a couple of drinks, which was a couple more than he intended. Now going to visit a friend of his. Well, friend's the wrong word. Old associate. They knew each other a long time ago. Back when they both had hair and good health. Been a while since Arnie Peterkinney had either of those. At least as long for Roy Bowles. Roy's a few years older than Arnie, mind you. Roy is sixty-six, Arnie three years younger.

Been a while since they had any kind of a conversation. Shouldn't be an issue. You go a long time without talking to people, but they don't forget who you are. They sure as hell don't forget what you've done. Not if they're any kind of smart. And Roy Bowles is all kinds of smart. That's why he's lasted so long in this business. So long since the police even looked twice at him. He knows what he's doing, and always has done. That's why he's the right man to talk to.

There's a reason why it's been a long time since Arnie spoke to Roy Bowles. Since he spoke to anyone in the business. Arnie takes no pride in some of the things he did to make money back in the day. Nothing too extreme. He avoided the worst of what could be done, but he made some extra money doing things decent people should frown upon.

He always thought he was decent. Always wanted to be. Spent most of his life doing legitimate jobs, working hard. But no great training, no great brain at work and no great luck. So he lost jobs. Never his own fault, but shit happens. Had to find some way of making money. On a few occasions he helped out old friends he shouldn't have been friends with.

One of those old friends was Roy Bowles. Roy was always sneaky. The quiet guy. You never quite knew what he did for a living. You knew it was illegal, and you didn't ask more than that. Arnie knew. It was guns. Always was. Bowles has been handling them for the best part of forty years now. Selling them to all kinds of scum. Doesn't care about the consequences, because the consequences have nothing to do with him.

Arnie didn't sell them for Roy, he collected them. When someone was selling a gun to Bowles, Bowles wanted a layer of protection. An employee who could go and pick the gun up from the seller. Someone smart enough to handle a nervous seller and tough enough to handle a dishonest one. There was never rough stuff for Arnie. Willing seller, willing buyer. But Bowles was a wary soul. So Arnie worked for him a couple of times over the years. Never for longer than he had to. Always glad to leave. You don't get a slap on the wrist for handling guns.

Now he's going back. Not for himself. He's approaching Roy's house to scrounge a job for someone else. Ringing the doorbell. Good lord, it's late. Should not have stayed in the pub. Needed to steel himself for this. It's going to be awkward. Begging. Never mind, one thing he learned about Roy is that Roy is not a fan of sleep.

Door's opening. A look of surprise from Roy.

'Arnie.' A pause. 'Good to see you.' Sounded almost like a question, the unconvincing way he said it.

'Roy. Too late in the day to have a quick conversation?'

They're in Roy's living room. He's insisted on making a cup of tea for them. Not what Arnie's bladder needed. They're sitting, talking a little about old times. Small talk. Tiny, in fact. Neither one of them cares at all about the conversation.

'So what brings you here in the dead of night?' Roy's asking.

'I knew you'd be up,' Arnie's shrugging. 'That never changes.' Roy used to be up all night, even when he was married. Even when he was married with a kid. Arnie would get phone calls from him at two o'clock in the bloody morning. That was the nature of his business. Not many people want to buy or sell guns in the middle of the day. It was a night-time pursuit, and Roy lived accordingly. 'I need to ask you a favour.'

Roy's frowning a little. Not easy to spot the frown on that lined face with the beady little eyes, but it's there. That was how Arnie used to start the conversations when he was looking for work. Roy remembers those reluctant conversations. Arnie hating the job but needing the money. Roy uncomfortable at having such an unhappy employee. He has a good memory. Another part of what makes him good at his work.

'Don't worry,' Arnie's saying with a knowing smile, 'it's not for me.' He remembers those conversations too. Arnie knows he's too old and too long out of the business to work for Roy now. Things have changed since he last did a job for Roy. Must be close to twenty years. Close to ten since they had more than a passing word to say to each other. Now he turns up looking for a favour. Yeah, he knows how that looks. 'It's for my grandson.'

Roy's nodding a little. Non-committal. He doesn't know anything about Arnie's grandson. Didn't know the boy was old enough to work. Better hear it out. You never know. Sometimes you end up unearthing a gem from these kinds of conversations. Rarely, but sometimes. 'Go on.'

'He's nineteen. He's a good kid. Sharp as they come. Needs to find some work though. You know how it is out there. There's nothing at all. The boy's living with me. It's not where he wants to be. He's desperate to get out into the world and do something, but . . .'

That's half the story. The half that Roy Bowles needs to know about. He doesn't need to know that Arnie's worried about the boy. Hanging around with halfwits like Alex Glass. Half-witted friends are no big deal. Where they lead you can become a big deal. As soon as Arnie heard mention of Marty Jones, he knew he had to do something. So here he is, doing something. Finding an alternative. Not a big leap up from Marty, but better. If Oliver insists on working for someone that isn't above board, it might as well be someone reliable. Someone who isn't going to end up inside, with Oliver in the next cell. Marty is a disaster waiting to happen.

'So he's looking for work. What's he done?'

This is where it starts to get awkward. Having to admit that Oliver's in no way the best person for the job. Times like this, so many people looking for work, Roy could have his pick. 'Not a lot so far. Like I said, he's a kid. But he's a smart kid. A good judge of a situation. Sharp, you know. Clean record. I know I'm his grandfather so you'd expect me to say this, but he's a kid who's worth a chance.'

Arnie's opinion was always solid, but that's not worth anything now. Arnie doesn't know the business now. And he can't be a proper judge of his own grandchild.

'Does the kid know you're here?' Roy's asking.

'No, he doesn't.'

'So how do you know that he wants to work for me?'

'He's desperate to make a start,' Arnie's saying. Thinking of him, hanging around people like Marty Jones. Sure, Arnie hasn't been around the business much these last twenty years. Doesn't mean he doesn't know about Marty and his kind. A fucking pimp. That's not the worst of it. A bloody debt collector too. Preying on the weak and vulnerable. Snaring them in a money trap and bleeding them dry. Ruining their lives. Anything is better than that. 'The boy will be thrilled with a job with you, Roy, I know it. He'll take the chance if you give him it. He's a good long-term option.' Throwing in the reference to long-term, because he knows Roy will like that.

Roy's pausing, thinking about it. His is a small operation, always has been. There are some who try to go industrial, but that doesn't work in a marketplace this size. You work in a city with just over a million people in it. That means the number of people who would ever buy from a man like Roy is relatively small. They want something cosy, trustworthy, long-lasting. Industrial doesn't reassure them. Only way you can sustain industrial is to be national, and Roy's never wanted that. He'll stick to his territory. Besides, you go industrial, and you get noticed fast. So he's always stayed small and that's always worked for him. One or two people helping him at any one time. No more than that. Right now, only one employee. Could do with a second.

'You know how it works, Arnie. I can't promise him regular work. Little stuff, now and again. I'll pay reasonable, I always do. Tell him to come round and see me tomorrow. I'll talk to him then. If that goes well, if I think he's up to it, I'll have something for him. Nothing regular to start, but we'll see.'

'Thanks, Roy. I do appreciate this.'

'You were lucky with your timing. I've only had one fellow helping for the last couple of months. I don't like using him as much as I do. I'd rather split the workload, safer that way. Draws less attention to each one. Still, I'm not guaranteeing anything until I've spoken to him.'

Arnie's out of the house. Walking down the street, wishing he had enough money for a car. His poverty embarrasses him. He's always been a grafter, but he's had health problems. Lack of circulation in the legs making them painful and bloated. Angina. Damaged lungs too, apparently, you can throw that one onto the list. Lifestyle. That's what the doctor said. Hard living, Mr Peterkinney, he said smugly. Bastard. He was right, but still a bastard.

Sixty-three years old and what does he have for all that living? A dead wife, a feckless son and a dependent grandson. No money, no job and no prospects. A small, damp flat, no car and a long walk home on his bad legs. He won't let this happen to Oliver. His son he did nothing for. But then, his son did fuck-all for himself. Ran off, left his wife and kid. Then the wife ditches Oliver with Arnie when the kid was thirteen. Good kid, but not what Arnie wanted in his life.

Now trying to do right by the boy. Find him work. Is this doing right by him? Setting him up with Roy Bowles? It's the last resort. Arnie spent months trying to find Oliver a legit job. Anything legit. The boy did his fair share of looking too. Just nothing out there. So it's this or Marty Jones. That's the only reason Arnie can justify this. The devil or the deep blue sea. Time to send Oliver swimming.

It was a long walk. Tiring and sore. He's grumpy by the time he puts the key in the flat door and steps inside. Cold inside. Always bloody cold inside. Switching on a light, and standing outside Oliver's bedroom door. These walls and doors are paper-thin. No privacy. Another good reason to get the boy out of the house. No sound from inside the room. Knocking and opening the door. Switching on the light. Little more than a box room. Not home. Okay, well, he's a young fellow, can't tie him to the flat. Out with his mate Glass, no doubt. Having a bit of fun. Fine. Lucky him. Arnie will give him the good news in the morning. For now, he's going for a long-awaited piss. Narrow little bathroom at the end of the corridor. Then bed. His bedroom larger than Oliver's, but small, damp and basically furnished. Struggling to sleep. Hoping Oliver isn't doing anything stupid.

8

Didn't sleep a lot last night. Doesn't sleep a lot most nights. Too much to think about. Plenty of work to do today. Bavidge has a small house, in a good area. Tidy, plain, predictable. The sort of house that hardly looks lived in. A house whose occupant has no interest in creating a home. He's a quiet neighbour, polite and well-mannered to all he meets. Occasional relationships. Never anything that lasts. He has too much sense to try to create a long-term relationship. Not with his work. With his lifestyle. That's just asking for trouble.

Does get lonely though. One of the reasons he doesn't much like being at home. Always alone there. He resents the loneliness that closes in on him here. No photos on the walls or mantelpiece. No hints of a hobby. No character. Just emptiness. Better to be out working. Day and night. On the streets, getting the job done. Make the money. Gain the security that comes with success. Then you settle down. Always persuading himself that that's the plan. That he'll see it through, and one day settle down with someone. Trying to persuade himself that that's possible for a person like him. It's a hard argument to keep having with himself. Cynical reality stamping on hopeless naivety.

A quick breakfast, and out of the house. Consumed by work. Into the car and deciding on his first port of call. Not Jim Holmes. Someone else can deal with that hopeless bastard. Patterson will get someone to fix his door. Patterson will call him and reassure him that they're doing all they can. Might calm his girlfriend a bit, hearing from the boss direct. The plan to ignore the kids and focus on bigger things won't be shared with Holmes. He's probably still sitting on his arse in front of his couch, doing what his girlfriend tells him.

His first job is to drive past the house of Potty Cruickshank. Not exactly a job. A hobby, until there's a plan. Big place. Old townhouse, where old money lives. Gardens too well maintained to be looked after by their owners. Estate cars and four-by-fours. Bavidge has no intention of doing anything to Potty yet. Leave him alone until Patterson decides otherwise. When that time comes, Bavidge will have to be ready.

For now he's getting an idea of the man. He's seen him around. Watched him waddle from the door of a shop to his car one time. Didn't look intimidating, but Bavidge knew better. The ones who look intimidating aren't often the ones you should be most afraid of. Big tough muscular guys are not the best fighters. They rely on their muscle. They fight with the confidence of superior size. It's the little ones, the smart ones. The ones that don't have limits. The ones that don't have size to depend on. People like Bavidge. And it's the ones that come with consequences. Like Potty.

Bavidge has heard all the stories that get told. As with most people in the business in this city, most of the stories are bullshit. The fantastic criminal tapestry of myth, half-truth and possibilities. A lot of the bullshit is spread by Potty and his people. They know how to build and maintain a reputation. But some of the stories are true. Enough are true to make Potty a very scary man. Enough to make him an exceptionally dangerous target. Patterson didn't say it, but they both know it. If you're going to take down Potty Cruick-shank, then you have to kill him. Leave nothing standing.

Won't be here though. Too many big houses. Too many people walking their dogs and bossing around their garden-ers. Too many people wary of threats and on the lookout for strangers. Big front gardens. Long driveway up to the garage. Potty isn't daft. He'll have all sorts of security at the house. Every inch down to the road will be covered. That makes the drive past worthwhile. Knowing that if they have to move in a hurry, this isn't the place you hurry to.

Turning at the bottom of the street and heading towards the west end. Work to do. There's a difficult collection that Bavidge knows hasn't been done yet. Other people are avoid-ing it. They have tough men collecting for them, but this one has been left simmering on the books too long. Has to be done. If he has to be the person that does it, so be it. Never bothered him much, the difficult work. If the job turns nasty, he turns nasty. If it's awkward, it's awkward. So what? You can't expect to work in this business and have no trouble. Accept that whatever is going to happen will happen, and face it. You either survive or you don't, and Bavidge isn't too concerned either way right now.

The guy's name is Jamie Stamford. Tough son of a bitch. Works as muscle for Alex MacArthur, which is reason enough to be cautious. Stamford's young and nasty. Thirty years old. Chucked twenty grand down a hole gambling on anything that moved and a lot of stuff that didn't. Patterson bought the debt for 50 per cent. Nobody else would touch something that poisonous, which is why it was going cheap. Hell, the two bookies he bought it from were delighted with 50 per cent. Just getting that much made Patterson their new best friend.

Finding Stamford isn't hard. One of Patterson's men knows the gym he goes to pretty much every day. Wait for him outside. Have a conversation. Got to find the bloody place first. Bavidge isn't one for gyms. His one impressive feat of agility was body-swerving the whole health and fitness movement. Not that he's unhealthy. He's trim because he works a lot and doesn't eat too much. But the gym? Watching yourself sweat and pant in a big mirror while running on a treadmill like a fucking madman? Running to nowhere. No thanks. More of a metaphor than he wants to stare at all day.

Took him a while to find the gym, but he did. Stamford's car is still in the car park. Swanky-looking gym, swanky-looking car. Gym membership won't be cheap. Neither is the car. For a guy with a twenty-grand debt, he seems to know how to spend money. How to waste it. That's because he thinks he can get away with it.

Stamford's been doing it for years. Gambling like a moron, throwing his money away. Getting into debt, and then hiding behind MacArthur's skirts. Being MacArthur's favourite muscle has gotten him off the hook on all sorts of debt. And every time, the debt gets bigger. This twenty-grand debt is the biggest yet. Addiction running further and further out of control. Nobody else wanted to buy it. Nobody else wanted to piss off MacArthur. Patterson basically bought it to make a good impression on the two bookies. But he figures it's worth trying to pick up.

Bavidge agrees. You let one thug get away with it and they all think they can. A free run for the stupidity collective. Stamford is an example the collection industry can't afford to set. So you go and get the money. You make an example of him. If he can't get off the hook, no one can; that sort of example. If MacArthur decides to get pissy about it, you ask him what he would have done. Shit, if the old man's dumb enough to have someone like Stamford close to him, that's his problem. MacArthur knows how it works round here. If you owe money, you bloody well pay it.

A few people have come and gone from the gym. All looking bronzed and vacant. All getting into their little mid-range sports cars or gaudy four-by-fours. Then Stamford. A bag slung over his shoulder. Wearing shirt and trousers, looking semiformal. Always a guy that likes to dress well. Those clothes won't have come cheap either.

Bavidge is out of his car and walking across to Stamford. Intercepting him before he reaches the safety of his car. Black Nissan GT-R, polished to a mirrored shine. Stamford's seen him coming. Been muscle long enough to know trouble when he sees it. But he's bigger than Bavidge. Taller, broader, firmer and with a longer reach. All the things he thinks matter. He doesn't know who Alan Bavidge is. Doesn't know what he's done in his life. And his financial management shows that he's a complacent prick with the judgement of a lemming. So Bavidge isn't worrying too much.

'Jamie. Good workout?'

Stamford's looking at him. Sneering, but with way too much effort to look anything other than dumb. 'What are you, cop?'

And Bavidge is laughing. A genuine laugh too. Not just doing it to piss Stamford off. Bavidge looks so much younger when he laughs. He can look so happy. It is hilarious that Stamford thinks Bavidge is a cop. Coming to question or arrest Stamford on his own? Yeah, right. He really is dumb muscle if he can't tell the difference between a collector and a cop.

'No, I'm not a cop. I just wanted to have a wee chat about some money you owe.'

'I don't owe any money,' Stamford's saying, moving to push past Bavidge to his car. Confident and dismissive and happy that this isn't a conversation he needs to worry about.

Lay down a marker. You let him push past you once and he keeps trying to push past you. You let him walk away from this conversation and you never get him back. The key to being a good collector is setting the tone. Do it early. Make sure the person knows who controls this. Make sure they know it's never going to be them.

So Bavidge is shoving hard against Stamford. Shoulder to shoulder. Stamford is bigger, but he's not expecting it. People don't shove back against him. So when Bavidge does, Stamford stumbles. And now he's looking at Bavidge. A little bit of disbelief. A lot of anger. Ready to lash out, which is why Bavidge is acting first. He's done this sort of thing before, you will have gathered.

'You throw a punch and this gets out of control fast,' Bavidge is saying with a snarl. 'I'm here to let you know how it's going to be. You owe exactly twenty thousand, one hundred and forty-two pounds. You are going to pay exactly twenty thousand, one hundred and forty-two pounds. No discounts. No deals. No getting off the hook. No hiding behind your boss like a pussy. We have your debt and we are going to collect. Other people might not collect on you, Stamford, but I will. You're fuck-all to me. No hiding. However far I have to go to get that money, I will go.'

Almost doesn't matter what you say. Chances are Stamford's heard some variation of this before, and it meant nothing to him then. He's wriggled off so many similar hooks, the words don't matter any more. It's all about tone. You have to sound threatening. You have to sound confident. You can't afford to sound like you're out of control. And you can't afford to sound like you're trying your hardest. He has to believe that you have several more gears of the tough-bastard routine to go through.

Stamford's taking a step back, which is good. Everything he says beyond this point means nothing. Point is, he stepped back. He's not trying to push through. He's accepted that Bavidge is controlling this conversation. It ends when Bavidge says it does.

'You don't know who you're fucking with, pal.'

'Not a pal. And I do know. Jamie Stamford. Slack-jawed piss ant for Alex MacArthur. Problem gambler. Using his boss to get off the hook. Not any more. This is a big debt and a big problem, Jamie. Twenty grand. You need to pay that money, before it buries you.'

Can't make it clearer than that. But with some people, you can never make it clear enough. Stamford is starting to laugh. Not the nervous laugh of someone trying to look strong in a weak position. The complacent laugh of someone who knows their boss is bigger than any collector in the city. Who knows he has enough standing with the boss to expect yet another bailout.

Kill that complacency. Fast. A punch in the stomach and Stamford is stepping backward. Not a great punch, but he wasn't expecting it, so it had impact. The second one's better. Side of the mouth. It'll definitely bruise, might even loosen a tooth or two. Always leave them something to remember you by. Always leave them with a mark they have to explain to others. Keeps reminding them how serious you are. It'll bruise Bavidge's knuckles as well, but he has no one to have to explain that to. Stamford still isn't down. He's set his feet well, ready to counter. But this is one of those rare occasions where Stamford is not the more experienced fighter. Bavidge is charging him. Catching him hard with his shoulder, right in the chest. Stamford is down. On his back, instinctively trying to get back to his feet quickly. Ignoring the pain in the back of his head where it hit the concrete to try and get vertical. Always stay on your feet. Golden rule. But Bavidge is on him. He didn't go down in the charge. That was the point. Now he's kneeling down. Putting his knee, and all his weight, on the side of Stamford's neck.

'You want to go running to MacArthur? Fine, you go running to him. I'll let you up and you can mince off to him now.

You can cry into his fucking lap. Tell him what I did to you. Every time you go to him, he thinks less of you. You do get that, don't you? You understand that every time he has to rescue you, he hates you a wee bit more? The more he has to help, the less he wants to. That's rule number one. Never beg from your boss. You've been doing that a lot, haven't you, Jamie?'

'Get off me. You're fucking dead.'

'Sooner or later,' Bavidge is saying, leaning in closer and lowering his voice, 'you're going to have to clean up your own shit. Start with this one. Impress the world by doing your own dirty work for once. Get my twenty grand. If I don't have it inside a fortnight, I'm coming back for you.'

Bavidge is getting up now. Two people have come out of the gym. They're standing close to the glass door, watching. Both dressed the same, so they must be staff. Must have seen it on the security camera. Bavidge is turning and walking back towards his car. He can hear the scuff of Stamford getting quickly to his feet. Waiting for the idiot to make a charge at him.

'Is everything okay?' one of the staff is shouting across.

Bavidge is ignoring them. So is Stamford. Bavidge is at his car. Dropping into the driver's seat, facing Stamford. He's beside his car now, angrily throwing his bag into the passenger seat. Watching Bavidge as he drives away. Didn't go brilliantly. Didn't go badly. Probably won't get the money, which is why he's going to have to pay Stamford another visit. Something else he won't bother looking forward to.

9

There are memories. They're vague, but they're definitely there. Some of them might be imaginary. Romanticized, at least. But Oliver Peterkinney can remember a few things about the night before. He remembers them as soon as he wakes up on the floor of Alex Glass's living room. Yeah, that was a good night. He's blinking heavily, and then looking around. Nobody there. Just him.

Ah, that's what that bang was. The front door. Someone leaving the flat. Who was it? Probably the silent girl. She didn't say a lot last night, even after the four of them came back to the flat. She seemed happy, at least. Sure as hell relaxed. And they had a good time. He thinks.

There was more alcohol. There was sex. There, the memories get a little confused. They were in the living room. Glass and his girl went into the only bedroom in the flat. Then there's another memory. On top of the silent girl. The other girl sitting on the floor behind him. His leg rubbing against the thigh of the other girl while she sat there. Did that happen? Maybe not. Probably not. He remembers the feeling of skin. That's about it.

He's wondering what the silent girl thought of him as he

finds the pile of his clothes on the couch. Why was he on the floor and the clothes on the couch? No idea. Never mind. What did she think? Not a lot, probably. He doesn't remember much about his own performance. Did he speak well? Was he intelligent and funny? Did he seduce her and perform manfully? Not bloody likely. He was drunk and high and has little experience with either state. That won't have helped. And she's a hooker, after all. How much experience of better men does she have? Ah well, she's gone anyway. He can make any assumption he wants, and she isn't here to contradict.

Into the bathroom. Grubby little bathroom. When he gets a place of his own, he'll keep it cleaner than this. His grandfather's flat is tiny too, but at least it's clean. A lot of cold water on his face. He's nearly woken up now. Feels like he needs a shower. Smells like he needs a shower. Not this shower. He'll get one when he goes home. Stand in the bath, then wrap himself in a towel and go sit on the radiator in his bedroom in the search for heat. For now, he just needs to be awake.

He's in the kitchen now, trying to find some coffee. Scruffy kitchen. Not dirty, just everything scratched and scuffed and poorly maintained. The cooker and toaster and kettle all old, on their last legs. The best Glass could afford, but the best isn't much. Peterkinney's thinking about Jim Holmes. Jesus, what a mess they made of that. Okay, they got away with it on the night, but come on. What a fucking joke performance. They made enough mistakes to fill a book with. He's shaking his head. You learn by doing. Learn by making mistakes. Last night they learned a lot.

And he's thinking about Marty Jones. Slimy bastard. Asking them questions in his brother's office. Trying to play the king of the castle. He's well connected though. Everyone knows that. Connected to Peter Jamieson. Everyone knows that much because Marty makes a point of telling them. That's his protection. People need to know how protected he is. The money he makes from parties like last night's is one of the reasons he has that protection. He might be slimy and an arsehole, but he always knows how to make good money. That's a trick worth knowing. A trick to be envied.

They were the victims of the sharp man's trick last night. Played them like the kids they are. He could have sent anyone to handle that Holmes job. Sent someone more experienced, who would have handled it better. But he didn't. He chose kids because he wanted someone he didn't care about. Someone that didn't matter. If Holmes had battered them. If the cops had caught them. Doesn't matter. Message is still delivered. Holmes knows that Marty's willing to try and get him. The quality of the job didn't matter, just the message. So he sent the kids.

Peterkinney's filling his mug when Glass wanders in. In boxers and a T-shirt. Grinning like a child at Christmas. Now he's stopping, looking around.

'Where's your girl?'

'Think she left,' Peterkinney's saying with a shrug.

'Ah,' Glass is saying, and tilting his head with exaggerated sympathy. 'Well, it's harder to keep them than get them. Some of us have that gift, some of us do not. Mine's still lying in bed, happy and waiting for a cup of that stuff.'

Just a little too smug to go unchallenged. 'Of course they're harder to keep than to get. They're prostitutes. That's the point. You're not supposed to keep them.'

'Hey, it's not like that,' Glass is saying. A little angry now. Peterkinney can be caustic when he wants. Has a habit of knocking down other people's good moments. Putting Glass on the defensive, because he knows he's smart enough to keep him there. 'Me and Ella were just talking about it.'

'Ella?'

'Her. The girl.'

'The prostitute?'

'Fuck off. We were talking about it. Look, it's not the way you think it is. They're not like hookers or anything. They go to parties. That's it. They go to parties and dance along with the guys. Keep them happy. That's it. It's not as bad as you're making it out. It's not.'

'That's not what you were saying yesterday,' Peterkinney's arguing. Keeping his voice down so the girl doesn't hear. He's incredulous at his friend, but he still has some manners. 'When Marty said we could go to the party after the job, you said we were on a promise. You said it was guaranteed. You said the girls had to. That's their job.'

'I said, I said, I said. The hell are you listening to me for all of a sudden, Captain Snarky. I said that yesterday when I didn't know. I was just going on the rumours and shit. Now I know. I've spoken to Ella and I know.'

Peterkinney isn't saying anything. Getting out of Glass's way so he can make another two cups of coffee. Seems pretty obvious that Glass knew better before the party. He said it was guaranteed and he turned out to be right. Apparently evidence isn't worth as much as a naked girl's point of view.

By the time Glass has finished making the coffee, she's come into the kitchen looking for him. She's four years older than Glass, but she looks and acts younger. Peterkinney can see the difference between her and the silent girl straight away. The silent girl was mature enough to see the misery in what she was doing. To see how it will all end if she keeps doing it. Not this girl. Not Ella. She only sees the potential upsides. Blind optimism.

'Here you go,' Glass is saying, passing her the cup.

She's wearing what she was wearing last night. Last night a short skirt and tight shirt open three buttons down was appropriate. Worked well in the club. Here it looks ridiculous. She's taking the mug and sipping from it.

'What are you guys doing today?' she's asking Glass. Glancing at Peterkinney to politely include him, but focusing on Glass. Talking sweetly to her new favourite person in the whole wide world.

'Uh, don't know really. Probably go see Marty,' Glass is shrugging, looking at Peterkinney. 'See if he has any work needs doing. You know, make ourselves useful, get some cash in our pockets.'

'So you work for Marty?' she's asking. She seems impressed by this. What's so impressive about it, Peterkinney can't guess.

'Yeah, we do,' Glass is saying. There's pride in his voice.

Peterkinney is looking at him, but not saying anything. If these two want to be so impressed by Marty, let them. Their mistake. They're all being used by that snake, only Peterkinney can see it. It's depressing to think that the other two aren't smart enough to see that. Fine, whatever, let them circle the drain hand in hand.

'I work for him too,' she's saying. Said with an enthusiasm she doesn't get to use often regarding work. Smiling at Glass, at this thing they have in common. The bond of working for the same guy, and not telling people what they do. The secret of success. Like working for Marty is a ticket to wealth, health and happiness that only they know about.

Where the hell is this pride coming from? What's to be proud of? Peterkinney's draining the last of his mug in one scalding gulp. Marty Jones is scum. Even Marty Jones knows that. The entire population of the world that doesn't know it is now concentrated entirely within this kitchen. A place Peterkinney doesn't much want to be any more.

'It was nice to meet you, Ella,' he's saying. 'I'd better head home. I'll call you later,' he's saying to Glass.

Ella smiled politely and nodded to him, but she could see he was faking the smile he gave back. He didn't like her, but he was leaving. Now she's turning to smile at Glass instead, because his smile is real. Glass is shouting to make sure he does call as Peterkinney pulls the front door shut behind him. He doesn't always call. There isn't always a reason to call. No guarantee that last night will change that. They did a bad job well enough. They got Marty what he wanted. Doesn't mean that Marty has any intention of using them again.

10

Arnie is sitting in the kitchen when he hears the key in the front door. He's sitting and waiting. Don't rush the boy. Don't start pelting him with questions. He doesn't like it. Always been thin-skinned and bloody-minded. Doesn't like being asked a question he doesn't want to answer. Never afraid to show you that he doesn't like it.

He's closed the door, coming along the corridor. Where he goes first is usually a good indicator of his mood. Into his bedroom and he's in no mood to talk. Nope. Past his bedroom door and along the narrow corridor to the kitchen.

'Hey Grandpa,' he's saying, giving an ironic twang to the word 'grandpa'. Knowing Arnie isn't thrilled about feeling his age.

'Funny hour of the morning to be coming home at night,' Arnie's saying.

'Yeah, good one. I stayed over at Alex's.'

He's getting a chocolate biscuit from a cupboard. That's breakfast out of the way. Now he's making his way out of the kitchen. There's hardly enough room for the two of them in here anyway. The old yellow cupboards dominate the space. There's a fridge-freezer, a cooker and a little table that's been there for over twenty years, always folded. You can sit a person on either side of the table when it's folded like that. Just enough. Arnie always sits on the far side, where he has a view of the door out to the corridor. Where he's sitting now. And that's it. That's all the furniture the kitchen can hold, and it still leaves not quite enough floor space for two people to avoid elbowing each other.

'I have some news,' Arnie's saying, calling him back. Not looking at him, because Oliver won't be thrilled about his grandfather sticking his nose into his business. Got that from his father. He had no business worth sticking your nose into, but he protected it jealously. Too bad, it's for Oliver's own good. 'I spoke to a friend of mine last night. Said he might have some work for a smart young man. If a smart young man is interested.'

'He is.' Peterkinney junior is standing in the doorway, looking down at his grandfather. Wary of what crappy job might be available to him. But enthusiastic, because a job is a job. A job is money, and money is a place of his own. A car. A life. Money is the one thing he's never had in his life, and has always wanted. Strange tone in the old man's voice. He hardly sounds thrilled with his achievement. 'Who's the friend?'

'Man named Roy Bowles. You ever heard of Roy Bowles?'

'Don't think so, no.'

'No. Well, that's because he's too smart to be known. Roy

is . . . Well, Roy's not a good person. I used to work for him, so I know. I've seen it all with my own eyes, what becomes of it. Listen to me, Oliver. If you go work for him, I want you to promise me something. I want you to promise that you won't stop looking for a proper job. Something you don't have to hide from people. What Roy does is rotten. Rotten from end to end.'

'Jesus, what have you set me up with?' Said as a joke, but the smile isn't entirely light-hearted.

'He buys and sells guns. Not legally, obviously. The stuff he'll want you to do, well, he'll want you to do donkey work. Go pick things up for him, that sort of thing. You'll have to be smart. And discreet. Very discreet. It'll only be now and again he uses you, so you ain't getting rich off this. You'll make something, and that's a start. But not riches. Hopefully, that'll keep you looking for something else.'

'Okay,' Oliver's nodding. Actually sounds like it could be useful. Occasional work, but the pay won't be bad. Something like that, there has to be decent money around. Come on, guns shift for good money. Could be little work with decent pay. 'When do I go see him?'

'Today. Afternoon. I'll write down his address for you. And the first thing you're going to do with any money you make is get driving lessons. You'll need a car to be taken seriously with something like this. You don't want people thinking you're just some kid.'

Watching his grandson leave the room. That felt wrong. It felt like he just kicked the boy into a hole. But what else could he do? What's the other option? Let him wander round the streets with Alex Glass, trying to impress people like Marty Jones? No fucking way. Not a chance. This is better than that. Has to be.

A shower. Struggling to get dry in a flat damper than he is. Finding some decent clothes to wear to go visit Roy Bowles. This is a chance. Then the phone's ringing out in the hallway. Arnie's out. Gone to the shops, as he often does. Goes out and gets a handful of things. Never just buys the week's needs in one go. He says it's about saving money. Oliver thinks it's about having an excuse to get out of the flat more often. Can't blame him. Picking up the phone.

'Hello.'

'Is this Oliver Peterkinney?' There's a slightly mocking tone in the voice, like the name is just too funny to say normally.

'Speaking.'

'This is Marty Jones. We should talk. Come round to the club, be here at twelve.' And he's hung up. Presumptuous bastard. Calling it the club, like he owns it. His brother is the manager, that's it. Neither of them owns that dive.

A look at his watch. He can make it for midday and still have plenty of time to go see Roy Bowles. He's out of the flat and running. Drenched in sweat is not the best way to turn up at the club, but he doesn't have time for a stroll. Marty obviously thinks Peterkinney has transport. That he can get to the club at the drop of a hat. Thinks he can even afford a bus fare, which he can't. Not without thinking long and hard about the other things he needs the money for. Oh boy, this amateurism is going to have to change.

He's got to the club before midday. Taking a few minutes outside to catch his breath. Let the panting stop. Hoping he looks halfway presentable. Then stopping. Chastising himself. Wasn't he just pissed off with Alex and Ella for fawning over Marty like he was a somebody? How is this different? Fine, this could be important. Could be a warning about last night. Could be something he really needs to hear. But the difference between five minutes early and five minutes late should be fuck-all to him. Get your head together. Remember who this is. Remember how little you care.

Into the club. Through the foyer and marching past the door to the dance floor. He knows where the office is.

'I help you?' someone's shouting from behind him. Gruff and deliberately unfriendly. It's a where-the-hell-are-you-going-without-my-permission offer of help.

'I'm here to see Marty. He's expecting me. Oliver Peterkinney.' Talking to some guy sticking his head round the door from the dance floor.

'Fine. Go on.' His tone making it clear that he doesn't care much either way. If you're here to help Marty, good luck to you. If you're here to stick a knife in him, hey, good luck to you too.

Through the heavy door and down the corridor. Knocking on the door. Hearing a shout to enter. Going in to find Marty sitting behind the desk. His brother nowhere to be seen. Marty looking at him and leaning back in the chair.

'Close the door, kid,' he's saying. Kid. Marty's thirty-three years old. He calls people kid because he heard it in a movie and thought it sounded cool. Made him feel senior to talk down to people. Starting to wonder why the really senior people don't talk that way. Starting to think that maybe he shouldn't. But it's a habit now, and habits are hard to break.

Peterkinney's closed the door. Standing in front of the desk, looking down at Marty. Quite happy to stay standing. Hoping this is going to be a short conversation. Thinking of his interview with Roy Bowles. Quite enjoying looking down on Marty.

'Jesus, take over a seat, man,' Marty's saying. 'Standing there like a fucking schoolboy.'

Peterkinney's giving him the kind of look Marty doesn't get often. A look that tells him he shouldn't be talking that way to the person in front of him. Peterkinney doesn't even know he's doing it. More a glance than a look. Instinctive and unrecognized by Peterkinney. Spotted by Marty though. Recognized as something rare and valuable. Peterkinney's going across and getting the chair, putting it down in front of the desk and sitting. Looking at Marty. Straight at him, holding eye contact. Keeping a cold expression.

'So you and your mate want to do more work for me?'

'If the work is right, yeah,' Peterkinney's saying. Shouldn't be putting in conditions, but he has that Bowles interview coming up. And he doesn't like Marty. And he's still pissed with himself for running to get here. There's a lot of reasons for the contempt that dripped off that sentence. Trying to establish some authority of his own is another, although that's subconscious. He's not thinking about authority over someone he doesn't want to work for.

'That's big of you,' Marty's saying. Saying it with a smile though, because he likes this. Doesn't hear it often enough. It's amusing. 'How would you feel about doing work alone?'

'Without Alex? This was all his big plan. He's the one that wants to work for you. If you're only looking for one guy, he's the guy you're looking for. He'll do whatever work you want done.'

'And you?'

'And I'm a little fussier.' Making it clear that he considers himself more discerning. Maybe too discerning to work for someone like Marty.

Marty's nodding. Impressed by the balls on this one. Talking to Marty like he's his equal. Hell, talking to him the way people in charge talk to him. That cold tone. People like Peter Jamieson and his right-hand man John Young use it all the time. Like they don't want to be in his company, but they'll suffer it. Stuck-up bastards. They'll take his money though. Oh yeah, you can bet on that. Real quick to take their cut, but don't want to hang around with him. Don't want to give him the opportunities to step up to bigger things that he's earned.

'Sounds like you handled Holmes well. And I heard about your wee confrontation with Neil Fraser last night. That wasn't too clever. Fraser's good muscle. John Young uses him. Not their favourite, but he's got a reputation. If you get the chance, you should thank Angus Lafferty for stepping in and saving you. Fraser's a nutter; he'd have stuck you, right there in front of everyone. But you had the balls to stand up to him. I like that.' Talking with the casual certainty of a man who knows. He knows who these people are, knows what they're capable of, knows how to handle them. The sharpness that makes Marty rich shining through.

'Okay.' A one-word response with no emotion. Can't think of anything else to say. Hearing a lot of names he only vaguely recognizes. Being told to do things he knows he won't do.

'I looked up your number, called you personally. That's because I want you to come and do a few jobs for me. What do you say to that?'

Peterkinney's shrugging. 'Depends on the work. Depends on the reward.'

Marty's smiling. 'Listen, kid. I called you up. I know where you live. I know you live with your grandfather, for fuck's sake. I know those flats. Small spaces, ain't they? You don't want to be there forever, do you? I know you probably had to take the fucking bus to get here. Riding along with the plebs. You enjoy that? There's good money in what I do. For a guy your age, life-changing money. I think you're the sort of person who can help me with it. I think you can handle it. I'm giving you the chance to move up in the world here, kiddo. Don't throw that back in my face. You might not get another chance.'

Said it like he was offering him the world. Sitting in the shittiest little office Peterkinney's ever seen in his life, and Marty thinks he can sound impressive. But it's not about the surroundings, they both know that. It's about the rewards.

'If the money's right, and if there's work for Alex too.'

'Your wee mate? I can find some work for him. Won't be much. You'll be getting the better stuff. I think you're cut out for the good stuff. Kind of things I have to be careful about. Takes brain, as well as brawn. And there will be real money. Money, parties, women. All of it. Think about that, huh. Last night? That was bullshit. I throw better parties than that every fucking week. You could be in that life.'

'Fine,' Peterkinney's saying with a reluctant nod. 'I'll do a few jobs for you, see how it goes. Can't promise anything, but we'll play it by ear. You know how to get in touch with me, obviously.'

'Excellent,' Marty's saying. Getting up and shaking him by the hand. As Peterkinney's walking out of the office, Marty's wondering how the hell that just happened. It was like he had to twist the kid's arm. In the end, it was like the kid was doing him a favour. Wrong way round, that was. Bloody hell. Got to keep an eye on this kid.

Peterkinney's out the front door and looking at his watch. Plenty of time to get across to the address his grandfather gave him. Could have two jobs by the end of the day. Two jobs, real money. This could be the start of a little something. A flat of his own. Lounging in the living room, watching the TV he wants to watch. Taking his time in the bathroom, because there's nobody grumbling outside the door waiting to get in. Privacy. Peace. A leap towards the life he craves. Now he's smiling.

PART TWO

1

Peterkinney knows the routine by now. He's done this four times in the last two and a half months. First time he did a job for Roy Bowles it was nerve-racking. Creeping around, terrified of being caught with a gun on you. Convinced that everyone knew what you were carrying as you returned the gun from the supplier. Not any more. You relax, when you know what's going to happen. You understand the routine. You understand how little the rest of the world cares about what you're carrying.

Bowles called him this morning, told him to get round to the house. That's much easier done now. He's got himself a little car. Doesn't have a licence, but he has a car. Cost him four hundred quid. Little blue Peugeot. Peterkinney should get along with it, because they're not far off being the same age. Mostly held together by bloody-mindedness, but it's faster than walking, just about. And he'll get that licence when he has time. No, really, he will. Next thing is a flat of his own. Gathering savings to pay for the essentials he'll need for that. Then a driving licence. It's all planned, and the plans are getting bigger.

He's been a busy boy, these last couple of months. Used

to have no job at all. Now he has two. And people say the economy's circling the drain. Marty keeps him busy. That's dirty work. Doing shitty collection jobs. Doing them well, but not enjoying it. Gets reasonable money, but smarty Marty's always trying to screw you. Always trying to persuade you to take anything other than money. Take some girls. Take some drugs. Take anything other than the money you earned. Marty understands the value of cash, understands that nothing matters more. That's why he hangs on to every damn penny. Peterkinney understands the value of paper money too. Always insists on cash. That's why he and Marty don't always get along.

Bowles is different. He has a different sort of business, a different way of handling it. Give your people the money they earn, keep your head down and your mouth shut. His is a business of silence. In many ways, he's the anti-Marty. Doesn't make him a good person, mind you. Don't make that mistake. Does make him dependable. Right now, dependable is attractive. Every job is well paid. Usually about a hundred and fifty quid for a couple of hours of easy work. The money reflects the risk, and buys silence.

Pulling up along the street from the house. Taking precautions, because that's what common sense tells him to do. Look around, play it careful. Not a lot of people know what Bowles does. He's smart and careful. But some people know. That makes working for him a risk. The police could find out.

They follow you on a job, pick you up after you've collected the gun. Automatic jail term. Years inside. You don't want your name connected with him.

Through the side gate and round to the back garden. Glancing across at the little wooden shed, wondering if there's a gun in there. That's where they're returned, when people are finished with them and don't want to keep them. See, most people, most professionals, only want a gun for a short time. Then, after using it the one time they want it, they're stuck with something incriminating. Why chuck it in the river and lose all your investment? It still has value, just not to the person who's used it. Take it back to Bowles, dropped inside the loose panel on the side of the shed. A few days later, you'll get some of your money back. Not all of it. Bowles still has to make a living. No charity in this industry, you'll find. But it becomes a rental fee, rather than a purchase. If you don't return the gun, Bowles keeps all the money.

Knocking on the back door and waiting. You do not go into his house without permission. You do not go into his shed at all. You do not ever deal with the people he sells to. You do not recommend him to anyone. You do not mention that you've ever even heard of the man. Keeping your gob shut is the key to being a good employee. He finds his own clients, develops relationships with them over time. Any verbal element to a job belongs solely to Bowles.

Door's opening. Bowles looking back at him, nodding for him to come in. This is all familiar. First time Bowles called Peterkinney to come and do a job for him, Peterkinney thought it was going to happen there and then. That's how it works with Marty. Marty calls you up. Tells you what he wants done. You go and do it straight away. Not Bowles. Bowles always gives him at least a day's warning, sometimes more. Different business, different set of rules. No set of rules is right or wrong. Frankly, Peterkinney thinks they could each learn something from the other.

They're into the living room, sitting in familiar seats. Bowles always does it the same way. Every single time, no matter the job. Continuity.

'There's a pick-up tomorrow,' Bowles is saying. Always speaks slowly. Always feels like he thinks you're an idiot, the way he talks to you. Just his way. Keeps everything slow and simple, making sure there's never a misunderstanding. Those are very dangerous. More dangerous than talking down to a tough guy. Besides, if he thought Peterkinney was stupid he wouldn't have him working for him. 'New fellow, a little twitchy. I'm not convinced by him, but he has good connections. I'm sure he can deliver the piece, but I worry. I want you to be cautious.'

'Anything specific?'

'No,' Bowles is saying, shaking his head. 'Just a feeling I got from him. I spoke to him on the telephone. He was unconvincing. Granted, as I said, he has the connections. He can get his hands on the piece. I have no doubt of that. He just didn't sound reliable. I don't like people who aren't reliable.'

Peterkinney's nodding. 'Where's the meet?'

'Tomorrow at two. I have an address. It's not residential. This is another problem I have with it. It's an old garage, terribly rough area. Industrial, no housing. I suspect he wants to meet you outside.'

'In the open?'

'That's what he suggested. Said he'd be waiting outside. I doubt this fellow has a key to get in. He's down on his luck, as they say. As though luck is the reason he's down. Desperate for the money, so I don't doubt he'll be there.'

Bowles researches people. Checks up on anyone he's going to buy from. Makes sure that they meet his definition of reliable. Not like him to even consider someone he doesn't fully trust. Having a piece to sell isn't enough to persuade a man like Bowles. All those years avoiding detection, he won't take a risk now. Yet this guy doesn't sound reliable at all. Must have very good contacts. Probably ex-military. A lot of them are. Or maybe someone with connections across the water in Northern Ireland. He's obviously convinced Bowles that he can deliver something worthwhile.

Bowles has gotten up to go and get the money, which means he has no intention of going into any further detail. If

Peterkinney wants to work out why this guy's unreliable, then it's up to him to do so. Bowles wouldn't tell him just because of a feeling, though. That's not him. Feelings intrude very rarely. He must know something that leaves him so worried. Keeping it to himself, for now.

Back in with the cash. A thick wad of used notes in a small white envelope. Passing it carefully, almost respectfully, to Peterkinney. Watching Peterkinney slip it into the inside pocket of his coat. Always have a pocket with a zip when you come visit Bowles for a job. He's going to give you money, and he's going to demand that the money be put in a pocket with a zip. Demanded it on the first visit, made it clear that he expected Peterkinney to remember that demand.

'His name's Howard Lawson. Apparently everyone calls him Howie. He's forty, skinny fellow, rather scraggly. Well, he should be the only one there, so you shouldn't have trouble picking him out.' A pause, thinking. 'Any sign of trouble, get out of there, Oliver. If he's not alone, leave, immediately. I specifically told him to be alone. He swore he would be. If you hear or see anything untoward, leave immediately. And of course, my name never comes up.'

That's always the cue to leave. The reminder that his name never makes it into a conversation, even with the person you're getting the gun from. It's always the last words he wants in your ears when he sends you out the door.

But the words that came before are what Peterkinney

remembers. Warning. But also, trusting. Trusting Peterkinney to make his own judgement on the deal. If he sees anything untoward, he must walk away. Up to him to decide what constitutes untoward. Not just Bowles playing careful, although he always does that. It's also a sign of trust. He considers Peterkinney smart enough to handle this job, to make this judgement.

Peterkinney's in his car. He'll go back to the flat first, stash the money. Would be nice to find out a little more about this Howie Lawson before he does the job tomorrow. No chance. Peterkinney doesn't know enough people in the business that he could ask. Not yet. Only been involved for a couple of months, mind you. He's learning fast and learning well. He has a few contacts of his own already, and he's picking up more as he goes along. He has the intelligence, and he has the attitude.

Would be nice to hang out with Glass for a while, but what's the point? He'll be with little Ella Fowler. Always with Ella these days. Living the life, is what Alex calls it. She practically lives with him now. Going out to parties all the time. She works a lot of parties. Glass goes along and has fun, apparently. Peterkinney still hasn't gotten his head round that. She's a very sweet girl, in a girly sort of a way. But she does get on his fucking nerves. All sweetness and light, giggles and mumbles. Glass has fallen for her big time. Fair enough, she's pretty, and she's obviously into him. Or some idea of him. A hooker and a jobless thug, trying to play happy families. Trying to pretend that they've got something unique going on. That's what gets on Peterkinney's nerves. They can't see how hard you have to work to get anything good in this business. He sees it. He's doing it.

Fine. Let her take Glass to her parties. Let them get hammered every night. Let them wallow in their childish idea of a loving relationship. Whatever keeps them happy. Not like he doesn't have other things to be getting along with now. Marty's given Glass a few jobs, but it's real garbage stuff, and it's only now and again. He always has something for Peterkinney, as long as Peterkinney's willing. Today, he is.

2

Last night was a good night. Lots of drink. Some coke that was given out free. Got home about two. Ella got back around six. Glass doesn't know where she went. Hasn't asked. Won't ask. She makes more money than he does. She seems to like it. She seems happy with her life. He isn't going to do anything to rock that boat. Why would he? This is what he wanted. What he always thought was the perfect life. Parties most nights. Drinking every night. Out with his girl. A pretty girl. A girl who loves him back. That's what it's all about.

Been like this for a couple of months. Honestly, he's pretty exhausted. And it ain't cheap. All the drink, all the drugs. That costs money. Sure, some parties have freebies. The big parties. Most don't. It's an expensive life. Money he doesn't have, going up his nose or down the toilet. Wouldn't be a problem if he could get more work from Marty. Marty isn't helping him out as much as he should.

This is another thing that pisses him off. Why is Marty giving Peterkinney all the work, and hardly any to Glass? That doesn't make sense. It was Glass that set up the job on Holmes. It was Glass who led the job. They did a good job. Must have, because Marty's using them both still. But he uses

Peterkinney all the time. Glass hardly at all. Occasional jobs that don't pay much. Not much use. Just doesn't seem fair.

He'd mention it to Peterkinney, if he ever saw Peterkinney. Hardly ever comes round these days. Seems like he's working hard to keep his distance. Obviously doesn't like Ella. Or doesn't like the fact that Glass has a girl and he doesn't. Or maybe just doesn't like the life that Glass and Ella are living now. A couple. A proper relationship. Hard to tell what his problem is. Probably because he doesn't like Ella, which is another thing to piss him off. Peterkinney could always be a bit snobby. Not much to be snobby about, but that's the way he was. Looking down his nose at people like Ella.

Ella's out of the bathroom now. Slept until afternoon. Hasn't spoken to her since some time last night. Can't remember anything they said since before they left the flat last night. There are a lot of episodes like that in his life now. Vague conversations. Lost evenings. Failed memories. Still, as long as she's a part of it, this is what he wants.

'Morning. How you feeling?' he's asking. He knows how to work the tone now. Took him a little time to realize that what you say is less important than how you say it. With Ella, anyway. Say it with a smile, a little charm. Don't let it sound anywhere close to an accusation. No judgement allowed.

'Little tired. Little sore,' she's saying with a weary smile.

She has a small cut on the top of her shoulder. He saw that when he was getting up in the morning. Wasn't there last night. He won't mention it. It's happened a few times. She's arrived home hours after him. She's had a bruise or a cut or something like that. And he says nothing because she doesn't want to talk about it. Upsets her to talk. It's a separate part of her life, she said the first time. Work and home, they stay apart. One doesn't talk to the other. So he doesn't mention these things, because they're work and he's home.

'Got anything on today?' he's asking. Trying to make it sound hopeful, like he wants to spend time with her. That'll keep her happy.

'I got to go see someone,' she's saying. 'But I'm not doing anything tonight. We should go out. I know a guy who can get us in at Fourteen. You been there before? It's a great club. Real classy. We should go.'

How does he say no? They've been together a couple of months. Long enough for him to know that she's out of his league. Long enough to know that he has to work very hard to keep a hold of her. You don't say no. That's the first rule. He's worked that one out for himself. No trial and error required. He knows. He has to say yes.

'Sure, that sounds great. I haven't been.'

'Oh, you'll love it,' she's saying. All casual and happy now. Her chirpy, flirty self. Going across to the fridge to see if there's anything that could pretend to be breakfast in there. 'I've been there a couple of times before. Great parties. But even without a party, it's a great night.'

'Sure. Great.' He's nodding. Happy to make her happy. Working hard to make this work. Oblivious to the fact that what she loves most about him is the chance of normality. The chance of a proper relationship and regular life. The parties, the nights out, they're just what she's used to. Part of the routine.

Thinking about the cost. Fourteen is a swanky kind of place. An expensive kind of a place. If it was just him, he would never have thought of it. Not his kind of hangout. Not the sort of club him and Peterkinney used to hit for a night out. Ella can only know it through her work. It's the sort of place those sorts of men go. The kind of men who can show her luxury Glass can't afford.

While she's making her breakfast at lunchtime, he's thinking about Marty. Needs to get in touch with him. Call him up, see if there's anything to do. Must be, surely. Could do with a little extra money. Actually, scratch the word 'extra'. He needs money. Right now his wallet contains a video rental card he hasn't used in two years. That's it.

He's left her to it, walking through to the living room. She likes to be alone when she's making food. A little bit obsessive about it. Started baking as well, the other afternoon. Made a banana loaf. It was okay. She loves that, cooking and baking. Likes to drag him round the supermarket, picking out ingredients.

He has a number for Marty, but Marty's fussy about

answering. He made it very clear that he doesn't want to be called all the time. Doesn't want every little nobody calling him every time they're short of cash. Well, Glass has been careful. He's only called once before, and Marty didn't seem to mind. So he's got his phone in his hand and he's tapping on Marty's name. Holding it up to his ear and worrying that he's pushing his luck. But he isn't. Truth is, Marty loves it when people call him up. Loves it because he gets to feel important. Tell people that he has work for them. Or tell them that he doesn't, and listen to them deflate.

'Hi, Marty, it's Alex Glass. Is now a good time to talk? Good, cool. Listen, do you have any work needs doing? I'm happy to do whatever, you know, anything at all.' Now he's standing there and he's listening. You wouldn't need to hear what Marty's saying to know that it isn't good news. You can read the expression on Glass's face. 'Okay. Yeah, that's fine. You know, whenever you need any work, I'll be around. You know I . . . Sure, I'll let you go. Bye, Marty.'

He's dropped his phone onto the couch and he's standing in the middle of the room. He can hear Ella moving around in the kitchen. She expects to go out to Fourteen. She wants to be there, and if he can't take her, someone else will. He can see how tenuous this is. He needs to keep impressing her. So he'll get the money. Hook or crook, he'll get it.

Ella's out of the kitchen with a poor excuse for a sandwich in one hand and a mug in the other. Not much effort went into that, but she's tired. Dropping into the chair that happens to have the TV remote on the arm of it. Looking up at Glass and smiling. He's standing there in the middle of the room, for no obvious reason. He smiles back and nods.

'Just going to head out for a wee while. Bit of work, maybe,' he's saying.

She looks disappointed. Always does when he does anything to compromise the domestic bliss. She hoped they'd have an hour together before she went to work. It's always nice to spend time with Glass. He's always nice. Always considerate. Always different from all the others.

'Right, sure. I'll be away in an hour. So, I don't know, I'll see you later.'

'Yeah,' he's smiling, and leaning down for a kiss. She likes that. Proper couples kiss goodbye.

He's getting his coat and his phone and he's out of the flat. Got to think about this. Think, man. Think of an alternative. There isn't one. He knows what he has to do; something he doesn't want to do. Got to make sure he gets this just right. Make the wrong judgement here and he's under the thumb for years.

3

You can make all the plans you want. Doesn't matter. Not a damn bit. Potty spent the thick end of two months trying to come up with a clever way of getting to Patterson. All through those two months, Patterson was growing and growing. Getting stronger, taking more clients away from him. All the time, Potty stewed. Trying to come up with some ingenious route to the heart of Patterson's business. Trying to find a weak spot and the silver bullet to exploit it. Two months wasted.

Then it fell right into his fat lap. Straight out of nowhere. A rumour that one of his muscle heard and passed on to him. Muscle didn't even know that it might be important. Dickhead. Even muscle should have the basic sense to keep their ear to the ground. To know what matters and what doesn't. Hardly brain surgery, is it? But some people . . .

Potty would have found out eventually. Everyone found out eventually. Not the sort of thing that could be hidden. Jamie Stamford ends up in hospital and the city gets to hear about it. Now, Stamford was the first one to try and cover the whole thing up. Didn't reflect well on him. Premier muscle, beaten to a pulp. But details leak out. People find out. They have to, otherwise the message Patterson was sending isn't heard. It was in Patterson's interest to make sure the story got out. But that was always going to piss important people off. Impressed some important people, no doubt, but pissed a whole bunch of other ones off.

So Patterson had sent one of his boys to smash up Stamford. Punishment for not paying a debt Patterson had bought. Potty was offered that debt. Turned away the two bookies that had come together to try and sell it. No way Potty was going looking for trouble with Alex MacArthur. Everyone knows MacArthur likes Stamford. One of the muscle he keeps close. He trusts. So you ignore his many debts.

Patterson made the mistake of buying it. Of thinking he could act without consequence. All men are equal, and all that. Nope. Not true. You don't treat everyone the same. You're never in your own little bubble. People won't accept your behaviour just because you're right. Being right means very little in this business.

Potty knew all that when he made the phone call to Alex MacArthur. He knew MacArthur would talk to him. The Cruickshank name still carries a lot of weight in this city. In the right circles, at least. And MacArthur is the master of his circle. Just about the biggest criminal network in the city. One of the big three. Not a man a little shit like Billy Patterson should be picking a fight with. Potty chatted to MacArthur. Mentioned Patterson's name just the once. Casual, in passing. The mention of a mutual problem. That got him an invite to one of MacArthur's offices.

A good office. You can tell a lot about what he thinks of you by the office you meet him in. He has a lot to choose from. Clubs and pubs, shops and companies. You name it, he's either got it or got access to it. He's been in the business so long. A fixture. One of those people you don't want to see leave. Not that anyone really likes him. Rasping, chain-smoking old egomaniac. But what replaces him? He's one of the few big old sharks that know how to keep order. If that goes, you don't know what'll step in to fill the gap he leaves. Nothing deserves greater fear than the unknown. Stick with this old devil, he's familiar.

Potty's being driven to the office block where the meeting will take place. Have a driver, have an expensive car. Make sure MacArthur can see that the Cruickshanks are still in the money business. The office block is nothing special to look at, but it contains the heart of MacArthur's operation. His office on the top floor is one of his favourite offices. Probably makes him feel legitimate. Potty knows that a meeting here is a sign of respect. It's MacArthur acknowledging that Potty is a man worthy of respect. Two big beasts of the old guard, meeting on equal terms. Up in the lift, and being shown through to the office straight away by a young secretary. More respect. It's a good start to the meeting.

'Ronald, good to see you,' MacArthur's saying. Standing

up from behind the desk in the office. There's always a desk for the boss to sit behind. Doesn't matter if he needs it. Doesn't matter if he never uses it. Sitting behind it makes him feel important. Makes him feel like he's in charge, the rest of the room facing him. Potty understands that. Does it himself. He does appreciate that they've put a large cushioned chair in front of the desk for him. Making an effort. MacArthur's domain, but Potty's welcome.

'Alex. How are you keeping, sir?'

'I'm a decrepit old bastard, Ronald. Can't say more than that.' Said with a smile, but nobody's going to argue with the truth of it. That smile is sad and knowing, not funny. Been rumours about his health recently. Smoking God knows how many a day will do that.

As will eating too much, Potty is thinking to himself. MacArthur's a skinny little fellow. Always looked weak, now looking frail. A little wisp of a man, aware that he's survived all the dangers just long enough to kill himself with his own lifestyle. Something Potty's doing, just at a faster rate. Should have taken up smoking instead of eating.

Ray Buller is in the room too, but he's sitting off behind them at a small table. Buller has been one of MacArthur's senior men for decades. If MacArthur's age and health are worrying, Buller won't make you feel any better. At sixty-four, he's two years older than MacArthur. His health is better, sure, but better is relative. Better doesn't mean healthy. He's not a replacement. That's probably why MacArthur keeps him so close. Nobody wants the man standing next to them to be eyeing up their seat.

It's quite the office. Paintings on the walls, furniture designed to look expensive. Good views, if you want to spend your time looking out the window. Even got a TV up in the corner of the room. Supposed to give a more casual feel to the place. A thin computer monitor and keyboard on the desk, no sign of the hard drive. No filing cabinets or stacks of paper, that would cheapen the place. This is an office in which you reflect on your success. There are other, more functional, offices where you go to earn the money to pay for this.

'I hope I'm not intruding with this wee problem I have,' Potty's saying. Careful to call it his problem, not theirs. You never imply that MacArthur has a problem, not unless he brings it up. Not some bullshit 'you must respect the boss' routine. Just good manners. Uncle Rolly always stressed the value of good manners around the wealthy and respectable.

'Never an intrusion. I've been interested in this Patterson kid for a while. Little shit's been running round without anyone slowing him down. Thinking he has the run of the place.' And that's as much of a mention as Jamie Stamford will get. MacArthur likes the boy. He's not going to embarrass him by discussing this in front of an outsider. Potty knows, and MacArthur knows. That'll do for detail.

'Well, I've been looking to do something about him for

months,' Potty is saying with a shrug. Trying to sound casual, but he knows he's leaving himself open to criticism here. 'Haven't had a chance. The lad has some mean bastards around him. Toughest crew I've seen coming up in a long time. He's been careful putting it together. I intend to do something about him, but I think it will take some support to wipe him out.'

MacArthur's nodding. He likes that Potty is talking about wiping this boy out. Not holding him down or setting him back. Getting rid. Clean out the filth; don't just shove it out of the way. Never mind that Stamford's always been a good boy. Never mind the personal insult delivered. The real issue is that people know Patterson had one of MacArthur's men put in hospital. Gave him a real kicking. MacArthur has to be seen to do something about it. If he lets this pass, everyone thinks they can get away with it. Come up with some flimsy excuse and start kicking lumps out of people working for him. Be seen to be weak once, and vultures will circle. Besides, whose fault is all this? Not Stamford's, that's for damn sure. It's the bookies' fault. If you have a guy with big debts, you refuse to let him keep gambling. Common sense. If they were too scared to refuse Stamford, whose fault is that? Theirs again, you'll find. MacArthur won't pay a price for another man's cowardice.

'What's the plan?' MacArthur's asking.

'Well, he has a group of guys around him that are tough.

Take them away and there's nothing left. I want to pick off the most important ones. Not all of them need to be attacked. One or two will be bought. If I'm sure of anything, I'm sure that there are always one or two that can be bought.'

MacArthur's smiling. Here's a man that shares his vision of the business, his understanding. Buy the people you can. Remove the ones you can't. There have been so many times in the past when that strategy has worked. Almost none when it hasn't. You just have to pick the right targets for each option. The key is making sure you don't miss anyone out. Either buy or remove them all.

'I want to start working on them right away. Pick away at it until he's good and exposed. Then I can get rid of him,' Potty's saying.

'You know I'd be more than happy to help you with that, Ronald. All the manpower you need.'

That's what Potty came here to hear. This was never about funding. Potty will have to pay for anything that costs money. But manpower is another matter. MacArthur has far more of that than Potty. He has people better equipped to do the kind of work that needs to be done. This is a union. An agreement that they will now work together to destroy Billy Patterson.

Potty is smiling by the time he gets back into his car. The rest of the conversation with MacArthur was small talk. Bull-shit. Two men of experience, chewing the cud. Remembering a few old stories about the good old days. This is a good day too. This is a day when he can start to stamp on Billy Patterson. Reinforce his position at the top of the collecting tree. A sloppy mistake. Thinking that they could target Stamford like that. Real sloppy. The kind of mistake that costs you your business.

4

They haven't had a happy conversation since the Stamford incident. Patterson thinks Bavidge went too far. He's right, of course. Bavidge knows it. He wasn't going to go that far. Stamford was actually trying. He was failing, but he was trying. He hadn't gone running to MacArthur this time. He was trying to put some money together. Working hard to solve his own problem. Trying to pay the debt, or at least some of it.

But Stamford's an addict. Can't stop gambling. He called Bavidge up, told him he had seven grand to put towards the debt. Bavidge was positive. Made it clear he still wanted the other thirteen, but seven was a decent start. Tried to sound encouraging. Said they would meet the following day. A handover. They met. Stamford had three grand. He'd gone gambling with the seven he'd accumulated. Thought he could double it, maybe more. Thought he could cover the twenty grand with a bit of luck. Lost four. Bavidge called him on it, told him what a moron he was. The meeting turned brutal. Two nasty men and a poisonous atmosphere made for an inevitable conclusion. Stamford learned how nasty Bavidge is capable of being.

Stupid thing is, if Stamford had called and said he had three grand, Bavidge would have settled for that. He doesn't expect a moron like Stamford to come up with every penny in one go. He should be getting it faster than he is, but he was trying. That was as much as Bavidge ever expected. It was the sheer stupidity of it. Throwing good money down the hole that sucked your wallet dry last time. That's what made him lose his temper.

He's into the little poker room, Patterson sitting at the table. Bavidge sitting opposite him. These have been awkward conversations lately. Patterson trying not to imply that Bavidge has gotten them into a shitload of trouble, when they both know he has.

'We've got a problem,' Patterson's saying as an opener.

Bavidge is grimacing, because he thinks this is going to be about Stamford. Patterson's smiling a little in response to the grimace. This isn't about Bavidge's mistake. This is about Patterson's.

'Jim Holmes,' he's saying. Sitting back and waiting for the reaction.

'Already?' Bavidge is leaning back in his chair. Not going to make any more of an issue of it than that. The boss makes a mistake, you don't rub his nose in it. Even if you saw the mistake coming. Besides, Patterson's been determinedly gentle with him over the Stamford beating. He's earned the right to the occasional mistake of his own.

'Already. Spent last night going through a few figures. He's been skimming a few per cent for a few weeks. In the last two weeks he's gone from about 5 per cent to around 20. He must know I'm going to spot it.'

'Does he have protection?' Meaning has he already organized to go work for someone else? Is this sabotage rather than stupidity?

'None that I've been able to spot. If he's gone to someone, then he's keeping quiet about it.'

'Doubt it,' Bavidge is saying quietly. 'Who would take the bastard?'

'Exactly. Which makes me think he might be about to do a runner. I don't think working for me has turned out to be everything he thought it would. Thought he could come here and be some big shot. I haven't let him have any important jobs. Gutter work. I think he might be ready to bolt. I mean, he ain't going to jump to skimming 20 per cent of my money without me knowing. Even he has to see that. He must have a foot out the door already.'

Bavidge is nodding. This is something that has to be done fast. 'Can we get the money back?'

'If it's in the house, great,' Patterson's saying with a shrug. 'Doesn't matter too much. He was taking 20 per cent of small jobs. Only took about a grand and a half. I'm not going to turn the city upside down looking for it. But I want a message sent. A real message.'

Patterson's messages are dark. Even by the standards of the inky-black collection industry. Might just be the most brutal part of the criminal industry, and he might just be the most brutal person in it. The most brutal person of influence, anyway. There are plenty of dickheads setting up shitty little operations, going too far and being shut down inside a few months. They don't count. Short term. Of the people that count, Patterson goes closest to the edge with his punishments. Bavidge is his favoured means of delivering those messages.

'It'll need to be done tonight,' Bavidge is saying. Then grimacing.

'Something wrong?'

'I have a date tonight. Shit, forgot about her.'

'Serious?' Asked with a hint of hope in Patterson's voice.

'Nah,' Bavidge is saying, shaking his head. 'Not really. She's shacked up with some driver for Peter Jamieson. Nice, though.'

Patterson's nodding. It's good that Bavidge has someone in his life, but it doesn't seem to be cheering him up much. Never does. He only ever goes in for relationships that he knows won't work. Never wants something that might matter to him. Depressing is what it is. Making his own life more miserable than it needs to be. He's never going to stop being a man to worry about.

Time might come, Patterson's thinking, when he'll need to interfere. Get involved in his friend's private affairs. If this girl is worth the effort, he might just have a word with the driver. After all, couldn't be hard to chase a driver away. Nah, works for Jamieson. Fine, set Bavidge up with someone else. Someone that can settle him down, make him happy. Not sure that's possible.

'Can you let her down gently?'

Bavidge is shrugging. 'I can let her down. I think she's getting used to it. I'll get this done tonight, before he has a chance to get out. I'll make sure it's very clear. He still at the same address?'

'He is.'

'Okay. Anything else?'

'No, that's it.'

A brief shake of the hand, and Patterson's watching Bavidge leave. He will do something about him. Has to. Wouldn't be much of a friend if he didn't. He needs to get away from his work. Patterson won't sack him. Too good to be sacked. Force him to take a holiday. That might be a start. Probably wouldn't work. A holiday wouldn't be enough to make him happy-go-lucky. Often thought about having a conversation about him, but how weird would that be? You don't sit down with a guy like Alan Bavidge and talk about feelings. Talk about the fact that he seems to be a bit depressed. If he doesn't laugh in your face, he'd punch you in it. He'd be right to, as well. If someone started that conversation with Patterson, it would be a short conversation.

5

Treading carefully, because he doesn't know this guy. Heard about him, never met him. Glass found out where his little office was, dropped by. Seems like a decent enough guy. They all do though, don't they. They want you to borrow money from them. They're selling, not you. There are plenty of people you can borrow money from, so they all have to be nice until they have their claws into you. That's when the reassuring smile fades.

Jefferson's looking across the desk at him. Another man trying to feel big behind his desk. Or trying to make the other person feel small. That might be it. Trying to make Glass feel that he's dealing with someone so much bigger than himself. Impress him. Make him more agreeable to the terms he's about to be offered.

But it's not the office that makes people feel small. The office isn't capable. Basic, would be the word. Small room, small desk. Everything a little scuffed and worn. Stacks of paper, an old computer monitor on the side of the desk. Gloomy, too. There's a window, but the dirty glass seems to be more than the sunlight can cope with.

Jefferson isn't intimidating either. But then, we've

already established that he's not trying to be. A man in his early forties, casually dressed. Smiling at Glass and treating him with exaggerated respect. He's not intimidating, but he knows what is. He knows that there's nothing so terrifying as money. Being without it is scary. Trying to find ways of acquiring it is demoralizing. And Jefferson has it. Sitting there behind his cheap desk, in his unimpressive office. He has what they want, and that intimidates them all.

'I really don't need much,' Glass is saying. He's been trying for nonchalant since he got here. Like this whole thing is all rather beneath him. Just because you haven't done it before, doesn't make it beneath you. 'Don't need it for long either. A few days.'

'You sound like the perfect customer,' Jefferson's smiling. Jocular, false. Doesn't mean it. The perfect customer is one who can't pay back in the short term. Then you get them long term. Build up the debt. But you say the right thing. Let them think this is only going to last days. 'How much are you looking for, Alex?' First names. Always first names. Try and make it sound like you're already their mate.

'Five hundred,' Glass is saying with a shrug. Still going for nonchalant. It comes across as a little bit dumb this time. You should know with certainty how much you need to borrow. If you've arrived at a point in your life where you need to use someone like Jefferson then you should know exactly.

'Five hundred then,' Jefferson's nodding. 'How long will you need to pay it back?'

This time the shrug is genuinely uncertain. Glass is trying to work out how long he can ask for. How long it would take him to come up with that kind of money. How long would it normally take to put together five hundred quid? Not long if you're Peterkinney. Much longer if you're Glass.

'A month. Maybe two.' Did he make five hundred quid in the last month? Just about. Five hundred with the interest rate he'll pay here? Nope, not quite.

Jefferson's looking at him with raised eyebrows. 'Shall we split it and call it six weeks?'

'Yeah, yeah, six weeks.'

'Do you have a job? A source of income, so that I can be sure you'll be able to repay?'

'Oh yeah, I have a job,' Glass is saying. Confident this time. He does have a job. A sort of job. He's thinking about his work for Marty. Occasional, and becoming more occasional as time passes. The more he thinks about it, the less of a job it feels. 'It's not always reliable, you know. Sometimes loads of work, sometimes hardly any. That's why I've been caught short.'

Jefferson's nodding. 'Sure. Not a problem. Cash flow, I understand. Just reassuring to know you have a source of income. I'm not prying.' Always so reasonable. 'Now the interest rate may seem rather high,' he's saying. Try to work out how smart the person borrowing is. If they're sharp, they know your rates are a fucking disgrace to decency. They will hate you for charging such an amount and they will become difficult. They'll justify their failure to repay because of it. If they're not too bright, you can convince them it's the best deal they'll ever get. They'll take it, be thankful and make every effort to repay. This boy's been around. Might not be too clever, but knows enough about the business to know he's not getting a great deal. 'It's about as good as you'll get from someone like me. And you have to remember, the 6,000 per cent is annual. You don't need to worry about annual. You're only borrowing for six weeks.'

Glass is nodding. He knows he'll get screwed on the deal. He knows he'll end up paying back more than he should. Or working it off somehow. But that's six weeks away. This is now, and now is Ella. Now is a night out at her favourite club. Now is proving to her that he can give her what she wants.

She'll be out of the flat by now. Off with some guy, probably. Getting her own money. She always manages to get some. She's always very careful to make sure that she doesn't mention clients. That she doesn't let him hear anything that would upset him. But she goes to these parties and he knows what happens there. And some afternoons she goes out. Doesn't say where she's going. Comes back with money. He knows.

Jefferson's unlocking a drawer in his desk. Taking out a

small wad of cash. Counting off fifties. As he peels them from the wad, Glass is thinking about Ella. Thinking about that first morning. The first morning, when Peterkinney was there. Never saw his girl again. The silent one. Ella knows her, but Peterkinney had no interest in seeing her again. He called Ella a prostitute. Glass argued. Said she was just a girl who went to parties. Worked them. No big deal. Not the same as being a hooker. He still tries to believe that.

Jefferson's sliding the cash across the desk. 'I want you to sign this contract,' Jefferson's saying. Contract means almost nothing. A piece of paper with no legal weight whatsoever. But it gets Glass's signature in Jefferson's office. Makes it feel official, which adds to the intimidation factor. Means Glass can't deny that he borrowed money from Jefferson. But that amounts to very little as well. If this comes to an argument, it's unlikely it'll be settled by the presence of that signature. They both know what happens if you refuse to pay. It's not the sort of thing a contract has any role in.

Glass is signing. Not reading it, just signing. The money's on the desk in front of him. He wants it in his pocket. He wants to get out of this office. Phone Ella. Tell her he has plenty of money for the both of them. Maybe she hasn't left the flat yet.

Jefferson's taking the piece of paper back, slipping it into the drawer. 'It's been good doing business with you, Alex. I hope the money serves you well. I'll put you down in the book. Let's say six weeks from today as the deadline. If you have the money for me before then, obviously, drop in. Sooner the better,' he's saying with a smile, and reaching out a hand. Sooner the better is bullshit. Alex knows that. They both know that. Sooner is the worst option. Keep the money, build up the debt. The longer it builds, the more the lender benefits. He can't lose.

They're both thinking the same thing as they shake hands. If this debt isn't repaid inside a week or two, it's going to become a millstone. Jefferson knows it and he likes it. He's not like a bookie. If a bookie lets you run a tab you can't pay back, the bookie loses that value. They need that value back, every penny. That's their legit profit. With a moneylender it's different. Your final debt is guaranteed to be a lot higher than your initial borrow. The lender can sell the debt to a collector, and as long as he gets more than his original outlay back, he's up on the deal. A five-hundred-pound lend becomes a three-grand debt. He sells the debt to a collector for a grand and a half. Triples his money without doing a damn thing. And he'll usually sell for more than 50 per cent.

Glass is thinking about that as he walks out of the little office. He needs this money for tonight. Try and spend as little of it as possible. If he can keep a hold of some of it, get a few jobs from Marty in quick succession. It could happen. He could have enough to pay it off inside three or four weeks. He'll have to pay three or four times what he borrowed.

When was the last time he made two grand in a month? Never has.

Getting his phone out of his pocket. Scrolling to Ella's name and tapping to dial. One hand holding the phone, the other holding the notes in his pocket. Come on, where are you? Pick up. Through to voicemail. Shit. Hide your disappointment.

'Ella, it's Alex. Listen, I just came into a bit of money. Got enough for a good night out. Couple of good nights out, you know. So, yeah, I thought I'd let you know. Give me a call, whatever. See you later.'

Hanging up, dialling again. Through to voicemail again. Hanging up. Phone's back in his pocket. Walking along the street, instinctively heading home. Ella will be gone. Peterkinney. He might be around. Phone out of his pocket. Trying Peterkinney's number. This person's phone is switched off. Shit. Might be a good idea to spend some time with Peterkinney in the next few weeks. Money seems to be gravitating towards him.

6

Getting dark. Good. That's what Peterkinney's been waiting for. Marty had a job for him. Go find Gordon Aird. He owes eight hundred quid. Tell him he owes a grand and knock him around a bit until he pays. Aird borrowed a couple of hundred, and has zero chance of even paying that back. Aird is a user. He borrows money, injects it, borrows from another lender to pay off the first debt. Always going round in one big depressing circle. Not even trying to solve his problem.

Marty doesn't expect any money to come back to him. He didn't say that to Peterkinney; you always cross your fingers and hope. But a couple of months is enough time for Peterkinney to know how this works. Marty likes to use people like Aird. If they can pay up then that's great. But people like Aird rarely can. And a guy like Marty knows that when he takes the debt. Aird is such a mess; he'll do whatever's asked of him to get through another day. All about survival. Marty likes that. He can use that. But first you have to soften them up. Make sure they know you're serious. That's where Peterkinney comes in.

Marty hasn't told Peterkinney that he's his best muscle these days. Peterkinney worked that out for himself. Being given increasingly awkward jobs. Getting more frequent work than most other muscle. It all adds up to Peterkinney being the best. Fine, whatever. He doesn't much care. This is short term for him. Make some money then walk away, best or not.

Working for Roy Bowles might be more long term, but it's not frequent enough. If Bowles came up with the work often enough, Peterkinney would settle for it. Ditch Marty and his shitty, scum-of-the-earth work. But that's not an option. Need the regular income. Bowles is so careful, keeps his workload down. The work is carefully plotted, reassuring. But there's so little of it. Peterkinney has to earn more than Bowles provides. He wants to get a place of his own. Needs to. Starting to climb the walls in that damp little flat of his grandfather's. The flat's no worse than it ever was, nor is his grandfather. But the more money he saves, the more he wants. The closer he comes to escaping the flat, the more desperate he gets.

Anyway, he's been waiting for the darkness to come. Shouldn't need to. Aird isn't going to make an issue of this. You get to his point in life and you don't make an issue of anything. Aird's living on the edge. He won't fight back. He won't argue. He'll take whatever's dished out to him. He'll be grateful for anything that stops short of pushing him over the edge. The challenge for Peterkinney is to make sure he doesn't go too far.

A guy like Aird is easy to misjudge. You knock him

around, maybe he panics. Maybe he turns up at Marty's office with the money. Marty doesn't want that. Can't use a man who pays his debts. Can't misuse him. Intimidate him, but don't send him running to another lender. Intimidate him enough to put him under pressure. Then, when a favour is requested, he'll be only too happy to oblige.

Peterkinney doesn't ask about the favours. Marty needs something done, he sends someone round to Aird to request a favour. Tells a man who owes a grand that he can have three hundred dropped if he does something useful. What constitutes useful in Marty's world is Marty's business. Peterkinney doesn't care. He can guess. Go rob a house owned by a rival. This car will be parked in this location. Go trash it. Use expendable, desperate losers to annoy and intimidate your rivals. That sort of thing. He's hardly going to give them important work, is he? Just risky, trashy, low-grade stuff that he couldn't persuade anyone else to do. If it's a woman who owes the money? That's different.

Aird lives in a shitty little flat in a rough part of town. According to Marty there might be a couple of other people living there with him. Might be. Marty doesn't know. Rumour has it that Aird doesn't live alone. Needs other people to help him pay the rent. But Marty can't be sure, because Marty can't ever seem to be fucking sure. It's always vague information and a demand for the job to be done as soon as possible. Not that Marty couldn't find out. He could, if he could be bothered. He just doesn't care about the risks his staff take.

Peterkinney's learned how sloppy Marty is at what he does by working with Bowles. Bowles is good. He knows how to handle these things. He understands the value of information. Understands the need for preparation. It's not just because Bowles has more experience. And it's not because what he does carries more risk. He does have more experience and gunrunning does carry more risk. But that's not it. Bowles cares about people working for him getting into trouble. Entirely selfish. He doesn't want them arrested, hospitalized or killed. That would raise awkward questions. But he also wants to make sure that good employees stick around. Marty doesn't care. Everyone's expendable to Marty. If Marty cared to make an effort, he could match Bowles for detail. Even exceed him. Marty has connections Bowles can't get. But Marty's only thinking about Marty. Not even taking the collection business all that seriously, it seems to Peterkinney. Too lazy, too distracted by the other strings to his bow.

That's why Peterkinney's already looking for a way out. Not desperately. He'll keep working for Marty until an opportunity comes along. But he won't settle for this. This won't be the rest of his life. No way working for someone like Marty can last. Too unpleasant. Sitting in his car, outside this block of flats. A street of four-storey blocks. Watching lights come on as daylight runs away. He has the address for the flat. Might as well get this out of the way.

He's not wearing a balaclava, although he has purchased one. One of the first things he did when he knew he was going to be working for Marty. Bought a balaclava and a pair of gloves. Ditched the gloves. They were a stupid idea. As seen on TV. Wearing a pair of actual gloves makes every part of the job harder. Some thug working for Marty tipped him off to thin surgical gloves. Sort of thing cleaners wear. You can buy them by the boxful in the supermarket. But he's not going to wear them either. Not tonight.

Tonight isn't a job that needs any sort of protection. Tonight is a job where faces can be seen and fingerprints left. There's nothing that Peterkinney could do to Aird that would make Aird go to the police. Not a thing in the world. Could torture the boy, he still wouldn't go to the cops. See, a boy like Aird lives in greater fear of the cops than Peterkinney does. Aird has a habit that will get him into trouble. He has probably resorted to paying for that habit by doing things he shouldn't. He won't want the police getting his fingerprints on file, comparing them to those found at the scenes of robberies and muggings. No, the police have no role to play in tonight's criminality.

Through the door of the building and along to the front door of the flat. Ground floor, which helps. Something else Peterkinney has learned. You don't know how fast you'll have to get away. Look, Aird should be soft. People like him almost always are. But there could be other people there, Marty said. One of them might decide that the best way out of debt is to kill the collector. Attack him at least. People react stupidly, violently. You have to know the way out. Need to have a clean run to the exit. That's easier if you don't have a dark stairwell to negotiate.

Knocking on the door. No need to kick your way in. That was a mistake Peterkinney only made once. Made it when him and Glass went after that Jim Holmes character. That was a fuck-up. A lucky fuck-up, but that doesn't make it any less of a fuck-up. Kicking down the door? Behaving like the bloody A-Team. You don't kick down doors. You knock on them. Even people who know they're in trouble answer the door. Even people in trouble know other people who might come visit. As long as you're not too late in the night, there's nothing suspicious about a knock on the door. You just have to know how to make the work easy.

The door's opening slowly. Looks like the description of Aird. Mop of thick black hair. Broad-shouldered but skinny round the waist. Brown bags under his eyes. Befuddled look. Doesn't cope well with the unexpected. Not a lot of people knock on his door. Someone new turns up, and it's likely to upset him.

'You Gordon?'

'Uh, yeah.' Had to think about that one.

'Good. I'll come in then.' Take the initiative. Never give them the chance to pull the strings of the conversation. Once they get used to the sound of their own voice, they'll try and fill the room with it. Make sure yours gets there first and takes all the space available.

Peterkinney's pushed his way inside. It's small, narrow, almost empty in here. Furniture is a luxury for people with the spare cash. Aird has something else to spend his money on. Smells like a small place, never cleaned and always occupied. Bloody freezing as well. Too bad. Aird has his life, Peterkinney has his. When this is done, Peterkinney will go home to his grandfather's flat. He won't give Aird and his little hovel another thought.

'You know that you owe money, Gordon.' Peterkinney standing in the gloomy corridor. Nothing on the walls but flaky white paint and damp. There's no bulb or shade on the light above them. The only light reaching the corridor is coming from the open door to the empty living room. Peterkinney stopping in the corridor. Good a place as any. Less space for Aird to wriggle out of a punch. 'Been a long time since you made any effort to pay.'

'Ah, shit, yeah.' Early enough in the evening for Gordon to know what he's in trouble for. That helps. You occasionally get people who are too far gone to remember who they owe money to. You knock them around. Following morning they wake up with cuts and bruises and no memory of how they got them. And still no memory that they owe anyone cash. They're not faking it. It comes as a shock to them to find out they owe anything at all. Almost no chance of gaining anything from those ones.

'So it's time to pay up. You owe a thousand pounds, Gordon.'

'A thousand. Do I owe a thousand? Shit. Thousand pounds is a lot of money, you know. I don't think I owe that. Do I?'

'You do. And you need to pay it, before it gets any bigger. Need to pay it now.' Putting a harsh tone into his voice. Don't let the junkie run the conversation round in circles. Confusion can be infectious. 'So are you going to pay?'

Aird is making a startled noise. The idea that he would have a thousand pounds on him is pretty startling. 'I don't have that cash. I don't. But I'll get it. I mean, I can. I can get it.'

No point hanging around here. Doesn't seem to be anybody else in the flat. Time to give the boy a fright and leave. Peterkinney's reached the end of the corridor, able to see into almost every room. There's nobody there, no chance of this spinning out of his control. As long as it's just him and Aird, it's under control. Turning back, and quickly punching Aird in the stomach. No warning. No pulling back of the arm. Quick little rabbit punch. Catch him off guard.

Thing is, a guy like Aird can't take a punch. He's young and he's broad-shouldered, but that counts for nothing. He's spent nearly a decade wrecking his body. He lives in terrible conditions. He is basically unhealthy. Undernourished, rotten teeth, broken fingernails. Pick a body part, and it's not in the condition evolution intended. One punch and he's dropped down onto his knees. That makes this more difficult. Peterkinney has to really scare him. One punch isn't enough for that. One punch won't even be memorable. Not when you've taken as many as Aird.

Now that Aird's down, he's awkward to hit. Peterkinney's shuffling to get his footing right. Leaning slightly. Swinging a second punch. Better backswing this time. Looking to hit him on the side of the jaw. Avoid the top of the head unless you want to know what broken knuckles feel like. You don't want to know what broken knuckles feel like. Neither does Peterkinney. It's an awkward punch. Not going to do a lot of harm. But it has shock value. Aird thought being down would protect him. It's sending him sideways, into the wall in this narrow corridor. It'll bruise. It'll make talking and eating uncomfortable for a few days. Nothing broken though. Wasn't able to hit him hard enough for that. Not in this stupid crouching position. But it'll remind him about the money he owes, every time he feels the pain of it.

Peterkinney's straightening up. 'You listen to me, Gordon. You have a week. One week from today. You pay up one week from today or there's going to be serious trouble. You under-stand me?'

'Uh-huh. Uh-huh.'

Peterkinney's stepping over Aird. Walking to the front door and out of the flat. No colder outside than in. Aird probably doesn't even know what day it is. He won't remember that he has seven days to pay. But he will remember that he has to pay. He might even try and do something about it. But before he has any chance to find the money, someone will come pay him a visit. Another one of Marty's men. Always a different one from the attacker. The attacker is the angry face you must fear. The man offering work will be the friendly face, helping you out of a hole. They'll tell him they've got an idea to help him. Do this little favour, and some of the problems will go away. And he'll be so desperate to help. So pathetic.

7

A different kind of job. A punishment. Bavidge is letting the clock tick a little further. Get closer to midnight. He's been seen in this area before. The neighbours gawked at him last time he was here. Couple of months ago. Long enough that most of them won't remember. Not going to take any risks though. A person with an empty life will remember the few interesting faces that pop up. He's borrowed a car. Patterson has a couple of them that he keeps spare. Rotate between them; use them on jobs like this. Bavidge is dressed plainly. He has a pair of thin gloves and a black cap on. Not a bala-clava, that shouldn't be necessary.

He's parked near the bottom of the street. Watching the street ahead. Looking for any sign of action. If Holmes is running then he might have people helping him. There might be a bunch of them at the house. Packing up, and helping him run. No sign of it. Just a few cars parked on the street. None right outside the house. A deep breath. Doesn't matter how many times you've done this, a deep breath always helps. Starting the car.

He's parking right outside the house. The shortest escape route. Looking up and down the street. Trying to work out if it's worth the risk or not. No, take the keys with you. If he thought he could get away with it, he would leave the keys in the ignition. Gain a few potentially precious seconds. Not this time. Shouldn't need that extra time, but hell, you should never need it. In this area, you don't gamble with your transport. Protect your escape route. Take the keys in with you.

This job requires all the thought you can give it. Not a normal job. A normal job is an attack on someone with only a basic idea of how to defend themselves. Of how to attack back. Not Holmes. He knows the business. Been doing this longer than Bavidge has. Not better, but longer. Long enough to learn the lessons. Long enough to make this a handle-with-care job.

Pulling the cap down a little and getting out of the car. Locking it. Looking at the house. There's a light on downstairs. Front window was the living room, if he remembers right. That means the thief and his woman are in there. Still up and about. Maybe packing up their stuff, if they have any idea of what's good for them. Amazing that they haven't run already. Stupid of them, and stupidity carries a price. Bavidge is walking quickly up the path. Ringing the doorbell. Be interesting to see how long they take to answer. A glance at his watch. Ten to midnight. Should take enough time for questioning looks and a reluctant walk to the door. If there's a rush to the door, then they might be expecting someone else. Someone to help them run.

Ten seconds. Twenty seconds. Finally the sound of the door being unlocked. Then opened. Hope to God it's not on one of those wee chains. Then you have to try and talk your way in. Bavidge can do it. Holmes knows him now. Knows they both work for Patterson. Bavidge could bluff his way in with that. And if the bluff fails, you have to kick it in, and the job's gone to hell before you've crossed the threshold. But he doesn't have to. The door's opening wide and Norah Faulkner is staring back at him. That same rough expression. The same dressing gown as two months ago, although Bavidge doesn't recognize that. Hair tied back, no make-up. Ready for bed. So not running tonight.

'Norah. Alan Bavidge, Jim home?'

She's relaxing. More than she should. More than he thinks she would if she knew Jim was skimming 20 per cent from his boss. Now that is interesting. She's nodding, and waving a hand for him to come in. Looking out the door behind him to make sure that none of the nosy neighbours are around and watching.

'Something the matter?' she's asking. Leading him through to the living room. 'Is it that Marty Jones again?'

'No, Norah, it isn't,' Bavidge is saying.

Holmes is in the living room. He was sitting in his chair watching TV, but he's getting to his feet. The look on his face started out intrigued, but that's been knocked out of the way by panic. Bavidge can see it. Holmes is scared. More likely to do something stupid. More likely that this is about to turn nasty.

Bavidge is moving fast. Has to, because of that look. Because Holmes knows why he's there. And because of Norah. He's one against two. She might not know what's going on, but she's going to work it out. She's going to back her man. Probably. And she's as tough as buggery, is Norah Faulkner. Dismiss her as the wife if you want, but a wife with a weapon is more dangerous than a man without. So Bavidge already has his hand in his pocket. Pulling out the Stanley knife. Clicking the blade up a single notch. Keep it short and manageable. Makes it much less likely to snap, which these blades are prone to doing. Moving round the side of the chair and closer to Holmes, before Holmes has half a chance to react.

Bavidge just doesn't get nervous. This is his life. Day in, day out. Dealing with people like Jim Holmes. Getting into violent and dangerous situations. You do it often enough, and you lose the fear of it. Bavidge lost that fear years ago. Only thirty-two, but he's been around this life long enough not to worry about it. Not to fear the danger he's putting himself in. Not to fear the pain that he might suffer if it goes wrong. Pain and suffering are part of the job. He'll think about it afterwards. Sometimes he'll even worry about it afterwards. But not at the time. Never at the time.

So the knife is in his hand. Slashing out. If you didn't

know what to look for, you might think it was a wild swing of the arm. It wasn't. He was aiming for the left cheek, and he got it. Not just got it, but caught it near the ear and is running the blade swiftly down towards the mouth. Not casual. Fast and certain. Finding the target with one swing. In the first couple of seconds afterwards, there's very little of anything. Not a lot of blood. Just a thin red line welling up on Holmes's face. Not a lot of reaction. Holmes has stumbled backwards a step, raising a hand towards his face but not touching the wound. He can feel the sting, but hasn't realized how serious it is. Staring ahead at Bavidge. Norah is still standing by the living-room door. Watching.

Now the reaction. Bavidge should have moved quicker after the slash. That was a mistake. Can't afford two of those in one night. Holmes is lurching forwards. Shouting something that only made sense in his head. Loud and big and throwing himself at Bavidge. Trying to use size to intimidate and overwhelm. Worked for him many times before. Bavidge is ducking sideways. Holding the knife outward, hoping for a glancing blow. But Holmes is past him, and stumbling towards the couch. Not looking to tackle Bavidge, just looking to get past him. Stumbling towards the drinks cabinet behind the couch.

Still shouting sentences constructed entirely of vowels. Like his fury is something the world deserves to hear about. And Norah joining in now. Screaming baffling words. A choir of panic. Bavidge is across to Holmes. Kicking the back of his leg and leaning in after the kick. Holmes going down beside the drinks cabinet. Hard on his knee, ignoring the pain. Still trying to reach for the little handle of the cabinet. There's something in there. A weapon he wants to go for. Something he knows would turn the tide of this fight. Not today. Should have had it closer to hand. That was his mistake. Bavidge is down beside him. On his knees. Grabbing Holmes's mouth in one hand and squeezing until the lips part. He saw a guy do this once. Years ago now: 'Gully' Fitzgerald. Tough bastard, had a lot of little tricks up his sleeve. Taught Bavidge this one. A good way to shut someone up and panic them. You get a man panicked, and the fight is yours. Quickly slashing the tip of the blade along the upper gum. Got a lot of tooth, but enough gum. Enough blood. As an injury, it's little more than nuisance value. But it's a scary nuisance for the first few minutes. A wound you can't see, but can taste.

Holmes is panicking. Thrashing around with both hands up to his mouth. The more he moves, the more the blood from the wound on his cheek spreads and spills. Now Norah's screaming something they can all understand.

'What did you do to him? What did you do to him?'

Bavidge is beginning to lift himself up from his kneeling position. Something hits him in the back. Something big and solid. Jesus, Norah, you're heavier than you look. Bavidge is taking a couple of steps backward. Straightening up and throwing her off. He's not strong, but she doesn't have much of a grip. No grip of anything at this point, to be fair. Bavidge needs to end this quickly before he totally loses control. Lost some, but has more than anyone else. Norah charging at him now. Bavidge pushes her back with his left hand, keeping the knife away from her. She isn't a part of this. Don't spread punishment any further than it needs to go. Basic rule. She's stumbled backward. Crashing into the big TV and the little stand it's on. The TV's back against the wall, so it only tips over slightly. Nothing broken. Norah pausing, wheezing, and preparing her next attack. Bavidge has to stop her.

'He was skimming money again,' Bavidge is saying. Loud enough to break through the cacophony of stupidity from the other two. Surprised by the edge in his voice. It almost sounds nervous. Definitely sounded angry.

Holmes is on his knees. Hands to his mouth. Ignoring everything and everyone. Forgetting about the old handgun he paid four hundred quid for and hid in the cabinet. Too late for that to do any good now. He's rumbled. It's been said. Norah's on her backside, one arm back against the slanting TV. Looking at Bavidge and shaking her head.

'No,' she's saying. 'I warned him. It wasn't him, it couldn't have been. I warned him.' She had no idea. Desperate for Bavidge to be wrong. Sure that he's right. It's broken them, silenced them.

'It was him,' Bavidge is saying. Quiet now. No need for

raised voices. 'Five per cent to start with. In the last couple of weeks he's kicked it up to twenty. He knew we would notice. He had to know, but he did it anyway. He's been preparing to run. Must have it all planned out.'

He was not planning to take Norah with him. She's shaking her head. Looking past Bavidge at Holmes. He's still on his knees. Hands to his mouth. Blood through the fingers. Looking across at Norah. Ignoring Bavidge. He's done all the damage he came to do. Delivered the message. One that will be seen and heard. The slash on the cheek lets everyone see the price of fucking with Billy Patterson. Holmes is looking at Norah. Norah's looking back. It's not a good way to end a relationship.

Bavidge has clicked the blade back down inside the plastic handle and slipped the knife into his pocket. He's pulling the dislodged cap back down over his head and walking out of the house. Leaving behind the mess of other people's lives. Whatever happens with these two is their business. None of his. He just wants out. Away. The neighbours will have heard that racket. How could they not? Even if they're scared of sticking their noses into Norah's business, one of them will call the cops. Bavidge is into the car, and relieved to be driving away.

Too late to call up his girlfriend. He'd already cancelled the date. Been doing that a lot lately. He'll go home instead. Home alone. A small house, in a good part of town. Quiet and simple, devoid of any good reason to want to spend time there. It's a house that's only ever been occupied by a single man. A man with no idea how to create something that even he would be happy in. He's parked outside, gone in. Standing in the kitchen. Remembering Holmes's house. Not the fight, not the screaming. The decoration and the effort. Norah, you could tell, made that house what it was. Nice and comforting. Homely. Bavidge is shaking his head. Of all the things to be jealous of. Have a couple of drinks and try to get some sleep. There'll be more of this to come. Plenty more. It's getting late.

8

It is late. Glass has been thinking about going home for a while now. Ella was right about this place. It is a nice club. There is a good quality of clientele. It is expensive. One of the reasons it isn't his sort of place. It feels more buttoned up. The music isn't so loud. The people are all a little richer than he's used to hanging around. He feels out of place. He assumes everyone else has noticed that he's out of place. These are smart people, they can tell. Ella hasn't noticed. She's having the time of her life.

She was delighted when she got back to the flat and found that he had some money. She had some too. She had as much as she had been planning on spending that night. When she saw his five hundred, she suddenly planned to spend more. That's why she's having the time of her life. This is an escape for her. The chance to come to a place like this with her boyfriend, and her money. Not work, just play. The amount of fun she has seems to be directly linked to the amount she spends. The same is not true of Glass.

His five hundred is shrinking fast. He should have borrowed less. He realizes that, now that it's too late. No matter how much he borrowed, she would have spent the lot. She's enjoying showing people that she has money to spend. He could have gotten away with a couple of hundred. Cursing himself for that. It's spoiling his evening, watching the money disappear. Knowing that he'll have to find it all over again.

Ah, fuck it. Just forget about the money. Concentrate on Ella. Concentrate on the good time she's having. See how happy she is. She's having that great time with Glass. Being happy with him. Nobody else there. Nobody else impressing her with their largesse, just Glass. They feel like a couple. A proper couple, you know. Not just two young people who spend a lot of time together. Not friends with benefits. It feels like they're together. Like they're the sort of couple that will stay together. These are the first blocks in building a life together. That's a good feeling. One worth paying for.

After midnight, memories start to get a little hazy. He'd been drinking. They'd done a line or two. They were dancing. There have been a lot of nights like that in the last couple of months. Drink, drugs, dancing and little detail. But this one was different. This was his night out as much as hers. This was something he was able to pay for. On this night, his night, he realized how humiliating it was to tag along when she was working. Never noticed it before. Never felt it. There were embarrassing moments, sure. But this was different. This was the night that made him understand that he wants Ella to stop what she does for a living. Made him understand that to be his, she couldn't be anyone else's.

He stayed way past the point that he was enjoying himself. He paid for this night. He was damned if she wasn't going home with him. This wasn't a work night. He can't remember going home. It was late. Later than it should have been. Club stayed open past time. He remembers walking along the street with Ella. The pair of them needed every inch of that pavement. They were both long gone, weaving all over the place. But everything was funny. They had their arms round each other, laughing at things that usually seemed so boring. It was nice.

They got home. Not sure how, but they got back to Glass's flat. He remembers what a great mood she was in. She wasn't tired. She wasn't moody. She does a good line in both of those when it's late at night and she's just gotten home. Nope, she was happy. He was happy. They had a happy half hour before they fell asleep.

It's morning. Well, technically it isn't. Technically it's five past twelve in the afternoon, but Glass has just woken up so let's call it morning. Anyway, Ella is still asleep. She always sleeps late. That's her habit, whether she's working or not. So he's in the shower. Then into the kitchen. Making a cup of coffee. While he's waiting for the kettle, he's walking through to the bedroom. Silently sliding his wallet out of the pocket of the trousers he wore last night. Tiptoeing back into the kitchen.

There's one hundred and ninety quid left. Where did the

other three hundred and ten go? No fucking clue. Might as well have thrown it into the air, for all he remembers. Yeah, he had a great time with it. But three hundred and ten quid of great time? Shit. That was more expensive than it should have been. Probably got ripped off by someone. Too late to care now. Last night is gone, and now he's looking down the barrel of the future. Now he has to worry about getting some money together. Get that debt paid.

Calling Marty. Can't think of any other source of money, so it's back to Marty. Aware that this phone call counts as haranguing. Turning himself into a boring nuisance, because he can feel the desperation creeping up behind him. Doesn't matter how long he has to pay the debt. He has to start collecting the money. As in, right now. It's ringing, taking a while to answer. Glass is filling his cup with boiling water, hearing the phone being answered. Hearing an annoyed voice on the other end.

'Yes?'

'Marty, this is Alex Glass. Listen, any chance of some work? Anything you need done, I'm there. Doesn't matter the work, I'm up for it.' Couldn't sound a great deal more desperate than that. Knowing it, and accepting it. Desperation might persuade Marty to fob him off with some garbage job he has lying around. Anything for money. Anything.

There's a grumble on the other end of the phone. Marty pretending that he's fed up of people calling him for favours.

He gets plenty calls from people looking for work, but that's always been part of the job. Used to it, not concerned about it. Be more worried if people weren't calling. It's a measure of how well he's doing. Reassuring, and important. Important to know that when you need people, they'll be ready and willing. Sometimes desperate.

Nobody else is as desperate as this boy. That usually means it's time to stop employing them. The desperate ones are the worst. They take risks. They get pushy. They screw things up for other people. You want someone who wants to do the job but doesn't really need to. Marty had no intention of hiring this kid anyway. He was always a little too enthusiastic. It was the other one he wanted. Glass's mate Peterkinney. He's worked out well. Did another fine job yesterday on that junkie. Stuck-up kid, but smart and tough. Little too smart and assertive for his own good, but profitable. Not this one. No profit from desperation.

'I don't really have any work for you right now, kid,' Marty's saying. That's not true. Once this call is done, he's going to call up one of his other boys. Got a couple of collections need doing. Needs three guys to work as drivers for a party on Friday, another two or three to work security. None of them will be Glass. This loser at a big party? Nah, wouldn't know how to handle it.

'I'll do anything that needs doing, Marty?'

Oh God, he's pleading. 'Listen, I don't have time for this,'

Marty's saying. Putting an edge on his voice. Make him understand. 'I got things to do. I already told you, I have no work for you. Look around. Find someone else that needs some work done. You don't just have to work for me. This was never exclusive. I don't mind if you find work somewhere else, long as you don't step on my toes. Okay?'

Could not have made it any clearer. He doesn't care if Glass goes and works for someone else. He doesn't care if Glass never works for him again. He wants rid of Glass. This is a sacking. Glass knows it. Shit. Shouldn't have called him. That only pissed him off. Glass is hanging up about half a second after Marty's already done so. Drinking that cup of coffee.

Fine, so Marty doesn't want him. There are plenty of other people he can go work for. Plenty of other ways to make money. He's resourceful. He's willing. He'll go and do whatever needs to be done. Hell, there's plenty jobs for a guy who's willing to work. He hasn't managed to find one before, sure. There aren't a lot of people hiring, the way things are. But there are jobs if you know how to do them. Look at Peterkinney. He's got two of the bloody things. One for Marty. Another one he doesn't talk about. Secrets and money, got plenty of both. Got enough money to go buy a car. Looking to get out of his grandfather's flat. Moving on to bigger things. Yeah, and leaving the rest of them behind.

Glass has his phone out, about to call Peterkinney, when

Ella plods into the kitchen. Wearing a T-shirt and nothing else. Her hair tied back and messy. Looking tired. Looking for a coffee.

'Morning,' Glass is saying with a smile.

'Morning, you. Last night was excellent,' she's saying, drawing out the word 'excellent' for no apparent reason. A happy little sigh and an impish smile. Last night was a great treat to her. Not something she expects or even wants every night. Just nice to have once in a while. Not a treat if you have it every day, is it?

'Yeah. It was. Listen, Ella. I was thinking, we should have more nights like last night.'

She's smiling, and shaking her head. 'It was good, Alex, but those places are expensive. We need to be careful. We got things to save up for. I want to decorate the bathroom. And we should get a new carpet for the living room, that one's full of holes and snags.'

'Yeah, sure. But I mean nights where it's just you and me. Having fun and all that, but just you and me.'

'It's always just you and me,' she's saying. Trying to keep her tone playful, but she can see where this is going. She's had this conversation before. Doesn't want this to become an argument. Doesn't want this flat to fill with memories of battles between her and Alex. Keep it happy. Keep it a home.

'No, I mean, nights where . . . Nights where it's you and

me and no work, you know. We should have a lot more of those. Lot less of, uh, other nights.'

She's stopped and she's looking down at the worktop in front of her. She isn't frowning exactly. She's gone from happy to no expression, which feels like a frown. 'So you want me to stop working?'

He's opened his mouth, but he's closed it again. It's a harder question to answer than it should be. The ice didn't look this thin when he thought about this. Seemed so simple. Not with the tone she's taken. He doesn't want arguments in here either. He fears that one argument could be enough for him to lose his grip on this relationship. Just doesn't realize how firm that grip is. Doesn't realize how simple it is to keep hold. Don't be a layabout and don't mention work. That's it. Everything else is happy.

'I think it would be nice if you worked less. I think we could be together more. I think, you know, we should both be looking for other work. You know, like work that'll last long term. That sort of thing. That's all I meant. Build for the future.'

She's shaking her head. 'I knew it would start eventually. You can't handle what I do. I make money. You're not bringing any in. I make money. We need that. We can't build for the future without it. Listen, Alex, we have to be realistic. I want us to get other things. I want us to have all the things you want us to have. The long-term jobs, all that. But . . . we don't have that. I don't know how to get that. I know how to do what I do. If you can find other jobs, then great. Until you do, I have to keep working.' Made every effort to stay calm throughout that. Kept her voice down, kept it away from argumentative. But there's an argument in there. Feels like there needs to be. Something to drag Alex towards reality. 'Unless you've come up with some way of making money . . .' she's saying. Trailing off and making it a question.

'No.' A little bit sheepish. Looking down at the floor. This has gotten away from him. He just wants it to end.

'No. So I have to keep working. Keep earning money. We don't have a choice, for now. You get that, don't you, Alex?' Stepping towards him, and putting her hands on his sides.

'Yeah. For now. But I'll look for something else. Look for better opportunities.'

'Yeah,' she's saying with a smile, 'better opportunities. They'll come, but we have to be patient. They'll come.'

She's gone back to making her coffee. He's gone back to finishing his. Wishing he hadn't started that particular conversation. He can try again, but not yet. He can only try again when he's in a position of strength. When he's making some money. Then he can pull her round to his way of thinking. He needs to find work. Finishing off the last of the coffee.

'I'm heading out, I shouldn't be too long.' He's reaching across and kissing her on the side of the head.

He doesn't see the look. The concern on her face. He's always running off somewhere or phoning someone these days. Trying to find something. A job. A way of making money. Running round all over the place and making nothing of himself. He's capable of better, if he would get real. You don't get rich quick, and there's no easy money.

Glass is out the door and walking. Go see Peterkinney. They've been best friends since they were in school. Since they were fourteen years old. Peterkinney has work. Has money coming in. Good money, probably. If anyone's going to help him out, it's going to be Peterkinney. Has to be.

9

Peterkinney's driven round the area a couple of times. That's standard, but Bowles's warning is still ringing in his ears. Something was making Howie Lawson nervous. It made Bowles nervous. Nervous enough to mention it, anyway. That's made Peterkinney nervous. So Peterkinney's driving a little more slowly, looking a little more closely.

It's an industrial area. Or was. Not much industry now. All warehouses and old buildings. Large buildings with nothing in there. Big wide doors on rusty hinges and broken windows. Most of the buildings have front yards for delivery, so they're not up against the wall. Makes it harder to see anyone peeking out a window or door at him as he drives past. Plenty hiding places. Doesn't like that. Better to do a handover of a single piece somewhere less isolated. Hiding in plain sight.

This is the sort of place you just know will be redeveloped soon. It'll be on the list. Especially this close to the river. Old grimy square buildings replaced by shiny angular ones. A place with potential, the redevelopers will say. The sort of place Peterkinney won't be frequenting any more.

Nobody out of place. Not that he can see. That's the first

thing. Nobody lurking around on the street, looking like they're waiting for him. Nobody around at all. Unless of course they're doing a very good job of it. Can't see into the buildings, obviously. Have to guess what is or isn't in there. Some of them are still in use, but none have activity around them. Big doors shut, nobody loading up or dropping off stock. So he's finding a place to park. Lawson wants to meet round the back of the large warehouse on the left. The dark-grey building with a row of broken windows close to the roof. No vehicles in front of it. Grass growing out of the concrete around the fence at the front. Looks like it hasn't been used in years.

This would be better if he didn't have to get out of the car. If he could drive it round the back of the building. No opening for a car. Even if there was, he doesn't want to be seen driving round there. Raises eyebrows, if anyone's watching. The only car in years to go round the back of that building. Do nothing that draws attention. So he's parking on the street and getting out. The street curves in the middle, so he can't actually see the end of it from here. Can see enough to reassure him. Nothing moving. Nothing grabbing his attention.

He has the money in his pocket. Tapping the pocket again, just to make sure. Feeling the shape of the envelope. Bowles has to be careful. He has to make sure that every penny finds its way to the seller. If he doesn't pay, he loses a seller. Worse, word might get round that he doesn't pay the agreed price. Then nobody sells to him. The seller has to trust the buyer as well, you know.

Peterkinney's found a gate that leads round to the back of the building. Seems to be on the property next door. Might have to find a way over the fence between the two. Along the fence and, yes, he is in the wrong place. Bloody hell. Fence is high, but it's easy to climb. Over it and dropping down into the yard behind the warehouse. Little jarring on the ankles, but not bad. Huh, weird layout. Big yard for lorries to collect stuff, but no way for them to get in or out. Obviously the land the fence is on used to be a part of this yard. People next door must have bought the strip of land from the warehouse owners. Or just taken it. Who really gives a shit?

He can see Lawson. There's a short wall running along the other side of the yard and Lawson's sitting on it. Wearing a dark hoodie, hood pulled up. That's a great way to look conspicuous, genius. A dry day and you're wrapped up like there's a snowstorm. When you're doing the pick-up on a gun, you need the seller to take the same precautions you do. You need them to have the same sense you do. To have some fucking sense, at least. Meeting outdoors at an unused location is not sensible. Sitting on the wall with your hood up in good weather is not sensible. At least he's alone.

Peterkinney's walking across to Lawson. Still keeping his eyes open. Don't get complacent. Not until the gun has been in Bowles's possession for at least eight hours. Then you can stop worrying about it. Then there's no chance of someone in a uniform knocking on your door. Well, not no chance. Less chance. There's never no chance. Not in this business.

'Howie?' Peterkinney's asking. He knows the answer already. Stopping four feet in front of Lawson. Far enough away to make sure Lawson doesn't do anything stupid. Because you never know that either. It was one of the first things Bowles taught him. With any new seller, you keep well back until you see the gun. They might be luring you there to take the money. Even after you see the gun, take nothing for granted. They might be planning to use it to take the money. Now Peterkinney's starting to understand why Bowles was so nervous about this.

'Yeah. You got the money?'

'You got the gun?'

Lawson's reaching under his top. Taking out a blue plastic bag. The bag is wrapped so tightly round the gun you can pretty much make out the outline of it. Not subtle. Lawson still has a lot to learn. Nervous, and making mistakes. He'll get better. He has connections so he can get the weapons. If he keeps delivering, Bowles will make sure he gets plenty of practice. Practice makes perfect.

'The money,' Lawson's saying.

Peterkinney's taking the envelope from his pocket. That nervous moment when you have to swap. Money for gun. Who lets go first? Lawson at least has the sense to see that the seller lets go first. He's handing the bag over. Peterkinney taking it in his left hand, now passing the envelope with his right. Pulling open the top of the bag and looking inside. He could tell from the weight already, but you check. A handgun, as advertised.

Now things are happening fast. Peterkinney's about to look up and tell Lawson he's done well, when he hears scuffing. Boots on the ground. Lawson is looking behind him. Suddenly he's spinning over the wall and running. Off in the other direction. The direction of the single uniformed cop running towards them. Idiot. Trying to get out the way he came in, no matter the obstacles. Peterkinney's thinking about the car. His escape. Turning and sprinting for the high fence.

But it's harder this time. Struggling to get the footholds, but struggling more with his hands. The damn gun. Can't drop it. Need to get out and need to get the gun out too. Can't come away empty-handed. Can't leave the gun for the cops to play with. But it's slowing him. He's looking behind him as he's swinging his leg over the top of the fence. No cop. He must have gotten Lawson. That's Lawson's problem. He'll only talk if he's dead from the neck up. Even someone desperate and stupid knows that you don't name the buyer. So the cop has Lawson to play with. Good, gives Peterkinney a better chance.

Peterkinney's dropping to the other side of the fence.

Jarring his ankles again. This time worse, but in a hurry. Ignore it and move. Something else Bowles told him. A uniformed cop is never alone. Always in pairs. And if they know there's a gun involved, there will be at least one detective as well. So there could be two more, and they could be close. Could be at his car. Play this careful.

But careful just took a jump out the broken window. There's a cop stepping inside the gate. Closing it behind him. Moving casually. Peterkinney's stopped. Back the way he came? Maybe run round the other side of this building and see how his luck holds. No idea what's there, but it's still an option. But he's not moving. He's standing, watching the cop come towards him. The cop's smiling.

'Well, young man, what have you got there?'

So smug. Happy as a pig in shit, as they say. And Peterkinney knows him. Learned this little lesson from one of Marty's boys. A guy he once did a collection job with pointed this cop out in a pub they went to. PC Paul Greig. Bent, the fellow told him. A fucking nightmare though. So bent he takes your money and still arrests you. You just can't rely on him at all. But bent. That's the important thing to remember here. It's Peterkinney, a gun and a bent copper. Now his mind's racing. Coming up with a new option.

Things are starting to make sense. Lawson was nervous about it. Bowles was worried that it might be a set-up. One cop came running after them. One, on his own. A situation with a gun, and only one cop came round the other way. Now Greig turns up. Nah, that doesn't add up to an honest situation. This is a stitch-up. Lawson probably in on it. They set up the sale to catch Peterkinney. Or any employee of Bowles. But that's not how they do things. Not when they're honest. One cop confronting Peterkinney, all on his own. Doesn't need to worry about the gun, the cop knows more about it than Peterkinney does. The cop will know there are no bullets to fear. But he shouldn't be here alone.

So Peterkinney's starting to talk. He's not going to fight his way out of this. Whatever Greig is, he's still a cop. Can't run. Doesn't know for sure what he's up against, although he's willing to bet now that there are only the two cops. Greig wouldn't be on his own if there were more. Best way out is talking.

'Can I help you, officer?' Pausing as Greig smiles a little. 'I'm sure I can do something to help you.'

Greig walking a little closer, standing a few feet away. 'You think so, huh? I think if I opened that bag you're carrying I'd find a gun. I think I could arrest you. Get you locked up for a few years. Very serious crime, carrying a gun.'

'You could do that. But what's the point? Another gun will replace it. Someone else will replace me. I'm sure you and me can come to a better arrangement than that. One that'll last. One that we can all benefit from.' His heart's beating fast. This, talking to a cop, is far more nerve-racking than collecting a gun or money. But his mind is still sharp. It's the good kind of nerves. Inspiring.

Greig's looking at him. 'So, what? You and me set up some scheme, huh? You and me take a cut of money away from the seller, that sort of thing? That your big idea?' Looking sharply at Peterkinney. Speaking sharp too.

This is where you pick your words carefully. What do you know about Greig? How do you judge what he just said? 'That sort of set-up wouldn't work,' Peterkinney's saying honestly. 'People would never sell to my boss if they heard people were being ripped off. But there could be another way. My boss would pay for protection. He would pay for . . .'

'Please,' Greig is saying, waving a dismissive hand. This isn't what he wants to hear. He needs to hear something convincing, and this ain't it. Roy Bowles will not pay a uniformed officer good money for limited protection.

Peterkinney's thinking. Remembering that conversation he had with one of Marty's boys. Greig still arrests you. He still does his job. He's still a cop who acts like one. That's why you don't trust him, apparently. But if you know he's still a proper cop, you can use that. Use it to get yourself out of this situation. Not like Greig's told him to shut up. They've both essentially accepted that a deal can happen. Now they're just negotiating.

'You keep the money from this sale, fine,' Peterkinney is saying. 'Maybe there's a way of sorting out other payments, maybe not. I'm sure we can come up with something. But look at it this way. You know there are much worse people than my boss moving guns in this city. Much worse. Much less careful. People like Mark Garvey. People like Robby Draper. You heard about this new kid Spikey?'

'I heard. So what?'

'So you know how my boss does his work. He's strict. He only sells to people in the business. Everything he sells is for use in the industry. None end up in civilian cases. You know that. Can't say that for the rest of them. Garvey will sell to anyone. Draper's been getting desperate. Losing business and selling to anyone who'll pay. This Spikey is a kid, selling to other kids. Street gangs. You want to keep these guns away from civilians, you need someone like my boss controlling the flow. Can't wipe out the trade, you know that. That's naive. If you can't wipe it out, next best thing is controlling it. There might be money in it for you, but what I'm talking about is worth more than that. I'm talking about taking charge of who does and who doesn't get guns in this city.'

Damn, that sounded good to Peterkinney. Can't believe how easily it all spilled out. Almost casual. The nerves are dropping too, because he knows he's right. Knows he sounds convincing. Knows that this is what Greig wants to hear.

Greig is looking at him. Not saying no, which is a start. Looking back towards the gate. Looking thoughtful. 'What's your name, kid?'

'Peterkinney. Oliver Peterkinney.'

'Huh. Well, Peterkinney, you may have stumbled onto something worthwhile. Your boss doesn't get a free ride. He steps out of line and I'll be on him. And I'll be watching you too. We'll be having regular meetings. You and me are going to get to know each other, you understand?'

Peterkinney's nodding. He means that Peterkinney's going to have to pay him regularly. The control thing might matter most, but don't forget the money. 'I'm sure it'll be a profitable relationship,' Peterkinney's saying.

Greig's nodding. Nice to meet a kid who gets it. Who understands the ways of the industry. He'll do okay, this one. Greig's nodding for the kid to leave. Watching him walk to the gate and out. Walking comfortable. Not running, not stiff. Walking like he's just done a perfectly normal thing.

10

Arnie's never quick to answer the door these days. More often than not bad news. Why rush? Just be someone he doesn't want to talk to. So the person is knocking a second time when he opens it. A young fellow. Takes him a couple of seconds to recognize. It's Alex Glass. Oliver's wee mate. Or he was. Don't see nearly so much of him round here any more. Which is a good thing, in Arnie's book.

'Hi, is Oliver about?'

The kid looks a mess. He was always a rogue, but at least he was a well-turned-out rogue. Now he looks tired. Looks like he hasn't had a shower after a long night. Looks nervy.

'No, he's out. You want to leave a message or something?' Kids these days. Don't need to leave messages. They got about a hundred different ways of getting in touch with each other. If you can't get through to someone it's because they don't want you to.

'No, no,' Glass is saying. Doesn't sound convinced though. Still standing there. Seems like a boy with something to say.

Arnie's about to close the door when the kid pipes up. 'Actually yeah, I do. Look, tell him to call me, yeah. Home or mobile, whatever. I really need to talk to him about work. It's important.'

That's got Arnie pausing. 'What work?' he's asking. The only work Arnie knows Oliver does is for Roy Bowles. Roy would not hire this unreliable moron. And he would not be happy to hear that one of his men has been passing work on to him. Or even talking about it, for that matter. This could be a sackable offence.

Glass is nodding, because he thinks he understands. Peterkinney has two jobs, and his grandfather wants to know which one he's talking about. The old man might be able to put in a good word for him. This could be a chance. 'Working for Marty, I mean. I know Oliver's been getting loads of work from him. I haven't been getting any. It's a struggle, you know. Trying to make ends meet. I was hoping he might be able to help me out, get some work.'

Arnie's nodding. His face has gone hard, but Glass is too wrapped up in his own problems to notice. 'Why don't you come in and wait,' Arnie's saying. 'Have a cup of tea. He's only gone out for a wee while. He won't be long.'

Glass has nowhere else to go, so he's stepping inside. Into the cramped kitchen. Taking a seat and a cup. Arnie sitting opposite him. Wanting to know about this Marty business, but not wanting to push it. He knows Glass will clam up if he thinks he's dropping his mate in it. So he has to pretend that he already knows. Pretend that Oliver doesn't mind him knowing. Even though Oliver's obviously been keeping it from him for a while. If he's been working for Marty since the first time Arnie heard mention of Marty's name then this has been going on for months. The boy lying to him.

'You not getting a lot of work then, Alex?' he's asking. Being friendlier than he's ever been to the worthless kid before. That should be enough to put the boy on high alert, but apparently not. He's just delighted to have someone show an interest.

'Nah. I think Marty's done with me. Says he doesn't have any work for me, but he's got plenty for Oliver. Plenty for everyone else. I was hoping me and Oliver could sort something out. You know, he takes a job from Marty, I do it for him. We split the cash. That sort of thing. Helps him take more work, helps me make some money. You know,' he's saying, then trailing off. Aware that he's been talking for a while, and feeling uncomfortable. He always had the impression that Arnie didn't like him much, and that memory has suddenly come back to him.

'You struggling for cash?' Arnie's surprising himself. He actually cares.

'Little bit, yeah,' Glass is saying, and shrugging. Looking down at the table. Looking awkward. Not the sort of thing he wants to admit. He's always been independent. Left home when he was eighteen. Always managed to keep his nose above the waterline. Been close a few times, but he's always been able to look after himself. Found work, earned money. Did a better job of looking after himself than his parents ever did of looking after him. Now he needs help.

A suspicion. Arnie frowning and looking at the boy. 'You in trouble here, lad?'

Glass breathing out heavily. The truth is tempting. And maybe the old man can put pressure on Oliver to help. Getting to the point where humiliating yourself in front of this old man is the only choice he's got. 'I . . . borrowed some money. Shouldn't have, but I needed it. So now I'm in a hole. I just need some work, that's all. Just a bit to get started, you know. I didn't borrow a lot, so I just need a little work to cover it. It's okay. Just a bit. Oliver can sort me out. He's well in with Marty.'

'I didn't know he was doing so well,' Arnie's saying, making it sound casual. Making it sound like he knew his grandson was working for that piece of shit, just didn't realize how successfully.

'Oh yeah, Oliver's doing great.' Thinking he's doing his mate a favour by talking him up. Looking Arnie in the eye, across the little table. They can't both put their arms on the table; their hands would meet in the middle. So Glass has his hands in his lap, feeling uncomfortable and looking childish. 'He gets a hell of a lot more work than me. Actually, I think he gets more than anyone. Marty likes him. I don't think Oliver likes Marty much,' Glass is saying with a shrug. 'Doesn't go in

176

for the lifestyle or anything like that, you know. But he gets the work, so . . .'

One thing to be relieved about. But it's a small thing. He might not live the life, but he works the job. That's bad enough on its own. 'Was it going in for the lifestyle that got you into a hole?' Arnie's asking.

Glass is smiling. He doesn't think about Ella as being part of the lifestyle. She's part of his life. 'Sort of,' he's saying reluctantly. Because he only met her through her work. Can't deny that. And her work is part of the lifestyle. Doesn't matter how much he wishes otherwise, it is and it will continue to be.

Arnie's about to pursue the point when he hears a key in the door. Oliver home. Hears him walking along the corridor and opening the door to his bedroom.

'Oliver, kitchen,' Arnie's shouting.

Oliver sticks his head round the door. Sees his friend and his grandfather. A slight frown that he manages to kill before it gives his mood away. He was happy coming in the door. Came out of that meeting with Greig about as well as he could have. The adrenalin may be fading, but he's still a little high. The thrill, the confidence that he handled a treacherous situation well. Can't beat that feeling. It's going to cost him. He's the one who'll have to pay the cop, because he isn't going to tell Bowles about it. Not yet, anyway. You don't tell the boss that you got cornered by a bent copper. You pay the cost yourself. You see if there's any way you can make it work for you. A guy like Greig could be very useful. A guy like Glass, not so much.

'Alex. Good to see you, man. Come through.' Nodding for his friend to follow him through to the bedroom where they can talk in private. Away from Arnie. Away from any conversation that reveals more than it should. Too late for that.

Arnie is still sitting in the kitchen. Waiting for Glass to leave and Oliver to come talk to him. Which he will, because he has to explain this Marty thing. Glass isn't smart enough to lie about what he told Arnie. They've been in there ten minutes now. At one point there was a raised voice. Oliver's, certainly. Harsh, it sounded. Almost mocking in tone. Now the bedroom door is opening. Now the front door, and someone's gone. Glass moved along that corridor quickly, leaving in a hurry and a huff.

Oliver's coming into the kitchen. Nodding to his grandfather. Looks grumpy, looks like he's ready for an argument. Arnie knows the look. Oliver gets it when he's annoyed with something, but he knows it better from Oliver's father. There was a fellow who never let a potential fight walk casually by. Always spoiling for trouble. Always in a howler. Had to handle him carefully, just like you do his son.

'I think that boy's in trouble,' Arnie's saying. Open with agreement. Something obvious. Something that Oliver can't possibly object to.

'I think so too.'

'Silly thing, to borrow money. Drags you down, that sort of thing. Never ends well. That boy needs a friend to help him out. Why don't you give him the work Marty Jones is giving you? You can concentrate on getting the hell away from Marty Jones, like you were going to.'

A sigh for an answer. Oliver standing with his back to the worktop, looking down at the table where Arnie's sitting. A grim look, already on the defensive and ready to defend with aggression. 'I've been doing a few jobs for Marty, yeah. Just a few. Now and again. I don't make enough money from Roy Bowles. You know how unreliable that work is. You know I don't make enough there. So I need something else. But it's temporary.'

'And how long has it been temporary?'

'Fine. You're right. I know you are. Marty Jones is poison. You don't have to tell me that. You really don't. Listen, right. I'll make you a promise: I will be out from Marty's business within the month, okay? I'll be gone in a month. I'm looking at another opportunity. Something better. I've been think-ing about it for a while. I did a job for Roy today. Made me realize a few things. Seriously, within a month. That enough to make you happy?'

Arnie's looking at him. Ignoring the snarky tone. The superior tone that's crept into a lot of what Oliver says these days. This time he meant it, but he doesn't always. There's been a tendency lately for him to speak down to his grandfather. Presumably because he's working and Arnie isn't. Gets on Arnie's nerves, sure, but he doesn't say anything. Why bother?

He wants to believe Oliver will get out from under Marty. He also wants to believe that when Oliver stops working for Marty, it will be for something better. Something legitimate. Wants to believe, but doesn't. If he has plans of his own then it'll be within the industry. What else does he know? But anything is better than Marty.

'Fine. You get away from Marty Jones; I'll say no more about it.'

PART THREE

1

This hasn't gone as quickly as he would have liked. Not as quickly as MacArthur would like either. But Cruickshank can see it for what it is. Cracking a tough little nut. Once you get inside, it'll be soft. Break through and things happen quickly. But Patterson has surrounded his business with a wall of tough employees. Loyal and hard. Also very private. Done an amazing job of keeping mouths shut, not giving away any detail they don't want people to know. That's a hard challenge, even with loyal employees. People speak, but not the people working for Patterson. Been difficult for both Potty and MacArthur to work out who's who in the Patterson organization. They've done so well in protecting themselves. Today will change some of that. Today Potty has a meeting with a lowlife scumbag with a big mouth.

Best part of three months since Patterson got rid of Jim Holmes. Sent someone round to slash him. Left a mark for all the world to see. Lets people know that Holmes is not a man to be trusted. Which is a good thing to tell people. Helpful. Appreciated. But that doesn't stop Holmes from being useful. At least, Holmes better hope it doesn't. Today, he needs to be useful.

They're meeting in the back of a pub that Potty has a share of. Little place. Reasonably upmarket, as these places go. Potty doesn't much like pubs. Never visits. But he has to have places like this. Lots of little businesses where his money washes itself clean. Can't justify all of the returns that his 'finance company' makes. Pubs are an easy sort of business to pick up these days, easy to work the books.

Holmes was early. Was here before Potty, and hit the bar while he waited. He was on his third pint when Potty's driver dropped him off. The landlord showed Potty through to the back, made sure he had everything he needed. A big, well-lit room with a small table. A large, cushioned seat for Potty, a small chair for the other guy. They have little events in here, put out a few tables. Just the one table for this meeting. The landlord showed Potty to his seat, asked if he wanted any-thing to eat or drink. Then went and got the waiting Holmes from his happy place at the bar.

Sitting opposite each other. Each thinking the same of the other. What a bastard. Everyone thinks Potty's a bastard. Principally because he is, and makes little effort to hide it. Potty thinks Holmes is a bastard for a couple of reasons. Both are that he's a little thief. Thieved from Marty Jones. Got caught. Thieved from Billy Patterson. Got caught. Three months go by, and now he's running to Potty, looking for help.

Potty's had Holmes's background looked into. Found out

what he's been up to for the last three months. Struggling, is what. Split with his woman. Left his house. Tried to run, but couldn't make life work anywhere else. Came back to the city looking for work. Couldn't find it. Now begging at Potty's door. Saying he has info about Patterson that could help. The shaggy-haired, bearded, overweight prick better, because he's on thin ice. Three strikes and you're out. Got away with thieving from Marty. Was lucky to get away from Patterson with scarring. Piss off Potty Cruickshank and it goes further.

Don't show your distaste. Fellow looks like he could use a wash. Hair is a little too long, beard that's probably only there to hide scars. Clothes look scruffy, but Potty's seen a good deal worse. You think he's pathetic and disgusting. You think he's the sort of person you shouldn't have to lower yourself to meeting. But you do. Information can come from anywhere, and sometimes you just have to hold your nose to get a hold of it.

'So, Mr Holmes, I'm led to believe that you have information you think I would find useful.' Said in a tone that makes it clear Potty doesn't believe him. That makes it clear he better deliver fast. Keep this conversation short.

'I do. I know all about Patterson. Worked for him for a couple of months. I can name everyone working for him. Everyone close to him. The lot of them.'

They know a few names already. They've taken action against a couple so far. A couple isn't enough. Not in three months. Especially when they're not at the top of the tree. You have to be seen to make a sustained attack. Less than one a month is not sustained. At times, it's felt like they shouldn't have bothered. Should have waited until they had three or four names and gone after them all in a week. You drip-feed it like this and you're the one who looks weak. Attacked the first guy. Beat him and set his house on fire. A little showy, but it sent out the message. Sent him scurrying off out of the business. Bought off the second guy. He was reluctant and expensive, but he took the money in the end.

'And what makes you think I would care about that?' Potty is saying. Throwing in the question because you have to pretend that you don't care. Make the bottom feeders think you have a thousand plates spinning. Make them think Patterson is no big deal to you. You don't want the likes of Holmes knowing your business, or even thinking he knows.

Holmes is watching him, mouth slightly open. Picking his answer from the short list of options running through his mind. Holmes is no fool. Been around the business too long for that. He knows that Potty doesn't want to hear that he's at war with Billy Patterson. You don't say that sort of thing out loud. Not to the guy in charge. Especially when the guy in charge isn't clearly winning the war.

'I thought it would be useful for you to know. Always good to know what a rival's got around him. Information, you know. Even if he ain't much of a rival, I mean.' Said with a shrug. Grasping for the right tone.

Potty's smiling. He's even more unpleasant when he smiles, but isn't that often the way. 'You have been around this business a long time, haven't you, Mr Holmes. Yes, that might be useful. And what would you want in return?'

Pick this one carefully as well. Don't trip yourself up here. A shrug to begin with. Get the tone just right before you throw the options back at Potty. And you do give Potty the options. He has to be the one that decides the reward. You don't demand anything, because you don't have the right to choose.

'I'd be happy with work. Happy with payment. Whatever it's worth, Mr Cruickshank, whatever it's worth.'

Potty's nodding. Holmes doesn't expect work. Maybe doesn't even want it. Happy to take money, bonus money. Go sit at the bar with it. He must know work's never going to come his way from a man like Potty. You skim from one guy, you still have a chance of finding work. You skim from two and you can forget about it. Two is a pattern. Two is the end of your career. Two is the last time anyone credible looks at you as anything other than filth. And Holmes knows it, because Holmes has indeed been around the business for a long time. He was skimming from Patterson because he was going to run. Never planned to come back. But here he is. Back, desperate, and looking for money.

'I would be willing to pay you,' Potty is saying. 'Information is a valuable commodity, and I'm a generous man. But it has to be the right information.'

'I know the people around him. I made a point of finding out. He keeps some things close, does Patterson. But you can always find out when you're in the company. They have to tell you something.'

'The key men?'

'He has it, like, I guess you would say a pyramid. It's all very carefully put together, know what I mean. Conn Griffiths and Mikey Summers. Those two are high up the chain of command. Very high. They oversee a lot of stuff. Organizers. Collectors as well, but they're more than that. They collect to make it look like they're not that important. Tough guys, too, so they can do it. Real tough, actually. But they're a lot more than collectors. Those two are important day-to-day. They're who you go to if you have a problem. Who you go to if you need to find something out about a job, or to find out what the job is. People would notice if they weren't there any more.'

Potty can sense the sting in the tail. Very clear from his tone that Holmes is building to something bigger, but that he wants Potty to ask him about it. Makes Holmes feel clever. Fine, we shall play the game, just this once. Only because these are good names. Griffiths was a name one of MacArthur's boys brought them, but only as a collector. They didn't know he was important. Summers is interesting. Potty remembers the name. Used to have a reputation as brutal muscle, one of the toughest in the city. Lot of people wanted to employ that boy, and then he went off the radar. Now he knows why. Anyway, back to the game.

'So these are the two I should be concerning myself with, are they?' Asked with an almost bored tone. Almost, but not quite. Don't put Holmes off before he's had the chance to show how clever and useful he is.

'They're important,' Holmes is saying, 'but they're not the most important. If you want to get to Patterson, the man you want is Alan Bavidge. He's the one guy with full access to Patterson. The one guy Patterson trusts with all his biggest stuff. That's who he goes to, every time.'

Potty's frowning a little. See, Potty had a good look at Holmes's background. He knows who attacked Holmes that night three months ago. Cut his face. Cut his mouth. Norah Faulkner dropped the name of Alan Bavidge. Young Mr Bavidge has quite a reputation for being a ruthless bastard. Rather a good reputation to have in this business. A man that a lot of people, Holmes included, have good reason to hate.

'I do hope you're not giving me this name in some attempt at revenge,' Potty is saying.

Holmes is frowning. Obviously didn't expect Potty to know who cut him. His right hand starts to make its way up to his face to touch the scar. A long ugly line, barely perceptible to the touch but very visible. The beard covers it, but imperfectly. He's realized what his hand is doing and he's bringing it back down to his lap. 'No. Not revenge. It's the truth. Patterson doesn't have a right-hand man. Not in the usual way. But Bavidge is the closest thing to it that he has. Bavidge still collects. Still goes out and does the shitty jobs. That's a cover. He's the one. He attacked Jamie Stamford because Bavidge is the key guy. He attacked me because of it. He's the one Patterson uses on every big job. Just the big jobs. Takes his advice on every big move. All Patterson's men know that. You get rid of Bavidge and Patterson's weak.'

It's not like this is the first time they've heard the name Alan Bavidge. They knew he attacked Holmes. There were suspicions he was the one who attacked Jamie Stamford. Stamford didn't confirm it, said he wasn't sure. Trying to cover his embarrassment. It was Bavidge. And now Potty's hearing that Bavidge is the most important person in Patterson's organization. He believes Holmes. Holmes has to be telling the truth, because he knows the price of a lie.

'Okay, Mr Holmes,' Potty is saying, and nodding. 'I can accept that as a start. I want your contact details. I may be in touch with you again. I'll pay for this. Half up, half when I know you've been honest with me.'

Holmes is pausing, but not for long. A man like Potty will pay. He might not be walking out of here with money, but he'll get something. Potty will pay the upfront money in the next couple of days. The rest will come when Potty sees how much damage he can do Patterson with the info. Doesn't serve Potty's interests to stiff someone on a deal. Even someone like Holmes. So Holmes is shaking Potty's fat hand and walking out to the front of the pub. Another drink or two before he leaves.

Potty's watching him go. Desperate. Maybe they both are, but Potty's hiding it better. This is what he was waiting for. Three names, all confirmed as senior movers. But it's Bavidge he'll go for. That's the star prize. A man close enough to Patterson to make an impact on the whole organization. And a man Alex MacArthur will be very happy to see the back of. There'll be no attempt to buy Bavidge. They will remove him instead.

2

He was in a hole. So he dug. Glass isn't proud of himself. Isn't proud of the situation he's found himself in. When he borrowed that money from Jefferson, he had every intention of paying it back. Pay it. Pay the interest. Cut the rope that the collector would hang you with. Never go back. But you have to have work. He could raise some money, but never fast enough. He paid and paid, but there was always more interest than he could keep up with. And all the time he was worried about losing Ella.

She never demanded that he bring in more money. It was never like that. That makes her sound like she was pushing him into it. It wasn't that. But there was a life she wanted for them both. Improvements to the flat. Even talking about finding a house. All these things that she wanted them to have, and she was the only one earning money to pay for them. She never pointed that out, but Glass knew, and it hurt. And he wanted to give her the lifestyle too. Parties, drink, drugs, fun. These things cost money, and he wanted her to have them. To have whatever made her happy. It was either that or lose her to someone who could pay for the life. See, she's pretty and popular. She knows a lot of men. Some of whom would give her that lifestyle. Glass was convinced that she wanted all that. Convinced that he had to help pay for it. So he borrowed more.

He was paying just enough back for Jefferson to lend him more. So he borrowed more, and the interest climbed higher. But he was able to get the things Ella wanted. They got a tumble dryer. They got a new carpet for the living room. And they went out a few times. Couple of times to a club, which is what Glass thought she wanted. Then the third time he suggested it, she said they should go to a restaurant instead. That was even better. The money was to make her happy. To make sure that, at the end of the night, she went home with Glass. And it worked, for a while.

Money runs dry. If you don't have work, it runs dry fast. So he couldn't pay for the life. Ella had worked less when he had the money. The money went, so she started working more. They didn't talk about it. She didn't say anything, because she didn't want to upset him. But she was working more, and he knew it. Glass begged for work but got none. So he borrowed a little more. But that was his last borrow. Hasn't paid a penny back to Jefferson in over a month now. Jefferson, understandably, is not happy.

No point looking to Marty for work. He wasn't interested before, and he sure as hell isn't now. Being a friend of Peterkinney has suddenly made Glass's name poison with Marty. That little falling-out makes Marty a no-go area for

Glass. Peterkinney stabbing Marty in the back cost Glass work. So Glass looked to Peterkinney. But Peterkinney has bigger fish to fry now. Doesn't need Glass any more. Oh no, no time at all for his friends. All Glass did was introduce him to the industry. Get him started with Marty. Set him off on the road he's on now. Only has what he has because of Glass. You would think that would mean something. You would think being a friend meant something. Does it fuck. Not in Peterkinney's new world. Nah, Glass is yesterday's news. He tried getting in touch. Did everything he could to reach out to Peterkinney. Didn't matter how often he called or went round to Peterkinney's office though. He got nowhere.

So now he's going to see Jefferson. Jefferson called the flat about eleven this morning. Ella was still crashed out in bed. She worked last night. Arrived home five hours after Glass. Collapsed silently into bed and fell asleep in her clothes. She's been doing that more lately. Glass knows. He remembers that first night. Shit, that was more than five months ago. Feels like years to him. It was thrilling. It was fucking brilliant. Now other men are having their first night with Ella. Doesn't matter that she always comes home to him.

He never told Ella that he'd borrowed money. She would only get pissed off about it. Say that he wasn't earning proper money. She would start saying that he was making matters worse when she was working to make them better. It would push her away. So he didn't tell her where he was going. Just went into the bedroom and told her he was going out. She grumbled something inaudible. Her mind was still lost in the mists of last night. It'll take a good hour after waking to get her head together.

So he's walking to Jefferson's place, because he still doesn't have a car. Couldn't hope to get the cash for one of those. Couldn't buy one, couldn't fill it with petrol even if he could. Not going to spend the money for a bus fare when he's not in a hurry. Takes him the best part of half an hour to get there. Not long enough. Hasn't thought of anything to say. He needs to buy time, but he has nothing to buy with. Only way to buy time is to pay some money to Jefferson. Money Glass doesn't have. Hasn't had in an age. All he has is words. The poor man's currency.

Through to the back office, sitting opposite Jefferson. Same as it was when he borrowed the first time. And the second, and third. Same as when he paid back. Plain little office, Jefferson behind the desk. This time the mood is different. Gone from friendly, to understanding, to weary, to angry. Jefferson looking across the desk at him, shaking his head before he says a word.

'I'm hoping you're here with money, Alex, but I doubt it.'

Glass is smiling a little bit. It's an unconvincing attempt at charm. 'Listen, thing is, I ran out of work. But I'm confident. I am, real confident. I have something lined up. Shouldn't need more than a couple of weeks and I'll be able to come up with something for you. Something substantial, you know. Not just pennies this time.'

Jefferson's frowning. 'Not the first time you've told me that. Said that last time and it turned out to be baloney. I don't see why I should trust you this time. Do you even know how much you owe me, Alex?' Asking just to put the pressure on. They never know. Not unless they have a head for figures and the fiscal discipline to work out their interest payments. People with a head for figures and fiscal discipline don't borrow from Gary Jefferson. They never know, and Glass won't either.

'I know that I owe you a lot. I know . . .'

'Do you know that you owe me six thousand two hundred pounds?'

A frown. But no arguments. He's borrowed over a grand from Jefferson. Makes sense that it would be up to over six thousand. Actually, he thought it might be higher than that. He has paid back about eight hundred, but not fast enough. Yes, it's a rip-off. He knew it would be when he came here the first time. Knew it would get worse with each visit. So six thousand isn't a surprise.

'Okay. I owe you six thousand two hundred. And I will pay you every penny of that. You know I will.'

'Excuse me, I do not know that. You are a client who's never paid a debt in full. Bits and pieces, but never in full. I do not know that you are capable of paying this.'

Another frown. This is moving into territory Glass is afraid of. The lender selling the debt to a collector. He has to make sure that doesn't happen. He couldn't cope with that. The beatings. The intimidation. The truth spilling out. It would ruin his relationship with Ella in a heartbeat. She'd be gone. They'd take everything from him. Just hang on to what you've got. This might be bad, but it's the best he can do for now.

'Listen, okay, listen. I have some things I can sell. I have a couple of favours I can call in. I swear to you. I will raise some money by the end of the week. Can you give me until the end of the week?' Pleading, and trying to sound like the most reasonable man in the world while he does it.

A reluctant sigh. 'Listen to me, Alex. If you don't have at least five hundred by the end of the week, I run out of patience. I have a business to run here. This isn't a charity.' How often has he spoken these words?

'Sure. I get that, I do. Trust me: I will have five hundred by the weekend. I swear on my life I will.'

Glass is up and shaking Jefferson by the hand. So enthusiastic, just because he thinks he's bought himself a week. They all get like that. Thinking they've done something brilliant. The great negotiators. Thinking a week will be enough to pay off the debt they've been building for months. Always thinking that something will come along and rescue them.

By the time he gets back to the flat and Ella, Glass is

feeling pretty good about things. He's got five days to put something together. To come up with some real money. Right now he has thirty quid to his name. That's everything he has in the world. Where to find work in five days. Where to find work that will pay him five hundred quid. Okay, that's a tough one. Begging to Peterkinney again. That has to be the first port of call. After that, he's out of options. Into desperation territory. Kind of territory where you don't earn money, you just take it.

'I'm going out tonight,' Ella's saying, sitting down beside him on the couch. 'Work.' Neatly dressed, made-up. Always ready to make a good impression.

'I'll come with,' Glass is saying optimistically.

'No, can't. I'm going to Heavenly. Adam told me you're not allowed. Marty's orders.'

Well, that's just fucking brilliant. Ella going to a private party and Glass isn't even allowed in the door. And whose fault is that? Peterkinney's. So he bloody well owes him a favour. A little work isn't much to ask. Not with the money Peterkinney's making these days.

3

There's a pleasure waking up in your own place for the first time. Not his parents' house. Not his grandfather's flat. A flat of his own. Small, sure, but he's the only one here. He doesn't have to wait for someone else to get out of the bathroom, or rush because they're waiting for him. He doesn't have to shuffle sideways to get past his grandfather in the kitchen. It's small, but it's big enough for one. And his own. All his own. Oliver Peterkinney, with his own place. His own privacy. His own life, at last. That's because he has the money for it. Because he's raising the cash to pay for this. Moving up in the world costs.

Did one shitty job too many for Marty. Got bored of waiting for Bowles to come up with more work. He knew he could do better than Marty. He could see how Marty was running his business. See all the mistakes he was making. Mistakes born from greed and complacency. Marty was too distracted. Had too many other things he was trying to make money from. Collecting was down his list, and that meant he took his eye off the ball too often. Peterkinney could do better than that; he just needed to take the initiative. So he did.

He had the connections. Knew plenty guys at the bottom

of the heap from the work he'd already done. Easy to find the other connections he needed. They came thick and fast as soon as he started looking. You start with Paul Greig. He was willing to help. He's a very well-connected man. So he gave Peterkinney a few names to help him get his business off the ground. After that, it was all about setting the right tone.

He'd thought Greig was going to be tricky. Not a bit of it. You just need to know what to say. Greig wants two things from any deal he does. He wants money, and he wants to feel like he's doing his duty. See, the money on its own isn't enough. Greig's bent, but he doesn't want to be reminded of it. That's what some people don't get. People like Marty, who Greig thinks is a monumental dickhead. You have to give Greig the sense that he's doing what's right as a cop. That was simple. Just repeat the trick he used with the guns.

They had a good thing going with the guns. Peterkinney paid Greig from his share, Greig kept Peterkinney safe. Even dropped the name of a new buyer in town. So Peterkinney went for two in a row. Told Greig he was looking to get into the collecting business. That he saw the mess a guy like Marty was making, and thought he could do it better. Do it cleaner. Do it in a way that contains it. A lot of talk about moneylending and debt collection these days. Economy in the gutter and all that. Greig liked the idea of containing that business. Didn't much believe in it, but he liked it enough to justify helping. To justify taking his cut.

Out of the flat and along to his new car. Nicer than the last one. Not much to ask. Not exactly top of the range, but one step at a time. Got a decent deal from a garage owner looking to cut a debt he owed. Peterkinney knows better than to be flash. It's smart to stay under the radar. He's already made an enemy of Marty, which he didn't want to do. Didn't want to make an enemy of anyone. Best way to make your way in this business is quietly. Grow without drawing attention until you're big enough to defend yourself. These early days are the riskiest. But he's been at this nearly two months and nobody's stamped on him. So far, he's in the clear.

He's got a little office. It was Greig that pushed him towards it. Peterkinney wasn't sure about the expense, but Greig made it clear. People want you to have an office. People expect you to have an office. If you want to look significant, you go get an office. You get a covering business. If people don't see those things, they think you're not serious. Nothing worse than people thinking you're some bumbling amateur. So Peterkinney has them, and the expense they bring. Can't argue with it though, people respect the property as much as the business. People like to see it. Peterkinney likes them to see it. Loves the feeling of power, of intimidation. Makes the job so much easier. Once you're behind the desk, on the proper side of the desk, you realize what it means. You see the power of the office. Of legitimacy. There's nothing more powerful than that. He loves it.

Used to belong to a van hire business. They had the little office and the big garage next door. They sold the garage to some storage company that hasn't started using it yet. The office they're renting to Peterkinney. They don't ask questions, they have more sense than that. They must know what he's doing. It's not a secret. Can't be if you want customers. They must know, and they turn a blind eye. As long as they're getting their money.

Peterkinney's not greedy. That's the key to his good start. He takes wafer-thin margins on the debts he buys. Sometimes he buys at a loss. A lot of his profit goes back out the door in buying loss-leaders. Doesn't matter. Let the profit go. It'll be back. And it'll bring friends. You get a reputation as a good buyer, and all the lenders get in touch. The first few months are defined not by the money you make, but by the impression you make.

But a good buyer needs to show that he can last. That's the second thing. See, the big lenders like to stick to one debt collector. Preferably for years. Common sense. Builds trust and reduces risks. So Peterkinney has to show that he's capable of sticking around. At least as capable as his competitors. Needs to work harder than anyone to prove that, given his age. That means having good people around you. Get a smooth start. No fuck-ups. Another tick on that one. Didn't get every employee he wanted. A few were out of his reach. A few that would have made a difference. Still needs to prove himself to get the very best. But he got good people to work for him. The rest will come, he's sure.

The good employees he did get were attracted by the office too. Here's a new guy, connected to Greig, setting up his own office. Still only twenty years old. The hot new thing. Something of a prodigy. Get one or two well-regarded employees, and the rest follow. Now he has a good little group around him. All busy, collecting. No mess made. They're tough with people, because they have to be. That's the job. He has to collect as much of the debt he buys as possible when his margins are walking on the edge like this. Needs every penny he can claw back. They're tough, but they've never crossed the line. Peterkinney made that very clear. First man crosses the line gets a dose of his own medicine. They respect that approach.

'Any news?' Peterkinney's asking John Kilbanne. Kilbanne works the office for him. Keeps the books. He's nearly twice Peterkinney's age, but that doesn't seem to be a problem. You just have to act mature, and people forget the age. You give them a reason to remember you're a kid, and you're in trouble.

'Nope. Few collections in. Three, actually. One of them paid in full. Other two are still on the hook, but they'll be good for it over time. Couple of jobs to do this afternoon. That's about it.'

He sounds bored. Probably is. Excitement comes from

being successful. Well, it does for Peterkinney. This isn't success for Kilbanne. A thirty-eight-year-old with a degree and ten years' work in accounting. Then a conviction for embezzlement. Then a year and a half inside. He did steal rather a lot of money. Stole it from a law firm, of all things. Then months of not being able to get a legit job. Then years of this kind of work. He doesn't like his work. He doesn't want to be doing this. But his name is poison, his reputation ruined, and this pays the bills.

Peterkinney understands that. It's one of his sharpest skills. He seems to have a knack for knowing what makes people tick. With Kilbanne, it's making sure he has a sense that there's something better on the horizon. Something befitting his old standards. He wants to kid himself that he can reclaim his credibility. So Peterkinney keeps feeding him lines about growing the business. About expanding into legitimate financial services. A wide variety of legitimate businesses that Kilbanne will run. And that keeps him happy. Bored, but happy.

The office is a small place. Room enough for a couple of desks and a filing cabinet. It gives the impression of being a busy place. Folders and sheets of paper on both desks and on top of the filing cabinet. The window's by the front door, a big whiteboard dominates one wall. Peterkinney's happy for people to think the whiteboard was his idea. Let them think they keep running tallies of debts there. They don't.

It was here when they moved in and they've never used it. But he likes it. Likes that it makes the office feel like a working environment. Better a blank whiteboard than some smutty calendar.

There's a little toilet out back as well, but it's temperamental. Not worth the risk. Little corridor that leads out the back door to a small yard that now belongs to the storage company. Kilbanne goes out there for a smoke, but that's it. Peterkinney keeps the door to the corridor closed whenever there's a customer around. Let them think it leads somewhere bigger. Let them think there are more offices back there.

'Your grandfather called again this morning,' Kilbanne is telling him. That's all he's saying. All he needs to say.

Peterkinney's dropping down into his chair. Looking across the small office at Kilbanne. He knows what Kilbanne thinks. Kilbanne thinks his dear old grandpa just wants to talk. Spend some quality time with his wee grandson. Kilbanne thinks that Peterkinney should call the old man back. Go round to see him. Spend some time with him. Arnie's been calling often, and Peterkinney hasn't called back once. Bad grandson. Naughty grandson.

But that isn't it. His grandfather doesn't want to spend more time with him. Living together was enough, thanks all the same. Arnie's about as glad as Oliver is that he's moved out. But Arnie still worries. And Arnie does not like

Peterkinney's new venture one little bit. That's why he's call-ing. Took him a little time to find out what it was, but now he knows. Now that he knows, he's pissed off. He was pleased when Peterkinney told him he had quit working for Marty. The boy keeping a promise. A little relieved when he found out he wasn't working for Roy Bowles any more. Thought the lad was going straight. Then he finds out he's set up his own collection agency. Well, that sent him off the deep end.

They had one argument about it. Only needed one. They've hardly spoken since. Won't either, if Peterkinney can help it. They're not living under each other's feet any more. Easy to break contact. Let the old man get used to it, then get in touch. If he can't get used to it, then he loses a grandson. He doesn't want to lose his grandfather, but this is Peterkin-ney's choice. This is his life and his future. This, he knows, is what he's good at. He won't be held back by anyone. Can't be.

It's afternoon when the call comes into the office from another person that'll only hold him back. Alex Glass. Been a long time now since they spoke. He's still shacked up with that cheap hooker. Ella something or other. There's a pair of them. Total halfwits. Running round after Marty, looking for scraps from his table. Now looking to scrounge from Peter-kinney.

Kilbanne's taken the call. Looking across at Peterkinney and getting a shake of the head.

'No, he's not in,' Kilbanne's saying. 'Can I take a message?

Okay, I'll tell him when he gets back. Goodbye.' Hanging up the phone and looking across at Peterkinney. 'Wants you to call him. Says he has news.'

Yeah, right. News. They always have news. Funny how quickly news turns into requests when people know you have money. Another one who needs to learn, before they can go back to being friends. He does care about Glass, but he won't be his safety net. He won't pay for Glass's mistakes. When Glass stops dreaming and gets rid of the girl, then they can talk. Peterkinney will find work for a friend, if the friend is mature. If the friend can help him.

4

He's been pacing around the office for the last ten minutes. You don't have to know him to know that the best thing to do right now is sit there and nod along. Don't say anything. For God's sake, don't open your mouth. Sit there. Nod when it feels like he's said something that requires agreement. Sit it out and wait for him to say something that requires an answer.

'I lifted him out of the gutter,' Marty's saying. Well, shouting. Hissing, occasionally. They're sitting in the office above a gadget shop that Marty owns. Or leases. Like a lot of Marty's businesses, it's cloudy. Only Marty seems to really know, and he doesn't share info on his businesses.

He uses this office for his collection business. It's his favourite collection point. The muscle bring the money back to this office. Door out on the street that opens onto the staircase. Up the stairs and the door on your left. Unmarked. An office that doesn't advertise its financial service. Big enough place, airy and bright. A few desks, but nothing on any of them. It's not an office where office work gets done. Just a collection point. A place to give out a few orders and collect the returns. The real office work is done somewhere else.

Somewhere the muscle don't get to see. No muscle coming in today. Today there are just the two of them in there.

Marty called Neil Fraser about an hour ago. Fraser arrived half an hour ago. All he's said so far was hello. That was ignored. Marty's on a rant. One that, even for him, is turning epic. Getting it out of his system, and there's a lot to get out. So Fraser's sitting on the comfy swivel chair at a desk, and he's dutifully nodding along in silence. Resisting the temptation to swivel back and forth while he listens.

'He was nothing. Nothing. Shit, wasn't even him I hired, it was his mate. That useless prick. What was his name? Doesn't matter. I hired him. I saw the potential. I gave him everything. Everything. Nobody in his life did more for him than I did. He was living with his grandfather in some shitty shoebox flat. I gave him everything he has. And he thanks me how? How? By fucking off and setting up in competition. Trying to cut me down. Then what does he do? Oh man. What does the bastard do? He grasses me to John Young. Me. The man who made him. And he's grassing me to Young.'

It needn't have come to this. Peterkinncy had no intention of picking a fight with Marty. He was going to walk away and hope Marty was smart enough to leave him alone. But Marty couldn't just let him be. Wounded pride. Bad PR. Marty wanted to be seen to bring down the man he had built up. Had to show the world that he took this sort of thing seriously. You let one bastard with big ideas set up against you, and the rest of these knuckleheads will try and do the same thing. They're impressionable. So he tried to take a few shots at Peterkinney. Undermine him with lenders. So Peterkinney decided to undermine Marty with the people that matter most.

Marty's position in the business is dependent upon the protection he gets from Peter Jamieson. We've established that. Marty couldn't get away with it all if he didn't have that protection. He can run his girls and his parties without Jamieson. He can run some of the other little businesses he has on the go as well. But collecting is different. Collecting is a business built on violence. Attack and defence. You need to be able to protect yourself, or have someone that'll protect you. Jamieson is the protection Marty hides behind.

Jamieson's right-hand man is John Young. Young handles the day-to-day stuff, including collecting their share of Marty's money. A reasonable cut for providing little-needed protection. The name – and reputation – Jamieson and his men carry is protection enough. But Peterkinney knew a little something. He knew that Marty held his private parties at his brother's club instead of Jamieson's because it meant he could avoid paying Jamieson his cut. Thought he could keep a little more for himself. That was greedy, and very stupid. So Peterkinney made a phone call.

'That little bastard calling up John Young. Dropping me right into the shit. Thinking he was being clever. Thinking they would stop working with me because of it. Huh, little bastard doesn't know how this business works. Doesn't know a fucking thing. Now I'll have to spend the next few months sucking up to John fucking Young because of this. He's not getting away with it. Nobody gets away with treating me that way.'

It's all clichéd ranting. In part, this is Marty trying to sound big and tough. Trying to reassure himself that he can sound big and tough. A brain-dead lump of wood like Fraser will believe it, and that boosts Marty's ego. But he also knows that nobody would grass a man they really feared. Nobody would grass Jamieson or Alex MacArthur. Nobody would grass men like Don Park or John Young. Even muscle like Nate Colgan and Mikey Summers would carry enough reputation to protect themselves from tattletales. But Peterkinney didn't fear Marty, and that worries Marty. People like Jamieson and Young see him as a profitable opportunist. People like Peterkinney see him as an unreliable party boy. None of them see him the way he sees himself. So he's going to have to persuade them. Prove that he's a man to fear. For that, he needs someone like Fraser.

Fraser's nodding along to every sentence. All this movie-mobster shouting sounds pretty good to his ears. This is the way a powerful person should talk, he thinks. This is a guy showing how tough he is. Fraser prefers this to the quiet, businesslike manner he sees in John Young.

'You know what we're going to do? You know what we're going to do about this?'

Fraser's opening his mouth, about to throw in what he thinks will be a convincing answer. Something he thinks will add to the conversation, if you can call it a conversation. But that wasn't a question that invited an answer. Fraser's only just gotten his mouth open when Marty starts talking again.

'We're going to send a message. You and me, we're going to send a message. A message to that shit Peterkinney. A message to everyone else as well. Let them see that you don't fuck with Marty Jones.'

Now he's looking for a response. Looking to Neil Fraser, a man who's never been quick with his responses. Marty picked him carefully. Picked him because he knows Fraser loves this bullshit mouthing off. Loves going to Marty's parties. Loves playing at being the big tough guy. Slow-thinking, but always willing to act. Willing to do what he's told, as long as the rewards are good. And Marty will make sure he gets a good reward for this. Parties, mostly. Drugs and women. That's what Fraser wants. A bit of money, sure, but it's more about the lifestyle.

Picked him for another reason, too. Marty remembers. Remembers who hates who. That's an important thing to remember in the industry. When you arrange parties, you get to meet a lot of people. Hear all the gossip. Marty knows how valuable that is. Fraser hates Peterkinney. It's been mentioned a few times. There was that scuffle between them. Was it a proper fight? No, hold on, Angus Lafferty broke it up before it turned physical. Another man people respect and fear. They do what he tells them, so the fight never really started. But Fraser was pissed off about it. Complained a few times. Made a few noises about what he would do if he saw Peterkinney again. Probably seen him again since. Did nothing. But now the opportunity is going to land right in his lap. He can't say no.

'Yeah,' Fraser's saying. 'We should go get him. We should make sure people know that he can't get away with it.'

Marty's nodding. This is what he wants to hear. Fraser not only agreeing, but being enthusiastic about it. He wants to be a part of this. He wants to go out and hurt Peterkinney. He wants to deliver the message and get himself closer to Marty. No reluctance. Which is dumb, by the way. Marty knows how stupid Fraser is being here. Fraser gets a lot of work from John Young. Young uses Fraser because Fraser is physically big and intimidating. As long as Fraser keeps his mouth shut and stays intimidating, Young's happy with it. But Fraser isn't happy. Fraser wants more, despite not being capable of handling more. He has ambitions he's not nearly smart enough to fulfil. Easy for Marty to exploit.

'Good,' Marty's nodding. 'Because I've got a plan. We're going to send him a real message. No fucking around, you know. Get the message out to him. Make sure everyone knows what a big deal it is to fuck with me, you know?'

'Yeah, sure.'

Marty's nodding and smiling. This is the hard bit. See, Fraser's muscle. That's all he is. He's big dumb muscle, and he goes out and beats people up. Cheap and nasty. This is going to be something else. Marty wants to push Fraser a little further. Wants him to do more than just beat Peterkinney up. Peterkinney isn't some little bastard that didn't pay his debt. Beating him up doesn't send anything like enough of a message. He has to be seen to suffer more than a rogue client.

'I want you to send the message, Neil,' Marty's saying. Standing in front of him. Fraser still sitting in the swivel chair, moving slightly back and forth. Marty trying to make a strong impression. 'I want you to go and pay him a visit. I want you to send a message that can never be ignored. You with me on that?'

'Yeah, sure, I'll go pay him a visit.' He still doesn't get it. He still doesn't see that this is more than just a beating. Marty's going to have to spell it out.

'You agree with me that it's not enough just to give the arrogant bastard a beating, right?'

'Yeah, okay. I do.' Nodding along, but a little less enthusiastic now. Doesn't like the edge that's come into Marty's voice. Obvious that Marty's trying to push this a different way. This is going to move in a direction he hasn't gone before.

'We need to make sure that he's out of this. That people see that if you fuck with me, you're out of the business. You know? So it's not enough to beat him, right. We have to do more. I say we stick him. You go out, find him alone and stick him. That'll send the message. You and me, Neil, sending the message. Then you and me celebrating, you know.'

Fraser's nodding. He wasn't nodding at the talk of stabbing Peterkinney. That's a little more than he's used to. But the talk of celebrating. That makes him happy. That's enough for him to start nodding along. He hasn't noticed that Marty kept using the word 'we'. It won't be we. It'll be Fraser going out and doing all the work. He will take all the risks. Do all the dirty work. The 'we' will start when the job is done. Him and Marty celebrating. But it's the promise of the celebration that matters.

'Good,' Marty's saying to the nod. Not letting Fraser talk about it. If he starts talking, he might start questioning. If he starts questioning, there might be a problem. 'I'll get you a list of addresses. The place he lives, his office. You go find him. Get it done quick. Listen, I've got a huge party coming up this weekend. Big thing. You and me are going to make it a hell of a weekend.'

And Fraser's bounding out the door. The big unit, happy as Larry. He's going to get the rewards. Marty's happy too.

The rewards won't cost him anything, because he's throwing the party anyway. He'll let Fraser hang around. Could be useful. A guy close to Young could really help at a time like this. Marty's struggling to keep Jamieson's protection because of Peterkinney. He grassed him up to Young. Marty's in the bad books. He hasn't been kicked out yet. Jamieson hasn't abandoned him. Not yet. Marty's too profitable to be ditched for a first offence. But he's not going to be as well protected as he was. He's going to have to win them back around. Fraser might help with that. Sending a message. That always helps. Marty's sighing as the energy of the performance drains from him. He used to enjoy this sort of thing. Performing, fighting, striking back. Now it seems childish. Seems like it's getting in the way of bigger things.

5

Took the best part of an hour for Jefferson to pick up the phone and make a call. Glass won't get the money. Tough shit if he does. He's had more chances than he deserves. He won't, anyway. Jefferson's seen the like so many times. They buy a little time, and then turn up at the end of the week looking for more. Glass will be the same. He won't get the money. He'll come back begging for more time. Might as well get rid of the debt now and save a week of waiting.

So Jefferson made the phone call. That took more thought than you might imagine. Jefferson is a man with his ear to the ground. Every good lender is. It's not just knowing who you can lend to and who you can't. You need to know who to sell the debt to. He's been selling to Patterson for a while now. A few months, and it's been a good few months. Productive for both parties. Patterson bought some poor debts. Gave good percentage. But times are changing.

Jefferson listens. Jefferson understands. Potty Cruickshank is making moves against Billy Patterson. Potty Cruickshank has Alex MacArthur helping him. That means they're big moves. That means it's time to make sure that Potty isn't still pissed off with him. He needs to rebuild bridges. Not that he thinks Potty will definitely win. He and MacArthur are taking such a long time to make any impact on Patterson. That's a sign in Patterson's favour. But you cover your bases, don't you? Cruickshank and MacArthur together is one big fucking tag team.

So Jefferson called up Cruickshank. Let him know that he has a few debts he's looking to shift. See how Cruickshank took it. Potty's an old pro. Potty didn't make any fuss about Jefferson making sales to Patterson. Didn't even mention Patterson. And now Cruickshank's car has pulled up outside the office. Making his way in. Fatter than ever, which is saying something. He's filling the doorway, looking out of breath already. Only taken a few paces from the car. Maybe it's the stress. A man like Potty isn't used to having to fight these battles. Not exactly in fighting condition.

'Gary, good to see you,' he's saying, smiling. Waddling across to the desk. There's an extra-large and extra-comfortable chair in front of the desk to accommodate his fat arse. Jefferson had to borrow it from a neighbouring office. Won't mention that, obviously. You don't mention the fact that you've had to take special measures to accommodate someone else's obesity. Potty's shaking hands with Jefferson and carefully lowering himself into the chair. The slow lowering of a man used to spilling over the sides. Used to straining the chair beneath him.

'Good to see you too. It only occurred to me this morning how long it's been since we did business.'

Potty's smiling. Play the game. Create the convenient little lie. Pretend that they never really fell out. That they never really stopped doing business. Let's pretend and get on with it. But if Jefferson's stupid enough to think that Potty will forget, there could be a nasty surprise coming down the road. Potty doesn't forget. Let's not get melodramatic: he's not going to do anything about it. Not right now. Maybe not ever. He won't try to make something happen. But if an opportunity lands in his lap to punish Jefferson, he will take it. No more than that. Another lesson learned from his uncle. People will line up to cause trouble; don't join the queue. Keep people happy until the chance organically arises. It usually will. You only take direct action when you really need to. So Potty's playing the game, and waiting.

'It has been a while,' Potty's nodding. 'Time to put that right, I would say.'

'Yes,' Jefferson's saying. Not too enthusiastic. Not when Patterson's still in the game. Not when he's doing such a good job of standing up to Potty. This meeting still comes with the risk that Potty might not win this battle.

'Let's look at the book, shall we,' Potty's saying. Leaning forwards to look at the debts that Jefferson's putting in front of him.

There are only a few debts on the book Jefferson's passing across the table. Keeping it soft. Mostly safe. Debts Potty can be sure of turning a profit on. Debts Jefferson's already made his profit on. He's put Alex Glass on that list. Right near the top. Right where Potty can see it. The ones at the top are the ones Jefferson wants rid of. The ones he hopes Potty will pick up, all in the name of rebuilding those collapsed bridges.

Potty's scanning them. Checking every name before he makes any sort of judgement. Another lesson from Uncle Rolly. Don't throw yourself at the first name on a list. When you're buying debt, you have to put yourself inside the head of the lender. There will always be debts he will want to sell you more than others. Of course, a lot of the time you'll just be negotiating for one particular debt. But when you're looking at the books, you look at the whole damn thing. Take in the detail. Spot the elephant traps, if you can.

Which is exactly what he's doing. Looking for names he recognizes. Ones he's dealt with before. Mercifully few of those. A few big debts here, a few small. Nothing to get wildly excited about. Occasionally you stumble across a debt that just blows you away. Impossible to understand how anyone could be so stupid as to get into that kind of trouble in the first place. Six figures, occasionally. That's usually gambling debts. People with a decent job and a house of their own who gamble more than they should. Keep getting credit extended because they've got that job and that house. In the end, they can't pay it back without selling the house. Won't sell the house. So Potty steps in and his boys persuade them. None of those today.

Eyes scanning back up towards the top of the list. Mid-range stuff. Again, all very ordinary. But these are the ones Jefferson wants to sell. So Potty will make the effort to be polite. He won't buy all of the names at the top. One or two out of the top three. Then a few from further down. Enough to make Jefferson happy. Enough to let him know that Potty has more generosity left in him if Jefferson behaves himself in the future.

'Anything I should know about any of these fellows?' he's asking. And they are all fellows, in case you're wondering. Not a woman on the list. Jefferson has women who owe him. Female debts to sell. But not to Potty. Other people will pay better to have a woman to collect from.

Potty wants to know if there's any good reason for him to avoid any of these names. If any of these men are connected to people that Potty would piss off by collecting on them. You don't want to be collecting from a Jamie Stamford without realizing it. Potty's smart, well connected. If any of these men were well connected he would know. But you always ask. Might be someone awkward, from lower down the chain. And if a problem turns up that Jefferson didn't warn him about, Jefferson's in trouble.

'Could be. I don't know how interesting it is to you. The boy Alex Glass, down for six thousand two hundred?'

'Uh-huh. What about him?'

'He used to be very tight with Oliver Peterkinney. You

know the boy Peterkinney. Little kid, set up his own collection agency?'

'I know of him,' Potty's saying. Of course he bloody does. Knows all about him. Keeping a close eye on that one. Got his fingers burnt with Patterson by not keeping a close eye on him. Won't make that mistake a second time. Keeping a close eye on the boy because he seems to know what he's doing. Everyone dismissing him as a kid. Like that matters. Doesn't matter how young he is, he's smart and tough. Smart and tough is worth watching. Managed to get some good people on board with him as well. Potty has a theory that there might be someone else in the background, pulling strings. Just a theory. Maybe Peterkinney isn't just the front man. Maybe he is the boss.

'Well, this kid Glass used to be his best pal. They ran together for years. Story is, it was Glass who got Peterkinney into the business. Got him a job with Marty Jones. Only in the last six months or so that they've grown apart. Glass doesn't work for him, so, I don't know. He doesn't work for him, needs to borrow money from me. Maybe they ain't that close any more. But they were. Close as brothers for many years.'

Potty's processing all that. Just sitting there, looking straight ahead. A slight smile on his face, but that's often there. Don't read too much into that. He's thinking. Thinking about Peterkinney, and about Alex MacArthur and Alan

Bavidge and all the other pieces of the jigsaw scattered before him.

'So the boy Glass did work for Marty, did he?'

Jefferson's shrugging. 'Did a bunch of scruff jobs for him. Low-end muscle work. Gofering. If he's doing anything for him now then it's not much. Certainly not enough to pay me off. His girlfriend works for Marty too,' Jefferson's saying. A sneer at the word 'girlfriend', turning quickly to a grin at the mention of working for Marty. Not hard to guess what a young woman working for Marty does. 'She must be making money, but, I don't know, not enough. Or they don't share the finances. Whatever it is, I've not had a penny from him in nearly two months.'

'So he doesn't have enough to live on?' Potty's saying. There's hope in that voice. The hope of a clever little plan. 'Shame.'

'I don't know about enough to live on. Not enough to live the life he wants to live. One of my boys saw him at a party. Told me all about it. One of those parties, if you know what I mean.' Hoping Potty does, because Potty isn't the kind of guy you spell these things out to in gratuitous detail. 'Expensive parties, those. I think the kid might be a user. But he was snorting his money away the night after he turns up here paying 6 per cent of what he owed me. Six per cent. So he's living the life all right. Or trying to.'

A whore for a girlfriend. A party lifestyle. A past of

working presumably violent jobs for Marty Jones. A childhood friend of the new kid on the block. Oh, this could work out nicely. Still has to play it the right way, but this could be the opportunity he's been waiting for.

Potty's buying up all three debts at the top of the list, because he's feeling a little happier about life. Buying a couple towards the bottom as well, just to round it off. They all seem reasonably safe. He'll turn a profit on every one of them, and rebuild his relationship with an important lender into the bargain. But that's just work. None of that is what makes him happy. What makes him happy is thinking of what Alex Glass will do for him. What he will have to do for him.

6

There's a different atmosphere when you're under attack. Not scared. Thrilled, a little bit. Nervy, sure, but that's not always a bad thing. If you're under attack and struggling, it feels bad. But that's not how Billy Patterson feels. He feels like he's doing rather well. That's where the thrill comes in. Someone's attacking you and you're standing up to it. Someone who considers themself a major player is failing to bring you down. Everyone can see it. Everyone knows. This could turn into the fight that confirms Billy Patterson as a serious force.

Potty's made moves against a couple of guys. Bought one. That was disappointing. Disappointing, but no more than that. People get bought in this industry. It happens. Patterson did a good job of keeping it quiet. Potty spread the word around, but it didn't seem to do a huge amount of damage. Truth is, it ended up being a relief. One man bought, nothing else happening. After the first attack, Patterson expected worse. Opening shot, followed by ever-increasing attacks. Didn't happen. Little while later they beat every ounce of snot out of Andy Leven and then set his house on fire. He was in hospital for a couple of weeks. No surprise that his wife decided for him that he wasn't going to work for Billy any more. Patterson understood, made no issue of it. Last he heard, the Levens were packing up their kids and moving out of the city.

That one was a win for Potty. It scared a few people in Patterson's organization. He knew it. He and Alan Bavidge did a lot of work to reassure people. Worked extra hard to keep their heads down. Made sure they didn't give Potty any more targets. For a while, there was worry. Then it all calmed down. Potty didn't do anything. Potty didn't know who to aim for next. That was when Patterson realized that the attack on Leven was Potty throwing a hissy fit. Only having one target and throwing the kitchen sink at it. Leven wasn't important to Patterson. Potty got a win because he showed people how angry he was, how hard he could hit. Then, by doing nothing to follow it up, he lost all the impetus. A win, of sorts, for Patterson.

Yeah, it's a worry that Potty's hooked up with Alex MacArthur. MacArthur seems to have some hard-on for the boy Stamford. Going out of his way to hurt those who hurt Stamford. He should learn to accept that Stamford is just bad news. Cut him loose. Surprising that MacArthur isn't doing that. Never known for his sentimentality, should've ditched the kid to make a point. No surprise that Stamford's already back in debt somewhere else. No surprise that the new debt is causing all kinds of bother for MacArthur.

Word is Stamford's down eighty grand to the Allen brothers. Eighty fucking grand? The Allens, who are actually first cousins, were stupid to let it get that far, but they did. They let him run and run, lose and lose, and now there's an eighty-grand wedge between them and Alex MacArthur. The Allens are involved in the drug trade, mostly outside of the city. But it's causing friction. Big fall-out between them and MacArthur. MacArthur telling his suppliers to stop supplying the Allens, even though they don't compete for territory. All because MacArthur is willing to let Stamford get away with his bullshit. Makes you wonder if the old man is losing the plot.

Potty isn't losing the plot. Chance would be a fine thing. So Patterson's having a meeting with Alan Bavidge. There are things they need to do. Make alliances. Create more protection for themselves. My-enemy's-enemy-is-my-friend can work, but you have to be careful. Alliances cost money, and your enemy's enemy may turn out to be a greedy bastard. They may also have connections to another rival. Everyone's connected to someone. Peter Jamieson, for example. He would be a great option. Rival of MacArthur. But he's too close to Marty Jones. No deal there.

Bavidge is arriving, taking his seat. Looking tired. Looking ten years older than he is. Still hasn't taken a bloody holiday. Hasn't had a girlfriend for a while. The last one ended it with him. Needs a strong woman in his life. Someone to force him into relaxing. Patterson can't do it. Tried and failed. Given up trying, for now. Later, maybe, he'll try again. When the timing is better. Right now, he can't afford to tell Bavidge to take a week off. He needs him.

'What do you think of arranging a meeting with Charlie and Ian Allen?' Patterson's asking as Bavidge sits at the little round table.

Bavidge is shaking his head a little. 'Don't see the gain. They can't give us anything. They won't come into the city to work with us. And we sure as shit don't need another Jamie Stamford debt on our books.' Said with real distaste. Even Bavidge can see how badly he handled the last Stamford debt. Doesn't want any repeat of that embarrassment.

'Okay. But I want to start making moves. I want people backing us up. Not safe to go into this one alone.'

'This one being?'

'I want to take down Potty Cruickshank.'

'Take down or take out?'

'Whatever works.'

Bavidge is leaning back in the chair. This is a bigger discussion. The right one to be having. Overdue, frankly, but still intimidatingly big. You don't just take out Potty Cruickshank. That's a move with a lot of loose ends. You have to remove the danger from all his connections and contacts. All the employees who think they're fit to step up and take his place. It's a dangerous move.

'You have a plan?' Bavidge is asking. Patterson wouldn't be mentioning the idea if there wasn't a plan to back it up. Something workable. Something he's confident they can put together.

'Lenders that crossed to us are starting to cross back to Potty. I know this. Not a lot, but they're selling to him again. Covering themselves in case we go to shit. If we don't do something, we could lose out a lot here. We have to be seen to do something.'

'That something being?' Bavidge isn't entirely convinced. Needs to be won round. They aren't losing much business to Potty. Frankly, Potty's doing a piss-poor job of getting at them.

'That something being that we make a hit against Potty. Set someone else up for it. Jesus, there are plenty of candidates. But we get rid of him and let someone else take the blame. We move in and sweep up his best lenders. We try and get a few of his employees on board too. Try and take over. We won't get it all, but we'll get some. We won't be the big enemy. They'll blame someone else.'

Bavidge is frowning. Sounds complicated, and complicated doesn't work as often as it should. 'I take it you have a plan in mind. Someone you think will carry the can.'

Patterson's smiling a little bit. 'I do, as it happens. How would you feel about working for Marty Jones?'

'Not good, funnily enough.'

'Fair enough. How would you feel about pretending to work for him?'

'A little better.'

'Good. That's my plan. You're going to set up a meeting with someone. A gunman. I don't know who yet. I'll work that out in the next couple of days. Freelancer, obviously. You're going to make it clear that you're working for Marty. That the hit has Peter Jamieson's backing. The person we have to worry about most is MacArthur. His reaction is the big one. He'll be willing to believe that Jamieson was behind it. Making a move against him. People will be willing to believe that Marty would pull a stunt like that. Well, if he had Jamieson's backing.'

It's not the worst plan he's ever heard. Sure, it has holes in it, but every plan does. It's bullshit to think you can work something like this and have it watertight. You always need a bit of luck. Even the big organizations have holes in a lot of their plans, and this isn't a big organization. This is a collection business with ambition.

'It could work,' Bavidge is saying, nodding his head. Then thinking about the holes in the plan. Trying to convince people that Marty was behind it. Need to leave a lot more evidence than an easily misled gunman. 'Could also go horribly wrong. Like, deadly wrong. Like Alex MacArthur sending all his boys round to drill holes in our heads wrong.'

Patterson's nodding and smiling. 'That's the fun of it, isn't it?'

Bavidge is smiling back, but it's a sad smile. He doesn't feel that sense of fun any more. The thrill that used to be there. Patterson's telling him that he'll give him a call soon. Work out what gunman to use. Someone who can get at Potty and get away. It's not a great plan, but it's a plan.

'Look at it this way, Alan,' Patterson's saying. 'A week from now, this'll be done. Potty out of the way. Us taking up some of his best lenders. Some of his people. Not all, but some. We'll get through the messy aftermath. Then we'll be looking forwards.' Sounded good to Patterson, but Bavidge is just nodding. Shaking hands and leaving. Patterson shaking his head. Best man he's got. Best muscle he's ever likely to have. And all the time he insists on looking all vulnerable, a man who needs saving.

7

Keep yourself busy. Don't spend all day sitting behind a desk. That's a good way to forget the things you need to remember. If you want to run a collection business then you need to be on the street. You need to know who's borrowing. You need to know what the lenders are doing. You need to see the business in action. Need to be seen by the people who owe you, the people who sell to you and the people who work for you. Peterkinney gets that. He's not going to become some fat bastard sitting behind a desk like Potty Cruickshank.

So Peterkinney's making a collection. He actually enjoys it now. Didn't think much of it when he was working for Marty. There was a difference. That money was going to Marty. Well, most of it. Peterkinney got his cut. Then Marty waltzed off with the rest. Sure, he had to kick a share up to Jamieson, but Marty was still getting more than he deserved. A man who never made a collection in his life. Spends his days hanging out with his dipshit brother. Picking up women for his other business. Coming up with ideas to make more money without working for it. Effort got in the way of Marty's work. Now the money is Peterkinney's, and that knowledge makes the experience of collecting it so much sweeter.

This should be an easy collection. That's another thing. Yeah, you're in charge, but you don't do the tough jobs. Your men don't like it if you do the tough jobs. Another lesson he learned from doing the muscle work himself. All the muscle want to do the biggest jobs. The toughest ones. The riskiest ones. They want to be able to say that they did the jobs that mattered. It's an ego thing. Their chance to prove themselves. Don't take that away from them.

But you do pick the job carefully. Don't just take something that doesn't matter to them. Take something that they don't want to do. Then they think you're a stand-up guy. So that's what he's doing. There are brutal jobs that the tough guys want to do. Makes them seem tough, on top of their game. The awkward stuff, the stuff that requires subtlety and brainpower, they prefer to avoid. That's why Peterkinney's here. Picking the most bloody awkward debt he has on the books, and going to collect. And he's still in a good mood.

Her name's Collette Duffy. Typical enough. Pretty young thing with a habit and a kid. No job, no prospect of one. Borrowing money with no hope of repaying. In the grand scheme of things, she's no big deal. Her debt isn't massive. She's easy to talk to. The problem is her brother. Her brother Liam is not a man you want to piss off. Does a lot of work for Chris Argyle, in what we will politely call the import business. Liam Duffy is not good people. Known to overreact to perceived slights.

Known to protect his little sister and her kid. That's why lenders are scared to refuse her. It's why collectors are reluctant to buy her debt. That's why none of the muscle wants this collection.

Peterkinney bought the debt as a favour to a lender. He has almost no intention of collecting on it. Two grand he won't see again. Not necessarily two grand poorly spent. It's a connection. Peterkinney's going to be as nice as nice can be with Collette. He's going to leave her flat after making her a happy little girly. Make a good impression. She shares this good impression with her brother. Her brother shares it with the people he knows. Peterkinney gets a reputation in the industry as a man who knows how to treat other people in the industry. Reputation is worth paying for. Even if it doesn't work, he made a good impression on the lender just by buying the debt. Can't lose entirely.

He's found his way to her flat. Small place, but not a bad area. Better than a girl with no job and a habit would normally have. That'll be the brother's influence, Peterkinney's guessing. Up to her door and knocking. Waiting ten or twenty seconds. Not going to rush her. Not going to knock a second time. You get a lot of people who owe money who are allergic to answering doors. Understandable. Usually you knock and knock. Maybe you leave a note letting them know this isn't over. Eventually, you push your way in. Not today. Not ever with Collette.

Peterkinney's about to walk away when the door opens. A young woman looking back at him. Pretty, as it happens. You can see why her brother would feel the need to protect her from collectors. A girl like that, there are ways she could repay the debt. Ways people like Marty Jones would be real quick to exploit. Wouldn't stay pretty for long. She needs protecting.

'Hi, sorry, I was just giving my little one her tea.' A giggly smile. She's nervous. A guy she doesn't recognize turns up at her door. That's worth worrying about when you're deep in debt.

'Oh, that's okay,' he's saying with a friendly smile. This is where looking young and innocent helps Peterkinney. He's non-threatening. People like Collette Duffy are willing to talk to him. 'I don't know if you know me. My name's Oliver Peterkinney.'

No flash of recognition. That's a good thing. If she knew him, it would almost certainly be because of negative things. She might have heard some stories that made her nervous. That scared her. Any collector has brutal stories to back up his work, his reputation. This way, he gets to introduce himself. He gets to set the tone of her perception of him. If the only profit from this deal is to enhance his reputation with people like Liam Duffy and Chris Argyle, then he needs to set the tone.

'I run a business that collects money,' he's saying. Not

using the term debt collector. Never use the term unless you want to frighten people. 'I've picked up your debt from the man you borrowed from.' Talking low, making sure no neighbour could overhear. 'I'm not here to collect,' he's saying quickly. Reassuring, friendly smile. 'But I thought it would be good to have a chat about the debt. See what we can do about it. Make sure we can sort it out without any bother, you know? Is now a good time? I can come back some other time.'

He's reassured her. He can already see it in her expression. He's said he's not here to collect money, which is a good start. She's seeing this as an opportunity. Here's a nice guy that's offering a chance to discuss her debt. This could be a chance for her to talk it downward. That's what she wants. She'll be glowing in her praise of him if that happens.

'I can talk,' she's nodding. Holding the door open for him to come in. A collector welcomed into the home of the debtor. All because of the nice way he talked to her. That baby face of his, paying off again.

She's leading him through to the living room. He can hear a TV in another room. That'll be to entertain the kid through her dinner. The ever-present babysitter. Into the living room. The carpet's thin and stained. There's a couch and one chair that doesn't match, and both have seen far better days. But there's a big TV, a Sky box and a Wii in the corner. There's an iPad resting on the arm of the couch. Strange priorities. But she's a junkie, apparently. Her priorities are going to be all over the fucking place. Can't be that far off the deep end though, can she. Holding it together enough to keep a home, keep the child. Seen worse, that's for sure. Not Peterkinney's problem. He's sitting down.

'Thing is, Collette,' he's saying, 'I now own the debt. But I don't want to start making a big deal out of it. I know how it is. You borrow a little and the interest catches you out. It's a lousy system.'

And she's nodding enthusiastically. Dark-brown hair bobbing up and down on her shoulders. Wearing a stripy vest and dark trousers. Shapely. Oh, the likes of Marty would have a field day with a client like this. Actually, Marty himself would be smart enough to keep away from Liam Duffy's little sister, but there would always be someone stupid enough not to.

'We need to work out a way that makes it easy for you to pay back. Something that doesn't stop you living your life. Something that doesn't get in the way of the other things you need to do.'

'Yeah, yeah,' she's saying, and nodding again. She has nothing else to say. She's hearing what she wants to hear and that's enough. Worried that anything she says might poison the well.

'So we need to look at how much you're earning. See what you can afford to pay. We'll do something about this interest, because that's not helping the situation. I also don't want you to think that there's any great urgency with this,' he's saying. 'I'm not in any great hurry about it. If we peg the interest, that'll give you breathing space.'

She's smiling and nodding. Unaware that Peterkinney wants this to last because it gives more chance of spreading the word about what a good guy he is. What a good industry man he is. That's where the value is for him. A young man who understands how to treat the family of other insiders. She doesn't see that. Honestly, she doesn't care. The value for him is irrelevant to her. He's welcome to any kind of profit he can get. She's only concerned about her position.

'Do you lend?' she's asking.

Jesus Christ, this isn't going to be easy after all. She's looking to borrow more. Hasn't paid a penny of her original debt, and she's hoping he'll hand her more cash. That's going to make it more difficult. He sure as hell isn't going to go buying up an unlimited amount of her debt just to make a good impression. Reputation is worth paying for, but everything has a limit. Might actually work in his favour, he's musing, before he answers. If she borrows from someone. They sell her new debt to someone else. She then has someone else to compare him to. Someone else for her brother and mates to compare him to. That could help.

'No, I don't lend. I just collect. Listen, Collette. Don't go borrowing just to pay off other debts. That'll make it worse. That's how you end up with even more interest, and even more debt. You and me should try and come up with a plan to make sure that you can pay this back. Make sure that you don't even have to think about borrowing again.'

She's nodding. She's uncertain, but she's not going to argue with him. He's here to help and she needs help. But she doesn't like the sound of not being able to borrow. Been a long time since she had an alternative money source. Borrow from lenders, get help from her brother. The lenders get rough and her brother sorts it out. That's the system that's kept her going for the best part of a year. Now Peterkinney's suggesting something else. But the other tactic that has served her well is nodding along with other people's ideas. She's just smart enough to realize that money doesn't flow from disagreement.

It's twenty minutes later when Peterkinney leaves the flat. Smiling and happy. He's gotten what he wanted. A payment plan that's so absurdly generous even she was surprised by it. All the time in the world to pay, interest suspended for the foreseeable future. She'll be very positive about this. Word will go around. It's a PR investment. She won't even meet the plan they've written out, but that's not the point either. Just gives him another opportunity to be all saintly when she fails to meet her obligations.

He's going back to the office. Put this on the file. Kilbanne will look at it and say nothing. He doesn't question. Too smart for questions. He'll look, he'll make a guess at the reasons for such an agreement, and he'll keep the conclusions to himself. And the business will get on with making money.

8

He has his coat on. Glass is ready to go. But he's scared. Properly scared, not just a little nervy. You get a telephone call straight from the mouth of Potty Cruickshank and you have a lot to be nervy about. A call from the blue. Telling him to come and visit Potty, right away. Giving him an address. A place Glass has heard of before. A little city centre club. Not a nightclub, but a private club. At least that's what he's heard it called. Never been inside. Just heard people talk about it. Like it's an exclusive little casino or something. Not a place for the likes of him.

Potty didn't give details. Made it clear that Glass had better be there. That he won't stand for being stood up. Or kept waiting. That it was in Glass's best interests to be there. Tried to make it sound at least a little bit friendly. Slimy, more like. So Glass will be there. He hasn't been told why, but he can guess. Jefferson sold the debt. Sold it to Cruickshank. But that doesn't tell him why he's been called to a meeting with Cruickshank himself. How many debts does Potty buy in any week? How many of them are worth his private attention? None, on average. But Glass is getting a call on a six-grand bill. Something isn't right.

He's delayed as long as he could. Hoping that Ella might come home. She's been out all day. Hasn't come back and it's getting dark. Dark is her work hours. He might not see her until tomorrow. Shit. It would be nice to have someone to talk to about this. But could he talk to her? Admit that he's deep in debt trying to keep up with her aspirations? That's a stupid thing to think. It wasn't her fault. He made the choices. Blaming her for it's just cheap. Get yourself together, and get to that meeting. Stand up for yourself. Stand up to the world. Can't be that hard when so many other people do it.

As he walks to the bus stop, he's thinking about Peterkinney. Maybe that's why he gets a personal meeting. Not because of the amount. Six grand is chicken feed to Potty. Someone pointed out Potty's house to Glass once. Big place you could get lost in without a detailed map and a bit of luck. Yeah, six grand wouldn't buy you much of that place. So Potty's interested in something else. The six grand should get one of his grunts at the door with threats of limb removal. Not a call from the fat man himself.

Oliver Peterkinney. Glass is thinking of trying another call. For what? To get fobbed off again by one of his minions? Best friends for years. Hung out most days. Partied together. Glass got Peterkinney started in the business. Yeah, doesn't take long for the ambitious to forget their friends. Maybe Ella got in the way of the friendship a little. Maybe. But that wasn't deliberate. And it's no reason for Peterkinney to be acting the way he is now. Like he's too good to bother with Glass.

Here's the bus. He's getting on, paying. Thank Christ the club, if that's what's even behind that front door, is in the city centre. Easy to get to. Closer he gets, the more he's starting to sweat. It's a cold evening, but temperature isn't a part of this. Potty Cruickshank. That'll be the biggest industry man Glass has ever met. Biggest in every sense, actually. But before now, Marty was the most important person Glass had come into contact with. Never got close to someone of Potty's stature. His reputation. Jesus, this has to be a step up.

As he's getting off the bus, he's trying to win himself round. Persuade himself that all is not lost. This might not be that bad. Walking towards the quiet street where the club is. Not so busy even in the busier areas. The brief time between shoppers shopping and drinkers drinking. But look at it this way. Potty wants to talk to Glass. Glass has that connection to Peterkinney. A guy like Potty knows that Peterkinney's in the collection business now. So he buys Glass's debt. Calls him along to a meeting. Maybe he has an offer. Maybe he wants Glass to be a go-between. Or he wants info. Could pay off a big chunk of the debt. Hell, maybe even all of it.

Back to being scared and miserable by the time he gets to the correct street. Back to reality. Info on Peterkinney. Talking to Peterkinney. That wouldn't be enough to pay off the debt. Info doesn't buy you freedom. Might cut the debt, but not by enough. If he has info, then Potty will want to keep him indebted. Keep him talking. Talking to Peterkinney wouldn't help either. If he's the messenger between the two, Potty will want him under his thumb. He'll keep the debt hanging over him. Use it. If Glass is any kind of useful, then it's common sense that Potty will want control of him.

By the time he's reached the door, he's just about terrified. This isn't his depth. Not even close. A big red door, no windows on it. A three-storey, mid-terrace brown stone building. It looks like an expensive house. But that's the point, isn't it. What goes on behind closed doors. Knocking on the door a couple of times. Jesus, please don't answer. It would be so nice if he had an excuse not to go ahead with this. But it's opening.

The first little piece of his curiosity is stamped upon. The guy answering the door is muscle. Stereotypical muscle. Tall, a little overweight, shaven-headed. Looks like he'd break his granny's neck if the price was right. Not the sort of person that answers the door at a swanky private members' club. The muscle's nodding for him to come in.

Inside it looks like a nice house too. Not some special place the rich come to play. A corridor, doors closed on either side. A staircase on the right-hand side of the hallway. The muscle leading him along the corridor. Thin, cheap carpet. There's a big scratch on the wallpaper above the radiator. So not some private members' club after all. That's a disappointment. This isn't some special meeting place. Just a city-centre location that a man like Potty has easy access to. Convenient, not special.

Places like this get their own mythology. A man like Potty is seen coming and going. It's a good location in the city centre. It's the sort of property that could easily be used for something exclusive. Something exciting. So it gets a reputation as some special place. That's what people want to think. They want to think there's something clever and dangerous going on behind these doors. Something glamorous. Fascinating fantasy trumps tedious truth every time. Truth is it was a good piece of property that Potty managed to come by on the cheap. Owner owed some money. Gave Potty a big price cut on the deal. A good little investment. Property is a good way to clean money.

None of this matters to Glass now. He's following the muscle along the corridor. Getting more nervous as he goes. It's silent behind the closed doors. There's nobody else here. Just him and Potty and this thug. It suddenly feels dangerous. Ominous. It was intimidating before, but he was sure he would have a chance to pay off the debt somehow. Now it feels like a set-up. It feels like he's never going to get out of here.

The muscle's opening the door, nodding for Glass to go in. It's a large room, well lit, white walls. There's a sink over against one wall, but that's the only giveaway that this used to be a kitchen. All the units and features have been ripped out to leave the place almost empty. Looks like they started a conversion and ran out of interest. There's a table in what was the dining area. That's all the furniture. A long dining table, with Potty Cruickshank sitting at the head of it. The muscle who was sitting along from Potty is getting up, moving towards the sink.

That's Glass's cue to take a seat at the table, which he's doing. Looking behind him at the sound of the door closing. The muscle who led him in is standing just inside the now closed kitchen door. There's a closed window behind Potty, and no other way out. The other muscle is leaning back against the sink, looking casual. Both of them watching him. Not watching Potty. Just Glass. Potty's taking a sip from the glass on the table in front of him. Not offering Glass any-thing. The state of this place would suggest Potty did well to get anything for himself, never mind a guest.

'I'm glad you made it,' Potty's saying. 'You and I need to have a very serious discussion.' His tone is sombre. No mess-ing around here. 'We need to have a discussion that I don't think you're going to like. But you're a strong person, aren't you, Alex? A tough guy?' Little bit of mockery crept in there, just at the end. The little mouth curling up at the edges, ever-so-slightly creasing those big cheeks.

It could be an offer of work. Wanting an old friend of Peterkinney to be seen working for him. It could be something else. Either way, you agree with Potty. 'I guess. Tough enough.'

Potty's nodding. 'Mm, good. Because what I have to offer you will require a tough person. It's an opportunity for you to pay off your debt to me in its entirety in one evening. The whole thing, gone. But it's tough work. Are you interested?'

It's not as if he can say no. Potty's just said that he owns the debt. He's giving him a chance to wipe it out. The man's offering a rare opportunity. A favour, it looks like. How often does Potty sit down with a man and offer one of those? Saying no is going to piss Potty off. Alone in a room with Potty and two of his muscle is not the time to piss him off.

'I guess, yeah. I'm interested.'

Another nod. Potty hearing what he expected to hear, and knowing how worthless that can sometimes be. 'Let me ask you, Alex. Do you know where your girlfriend is right now? Where Ella is?'

Glass is looking at Potty with alarm. His mouth is open, but his brain hasn't found a word ready to head out there yet. The fear turning to anger. He's about to get emotional when he remembers who the fat guy sitting in front of him is. Remembers the two thugs that are in the room with them. Watching him. And the fear returns. He's shaking his head. Not saying anything because he doesn't trust himself to speak. Just shaking his head.

'No,' Potty's saying. 'But you can guess. Don't take this as a threat. I just wanted to know if what I'd heard was true. What I'd heard about her occupation. So one of my boys tracked her down. Offered her money for her work. She agreed, of course. It's some money for you both, I suppose.' Said with a smug shrug. 'But what of you, Alex? Are you earning any money? Helping her out of this life she lives?'

Another shake of the head. If they were alone it would be different. If they were alone he would threaten and shout. He might even throw a punch. He's beaten people up. He knows how he would do it here. Charge all his weight at Potty. Knock him off the chair and onto the floor. Once you get a man that big onto the floor, it's easy to keep him there. But no. They're not alone. Potty's never going to let that happen. And Glass is never going to do anything. Just shaking his head until Potty starts talking.

'So she's the one bringing the money in. Doing all the work for the both of you. And here you are with a large debt. A debt you now owe to me. I'm going to offer you a chance to remove that. To wipe your slate clean. Isn't that what you want?' Talking quietly, confidently. Elbows on the table, chin resting on his folded hands.

Get him to agree to the job before he even knows what it is. It's a good tactic. Make it as hard as possible to back out. If he was thinking clearly, Glass would realize how big this is. Threatening Ella. Threatening him. Trying to force him to accept without details. It should tell him a lot about what's coming next. But he isn't thinking clearly. The threat to Ella made sure of that. All going to plan for Potty then.

'I do want that.'

'Of course you do. Strong young man like you, you want to do the right thing for yourself and your partner,' Potty's saying, and leaning forwards against the table. 'I am going to give you an opportunity that can clear your debt. That could make you very popular with me. You do understand how valuable that could be, don't you, Alex? Being popular with me? It could serve you very well. Will you do it?'

'Yes.'

'Good. One of my boys will give you a knife. You are going to go to this address. You are going to kill the man who lives there. Do you understand me? You are going to kill this man. You are going to do this.'

There's a slight shake of the head. Watching as Potty passes a quarter of a page from a phone book. One name and address ringed in blue ink. Sliding it across the table. Potty saying nothing, just glaring back at Glass.

'I haven't . . . I don't know how. I couldn't.'

Potty frowning. 'Are you refusing to help me?' Asked quietly, with a sad expression. That's the nod for the guy by the sink to stop slouching and stand up straight. Take a noisy scuffed step towards the table. Let Glass know what pressure he's under.

'No, no,' Glass is saying. 'It's just, I haven't done this before. I don't know how. There must be someone better.'

Potty's smiling and shaking his head. 'First-night nerves. You'll get over it. You're the best person for the job. Tough lad like you, of course you are. You go there right now. You knock on the door. He answers and you do it. Then you get out of there. It's really rather simple. Don't overcomplicate it, Alex, that's where many people slip up. Do it quickly and keep it simple, and you'll be fine.' Said with a quietly reassuring tone. Just about sounded like he cared. There's a pause. 'You understand that I will be very happy with you if you do this well. I will be very angry if you don't.'

Glass is looking at him. You can see that he means it. Potty Cruickshank doesn't have time for idle threats. Potty's never lived in a world of idle threats. Too busy issuing real ones. He's threatening Glass. Letting him know that he will be the one impaled on metal if he doesn't do the job. Probably be killed right after they do something to Ella.

'I know,' Glass is saying. 'I'll do it. Tonight.'

'Good lad,' Potty's saying, and smiling a smile so false it's an insult. 'Show Alex out, would you,' he's saying to the muscle at the door.

The muscle's walking Glass back along the corridor. Taking out a long thin knife from the inside pocket of his fleece. Passing it to Glass. Glass holding it and looking at it.

'Put it away,' the muscle is telling him harshly, then opening the front door.

Back out into the cold night. The metal feels heavy in his pocket. That's the handle, rather than the blade. He's walking slowly along the street. He knows where he needs to go. Taking his phone out and calling Ella. Her phone's switched off.

9

He started tracking him at his office. Parked across the road from it, watching a few people come and go. Little place, doesn't look like much. Peterkinney arrived in his car. Got out looking happy with himself. Little shit. Went into the office and stayed in there for about twenty minutes. He thought about going in then with the knife, but he didn't. Too much chance of being seen. Marty wouldn't want that, so Neil Fraser sat in the car and watched.

See, people are always treating Fraser like he's some idiot. Like he doesn't have the subtlety to do anything important. Young's always treating him that way. Only ever takes him along to look mean and be quiet. Finally someone's giving him a job that matters. That'll let him show people how good he can be. Staking the place. Tracking the target. Waiting for the right moment to strike. This'll show them what a pro he is.

He sat patiently and watched the office. Patiently, you see, patiently. He can do this. And Peterkinney came out, got in his car and drove home. And Neil Fraser followed him. Thought he did a pretty damn good job, too. There was a spell where he was right behind Peterkinney's car, but so what?

Even if Peterkinney looked in his mirror, he probably wouldn't have recognized him anyway. So Fraser followed him home, parked a little way along the street from his flat, and waited.

Nice little street it is too. You can see the boy's moving up in the world. Sort of place for the young middle class. People with rich parents. Well, that ain't Peterkinney. But young people with money. Don't need a lot of space, but want to be in a nice area close to the places that matter in the city. Yeah, he's done all right out of screwing Marty, Fraser's thinking. Looking at the buildings. Thinking it would be nice to live in a place like this. Maybe he should screw Marty too. But he wouldn't know how. Nah, do this job, and trust Marty to reward him. Marty sees his potential.

Fraser waited there for nearly an hour, which was pretty damn patient. Then got fed up waiting. There's really no need to spend forever waiting for a better opportunity. Take the opportunity that's in front of you. So he got out of the car and started to walk to the door of the flats. Casual, trying to look like he belonged. Then the door of the flats opened and Peterkinney came out. Down the steps, looking relaxed. Didn't look at Fraser. Just walked to his car at the side of the road and got in. Fraser stopped halfway along the pavement. Trying to work out what he should do next. Keep on walking to act casual, or turn back to his car and maybe catch the boy's eye. Frozen on the pavement, unsure of himself.

Peterkinney's starting his car and pulling away. Fraser, without waiting for Peterkinney to turn the corner at the bottom of the street, has turned and is running back to his car.

Okay, so he handled that badly. He knows it. Doesn't need you ramming it down his throat. But he managed to follow Peterkinney. Caught him up and kept close. Driving into the centre, lot of people around. Parked close behind him. Watched Peterkinney stroll along the street and into a cinema. So Fraser hung around outside the cinema, for the best part of two hours.

Two fucking hours, standing in the street like an idiot. Just lurching around, people coming and going. Getting hungry, but nowhere he can go to grab something to eat. Nowhere that he could still see the cinema doors from. People are seeing him, hanging around. Bloody stupid, this is. But he can't go in, he knows that. Got to hang around and wait. Keep watching the door. Keep your distance. Be smart.

He was impatient by the time Peterkinney came out of there. Walking along a busy and well-lit street. Fraser knows better than to attack now. But what if this is the perfect place to attack? This is the last place anyone would expect him to attack. They always say that's the best time. No, not here. Too many people around. Wait until it gets quieter. There'll be a better chance. Back on the street where they're both parked. He can just walk up behind him and stick the knife in him. Keep walking to his car. Yeah, that's the perfect way to do it.

Except Peterkinney isn't going back to his car the way he came. He's taken a turning away off down an adjoining street that takes them further away from their cars. But that's okay, because he's walking to a quieter area. There are fewer people, it's darker. There are more little alleyways down this way. Peterkinney's leading him closer and closer to his chance. Turning again, into what's basically a wide alleyway between shops and a multi-storey car park. Fraser keeping close, but not too close. Nobody else down this alleyway.

Must be going to meet someone. Shit, might be going to meet someone tough. Better get a move on. Get this done and get back to the car. That's common sense. If your target is going to meet up with someone else then you get to them before the meeting. Even Fraser knows that. He's turning into the alleyway, wide enough to drive a delivery lorry down, and picking up the pace. Watching the back of Peterkinney as he turns again, out of view. Fuck, must be another alley there. Some little cubbyhole between the shops where Peterkinney can do a deal. Fraser's jogging now.

Down the alleyway. More aware of the darkness. More aware of how isolated he is. But he isn't stopping to think about that. He never stops to think about these things. Some people mistake it for bravery. It isn't. It's a failure of brain to keep up with action. Some dumb people get away with it because instinct takes over. Not for Fraser. Instinct is way in the background. So he's reached the corner. Hardly slowing as he runs round it.

A hand thudding out and into his side. A cold blast running up his side to his head. A flush of adrenalin, causing him to jump backwards. The adrenalin washed away in blood, and he's slumping down to his knees. Now onto his side, clutching at the wound.

'Oh Neil, you are so predictable.'

He can hear Peterkinney. Hear him loud and clear. Not fuzzy or distant. He sounds like he's standing over him, which he is. Fraser had dropped to the ground, but he knows better than to stay there. Now turning over, getting back onto his knees. There's blood coming out of a slit in his jacket. He has a hand over it. Got to move. Got to react. Got to do something. Think of something to do next. Come on, hurry up. His mind racing to get there, but always running in the wrong direction. Only a few thoughts entering his head, and most of them come back to dying in this alley.

'You think I didn't know what you were up to? Huh? You think I'm fucking blind?' Peterkinney doesn't sound upset. Not emotional at all. Calm, relaxed, satisfied. Happy with his night's work. 'You think I'm as stupid as you are?' Having fun and taking his time. Not intimidated by Fraser. Not intimidated by the thought of being caught behind a shop with a man he's just stabbed.

He had the chance to look around and make sure this

place was safe. The car park on one side is lit up, but empty. Nobody moving around in there. The shops behind them are in darkness now. No windows from the shops look out onto this little loading bay anyway. Big doors, covered by corrugated sheeting to deter burglars and encourage graffiti. Silent, dark and perfect for this.

Fraser's not listening any more. He's trying to get his own knife out of his pocket. He's got his hand on the handle. Taking it out. Struggling for a grip because there's blood on his hand. Peterkinney's seen it and he's laughing. Fraser's trying to get up to get a slice at him. Putting weight on his feet, but as soon as he starts to push up the pain shoots through him. Up his side, through his neck, up behind the ear. It's like being stabbed again. So he's slumping back down. Hand out, trying to prevent him from rolling onto his side.

Peterkinney's laughing again, just a little. You'd have to know him well to know that he's faking it. Good actor. But the laugh has turned hollow; he doesn't find this funny any more. Time to wrap it up. 'You tell Marty that this is what'll happen to anyone who tries to stop me. You understand me, Fraser? You tell him that he can't lay a finger on me. That he better not try again, or he might be next. You got that?'

And Peterkinney's turning and walking away. Back out into the alley from the loading area at the back of the shop. Along the alleyway and out onto the lit street. A bloody knife in his pocket, but that's okay. He'll ditch the knife and the top he's wearing. But this was a good day for him. This message will be enough to deter Marty. Marty isn't a man to risk failing twice. He doesn't care enough. If this was about his core business, women, then he would try again. Keep trying until he succeeded. But he's not going to rock the boat with a second attempt after pissing off Jamieson and Young already this month.

This was in Peterkinney's mind from the moment he saw Fraser parked across the street from the office. Not parked nearly far enough away from the office. They have a large window looking out onto the street, for Christ's sake; easy to see everyone parked on the street. Fraser following him home. Driving right behind him. Right behind him. Unbelievable. Obviously never done something like this before. Marty picked him because he's expendable. Because people don't think of him as being one of Marty's boys. Because he was the only one stupid enough to do it. Stupid enough to carry a grudge from some party months ago. Feels like a lifetime ago. Probably not for Fraser. He hasn't done much of note since then.

Only question was what weapon Fraser was planning to use. You don't bring a knife to a gunfight, that's movie cliché number one. If Fraser had a gun, then this wouldn't have happened. But Peterkinney decided to take the risk that he wouldn't. Let's face it, even Marty wouldn't be stupid enough to arm Fraser with a gun. Fraser is no gunman. Gunmen are a different breed. If Marty used a real gunman, Peterkinney would be dead now. He knows that. So he made the decision that Fraser only had a knife, and he was right. Predictable enough. That made it an even fight. All he had to do was pick the location.

Best thing is, Marty won't make a fuss. Can't. Fraser isn't his employee. Which is a good thing if Fraser does the job properly. Nobody can prove Marty was behind it. It becomes a bad thing if Fraser botches the job. Uh-huh, should have seen that coming. Fraser works for Peter Jamieson. Marty just got a Jamieson employee stabbed. Marty won't admit to being involved. Fraser won't grass him up either. Fraser will use his mobile to call for help. He'll be taken to hospital. One of Jamieson's more intelligent men will go and get him out of the hospital before the police can bamboozle him with anything so fiendish as a question. And nothing more will be said about it.

Peterkinney's back to his car. Looking up and down the street to make sure that Fraser didn't have company. A safety net for the job. Of course he didn't. That would have been the sensible thing to do. Fraser wouldn't organize that. Nor would Marty. It's a two-man job, but he can send one moron instead. It's cheaper. It carries less personal risk to Marty. Those are the things that matter most to him.

By the time Peterkinney's ditched the knife and top and gotten home, it's pitch black. Still, he's feeling good. Into the flat and looking around. His flat. His space. His company. Making money for him. This is what he should have been doing ages ago. Never having to live in someone else's pocket. Bumping into his grandfather every time he opens his bedroom door. Embarrassing himself with crappy jobs for Marty. That's no life. The good life is the life you make yourself, any idiot can see that. This is the life.

10

He's gone back to the flat first. Shouldn't have. Should have gone straight round to the address and gotten the job done. That's what Potty wanted him to do. Get there and do it without thinking about it. You dwell on it, and you're going to think of all the reasons why you shouldn't do it. All the things that can go wrong, and there are plenty of those. But Glass couldn't rush it like that. Had to come home first.

He's called Ella three times and gotten no answer. She's with one of Potty's boys. Maybe Potty's boy is going to keep her there until they know Glass has done the job. Maybe that's the point. He's not experienced enough to know. Never been here before. Hopefully she doesn't know what's going on. He doesn't want to think of her being held against her will. Being scared, or even hurt. Sooner he does the job, less chance there is of that happening.

Walking through the flat. The knife is still in his pocket; he hasn't taken his coat off since he got home. He can feel that knife weighing him down. Walking from room to room. Not looking for anything. Not expecting to find anything. Just wanting to burn off some nerves. He's going to kill a man. He has no choice. If he doesn't, Potty kills him. Maybe Ella too. That was the threat. What choice does he have?

What choice? There could be a way out. There could. He's looking at this from a different angle. There are people out there who would like to know about this job. Who might just want to get involved in this little adventure. Throw a spanner in Potty's works. Except he only knows the phone number of two of them. And neither of them will answer his calls.

He's calling Peterkinney first. They were friends. This was the sort of thing they would have told each other about. That they would have helped each other with. Times have changed. Not thick as thieves any more. But this matters to Peterkinney. This is something that he needs to know about. He's part of the industry now, after all. But the phone's ringing and ringing and nobody's answering. Typical. Just bloody typical. Thinking he's too good for Glass. Well, he's the one who's going to lose out.

Calling Marty. This is a chance for Marty. Get involved in Potty's business; trip him up in something important. Surely Marty will want that. And a chance for Glass to prove to Marty that he can still be useful. This could be a way in. You deliver information like this, and it can lead to permanent work. Shows Marty how useful he can be, and how much he wants to work for him. Hell, it even involves Ella, and she's one of Marty's girls. He has to take an interest. He has to be willing to help. The phone's ringing. Two rings and it's answered. That has to be a good sign.

'Yes?' An aggressive yes.

'Marty, this is Alex Glass. I want to talk to you about something important. Something that's happening right . . .'

'Oh, I get it. Yeah. Get his wee bum chum to call up and take the piss. Is he hanging over your shoulder listening to this? Is he? Are we on speaker? You tell him from me, okay. You tell him he can go fuck himself, all right.'

'Marty. Marty, it's Alex Glass. Alex Glass.' Thinking that Marty doesn't know who this is. That he's got him mixed up with someone else. Must have. What else could explain this outburst? 'I used to work for you. I'm Ella's boyfriend.'

'I know who you are. And I know what your mate did tonight. You just tell him that this ain't the end of it. One of Jamieson's boys got to the hospital. They won't let this lie. Neither will I. There'll be a price to pay for this. Can he hear me? A price to pay. I'll get that little prick. You tell him that.'

Marty was practically spitting into the phone before he hung up. Not raging and ranting. A cold hatred, hissing out of him. Glass is staring at the phone. Doesn't know what to do now. Marty's up a tree about something. Something's happened and it's pushed him beyond anything as showy as anger. Glass has no idea what this is about. He mentioned Jamieson and a hospital. That has nothing to do with Glass. Nothing to do with tonight. Maybe it has something to do with Potty. That could be it. Marty thinks Glass is working for Potty already.

Still walking round the flat. Trying to make sense of something that doesn't want to be understood. Grasp at any passing straw. Phoning Arnie Peterkinney. He needs help. He needs to get through to Oliver.

'Hi, Arnie, this is Alex Glass.' Feels weird calling him Arnie. Not like they're close or anything. 'Do you have Oliver's new home number?'

There's just a little pause. 'No, I don't. You can get him on his mobile though.'

'Uh, yeah. I tried. Never mind.'

'Alex, lad, are you okay?'

Didn't realize how emotional he was sounding. That he's close to tears. He knows that if he doesn't get help, he's going to be killing a man in the next couple of hours. Or maybe his target will kill him. Why not? Chances are the target's a damn sight more experienced at this sort of thing. Most people in the business are more experienced than Glass. He's been close to tears since he left Potty's house, but he didn't realize it. Marty was too excitable to notice.

'I'm okay. Just . . . a few things, you know. Stuff. I was really hoping I might get through to Oliver though. I thought he might be able to help me out. I could use a wee bit of a hand with something tonight, that's all.'

'Anything I can help you with?'

It's weird how much it hurts to hear him ask that. Arnie Peterkinney never liked him. Glass knows that. He knows that Arnie always thought he was a bad influence. And he was. Damn right, old man. Look at where Glass's influence has gotten them. And yet the old man's offering to help. The only person who has offered to help him. The only person who would actually sound like he means it. That's pushing Glass closer to the edge. The only person who wants to help and there's nothing he can do. Shit, even if he could, Glass wouldn't let him get involved. The one person who cares enough to offer, you don't drag him down with you.

'No, no. I can handle it. I just thought it was something Oliver might want to know about. Thought he might benefit from it. Be good, uh, if I could help him out. Listen, it's no big deal.' Pulling himself together. Making a show of how small a deal it is. Trying too hard. 'I'll sort it out. But thanks for the offer.'

'Okay. Well, take care of yourself, kid.'

Standing by the front door. Mobile phone tucked back into his pocket. Eyes dried, because you can't go wandering the streets with tears in your eyes. People will see that. They'll spot him and think something's wrong. You have to look like there's nothing happening. Like it's no big deal. Biggest deal of his life.

Out of the flat, into the street and walking. Cold. Bloody freezing. How many things is he doing wrong? How many mistakes is he making that'll get him caught? Hundreds, probably. The sort of mistakes someone like Peterkinney would laugh at now. Ridicule Glass for it. He had a head for this. He could probably do something like this without even batting an eyelid these days. The quiet one. The nice one. Now the one Glass wishes he had at his side to help him.

He's been walking for more than half an hour. Didn't want to take the bus. Didn't want to be seen. Seemed like a smart idea, although he's exhausted now. He's on the right street. Quiet place. Expensive-looking houses, terraced. Not huge, but the area is good. There are trees on the little verge between the houses and the road. Everything clean and well maintained. Tiny little front gardens, an excuse to give the residents a front gate of their own. Good cars parked outside each house. A good place. Sort of good place Glass shouldn't be. Sort of good place this shouldn't happen. It's quiet. It's late enough to be quiet.

Glass is shaking. Not from the cold. That doesn't matter any more. He's shaking anyway. He can just about hear his heartbeat. He has a strange feeling, like he's disconnected from all this. Not out of body or anything like that. That would make it easier. Still very much there. Just not controlling himself any more. Watching over his own shoulder, wishing he could take control.

He's walking slowly along the street. Looking at numbers on doors. Nothing could be worse than getting the wrong number. He's found the house. The right number, according to the phone directory. A deep breath. A second deep breath, catching in his throat and almost turning into a sob. Then a moment of panic as he wonders if anyone's watching him. Glancing frantically round, looking for witnesses. Nobody on the street. Looking for lights in windows, people lurking behind curtains. Can't see anyone. Pulling up his hood and walking the three steps from the pavement to the door.

Knocking once. Waiting. Nothing. Knocking again. Come on. Knocking a third time, louder now. Worried that he's drawing attention to himself. But nobody's coming to the door. Nobody's at home. Shit. Potty didn't tell him what to do if this happened. He doesn't know.

Back out onto the street, walking down to the corner. There are no lights on in the house, but that doesn't matter. It's late. Might be asleep in bed. Might be lights on at the other side of the house. Maybe he just doesn't answer the door this late. A man in his position, you wouldn't, would you. You don't rush to answer the door if you know a lot of people are out to get you. If he knows people are out to get him. Shit, of course he does. He knows, and he could be in there, waiting for someone like Glass. Or he could be out at work. These would be his work hours, probably. So Glass is standing at the corner. Trying to work out what he's supposed to do next. Go home. Stay and watch for someone arriving. Or try and force his way into the house.

Not the last one. Doesn't know how to do that without causing a scene. And he won't go home. Potty will want to know why he went home so easily. He'll accuse Glass of chickening out. And he'd be right. There's relief coursing through him right now. The glimmer of hope that this might not happen. But he won't go home. He'll hang around on the street. He knows what the target looks like. Seen him before. He'll keep watching. He has to. He just has to. For Ella. For himself.

11

Bavidge just had another meeting with Patterson. He's narrowed down a list of freelancers he's thinking of using. Has to be careful. Has to be someone with a bit of talent. There aren't that many to choose from. Has to be someone they can trust to do a good job. Won't be someone they trust with the truth. Nobody will get the truth. So it needs to be someone who isn't too inquisitive. Won't go looking for facts they're not supposed to know. Only Patterson and Bavidge will know the truth. They'll try to persuade the gunman that he's working for Marty. Try and make sure word gets out. Drop Marty in it. Maybe drop the gunman in it too. That's the risk of his job.

But it doesn't feel like a safe plan. Feels like there's too much outside of their control. Make or break, probably. Either get rid of Potty or be destroyed by him. The way of the world. The way of the business. But they should have something more solid than this to base the risk on. Bavidge is driving home. Get some sleep. It's the only time he's not working. Right now, his work makes him unhappy, so sleep is a good idea.

Pulling into the street and parking outside the house.

Usual spot. This isn't even his car, it belongs to Patterson. Bavidge will use it for the next few days for meetings with the gunman. Using a car that can't be linked directly to him as a precaution. They can't be sure that the gunman won't try and get in contact with Marty. That he won't smell a rat and go looking for answers. So you take the precaution of using a different car so that you can start to deny things. Pretend it wasn't you. Always fucking pretending.

Not looking at the world around him. Trying not to think about it. The holes in the plan. The fact, and Bavidge is convinced it is a fact, that something's bound to go wrong. If something small goes wrong, they'll be okay. Something big and all the little precautions in the world won't help them. Forget it. He just wants to get into bed and try to forget that the world exists. Opening the car door and stepping out onto the pavement without checking.

He can see the movement before he feels it. Someone lurching at him. Coming round the back of the car and getting beside him, their hand reaching out. Something jabs at Bavidge's arm. He knows straight away. It's a knife. This is the end. He doesn't have anything to defend himself with. Some kid with a knife. All he can do is throw himself at the man. Try and fight back. But the man isn't thinking properly. He isn't trying to pick his stabs. He's flailing wildly. The knife comes down across Bavidge's face. Another swing across his stomach. This time a jab that goes deep into his stomach.

Glass has let go of the knife, leaving it in just below the ribcage. Bavidge is still standing. Beginning to slump backwards. Glass is reaching out, grabbing him. Steering him back down into the driver's seat of the car. His legs out on the pavement. Then panic. Nothing but panic. All Glass can think about is leaving the body here. He can't do that. He shouldn't do that. People will see. They'll see him. This is . . . wrong. He has to do a good job for Potty. This is wrong. Just move it. Get it into the car.

He's lifting up the legs, forcing them into the car. Bavidge is still alive. Groaning a little. But he isn't resisting. Doesn't have the strength. His head is across on the passenger seat now, his body across the centre console. He's trying to say something. Something Glass doesn't want to hear. He wants to get out of here. His hands have blood on them. Jesus, he's going to be sick.

Lights. Coming round the corner at the far end of the street. Coming towards them. Glass is frozen. Standing, watching the car approaching. Passing them. The driver looking at him. Looking right at him. Eye contact. And now slowing down. He's gone twenty yards past them, but he's slowing to a stop on the road. Not pulling over. Stopping in the middle of the road. Stopping to intervene.

It's just panic. Crazy, think-of-nothing panic. If that guy comes over and demands to know what's going on, Glass won't have an answer. All he'll have is bloody hands and a body. He's getting into the car. Didn't think about it. Just getting into the car. Sitting in the driver's seat. Bavidge's legs are still in the footwell of the driver's seat. Hardly enough room for him to close the door. Glass is pulling the door shut, forcing himself in.

'Come on,' he's growling. Crying. Properly this time. His shoulders rocking. His eyes filled. 'Move over,' he's pleading to Bavidge.

Bavidge making some sort of response. A low groan, but trying to pull his legs across. Closing his eyes hard and whimpering at the pain of effort. Glass pushing Bavidge's legs across the gearstick and into the footwell on the passenger's side. Bavidge reaching out a hand. The keys. He has the keys in his hand. He's giving them to Glass. And Glass is taking them. Starting the car. Looking in his mirror as the driver's door of that other car opens. A man getting out onto the road and walking slowly towards them. Glass has the car started, and he's pulling out. Racing down the street.

It's taken him three streets to remember to put the lights on. He hasn't stopped at a junction. If this was any other time of the day, he'd have hit something by now. But we're past midnight, and the streets are just quiet enough. Driving. No idea where. Just going straight ahead. Driving to nowhere. Getting distance between himself and the witness. Now looking at Bavidge and realizing that he should have run. Should have left him to die in his car, and run. Now he's with a dying man, driving through the city. This is much worse.

'I don't know where to go,' Glass is saying quietly. 'I don't know.'

Bavidge isn't answering. He's slumped against the passenger door. Bent over, his eyes shut. His mouth is slightly open; he's making groaning noises every now and again, but less and less often. He doesn't seem to be aware. Not hearing or seeing or understanding any more. So Glass has to make the decision. But he has no idea. He's just driving. Checking his mirror to make sure that other car hasn't tried to follow. Trying to work out where he is now. Trying to drive the car properly. Too nervous to focus on any one thing. The pedals a little too far away with the seat pushed back the way the taller Bavidge likes it. The blood on his hands now on the gearstick, meaning it slips from his hand every time he tries to change gear. And still that disconnected feeling, like this is something he can do nothing about.

It's taken him too long to realize that he's driving into the city centre. Now that he has realized, he's also realizing that he has to get out of the car. Get away from Bavidge. Get away from the whole situation. The smell, the silence, the fear of it. Get away. Potty told him. He said to get him on the doorstep. Hit and run. Don't hang around. Get it done and get out of there. But he's still here. Ten minutes after stabbing him and he still has Bavidge sitting beside him, bleeding onto the floor of the car.

Now he's just thinking about stopping. Can't think of anything else. Find somewhere, anywhere, to stop. Anywhere that doesn't have people. That's all you need. Indicating to turn right at a junction. Realizing that it's quieter left and going that way. He hasn't even thought about CCTV. He won't either. This is desperation. The only thing that will save him is luck.

Onto a narrower street, going downhill. Doesn't seem to be anyone around. That's a start. Looking left and right as he drives. Lots of little shops with flats above them. Nondescript. Not the sort of place people hang around late at night. No pubs or clubs, although Glass hasn't picked up on that. He just likes the loneliness of it. There. A gap between two buildings. Leads to the rear of the buildings. Leads out of sight. You can get a car into that gap. Course you can. He's turning. Into the alleyway. But there isn't room for a car behind the buildings. It's just a pathway behind the buildings with a high wall. He has to park in the alleyway. Shaking now, struggling to keep a hold of the steering wheel. Stopping too close to a wall on the passenger side. Now he won't be able to get Bavidge out that side. Reversing back and straightening, to give himself more room.

Switching the engine off. Leaving the keys in the ignition. Surprised by the intimidating brightness in the alleyway.

Switching off the lights. Getting out of the car and going round to the passenger side. Just as he's opening the passenger door, a car goes past on the street. It goes past, doesn't sound like it's slowing down. Bavidge is now leaning halfway out of the car. Groaning louder.

'You have to get out,' Glass is saying. Reaching down and trying to help him out. Trying to lift him by one arm and giving up. His nerves have exhausted him.

Bavidge is trying. He is. Willing to go wherever he's led. Long past the point of resistance. Long past the point of caring what happens, just hoping it happens soon. He wants this to be over. That's the only thought in his head now. Finish it. But he can't lift himself out of the car. Can't put weight on his legs.

'Please, help me,' Glass is saying. Pleading.

Another car goes past as he's dragging Bavidge from the car. Taking Bavidge under the arms and dragging him out onto the concrete. Pushing the passenger door shut to make room. Dragging him round in front of the car and laying him down slowly. Trying to be careful. Trying to be gentle. Looking down at the young man he's killed. Bavidge looking aimlessly past him. Looking at the sky above. Blinking heavily. Breathing short and fast. Too much effort.

'I'm sorry,' Glass is saying. 'I'm so sorry.' He doesn't know if Bavidge even heard him. Doesn't seem like it.

He's three steps past the car when he decides to take it.

He needs distance between himself and Bavidge. Doesn't matter if someone sees him in the car. He doesn't care about precautions. He just wants to be away. He's turning back and opening the car door. Bavidge is moving. He just moved. Trying to pull himself somewhere. Groaning. Glass can't watch this. Can't take any more of it.

Into the car, the seat still wet with Bavidge's blood. The passenger seat and footwell are thick with it. Stinking. Turning the key, into reverse. Lurching backwards out of the alley, almost catching the wall. Turning on the road. A screech of brakes behind him and the honking of an angry horn. A glance in his mirrors and he can see that he's pulled out into the path of an oncoming car. Lucky it didn't hit him. It's seen him though. Seen him and will remember him. The idiot rushing out of that alley late at night. But Glass isn't thinking about that. He's just putting it into first and hitting the accelerator. Getting away from Bavidge.

He's driven for the best part of three minutes before he remembers to switch the lights on again. Went past plenty of other cars and pedestrians in that time. All of them will have noticed the car with no lights. Now the panic of getting away from Bavidge has been replaced with the panic of getting rid of the car. Looking for anywhere to park. Doesn't matter where. Just anywhere.

The car park of a supermarket. Pulling in and stopping. Switching off the lights and the engine. Jumping out of the car. Slamming the door shut behind him and taking two steps back, looking back at it with disgust. He's parked as far from the building as he can. Now walking slowly over to the shrubbery at the edge of the car park. Bending over and vomiting. Twice. And then a rush of relief. It's gotten rid of the some of the nerves. It's forcing him to realize where he is.

A long way from home. Wearing bloodstained clothes. A knife with his prints still embedded in Alan Bavidge. Fingerprints and DNA all over a blood-drenched car. And he's crying again. Hunching down and crying loud. Shouting between sobs. There's nobody here. He wouldn't care if there were. This is over. Everything's over. He just killed a man. Stabbed him and left him to die. His life is over.

PART FOUR

1

It's only the third time he's seen him since he moved out. Three times in, what, over six months. Didn't expect to see his grandson every bloody day. Glad of a little space, to be honest. The tiny flat has felt more like his home since the boy moved out. Not having to make room for the lad, not having him hear every conversation. The walls have always been paper-thin; a little privacy is worth a lot. But he didn't expect to have to track him down like this. Didn't expect that his grandson would avoid him the way he has.

Everyone says he's changed. They say he's become tough, a little schemer. Everyone who knew him before and knows him now. Aren't many of those. Oliver seems to be doing his damnedest to ditch anyone who knew him before. Arnie isn't so sure about this great change. Oliver was always sharp. Always wanted more for himself than he could get. He wasn't the toughest kid, but he was never what you would call sympathetic. Never emotional. Kept people at a distance. That's probably what makes his work so easy for him. Doesn't think of people as people. Arnie blames his parents. Always did. Ditching the kid like that. Feckless pair of bastards.

Now he's running this business. A business that benefits

from his way of thinking. Creating a completely new life for himself. Know what? Arnie would be fine with that if it was the right kind of life. There's something admirable about a young man striding off into the world and building a new life for himself. If he felt he needed to cut old ties to do that, Arnie would respect it. A young man, just gone past his twenty-first birthday, and he already has his own little company. His own flat. His own life. But it's a rotten life. And that's why Arnie's tracking him down.

Arnie knew what Oliver was doing. He knew he was debt collecting. Scraping the bottom of the barrel. Arnie sat in his little flat every day and felt disgusted. Felt ashamed. But he did nothing. Did nothing because he hoped it might not be true. Hoped that maybe it was a short-term thing. That happens. A kid making money. Then the kid finds another way to make some dough. A better way. Maybe a more glamorous one. Less risky. And he moves away from the dirty side of life. But that's six months, and the stories he's hearing keep getting worse.

There's a middle-aged woman who lives in the next block of flats along from Arnie's. He doesn't know her, but he knows of her. Friends of friends, that sort of thing. Anyway, this woman borrowed money. Stupid thing to do, let's be honest. Arnie despairs of people who would borrow in the first place, given what happens. Always ends badly. Mind you, moneylenders can advertise on TV now. See it all the time. It's in danger of becoming acceptable. They're letting the sharks play in the swimming pool.

So this middle-aged woman, Kirsty something or other. She borrowed money and didn't pay it back. Couldn't, at the rates they were charging. The lender sold the debt to a collector. The collector sent someone round to intimidate her. She still couldn't pay. You can intimidate someone as much as you want; fear doesn't make money. So they started taking her stuff. Furniture, that sort of thing. She tried to stop the two thugs who had barged into her flat. So they beat her up. Not life-threatening or anything like that, but they knocked a couple of teeth out of her head. Left her all cut and bruised. Just about scared the life out of the poor woman.

Arnie heard the story and he shook his head. What kind of people would do that to a woman? Two days later he heard the story again, and it had grown a few hideous details. Grown to include the name of the collector who had sent his men round to steal her furniture. Who sent another one round when she was back from hospital the day after the beating to warn her to keep her mouth shut. They were saying it was Oliver Peterkinney.

Shame? He's never felt anything like it. His grandson sending nasty bastards round to beat up women. Never felt so humiliated in all his life. Let's make no mistake about it: he's done some things he's been ashamed of in his time. Things he wouldn't admit to, to you or to anyone else. But they were minor compared to this. The boy he helped raise, doing a thing like this. It's a humiliation. He knows it, and so does everyone else.

Which is what's brought him here. Walking across the road and towards the entrance of Oliver's office. His own little office building. Been here a while. Established, is what they call it. Beyond the point where he's a newbie who might fail at the first hurdle. Nope, he's past that hurdle and halfway down the running track. He's established now. That means people take him seriously. Fear him. Huh.

Arnie didn't want to come here. Would rather have met Oliver anywhere but here. Wanted to meet him at his flat, but he's moved again. Got a new address that he didn't bother to share with his grandfather. Moved again about a month ago. Moved to another flat in a more upscale part of town. Going up in the world, and obviously wants his home to show that. Bringing in a lot of other people's money. Wants the world to see how upwardly mobile he is. Wow the world with his success, like it's something to be proud of. Didn't bother to tell his grandfather where he was going.

Couldn't turn up at his flat. Called the office and got fobbed off by that nasal little lickspittle he employs. So this is the last resort. Turning up at the office and giving the boy no option but to talk. Because, by God, he is going to talk. He is going to explain himself. If he can't explain himself very well indeed then he is going to listen.

Arnie's across the street and opening the door. Stepping into the little office. Small place, but that's all you need when your job is intimidating the vulnerable. That doesn't take much space, does it? But they won't be here long. Arnie would bet on it. They'll stay in the area because people associate them with this area. But they'll get somewhere bigger. Somewhere they don't even need. To look big and clever. Intimidate people with their growth. And to cover their tracks. How much of this money has to be laundered? What other filthy practices do they use to get that done?

The two of them are in the office. Oliver behind his desk, the other fellow taking something out of a filing cabinet. Jesus, they almost look respectable. A pair of office boys. The other one's looking at him without a hint of recognition. Oliver's slumping back in his chair. A look of displeasure on his face. Rolling his eyes to the ceiling and then glaring back towards the door. Doing his best to make his own grandfather feel unwelcome.

'Can I help?' the other one is asking, sliding the drawer of the cabinet shut.

'Not you, son, no,' Arnie's saying.

'What do you want?' Oliver's asking him. 'You should have phoned. I don't have time for catching up. I'm busy.'

'Phoned, that's a laugh. I phone here and all I get is this wee bugger telling me you're not in. You're never in for a phone call. Disappear on the first bloody ring. I figured the only way you were ever going to be in was if I was in with you. No pretending then. So we can talk. Because we need to talk, Oliver. We do.' Trying to sound reasonable. Started with an irritated tone, but worked hard to calm it before he stopped talking. He doesn't want this to turn into an argument any earlier than it has to. Inevitable that it will at some point, but he has to try.

'Listen, I need to go out and . . .' But Peterkinney's trailing off, because Arnie's already turned round to look at Kilbanne. He's standing behind his desk on the other side of the room now.

'You can go make yourself scarce. Get lunch. Get lost. I don't care. Just get yourself out. This is a private conversation. Family talk.' Not bothered about being polite with him. The amount of times he's been lied to by this snivelling bastard, he hasn't earned politeness.

There's something remarkably intimidating about an angry old man. Arnie's not that big, looks unhealthy and sounds a little wheezy these days. But when he points and barks at you, you pay attention. Kilbanne is looking across at Peterkinney. Waiting for instructions from the boss. Maybe Peterkinney doesn't want to be left alone with this old guy.

'Go. Come back in fifteen,' Peterkinney's saying. 'This won't take longer than that.'

Kilbanne's leaving. Arnie still standing in front of Peterkinney's desk. Looking down at his grandson. Looks a little fuller in the face than he did. A little older. A little more rugged. Like he's lived something of a life now. Yeah. And at whose expense? Arnie's shaking his head.

'Why haven't you been willing to talk to me?' he's asking quietly.

'I've been busy. Working, you know.' Said with a hint of sarcasm. Pointing out the fact that Arnie hasn't had a job for some time now.

Oliver still hasn't asked him to sit down. Not that Arnie wants to. He wants to stand over the boy when the argument starts. Feels like a position of strength. But he's noticed Oliver's making no effort at being welcoming. He still doesn't want to talk. Doesn't want his grandfather to be a part of his life any more. The man who took him in. Gave him a home. Did his best, such as it was, to raise him. Don't throw that at him though. That's not the way to win this argument. Oliver clearly feels no sense of debt.

'I know what work you do.'

'Uh-huh. Not a secret.'

'No, it isn't, is it? Everyone knows. Everyone's talking about you. Talking about how you had your thugs beat up some woman along the street from me. That you don't give a shit about the law or anything else. Tough little bastard, you are. That's what they say. How tough you are. Hiding behind your thugs. Stealing money from the weakest people you can find. Yeah, everyone's talking about you all right. Tough little nut, uh? Very scary.' Damn it. Didn't want to go off on a rant this soon. Wanted to make a persuasive argument, not an aggressive one. Just couldn't control it. Months of knowing what his own flesh and blood was doing. Months of doing nothing about it. His own embarrassment at not doing this sooner was to blame. There was just too much locked away in there that needed to come out.

'You here about her? I heard about that, already repri-manded someone for it. It was a mistake. An accident. Shouldn't have happened. I'm sorry, okay? We done?'

It's a funny thing. Really is. You live with someone for a few years and you get a pretty good handle on the sort of person they are. You lose track of them for six months. Catch up with them again and they're someone else. Completely different person. Oliver was distant, and he could be cold. He wasn't always an easy boy to love. But he was respectful, because he understood that that worked best. He was never a dismissive, arrogant little shit. He understood what it meant to be a good person. He could be morally hazy, sure. Arnie wasn't going to judge him for that. Anyway, he was a kid, a little bit immature. All kids make mistakes. Follow the wrong path once in a while. Didn't make him a bad person, not at heart. He was a decent person, when push came to shove. Now look at him. He's someone else.

'It will kill you, you know,' Arnie's saying. Saying it quiet.

Saying it with genuine regret. A sadness that catches Oliver out.

He's looking up at his grandfather. A puzzled look. 'What?'

'This. All this. The work you're doing. The life you're living. It's going to kill you. You won't be the first one, oh no. It'll destroy anyone innocent first. That's what it does, this life. It kills the good people first, then the bad. This life of yours is poison. That poison will catch up with you. It will. Has to. You mark my words, boy. It will catch up with you and it will kill you. I've seen it. People being murdered. Or getting into drugs. Some stupid thing. And I'll have to go. I'll have to go to your funeral and stand over your grave and know that I didn't stop you. Couldn't stop you from doing it to yourself.'

He's stopped talking. He was rambling and he knew it. His voice was quivering with emotion and Arnie isn't the kind of man who likes to hear that in himself. Old school. He came here to be strong. He didn't come here to be emotional.

'I think you should go.' Oliver sitting there, looking up at him. There's a look of shock on his face that he's doing a poor job of hiding. Never heard his grandfather talk like this before. Never seen that sort of emotion from him.

Arnie's looking down at him. Scowling to cover the emotion. Shaking his head, because he just can't think of anything else to say. Wishes there was something convincing to say, but there isn't. He's turning and walking to the door. Pulling it open, but stopping. Looking back at Oliver. Just looking at him, because he's scared he might never see him again. And leaving, because he can't help a man who doesn't believe he needs help. Who won't realize until it's too late.

2

Furious. Actually, furious doesn't begin to sum it up. If he had the mobility, he'd be bouncing off the walls. Potty Cruickshank has never been so angry. Never in forty-eight angry years. Six hours ago he was arrested. First time in his life. Some detective and a couple of plods turned up at his house and arrested him. Led him out into the street for all the neighbours to see as they loaded him into the back of a police car. Deliberately embarrassing him. Suspicion of laundering money, they said. Took him away to the station. The thing he was most angry about? They were right.

He's always been so careful with his money. That was hammered into him by Uncle Rolly. The money is the easiest way for the cops to get you. You always hide it away. You take every last precaution to make sure it's well out of view. Someone grassed. Someone who knows about his systems went to the police and spilled their guts. It's the only way. They couldn't have known what they did without inside info. So now he has to find out who.

They haven't charged him yet. Questioned him for a few hours. A lot of questions he genuinely didn't know the answers to. He doesn't know every exact detail about every penny that gets hidden. He hires people to handle that. He has deniability on the details of it. A few questions he did know the answer to. Those he chose not to answer anyway. It did give him a few clues about timing. They only seemed to be asking about money that was moved within a certain period. About a year ago until about six months ago, give or take. That's interesting. That's a place to start investigating.

The cheek of them. Arresting a Cruickshank. Didn't even have enough to charge him with. That's what he thought. Not what his lawyer thought. In the car on the way back to his house the lawyer had a different idea to share. After five hours in the station, Potty wasn't thinking straight. So the lawyer put him right.

'They brought you in to scare you. See if they could trip you up. They'll be arresting other people. Must be, the evidence they have. I think they will arrest you again, Mr Cruickshank. They're setting you up to arrest you a second time, and this time they'll charge you.'

He was right. Potty's been at home for nearly an hour. Taking that time to try to calm down. Not happening. This kind of fury will take days to calm. He needs to find out who grassed him. Find out what damage has been done. There's an easy place to start. The police were asking about money from that period of time. Time to get in touch with the man who was moving his money around at that time.

Potty has two different men who handle the money, but

neither of them is young any more. One of them, Willie Caldwell, has hardly done a hand's turn for a year and a half. The man's seventy and had treatment for cancer. He was Uncle Rolly's moneyman for many years, just carried on working for Potty. He's started doing a bit of work again in the last three months, but nothing as far back as six to twelve months. Which just leaves Steven Wales. Sixty-three, and amongst the most dependable criminals that God ever placed on this earth.

Potty's calling his house. It only rings twice and there's an answer. A woman's voice. That'll be Mrs Wales then. The often-mentioned, never-seen spouse. Potty's never met the woman, for all that he's heard Wales talk about her over the years.

'Hello, I'm looking for Steven Wales. Is he home?'

'No. No, he isn't. Who's calling, please?'

The woman sounds emotional. Potty doesn't have the patience for emotional. Not in the mood. 'This is Ronald Cruickshank.'

'Oh, Mr Cruickshank,' she's saying. There's relief in her voice. Something Potty doesn't like to hear. Usually means someone expects you to do them a favour. 'Oh, Mr Cruickshank, they came to the house this morning. The police came and they took him away. They said they were going to question him and he hasn't been back yet.'

Potty's grimacing, but in a sense it's good news. They've

arrested Wales, which means Wales isn't the grass. Wales is the one who knows the most. He was the one cleaning the money. So long as he keeps his gob shut, that'll prevent the police knowing the worst of it. So the grass is someone else. Someone a little further away from the centre. Someone who knew that Wales did work for Potty. Knew at least roughly what that work entailed. Specifically from that time period.

'Now you listen here, Mrs Wales. I will do all I can to make sure your husband is well treated. I'll get my lawyers on it right away. Your husband won't be in any trouble if I can help it.' He can't say that her husband has done nothing wrong because, well, he has. She must realize it. There may be trouble that Potty can do nothing to stop.

'Thank you, Mr Cruickshank. It helps to know.'

Wasn't Wales. Then who? Sitting down and thinking things through. Considering the options. And there's one there. Lurking in the back of his mind, elbowing its way forwards. Someone who was around a lot back then. Helped him out. Someone who's been drifting away from him for no good reason in the last six months.

He's made three phone calls and come up short. Nobody knows just what exactly PC Paul Greig is up to these days. Conflicting reports. One person saying he's working for Shug Francis. Another person saying he's working for Alex MacArthur. So now Potty's calling Alex MacArthur.

'He isn't doing any work for me,' MacArthur's saying. There's an edge to his tone. Their relationship has been good these last few months, since the Bavidge thing. But this call doesn't seem to be welcome. Sounds like the old man's distracted. 'I think he's been doing work for Don though. Call Don if you want to ask about him.' Didn't say Don Park's name with any great love. One of his own men. Sounds like the old man is finally getting wary of potential successors. They all do, in the end.

Calling up Don Park. Getting a chuckle at the mention of Greig. Smooth little operator this one. One to keep an eye on if MacArthur's health gets worse. 'Working for me? Not exactly. Working for everyone. You know what he's like. Doing work for me and doing work for Peter Jamieson. Doing work for you and doing work for Oliver Peterkinney. That's Greig. A finger in every pie.'

That's as much as Potty needs to hear. Greig doing work for Peterkinney. Of course he fucking is. A new kid turns up and starts making an impact. Growing untouched. Getting good deals. Knowing where to go. Contacts that others take years to find. Needs experienced people to point him in the right directions. Help him along. People very much like Greig.

Starting to make a lot more sense now. Peterkinney gets Greig onside. They strike a deal. Greig helps Peterkinney by removing the opposition. Good Lord, Potty didn't take the kid seriously enough. Some little bastard who worked for Marty

295

and set up his own business. Not like he would have learned much from Marty. He did mean to watch him. Had every intention of doing something about him sooner. Should have. Would have. Too busy pulling the rug out from under Billy Patterson. This is what happens when you take your eye off the ball. Slap on the wrist for Potty, move on.

Move on and work out what he's going to do about Peterkinney. What he's going to do about Greig. Don't let personal feeling get in the way of a business decision. Be very careful with Greig. He's a cop. A lying, cheating bastard, but a cop. You don't pick a fight with a cop. Not unless you're on solid ground, which Potty isn't. No way he can make a convincing allegation against Greig without implicating himself. No way he can bring down Greig without Greig making life even more difficult for him.

But Peterkinney. He's a different business. He can be taken down. There are things that Potty can and will do to teach that wee boy a few lessons. The first lesson being that you don't pick a fight with a Cruickshank until you're 100 per cent certain of victory. So now Potty's plotting. Trying to work out ways of getting at Peterkinney. He tried once before with the Bavidge thing. Didn't work out perfectly, but that didn't matter much at the time. Peterkinney didn't end up getting any of the blame, as Potty intended. But that was always a bonus to the main event. This is different. Now Peterkinney's going to be the main target.

3

Glass didn't leave the flat for days afterwards. Spent the whole time waiting for a knock on the door that didn't come. Only person who came to the flat in that time was Ella, and she has a key. She spent some time with him, trying to work out what was wrong. He wasn't responding to her. Lying in bed, refusing to tell her what had happened. She made an effort. A week of treating him like an invalid. Cooking for him, getting him to shower. Never forcing him to share anything, but trying to coax it out of him. Nothing she did made an impact.

It upset her, seemed like he was deliberately pushing her away. So Ella made a decision. Try and shock him into action. Get him out of his bed and into the world again by giving him no other option. She stopped coming to the flat, and he was completely alone. The idea was that it would compel him to get up. Go out and get some food, get into the world. Didn't work. She waited a week, and no phone call came. Went past the flats a few times and saw no sign of life. When she went back in, he was the same as ever. He'd fed himself, yes, because he had to. But he was eating food way past its sell-by date. Unwilling to leave the flat even for that. She cried over it, and went back to playing nursemaid, fitting it around her work.

One thing Glass made the effort to do was constantly check websites and local TV news. They found Alan Bavidge's body the following morning. Multiple stab wounds, is what was reported. Knife found at the scene. Didn't say that it was still in his body. Said they were hopeful of progress. Glass knew what that meant. Meant his fingerprints were on the knife. Meant they had all the evidence they needed for a conviction; all they had to do was track down the killer. But time passed and they didn't track him down. They had his fingerprints on the knife, but nowhere else.

But there was so much else. The longer he lay in bed thinking about it, the more he remembered what he had done wrong. The people who had seen him. The CCTV cameras that must have picked him up. Leaving the car in a car park. A bloodstained car with the number plates still on it. Would take them all of ten seconds to put two and two together. But nothing. No knock on the door. Nobody coming to tell him that he was being charged with murder.

He'd already decided that if they came for him, he would confess. No point in denying it. He couldn't claim innocence, so he would confess and hope they were gentle with him. He wouldn't tell them why. He'd decided that. If he grassed Potty then Potty would take revenge. Could kill him. No, he would say that he owed money, and that he thought Bavidge was going to collect from him. Something like that. Take all the blame for himself. Looking at a long time inside. Thinking about how he would survive it. Twenty years. Thirty, maybe. But the knock on the door didn't come. It was like they didn't check the CCTV. Like they didn't interview the witnesses. Like they never found the car.

Which they didn't. Not the police's fault. The witnesses never came forward. Not one. Not even the guy who stopped and got out of his car outside Bavidge's house. He went home and decided to forget about it. If he saw the report of the dead body found behind the shops, he either didn't connect the two things or didn't want to get involved. That's the thing. People don't want to get involved. Not if they can avoid it. So the driver of the car that Glass nearly reversed into pulling out of the alleyway said nothing. They must now realize that they saw the killer leave the scene, but he or she is keeping it to themselves. Scared of getting tangled in a gangland dispute.

Without witnesses, the police don't know what they're looking for. Don't know what car. It wasn't Bavidge's own car. That was parked outside his flat. This was a company car belonging to Patterson, but the police don't know that. They're convinced the body was moved, but they think in the killer's car. So they've gone through the CCTV around the scene, but more than half the cameras don't work. They've come up with no reliable image of the car that took Bavidge to the scene.

And they never found the car. Nobody did. A couple of

hours after word spread that Bavidge was dead, the car was gone from the car park. Disappeared off the face of the earth. Glass doesn't know that. Didn't know it for those few weeks he spent hiding from the world. Assumed the police had found it. Assumed they would be knocking on his door any minute now. But the car was gone. The evidence they needed, spirited away. Nothing for the police to use. Their investigation undermined. Glass's freedom saved.

After three weeks, he started to re-engage with planet Earth. Enough time passed for Ella's pleas to become convincing. She didn't know what he was scared of, but she kept saying that it had been weeks and nothing had happened. Weeks when he thought he was in danger but was safe. Surely it was time to get back to normal. Three weeks was sufficient for his fear to shrink just enough for him to see other people's problems. To see how much he was upsetting Ella. So he made the effort. Out into the big scary world. Afraid of every step. Waiting for a hand on the shoulder. Waiting for someone to say or do something. But nobody did. Nobody cared about him in the slightest.

It was a weird couple of months thereafter. He gradually got used to living again. He knows he was childish about it. Living in fear, needing to be looked after. Even in the month after he started going out again. Ella nursed him through it all. But it hasn't been the same. Hasn't been the same with Ella. Hasn't been the same with anyone. Still living with that fear. Always will. Knowing that he did something he ought to be punished for. Knowing that there are people out there who will seek to punish him. Worse people than the police.

He was waiting for the police, because they were the first fear his mind turned to. Still are. Getting to a point where it would almost be a relief if a copper did come for him. But there are more dangerous people out there than the police. Alan Bavidge worked for Billy Patterson. Everyone knows Billy Patterson is a tough little bastard. Everyone knows he punishes hard. He has to be looking for the person who killed Bavidge. When he finds that person, he's going to kill them. Torture them and kill them. When the police find the killer, Patterson will still try to kill them. You live with that sort of fear, that sort of expectation, and it changes your behaviour.

Glass basically stopped caring. If you're going to be arrested or killed tomorrow, it doesn't much matter how you behave today. So he started going out with Ella every night. Even when she didn't want to go, he insisted. She only went because she was worried about him. Thought he needed her there to stop him doing something stupid. Still nursing him, because he was obviously still sick. Living every night like it was his last. Could have been. You never know. So he lived it that way. Drinking a lot. Using a lot more drugs, because that seemed to help. Kill reality.

You know what's funny? He doesn't remember going

back to Jefferson for another loan. No recollection at all. Doesn't even remember spending the money. Jefferson happily gave him the money when he asked. He knew that Glass had paid off Potty. Had done something to wriggle off the hook. Potty was happy with Glass, so Glass got another loan. Jefferson working on the assumption that he can sell this one to Potty as well. Glass doesn't remember asking for the money. Doesn't remember spending it. Doesn't remember going back and asking for more.

That's what it's been like. Months of blur. That's the way he wants to keep it. Life doesn't feel real, so life stops being something he needs to care about. His relationship with Ella is suffering for it. She cries a lot, shouts at him. Shouting about things he barely understands. Something about a carpet the other day. He didn't understand that she had been saving up for a new carpet in the living room, and he blew the money on drink. Doesn't understand that she's trying to create a stable home, and that he's destroying it. But that doesn't matter to him. Nothing does.

Jefferson's been calling. Glass is heading round there now. Not thinking about it at all. He doesn't care what Jefferson wants. Doesn't care what he demands or threatens. Jefferson's nothing when you stand him next to Billy Patterson.

Into Jefferson's office. Jefferson actually seems surprised that he's turned up. Raising an eyebrow and slowly nodding his head. Seen this before. Borrowers who just don't care. Don't even try and hide from the problem any more.

'You came. Good. Sit down.' There's a pause while he looks at Glass. Glass has the look of a man who slept for three hours last night. Who didn't shower this morning. Stubble, tousled hair, scruffy clothes. 'You look like shit,' Jefferson's saying. A hint of concern. Not about Glass. He doesn't care about Glass's well-being any more than Glass does. He's concerned about the debt. If Glass can't look after himself, he can't look after the debt. The boy's really gone downhill in the last few months.

'Thanks a lot. What do you want?'

Jefferson's frowning now. 'What do I want? I want my fucking money, is what I want. What did you think I wanted? You owe me money. You owe me four thousand one hundred pounds. You haven't paid back a single penny.' That's why he's calling it in. This new debt hasn't been running long, but at least last time Glass showed signs of paying. Not this time. This time, not a damn penny. No money paid, no effort made to pay. So he's calling it in early.

'I don't have any money.' Glass saying it like it's no big deal. Like he doesn't care at all. And he doesn't. Last time it worried him sick. This time he has it in perspective. Money is nothing. If he's dead tomorrow, the debt dies with him. If he's locked up tomorrow, the debt gets locked up with him. The debt is a long-term problem in a short-term world.

'You think you're going to get off with this? You think you've bought yourself some sort of credit? Huh, is that it? You think Potty Cruickshank will bail you out a second time? He won't. Let me tell you that now. He won't. Seems like he isn't interested in you any more. Yeah, I called him. Yesterday morning. Called him up and said I had another debt of yours I was looking to shift. Thought he might be interested. He said no. Not interested at all, thanks for calling. So you're out on your own. You need to come up with that money, because there's nobody in this world that wants to help you.'

Glass is laughing. Nobody ever wanted to help him. He never thought for one second that anyone did. Potty? Wanting to help him? That's a laugh. Jefferson's frowning again, and he can frown all he wants. Glass didn't borrow because he thought there was a way out. He borrowed because it doesn't matter to him.

He's out of the office and making his way back home. Pointless meeting. Back to the flat. Maybe get some sleep in the afternoon. Spend a little time with Ella. But she's not there when he gets back. Gone off somewhere without telling him. She does that more now. He hasn't thought about why. She's working more to try and earn more money because he's throwing so much away. She's trying to keep the dream of a good life alive. The dream they used to share.

4

It shocked him, how much it hurt. Billy Patterson is a tough man, make no mistake. He's thirty-nine, and people have come and gone in his life. People he cared about. Didn't slow him down. Always hurts to lose someone you care about, sure, but he coped. Coped well. Shut the emotions away and got on with being his usual hard self. So he didn't expect losing Bavidge to hurt the way it did.

Partly because he blames himself. Never blamed himself before. He's been responsible for people dying before. Two people. Didn't carry out the killings. Didn't order them either. But sent people round to beat these two up. They didn't take the beatings well. Died. Patterson didn't take that hard. That was the job. Some people can take a beating. Some people can't. The risk you run when you're dealing with collectors. This was different. This actually felt like his fault.

Bavidge was a friend. They didn't hang out socially, but that wasn't the point. They were friends in a way that mattered more than socializing. They were on the same wavelength. Patterson sent Bavidge out into the world to do bad things. Bavidge did them, never questioning the role he played. He was honest, and he was reliable. He understood.

It was Patterson who sent him out to do those bad things, and one of them caught up with Bavidge. Strange thing is, this is what he expected. He had always viewed Bavidge as a man destined for an early death. He knew that, and it didn't stop him using Bavidge. And that got him killed.

He heard the news from a contact in the police. A civilian, doing office work. They called him up, told him that the police had found Bavidge's body. Gave all the details. They were confusing. Multiple stab wounds to the arms and stomach. The knife was still in him. He was found behind some shops in the city centre. Made no sense. Body had been moved. Probably attacked outside his house: some blood had been found on the pavement by the officers sent round to check the place. The police searching for the car that moved him. Patterson was stunned by it. Took him a few minutes to pull himself together. Then he acted fast.

Sent someone round to Bavidge's house. Wanted to see if the police had found the car Bavidge was using. That car was the link to Patterson. A link Patterson couldn't let the police find. Car wasn't there. Police were. At first he feared the police had found the car and taken it away. Reassurance from the contact. The police still hadn't found anything. Bavidge's own car on the street, but nothing else of interest. So all his people were sent out to look. Find the car. It had to be what the body was moved in. Had to be. It was luck that they found it so soon. The muscle searched car parks and one of them stumbled across the car. Inside soaked in blood. It's been destroyed. Nothing to link the murder victim with the debt collector he was planning crimes with. How could Patterson explain the use of that company car to the police? Admit that they were using it to try and trick a gunman into killing Potty Cruickshank in an attempt to set up Marty Jones? Yeah, good one. The car had to go.

That was the clean-up. The following couple of months were awkward. Just trying to get the tone right. People in the business knew they were vulnerable. Had to know. They knew that Bavidge was an important man and now they know he's dead. So Patterson went into reassurance mode. Making sure all his men knew that they weren't going to be crushed. This was a one-off, not dominoes falling. That meant keeping their heads down. No drawing attention. If people don't look at you, they don't see your vulnerability. Let everything calm down before you launch a counter-attack.

Truth is, if he'd been in a strong position, he would have hit back straight away. He wanted to. Would have loved to do something about it. He was burning to punish someone. Two problems. Couldn't be sure who had done it. The hit was a mess, and that pushed him towards thinking it was someone amateur. Someone a bit dumb. Maybe someone Bavidge had collected from. Or a jealous husband. But the main target still had to be Potty Cruickshank. He was the obvious candidate.

Would never put it past him to use some amateur to cover his tracks.

But Patterson wasn't strong enough to fight back. Not yet. He needed to regroup without Bavidge. He needed to find answers. He needed to build strength. And he's been doing that. Tough, but not dumb. He's been working silently. Giving people the impression that he's weak. Giving people the impression that he's slowly losing business. Letting them believe what he wants them to believe. Pulling his inner circle closer and getting them to work.

Today is one of the first big steps in his plan. He will take down Potty Cruickshank. He will. He will because he knows. Doesn't know everything, sure, but he knows enough. Suspicion has hardened into certainty. Potty and MacArthur were working together, and MacArthur has a big organization. A lot of people who find stuff out. A lot of people who can talk about it. And they did talk. Conn Griffiths got a lot of good info about the Bavidge killing yesterday. Organized by Potty. No doubt about it. Potty and MacArthur were rather pleased with themselves about it. Jamie Stamford, weirdly, wasn't that happy. Probably didn't like someone else publicly cleaning up his mess. But it was Potty. Everyone in MacArthur's organization is saying so.

Still haven't found out who actually carried it out. Working on that. Won't stop looking until he finds them. And when he finds them, he'll kill them. Potty's the big one. Potty's the one who made it all happen and he's the one who has to pay for it. The person who carried it out has to be seen to be punished. But that takes help. Patterson's been lying low. He's using fewer people now, buying fewer debts. That's deliberate. Self-preservation. If you're too small to win the fight, get so small the opponent thinks they've already won. Potty will think that he's won. Beaten Patterson. But he's got a surprise coming.

Patterson's meeting with Marty Jones. Polite little meeting in an office above a shop. Talk with Marty about helping each other out. Marty will think he's the big half of the meeting. He'll believe Patterson is small now too. So he'll be willing to do a deal because he'll think he can dominate this. That's fine. Let him think that. If Bavidge had lived, Marty would be carrying the can for a hit attempt on Potty right now. Just don't underestimate flashy Marty. Doesn't matter how scatty a shark like him looks, he still has bite. Patterson's increasingly convinced that that's all part of Marty's own self-preservation. The lifestyle. The parties and the women. Profitable, sure, but a smart way to look like a cheeky rogue, rather than a ruthless gangster.

'Good to see you, Billy,' Marty's saying. Sticking his hand out and pretending to be a friend. Sitting behind one of the desks in the office.

The office is practically empty. Desks and chairs and very little else to get excited about. Easy to guess what Marty sees

309

in this place. It's on a busy street where he can come and go without standing out. Have meetings like this. Collect things here. Kind of good little office Patterson could do with.

'Good to see you too, Marty.' Very disingenuous, but Marty must encounter so many bullshit merchants that he doesn't bat an eyelid. 'I think we ought to have a little chat about what we can do for each other.'

Marty's smiling and nodding. A guy comes to you and says you should help each other out. A guy who's been under attack. A guy whose business has been shrinking. Of course Marty's going to think that this is a golden opportunity for him. Of course he's going to think that he can take control of this. That's what he's supposed to think.

'Well, I guess maybe we can,' Marty's saying. 'Although I'll be honest with you here, Billy, I'm not seeing what we're going to be able to do for each other. You and me, we're not exactly the best possible fit.'

'See, I think we are,' Patterson's saying, getting in there before Marty has the chance to follow that train of thought down the tracks. 'I think there's a lot we can do for each other. I think we're as compatible as two men in our business can be. Not a perfect fit, maybe, but you'll never find one of them. You have specific skills and connections that I don't have. I have specific abilities that you don't. And we both have common enemies.'

Marty's nodding to that. They sure as hell do. But Marty's

been thinking about that bastard Peterkinney a lot, and he's guessing that's not who's on Patterson's mind. He'll be more interested in Potty Cruickshank. Everyone knows he took on Potty and lost. Potty hooked up with Alex MacArthur. Now things are falling into place. Ah, Patterson, you smart little bastard. Potty hooks up with Alex MacArthur. Marty is under Peter Jamieson's protection. That makes it hard for Marty to say no.

But Marty's instincts are telling him to say no. He wants to say no so that he won't get dragged into something big and dangerous. This is a man who's built his career on exploiting the vulnerable, not fighting the strong. He knows what fights to pick. His instincts are razor-sharp on that front. This doesn't look like a good one. But he has to say yes. Jamieson's setting up a run on MacArthur. Everyone in the know knows. Or at least suspects. It's the next natural step. This will help to hurt MacArthur, and Marty still needs to wriggle his way back into the good books. Looking for every opportunity.

'You need to tell me something concrete,' Marty's saying. 'You give me something concrete, and I can get behind it. I'm not going to throw myself in front of a bus for you, Billy boy, but I could help you.'

Billy's turn to smile. Marty's good at this. You have to play him careful. Tempting to believe all the bluster and bullshit, but he's smart. Didn't get where he is by accident. 'I want Potty Cruickshank's fat head on a spike. I want the

Cruickshank business in ashes. I want that family name to be a distant memory. An old joke. I think that would serve you well. I also wouldn't mind cutting the legs off Oliver Peterkinney. I've watched him grow. He's dangerous. Would be smart to do something to stop that, sooner rather than later. You and me could carve this business up between us. If we're smart. If we're tough. If we use the advantages we have. We could undermine some important people into the bargain. Help bigger players take down bigger rivals. I have the men to go to war with Potty. Don't be dumb enough to believe that my shrinking the business was anything other than preparation.'

Marty's looking at his watch. He really does need to hurry this along. 'Okay. Listen, Billy. I ain't saying yes. Not certainly. But I'll think about it. Give it some, you know, proper consideration.'

'You know that Potty Cruickshank was arrested this morning?' Patterson's asking. Casual tone, making no effort to get up and leave.

Marty looks shocked. He didn't know that.

'The cracks are starting to show,' Patterson's saying, getting up from his chair now. 'You think about what I said. Give it proper consideration. Potty was arrested because your old employee Peterkinney is moving against him. Dangerous kid, that one. Taking on a man like Potty. Would serve you well to have some extra men around you. Men like my crew.'

Sticking his hand out to shake. Then turning and walking confidently out of the room.

Down the steps and out through the door onto the street. Marty has to say yes, and he will. He would have anyway, without knowing about Potty's arrest. He would have said yes because he needs to make the moves that make Jamieson happy. But Potty's arrest tips it over the edge. Doesn't matter who you are, an arrest makes you look weak. Once you look weak, you look like a target.

5

His grandfather's still on his mind. Shouldn't bother him at all, but it does. He never exaggerated their relationship. He was already a teenager when he went to live with Arnie. Arnie didn't have any profound effect on making him the man he is today. He didn't mould him. Always seemed to Peterkinney that his grandfather was counting the days to him leaving. Tried to push him in the right direction now and again. Never openly begrudged the expense of having Oliver there. Tried to bring him up with the least possible effort.

Now he's all over him. Giving him an earful. Captain fucking Morality. Where did that come from? Jesus, think back. Who was it that set him up with Roy Bowles in the first place? Bowles the gunrunner. That was his grandfather's grand plan to steer him away from Marty Jones. Get away from that frying pan and into the fire. Please. Coming over all moral now. Gets on his nerves. Really does.

And he's still angry as he pulls up at Jazzy Jefferson's office. Shoving his car door shut and walking briskly inside. Late in the day for a business meeting. It was Jefferson who called him up. Asked him to come round to have a look at the books. Might be a good deal or two in there for him. Sounded a little too pleading. Sounded like Jefferson was having a hard time shifting some debts and wanted the always-generous youngster to help him out. Well, the youngster is more established now. Less need to be generous. And he's not in a helping mood.

'Oliver, good to see you,' Jefferson's saying. Smiling so broadly you would almost think he meant it. Smiling so broadly he's beginning to look like he's in pain.

'Sit down, let's see these books.' No mood for pleasantries. Not with Jefferson anyway. Like Peterkinney doesn't know what Jefferson's been up to. Like he doesn't keep a keen eye on people like him. Any sensible collector keeps a beady eye on the behaviour of lenders. He knows Jefferson's been pawing at Potty's door again. Looking to keep onside with the fat man. They've all heard the stories about Potty teaming up with Alex MacArthur. Squashing Billy Patterson. Big deal, very impressive, whoop-dee-doo. Peterkinney's one of the few who doesn't seem to be impressed by these old farts squabbling. No surprise that Jefferson's gone running back. He really shouldn't be so naive as to think Peterkinney wouldn't realize.

Jefferson's passing the book across the desk. A hardback notebook, very neatly kept. You're always looking at the first page. All previous pages carefully cut out with a razor blade when they've been used. Peterkinney knows the debts Jefferson wants to shift are at the top of the page. There's one up there that's leapt straight out at him. But he's making a deliberate effort to ignore it. Not letting Jefferson see that he's noticed. Making a show of scanning down the page.

'Not a lot of fruit in the garden,' Peterkinney's muttering.

'There's a few in there that are as safe as houses. A few where you can't go wrong. Easy profit. Rest of them just need the sort of nudge I can't give them. Nothing there you wouldn't turn a profit on, Oliver, I'll tell you that now. Good list.' Selling too hard, realizing and backing off.

Peterkinney looking through them. Looking at the name, the address, the amount, the borrow date, the amount repaid, employed or not employed, known assets. Last one's a key indicator. Do they own a house or a car? If not, and they don't have a job, you're going to have your work cut out. Jefferson's good at detail. Plenty there to read through. Some aren't. Some lenders think you only need a name and an amount. But Peterkinney's eyes keep creeping back up the page. Creeping back to the name Jefferson has put there in the hope of him seeing. The hope of him buying. Alex Glass.

Everyone knows Glass was his best friend. Jefferson only put the name on the list in the hope that friendship would make him buy. No point pretending he doesn't recognize the name, although he has little inclination to purchase. He knows Glass's situation. Still in thrall to that hooker. Pissing his life away, is what he's heard. Heard he was drinking and using heavily these days. No job. No assets. No prospect of paying that debt. Still, Jefferson expects him to ask about it, so he'll ask.

'Alex Glass, what's his condition? Doesn't look good here.' Borrowed and didn't pay back a penny. Never a good sign when they don't pay anything at all. The ones who aren't trying are the ones you can't turn a profit on.

'I won't bullshit you, Oliver,' says the professional bull-shitter. 'You'll struggle to get your money back on him. That's if you go the conventional route, anyway. I put him on there for a couple of reasons. First is that I know he's your mate. Won't yank your chain on that one. I thought you might want to know what the situation is. Try and stop him being in debt to someone who might think it's a good idea to get at you through him, you know. Other people might use him to hurt you. Second thing is, he had a debt with me before. Little bigger than this one. Okay, he was in better shape then than he is now, but still. I sold that debt to Potty Cruickshank. This is going back a ways. Few months now. You'd only just set up your own business around then. But he paid Cruickshank off in full. Don't know how. Heard he did some sort of job for him. But he got the debt settled in full. Potty was happy. There might be something there for you. Must have some sort of skill that he used the last time. A chance to get him working for you.'

You have to admire Jefferson. You really do. Initially Peterkinney thought Glass had been shovelled onto the list in some desperate attempt by the lender to play on emotions. Try and get him to help out an old mate. That wasn't going to work. Not today of all days, when any part of his old life is a foul reminder of his grandfather. But Jefferson had a backup plan all along.

Jefferson's giving him a route to Potty. Not telling him outright that Glass did something dubious for Potty. Not saying that having Glass under his thumb on the debt could prove useful in attacking Potty. Jefferson would never come out and say something like that. That would look like picking sides. He's too smart for that. But he'll hint at it. He'll talk about Glass doing a single job for Potty that was enough to pay off a large debt. Something that made Potty happy. That's a hint Peterkinney can't ignore.

Potty is a big target. No sniggering, this is serious. He's big. Too big for a young guy like Peterkinney to take on directly. But any time you get a chance to take a shot at him, you have to. Bring him down a peg. That's what Peterkinney's focusing on. If Glass knows something big. If he was involved in something that Peterkinney can use to keep chipping away at Potty. Well, you don't let a chance like that fly by, do you? He's not in a mood to make people happy though. Doesn't want Jefferson thinking he's done something clever. But he has, the bastard, and this opportunity is too good to miss.

'Okay then,' Peterkinney's saying. And saying no more

about it, because Jefferson isn't going to give him any more detail than that.

They've talked for another few minutes. Peterkinney's asked a few pertinent questions about a couple of other names on the list. Just going through the motions. In the end, Peterkinney's buying two debts. One that he knows he can turn a quick profit on. The other belongs to Glass. Jefferson does look pleased with himself. That's the downside.

Peterkinney's back in his new flat, feet up. Relaxing in nice surroundings. This is what his grandfather doesn't understand. An old man, spending his life in some shitty little flat. Cramped, damp, dark and hopeless. Thinking that because he spent most of his life on the right side of the law he deserves some fucking medal. Most of his life, not all of it. He strayed from the righteous path as well. Never forget that. Standing in that office and lecturing him. Shit, makes him angry to think.

Walking through to his kitchen. Comparing it to the tiny little kitchen in Arnie's flat. The ancient wall units and the grotty little washing machine that sounded like a struggling helicopter. If that's what your flawed attempts at honest living get you, you can keep it. Peterkinney isn't going to live that sort of life. He knows that if you have the guts, you can have more. You can have the good life. You just need the courage to take it. You need the smarts to take advantage of every opportunity that comes along.

6

It feels like morning. It's morning, right? He's opening his eyes. Still seems dark. And wet. And he's beginning to realize that something's amiss. Slow awareness that he's not where he should be. A few more seconds. Now Glass is coughing loudly. Trying to sit up, but everything hurts. His stomach, his shoulder. Feels like there's something pressing at the back of his head.

Then a few minutes of nothing. Somewhere close to sleep. Now he's suddenly awake. Suddenly very aware of where he is. Lying in the alleyway behind Fourteen. Lying on the wet ground. The pain in the back of his head is from lying on the tarmac. The pain in his shoulder and stomach? They'll take a bit more memory work. First challenge is to get to his feet. Struggling up.

Damn it all, he's soaking. Not just rain, either. They must have dumped him in a puddle. All down his back is wet. Shaking his head, and remembering how he ended up here. Stopping shaking his head, because it makes his shoulder hurt. Coughing hard again. He feels like throwing up. Yeah, that would just about top it off.

Ella wasn't at home when he got back to the flat after

meeting Jefferson. That pissed him off a bit. He wanted to be with her. Spend some time with her. So he called her. Didn't get through first couple of times. Got through to her on the third call. Demanded to know where she was. She was oblivious to his tone. Didn't get that he was angry with her for not being there. That he was angry with everything for reasons he couldn't put his finger on. She told him she was at Fourteen. Said she would be home late. He said he would come see her there.

Managed to get into the club. Found Ella. She gave him some attention. She was nervous, and that annoyed him. They had a few drinks. They danced. It was going okay. Then she went off to speak to someone. Some guy, he remembers. Must have been the guy she was there to work. Can't even picture him now. Older than Glass, for sure. Some rich-looking bastard. Glass let it slide. It was her work. What she was there for. He remembered feeling rather mature. Sitting there. Letting her have her conversation with this guy. Not letting his jealousy show.

Can't remember what sparked the argument. Way too far gone at the time to remember it now. They were sitting together. She said something. Something about another guy in the club. That was it. Something about him being a nice guy. It was her way of implying she needed to get back to work. Glass made a snide comment. Ella said something to try and calm him, there was shouting. Then the guy from the earlier conversation came across and intervened. Trying to do the decent thing. Protect a young woman from her scruffy, angry boyfriend.

Punches were thrown. Glass must have thrown some. Can't for the life of him remember connecting with any of them. His knuckles aren't scuffed, which suggests if he hit anything, he didn't hit it hard. More than one person hit him. The guy who was intervening in the fight, and at least one other person. A few hits in the stomach. Then security came and dragged him out through the back. They gave him a few hits as well. Then threw him into the alleyway. He fell over, remembers that. That might be where the shoulder injury came from. Then he passed out.

Glass has spent five minutes just standing in the alley, staring at the ground. Trying to remember. Wishing he still couldn't. The more that comes back, the more upset he gets. It's just humiliating. If the police are going to come and get him then they should hurry up about it. If Billy Patterson wants him killed then he should bloody well do something about it. Living day-to-day, and every day is getting worse. Can't have many more days like today.

No idea what time it is. No watch on. No sound of life from the club. It's still dark though. The sort of quiet dark that suggests everyone else has gone to their bed. Sort of quiet dark that makes him wish he was in his. So he's starting to walk, trying to find a way out of this alley. Never been here before, but you don't need a map to find the end of an alleyway.

One step and he's wincing. The pain in his stomach, mostly. He's cold and stiff and his shoulder doesn't like him much either, but it's the stomach pain that flares the most when he moves. Muscle damage, he's telling himself. Like he knows. Doctor Glass. Another step, and another. Pain doesn't get any weaker. Home. That's a long way away right now.

Out onto the street and looking around. Not a single person on this busy street. Must have been in that alleyway for a few hours. Coughing again, and by God his stomach hurts when he coughs. He's bending over slightly in the hope it'll help, but that's getting him nowhere. Shuffling slowly towards home and stopping. What's the point in trying to walk home when you know you won't make it? He has no hope. Not in this state. Walking just to collapse in the street. Doesn't have his phone on him any more. Not a penny in his pockets. He needs to find a shorter journey.

Only one place comes to mind. Only one place that he thinks might be welcoming. And a lot closer than his own flat. Shambling along, pathetic and knowing it. Walked past one person on the way. Glass walking hunched, struggling to keep any sort of pace. The person looked at him and walked past. Didn't slow down. Didn't want to engage with him. Didn't want to get involved. They never bloody do.

The walk should have taken ten, fifteen minutes maybe.

He doesn't know how long it took, but it was fifty minutes and felt like two hours. Having to stop every hundred yards. A new challenge when he reached the block of flats and had to take the stairs. Every time he pushed up, the pain shot through him. But he's there. Knocking on the door of the flat. Another humiliation. Another desperate act. He's starting to cry. Out of nowhere, he's crying. It's such a weak thing to do. Makes him feel so pathetic. Humiliation piled on top of humiliation. He wants to stop crying before the door is opened. He wants to be able to maintain at least a tiny bit of dignity. But it's gone. Running down his cheeks and out of sight.

A light's come on through the frosted glass. Movement behind the door and it's being pulled open. Arnie looking back at him. He looks so small and old in a T-shirt and pyjama bottoms. Unshaven and on alert. Scowling at first, and then looking concerned when he sees who's at the door.

'Bloody hell, lad. What happened to you?'

'I need help. I need somewhere to sleep tonight. Can I?'

Arnie didn't even ask why. Just brought him into the flat. Through to that little kitchen of his. Sat the boy down and told him to get some of his wet clothes off. Got him a towel, made a hot cup of tea. Instructed him to show him the injuries. Bruised shoulder, very bruised stomach. Arnie's no doctor. Has no idea what sort of damage might have been done. But that's one hell of a bruise on the stomach. Two or three bruises holding hands, more like.

'I'm not going to ask for details,' Arnie's saying. 'Not my place. But if you're in some sort of trouble, you can tell me. I'm no grass. If I can help you, I will.'

Glass is shaking his head. Sitting at the kitchen table, an old jumper of Arnie's on, sipping his tea with shaky hands. 'There's nothing you can do. Too late for me. Doesn't even matter.'

'Now come on,' Arnie's saying. Surprisingly aggressive. Talking with the authority of an old man who thinks he's seen it all. 'You got no business talking that way. You're a young man. Whatever problems you have, there's always an answer. You got time on your side. Don't piss away the next fifty years just because you had a bad few months.'

'It's more than that,' Glass is saying. Struggling not to cry again. Thinking about Ella a little. Why didn't she come after him last night? Out into the alleyway to help him. She's spent months helping him, why stop now? Fed up of him, maybe. Or maybe her client wouldn't let her. But it's not her he's thinking about most. It's Alan Bavidge.

'Is it your girlfriend?' Arnie's asking. There's no diplomatic way to ask if her being a prostitute is getting the boy down. He'll leave the question as vague as that. But if it is her, then there's a simple solution that needs to be drummed into the boy.

'Not just her. Not really her at all. She's been so good to me. There's something else.' Just about crying now. Crying because he doesn't like to think about what he did. Crying because someone actually cares enough to ask. The first person who has since it happened. Ella kept asking until she realized how big it had to be. Then she avoided it. Didn't want to know something that could ruin their relationship. Another humiliation.

'Tell me, lad. It might do you the world of good.' Knowing it almost certainly won't. A problem shared is a problem spread.

Glass is crying properly now. Letting it out. His shoulders rocking, ignoring the pain it causes. 'I killed someone. I killed him.'

'Tonight?' Real shock in Arnie's voice.

'Months ago. I killed him. They made me. I owed money. I had to do it to get rid of the debt. I did it. I stabbed him. I didn't want to. I really didn't. I only did it because I had to. They would have killed me. They would have hurt Ella.' Breaking down now, head on the table.

Arnie's reaching across. Not saying anything. Just putting a hand on the boy's shoulder. If it was months ago, the police aren't likely to be battering down his door tonight. He can take his time with this. Let the boy cry. Let him suffer a little. Do him good to get it out, because he obviously hasn't before. And he is suffering. You can see it. Shoulders bouncing up and down, struggling to catch his breath as he cries. Holding onto his stomach, which is hurting.

Five minutes of silence before Arnie breaks it. 'Do you want to tell me about it? You don't have to, but it might help.'

Thirty seconds before Glass responds. 'I borrowed money. I had to pay it back but I couldn't. They said if I did this thing for them, I'd be off the hook. They said if I didn't, they'd be angry with me. I knew what that meant. They talked about Ella. They were threatening her too. One of their guys was . . . I don't know. So I did it. Stabbed a man. A gangster or something. He died.' Doesn't want to go into any more detail about it. No detail about the night itself.

'Okay,' Arnie's nodding. 'Okay. Have the police been sniffing around you?'

'No. Nobody has. Nobody seems to know it was me.'

Arnie nodding. 'Was Oliver involved in this?' A hard edge to his voice. The question he's wanted to ask since the words came out of Glass's mouth.

'No,' Glass is saying with honest certainty. 'It was nothing to do with him. Nothing at all. It was my fault. It was all my fault. It was so stupid and pathetic. So pathetic.'

Wasn't immediately obvious in the end whether he was talking about the killing or about himself. Pathetic seemed to apply to both in his mind. Arnie sent him to bed. Told him to get some sleep in Oliver's old room. Told him it would be a better world with some sleep behind him. Kid didn't seem to realize the time. After four in the morning. Kid doesn't seem to have a keen sense of anything any more.

Arnie won't sleep again tonight. Might as well get dressed and sit in the kitchen wondering what the world's coming to. Been doing that a lot lately. Now he's got Glass asleep in Oliver's room. Saying that he killed a man. He can't help his grandson, no matter how hard he tries. But he can help someone. Someone who wants to be helped.

7

Marty's been there since half six. Say what you want about him, but the man puts the hours in. He's willing to get up at an ungodly hour to make the money flow. People see the women and the parties and they think of Marty. But Marty's a man of fourteen-hour days, seven days a week. A man of effort. Been in the office now for nearly two hours. Sent out a couple of collectors who won't be back for a while. Took a phone call from a counterfeiter who likes to use this office as a drop-off point for his products. Always helps to keep people like counterfeiters happy. Never know when you might need them. Especially when you run a business like Marty's with a number of foreign employees. Girls who might not be as legally welcome in the country as Marty needs them to be. So you let the counterfeiter use the office, free of charge.

Marty will clear out of the way when the counterfeiter gets here. Before then he has another meeting. One he's actually a little nervous about. He won't show it. He's Marty Jones, he doesn't show nerves. He's always the most relaxed man in the room. He thinks it makes him look cool. Makes him look like a man who can handle any situation. Most other people think it makes him look like the most nervous man in the room, trying to look cool. They don't tell him that though. You don't tell a profitable and dangerous man things he doesn't want to hear.

This meeting brings nerves because it brings Potty Cruickshank. First time they've ever had a meeting. Not the first time they've met, but casual encounters don't count. This is a proper meeting. Potty calling ahead to set terms. Making sure a meeting is a safe thing. Then agreeing to come to the office. That's a feather in Marty's cap. Potty's coming to him, not the other way round.

Just a question of what he wants. Potty wants whatever's good for Potty. Marty wants whatever's good for Marty. Not impossible that those two things could overlap. Not impossible, but not pleasant either. There's something about Potty that just doesn't sit well with Marty. There's nothing in common there. Nothing that fits between them. Different kinds of people. Different backgrounds. Potty had everything handed to him by his uncle. Marty started with nothing. Fought for everything he's got. Fought hard. But that gives you the image of a scrapper, someone of low rank. New money. People like Potty tend to look down their nose at people like Marty.

Marty's at the window, looking down into the busy street. Quarter past eight in the morning and there are streams of people on either side of the street. Shops on both sides of the street, offices above a lot of them. Always busy this time of day. Marty's on his tiptoes, looking down at the parking spaces in front of the building. There's one beside the door, thank goodness. A large car's pulling up as he looks, stopping in that space. A big fat guy getting out of the back seat. Jesus, what a state. Big expensive car with his own driver. Potty sitting in the back seat like the fucking prime minister. Clambering out and waddling towards the door. He is actually getting fatter. Who would have thought that was possible?

The buzzer goes. Marty across and pressing the button to unlock the door, and waiting. And waiting. And still bloody waiting. It's one flight of stairs. Fourteen of them, Marty knows. Fat bastard must have conked out halfway. Too much effort to reach the top in one go. Making base camp. Jesus, imagine if he fell down the stairs. Imagine if that fat dickhead fell down the stairs in Marty's office and broke his neck. If he died there, nobody would ever believe it was an accident. They would think Marty had planned it. You don't get accidents at meetings like this.

A pang of relief when Potty eventually pushes open the door. A little disappointment as well. The world and the industry would be rather better without this wheezing ball of shit. Marty is too well-mannered to say such a thing. Too well-mannered even to acknowledge that Potty is wheezing.

'Good to see you. Come, sit down,' Marty's saying. Almost said take the weight off, but stopped himself. Manners, you see.

Potty's waddling across to the chair in front of Marty's desk. It's not a big chair, not as big as would be ideal for the arse that's about to occupy it. Marty didn't have anything bigger, just office chairs. So Potty will have to make do. Seems relieved just to be sitting.

'So what can I do for you?' Marty's asking, spreading his arms. Making himself seem as available as possible.

'I think, Mr Jones, that it's time you and I recognized a truth.' Potty's voice still has a wheeze in it. Doesn't sound as impressive as he wants it to, which annoys him. 'You and I are experienced men. We understand this industry. We both know that to gain strength in this business, you occasionally must consolidate. You understand?'

Ooh, that's not a good start. Marty knows how people see him. They think he's a bit of a clown. Running around with whores and dealers, making money on the side as a collector. They don't take him seriously. Or seriously enough. They don't seem to understand how brutal you sometimes have to be in Marty's other chosen professions. So they think he's a bit dumb. Bit of a soft touch perhaps. Sort of boy who might not understand what consolidate means. They talk down, and that pisses Marty off.

'I understand,' Marty's saying. Keeping the always-playful tone in his voice. Don't let a man like Potty see that you're not happy with him. Play him along. Use his ignorance to mask your anger.

'Good, good. You, I'm sure, can see that there are issues we need to resolve. We are competing in the same market-place, with the same product. We are stepping on each other's toes when we should be helping each other along. There's an opportunity here. I'm sure you can see it. We work together. We work together to remove competition. When we have removed it, we have the place to ourselves. You have your areas, I have mine. Very simple, very effective. Our combined strength could quickly and easily remove the problems we both have.'

He speaks so well, does Potty. So comfortable and con-fident in what he's saying. But he can't be that comfortable, can he? Wouldn't be here if he was. Marty can work that out. Potty doesn't come looking for consolation unless he has problems. And everyone now knows he has problems. He was in a police station yesterday. That's a pretty big problem. There's a whiff of desperation in the air, and Potty's trying to cover it with his self-confidence.

Marty's leaning back in his chair. 'Of course I'd love to help you,' he's saying, looking to pick his words carefully. 'There could be a problem, though. I mean, word on the street is that you're a good friend of Alex MacArthur.' Letting that hang. That should be enough.

That's Marty's get-out clause. You're with MacArthur, I'm with Jamieson. Even if those two are playing at being on good terms, doesn't change how we behave. They're just playing.

We keep our distance from each other, because common sense says that they will fall out. That's the business. They have to fall out so that they can try to take market share from each other. And they have to take market share from each other. Have to be seen to be growing, otherwise they stagnate. Stagnate, and you become a target. The industry turns on rivalry. Everyone knows this.

Neither of them will mention the arrest because Potty doesn't want to talk about it. It's a sign of weakness, and neither man will acknowledge it. It's another very good reason why Marty doesn't want to be anywhere near Potty. But he can't publicly use it. Needs the MacArthur excuse instead.

Potty's nodding. 'I can see why you might view that as an issue. I do understand. I think you and I need to rise above that sort of thing. I think you and I should be able to seek our own advantages without having to worry so much about the reactions of others. Essentially, this is nothing to do with them. I shouldn't imagine anyone outside of the collecting business would be at all concerned with it.' A little smile on his face, trying to make it seem so obvious. Trying to make Marty feel small.

Easy for Potty to say that other people can be ignored. He doesn't need MacArthur for protection. MacArthur was just a useful friend to attack an enemy with. Marty depends on Jamieson. He needs the strength of the Jamieson organization to keep him safe. Potty wouldn't be risking anything with an association. The risk would all be Marty's.

'I'm not going to sit here and say no,' Marty's saying with a smile. 'But I am going to ask for a little time. There are things I would need to check out first. You know how it is. I mean, I need to take a few more precautions before I do anything, my business being smaller.' Saying it with a self-deprecating shrug, and knowing that his businesses combined make nearly the same money as Potty's. The collection business is smaller, sure, but collecting is all Potty does.

'Of course, of course. I'm not going to bounce you into anything, Marty,' Potty's saying. Trying to sound generous, something he's never been. 'But I will need a quick decision. You know this business. You know how fast the swings and roundabouts move.'

Marty's nodding. This is Potty pushing him into a corner. A corner he doesn't want to be in. Looking at his watch. Making a show of it, but he does need the office cleared. Grateful for the excuse to get rid of Potty, before he's forced into making a decision. Making a commitment.

'Damn it. Listen, I have a fellow coming to use the office. Good guy, doesn't like to have other people here when he's having his wee meetings. It'll scare him.'

'Of course,' Potty's saying, struggling to his feet. No arms on the chair for him to use as leverage. Might be an excuse, might be genuine. Sort of thing he can understand, people looking for a good office to use. Hard in this business to find a reasonable place. 'But you let me know when you've made a decision.'

Marty nodding. Trying to seem all enthusiastic. Walking Potty to the door and opening it for him. Not going to walk him down the stairs. Doesn't have the time for that. Besides, Potty won't want someone like Marty treating him like he's disabled. He's not, he's just fat. Marty's back across to the desk and sitting in the chair. Both hands on the top of his head, leaning back in the chair. Potty coming to him for a union. Talking about what they could do together, like it's that easy. They wouldn't be a great fit. And why go looking for any help at all? MacArthur's his buddy. Why not use MacArthur for protection? Must be because MacArthur isn't willing. Must be. Potty's under attack and he doesn't have cover. So he's desperate.

A desperate Potty Cruickshank. He could use that. He could. It would be fantastic, if the best-case scenario played out. He could have Potty under his thumb. He could use Jamieson's influence to force Potty under control. He could make a killing. But he won't. Won't because he doesn't trust Potty. Won't because Jamieson would never trust Potty. Wouldn't want him anywhere near his business. Won't because he has a better offer. A tough bastard like Billy Patterson is an excellent weapon to use against Potty. A man with no other baggage, a man with reason to try and make this work. Marty and Potty would be a bad fit. Marty and Patterson? That could work.

8

He's early. And now he's complaining about where they're meeting. This isn't like Paul Greig. Making a big play of the house they're meeting in, like it's the worst option he's ever seen. Like he's used to so much better. He seems tense. Peterkinney isn't saying anything. This is a routine meeting, nothing more. Routine for Peterkinney, anyway. Whatever's crawled up Greig's arse is Greig's business. He should be professional enough to leave it at the door.

'You need to start thinking bigger,' Greig is saying, slumping onto the couch.

Little bit over a year ago Peterkinney had no job. Now he has a business of his own. An established, credible collector. And he's still only twenty-one. Now Greig's shouting at him to think bigger. Doesn't make any sense at all, but you have to let people rant.

'I'm thinking big,' is all Peterkinney's saying. Saying it calm, a little disinterested, wanting Greig to get down to business.

'Thinking big. Aye right. You don't know what big is.' Saying it with a mutter and looking down at the floor. Making no effort to hide the fact that there's something very wrong in his life.

'Problems?' Peterkinney's asking. Not concerned at all. Sounding a little smug. A man with no problems of his own. Sounding like a man who disapproves of Greig bringing his problems to work with him.

Peterkinney hasn't earned the right to talk in that tone to Paul Greig. Not yet, anyway. Boy has potential, but you don't act superior to a guy like Paul Greig this early in your career.

'Problems?' Greig's saying. 'Yeah, I got problems. I got problems all over the fucking place. I'm under pressure and I need a little support. Am I getting it? Am I fuck. You help people your whole life, soon as the going gets tough they disappear. You're no different. Don't you go pretending that you are. Don't you go pretending with me. Would you go into battle for me?'

'Do you need me to?' Peterkinney's interrupting. Fed up of hearing this, wanting an end to it.

Greig's laughing at that. 'You couldn't if you wanted to, kid, couldn't if you wanted to. Forget about it. Let's just focus on what we're here to talk about. Just so you know, there are things going on. I'm under pressure. I might need to lower my profile for a while if I get through this at all. Don't get all shocked if I go off the radar for a while. A long while, maybe.'

Peterkinney's nodding. Making an effort to look concerned, but he couldn't care less. He's long past the point of thinking someone like Paul Greig is important. Greig is helpful, but he's nothing more than that. Most of what Greig will ever do for him, he's already done. Peterkinney remembers that first meeting. The pick-up with Howie Lawson. Lord knows what's happened to him since. Meeting Greig and being so impressed with him. Not any more. It was good to have his guidance in the early days. Still good to have a police contact. But let's not pretend Peterkinney still sees Greig as important. Certainly not as important as Greig sees himself. And would he go into battle for him? No. No, he wouldn't.

'Okay, well, anything I can do, let me know,' Peterkinney's saying.

Greig's waving a hand. 'Forget it. I'll let you know if there's anything you need to know.' A dismissive hand for a man who can easily be dismissed. Wouldn't have dismissed Potty Cruickshank that way. Might have tried to use Cruickshank's help. Cruickshank is connected enough to make a difference. Not this kid. Not yet. Greig's own fault. Wanted someone younger that he could better control. The price of that is that he hasn't built enough strength to use yet.

'So what's the news?' Peterkinney's asking.

'They arrested Potty yesterday morning. You probably heard. Let him go yesterday afternoon. Plan is to try and gather more evidence and arrest him again. Seems like the accountant isn't as feeble and talkative as I thought he'd be. He's keeping his trap shut, for now. That could change.

The way things are stacked, the info we already have, there should be a second arrest on Potty. Should be charges against him.'

Peterkinney nodding. That's the news he wanted to hear. He wants Potty weak. He wants to make some serious moves. Getting an itchy trigger finger. You start fast, and things inevitably slow. This is the challenge now. The need for patience. The earlier in the process, the faster you grow. The more you grow, the harder it is to grow much further. Peterkinney can feel it slowing down. Not that it's going badly. Just that that breakneck sense is waning. He wants it back. The sense of momentum. You get it back by taking on opponents. Taking their business. You lurch forwards by swallowing them. That's what Peterkinney wants. That's why he wants to bring down Potty. More business, more money, more success.

'You have to be careful,' Greig's warning him. There's a depressed tone. Like he's about to say something he learned from painful experience. 'Doesn't much matter who brings Potty down. I mean, good that someone does, but that's not the pay-off. Him out of the business isn't the prize. The prize is taking his share of the market. You won't be the only one aiming for it. There'll be a queue.'

'And I'll be at the front of it.'

Greig's shaking his head. The boy's getting a little bit too confident now. 'You won't be at the front. It won't be some orderly line. Never bloody is. It'll be a mad scramble. And it won't just be the usual suspects either. It'll be people who worked for Potty, wanting to start on their own. Thinking their inside info will serve them well. It'll be every opportunist little shit in this city. It'll be big people like Alex MacArthur thinking they might as well take a slice of the business if it's going free. No bigger opportunists than the big organizations.'

Peterkinney's shaking his head. This isn't the conversation he wanted to have. 'So you're saying I take Potty Cruickshank and in return I get fuck-all. Actually, less than fuck-all. In return I get a bunch of other people who might try to take me down?'

Greig's shaking his head. Not the boy taking Potty down, it's Greig. But he'll let that slide. 'If you wait, yeah, that's what you get. What you want to do is take advantage now. Start pulling business away from Potty now. He'll know you're doing it, but that's the gamble. He'll come after you, but when the second arrest comes, he's finished anyway. If you're willing to take the risk, then you move now. He's weak, but he'll try and hit back. Try and damage you. You just have to hold out until he gets arrested.'

'Hold out?' Peterkinney's saying with a confident smile. 'I can do more than that.'

'No,' Greig's saying loudly. 'Don't be some fucking idiot about this. He attacks you once so you attack him twice.

That's all bullshit. You don't fight back. You don't do anything. You get into a war with that fat bastard while the police are investigating him and you get swept up in the arrests. Us cops aren't fucking blind, you know. A guy we're investigating is being attacked and we'll see it. We'll do something about it. You hold out. You take his business while everyone knows he's weak. You make him look even weaker. Then you sit back and let the police take him down for you. You get rid of him without breaking sweat.'

There's a pause while Peterkinney considers this. The idea of getting rid of Cruickshank without even having to attack him is nice. But there's a problem. The problem of PR. 'People see me taking shit from him without hitting back. People think I get lucky when the police put him away. That doesn't help my image.'

'No, people in the business will think you were playing it this way from the start. They'll know it. They'll respect it. It's not about winning. It's about winning with as few losses as possible. That's what people respect. Don't . . .' Pausing as he lets his frustration with Peterkinney slide. The boy's still young. You have to be patient with him. Ambitious and determined, but a little naive. Trying again now that his tone will be calmer, less aggressive. 'Look, you're smart. You get it. A lot of people will tell you that you have to look strong. How the way other people see you is important. That's true, but not at any price. See, the people that really matter are the people you do business with. The people you do business with know the business. They know that someone who takes advantage of a guy getting arrested before he gets arrested is well connected and smart. They will like that. They'll be impressed and they'll be intimidated. See what I mean? That's the PR you want.'

Now he's got Peterkinney nodding. This is something he can get behind. You might sacrifice a little of your image with the muscle, but you gain more from the moneymen. He can handle that. He's agreeing with Greig. He'll work to take business from Potty. He won't strike back if Potty moves against him. Which he might not, because he knows he's being watched by the plod. Although he might try one or two sneaky manoeuvres. Take it. Survive it. Then profit.

Greig's up and walking to the door. 'Listen, this stuff about me going off the radar. It's not a maybe, it's a definite. There's a lot of stuff going on. But I'll still be around, sort of. I'll keep in touch, now and again.' He can see that Peterkinney isn't bothered by that. He can see the boy doesn't think he's important any more. Which is fine. Happens with all of them eventually. They think a cop as a contact is a great thing at first. Then they get blasé about it. Finally they start to resent you because you don't do everything they want. So be it. Important thing to Greig is getting someone like Potty Cruickshank off the streets. That fat scumbag and his family have done so much damage in this city. Potty won't survive a year in prison, and he'll get at least that. The collection industry will be better in the hands of someone more controllable, like Peterkinney.

Greig's gone. Peterkinney sitting and waiting a decent amount of time before he leaves. Doesn't matter what his grandfather thinks. Doesn't matter what any of them think. He has a plan. He's going to take down Potty, and then all the rest of them. He'll have the whole collection business under his control by the time he's twenty-five. Then what? Ha. Easy. Then he goes looking for other challenges. Shit, he could have the city under his thumb by the time he's thirty. See what his grandfather thinks of that.

9

He knew Glass would sleep late. Physically and emotionally drained. Arnie had been to the shops and back and started making lunch by the time he showed his face. Not a great face to show. Tired and haggard. If you said he was thirty-five, Arnie would believe you. Kid looks a mess. A mess of his own creation. Walking gingerly, still clutching that stomach.

'How are the wounds?' Arnie's asking.

Glass dropping slowly down into the chair at the kitchen table. 'Shoulder's a bit sore but not as bad as it was. Stomach still hurts when I move around.'

'You hungry?'

'Yeah, really hungry.' Trying to remember the last time he ate something, rather than drank or snorted it. Can't. Yesterday, probably. Might have been the day before. No, yesterday morning. Before he went to see Jefferson. Hell, was that only yesterday. Time slows down when you're waiting for it to stop.

Arnie's pottering about in the kitchen. Working silently between frying pan and fridge. Getting the lad something wonderfully unhealthy. Looks like he needs it. Looks skinny, which he didn't before. Never fat or chubby, but used to be healthy-looking. Now he looks thin, weary and beaten.

Arnie's putting the plate down in front of him. Watching silently as the boy eats. One of them has to bring it up. One of them has to mention the fact that last night Glass admitted killing a man. Someone certainly has to mention the fact that he turned up in the middle of the night with lumps kicked into him.

'Do you remember who gave you the beating?' Arnie's asking. Ask the safe questions first. A beating is an easy conversation opener compared to murder.

'I do,' Glass is saying, slurping tea before he goes on. 'Bouncers at a club. Ella was there. We had an argument. Some guy got between us and there was a scuffle. I think him and his mate landed a few blows. I think the bouncers probably did too. Threw me out the back of the club. I passed out. Couldn't make it home after that.' Said quietly and apologetically.

Arnie's actually relieved. This sounds like no big deal. A few punches thrown in a nightclub. Bouncers chucked him out. Chances are nobody even called the cops. As soon as the door was shut behind him, they all forgot him and got back to their partying. The odds are slim that last night's incident will draw the police to Glass, which is good. This boy wouldn't cope with a police interrogation. If he burst out crying and confessed to Arnie, what would he be like with

347

some rough detective barking at him? He'd crumble. He'd tell them everything. He'd end up looking at fifteen years, minimum. Worse than that, he would grass the people that made him do it. Then he'd be a walking target.

Let him finish eating in peace. Let him sit back in the chair, a little uncomfortable at having a full stomach for the first time in a long time. A boy making no effort to look after himself. Holding those bruises on his stomach. They did look bad last night. In normal circumstances, Arnie would insist on him going to see a doctor. These are not normal circumstances. Glass won't go to a doctor. Won't go near anything that looks like authority.

It's Glass who breaks the silence while Arnie washes the dishes. 'About what I said last night,' Glass is saying. You can tell he's thought about how to bring it up. Tried to work out the best tone to use with Arnie. 'About, you know, killing that guy. I don't . . . I would appreciate it if you didn't tell anyone.'

Arnie's looking at him with a raised eyebrow. 'Of course I'm not going to tell anyone. It never occurred to me for one second to tell anyone. But you have to do me a favour in exchange.'

Glass is looking at him. A little bit crestfallen. Didn't expect Arnie to be demanding favours from him. 'Okay.'

'You have to promise me that you're going to get your life in order, okay? I mean, come on, look at you. You're in a bad place right now, and I don't like to see that. I want you to sort yourself out. I want you to get your life back under control. I'm willing to help you, lad. I am. But you have to be willing to help yourself. You have to want to change this life of yours.'

Glass is crying again. This time it came from nowhere. He had no intention of crying. Wasn't emotional. Just suddenly came bursting out of him. Someone offering to help. Someone who cares enough to help. Not wanting anything in exchange. Just wanting to help.

Arnie's no social worker. He's no good at the old give-us-a-hug stuff. He's standing back at the sink and letting the boy cry it out at the table. When he's quite finished with the emotional stuff, Arnie will start talking again. They'll try and come up with something. A plan that'll direct Glass back onto the right path.

Strange to see him this way, young Alex Glass. He was a strong and independent kid. Always in trouble, which is why Arnie didn't like Oliver hanging out with him. But he was independent. Went and got a place of his own when he was eighteen. Always seemed to earn enough money to keep him going. Not sure how, but he always did. He seemed like a kid who knew how to point forwards. But now? Now is different. Now he's stuck in the spiral.

They spend nearly an hour talking round in circles. They both want the same thing. Neither has any clear idea on how they're going to get it. Glass is walking home now. His stomach still hurts, but he can walk without bending over. He's not the wreck he was last night. Back to the flat. Not expecting to find anyone there. Surprised to find Ella sitting on the couch in the living room, her phone in her hand.

'Hello,' he's saying. Uncertain.

'Where have you been?' she's saying, getting up from the couch and walking to him. She said it louder than she intended, more emotional than she realized. 'I didn't know where you were. I went back to the club. I looked around for you. I was going to call the hospitals, or the police, I don't . . . Where have you been?'

'I stayed at a friend's,' he's saying, nodding slowly. 'Didn't want to, uh, walk all the way home last night. I was pretty out of it. His place was closer.'

There's an awkward silence. Each filling the silence with thoughts of what the other's just said. Ella said she went back to the club looking for him. Back to it. So she went with the guy. Left him there and went with the guy. Has to do her work. Has to earn money. She's thinking about Glass, not being able to make it home.

'How are you now?' she's asking quietly.

Glass is nodding. 'I'll be okay. Little bruised, nothing more than that.'

'Okay.'

More of that silence. Both building up to a big conversation. Just a question of who gets there first. It's Glass.

'Can we sit down, and talk?'

'Yes,' Ella's nodding. She's not sure if this is promising or ominous. They're both on the couch now.

'Listen, Ella. Thing is, last night. I . . . well, thing is, it was like, a wake-up call. That's what I'm trying to say. Last night, it was a wake-up call for me. We need to look at, uh, the way we're living.'

'Yes,' she's saying, and nodding her head enthusiastically. This is what she wants to hear. Glass accepting that he's been behaving poorly for the last few months. Committing to changing that behaviour.

'Yes,' he's saying, and smiling. 'Good, yes. And I think we can. We might need a bit of help, but we can get that. And we're both young, we can do what we want to do. I'll go find something serious. Something proper. Make some real money. And you can find something as well. It'll be so much better.'

She's not nodding now. She's frowning a little, because she thinks she can see what this is. This is Glass trying to come up with some conniving way to get her to change her job. Stop her doing what she's been doing. If that's what the last few months have been about . . .

'How do you think I'm going to change my job?' she's asking quietly. 'What am I going to do? We have no money. You're not earning anything. You haven't been able to find anything for ages. And I won't be able to find anything else. Not for a while, anyway. So what are we going to use for money in the meantime? Alex, you're not thinking.'

'But we need to change.'

'I know that,' she's saying, voice rising. 'I know that. And I want to. But we have no money, and we need to have money. I have to work. If you're not working then I have to, and this is the only thing I know how to do.'

'I will find something,' Glass is shouting. 'I will. I will find something, okay.'

This shouldn't have turned into an argument. Glass is sighing. Ella's getting up from the couch, going through to the bedroom. Her relief at his return has been wrecked. Felt like he was blaming her. Glass is sitting on the couch, wishing he was better at explaining the things he wants. The things he's sure they can get. He has Arnie to help him now. They have the chance at a life they can be proud to live. A life that isn't lived under a ticking clock. Waiting for time to run out.

10

You make sacrifices. That's how you do it. That's how you help people. Especially people who are in real trouble. They need help. You give it. You lose a little something along the way. Dignity, for one thing. Something you spent sixty years clinging on to. Believing it's the one thing of value you have left. The one thing you have to protect ahead of everything else. Arnold Peterkinney has clung on to his dignity long past the point anyone else noticed he still had it. Now he's going to let a little go.

He's telling himself that he's doing it for the right reasons. That's supposed to make it easier, isn't it? When you're doing it for someone else. Doing it to help them. Your sacrifice becomes something noble, rather than something pathetic. Doesn't help. Not a damn bit. It's humiliating, and that's all it is.

He's been standing across the road from Oliver's office for more than ten minutes. Making sure his grandson's in there. Hoping that other fellow in the office will leave. Oliver's there. So is the other one. Some poor-looking bastard went in a few minutes ago. Arnie's waiting for him to leave. Doesn't want anyone else in there. Not unless it's unavoidable. He'll tell the other one to leave as well. Just him and Oliver. But then, it's only Oliver's opinion he cares about.

There was a day that boy wouldn't have sneered at him. Wouldn't have dared. Wouldn't have wanted to. Today he'll be in his element. Revelling in what Arnie's going to ask. He'll be one snide remark away from a punch in the mouth. Arnie might be older than him and smaller than him. He might love the boy. But he will punch him in the bloody mouth if he pushes his luck.

The fellow who went in looking sorry is coming out looking sorrier. Actually looks scared. Went in looking for a favour and didn't find any waiting. Poor sod. Another one like Glass. Another one who couldn't see another way. Ah, the hell is he standing here thinking this for? Get in there, get this done. The sooner it's over, the sooner he can go home and punch a wall.

Across the street and pulling open the office door. Oliver and the other one are in the same seats they had yesterday. They're both looking at him as he comes in. There's a glare from Oliver. Not welcome. Did the other one roll his eyes? Looked a bit like it to Arnie. Probably fed up of being sent out of the office. Well, he's going to take another walk today. Either he walks, or Oliver doesn't get to hear what he wants to hear.

'Get rid of him,' Arnie's saying quietly to his grandson.

Oliver's sighing. This is tricky for him. He sends Kilbanne

away every time his grandfather shows up and it looks like he's under the old man's thumb. It also makes him look like a childish amateur. Papa's turned up to tell him what to do. But he'll do it this one last time. Not because he owes it to his grandfather. He doesn't. He'll do it because he's intrigued by the old man's tone. Because he's intrigued about him coming back so soon. Yesterday's conversation seemed like a goodbye.

Oliver's looking across at Kilbanne. Nodding just a little. There's an audible sigh and very clear shake of the head from the older man. Not happy at his young boss's behaviour. This is not how you run a business. Not the successful sort of business they both keep saying they want. But he's getting up because the young guy making the error is still his boss. Getting up and walking out of the office. Going for a ten-minute walk from which he will gain absolutely nothing. He'll negate the health benefits of walking with a couple of cigarettes along the way.

'So what do you want today?' Oliver's asking as soon as the door shuts behind Kilbanne. Little bit of sarcasm. Oliver wants this over fast. Another awkward goodbye.

'I want to talk to you about something, and it's a little awkward.' Arnie sitting down this time. Didn't do this yesterday. Suggests this is going to be a long conversation, which isn't what Oliver wants.

'Go on.' Hurrying him up.

'I need to ask you a favour. It's just come up. It's not for me. It's for your little friend, Alex Glass. You remember him? You two were like two peas in a pod. Now he says he never sees you.'

'Uh-huh.' A cautious response. Now he is intrigued. How the hell could he know that Oliver bought the debt yesterday? How could he have found out this fast? How could this old fart have found out at all? He's never shown any interest in Glass before. Always hated him, it seemed to Oliver.

'Well, Glass showed up on my doorstep last night. I won't go into detail. It's none of your business. Let's just say he was in no good condition. Me and him had a good long chat. The boy's in all sorts of a mess. He needs someone to help him. I want to help him. So that's why I'm here.'

'Uh-huh.'

'The boy's in debt. It's the second time he has been, and it's pulling him down. See, anything he does is ruined by the debt now. We get him back clean and sober and working, and that debt is going to drag him down.'

'But you can't expect the debt to just be written off,' Oliver's saying. 'He borrowed the money. He has to pay it back. You can't just wipe out a debt like that.' His tone is incredulous. A little confrontational.

'I know, I know,' Arnie's saying. Getting tetchy himself. 'I'm not saying he shouldn't pay it off. I'm saying that he needs to be given time and space to pay it off. Let the boy have a fair chance. That's why I'm here. The debt is with a guy called Gary Jefferson. I want you to buy it from him. I know how these things work, and I want you to do this as a favour to me and to Alex. You buy the debt, and he'll pay it back. Not with that bullshit interest you people put on it. But you can work something out. Something that gives him the time he needs to rebuild his life.'

He managed to stifle the smile. Wasn't easy, but he did it. He almost wants to tell his grandfather the truth. Wants him to see that with enough hard work, everything falls into your lap. The old man wouldn't like hearing it, but Oliver would sure love telling it. But he won't say it. Works out better if he doesn't. Think about it. The one thing that's been playing on his mind is his grandfather. That part of his past. This gets that under his control as well. Jesus, everything falling into place.

'You want me to buy Alex's debt? Despite the fact that he doesn't have a job and probably couldn't pay it off?'

A little sigh. 'He doesn't have a job just now, but that's going to change. He's going to get his life together. He is. He's committed to it.'

'Please, he hasn't had work in months. Not qualified for anything either. And he's got that wee girlfriend of his. A hooker, working for Marty Jones. Come off it. I'm telling you, if you want to help him, you need to get him away from her.

He's obsessed with her and she'll drag him down. Been that way from the start.' That sounded surprisingly personal. Sounded like he actually cared. He was there at the start of Glass's relationship with the girl. Saw it for himself. Maybe he knows better than Arnie on this subject. Arnie hasn't even met the girl, so he'll accept Oliver's word on this one.

Arnie's nodding. 'Sure. I know it's not going to be easy. I'm not naive about this. But the boy needs help and he has nobody else to help him. I know you're not a charity, but this is a chance . . . to do some good.' Looking around him at the office. Thinking of the sorry sap who sauntered out of here while Arnie was watching.

Oliver's shaking his head a little. 'I need to know that he can pay it off. If I take it on and get saddled with however many thousands he owes, it kills my profit. I can't put myself out on the street just to help you out.'

'He had a debt before,' Arnie's saying. 'Bigger than this, and he paid off the whole thing. He can do it again.' Desperate now. Trying to use the old debt as a persuading factor in the purchase of the new one. Arnie knows what Glass did to pay off that old debt. But he won't tell. He'd rather walk out of here with no deal.

Oliver's nodding. Now we're getting to what matters. All the hints Jefferson dropped about Potty. 'Managed to pay it off. Pay it off or work it off?'

'Paid it off, I think,' Arnie's saying with a shrug. Such a terrible liar.

'All right, then. I'll buy the debt. But you have to keep him honest. You got to make sure he pays me back; otherwise I look like I'm doing favours for friends. I look weak. That gets me into all sorts of trouble.'

You can see Arnie fighting to keep his temper in check. Oliver can see it and he loves it. That's basically why he said it. Wanted to get the old man's hackles up. See how he reacted to the suggestion that he was the one getting Oliver in trouble. That someone else needed to be kept honest. After all the moralizing yesterday, today Oliver has the chance to accuse his grandfather of causing trouble.

'I'll keep him straight,' Arnie's saying. 'You'll buy the debt?'

'I'll try.'

A nod. 'Okay then. You can be in touch about paying it off. I'll, uh, hear from you, then.'

'You will.'

Peterkinney's leaning back in the chair as his grandfather disappears out the door. This time with his tail between his legs. Ah, good old Alex Glass. You always had a head full of nonsense. Fancy turning up on his grandfather's doorstep looking for help. What a tool. Now Peterkinney has the debt under his control. He has his grandfather's permission to use it. His grandfather, for Christ's sake. And he has something to use against Potty Cruickshank. Don't know what it is yet, but it's something. Yep, today is a good day for Oliver Peterkinney. Know what? It isn't over yet.

11

Patience is an uncommon virtue. Patience is often profitable.
In this business, people like to rush things. They worry that
if they play a long game, someone else will blow the final
whistle before their pay-off arrives. Peterkinney's been smart.
Playing the long game whenever that was his best chance of
profit. Won't always work. A long-play failure is the worst
kind. You put money and effort into something over the
course of months, even years, and it yields nothing. That's
infuriating. But not this time.

When he bought Collette Duffy's debt, he was playing the
long game. Looking to make the right connections. Profitable
connections. For a few months, nothing happened. Just
Collette being a hapless liability. A tenuous grasp of real life,
that one. Didn't seem to realize that she still had to pay off
the debt, just because he was being nice to her. But he was
patient, and kept being nice, kept letting her off the hook.

It was about three weeks ago that her brother got in
touch. Told Peterkinney that he knew about the debt. Told
him he was doing the right thing by playing soft with Collette.
Didn't exactly sound thankful because that's not Liam
Duffy's way. Gratitude is a form of weakness. But he made

it clear that he was aware of Peterkinney's behaviour. That he was happy with it. Peterkinney was making the right impression with the right people.

Week after that, Liam Duffy suggests a meeting. Something casual. No big deal. The two of them met in a pub. Liam was a little less frosty this time. Talked about his sister. Actually paid up a little of her debt. Made it very clear indeed that if Peterkinney kept behaving to this high standard, there could be a profit in it for him. Duffy didn't say it was his boss he was talking about, but he said the right people were taking notice. People who could put good work Peterkinney's way. That was an easily deciphered code.

Couple more brief meetings with Duffy after that. They were obviously attempts by Duffy to make sure Peterkinney was a serious guy. Scouting him out. Scouting out his business. Asking a few pertinent questions about a man his boss might want to work with. Surprising that Duffy was as smart as he was. Surprising that Chris Argyle gave him so much responsibility. But there you go. People talking about a shake-up in the import side of the market. Big dealers falling out with each other and putting pressure on suppliers. Maybe Argyle is making changes as well.

Peterkinney hopes so, because he has his first meeting with the man tonight. Going round to his house. Going to have a nice polite chat about the kind of people Argyle would want pressured. This won't be as straightforward as a normal collecting agreement. Argyle doesn't have the usual supply of dimwits and suckers owing him money. Anyone in debt to Argyle is likely to be a serious person. They're the only sorts of people Argyle does business with in the first place.

It's a gamble. If Peterkinney suffered from self-doubt these days, he might worry that he's not ready. This won't be conventional collection. He won't be buying the debt from Argyle and going after the target for himself. He'll have a business agreement with Argyle to collect money on his behalf. He'll get the protection that someone like Argyle can offer, but he will have to deliver. He will have to go and collect money from some real tough bastards. He will have to get that money, because most of it will go directly back to Argyle. He'll need to collect every penny owed. Drop the ball, and Argyle gets angry with him. A failure here could be the last mistake he makes. But he's ready. He's sure his business is ready.

Going to Chris Argyle's house. Shit, imagine. A year ago going to Marty Jones's house would have seemed like a big deal. How small does that look now? Argyle has a big place north of the city. A rich bastard surrounded by a lot of other rich bastards. The very sort of place Peterkinney intends to land in one day. Big front garden and a wide driveway. Parking in front of the double garage. He's never had a meeting of this scale before. Of this importance. He ought to be shitting his pants right about now, but he isn't. He's ringing the doorbell and taking a step back, looking back at the mani-cured front garden. Dressed for the occasion, shirt but no tie. Smart casual. He feels important. He feels good.

It's Duffy who opens the door and welcomes him in. Seems in good spirits. Better than his usual grumpy self, anyway. Leading him through to a living room. Looks like a room that doesn't get used much. For guests and business meetings, probably. Couple of couches, a big TV and a coffee table in the middle of the room. Big window looking out on the side garden. But no personal touches. No photos, no magazines or newspapers left lying around. A useful but little-used room. Argyle's there. Sitting on one couch, staring idly towards the door. Looks like a man who's just sat down after waiting in another, more entertaining room for the doorbell to ring.

Peterkinney doesn't know a lot about Argyle. Knows what he does for his money. Knows the basics about his business and how he runs it. Doesn't know any of the personal stuff. Middle height, thin on top, thicker around the middle. Not fat, just slack in the gut. He looks like a guy in his early fifties, which he is. Looks like any normal kind of guy. Could be a lawyer or a doctor. Some git working in a bank. Looks perfectly ordinary, which is probably the point.

'Oliver, good to meet you, take a seat.' Sounds like a bank manager too. Doesn't have the thick accent that Peter-kinney's used to dealing with on a daily basis. Sounds like a well-educated, well-spoken sort of chap. A good egg. 'Let's talk business, shall we.'

The first few questions are all very normal. A few repetitions of things Duffy already asked. Just making sure he gives the same answers second time around. They want him to be consistent. Which he is being. Answering every question accurately. Answering them all with confidence. Displaying the fact that he is a man who knows his business. Which is exactly what they want to see.

'If you and I have a business agreement,' Argyle is saying, 'then it will be different from anything you have now. You'll be collecting from people who are willing to fight back. From some people who are determined to fight back. There are people who simply choose not to pay what they owe because they'd rather try a fight. People will rip you off on a deal, and believe they can handle the consequences. These will be people who have been preparing to fight for a while. It will take more than grunt to overcome them.'

'I understand that,' Peterkinney's saying. 'I've always employed on that basis. Make the assumption that people will fight back. Make the assumption that you need the best people around you. A good collection business isn't about muscle, it's about smarts. I have good people. People who can be subtle and use their judgement, as well as being tough.' Saying it because it's true. Saying it also because it's what Argyle wants to hear.

Argyle does seem happy with that. He likes a lot of what he's hearing from Peterkinney. The more they talk, the more Argyle understands that Peterkinney is ready. Duffy was right. This boy can go and fight battles for them. The business he has, the people he has around him, are good. Solid. He's not some five-minute wonder. His age was a worry, but not now. Now his age is a strength. Gives him greater potential for longevity and growth.

After an hour or so of conversation, Argyle is convinced. He'll give Peterkinney a couple of jobs. People he's given supplies to who haven't lived up to their end of the bargain. They were going to pay him back with money made from sales, but they didn't get the sales they were looking for. Too bad. This is business. They still have to pay. They haven't, and someone needs to persuade them. A simple enough job to start with. If Peterkinney does well with that, there could be more for him. Big jobs, big responsibility, big profit.

A cordial shake of the hand before Peterkinney leaves. As soon as Duffy has closed the front door behind him, Peterkinney is grinning. Wants to punch the air, but someone might be watching. There are a lot of windows in the house for someone to look out of. Probably cameras as well, although they're not immediately visible. Argyle keeping his security low-key, so as not to alarm his neighbours.

He has music on in the car as he drives back south. Heading home, tapping the steering wheel happily as he does.

Another leap forwards. Two in a day, when you think about it. Well, two in two days, but that's being pedantic. This thing with Alex could give him a shot at Potty Cruickshank. With Greig doing his business and the second arrest coming, Potty's looking nice and vulnerable. Now a deal with Chris Argyle. Yep, today was indeed a good day.

PART FIVE

1

Everything changed. It's amazing to look back four months and think about it now. One ordinary day, the news started to filter around the city. People began to hear all about it. Made the news. Charges were brought. More arrests expected to follow. Peter Jamieson. John Young. Hugh 'Shug' Francis. David 'Fizzy' Waters. Shaun Hutton. All important men in their own right. Either important for what they'd done or for what they knew. A major player like Jamieson, with a string of charges against him. None of the really big charges. Not yet. But he'll get time inside, everyone knows it. In one afternoon, without any warning, the industry in this city changed.

People had to change with it. Things you'd planned for months went out the window. Everything was different. Everyone was paranoid, for a start. If it could happen to those guys . . . Other organizations started to look weak. Alex MacArthur, arrested. Unbelievable. Un-be-fucking-lievable. They let him out, but he was weak. Straight away, people were talking. Don Park is moving to take control of the organization. That was the rumour then. Still the rumour now, months later. Park hasn't taken over, but the stench of weakness from that organization is sharp. Jamieson and MacArthur in trouble. That unnerved everyone.

Of course, some people thought it would be all change. Those guys would fall and there would be a new order. Bright young things would step up and fill their shoes. That's despite the fact that Jamieson was the bright young thing right up until he got arrested. But that wasn't what happened. Never is. You don't build something as big as they had without putting some safeguards in place. MacArthur was back on the streets and acting the boss. Even if Park was still trying to take control, he wasn't doing it publicly. That would damage the very thing he was trying to take control of. So MacArthur's organization kept on operating as it had, and pretended the rumours weren't whirling around its head. And Jamieson's organization. That was the most interesting.

Most interesting to Billy Patterson, anyway. Jamieson, the boss, was inside. His right-hand man, John Young, who should have stepped into his shoes, was inside too. That was the clincher. That was why everyone thought his business would fragment and disappear. Everyone would look for a different boss without Jamieson or Young to hold them together. But it didn't happen. Didn't happen because a group of senior men in the organization got together and did something nobody thought they would. They worked together effectively, loyally and intelligently. Most remarkable of all, to those on the outside, was that Marty Jones was one of those men.

He would have been a junior player at that first meeting. People are already talking about that meeting like it was something legendary. Was only three months ago. People love to mythologize these things. The meeting in the office above the nightclub. A big table brought into the office for the occasion. Extra security put on. All very Hollywood, to hear the story. Wasn't actually like that at all. No big table to sit around, looking menacing. Just the chairs that were already there. No extra security, just the drivers and sidekicks of the men at the meeting. That lot all stayed outside the office, playing snooker. So not dramatic in presentation, but still vital.

Jamieson and Young had been inside a month, things were starting to settle and the organization needed a plan. It needed organizing. Marty got an invite. But he can't have been an important part of it. Angus Lafferty, he was there. He would have been a big part. Kevin Currie was there too. He would have helped lead the way. Two or three other senior guys. But Marty was in the office, and that's what mattered.

The last three months, Marty's seemed like a new person. Seemed like it, but he doesn't think he's changed at all. Treating the world the same way he always did, it's just that now these things matter more to others. People are paying more attention to him. In a way, this is what Marty always wanted. To be taken seriously. To be given responsibility. Didn't want his bosses being arrested. Didn't want to lose the protection they provided him. But it put him in a position where he had the chance to step up and perform, and he has done just that. You can bet the big players are treating him more like an equal now. You can also bet that he loves that, so he'll keep performing.

He's been working like a Trojan. No more messing around. The parties still happen; the women are still a part of his business. That's not going to change, because they're still profitable. Profit is what makes Marty a big player at a time like this. But Marty isn't at the parties any more. He has minions to run those things for him now. Marty's making a serious effort to look serious.

Patterson's got a meeting with him this lunchtime. Marty might be the same guy he always was, but the changed circumstances mean you have to treat him differently. He's given up any hope of manipulating Marty. Treating him as the junior party. Thought he could at the start of this alliance, but that's not going to happen now. Even if he could manipulate Marty, the other senior men in the organization wouldn't let it happen. Hurt Marty, and they'll hurt Patterson. They're all protecting each other, because they have nobody above to protect them.

Marty's taking the collection business seriously now.

He's taking everything seriously. No more short-term money-grabbing. Everything is long-term now, for the good of the organization. He's also gotten ruthless. Much more willing to strike against the competition. Not petty beatings using people like Neil Fraser. Marty's willing to do the real dirty work to protect the organization, because there's no protection above him now. Everyone's gotten a little more brutal, because of the uncertainty. Twitchy, ready to fight.

Patterson's pressing the buzzer up to the office. Marty doesn't use this place often now. He's got a few other offices he uses. Not particularly impressive places themselves, but he needs more of them. Needs to move around more. Needs to take his own security more seriously than ever. He's a senior man in an organization some still see as vulnerable. Also has more money to hide, which means more legit places as fronts. But this is where he always meets Patterson. This is where he'll keep meeting him. Not letting Patterson get a taste of Marty's other businesses. Keeping Patterson in his place.

Patterson's up the stairs and through the door. Into the office to find two other men leaving. One of them he doesn't recognize. The other one is Ray Buller. He'd bet his right arm on it, and he's right-handed. Ray Buller, slouching out of a meeting with Marty Jones. A senior man for Alex MacArthur. One of his best friends for decades. Meeting in Marty's office. Bloody hell, Marty is moving up. Working this old bastard as a contact. Buller's giving Patterson a brief glance. Poisonous, angry that Marty's allowed someone to see him here. That's deliberate. Marty wants him to be seen. Wants a witness to the meeting.

Patterson's furiously putting two and two together as the door closes behind him. This must be an early meeting between them. Marty organizing a witness to make sure Buller can't back out of whatever corner Marty's boxed him into. Killing Marty won't now be enough to hide the betrayal. He'd have to kill Patterson too. And then kill anyone Patterson told. An ever-growing list that makes compliance so much easier than killing. Clever little Marty.

'How are you, Martin?' Patterson's asking, shaking his hand. Started calling him Martin as a joke, like he's too serious for a nickname these days. Suits him though.

'Good enough,' Marty's saying. No small talk about parties or women. No bullshit. Just get on with business. No time for dicking around. 'We need to talk about Potty Cruickshank. He's going on the offensive. Shame the police dropped their interest in him, but that's how it goes. Lot of good opportunities fell off the table back then. Means we have to do the job instead. If we leave him doing what he's doing, he's going to take serious market share from us. Time to deal with him.'

'Agreed,' Patterson's saying. Past time to deal with him, in fact, but that couldn't be helped. Marty had other things to deal with. Bigger games to play. Patterson doesn't begrudge that.

'I know for a fact that Potty is going to Alex MacArthur tonight. Going to look for a deal with his old chum, but he won't get it.' Not mentioning Buller, not going to mention him. Patterson already knows and these things don't need to be spoken about. Marty no longer needs to brag about how clever he is. 'MacArthur doesn't want to get involved in other people's squabbles. He's got plenty shit on his own doorstep. That's going to leave Potty isolated. Now is a really bad time to be isolated. Then, tomorrow, I'm going to visit Potty. I'm going to arrange a big meeting.'

Patterson's nodding, but not with enthusiasm. It's the slow-motion nod of a man who doesn't like where this is going. 'A meeting. Okay.'

'You, me and Potty. We're going to sit down and come up with something that makes me happy. A private meeting, away from prying eyes. We'll have an agreement.'

Patterson's fuming. Trying to keep it under control. He knows what happened to Alan Bavidge. Still doesn't know exactly who carried it out, but he knows exactly who organized it. He will make Potty suffer for one. One day, come hell or high water, he'll make sure Alan Bavidge gets payback. 'And if we don't get a deal that makes you happy?' Spoken through gritted teeth.

Now Marty's smiling a little. Just a little, but it means a

lot. It means Marty's already thought that far ahead. It means Marty already has a plan for that. 'You know what? I have a funny little feeling that we won't come to an agreement. Too much distance between you and Potty. I have a feeling we may have to settle the issue there and then. Goes without saying, you and I will be the ones making the demands. I think you and I are very close in what we want. You might want to bring a couple of your best with you, just in case there's tension.'

Patterson's not fuming any more. He likes the sound of this meeting now. Sounds like it's going to be the meeting he's wanted to have with Potty for a long time. Agreement is made. The meeting place. The people they'll bring with them. The timing, which means so much. By the time he leaves the office, Patterson's a very happy man. Happy with Marty. Happy to be led by him.

2

It's just not good enough. Not any more. Not for Peterkinney.
Not for the business he has now. You just can't have these
little debts getting in the way of the bigger work that needs to
be done. Makes you look small-time, something he no longer
is. His contract with Chris Argyle has been successful. He's
making more money than he thought he would at this point.
Well ahead of schedule. He's becoming influential within
Argyle's business. Handling all of his awkward muscle work.
And throughout it all, that debt is still there.

He's arranged a few meetings with his grandfather and
Alex to talk about it. The first one went well. Glass said he
would do whatever it took. Said he'd work the debt off,
whatever. Made it seem like there was nothing he wouldn't
do. Except there was something. Just one thing. The thing
Peterkinney wanted from him. The truth about how he paid
off his first debt to Potty. There's nothing else Glass has to
offer. Doesn't have any skills. Sure as hell doesn't have the
money. Only thing he has is information he won't share.

A few meetings since, and Glass has come up with nothing. It's stopped feeling awkward to Peterkinney, organizing
a meeting with a former best friend. Used to be he dreaded it.

Calling him up, having the meeting. Trying to make polite chat. Make it seem like they still had any sort of relationship. Not awkward any more. Now he doesn't feel like he knows Glass. Doesn't feel like he wants to know him. So it's a formal meeting. The kind he has every day. But no more. Glass has run out of chances.

All he had to do was tell Peterkinney what he'd done for Potty. Tell a little story. Simple as that. Every time they met, he refused to talk about it. Got angry whenever Peterkinney brought up the subject. No point pushing it. He won't talk. And he won't pay either. No matter how many times Arnie tries to cover for him. He's paid off some of the debt. But it's slow going. Glass can't get a permanent job. He's getting odd jobs here and there. Putting some money towards the debt, but it's slow. Never going to be fast enough.

And that hooker's still around. He warned his grandfather about her. Girls like that, they're always a drain. Always going to keep Glass trapped in a world of parties. But Arnie didn't get rid of her. Now, Peterkinney would have been good enough to turn a blind eye to that, if Glass had been smart about it. But no, he had to do the usual idiot act. One of Peterkinney's boys saw it. Glass out at a nightclub, with his expensive little girlfriend. Expensive nightclub to be hanging around. She was there to work, and Glass wasn't actually spending money, but Peterkinney's boy didn't know that. Just saw Glass in a place a poor man shouldn't be. Told

Peterkinney about it. Peterkinney arranged a meeting with Glass. Glass told him he was skint. Didn't have a penny to his name. No, because he spent it all in some shitty club the night before. Idiot. Thinking he can play Peterkinney for a fool. Nuh-uh, doesn't work that way, old pal.

Makes Peterkinney look bad. Makes him look like he'll let a debt slide if you happen to be a mate of his. Can't have people thinking you're soft. All of his people knowing about it. If your own staff think you're a bit soft, they'll try to take advantage of it. They all know he's doing good work for Argyle, but even a small debt can undermine that. It can be the chink in the gleaming armour. So he's going to do something about it.

He's called in one of his more junior muscle. New fellow they hired a couple of weeks ago. James Holmes, his name is. So many names come across Peterkinney's desk. His world is full of new faces. Doesn't remember this one. Looks rough as all hell. Got a scraggly beard and bags under his eyes. Thick dark hair that could seriously do with a wash. Doesn't seem to play well with others. Quiet and miserable. Looks like a boozer. Tough bastard though. He'll do for a job this simple.

'Here's the address,' Peterkinney's saying. Passing a slip of paper across the table. Not bothering to say hello. 'Name's Alex Glass. Lives there with his girlfriend. She works, he doesn't, so most likely he'll be there and she won't. He owes about three and a half grand now, but the debt's gone on too long. I want you to make it clear that it's time for him to take this debt seriously. He's been spending money elsewhere, and I want him to know that that just won't do. You understand?'

'I understand,' Holmes is nodding. He knows exactly how it works. Go round there and kick some sense into the boy. What could be simpler?

Holmes remembers Peterkinney. Remembers being kicked down the fucking stairs by him. Oh yeah, he remembers. All too well. Remembers his life plummeting down the toilet after that. Needed work. Needed something he could do that would pay fast. Weren't many places left he could go looking for work. Not many places where he hadn't burnt his bridges. This was one of the very few. And everyone knows that Peterkinney's expanding. Everyone knows he's taking on new people. If you're tough and willing to do dirty work. If you're willing to put your life on the line. Some of his collections are from very dangerous people these days.

He thought Peterkinney would remember him. Probably a sign of how well the kid's doing that he didn't. Holmes doesn't look the same. Lost a bit of weight, grew the beard to cover the scar. Peterkinney gave Holmes a couple of jobs to do. Holmes did them well. He's past caring about his security these days. In debt. Drinking heavily. Shifting from place to place, waiting for the council to find him a flat. Was in sheltered housing for a few weeks. Slept in a car park for three nights. Now he's willing to risk the last thing he has left, his life. Do it for some money. Enough money to drink himself to death, hopefully.

'Get it done later this afternoon, let me know how it goes,' Peterkinney's saying. 'I want detail on this one.' He knows he's going to get a call from his grandfather. Or a visit. Those are always fun. Talking awkwardly. Arguing. Each pretending he doesn't owe the other anything. Arnie will be furious, and Oliver will have to defend himself. For that, he needs detail.

Holmes has left. Scruffy-looking bugger, Peterkinney's thinking. Might have to tell him to tidy himself up. Not yet. Not while he's doing garbage jobs at the low end of the business. The people he's collecting from look even worse than he does. But he'll have to clean himself up if he wants to work the bigger jobs. Presentation matters. You need to look professional and decent. If you're collecting from a rich man, you need to look rich in his presence. At least look respectable.

Kilbanne is back from his lunch. Seemingly happier in his work these days. He knows what he's doing is still fundamentally crooked, but now it's on a big scale. There's something exciting about that. Peterkinney's starting to talk seriously about legitimate businesses. That's what it is. That's what gets Kilbanne excited. The thought that they're making so much money, they can start to look at buying legit concerns to hide it all behind. Then Kilbanne can hide his guilt behind the legitimacy.

'I know pubs, clubs and bookies are clichéd,' Kilbanne's saying, 'but they're a great place to start. Easy to manipulate the figures coming in. But there are other things we can do. Things that will raise less concern. They are more complicated, though. Probably more expensive to get off the ground, as well. Worth it though, long term.'

'Right now we need something that's going to work fast,' Peterkinney's saying. They've had this conversation before. Often. Peterkinney wanting to go the obvious route, Kilbanne wanting to do something unnecessarily clever. Right now they need to come up with ways of cleaning up their cut of the Argyle money. Doesn't matter how clever it is, it just needs to work. Sooner the better. Money's starting to pile up and it needs to be cleaned and put somewhere safe.

'I'm going to start moving some money,' Kilbanne is saying. 'Need to have it to purchase with. I mean, you're right; we should go for the simple stuff first. I'll start looking around. There's always pubs shutting down. Should be easy pickings.'

Easy pickings. Two best words in the criminal lexicon. Often the two most misleading, as well. These things are almost never easy. Peterkinney isn't naive about that. The economic situation will make it easier for them to find struggling places willing to sell. They'll either buy the whole place or a share. More likely the whole thing. Only buy a share if you can rely on the other shareholder to keep their mouth shut. Peterkinney isn't willing to trust people he doesn't know. Not big enough to scare people into silence yet. Kilbanne will take control of the books. Filter dirty money through them.

By the end of the afternoon, Peterkinney's in rather good cheer. He knows to expect his grandfather. It'll be a call now, because they're going to lock up the office. His grandfather's never been to his flat. Might not even know where it is. So he'll telephone and bitch and moan, and Peterkinney will have to explain the way the world works. And he'll rather enjoy it. It's about time Arnie Peterkinney found out that his Good Samaritan routine is a shambles. Worthless and ineffective.

3

He's nervous. Potty's actually nervous about this. It's because things are so different. Until a few months ago, this would have been routine. And even if this didn't go his way, he'd still have other options. But not now. The whole industry is changing. You can't take anything for granted now. Even he's trying to find a foothold in the shifting sands.

It started out looking like good news. Potty thought he was going to be one of the big beneficiaries of this turmoil. Some gunman belonging to Peter Jamieson blabbed to the cops. Dropped a lot of people in the shit. Somehow or other, that involved Paul Greig. PC Paul Greig wasn't a PC any more. He was quietly shunted out of the force. Police didn't want the embarrassment of it going to trial. His superiors would have had to admit that they knew some of what he was doing. But all the evidence he'd provided them with was suddenly useless. The cases that hinged on his evidence were quietly dropped. Including Potty's.

Throw in the fact that Jamieson and his organization looked like they were finished, and it seemed like a good day to be Potty Cruickshank. For a start, that would be the end of Marty Jones. Marty was never a major concern, too much of a playboy, but this would get rid of that nuisance. Without Jamieson's protection, he couldn't possibly survive. And Jamieson's fall would make Alex MacArthur stronger. Potty had been cultivating his relationship with the MacArthur organization. So good news all round. Three cheers for the gunman who talked.

But it didn't turn out that way. MacArthur was arrested a couple of days later. It didn't go anywhere, but that doesn't matter. He was weak. That was the opening the ambitious younger ones had been looking for. People like Don Park, looking to take control. For the last few months, it feels like it's been silent civil war in the MacArthur camp. People trying to slice each other, without the outside world hearing about it. Potty hasn't been able to get a meeting. Hasn't been able to get anyone to pay him any damn attention. To top it all off, that bastard Marty Jones seems to be going from strength to strength.

He's finally got himself a meeting with Alex MacArthur. Was offered a meeting with some junior a couple of weeks ago. Turned that right down. Don't they remember who he is? Don't they remember the respect the Cruickshank name commands? Whatever their internal problems are, they're no excuse for disrespect. Maybe they remember him now, because MacArthur's agreed to see him.

He's sitting in the back of the car. Sweating, which isn't good. He needs to look relaxed when he goes into

MacArthur's office. It's a small office they're going to. That's a bad sign. Might be more to do with MacArthur's recent struggles than Potty's. The old man moving around more to stay safe. Not using his preferred meeting places so often. Maybe it's not another sign that he doesn't take Potty seriously. Maybe. Still, it's a negative to focus on and make him sweat a bit more.

He needs this. Needs an alliance that can protect him through the storm. With Marty growing and seemingly pairing with that shit Patterson, Potty's feeling the pressure. Peterkinney's growing, becoming a serious player and a serious threat. Potty seems to be the only one standing still. The only loser in this little game. He needs support. Cut MacArthur in. Give him the chance to open up a new avenue of revenue, something he ought to want to do. Should want it even in good times. He should be bloody grateful for this chance now. Someone of Potty's stature coming to him and making him a generous offer. He has no right to turn it down.

Pulling to a stop in the sort of area a car like Potty's doesn't stop in often or for long. The driver will stay with the car. Potty's getting out and waddling slowly towards the door. It's a small building in an industrial area. The parking's tucked in just off the road. Up a step and pulling open the glass door. There's a small reception desk inside and the young woman behind it is asking if she can help him. She doesn't even know who he is. Bloody cheek. He's telling her, and now he's having to stand there waiting while she makes a call.

He'll put this down to MacArthur's increased need for security. He'll forgive it, which is generous. They should not be making a man like him stand in some waiting area like this. She's hanging up the phone and smiling at him.

'If you'd like to go through, the office is second on your right.'

Not even going to show him the way. Nobody coming to meet him. This really isn't the way to treat a person. Treatment like this is remembered. Alex MacArthur should know that. He wouldn't accept it, and he shouldn't hand it out. Potty's pushing open the door at the side of the woman's desk and walking slowly along the corridor. Finding the appropriate door. Two knocks and then opening, not waiting for an answer. Potty Cruickshank doesn't need to wait for answers.

MacArthur's sitting behind his desk. Ray Buller is sitting in a chair in the far corner of the room from MacArthur, and there's a chair in front of the desk. It's a small office. Not the sort of place you would expect to find a man with the business concerns of Alex MacArthur. Yeah, that would be the point, smart guy. MacArthur's hiding himself away.

No wonder he looks miserable. Looks even older and frailer than the last time they met, and that was only a few months ago. A man of his stature should not be hiding away in wee places like this. It's embarrassing for him. It makes him look weak, and he did not get where he is by looking weak. Does beg the question, just who is he hiding from? No stories about people outside the organization targeting him. Bloody hell, is he in here hiding from his own people? Bang goes any chance of a deal worth having.

'Mr MacArthur, how are you, sir?' Potty's asking, and regretting it. You don't ask an obviously sick man how he feels. That's the last thing MacArthur will want to dwell on.

'Good enough. Sit down, Ronald. What do you want?' Said with obvious impatience. An implication that Potty couldn't possibly have anything useful to talk about. This is all a waste of an important man's time.

It's an insulting way to speak to a man like Potty. This whole visit has been one long insult. Longer it goes on, the more Potty thinks he shouldn't be here. Thinks MacArthur might not be capable of helping him. Might have been wiser to try and start a relationship with Don Park instead. Too late. He's in the chair in front of MacArthur's desk, so he might as well play to the end.

'I have a business proposition for you, if you care to hear it.' That was a slightly snide way to end a sentence. Potty's struggling to hide his impatience. Should always maintain your manners around people like MacArthur. Doesn't matter what you feel or think about someone, you stay polite. Then, if you need to move against them, they're less likely to see it coming. Good manners cost nothing. Bad manners can be very expensive indeed.

'I care to hear it,' MacArthur's saying. His voice is weak, almost whispery. Makes his tone seem even more dismissive.

'We both know that the city is changing. Things have happened . . .' Potty's saying, and trailing off. Hardly needs explaining. Few people know better than the man in front of him. 'I'm offering a chance to open up a new revenue stream. I know you're not involved in the collection business in a big way. It's a potential new source of revenue for you. It offers me an opportunity of growth that will protect my business through this time of upheaval. It's good for both of us.'

MacArthur's making a good effort at looking unimpressed. He's about to say something when he starts coughing instead. A long-drawn-out wheeze of a cough. If Potty had heard that cough before he came here, he wouldn't have come. Everyone knew MacArthur was ill, but he's been ill for so bloody long, people assumed it was no big deal. One of those things that last long enough for something else to kill him. Now it looks and sounds like a big deal. Now he seems like the wrong horse to back. Truth is, if he was a horse they would shoot him. Someone still might.

'I'd be looking at providing you a cut of 25 per cent,' Potty's saying. As he'd come in the front door of the building, he had been committed to offering forty. Now he's not sure he wants MacArthur to accept his offer. Forty might have been enough to win him over. Twenty-five shouldn't be.

MacArthur's looking at him. Then looking past him at Ray Buller. Then back at Potty before he answers. And that look tells Potty a lot. The old man struggling. Not sure who he can trust. Pulling his friends close. Looking to people like Buller for more advice. Because he's not sure of himself any more. Giving them more power because they're the ones he would like to hand over to. Because they're not Don Park.

'I don't think so,' MacArthur is saying. 'Timing isn't right. I'm not saying never, but not now.' Said with finality.

A finality Potty has no interest in arguing with. 'If that's your thinking,' Potty's saying, and getting slowly to his feet. 'Hopefully times will change,' he's saying, a sentence that could mean just about anything. He's reaching out a hand to MacArthur. His fat hand swallowing the bony hand offered. Feels cold. Feels like goodbye.

Potty's nodding to Buller as he leaves. No handshake there. Buller was the one who said no. He was the one who made the decision. Maybe he should shake his hand. Thank him for killing the deal with a shake of his head. But Potty's already out the door and making his way along the corridor. Feeling the effort by the time he ignores the receptionist and pushes his way out the front door. Relieved to drop into the back of the car and be driven away.

Dodged a bullet, sure, but for how long? The deal with

MacArthur could have been a bad deal, given how weak the old man looks. But what's the alternative? Stand alone? No, that won't do. No deal is worse than a bad deal. He needs support. He needs to be able to survive these changes. By any means necessary. Dear God, he just needs to survive.

4

Peterkinney told him to do it this afternoon. And he meant to. He really did. But he got sidetracked. Happens to Holmes a lot these days. Life is a pursuit of the bottle. Everything else is a means to that end. Working to make money to drink. And he has some money. Not a lot. Money never lasts long for Holmes these days.

He wandered into a supermarket, is the short version of why he's late. Bought a half-bottle and six cans. Took it back to the flat he's in now. Blotted out the world for a little while. Blotted out what he's on his way to do now. The memory of that night when those two little bastards smashed their way into his house. His house. Man, if you could turn back the clock. He had his own house. Wasn't much to look at, but what does that matter? He had Norah. She wasn't much to look at either, but she was his. All gone now.

His things. Didn't realize that he cared about them until it was all gone. Until he had nothing. Stupid cliché, but that's all that's left. Into the bathroom to splash a little water on his face before he goes out. That straggly beard. Hair's too long as well. Needs a haircut, but that's money he could spend on something wet. Could trim the beard himself. Hates it. Only has it to cover the scar. The scar's ugly, but he stopped caring about that a long time ago. The long, thin red line is a reminder. That was the real punishment. Lets the world see his failure.

Can't hide the bags under his eyes. The sag of his chin. Jesus, he looks like his grandfather. Bloodshot eyes and loose skin. Same bad teeth the old man had. Same reason. It was booze that eventually killed Grandpa Holmes. Took its time though. Holmes can't wait that long. Won't wait. All those dreams of the good life. A better life than the one he had. Skimming money because he thought he could have a better house. A better woman. He'd give everything he has to get back the home and woman he lost, but he has nothing to offer. Fuck it: staring in the mirror is only a guarantee of misery. A splash of cold water and he's leaving. Little bit drunk, little bit angry. Nothing new.

He threw away the slip of paper with the address on it. Doesn't need it. Born and raised round here. Knows the place like the back of his hand. Spent his working life pounding the streets, finding and punishing people. If it's a shitty part of town, you can bet Jim Holmes knows it well. It's starting to get dark. Damn, must be pretty late. Doesn't have a watch to check. Never mind. Peterkinney won't care too much about the timing. He'll just want to know that it's been done.

It's a small block of flats, four storeys high. Not the best exit when the target's on the third floor, but Holmes doesn't care. This is going to be simple. One target. Only other person likely to be there is the girlfriend. And the boy isn't expecting him. That's always the difference-maker. If you don't expect it. If you aren't ready. If Holmes gets the first punch in, he'll have no problem here.

Up the stairs and along to the front door. A quick knock on the door. Then, thirty seconds later, another one. He's not patient. He doesn't want to have to come back a second time. Too much like hard work. Also, being seen repeatedly in the location of your crime is a dumb move. Holmes knows that. The old instincts are still there.

He has to wait another twenty seconds before the door slowly opens. It's a young woman looking back at him. She looks scruffy but pretty. Didn't someone say she was a hooker for Marty Jones? Wearing a T-shirt and jogging bottoms. Greasy dark hair tied back. She has a cloth or duster in her hand. Looks like she's been cleaning up. A woman taking care of her home. Quaint. A reminder of Norah. Not quaint. Hard to take.

Disappointing that the girl's here. Always easier without some squawking woman thinking she has to defend her man. That's the problem with them. They always defend their man, even when he's wrong. And even if they don't get physically involved, they can raise the dead with their shouting. Certainly raise the alarm. That's Holmes's experience of them, anyway, but his experience with women has made him sad. Not bitter. He knows it was his own fault.

'I'm looking for Alex Glass,' he's saying. You wouldn't know he was drunk to hear him. Maybe if you knew him well, but otherwise he would sound strong and in control. Takes a lot of practice to be able to control yourself that well whilst brimming with alcohol.

'He's not in,' she's saying, and moving to close the door.

You don't take them at their word. That's not instinct, that's just common sense. People who owe money become good at hiding. Practice makes perfect there too. They know when to shut the door and when not to. They have instincts of their own. Holmes is sticking his boot in the door and shoving into it shoulder first. He's not as big as he used to be. Lost a bit of weight. Not eating properly. Still a lot bigger than Ella, doesn't take much force to push her backwards.

'Hey. Bastard.' She's stepping back and letting him in. She can complain, but there's no point fighting back.

Holmes is inside the flat, looking around. Not much of a flat. Door opens into the living room, and you can see the door through to the small kitchen. No hiding places. There's a little corridor off to the side that he'll have to check. No sign of Glass at first glimpse.

'Where is he?'

'I told you, not here. He has a job. Something or other, I don't know what. Just for tonight. I don't know where.'

Holmes is ignoring her. If the answer isn't within the flat, then he doesn't want to hear it. He's going into the kitchen. Dishes in the sink, but no Glass. Out into the living room again. Along the corridor and pushing open a door. A bedroom. Small, with only a single bed in it. Doesn't look like it's used. Pushing open another door. Bathroom. Nobody hiding there. Into the final room. Second bedroom. Bigger, more furniture, a bed with a dishevelled look about it.

If he's hiding in the flat, then it's in this room. No room under the bed. Lifting up the quilt and looking under. Nope. Last-chance saloon is the wardrobe. Otherwise he's not here and Holmes is going to have to make a return visit. Opening the wardrobe doors and finding nothing but clothes inside. Damn it all. Shit. They can never just make it simple. Now he'll have to come back and go through this again. He'll get the job done late. Might not even get it done tonight. Then Peterkinney will be pissed off with him, and he'll be struggling to hang on to another job.

He's slamming the wardrobe door shut. It's not a door designed to be slammed. The wardrobe is shaking and doing its level best not to fall apart under the assault. Holmes is marching out of the bedroom, along the corridor and into the living room. Looking furious. Ready to pick a fight with anyone over anything. Just a good old-fashioned fight. It would make him feel better.

'Where is he?'

'I told you. I don't know.' She's getting fed up of this now. She doesn't know, and even if she did, it's obvious she wouldn't tell this gorilla.

'When's he going to be back, huh?' Almost shouting now.

A sigh. 'I don't know. Don't know where he is, don't know what he's doing, don't know when he'll be back. He's doing a job. Trying to make some money, okay. So that he can pay some back. But it was all rushed, and I don't know what it was.' Trying to be persuasive, but running out of patience. 'He shouldn't be long. You can come back in an hour. There's no need to be so angry about it. I don't know what your problem is.'

That's it. That's just enough to spark a rage. 'You don't know what my problem is? Do you want to know? Eh? Will I tell you what my fucking problem is? It's people like you and your wee guy. Your Alex Glass. Borrowing money you can't afford to pay. And then I have to come and collect it cause you're all so fucking daft. And your fellow ain't here to pay. Big fucking surprise there, eh. Always hiding. Always hiding.' He was shouting at the end, spitting as he did.

Ella's just glaring at him. 'He's trying to earn money to pay you back. And you don't need to be shouting at me, I don't owe you anything.'

Defiance. Not much, but enough for Holmes. 'Oh, you don't? Well, your man does. He's yours and so is his debt. You owe.' He's moved towards her, pushed her shoulder. Not violent, but looking to provoke violence.

'Stop that. Just leave. Please, just get out.'

'What did you say to me? You telling me to get out? That what you said?' Lashing out with a slap, catching her hard on the side of the head.

She didn't see it coming. Holmes was always a fighter, since he was a little kid. Always had a quick hand. It's the surprise as much as the force that's knocked her sideways. Knocked her off her feet and onto the floor. Lying on her side. Shaken, sore, but no permanent damage. But she's staying down. Convinced that if she gets up, she'll get hit again. She's been hit before. She knows how this works. Let them see they've won. Let them see that they're more powerful than you. When they see they've won their power game, they can back off. So she's staying down and hoping that'll be enough for him.

But it won't. Not for Holmes. He's not like her clients. Not trying to make himself feel big. Feel like a winner. He already knows he's lost. He's drunk and angry and remembering that time Glass smashed his way into his house. He's remembering all the failure that followed. Remembering Glass and Peterkinney at the bottom of the stairs in the old house. Standing there and kicking him while he lay on the floor. Now he can make one of them suffer.

He's lashing out with his boot. Not holding anything back. Hitting her in the stomach, his boot scuffing along her side. Didn't catch her square, but it felt good to him. Good to be kicking out. Good that he can make Glass suffer.

'You feel that?' he's shouting. 'You ask your boyfriend if he remembers. You ask him. I remember. You ask him if he does.'

Kicking her again. Hard as he can, all his weight behind it. Square in the stomach this time. Knocking her onto her back. She's rolled onto her other side and stopped moving. He's making to kick her in the back this time, but stopping. Instinct. Walking round to the other side of her. Looking at her face. Her eyes are half shut, her mouth half open. There's no movement. Her arms are down on the floor, not raised to defend herself.

'Come on. Come on, get up. Come on.' Holmes is bending down, grabbing her by the hair. Lifting her head half an inch and letting it drop onto the floor. There's a faint groan. Her eyelids flicker. But that's it. 'Shit, come on. I didn't . . . you're not that badly hurt. Come on.' Getting angry with her now.

Taking a step back and looking around. A deep breath. What do you do? Instinct says run and right now instinct is all he's got. He's out the front door, just aware enough to pull it shut behind him. Down the stairs and out into the night. Breathing heavily, in real need of a drink. This need isn't just pesky old alcoholism. This is fear that needs to be drowned before it hurts him. That girl was in trouble. He went too far.

5

Arnie's sitting in his living room, watching TV. Skimming through the newspaper for reasons of habit. A boring quiet night, until the phone starts ringing. He's looking at it with suspicion. Nobody phones him in an evening. There aren't many who phone him at all. This is going to be something annoying, he's sure of it.

'Hello, Arnold Peterkinney.'

'Arnie? Arnie.'

He knows already that it's Glass. Young voice, emotional. Sounds like he's looking for help.

'Alex, is that you? What's wrong?'

There's a pause and heavy breathing. 'It's Ella. She's not moving. She's just lying on the floor and she's not moving.'

He instantly assumes drugs, and then stops himself. She's a good girl. Didn't think she would be. Thought she would be the biggest problem in Glass's life. Nope, not her. She was helping Glass. She was the one with sense in the relationship. Okay, she does a job she shouldn't. Arnie doesn't like that. Doesn't like to think about it. Knows what it does to Glass to think about it. He tried to talk her into changing career, but she wouldn't. Stubborn wee thing.

Only way she knows to make money. But she wasn't a waster. Not a boozer. Not a druggie. Oliver was wrong about her. She wasn't the problem. So not drugs. Must have been a client.

'Listen to me now, Alex, listen carefully. What happened? How did she end up on the floor?' Worried now that Glass might have been involved. Worried that something bad could be about to turn into something horrendous.

'I don't know. I don't know. I just came home. I did that job for Mr Currie that you got me. I parked the van where he told me to and walked back. I came into the flat and she was just lying there. Lying on the living-room floor. She's not moving. She won't wake up. She's not . . . She won't move for me, Arnie.'

'Okay. Steady on, now. Listen to me. You have to hang up and call an ambulance. Dial 999 and tell them what you told me. You got that now, Alex. Call an ambulance. I'll come round to the flat, okay. I'm on my way now.'

'Okay. Okay.'

Arnie's hanging up the phone. Running to the hall, grabbing a coat. Out of the flat and along to his neighbour's front door. Knocking loudly, making sure they can't possibly ignore him. The door's opening, a confused neighbour looking back at him.

'Arnie?'

'I need to borrow your car. It's an emergency, really, or I wouldn't ask.'

The neighbour's nodding. Arnie's a reliable guy. He's not going to go off and trash the car. And he doesn't ask for much. Doesn't ask for anything, actually. If he was the sort of neighbour who borrowed a lot, Arnie might not get what he wants right now. But the neighbour's fishing in his pocket, pulling out a set of keys.

'I won't keep it long, I promise,' Arnie's saying. He was going to say something about filling up the tank before he takes it back, but he hasn't. Too much of a hurry. Also, it's a nice thing to do, and nice things cost money. He's not sure he has any of that on him.

He's down to the front of the building and into the car. Driving quickly through the streets, hoping he can get to the flat before the ambulance does. He wants to see Glass. Wants to see the situation. It's a terrible thing, but he's hardly thinking about Ella at all. He's only thinking about what this might do to Glass. How he might react to this. Worried that he might get into all kinds of trouble if this is serious.

Little traffic, and he's there quickly, but he's not there first. There's an ambulance outside the building. Arnie's parking out of the way and running up the stairs. Struggling a bit. Wheezing as he gets to the door. The two paramedics are down on the floor, on their knees beside Ella. One of them is talking to her. The other one is fiddling around her mouth and neck. Glass is standing behind them, hands at his sides, just staring.

Arnie's walked past the paramedics, over to Glass. Putting an arm on his shoulder. Glass is noticing him for the first time. Just looking at him and looking back at Ella. He doesn't look emotional. Doesn't look like this has hurt him. But that's what worries Arnie. This kid was emotionally all over the place after getting beaten up in that nightclub and turning up on his doorstep. Now he's not reacting at all. Before he was damaged. Now he's broken.

The girl looks bad. Can't see what's wrong with her. The medics are still working on her. One of them is lifting her T-shirt. Arnie assumes they're looking for puncture wounds, but they're not. They're looking for a larger injury and they've found one. Her stomach and side are red, heading for purple. The medics are talking in whispers to each other. One of them getting up and running down to the ambulance.

'We need to get her to hospital now. Have you a car to follow in?' the remaining one is asking Glass. Doesn't have a friendly tone in his voice. He knows what caused this injury. He suspects he knows who. Usually domestic. That's why he wants the boy in a car, not in the back of the ambulance with the girl.

Glass is nodding. Unsure.

'I do, I'll take him,' Arnie's saying. He wants to stay near Glass. Wants to make sure he doesn't react badly to this. Start talking and get himself in trouble.

The medics are moving her down on a small stretcher.

Going fast. There's a new sense of urgency about them now. Glass staying close, Arnie close to Glass. Arnie's watching them put her in the back of the ambulance, Glass standing beside him. Watching his girlfriend. Watching them close the ambulance door.

'Come on. Alex, let's go,' Arnie's saying. Needing to provoke him into action. Glass is following him to the car. They're driving behind the ambulance, through the quiet streets of the city.

The next hour is a disquieting blur to Arnie. They rushed her in and about ten minutes later a doctor came out to talk to them. Came out to tell them that Ella had died. That she had suffered internal injuries after a blunt trauma. There was silence for a long time. Arnie and Glass sitting together in a private room in the hospital. Arnie didn't know what to say. What do you say?

'Someone killed her,' Glass is saying eventually. Talking in a whisper.

He's right, but Arnie doesn't want this conversation to go any further in that direction. He knows where the road goes. Someone went round to the flat and killed her. Not like there are many obvious candidates. There's an obvious candidate that Arnie doesn't want to think about. He wants to move Glass in another direction.

'Would she have had someone back to the flat?' he's asking quietly. Trying to put the thought in Glass's head. Try and persuade him that it might be a client of Ella's. Try and persuade him that the dead girl introduced her own murderer into the situation. Anything to convince him that it's not the obvious option.

Glass is shaking his head. 'No. She never would have. Never did. Home was separate. Home was home.'

Ella never took men back to the flat. Not once. It was the place of safety that she clung to. Meant so much to her. She put so much into that flat. Little poky place, didn't deserve someone like her to take so much care of it. Mattered to her though. Proof that she could have normality. Safety. Something nice and neat that she was responsible for. Something grown up.

There's another period of silence. Arnie has to change this. Ella is dead. The girl is gone. They both know who's responsible. Who's almost certainly responsible. They need to get out of here. The hospital is just a reminder of death. Even this private room, that tries to be so nice. That tries to be so reassuring. It isn't. It's just death in nicer packaging.

'Come on. Let's go back to my flat. It's late, you need to get some sleep,' Arnie is saying. 'There's nothing we can do here.' Get him home. Get him sleeping. Emotions will be less bloody and raw in the morning. There will be a better chance to sort this out.

Arnie's given his address to the girl at the accident and emergency reception desk. If the police want to get in touch, they'll know where to find them. Arnie's driving them home. Going in silence. Glass doesn't want to talk. Arnie doesn't know what to say. Leading Glass up to the flat. Patting him on the shoulder and saying goodnight. That's all they've said. Goodnight. Glass disappearing into Peterkinney's old bedroom to try and sleep.

Arnie still has the car keys in his hand. Bouncing them up and down in his palm. Thinking about giving them back to his neighbour. He's spent ten minutes standing in the corridor. Listening at Glass's bedroom door. No sound from in there. He might be sleeping. Hopefully. A glance at his watch. Half an hour. That's all it would take. Get there, ask a few questions, get back before Glass realizes he's gone. Take the chance. He has to know. That's why he's sneaking out of his own flat. Pulling the front door shut behind him as softly as possible and jogging to the car.

6

Marty still hasn't left the office. Third office he's been in today, mind you, so technically he's left two already. But he's still there. Still working. Trying to figure out how the hell the Allen brothers, who are still just cousins incidentally, managed to pull off some major deal that has them selling all over the city now. Marty knows a little about the brothers. Used to know Charlie Allen a little bit. Charlie came to a few parties.

They were small. They were smart and tough, but they stuck to their own patch and they knew how to avoid pissing off big people. Marty heard stories about them looking for new suppliers back in the past. That was a legit story. They had a falling out with Alex MacArthur over one of his muscle owing them money, something like that. So it makes sense to Marty that they would have changed supplier.

What doesn't make sense is them suddenly having enough gear and enough backing to expand rapidly. Angus Lafferty is pissed off about it. You can bet the hair on your head, if you have any to gamble, that in a jail cell somewhere Peter Jamieson is pissed off about it too. Someone thinks they can force their way in, and they're using Ian and Charlie Allen to do it. That's got Angus worked up. Got him looking for answers. Got everyone in the group that runs the organization trying to find out the truth behind it. And they will. Marty's sure of it, because this group is good. By spreading their talent like this, they're getting results. And he loves being a part of it. Loves it. Loves what he's going to do next.

Out of the office, at last. Standing on the street for a few seconds, breathing in some sort of fresh air. Into his car and driving. Doesn't have a driver of his own. Not permanently. Uses one now and again, when he needs it. Doesn't need it tonight. Doesn't want it. This is going to be a private meeting, and he doesn't want anyone knowing about it. Not even a driver.

Nice street, nice area. Better than Marty's living in right now. He could afford to move up in the world. Not a question of cash. Question of time. Hasn't had the opportunity to look around at new houses, pick a bigger place. He should. All part of the image. Lets people see that he's more successful, moving up in the world. Also lets the other guys running the organization see that he's moving up. That's important too. Always that need to prove that he's one of them. To prove that he's a senior man. And when he does move up, it'll be to somewhere like this. The sort of street that Potty Cruickshank lives on.

He's parked outside, getting casually out. Looking up at Potty's house. Potty will be back from his meeting with MacArthur. Will have had a few hours to think about it.

Potty's a thinker. He'll have worked out every angle of his position. He must know that he needs protection. He must know that he needs to make a deal with someone. He must know that he's fast running out of options. His own men will be getting nervy about how exposed he is amongst the turmoil.

MacArthur probably wouldn't have taken the deal anyway. He's not in a position to do anything that might lead to trouble externally. He has way too much going on trying to keep possession of his throne from his own young pretenders. But there was a risk he would have seen this as flexing whatever muscles he has left. That's why it was reassuring to see Buller turn up and spill the beans. Reassuring that all the work he did setting up the meeting with Buller paid off. More reassuring still that Marty's judgement on MacArthur's situation turned out to be correct.

Up the front path and ringing the doorbell. He knows what the initial reaction is going to be. He knows that Potty won't be happy to see him. Might be nervous, scared about it. But Marty's very deliberately on his own. Unarmed. Coming to Potty's house, so it's a location Potty can feel comfortable with.

Takes a little while before the hall light comes on and the door opens. Potty looking back at him, frowning. Glaring at him for a few seconds before he recognizes Marty. The look moves from frustration to worry. His eyebrows are raised.

He's opened his mouth, but nothing's come out. Too busy looking past Marty, trying to see if there's anyone with him.

'Hello, Ronald,' Marty's saying to him. 'Can I come in? I think you and I need to have a grown-up, man-to-man chat about the way things are going.'

You can almost see the wheels turning. Potty standing there, thinking it through. Nodding his head slowly. Doesn't matter where this goes, but he can't leave Marty standing outside. Has to invite him in.

They're in the living room now. Potty in his usual seat, Marty sitting opposite him. Potty offered a cup of tea or something stronger. Marty made a point of refusing any alcohol, pointing out that he has to drive himself home. Letting Potty know that there's nobody outside. Just the two of them. Marty's making a point of not looking around at the living room. A feminine room. Must have been his ex-wife who picked out everything in here. Just seems ludicrous with Potty living here alone now.

'I want to talk about you and me getting together. Working out a little deal that I think can make life easier for both of us.'

'Well, of course I'm interested in anything that may benefit us, Marty,' Potty's saying, 'but you'll have to furnish me with more detail than that.' Sounding like he's humouring Marty. Going for a superior tone he wouldn't have dared use to Alex MacArthur.

'Well, of course,' Marty is saying. Not saying it in a sarcastic tone, but it might just be sarcastic. 'You and I have common enemies,' Marty's saying. 'We have common solutions. You're a smart man. You know how things are changing right now. You and I together could be strong. That's what you need. It's what I need. It's what my organization wants. We want strong people on board with us.'

'On board?' Potty's saying. Letting his enthusiasm for that suggestion get the better of his silence.

'On board,' Marty's saying. Knowing now that he has the fat fish halfway into the boat. Only has to clobber him over the head to seal the deal. 'See, my role has changed. I need to bring as much money to the table as possible. I have other ways of doing that. Collection is tough work, better suited to a specialist. I'm spread too thin. I can bring more money into the organization if I get you on board. You take over my books. I step out, and the organization takes a third of your profits. I'll be working on other things that you don't need to concern yourself with. There won't be overlap. You can expand your business, make more money than you are now and have the protection of the organization.'

It's a good offer. It's as good an offer as Potty could possibly hope for. A third of his profits is a little more than he'd like, but, Jesus, he'd have given a strong MacArthur 40 per cent. It's not unreasonable for Marty to demand it. The upper end of reasonable, given that profits will surely increase. With Marty's books merged into his, that covers much of the 30 per cent. Marty's books are smaller than Potty's but they're not thin. And with the backing of the Jamieson organization. Now, there's the risk. It's not the Jamieson organization as long as Jamieson's rotting in a cell. He'll be sitting in that cell for another year and a half, minimum. The leadership is ragtag. Only takes one falling-out and all the protection his 30 per cent is supposed to buy him falls apart. So there is a gamble. But the gamble of no deal is bigger.

'I would be open to the suggestion,' Potty is saying. 'I'll want to see the small print, obviously, but I'm certainly willing to discuss this further. One question, Marty: these common enemies. I presume you have a solution in mind?'

Not hard to understand why Potty's concerned. It's easy for people to promise solutions to your problems when they're trying to get you to do a deal. You do the deal, and suddenly the promises are forgotten. Happened to other people before. Marty promises that the big organization he's a part of will take care of these problems. Once Potty's on board, they're Potty's problems. Marty's off dealing with other things.

'Oh, I do. Billy Patterson is the first one I'm going to deal with. I think that would benefit us both. I'm actually going to deal with him tomorrow night. You know what, might be a good idea for you to be there. The first step of bringing you in. You interested?'

'Absolutely,' Potty's saying, because he can't say no. Wishes he could, but he can't. Marty wants him to be there for good reasons. If they're going to do something serious with Patterson, Marty wants Potty to see it. Wants the commitment that being there shows. Make Potty as culpable as Marty. It's a reasonable thing to demand. Besides, much as Potty is repulsed by the idea of watching Marty do dirty work, it might be nice to bear witness to Patterson's ending.

'Good,' Marty's saying. 'I've got Patterson to agree to come meet me in an old pub Kevin Currie just bought. I'll send you some details in the morning. Agreements, that sort of thing. The pub's on the south side, I'll send you the address. Come alone, of course.'

'Of course.'

A few minutes of small talk. Now Marty's leaving the house. A shake of hands on the doorstep. Potty seemed happy, seemed enthusiastic about the agreement. Marty's into the car, got another visit to make. A long-arranged meeting with Kevin Currie. Chance to kill a few birds with one stone here. Needs to get a set of keys for that old pub Currie bought. Going to tart it up and run money through it. But Marty has a little plan for it first. Going to need a few people to come help him make that plan work, as well. Lots of calls to make.

They'll be fun calls to make, though. Nobody ignores his calls any more. Nobody ever sounds reluctant when he puts an idea to them. It's a funny thing. He's pretty sure that most of his ideas are no better now than they were six months ago. How could they be? He's learned a lot in the last six months, but not so much that he's suddenly a strategic genius. No, people just respect him now.

He's pulling up outside one of Kevin Currie's offices. Currie's a senior man. Always brought a lot of money into the organization through booze and fags. Rips off the taxman no end, and the organization makes a good profit on it. Not just booze and fags though. That's the thing. People think that's all he does because in the old days that's how he started. That was all he needed back then. It made him rich. But now he has a good grip of every aspect of the counterfeit industry.

Into the office; Currie and a couple of others already in there. Marty the last to arrive, but not late. Nodding hellos, and stepping to the side of the room to talk to Currie with a little privacy. The other two guys work for Currie, and if he wants to share these details with them then he can go right ahead. But you don't risk blurting out details in front of people who may not be very important.

Currie is quite happy for Marty to use the pub. Telling him where he can get the keys whenever he wants them. One of Currie's men has a duplicate set he can use. Asking hardly any questions about it. That's another big change. Used to be a man like Currie would have swamped Marty with his suspicions. Not now. Now there's trust.

'I'll be using it for a job, Kevin. What we discussed at the last meeting. Cleaning up the collection business.'

'Ah,' is the response. A slight pause, but only slight. 'You have the men you need to get it done?' And that's all he's asking. Not demanding more detail. Not suggesting that Marty isn't senior enough to pull this job without one of them there to oversee. Just offering his own men to help.

'I'm fine. It's all set up, ready for tomorrow night. Should be clean. Should be simple.'

The two of them rejoining the group, and going through the business of the week that needs to be discussed. This is just a small meeting. Currie and Marty the only two senior men. There's a business opportunity Currie wants to pursue that he thinks Marty can help him with. That's why it's just the two of them, and Currie's men. Talk of money. Talk of putting pressure on people. The talk of senior men.

7

Arnie knows the address, but doesn't know the area. He's driving round for the best part of twenty minutes before he finds the right street. A nice little area. Sort of place Arnie's never lived a day of his life. And it hurts a little. His own grandson. He should be proud of this, not ashamed. Driving into this area that was always above him. Going to see his own grandson, his own flesh and blood. That's a thing that decent people get to be proud of. Maybe Arnie isn't a decent person. Maybe this is his punishment for never being quite good enough.

He's on the street, stopping about ten yards from the front door of Oliver's building. A nice street. Three-storey buildings, all made into large flats. Coming to live here doesn't come cheap. This battered old car doesn't belong here any more than the battered old man driving it. Ninety-nine per cent of him wants to drive away. Forget it. Take the coward's way out. There's nothing to gain from being here anyway. This is going to go badly, and there's no way around that.

Sitting in the car for nearly an hour. A couple of people have walked past. Arnie still sitting there, still trying to persuade himself that he shouldn't be here. But that one per cent just won't be won over. The one per cent that says it doesn't matter how fruitless this is. Doesn't matter if it only confirms your worst fears. You have to know.

He's gotten out of the car. Walking up to the front door of the building. There are doorbells at the side, names of the owners beside them. Closing his eyes and pressing the buzzer. Hoping to God that nobody answers. Then he won't have to find out.

'Yes,' comes the voice.

'Oliver?'

'Yes,' is the reply through the intercom. One word of annoyed recognition.

'Can I come up? We need to talk.'

There's a pause of a few seconds. Arnie not sure if Oliver heard him or not. 'Fine, come up.'

There's a buzz and Arnie is pushing open the front door. Stepping into the building and taking a look around. A tiled floor, a large staircase in front of him. So this is what that sort of life pays for. Yes, it sure is nice to look at. Up the stairs into the corridor. A nice carpet on the corridor, which would last about a day in Arnie's building. Finding himself in front of Oliver's front door. Is a pretty home worth it? Does it matter that much?

The door's opening just as Arnie is raising a hand to knock. His grandson staring back at him. There's an angry look there. Peterkinney wasn't expecting his grandfather to turn up at the flat. Thought he would phone to complain. Whinge about the warning given to Glass. The fact he's here means it's been delivered. The fact he's here rather than phoning probably means he's very angry.

'What's up?' Oliver's asking. Standing in the doorway. He'd like to get through this without having to let his grandfather inside. Let the old man vent on the doorstep and then piss off home.

'Can I come in, please?' Arnie's asking.

There's something disconcerting about a man who should be angry and isn't. Peterkinney was waiting to hear venom in the old man's voice. An angry tremble. Thought he'd start shouting straight away. But he hasn't. He just sounds weary. Sounds like he's gone beyond the point where angry would do any good. That could be a good thing or a bad thing.

Peterkinney's stepping aside, pulling open the door. Letting his grandfather in for the first time. Arnie's stepping inside and stopping. Doesn't know where to go. Oliver's shutting the door and walking past him, leading him through to the kitchen. Large kitchen, wide-open space and everything in white. Seems appropriate, somehow. When he thinks of conversations with his grandfather, it's always in the kitchen of the flat.

'You're up and about late,' Oliver's saying. Polite conversation. Try and keep the tone civil for as long as possible.

'I have reason to be,' Arnie's saying.

Oliver's sitting down at the unnecessarily long kitchen table. Gesturing for his grandfather to take a seat opposite, but Arnie's shaking his head.

'I won't sit. What I have to ask won't take long. I don't think you'll want me to stay long anyway. I need to know something, Oliver. I want you to be honest with me. Did you send someone to Alex's flat today? Someone to collect money, or give a warning?'

Seems like Arnie is going for the old 'I'm so disappointed in you' routine. Fair enough. Oliver will counter with a well-practised 'I had no choice, what could I do?' performance. Hopefully they can keep the conversation calm and it'll all be over in a few minutes.

Oliver's starting with a sigh. 'Look. I have a business to run. I made that very clear from the start. I needed to know that Alex was making an effort. That he wasn't messing me around. Playing on our old friendship. And I found out he was,' Oliver's saying with a shrug. 'I found out that he was out partying with his girlfriend. Spending all kinds of money to keep a smile on her face. Not spending any to put a smile on mine. He went out and spent bucketloads the night before he came to me and said he was skint. What am I supposed to do, huh? Makes my business look weak, and makes me look like I don't know how to run it. I had to act. What other choice did I have?'

'You sent someone round to beat him up. Deliver a warning.' Not a question. Just a sad acceptance that his worst fears are correct.

'I had no choice,' Oliver's saying. Saying it quiet. Less and less sure of his position.

'Your fellow went round to the flat and Alex wasn't there. Did you know that?'

Oliver's shaking his head. 'I haven't heard from my man.' A shrug. 'Lucky for Alex then.'

Arnie's looking at him and there's disgust on his face. This is closer to the anger Oliver expected, although its reason remains unknown to him. 'Lucky? Lucky, you think? Lucky for Alex maybe, not so lucky for Ella. She was there. She was there on her own.'

Oliver's looking down at the table and shaking his head. 'Shit, well, that was unlucky.' Some muscle will take advantage of women in these situations. Treat them in ways they shouldn't. If the scruffy bastard he sent did something inappropriate, then he'll ditch him. Doesn't want his company having a reputation for things like that. Would make him look grubby in the eyes of men like Chris Argyle. 'Shame for the girl,' he's saying, 'but it was Alex who put her in that position. Borrowing money he couldn't pay. If she wasn't badly hurt, then I don't know, she might consider herself lucky as well.'

Arnie's just staring at him. Looking down at the seated Oliver. His grandson, but it doesn't feel like that any more.

The words coming out of his mouth would never have come from the boy he knew. The boy he helped raise. This little bastard is someone else entirely. Someone he can no longer bring himself to care about.

It comes without warning. Arnie looking at his grandson. Not intending to react. And then lurching at him, throwing a wild punch. Arnie's knuckles brush through Oliver's hair. Doesn't catch him. Doesn't do any damage. But Oliver's dipped sideways to avoid the shot, and is now on his knees on the floor. Looking up at his grandfather. A shocked expression. In a normal situation, he would fight back. Start throwing punches, aim to hurt. He's done collection work, he knows how to fight. But not this time. This is still his grandfather. The same old man he always was.

'She's dead, you silly little bastard,' Arnie's saying. Saying and not shouting. Keeping it quiet. Fighting so hard to resist the urge to punch again, because what good is that going to do? 'The thug you sent beat her to pieces. Killed her. The girl's dead and you ordered it. It was you, Oliver. You did it. You killed her.'

Know what? It's not the suggestion that he killed her that annoys Oliver. It's the suggestion that he made a mistake. He didn't kill her, the muscle he sent did. The muscle blundered, obviously. Last thing you ever do is draw police attention towards your boss. Oliver knew that back when he was working for Marty. Knew it as sure as he knew anything when he worked for Roy Bowles. The man his grandfather got him a job with. The moralist standing over him and the gunrunner he got Oliver a job with, now in jail after the Jamieson shit-storm.

'I didn't mean for her to be harmed. That was never my intention,' he's saying. He wants to sound sorry, but he doesn't. Can't quite control his tone. He sounds annoyed and he sounds a little dismissive, but he doesn't sound sorry.

Arnie's looking down at him, Oliver still on his knees. It would be so easy for the boy to look sorry. So easy for him to sound like he knows what regret is. Just fake it. Just this once. But he can't even be bothered. On his knees, and he can't make the effort to be sorry. A shake of the head.

'I don't know you any more,' Arnie's saying. Turning and walking out of the kitchen. Along the corridor and opening the front door. He knows his disapproval means nothing to Oliver. Doesn't care. Oliver just stopped meaning anything to him.

8

Arnie was sitting in the kitchen with a cup of coffee when Glass got out of bed. Had a shower, put on last night's clothes. Went into the kitchen and started making a cup for himself without saying anything. Doesn't feel like talking. Not to Arnie. Not to anyone. If the world stayed silent forever, Glass would be happy with that. Talking will remind him.

He heard Arnie leaving last night. Heard him coming back. He was gone a while, longer than Glass expected. When he heard Arnie leaving, he guessed where he was going. Going to see his grandson. Going to confront him with the news of Ella's death. That's what Glass would have done. Makes sense. Oliver's family. Go and warn him about the inevitable police investigation. Go and warn him that he crossed a line, perhaps. But that would have been a short visit, and Arnie was gone for a long time. Doesn't occur to Glass that he spent an hour sitting outside Oliver's flat before he plucked up the courage to go in. But Glass won't ask. Doesn't want to know.

'You sleep?' Arnie's asking him. Painfully obvious that Arnie didn't. Would be obvious to Arnie that Glass didn't either if he was alert enough to see it. It's been too long a night to be alert now.

'Little bit,' Glass is saying. 'On and off.' Stirring his mug and sitting opposite Arnie. Not looking him in the eye.

A few moments of silence. 'The police will want to talk to you,' Arnie's saying. No doubt they won't be far away.

Glass is sighing. Taking another sip of coffee. Doesn't want to speak to the police. Doesn't want to have to tell them the truth. For so many reasons. The fact that Ella dying was his fault. He borrowed money he couldn't pay back. She ended up paying for it. Doesn't want to be a coward either. They'll ask him if he knows who was behind the beating. He'll say no. Has to. If he says yes he's a grass. He'll be punished severely. Doesn't want that. He's afraid of that. And he doesn't want to talk to the police anyway. They might ask about Alan Bavidge. So that's plenty of reasons. Add the fact that he doesn't want to hurt Arnie by having Oliver arrested. All adds up to a justified silence.

'I don't want to talk to anyone,' Glass is saying.

'You'll have to, eventually,' Arnie's saying. His tone serious. 'You need to think about what you're going to say.'

Fishing for a clue. Wanting to know what Glass plans to tell the police when he speaks to them. Wanting to know out of concern for Oliver, Glass assumes. Assumes wrong. Wanting to know out of concern for Glass. Arnie's terrified that Glass will say something stupid. That he'll confess all about the man he murdered and get himself put away. He's prone to emotion. He might blurt something out during a difficult

426

interview. There's no need for him to throw his own life away over this.

It's a horrible thing to think. Arnie knows it, doesn't need to be told. But he has been thinking that this is an opportunity for Glass, if he's smart enough to take it. This is a chance to separate himself fully from his old life. Didn't want it to be this way. Didn't want to see the girl dead. She was a nice girl, and she was desperate to help Glass. But she lived in the criminal world, and didn't seem to know how to live any other way. Being separated from that is a chance. Arnie won't say that, obviously. He's not that crass. But this is an opportunity that he won't let Glass squander.

'I don't know what I'll say,' Glass is saying quietly. 'I think I want to go out for a walk. Clear my head, you know.'

'Sure,' Arnie's saying. 'Take your phone. If I hear anything, I'll call you.'

Glass is just happy to be out of the flat. Thinking about Ella. She's gone. She was what it was all about for him. The life, the thrill, the money, the danger. It was all encapsulated in her. She was the life. Worth every risk, every sacrifice. He destroyed that. Destroyed her and destroyed the life. He knows it's his fault. His and Peterkinney's. Can't get away from that. Peterkinney sent someone to collect the money and they killed Ella. Glass doesn't need to be told to know. There was nobody else who would have done it.

And he'll get away with it. Like he always does. People like him always fucking do. They get away with it. They live their lives getting away with the sort of things that people like Glass have to pay the price for. How is that fair? A man like Peterkinney can get away with this. A man like Glass never would. People like Peterkinney have protection. Connections which keep them safe. Other people willing to shield them for the right price. There's always a price they can afford to pay. Not Glass. He can't pay any price at all.

He was walking aimlessly, but now that he's found himself in the vicinity of a pub he knows, he might as well go in. Getting a drink, sitting down. Alone in the corner. Nobody will bother him here. The background murmur of other people's conversations doesn't bother him. This is as close to silence as you get in the city. Close enough to silence for Glass to think about his position.

He has enough money in his pocket to sit in that pub for a few hours. So he does. Sits there nursing his drinks. Tells himself that he's thinking about his position. Thinking through all of his options, but he isn't. He doesn't have a lot of options. If he was sober and smart, he would realize that he's always known what he's going to do. Known it since he left the flat.

Instinct. Everyone has it. Some instincts are better than others. Some people are a lot better at listening to their instincts than others. If this was Peterkinney, he would have spotted what he was going to do within seconds. Acted on it within minutes. Not Glass. He's been trying to drown his instinct in booze. Trying to pretend that he isn't going to do what he knows he's going to do.

He's just drunk enough. Not so drunk that he can't walk from A to B. Not so sober that he'll be able to talk himself out of this. He's out of the pub and realizing how much time has passed. It's gloomy now. Afternoon long since killed morning. Afternoon falling to evening. And he's starting to walk. Knowing exactly where he's going. Knowing exactly what risk he's taking.

Back to his flat. Convinced there should still be cops there. There aren't. They've been and gone. Not a lot of flat for them to look around. They'll have done everything there is to do before looking for people to interview. That'll be the last part of their investigation. Interviewing people like Glass. That's where their good information will come from. Glass doesn't know it, but they found fingerprints in the flat that have got them excited. Known violent offender James Holmes. They're now trying to find him. Find out who he works for. They're going to look for Glass as well, but Holmes is the current priority.

There's nobody to stop him unlocking the front door. Nobody inside the flat. He's standing inside the door, looking at the spot on the floor where she was lying. Last time he came in this door, he found her lying there. Panicked. Didn't know what to do. Maybe if he'd acted faster . . . No. Don't

429

start thinking like that. You know what you're here for. Get it and get out.

Through the living room, down the corridor and into the bedroom. Their bedroom. Turning to the wardrobe. There's something on the door. Markings that weren't there. Some police thing, he figures. Why on the wardrobe, he doesn't know. Then he's stopping. Damn it all. They'll have gone through the wardrobe and taken the money. The little money Ella had set aside. She kept that money to cover emergencies. The ones she knew about, anyway. They'll have taken it when they searched the wardrobe.

But they haven't. They found it. The two shoeboxes on the floor have been opened and emptied. The shoes put back in both. The little bundle of money taken out of one. Placed back on top of the shoebox. Obviously not enough that they would consider it significant. It's not suspicious. There isn't enough of it to be evidence.

Glass is picking it up. Looking through it. There isn't much there. He never counted it before. Knew it was there, but it was hers and not his. He respected that. She didn't talk about it to him. Didn't hide it from him, as such. He saw her putting money in there, she let him see. It was for a rainy day. Pay bills that crept up on them, maybe. Or maybe it was for a treat. Saving up to get something nice, something she could be proud of.

One hundred and eighty quid. He thought there would be

more. Seemed like the bundle was bigger in the past. Enough for them to live off for a little while. Maybe there was more. Maybe someone took it. One of the cops? No. If there was ever more, Ella spent it. Something came along and she had to dip into her savings.

So it's a hundred and eighty quid. There's another twenty in the biscuit tin in the kitchen. Two hundred quid. Not enough. Not even halfway to being enough. But he has to try. His instinct has been trying to tell him for hours now. He's come to realize it eventually. No matter how much or how little money he has, he has to try this. Won't ever forgive himself if he doesn't. Won't ever stop regretting it. He's stuffing the money into his pocket and making his way out of the flat.

9

Marty told him to bring a couple of his men with him. Patterson's taking him at his word. Called up Conn Griffiths and Mikey Summers. His two best. Griffiths has become his senior man since Bavidge's death. Not as sharp as Bavidge, and there isn't the same bond there, but it's a good relationship. A man he trusts. Smart, tough and always willing to put the business first. Summers is tough. Properly tough. One of the best muscle in the city. You could have a conversation about who stands as the best muscle in this city. Nate Colgan would get a lot of mentions. Jamie Stamford has profile. Patterson rates Summers as high as either of them.

He feels he needs them both. Would be more comfortable with more than just these two. It's late afternoon and he's meeting Griffiths and Summers. They'll travel to the pub together. Ex-pub. Future pub. At the moment it's just a convenient empty location, in a quiet area. Businesses around it, all of which will be closing right about now. They'll be perfectly silent by the time the meeting starts. A good choice of location by Marty.

And that's what makes Patterson nervous. This has all been organized by Marty. Patterson's been tied to Marty for months now, but it takes more than that to erase years of mistrust. He would feel better if he'd seen the location beforehand. Would feel better if he'd sat in on Marty's conversation with Potty. All Patterson knows is that the conversation happened, and Potty is going to be there.

They're in the car together. Griffiths driving, Patterson in the passenger seat, Summers in the back. The usual silence that comes before a big job. They're all familiar with it. They've all done big jobs in their lives. They've all learned that the time to ask questions has passed. If there was something you wanted to say, you've missed your chance. Summers wanted to suggest taking guns, even though he knew it would be refused by the other two. Griffiths wanted to know more about who Potty would take with him. He always has someone with him, even if it's only his driver. Doesn't want to walk into an ambush. This could be a good chance for Potty to decapitate Patterson's business. But they didn't ask before the journey began, and now they never will.

Griffiths knows the area, says he knows where the pub is. These moments, you start to doubt everyone. The last couple of minutes before you reach the destination. Can you trust Marty? Can you even trust Griffiths and Summers? People who have given you no reason not to trust them. That's the nature of the business. People give you no reason to doubt them, and then promptly let you down. It's what a good set-up looks like.

433

'That's it, up there on the left,' Griffiths is saying. Slowing down the car before he needs to. Buying Patterson a few seconds to take in the scene.

Not much to look at. A lot of small buildings seemingly scattered at random. Less a street than an accident of bad planning with a road through it. The pub is a small, flat, single-storey building. Even by the standards of this street, its architect was one lazy, talentless bastard. Patterson's shaking his head. What a terrible place to build a pub. Who the hell would drink there? Nobody, and it doesn't matter a jot. Currie's bought it to pretend that people are drinking there. Helps him explain his earnings.

There are three cars parked out on the street. One will belong to Marty. One will belong to Potty. The plan was that Potty should get there first. Get him into the building before he knows Patterson's going to be there. Stop him getting spooked. That's what Marty said. The third car? Marty said he was going to bring some people of his own, but surely not two carfuls of them.

'Pull up behind them,' Patterson's saying. They've come this far. Spent months cultivating the relationship with Marty. He's put his eggs in this basket. Has to go for it now.

They're getting out of the car. Griffiths making a little noise and then nodding to the car in front when Patterson looks across. There's someone inside. Patterson's on the pavement now, ducking slightly to look into the car. Summers is doing the same thing, neither of them acting with the kind of subtlety they ought to pride themselves on. The driver is sitting in the car. Looking straight ahead. Looking bored. Making every effort not to look at the people who have just turned up. He knows better than that. Potty's driver. Has to be. A man experienced enough to know that you don't stare back at men like Billy Patterson and Mikey Summers.

The three of them are stopping outside the front door of the pub. No reason. Just seems like a smart idea to stop for a second, gather breath, and prepare yourself. Patterson's turning and nodding to the two men behind him, and pulling open the door. The three of them disappearing inside.

It's not a big place. And it's not glamorous. Dingy, cold and unwelcoming. To be fair, it's been shut for six months, although it doesn't look much worse than it did when it was open. The bar directly in front of you. Tables to the left of the room. Stained benches under the stained window opposite the bar and beside the door. The kind of benches a hygienic person steers clear of.

Not that the layout or the decor matters to Patterson. It's the people. Two large men sitting on stools at the bar. Both staring at the door, obviously waiting for the new arrivals. Another large man standing in front of the benches. Patterson doesn't recognize any of them. Sitting at a table, off to the left, are the two men he does recognize. Marty Jones and Potty Cruickshank. Sitting side by side behind a table, their

chairs facing the door. Both waiting for Patterson. Both looking rather pleased with themselves.

'Billy,' Marty is saying loudly, 'come over and join the
conversation.'

The invitation was to Patterson alone. Implied, an order
for Griffiths and Summers to stay where they are. Show no
hesitation. This was always supposed to be part of the plan.
There's nothing here he ought to be concerned about. Unless
some of these men belong to Potty. Then he has a lot to be
worried about. That smile on Potty's flushed face is worthy of
concern.

Patterson's across and pulling up a chair at the table. Sitting facing both men. Potty looks smug, as per usual. The
biggest man in the collection business, pun intended, who
didn't have to earn any of it. Was handed to him on a plate by
his uncle. He looks comfortable where he is right now. Sitting
next to Marty and opposite Patterson. Marty, he looks a little
different. He has the ebullient, playful look of the young playboy. The look he used to have a lot. The look of a man playing
a game he wrote the rules to. The look that had disappeared
these last few months.

'Well, this is a good opportunity, wouldn't you both say?'
Marty's saying. All the enthusiasm he can muster. 'Let's talk
business. Billy, why don't you start?'

That got a glance from Potty. Wasn't expecting Patterson
to get the first go at this, but that's okay. Marty's been the

perfect host since Potty arrived. Made it very clear that tonight they will wipe Patterson and his best boys from the equation. Let him have his little moment first.

'You killed Alan Bavidge,' Patterson's saying to Potty. Got caught on the hop by Marty. Wasn't expecting to be thrown in quite like this. Should have had something smarter to say.

'Perhaps I did,' Potty's saying. The fat man's sweating, but he still looks relaxed. 'You understand the nature of this business, Billy. Sometimes these things have to be.' Smiling, like he knows the words coming out of his mouth are bullshit. Like he knows it doesn't matter.

'The only thing that will pay for that is a 100-per-cent cut of your business,' Patterson's saying. No idea if he's on solid ground here or not. Glanced briefly at Marty before he said it, but Marty was looking happily at Potty. Marty might be about to chuck him under a bus. Cut a better deal with Potty. That's what it feels like. If those guys behind him belong to Potty. Jesus, this could be it. His last words could be idiot bluster.

Potty's laughing. 'A 100-per-cent cut, is it? That is terrific. Is that all you're looking for? Well, you should have asked sooner. Ha, that's terrific. Why don't I give you my firstborn as well, eh? Young man, you are in for one nasty surprise.'

Potty's turning to look at Marty. Looking into the smiling face of Marty Jones. Marty raising his eyebrows slightly as he realizes both men are looking at him. Marty turning his head and looking at Patterson, still smiling happily.

'Surprises. Yeah. Thing is, Potty . . . You don't mind if I call you Potty, do you? Thing is, you did have his man killed. A good man, by all accounts. Did you no harm. That's what I heard, anyway.'

Potty's laughing again, but he can't hide the nerves this time. The mood with Marty was so positive when he arrived. They chatted, they joked around. Marty still has that smile on his face. But there's something more sinister there now. He isn't laughing with Potty. He's laughing at him.

'Well, now, hold on,' Potty's saying, trying to meet Marty's smile with one of his own. This might be some sort of game of Marty's. Lulling Patterson in. 'The business is the business. These things have to be done.' Turning now to face Patterson. 'I apologize for your loss.' Said with such sarcasm. Then looking back to Marty, who isn't smiling now at all.

Marty's shaking his head. A quick glance over Patterson's shoulder at the men there, then looking back at Potty. 'I don't think sorry is going to be enough,' Marty's saying. 'See, we have a problem here. Three people. That's one too many. We need to reduce the numbers. Better for the industry as a whole if we do. I need someone who can take over my books while I focus on other things. Someone I can trust.' Trailing off and looking back and forth between Patterson and Potty.

Now Marty's laughing. Laughing enough to unsettle both Potty and Patterson. Both are looking at him, waiting for some explanation. Marty's getting serious now. This is fun for him. This position of power. He worked so long and so hard to get here. These two will never appreciate that. They both think he played his way to power. They'll never appreciate the shit he had to wade through. The bodies he had to climb over. Done a lot of things he's working hard to forget, and they'll never respect that. Oh well.

'There's a problem, Potty. A serious one. A lot of people don't like you. See, it's not just Billy here. He has every reason not to like you. Getting someone to kill his mate like that. That was too much. But other people don't like you either. Other people see you as part of the old guard. They don't like the old guard. Complacent old men who held everyone else back. Our organization has to show that it's still fresh. We got to make people see that we're the future. Sorry, big man, but you don't belong in the future.'

Marty's getting up from his seat. Nodding to Patterson to follow him. They're both walking across the floor of the pub towards the door. Neither man looking back at Potty. The large man sitting on the small chair at the table. Not moving an inch. Watching them go. Watching as the two men who had been sitting at the bar move to block the exit. Potty watching them. Knowing this is the end for him.

Marty's politely holding the door open for Patterson, Griffiths, Summers and the guy who had been standing at the benches. Out onto the pavement. The guy from the benches is getting into the passenger seat of Potty's car.

'Don't worry about the driver,' Marty's saying to Patterson. 'He's bought and paid for.'

Two men are getting out of a car that wasn't here when Patterson went in. One he doesn't immediately recognize. Late thirties, maybe early forties. That's a guess. That fellow's looking at the ground as he walks silently past them and into the pub. That's when the penny drops. Russell Conrad, freelance gunman. The bigger one behind him Patterson recognized instantly. That was Nate Colgan. Patterson's watching him go in. A few seconds after the door closes behind them, it opens again. The two men from the bar make their way out and over to the extra car. Colgan and Conrad must be the kill squad. No one else required.

'You could have warned me about the performance,' Patterson's saying quietly.

Griffiths and Summers are making their way back to the car, mumbling to each other. If you listen carefully, you can just hear Griffiths use the words 'fucking heart attack', but you'd have to be listening carefully. Doesn't want Marty to hear him complain.

'Yeah,' Marty's saying. 'I guess. But you didn't really think I would ditch you for him, did you? That reptile? The one who just went to Alex MacArthur for support?'

Patterson's shrugging. 'It's an unpredictable business.'

Marty's laughing. 'It is that. We need to get together and discuss you taking control of my books. Not like they're all that huge, but still, best to be prepared. You might want to take one or two staff of mine on board as well. Although there's a few you can ditch. Good opportunity to clear out the shit. Have to move fast to grab some of Potty's business as well.'

He's about to say more when his phone starts to ring. Taking it out of his pocket and looking at it. Frowning as he sees the name on the screen. 'I better take this. I'll call you tomorrow morning, set a time for the meeting.' Taking a few steps the other way up the street and answering the phone. A private conversation.

Patterson's made his way back to the car. Dropping into the passenger seat. Griffiths is starting the car, pulling out. Potty's car has gone, Marty's muscle are pulling away. Three men exhale at once, and then laugh a little. Tension making its happy departure.

'That was a bit more drama than it needed to be,' Griffiths is saying.

'It was,' Patterson's agreeing. But they got what they wanted. A deal with Marty that makes them the only collection business in the Jamieson organization. With Potty gone, they're very close to being the biggest in the city. But it's more than that. It's revenge for Alan. 'It was worth it though,' Patterson's saying quietly.

10

Instinct has carried Glass this far. No reason to rely on anything else now. There are a few places he could go, but he's settled on Mark Garvey. Nobody likes Garvey. A complete bastard and an absolute show-off, but he's the one Glass is going to. Not sure why, but instinct tells him that Garvey will take two hundred quid. Can't think of anyone else who would sell to him at low price.

It's not as though Glass knows a lot of places he could go for help. Spikey Tokely for one. But Spikey wouldn't help him for two hundred quid. Might not help him at all. You go to the person you're sure is willing to give you a hand. Someone who won't apply any standards to their sales, so long as the money is paid.

He's been walking for longer than he thought. Feels like hours, but it probably isn't. Lost track of time ages ago. Sitting in that pub. It's getting dark now. Must be early evening, he figures. Time doesn't matter. Just distance that matters. He's got a lot more walking to do, and the backs of his legs are already beginning to hurt. He's not used to this much effort. He'd rather be back at the flat, warm under the covers in bed. But that's not an option now.

That life, it's gone. All of it. You can't just take Ella out of his life and expect him to keep living the rest of it as normal. Doesn't work that way. In Glass's mind, all of it was tied together. One part of it falls, it all falls. Ella, the flat, the life. He'll never go back to any of it. Couldn't bring himself to. It's all gone now, and he has to move on. Has to move on by cutting all those ties to that life.

That's what he's doing now. Yeah, he's a bit drunk, so it sounds much nobler to him. But he knows it has to happen. What he's going to do tonight has to be done. Otherwise this follows him for the rest of his life, however long that happens to be.

He's nearly there now, which is a relief. He's feeling the tiredness of too little sleep and too much effort. He won't rest though. If he stops to rest, he won't start again. He knows that. Knows he's too much of a coward to motivate himself a second time. Now or never, as they say. So he's pushing on. Onto the right street. Knowing which house it is. Everyone knows where Mark Garvey lives, and what he sells from that house. As long as Garvey hasn't moved, he'll be okay. Now he remembers who pointed out Garvey's house to him. Told him it might be useful one day. Oliver Peterkinney. One of the last times they hung out together. That wasn't long after Peterkinney started working for Roy Bowles. Man, that feels like a long time ago now.

Glass is walking up to the door. Knocking twice and

443

stepping back. He doesn't know how Garvey will react to this. Instinct said this was the guy to try. No better option. But it's late and he might not react well to a drunk young man turning up on his doorstep. But then, how else does a man like him make a living?

The door's opening. Garvey looking back at him. A deep frown because he doesn't immediately recognize the young man before him. Then a creeping recognition, although he's still not quite sure.

'I need to buy a gun from you,' Glass is saying.

Garvey's leaning his head out the door and looking up and down the street. Letting Glass know that that's not the sort of sentence you blurt out on a man's doorstep. 'That right?' he's saying.

'Yeah, but I don't have much money. But I need it. I really do. I have two hundred quid.'

Garvey's snorting. 'I think you came to the wrong house, kid,' he's saying, and moving to close the door.

'Please. They killed my girlfriend last night. I need that gun. They killed her and I need the gun.'

Garvey's looking down at him. Pausing. Thinking this through. Some dumb emotional kid running round with one of his guns is usually bad news. Sort of thing he's careful to avoid. Only sell to people you trust. People who know how to use and then safely get rid of a gun. Only sell to people you're sure won't be caught and blab about where they got the gun they were caught with. But chances come along. The opportunity to ingratiate. You don't pass that up.

'Hold on there. I'll be back in a couple of minutes,' Garvey's saying. Closing the front door and bounding upstairs to the spare room. Getting one of his mobiles out from the drawer in his desk and ringing the only number stored on it.

Takes a while for Marty to answer it. Must be busy. Always busy these days. Answering the phone with a curt hello. Sounds like he's outside; there's a car driving past.

'Marty, Mark Garvey. Listen, I got a kid at the door you might be interested in. The Glass kid. Remember him? Wasn't he pally with that Peterkinney boy you were after?' Marty told Garvey the story at a party. How Peterkinney screwed him over. His way of making sure Garvey knew that Peterkinney was *persona non grata*. That any man who sold him weapons would be an enemy of Marty's.

'He was. What does he want?'

'Says someone killed his girlfriend last night. Looking for a gun he can't afford. Revenge, probably.'

There's a pause while Marty thinks about it. Garvey allowing him the time to work it out. If it was one of Marty's boys that killed the girl then this is a warning. Letting him know that Glass is on the prowl. If it wasn't one of Marty's then this might be an opportunity for him. Let Glass cause problems for someone else.

'Sell him the piece. I'll make up the difference.'

'You don't need to do that, Marty. Just thought I'd clear it with you first. I'll catch up with you sometime,' he's saying. His way of saying that he's doing Marty a favour here and that he expects something in return.

'Sure,' Marty's saying, and hanging up. Obviously it's not one of Marty's boys that did the deed then.

Garvey's out into the corridor and pulling open a cupboard door. Opening a suitcase on the floor and taking a small handgun from the inside lining. He doesn't make a fantastic effort to hide his stock. If the police come calling, they'll turn the place upside down anyway. No such thing as a good hiding place. You make a little bit of effort to hide the stuff, but you're just inconveniencing yourself to do more.

He's wrapped his hand in a cloth before he handles the gun. Now he's stuffing it into one of the large Jiffy bags he keeps in the cupboard. Making his way quickly downstairs. Opening the front door. Glass is still there. Looks like he hasn't moved an inch. Perfectly still and perfectly miserable.

'Let's see your money,' Garvey's saying quietly.

Glass is reaching into his pocket and pulling out a bundle of notes. Some twenty-pound notes, some ten, some five. Always a sign that the person wasn't prepared for the purchase. That this is a rush job, bringing together any note they can lay their hands on. Garvey's reaching out and taking it, handing the Jiffy bag to Glass.

'It's loaded,' Garvey is telling him. 'If you get caught with it, you do not tell anyone where you got it from. You got that?'

But Glass has already turned away and is walking down the front path to the gate. No desire to stay and chat. No desire to stay and hear a rule book he already knows. He'll never talk to anyone about the gun. Never would. He's not even thinking about it. Just walking along the street with the Jiffy bag in his hand for all to see. He knows exactly where he's going now.

11

Arnie's waited and waited. Hoping that Glass will come back to the flat of his own free will. He wasn't emotional when he left. Just worried about the police coming to talk to him. Something they will eventually do and something Glass will have to face. Needs time to get used to that idea. Just wait and the boy will come back.

Sitting in the flat, waiting for the phone to ring. Waiting for the police to demand some answers. They should have called by now. Maybe they didn't think to ask the receptionist at the hospital. Well, if they're that desperate they'll put out some sort of appeal. Arnie worried about what Glass will tell them. What moronic act of self-sabotage he might be drawn into. But that's not the only worry.

What will Arnie tell them? They'll question him too. They're not stupid. Well, the ones that ask the important questions aren't. They'll spot the connection to Oliver. They'll begin to piece it together. Sitting in his armchair, wishing there were other people in his life. Sixty-four years old and he has so few people to care for. Even fewer who care about him. It would help if there was someone else he could talk to. Tell them about this. A different perspective.

But there's nobody. There's Arnie, there's Glass and there's Oliver, and that's the end of it.

It's well past teatime. Getting dark out there. A silent day. No Glass. No police. He wants to do something. Needs to do something. Needs to go and find Glass. He could be sitting in a police station right now. Might have gone straight there in the morning and started talking. Arnie's phoning Glass's mobile. It's ringing, but there's no answer. Calling again and being ignored a second time.

It would be switched off if he was in a police station. A deep breath. Think about it. Where would he have gone? An emotional boy, who just lost his wee girlfriend. He would have gone back to their flat. That's an obvious answer. He wanted to be away from everyone. Away from the world, and living in silence. His own flat would be a good place to do that. Time of crisis, flee for home. The right place to check first.

Going to his neighbour's flat first. He could take the bus, but there's a feeling of urgency settling in his guts. Wherever Glass is, Arnie wants to be there fast. If the kid doesn't know what he's doing, then he has to be stopped from doing it. His neighbour is still willing to lend the car. The more Arnie asks, the less willing he is, but Arnie's built up a decent store of goodwill.

Driving through the city, but the going is slow. End of the working day. Everyone eager to get away from whatever place they call work. Not all so eager to get to whatever place they call home. Arnie's struggling to get through the traffic. Not getting impatient though. Glass has had hours of a head start. Could be anywhere he wants to be at this point.

Parking outside the block and going inside. Up the stairs and along to the front door. The door of the next flat is wide open, although there's nobody there. Arnie's knocking on Glass's door. Standing back and waiting.

'Not in,' a voice is saying gruffly to him.

Arnie's looking to his right. A man of roughly his own age is now standing in the open doorway of the neighbouring flat. Stocky, wearing a T-shirt and tracksuit bottoms. Lighting a cigarette, which is presumably the reason he's standing in the corridor.

'Has he been here today, do you know?'

'Uh-huh. Here a while ago. Came and went . . . The girl died.'

'I know,' Arnie's nodding. Not sure whether this man has any idea who he is, or whether he's just making bad conversation. 'You don't know where he was going?'

'No. Came and went. Didn't have anything with him when he left . . . He do it?'

Arnie's looking at the man. Angrier than he should be. Hardly a surprise that people are speculating on who killed Ella. Hardly a surprise that people want to point the finger at Glass. He's an obvious target. A young man with no job and known connections to criminals. Too easy a target to miss.

'No, he did not,' Arnie's saying. Letting the anger rumble out. Turning and walking back along the corridor, leaving the neighbour to raise his eyebrows in barely bothered response.

Down the stairs and back out to the car. Glass came to the flat and then left. Why would he come to the flat? Maybe to collect something. Well, that doesn't take a lot of working out. What would he have in the flat? A weapon? No. Any weapon in the flat the police would have taken. Money, maybe. Money to drink. Money for drugs. Or money for a weapon, if you want to wake up and get real here.

Arnie's standing beside the car, hands on the roof. Take a deep breath. Think clearly. Would Glass do it? He's come to think of him as such a likeable boy. Always thought he was a loser when he was pals with Oliver. Thought he was a bad influence and a waster. Got to know him and decided that he was a waster, but one that could be saved. A goof with a good heart. And he's tricked himself into thinking of Glass that way ever since.

But he's thinking back to that night when Glass turned up at the flat. Thinking of that conversation. He can be as likeable as he wants, but Alex Glass has killed before. Killed because he was in debt and that was his way of getting out. Essentially, killed for money. This isn't money. This is something more powerful. He could do it again. Don't kid yourself, he could do it again.

Arnie's getting into the car. Heading for Peterkinney's flat, cursing himself for not going there first. Because he's a coward. That's what he's telling himself. He's a coward, and if he wasn't, he would have gone to Oliver's flat first. Even just to warn him. But he warned him last night. Told him what had happened. That was a warning. Ah, stop trying to persuade yourself that you've done enough. Stop hoping that the worst-case scenario won't play out. You're going to get what you deserve, and you deserve the worst.

He's turning onto the street where Oliver lives. No sign of drama at first, but as he pulls to a stop outside the building he can see something. People on the street. The front door to the building wide open. Arnie's jumping out of the car, leaving the keys in the ignition. Running to the steps at the front of the building. There are four or five respectable-looking people standing nervously around, some in their nightclothes. Not the sort of people to be seen in public in their nightclothes unless they had a very serious reason.

'You shouldn't go in there,' one of them is shouting at Arnie as he bounds past. Which is when Arnie knows he should go in. Knows he should have been here hours ago.

He's at the top of the stairs, struggling to catch his breath. He can see the door of Oliver's flat, ajar. Something lying on the floor outside the door. Looks like a big envelope. He's walking slowly towards the door when he hears the bang. A single gunshot, muffled and shocking. Arnie's stopped. Standing in the corridor, waiting for something else to happen. Taking baby steps towards the front door. Pushing it open. Nothing in the corridor before him. Walking slowly forwards. Pushing open the door to the kitchen, praying that his instincts are wrong.

12

Glass's legs are aching now. Walking through the streets with the Jiffy bag in his hand. Nobody cares. Nobody paying him attention. Just some young guy wandering the streets with a large padded envelope. Why should anyone care about that? There are stranger things to see in this city at this hour. Glass can walk without raising an eyebrow, even if he's walking unsteadily. Weaving a little, on autopilot.

He bumped into a woman. She said something to him, shoved him sideways. He said nothing. Kept on walking. Doesn't want to be stopped by her or by anyone. It has to be tonight. There won't be a second chance. If he gets into an argument with someone, they'll stop him. Maybe call the police, and then it'll never happen. He'll never be able to finish this. Never be able to give this the ending it needs.

Onto the right street. He knows it. Ewan Drummond told him where the building was, one night in a pub. Ewan seemed impressed. Been along here a few times in the last few months, just to see. See where his mate ended up. See what he left the rest of them behind for. Nice street. Nice buildings. Seems like it would have been worth leaving a lot behind for. The sort of place he always saw himself being in the future. Him and Ella. Maybe with kids. Both making good money in jobs they didn't have to be ashamed of. With loads of friends. This was where he saw it ending up. It started with the fun lifestyle they had in the beginning. It ended with the sort of life you live on a street like this. It was the bit in the middle that he never figured out. How do you get from one to the other?

Walking up the steps to the front door. Names next to numbers next to buttons. O. Peterkinney. Pressing the buzzer and waiting. It's dark now. Must be night-time. Wait a little longer than you usually would before you press the buzzer again.

A crackle. A voice. 'Yes?'

Doesn't know what to say. Hadn't thought this far ahead. 'It's Alex,' he's saying in response.

There's a long pause before Peterkinney's voice comes back at him. 'It's late.'

'I know. But . . . but we need to talk. We do, don't we?'

There's a pause. Another long one. Peterkinney is getting a lot of practice at these. 'Come up,' he's saying, and the buzzer on the door goes.

Glass is pushing his way inside. Out of the cold and into the building. He doesn't know where in the building the flat is. Walking along the short corridor and looking at the numbers on the doors. Neither of these. Turning back and going up the stairs. Slowly. By the time he's reached the top of the stairs, Peterkinney has opened his front door. Standing in the corridor waiting for him, wondering what's taking so long. The conversation with his grandfather was tough. This will be worse. Hurry it up, get it over.

Watching Glass walking the few steps from the top of the stairs and resisting the urge to shake his head. He looks a mess. Not just rough, but like he's aged a decade. Okay, sure, he's had a tough day or two. But there's something else. He looks wasted. Like he's staring just off-centre. He's got a big padded envelope in his hand. Carrying something around. Probably something belonging to Ella. Pictures, Peterkinney's betting. This is going to be one of those tearful look-at-what-you've-destroyed conversations. Glass has had a breakdown, Peterkinney's sure.

'Alex. You want to come in?' Better to have this conversation away from the neighbours. There might be shouting. There'll almost certainly be crying on Glass's part. He looks halfway to tears already, and they haven't started yet.

'I didn't want to do this, Oliver,' Glass is saying and shaking his head.

Pitiful. 'All right, okay. It's been tough, I know. Why don't you come in, we'll talk about it.' Doesn't really want this wreck in his flat, but it's the only option. He can talk to him. Maybe win him round. Make sure he leaves here with the right message to tell the police next time they're talking to him. He's smarter than Glass. He can get him under control.

But Glass isn't moving to come into the flat. He's still standing there, looking at Peterkinney. Then, like he's just realized he still has it, looking down at the Jiffy bag. Holding it in front of him and stuffing his free hand inside. Great, here come the photos or some other trinket of the past. Something that's supposed to provoke guilt and regret. Something that's supposed to drag Peterkinney down to Glass's emotional level.

Glass is pulling out the gun, holding it in front of himself for a second. Then dropping the Jiffy bag on the floor and pointing the gun at Peterkinney. Weird thing is, as soon as Peterkinney sees the gun, he's thinking about the Jiffy bag. He knows that the gun must have come from Mark Garvey. He's the one who uses those padded envelopes rather than a carrier bag. Takes him a few more seconds to realize that an emotional Glass is pointing a gun at him. He just doesn't associate Glass with danger.

'Come off it, Alex. Look, come in, we'll talk, okay. This? This isn't the right way to do this. Come in, okay. We can talk.'

Glass taking a step towards him, but not lowering the gun. He's not following Peterkinney's instructions; he's pushing him backwards with the point of the gun. Trying to take control of the situation. Neither of them spotting the neighbour who's emerged at the top of the stairs. He's seen the gun. The Good Samaritan who'll get everyone out of the building. Peterkinney's stepping back, leaving the door open for Glass to follow him in. Still doesn't feel dangerous. After all, it's Alex Glass. His old mate. He's harmless. He can be talked round.

'Inside. Go on,' Glass is saying, nodding in the direction of the first door he sees. The kitchen. Peterkinney's going slowly. Glass trying to shove the front door shut behind him, but not closing it all the way. Draught excluder at the bottom always catches on the carpet. You have to give it a good shove, which Glass hasn't. Doesn't seem to care. Walking along the corridor, gun still raised.

Peterkinney's walked backwards into the kitchen. Trying to work out how to get the gun away from Glass. Glass might be harmless, but the gun isn't. Only takes one slip and this goes south fast. He's obviously emotional. Went and got a gun and wants to show it off. Wants to scare Peterkinney. Fine, scare away. That's a reasonable punishment for the suffering Glass is going through. But let's get that gun out of emotional hands as quickly as possible.

'I heard what happened to Ella,' Peterkinney's saying. 'I really am sorry, Alex; I know how much she meant to you.'

That was supposed to calm things down, but it hasn't. It's gotten an angry reaction. A frown from Glass and the gun raised to point at Peterkinney's head. Peterkinney's taking an extra backward step. Raising both hands.

'Okay, look, why don't you tell me what you want to say.

You have something to say, right? Well, you go ahead and say it.'

Glass hadn't thought this far ahead. There was no plan to say something. Just to shoot. But he does want to talk. Suddenly, for no good reason, he wants to talk. He wants to get it out before it's too late.

'You don't care what I have to say,' Glass is saying. 'You just want to delay me. You want to sucker me into giving up the gun. I'm not stupid, Oliver. I'm not one of your dumb muscle. You remember when we met? I was the one that led the way. You were all quiet. Riding along on my coat-tails. I was the one got you into this business. My own fault. But I got you in, because you didn't have the guts to get yourself in. Have the guts to make money from other people's effort, yeah. Never the guts to do it yourself. I did it. I was always the one with the guts.'

'Okay. Yeah, you're right. You are. Nobody's saying you don't have guts, Alex, you do.'

'Shut up!' Shouted this time. Fed up of hearing that smug voice coming back at him. Telling him what he wants to hear without any genuine meaning. 'You lost it, Oliver. You got so far away from that guy you used to be. You ended up killing Ella.'

'I didn't kill her, Alex. Honestly, I didn't.'

'You did,' Glass is saying sadly. Lowering the gun half an inch. 'You killed her. I killed someone too. Yeah. Know what?

It's horrible. Worst thing you can do. It is. It's horrible. And when you do it, you have to pay a price. That's how it should be.'

He hasn't lowered the gun much, but it's enough to be a temptation. Enough that an impatient man would make a grab. Peterkinney's taking two steps forwards. Looking to grab the gun, pull it away. Thinking that Glass is just too emotional to stop him. But he isn't.

Glass was waiting for it. Knew that Peterkinney would be arrogant enough to try something like this. Thinking he could take the gun from Glass. Peterkinney's made two steps, but not a third. One shot, and he's falling backwards. It was loud. The shock of it has knocked Glass back a step. A tingling pain in his hands. Watching Peterkinney tumble to the kitchen floor. Holding his hands up to his chest. Breathing so loudly, trying to catch his breath.

Glass is walking towards him. You can see the blood spread out on his shirt, through his fingers. Glass is standing over him, looking down. Waiting for Peterkinney to look at him. Waiting to catch his eye. This matters. It matters because he can't stop thinking of what was going through Ella's mind when she died. The confusion and the fear. Knowing she couldn't defend herself. Peterkinney has to feel that.

Takes the better part of ten seconds for Peterkinney to look up. To look him in the eye. Glass is pointing the gun again. This time at Peterkinney's head. This time he pulls the trigger twice. There's no movement from Peterkinney. No reaction. Silence and stillness.

Glass is ignoring the sound of the neighbours shouting in the street. Ignoring everything. He isn't finished here. If he leaves this flat, he'll never finish this. Not the way it ought to finish. He won't move another step.

The horrible thing, what really gets to him now, is that this didn't feel bad. Didn't feel good either, but it didn't feel as bad as killing Bavidge. This should be worse. His friend. But it isn't. It's nothing. Maybe because he knows the ending. Ella gone. Peterkinney gone. The end of the life he thought he would have. The only life he wanted to live. Raising the gun and awkwardly putting the end of the barrel in his mouth. A little fumble. Pulling the trigger.

If you enjoyed **The Night the Rich Men Burned,**
you'll love the new novel from Malcolm Mackay
EVERY NIGHT I DREAM OF HELL

*Nate Colgan: a violent man; 'smart muscle' for the
Jamieson organization; someone to be afraid of.*

But now, with its most powerful individuals either dead or behind
bars, things within the Jamieson organization are beginning to shift.
When Nate, long working on the fringes of the business, is reluctantly appointed it's new 'security consultant', he can little imagine
how things are about to unravel.

It begins with an execution, a message; and soon the various fac-
tions within the organization are in chaos. Out of the confusion
comes one clear fact: a new group has arrived in Glasgow, and in
their quest for power they are prepared to ignite a war. But who is
behind the group? And why is the calculating Zara Cope – the
mother of Nate's child – suddenly back in town?

Meanwhile, DI Michael Fisher, buoyed by his recent successes in
finally jailing some of the city's most notorious criminals, is prowl-
ing on the edges of these latest battles, looking for his chance to
strike – before all hell breaks loose . . .

Out now

An extract follows here . . .

1

'People are terrified of you. You've given them good reason. We know how valuable that is.'

I sat listening and didn't say anything. This was the pre-amble to the subject that mattered: business. I already knew what was coming next. We were sitting in Kevin Currie's office, and I was listening to him speaking someone else's words.

'I don't need to tell you that there's a lot of stuff going on, a lot of stuff that needs to be sorted out,' Kevin went on.

I liked Kevin, but he was wasting my time. I knew there was a lot that needed sorting. He knew it. If he'd stuck his head out the window to alert a passer-by, there was a good chance they would already have known. Peter Jamieson ran the criminal organization Currie was a major part of, but Peter Jamieson was in jail. That meant people were trying to pick scraps from the organization, profit from temporary vulnerability while it still existed.

'There's a lot of little stuff,' Kevin went on, 'but even that's become more complicated. A man with your reputation, you can simplify all that. That'll be the first thing we want from you.'

There were shelves on the wall behind Kevin, and most of them were filled with what looked like folders. Supposed to make him look like the legitimate businessman nobody was dumb enough to believe he was. Maybe once he could fool people, but not since Jamieson went away. That change had made Kevin a bigger player than ever, one of the group of men running the organization day to day. So the neat little office of a legit businessman probably wasn't cutting it any more.

But it wasn't the folders I was watching. There was a little gold trophy at the end of one of the shelves, tucked in behind a leaning folder. Looked like the sort of thing you would give a mediocre amateur sportsman. I couldn't stop myself wondering what that was for. Kevin wasn't a sportsman; he was a guy in his late forties getting slowly fat and jowly.

'None of that sounds like a problem,' I said. I wasn't looking to sound nonchalant, but he was reading from a not particularly interesting script.

It was obvious what had happened, I probably don't even have to tell you. Peter Jamieson knew that I, Nate Colgan, was already doing work for the organization, and doing it well. He knew that he needed someone with a reputation to start throwing some weight around on his behalf, scare away the vultures. The serious attacks needed more defending than I could provide alone, but getting rid of the opportunists would remove the sense of weakness. So he made a call to

Kevin, told him to hire me permanently and told him what to say.

'I didn't figure it would be,' Currie said, nodding his head and letting his relief show. 'We need good people around us right now, Nate, we really do. Feels like we're taking shots from every side and I don't know where the next one will come from.'

'Anything new?'

He looked left and right, like someone might have snuck into that cramped little office. 'There is something. I mean, Jesus, you know what people are like, always complaining about something or other, but this seems different. We've had a couple of guys complaining about being pushed off their patch. Couple of other guys seem to have crossed over.'

'To?'

'Don't know. That's the problem. Well, we sort of know. Outsiders. Can you believe it? Like there aren't enough local sharks in the water. Some English guy seems to be trying to pick off business in the city.'

'You have an ID?' I asked. Knowing who the threats were was a big part of my job, and this was the first I had heard of this one. For the first time since I arrived in the office, Kevin had my interest.

'Just a name, Adrian Barrett. You heard of him?'

I shook my head, which I didn't like doing.

'English guy, like I said. We're trying to work out where he was before, who he might be working for, if anyone. Seems like he's putting the word around that he's in charge, but that could be a screen. The guy in charge doesn't turn up to do the donkey work, does he?'

Asking me, because he didn't know for himself. Kevin ran a counterfeit operation, a good and profitable one. The man knew how to run a business, let's make that clear right now. But he hadn't been involved in the dirtiest corners of the business until Jamieson's arrest pushed him there. Now he was up to his armpits in the filth and didn't know where to swim for safety.

'Not usually,' I said. 'Depends how big he is to start with, I suppose.'

'Aye, well, he's becoming an issue. Everything's becoming a fucking issue.' He was shaking his head and looking tired. The small things were mounting up, because the organization wasn't a well-oiled machine any more. It was causing the sort of frustration that coaxed a rare sweary word out of Kevin's usually pristine mouth. 'We have so many things we need to clean up,' he went on. 'There's stuff that still hasn't been done from months ago, stuff we should have gotten out of the way but we were too busy keeping our heads down. There's new stuff coming along all the time. You'll have to get on top of a lot of that.'

'Sure. What's my title?'

'You'll be security consultant, the job Frank MacLeod was

doing before he disappeared,' he said. 'You remember old Frank?'

I smiled a little and nodded. If you've been in the business in Glasgow at any point in the last forty years, you know of Frank MacLeod. I'd been in it for nineteen years, since I was eighteen. Disappeared was business speak for killed off and buried without the body ever being found. We knew he had been murdered on Jamieson's orders by a hitman called Calum MacLean, who then told his interesting little story to the police. But they couldn't peg the killing on Jamieson in any way, so that was another crime for which he wasn't convicted, despite the few for which he was.

'You'll be providing security advice for the club, some pubs, some bookies, some of the legit stuff that Jamieson has. You don't have to do anything though; the security mostly takes care of itself. We have people for that. Just put in the occasional appearance; I think that was all Frank used to do. Make sure the legit employees know your official job title in case the police ask them.'

That all made sense, but I'll admit I was a little uncomfortable having to step into Frank's shoes. I wasn't going to be doing his job, not his real job. He was a hitman, and that was a line I'd never crossed. But people would see me doing the 'security consultant' job he did and they would make the comparison. They would think I was now as important as Frank had been, and that would make me a target.

'Listen,' Kevin went on, 'there's a job I want you to start with, and I don't want you to laugh.'

I raised my eyebrows. When you're a freelancer, you can be choosy if you really want to be. Won't do much for your reputation, and your reputation is what's going to get you work, but it's up to you what jobs you do. If you can afford to say no and you want to say no, then go ahead and say no. Not when you're an organization man. When you're on the payroll, you have to do the jobs you're given.

'I want you to go round and kick seven bells out of Kirk Webster. I know that's a pathetic place to start, but it still hasn't been done and it needs to be.'

'Is that all that needs to be done?'

'Well,' Kevin shrugged, 'for now it is.'

I stood up and I shook his hand, like a new employee delighted to get through the job interview. There was something about that little office that made me want to play at being legit. That feeling had passed by the time I was out on the street, getting into Ronnie's car.

He had his little Astra parked in the single line of parking spaces in front of Currie's place. The car was too clean, I thought, maybe too new as well. It was a work car that nobody should ever spot. We were in Hillington, not far south of the river in an industrial area full of engineering firms and warehouses. Currie's was a single-storey white building, brick front and corrugated roof, the office at the back of a large warehouse, surrounded by respectability on a street lined with trees. Nothing to suggest that the warehouse was crammed with tremendously illegal goods.

'So?' Ronnie asked me.

'I'm on the payroll.'

'And me?'

'My first job will be to hire you in a security role. Congratulations.'

He started the car and we pulled away, me telling him about Kirk as we went. I'll tell you about Kirk in a minute, but first I want to tell you about Ronnie Malone. I'd met him a good time ago, when he was working in a grubby little hotel near Central Station. He was there for Currie, helping his men get rooms for whatever little business they wanted to hide from others. He was wasted there.

Ronnie was smart, and smart shouldn't be left booking rooms in a half-empty hotel for barely important counterfeiters and suppliers. I persuaded Currie to move him into my employ, let me work him into something more usable.

'You come and work with me, and we'll make good money together,' I had told him. 'You'll have cash, you'll have interesting work, you'll have the chance to move up fast.'

He'd looked at me like he was trying to find the world's politest way to say no. I wasn't there to hear no, however polite, so I leaned a little more heavily.

'All you're getting now is beer money, but you still go

down if someone points the finger at you. You've helped dangerous people do terrible things. The dough you're making isn't worth that. Let me help you make more, help make the risk worthwhile.'

He still looked reluctant, but he was a good boy, smart enough to realize that yes was the correct answer. So he came to work for me, and he was doing a decent job of it. Had a few little missteps, but every kid does when they're starting out. Kid: Ronnie had just turned twenty-six a few weeks before Currie put us on the payroll.

He drove me back to my house. 'You go look up Kirk Webster, find out what rock he's living under. Come pick me up when you've found him. I'll handle him. It won't be a two-man job.'

We were still at the point where Ronnie was doing the set-up and I was doing the dirty work. The process of educating him on how to get bloody was a slow one. He had to learn, because that was his job, but you don't rush a kid into it if you don't have to. I was taking my time, teaching him, because I enjoyed it that way.

2

I had a small terraced house in Balornock, on a long curving road in an area that wasn't quite as rough as it looked at a glance. Used to have the Birnie Court flats looming at the end of the road, looking ready for a fight. They had picked one with a demolition team and were gone by the time this happened. My house was the sort of place you would accept a man on a low income lives in. I wasn't on a low income, but I was happy for the world to make its usual assumptions and move quietly along. I needed just enough space for me and my few possessions and I wasn't fussy about location, location, location.

Don't get me wrong, I would have liked to share my home with someone else. More than one, actually, but there was no way I was going to let that happen. I was bursting with faults, some of which I may find time to tell you about, but that kind of selfishness wasn't one of them. I would have loved to have my daughter living with me, but I knew she was better off living with her mother's parents. I wasn't the man to bring up a young girl. And I would have liked to have a woman in my life, but that wasn't happening either. I was short-tempered, generally surly and lugging around a reputation that made me good at my job and bad at everything else. People were scared of me, and that cut bad as well as good.

There was someone sniffing around, a girl I liked, a girl I admired. Her name was Kelly Newbury, and because I liked her I was making a conscious effort to stay away from her. She wanted the security a relationship with me could give her. Have me be scary on her behalf. It was an invitation to trouble and other good things that I couldn't afford to get tangled in. Not with all this going on.

I took a sly look up and down the street as I made my way up to the front door because the habit of caution is a priceless gift. There was nothing out of place that I could spot, even if my eyesight isn't as good as it once was. It'll have to stay below its best because a guy like me doesn't turn up to his work bespectacled.

I pushed open the front door and stepped inside, already seeing something I didn't like. There was a folded piece of notepaper lying on the mat just inside the door that someone had put through my letter box when I was away getting gainfully employed. In the few seconds it took me to pick up the piece of paper I wracked my brains trying to think of any good news I had received in this way. None, ever.

Just needed a glance at the handwriting to know that this was more than bad news. This was a disaster waiting to happen. This was Zara Cope's handwriting. Messy but confident, her name scrawled across the bottom of the paper, the

Z much bigger than the rest of it, like a dyslexic Zorro.

I sighed my disapproval loudly to the empty corridor and wandered through to the living room. Putting music on always made it less likely that I would lose my temper, so I sat with a guitar being gently strummed in the background and read the note.

> *Nate,*
> *I was at your door but I guess you're not home.*
> *I don't have your number so I'm leaving this note instead.*
> *We need to meet. There are things we have to discuss,*
> *like the delivery I made for you some time ago.*
> *Remember that? There are other things to talk about*
> *as well.*
> *Zara*

There were little digs in there that were designed to annoy me. Let's start with the 'I guess you're not home' comment, as though I was hiding behind the fucking couch to avoid her. Even mentioning the delivery was uncharacteristically stupid. What if someone else had found the note before I got to it? And saying there were other things to talk about was just a cheap tease. There was a lot more to the letter than the words.

She was desperate, was the first obvious thing. Mentioning what she had delivered to me before she was arrested was her charmless little shot at reminding me I owed her money.

I didn't need to be reminded; the money was sitting in an account waiting for her to adopt it. The sooner she got it out of that account and into one of her own the happier I would be. I didn't want it anywhere near me. The money had started out its life attached to Lewis Winter, a walking catastrophe who had strolled to his early death when Zara was with him.

I should maybe give you a little history lesson at this point. Zara was the mother of my nine-year-old daughter, Rebecca. Zara hung around the business, using her looks and her smarts to make herself a fine little living. Or a living, anyway. She was a cut above the usual hangers-on, sharp as anything that's ever cut me. I fell for her hard; we moved in together; she had Becky. Didn't last though, and it was mostly my fault. Zara was twenty-one, looking for a fast life, and I was an angry and dangerous twenty-eight-year-old who wouldn't accept the world not constantly bending to my will. We were too young. She ran, and I let her. Becky went to live with Zara's parents, and it's been that way since.

Zara shacked up with Lewis Winter, a mid-level dealer, and when he was knocked off she came to me with some of his dirty cash and the last of his supply. The drugs needed selling and the money needed hiding until the dear Scottish police service kindly stopped looking for it. I did what I could to help her, because that seemed like the right thing to do for the mother of my child, and because I still didn't know how to say no to Zara Cope.

She was a special woman, one who had a power over me no other person has ever had. That didn't help her a damn when she got a three-month sentence for perverting the course of justice. Slap-on-the-wrist stuff for someone inside the industry, but she was no more than a hanger-on, and the sentence would have hit her hard. She got out and went off the radar for a while, didn't even come looking for her money. I knew she'd been away from the city for a lot of that time because I kept an eye out for her. Now, evidently, she was back. And yes, I did recognize her handwriting after all those years. There was almost nothing of her I had forgotten.

I turned the piece of paper over and saw that she'd scrawled a phone number on the back of it. A mobile number, underlined twice as though that would be the clincher if I was undecided. I was going to call her; she would gnaw at the back of my mind if I didn't. She could also cause trouble for me, and I had enough of that to keep me company already. Zara was on first-name terms with some of the skeletons in my closet, so I had to keep her smart mouth shut. And she knew that I'd organized the sale of drugs on her behalf, and the cleaning of the money it raised.

If you're interested in how, I had taken that little stash of drugs and dirty money she turned up on my doorstep with to Ross Kennedy to handle. He worked most closely with Angus Lafferty, Peter Jamieson's biggest drug importer, but his loyalties were made of smoke. He bought the drugs from me for less than their street value but as much as I could get in a hurry. He also cleaned the money for me, because making dirty things look respectable was always his greatest talent. Since then the money, about four and a half grand in all, had been gradually filtered into an account I'd opened to house it, waiting for Zara.

I was looking at that number and looking at the phone, wanting to call and wanting to crumple up the paper and pretend she had never existed. But I was going to call, both because I had to and because I wanted to hear her voice. I wanted to know that she was doing okay. Since she'd left the city she'd left my professional radar, so I had no idea what sort of state she was in.

The phone rang for a while before she answered it and I heard her voice, cold and flawless.

'This is Nate,' I said to her hello.

There was silence on the other end, the kind of heavy pause that insinuated horror. She wanted me to call so I was calling; it was up to her to say something next.

'You got my note.'

'It was inside my front door, so yeah.' Talking to Zara always ripped me in half. Part of me wanted to be nice to her, let her know that I still cared. The other part wanted to make sure that she kept her distance, stayed away from me and stayed away from Becky. That was the part that usually won, because protecting Becky from Zara's influence was my priority.

'Yeah. Well, we need to talk. I take it you still have the money you owe me?'

Needling away, emphasizing the word *owe* as though she had done me a favour. She hadn't; she had nearly led the police to me and had indirectly tied me to Lewis Winter through his product. It was a dangerous thing to be tied to a man whose murder was part of the MacLean confessions. It was hard to think of the last time Zara had done me a favour. Becky, I guess.

'The money I raised, cleaned and hid for you is sitting in a bank account, waiting.'

'Good.'

'You want the bank details? We can make this nice and simple and you can take the money without any fuss.'

This was me giving her the opportunity to keep her distance, something I didn't really want but that I thought we were both smart enough to understand was the best option. But she didn't keep her distance; she kept barrelling right on into my life.

'I want to see you,' she said, like it was a sudden revelation. 'We should meet up. There's stuff we need to talk about.'

I sighed, but I kept it light enough to make sure she didn't hear. I wasn't looking to provoke. Maybe ten per cent of my worry was about my own feelings at seeing her again, another twenty was about whatever trouble she was going to try and drag me into and the other seventy was the ever-present fear that she would want to talk about Becky. Whatever the split, it was still a hundred per cent of worry.

'Where and when?' I asked. I knew I was walking into trouble; this isn't me looking back and thinking I could have done something different. I knew it then every bit as much as I know it now. I went along with it because that was all I could do. The alternative was no, and no meant conflict with a dangerous woman at a dangerous time.

'Um, Wednesday, how about? I can come round to yours.'

'No,' I said, a little too quick and a little too hard. 'Wednesday, fine, but we'll meet somewhere.'

'Neutral territory, huh? Fine, if that's what you want. You know the Greek place right on George Square?'

'I do.'

'Midday?'

'Fine.'

She made a big effort to sigh down the phone at me. 'It's always a pleasure to talk to you, Nate.'

She sounded like she was about to say something else but she stopped herself and I heard a door closing in the background.

'You have company,' I said.

'Yeah, well, maybe now I have a chance of a grown-up conversation. I'll see you on Wednesday.'

I hung up without saying goodbye because I was feeling petty. Resentful might be a better word for it, and disturbed by the fact that I was jealous of whoever was having the conversation with her right now. Some new man in her life, hopefully giving her a good sort of life. I looked at the letter and I thought about its desperate contents, and I knew that whatever he was giving her, it wasn't a good life.

extracts reading groups

competitions books new

discounts extracts events

competitions extracts discounts

books new reading groups

events books extracts

extracts books reading groups

interviews events new books

events extracts

discounts new events interviews

new books events interviews new books extracts

events new

discounts extracts discounts books

www.panmacmillan.com

extracts events reading groups

competitions books extracts new

Please return/renew this item by the last date shown

**Herefordshire
Libraries**

*Herefordshire
Council*

Diana

SARAH BRADFORD

PENGUIN BOOKS

PENGUIN BOOKS

UK | USA | Canada | Ireland | Australia
India | New Zealand | South Africa

Penguin Books is part of the Penguin Random House group of companies
whose addresses can be found at global.penguinrandomhouse.com.

First published by Viking 2006
Published in Penguin Books 2007
Reissued with a new Afterword in Penguin Books 2017
002

Printed in Great Britain by Clays Ltd, St Ives plc

A CIP catalogue record for this book is available from the British Library

ISBN: 978-0-241-98070-5

www.greenpenguin.co.uk

MIX
Paper from
responsible sources
FSC® C018179

Penguin Random House is committed to a
sustainable future for our business, our readers
and our planet. This book is made from Forest
Stewardship Council® certified paper.

For William.

Contents

List of Illustrations   ix
Picture Credits   xiii

1   The Country Girl   1
2   A Norfolk Childhood   12
3   'I'm Lady Diana'   29
4   Enter the Prince   48
5   'Whatever Love Means'   63
6   The Beginning of the 'Fairy Tale'   91
7   'Di-mania'   107
8   'The Best Double Act in the World'   126
9   'Charles has gone back to his Lady'   144
10   A Dying Marriage   160
11   Diana Fights Back   180
12   The War of the Waleses   197
13   The Volcano Erupts   216
14   The First Step Towards the Abyss   233
15   The Inconsequential Years   254
16   Towards a New World   269
17   Fall from Grace   281
18   Out on a Limb   301
19   Stirring Beneath the Surface   321
20   Diana the Hunted   338

21 Fatal Summer   356
22 Death in Paris   373
    Diana: The Legacy   389

    Source Notes   395
    Select Bibliography   417
    Permissions   421
    Acknowledgements   423
    Index   425

List of Illustrations

1 Park House, where Lady Diana Spencer was born on 1 July 1961.
2 Diana's father, Johnnie, Viscount Althorp, with his bride-to-be, the Hon. Frances Roche, in 1954.
3 Diana's paternal grandmother, Lady Cynthia Hamilton (1892–1972).
4 Sarah Jennings, 1st Duchess of Marlborough.
5 The Spencers at Park House in 1972.
6 Diana as a child outside Park House.
7 Nine-year-old Diana goes to board at Riddlesworth Hall.
8 A pensive Lady Diana Spencer at the wedding of her eldest sister, Lady Sarah, to Neil McCorquodale in May 1980.
9 The 8th Earl Spencer and his second wife, Raine, in front of Althorp.
10 Lady Diana Spencer surrounded by press photographers outside her flat in Coleherne Court shortly before the announcement of her engagement to Princes Charles.
11 'That dress': a buxom, newly engaged Lady Diana Spencer with Prince Charles and Princess Grace of Monaco at a gala at the London Guildhall.
12 'We're all delighted': Charles and Diana posing with the Queen after the Privy Council granted the couple permission to marry.
13 The two women in Charles's life: Camilla Parker Bowles and Lady Diana Spencer at Ludlow racecourse.
14 Prince Charles with another close woman friend – Lady Tryon, known as 'Kanga', at the christening of her son, Anthony.
15 Prince Charles and Lady Diana Spencer attending a final wedding rehearsal at St Paul's.
16 The balcony kiss.

17 Wifely tenderness: Diana adjusts her husband's tie on arrival at RAF Lossiemouth, Scotland.

18 Charles and Diana on their Balmoral honeymoon.

19 The Prince and Princess of Wales wave from Caernarvon Castle on their first public engagement, a three-day tour of Wales in October 1981.

20 Diana riding with the Queen at Sandringham.

21 A heavily pregnant Diana with the Queen watching polo at the Guards Polo Club, Windsor.

22 4 August 1982: Diana holds the newly christened Prince William Arthur Philip Louis.

23 Diana looking gaunt less than five months after William's birth.

24 Australia, March 1983: the beginning of 'Di-mania'.

25 The Prince and Princess of Wales leaving hospital with Henry Charles Albert David – Prince Harry – born on 15 September 1984.

26 June 1985: an apparently spontaneous moment of affection – Charles kisses Diana after she presents him with a prize at a polo match in Cirencester.

27 The 'surprise' Diana prepared for Charles's thirty-seventh birthday: performing with Wayne Sleep at Covent Garden.

28 July 1986. 'Happy families': Diana and Charles pose with William and Harry at Highgrove.

29 June 1985: an angry row between Diana and Charles at a Windsor polo match.

30 1985: watching a polo match at Smith's Lawn with police bodyguard Barry Mannakee.

31 May 1987: Charles and Diana arrive at the Cannes Film Festival. Charles has just told her that Barry Mannakee had been killed in a motorcycle crash.

32 1987: 'The Merry Wives of Windsor': the Duchess of York and Diana at the Derby, Epsom.

33 Charles and Diana at the Saudi Experience, London, 1986. The strained relationship between the couple is all too evident.

34 August 1989: Diana and James Hewitt at the Inter Regimental Polo Championship.

35 Diana and William photographed with Dodi and Mohamed Al Fayed at a polo match in 1988.

36 June 1989: Charles and Diana with William and Harry prepare for a cycling trip in Tresco during their holiday in the Scilly Isles.

37 Diana returns to her old school, Riddlesworth Hall, and walks in the grounds with pupils and her former headmistress.

38 Diana and Charles at an Arab feast on their tour of the Gulf States in March 1989.

39 The notorious AIDS handshake that made the headlines.

40 Will Carling and Diana at Twickenham.

41 James Gilbey pictured post-'Squidygate' revelations.

42 Charles and Diana walking in Highgrove, 1989.

43 1 July 1990: Diana collects Charles from Cirencester Hospital, his arm in a sling after a polo accident.

44 Diana and William share a tender moment.

45 Brazil, April 1991: Diana visits a hostel for abandoned children, many of whom are HIV positive or suffering from AIDS.

46 India, February 1992: Diana visits Mianpur Old Age Welfare Centre and has her feet touched as a sign of respect.

47 Lech, Austria, 30 March 1992: Diana and Charles leave their skiing holiday after news of Earl Spencer's death.

48 Public sympathy causes Diana to break down as Andrew Morton's book, *Diana: Her True Story*, is serialized.

49 Oliver Hoare, 1994, pictured as the news breaks that Diana has been making anonymous telephone calls to his house.

50 Diana and her sisters, Sarah and Jane, after a night out.

51 South Korea, November 1992. 'The Glums': Charles and Diana on their last official trip together.

52 Diana enjoys the freedom of Nevis – her first holiday after her separation.

53 Diana is painted by Nelson Shanks as she sits for her first portrait as a separated woman.

54, 55, 56 In 1994 Diana gave up police protection, which made her increasingly vulnerable to the ever-merciless paparazzi.

57 Diana accepts an award from Henry Kissinger at the 'Humanitarian of the Year' awards ceremony, New York.

58 1996: Diana watching heart surgery at Harefield Hospital, Middlesex.

59 Diana with Imran and Jemima Khan and Lady Annabel Goldsmith in Lahore.

60 28 August 1996: Diana on the day of her divorce from Charles, accompanied by Lucia Flecha de Lima.

61 Hasnat Khan.

62 New York, June 1997: Diana at a gala party to launch the Christie's auction of her dresses.

63 Diana visiting the Lord Gage Centre for old people, a Guinness Trust home in Newham, east London.

64 London, June 1997: Diana at the Christie's pre-auction party.

65 1997: Diana comforts a grieving mother during her final campaign to ban the use of landmines in Bosnia.

66 Angola, January 1997: Diana at an orthopaedic workshop in Luanda.

67 August 1997: Diana and Dodi on the yacht *Jonikal* in St Tropez.

68 Diana and Dodi leave the Ritz moments before their fatal accident.

69 6 September 1997: the funeral of Diana, Princess of Wales.

70 Tribute to the 'People's Princess': flowers and wreaths outside Kensington Palace after the death of Diana.

Picture Credits

Alpha Photo Press: 54, 57, 58, 65.

From the Collection at Althorp: 3.

Camera Press: 1, 8; SPEN/AL: 6, 7; Diana Memorial Fund: 17, 24; Ian Burns: 34.

Daily Mail/Associated Press: 16.

Colin Davey: 52.

Empics: 12, 13, 25, 36.

Getty Images: Central Press/Hulton: 2, Fox/Hulton: 22; Keystone/Hulton: 5; Ian Tyas/Hulton: 10; Tim Graham Photo Library: 9, 11, 18, 21, 23, 26, 28, 30, 31, 43, 45, 46, 47, 51, 59, 62, 63, 64, 66.

Liverpool Post & Echo/Stephen Shakeshaft: 19.

Mike Lawn: 37.

Mirrorpix/Mike Malonay: 15: Gavin Kent: 38.

National Portrait Gallery, London: 4.

Rex Features: 14, 20, 27, 29, 32, 33, 35, 39, 40, 41, 42, 44, 48, 49, 50, 55, 56, 60, 61, 67, 68, 69, 70.

Photograph by Leona Shanks: 53.

1. The Country Girl

'In the Spencer family the gender issue is a big one . . . Women are very much second-class citizens' (a Spencer cousin)

Diana Spencer was born to the sound of applause. Her birth took place at 7.45 p.m. on a warm summer evening, 1 July 1961, in the bow-fronted bedroom where her mother had been born before her, overlooking the lawn where the annual cricket match organized by her father was nearing its end. Yet far from being a cause for applause, Diana's birth was regarded as a disappointment. As a girl she could not be the heir to the Spencer name that her parents so desperately wanted. Moreover, she was the third girl born to her parents, Frances and Johnnie Althorp, heir to the Spencer earldom, and had confidently been expected to be a boy, so much so that at the time of her birth the local newspaper reported her father as saying 'they had not yet decided on a name'. Since all Spencer male heirs were traditionally christened John or Charles this was understandable in the circumstances. The new girl's Spencer namesake, Diana (1735–43), was the short-lived sister of the 1st Earl Spencer.

Diana's father's family, the Spencers, was one of the most aristocratic in England; her extraordinary bloodline included the children of two Kings, a Duke, and a saint. A web of titled ancestors made her an eleventh cousin to the heir to the British throne, Charles, Prince of Wales; she was even distantly connected to the first President of the United States, George Washington. (Through her grandfather's marriage to American heiress Frances Work she was a seventh cousin to both Humphrey Bogart and Rudolph Valentino.)

Diana's family connections and the location of her birthplace could be said to have determined her royal future. Park House, where she was born, was the property of the Queen, and had been leased to Diana's maternal grandfather, Maurice Fermoy, in 1931 by King George V. It stood on the Sandringham estate in Norfolk about half a mile from the main house where the Royal Family frequently spent their holidays and the church where they worshipped. Diana had connections on both sides with the Royal Family: Lord Fermoy had been friend and shooting companion to Kings George V and VI, her father had been equerry (a privileged position as royal dogsbody reserved for members of the armed forces) to the Queen, Elizabeth II, and was a frequent guest at Balmoral shooting parties. Both her paternal grandmother, Cynthia Spencer (born Lady Cynthia Hamilton), and her great-aunt, Lady Delia Peel, were close friends and ladies-in-waiting to Queen Elizabeth, the Queen Mother, as was her maternal grandmother, Ruth, Lady Fermoy. Another Spencer great-aunt, Lady Lavinia White, who died in 1955, had been a close childhood friend of Queen Elizabeth. Park House could even be seen from the top windows of the Big House at Sandringham. She was, in a very real sense, 'the Girl Next Door'.

The Spencer family estate was Althorp in Northamptonshire but Diana rarely went there as a child; her fierce grandfather, Jack Spencer, the 7th Earl, and his heir, Diana's father Johnnie (Viscount Althorp at the time of Diana's birth), did not get on. She grew up with her roots in north Norfolk, a remote corner of one of the most isolated and rural parts of England, a county of gently rolling countryside under a vast sky. The Sandringham estate surrounding her birthplace is, in contrast, a sandy heath dotted with towering pine trees. The cold grey North Sea with its sand dunes and reeded marshes lies a short distance from Park House. North Norfolk is the territory of large estates and ancient families living the sporting and social life of a closed circle, largely barred to outsiders. Diana's parents, Frances and Johnnie Althorp, fitted perfectly into this background.

On Diana's mother's side the family were Anglo-Irish from County Cork: their name was Roche and their title Baron Fermoy.

Diana's great-great-grandfather, Edmund Burke Roche, was elected to Parliament and made a baron in the mid-nineteenth century; his second son, James Boothby Burke Roche, 3rd Baron Fermoy, married, in 1880, an American 'Dollar Princess', Frances 'Fanny' Work, daughter of a successful Wall Street broker. It was the usual alliance of American money in exchange for European title which became current practice in the nineteenth century and, as so many of such marriages were, it was unhappy and ended in divorce in 1891. Fanny's father, Frank Work, had little use for Europeans and after the divorce he told his daughter that her children would only inherit his fortune if they became Americans. Fanny's twin elder sons, Maurice and Francis, were sent to the cream of American schools and colleges, St Paul's School, Concord, New Hampshire, and Harvard, but despite this they refused to become Americans on their grandfather's death in 1911 and successfully challenged the conditions of his will. With $2.9 million (roughly £28–30 million today) apiece they turned their back on America and in 1921 left for England where Diana's grandfather, Maurice, now 4th Baron Fermoy, settled in Norfolk, becoming Member of Parliament for King's Lynn; a position he held from 1924 to 1935 and later from 1943 to 1945. On a trip to Paris, he met the beautiful, talented and ambitious Ruth Gill, a paint manufacturer's daughter from Aberdeenshire. Ruth was studying to be a concert pianist at the Paris Conservatoire but without much hesitation she gave up her career to marry Maurice, who was attractive to women, extremely wealthy and had a title to boot. They married in 1931, when she was twenty-six and he forty-six, and had three children: Mary, born in 1934, Frances, Diana's mother, born in 1936, and Edmund, born in 1939.

Maurice and Ruth Fermoy settled at Park House, a convenient base for Maurice because of its proximity to his constituency. He was outgoing, jovial and much liked by his constituents, a notable communicator, willing to burst into a speech at any time; on visits to local hospitals he would sit on the side of patients' beds and chat happily away with them. Ruth, backed by the Fermoy money, was a generous and skilful hostess. 'They had wonderful tennis

parties and things like that which nobody else had in those days,'
a Spencer relation recalled. 'Because of the American money they
lived in a style that nobody else seemed to then.' There were
rumours that some of the Norfolk grandees sneered at the couple,
at Maurice for his 'American trade' connections and at Ruth for
her modest background. 'The sort of Norfolk hierarchy – dubbed
"county-bound" by a Spencer contemporary [Lady Margaret
Douglas-Home] – wouldn't have anything to do with them, and
rather rejected them,' said an aristocratic contemporary of Ruth's.
'And because they lived at Park House [so close to Sandringham]
the King and Queen took them up. Queen Elizabeth never liked
that sort of ostracism and snobbery.'[1] Diana's mother, Frances,
was born on 20 January 1936, the day of King George V's death
at Sandringham; even at that stressful time, his widow, Queen
Mary, noted 'the birth of Lady Fermoy's baby' and sent Ruth a
congratulatory note.

Diana never knew her grandfather, who died in 1955, but her
grandmother, Ruth Fermoy, was to play an important part in her
life, not least for her close royal connections based on her valued
friendship with the Queen Mother whose woman of the bedchamber she became. Like her friend the Queen Mother, Ruth
had a Scottish steel about her. 'She was a very, very mysterious
woman,' the Spencer relation said, 'always very elegant and gentle
and quiet but there was another side to her – less gentle.' Ruth
Fermoy was socially ambitious, adopting the attitudes of the aristocratic circles she had joined on her marriage. She was delighted when
her daughter Mary married Anthony Berry, the son of Viscount
Kemsley, ecstatic when Frances became engaged to Johnnie,
Viscount Althorp, only son and heir to the 7th Earl Spencer, with
vast acres of Northamptonshire, and an historic stately home,
Althorp. Now titled herself, very rich and outstandingly beautiful,
she turned her back on her middle-class Aberdeenshire background
to cultivate her royal and aristocratic connections. Her rigid adher-
ence to the conventions of her adopted class and of the courtier
circle was to have dramatic repercussions on Diana's early life.

Frances Burke Roche, whom Diana was to resemble both in

looks and character, was a beauty with fine features, luminous blue eyes, long, slim legs and blonde hair. She was also as strong and independent minded as her mother, Ruth, if not quite as tough. Frances herself said of Ruth, 'I don't think I've ever known anyone with as much confidence. She made up her mind and went for it. She didn't waver over anything.' The same words were echoed of Frances by her friends. 'Frances was the strongest character of anyone I've ever known,' said one. 'She was forcible, dynamic, energetic and very intelligent – had she had a better education she would have been a very contributive person – she had leadership qualities. She had terrific power over men – she was funny but one of the most dominating female characters I've ever known and she was like that at seventeen.' And at seventeen, what Frances wanted was Johnnie Althorp as he then was; she had first seen him when he visited her school, Downham, when she was just fourteen. At seventeen and just after leaving school, her parents launched her on the marriage market for upper-class girls known as the London Season, a daily round of balls, cocktail parties, house parties at weekends and certain sporting events such as the unmissable Royal Ascot. During that Season, Frances met Johnnie again, they fell in love and became engaged, despite the fact that Johnnie had been expected to marry the beautiful and charming Lady Anne Coke, daughter of the Earl of Leicester, owner of a great estate, Holkham, in Norfolk. As head of the great Norfolk family, neighbours of the Royal Family at Sandringham and close friends of the late King and of Queen Elizabeth, the Leicesters were leading lights in the hermetic world of north Norfolk royal and aristocratic society. Lady Anne confessed that she 'adored' Johnnie, though many of her friends did not, finding him 'unkind'. Still less did they like Frances who ruthlessly cut Anne out and took her man.

Johnnie Althorp liked dominant women. Tall, handsome in a bucolic way, charming and impeccably bred, he was a catch in social terms despite the tight financial lead on which his father, the 7th Earl, kept him. Any available money – and there was not a great deal – was devoted to the maintenance and restoration of Althorp. (The exception was the sale of one of the jewels of the

Spencer collection, a magnificent Holbein portrait of Henry VIII, which paid for Johnnie's Eton education, and is now in the Thyssen collection in Madrid.) As was the case in many aristocratic families (and indeed, historically, the British Royal Family) the heir and his father did not get on. Jack Spencer was irascible, difficult and eccentric: his nickname in society was the ironic 'Jolly Jack'. His passion for the family house, Althorp, seemed to have left him little room for other affections and the thought of passing on his treasure to his son was painful in the extreme. Althorp was his temple, and as its custodian he regarded himself as the temple priest, spending hours polishing the silver in the butler's pantry although he had a butler to do it for him. Unlike his son, he disliked human contact, particularly with those he regarded as 'the lower orders'. Among the numerous bees in his bonnet was an aversion to his driver looking round when he got into the car, the signal for departure being the sound of his door slamming shut. As Lord Lieutenant of Northamptonshire he used an old Rolls-Royce with chauffeur; on one occasion after an official dinner, Spencer got out to relieve himself, the wind slammed the door before he could get back in and the driver, knowing perfectly well what had happened, gleefully drove off leaving him in open country in the dark. He was a crashing snob with a dread of anything middle class. Once, lunching at Clarence House, he told Queen Elizabeth that he would never go into a house where people ate fish with fish knives because it was so middle class. 'Whenever he came to lunch after that,' said one of Queen Elizabeth's circle, 'we always had fish with fish knives.' 'He induced respect in many, and fear in almost all,' his grandson Charles Spencer wrote.[2] Unsurprisingly, Johnnie's childhood memories were not happy ones. He used to dread the train journey home and would hide in the shadow of the carriage, hoping his father had forgotten to collect him. At Althorp, when he felt the atmosphere thickening, he would climb into the false ceiling of a bathroom and hide there with his terriers as companions. 'I fear these solitary moments were relatively frequent,' his son wrote.[3]

Jolly Jack's wife, Cynthia, daughter of the Duke of Abercorn, was his complete opposite, beautiful, sensitive, charitable and greatly loved. 'I have never heard anyone say a word against her memory,' her grandson wrote, 'and she is still very much alive as a paragon of sweet nobility ... The word most often used to describe her is "saintly".'[4] She had served the Queen Mother as lady of the bedchamber but even more the local people for whom she had done an enormous amount of voluntary work. When she died in 1972 of a brain tumour, the county's hospice was named after her. Johnnie, who had loved her deeply and seen her too little because of his difficult relationship with his father, was devastated. Some of Diana's gentleness and empathy with the sick and suffering came from Lady Cynthia, whom she resembled in looks. Diana, aged eleven, came to believe that her grandmother Cynthia watched out for her as her guardian angel.

Diana's father was a typical product of his age and class. He was educated at Eton, served as an officer in the Royal Scots Greys and, on the strength of his family connections, had acted as equerry to both King George VI and Queen Elizabeth II and accompanied the Queen on her post-Coronation Commonwealth tour in 1953. By then he was engaged to Frances; they married on 1 June 1954 in a grand society wedding at St Margaret's, Westminster, attended by one thousand guests including the Queen, the Duke of Edinburgh, the Queen Mother and Princess Margaret. The young couple were very much in love but their circumstances were unequal from the start. Frances would have to finance the marriage. Johnnie, once described by his commanding officer in the Royal Scots Greys as 'very nice but very stupid', tried to find a job as a banker but was turned down by his old friend and partner in Hoare's on the grounds that 'mathematics was never his strong suit'. He then enrolled as a student at the Royal Agricultural College at Cirencester, the traditional option for the landed gentry and aristocracy (unkindly dubbed 'clotted cream': rich and thick). They lived first at Rodmarton, Gloucestershire, in a rented cottage and then at Orchard Cottage on the Althorp estate in uncomfortable proximity to Jolly Jack.

Happily for them, after the death of Frances's father, Maurice

Fermoy, in 1955, his widow Ruth had offered to let them take
over the lease of Park House. At the same time Frances, having
inherited her share of her father's fortune, generously bought
Johnnie a 600-acre farm at nearby Snettisham for £30,000. While
Johnnie farmed at Snettisham and the family land at North Creake
and looked after his charities, particularly the National Association
of Boys' Clubs, Frances set about the business of producing babies.
The pressure was on her to bear the male heir but her first two
children were girls: Sarah, born in March 1955 nine months after
the wedding, and Jane born in February 1957. She had a miscarriage
but when finally a son was born, on 1 January 1960, it was not
a triumph but a tragedy. John Spencer was born malformed: he
died ten hours later, unable to breathe, having been taken away
from Frances before she could hold him. It was a pain she never
forgot.

Something in the relationship fractured after John's death.
Johnnie Spencer insisted that Frances was responsible for her continuing failure to bear a healthy boy and she was sent to a Harley
Street gynaecologist for humiliating tests and treatment. 'It was a
dreadful time for my parents,' Charles Spencer said, 'and probably
the root of their divorce because I don't think they ever got over
it.' A Spencer cousin and a friend of Frances, said: 'The death of
John was a deep tragedy in their lives. Afterwards there was a
sadness in both of them which had not been there before.'

Diana was intended to be the replacement child, the longed-for
heir. By the time she was born, her parents' marriage was in
trouble, which the arrival of yet another girl did nothing to improve. The Norfolk married life which may have suited Frances
as a young bride became confining for a woman with wider
horizons. Her dashing husband had become considerably less
dashing as time went by, settling all too comfortably into his
country squire surroundings. 'Johnnie was the best company when
he was a young man,' his former fiancée Lady Anne Coke said,
'but then he just became boring, wrapped up in his children and
his country life.'

Diana convinced herself that she should have been a boy and

that, being a girl, she was a disappointment and regarded as a lesser
being. 'I do know that in the Spencer family the gender issue is a
big one and even when there was a son and no pressure to produce
an heir, the female children are of less account than the male.
Women are very much second-class citizens in the Spencer family,'
a Spencer relation said. By the time the longed-for heir, Charles
Spencer, was born in May 1964, the marriage was beyond repair.
Johnnie, as long as his irascible, eccentric father lived, had virtually
no role to play beyond gentlemanly farming, cricket and shooting.
Essentially a weak man, he resented the intellectual and financial
dominance of Frances. There were rows, sometimes, it is said,
descending into violence. Frances was bored with her husband and
her life in staid, enclosed, predictable Norfolk society. She was
only twenty-eight and wanted to spread her wings.

The inevitable happened: she fell in love with another man,
Peter Shand Kydd, whom she had met at a London dinner party
in 1966. They met again on a joint skiing holiday with their
respective spouses early in 1967. This time interest turned into
powerful attraction and they began a secret affair. In the summer
of 1967 Frances and Johnnie agreed on a trial separation: with the
two older girls now at school, Frances would take Diana, aged six,
and Charles, aged four, to London for the weekdays. Both were
enrolled in London schools and returned to Park House and their
father for weekends. The family were reunited at half-term in
October and again for Christmas. By then the thought of continuing with life at Park House had become intolerable to Frances.
She was headstrong, a character trait that Diana would inherit, and
at Christmas 1967 she confronted Johnnie with a request for a
divorce. An affair, however, was one thing, divorce quite another.
It was a tradition in English upper-class families at the time that
everything should be done to keep the family together and to
avoid the scandal and humiliation which the request for a divorce
by the wife would involve. Johnnie was not merely hurt but
bitterly angry, determined that Frances should be punished and
seen to be so. She would not be allowed to profit from her crime
by keeping the children. She could leave, but as an outcast. He

declared that the children would be sent to school in King's Lynn, that they would stay with him and not return to London.

In the subsequent custody case, Ruth Fermoy took her son-in-law's side and gave evidence against her own daughter. The deep-seated reason for this apparently cruel action seems to have been a combination of shock at her daughter's behaviour and extreme snobbishness, manifested in her determination to take the Spencer side: 'It was the name and the shame,' a Spencer relation who knew Ruth well said.[5] 'When I asked her why she did that,' a friend said, 'she said it was because Charles must be brought up at Althorp . . .' 'She had a very ruthless streak. It was the most extraordinary thing to do. It split her family. Ruth's funeral was one of the saddest and creepiest I have ever been to. We sat on one side of the church with Charles and Diana – who had separated, I think, but came together for the day – and on the other side of the aisle was the Fermoy family, and there was Frances, and they didn't talk to each other, husbands and cousins who were all not talking to her. It was the most terrible thing.'[6] Ruth, she said, in a phrase which was to become a litany in court circles later on, blamed the 'bad Fermoy blood' for Frances's behaviour. 'I remember Ruth saying that the trouble was her husband's family. They are what you call "bolters". They were all American bolters. A very unfortunate gene.'[7]

Diana, six at this time, was old enough to sense the strained atmosphere and, as she later recalled, to overhear the bitter rows. Opinions are divided as to whether an overwrought Johnnie actually hit his wife or not. Both are now dead so the truth cannot be known; the rumour that he did may have arisen because Frances later based her grounds for divorce on a plea of cruelty. Frances had come back for Christmas with the intention of having the children with her in London but, when she left this time, she left for good. Years later Diana, pouring out her heart on tapes for Andrew Morton's explosive book, *Diana: Her True Story*, remembered as a defining moment the crunch of tyres on the gravel as her mother drove off. 'I'll be back,' Frances told her, but she never did return to Park House.

The happy, undemanding childhood life at Park House fell apart. Diana saw her father unhappy and withdrawn, couldn't understand why her mother was no longer there, heard her little brother Charles sobbing for his mother in the night. Her longing for love and her fear of abandonment, her horror and fear of divorce and determination that it should not happen to her and to her children was born at that moment. Torn between love for her devastated father and her absent mother, Diana suffered what was to turn out to be a deep and psychologically crippling wound.

2. A Norfolk Childhood

'She has been accused of making too much of losing her mother through divorce in the late 1960s, but in truth the loss ran deep within her'
(William Deedes[1])

Diana's despair at the departure of her mother would be at the root of her later view of herself as a 'victim', something to which she returned over and over again, particularly when faced with a television camera or a tape recorder. She had a strong streak of fantasy and self-dramatization in her make-up, and as a child had a reputation for lying: one day on the school run, a local vicar's wife told her: 'Diana Spencer, if you tell one more lie, I'll put you out of the car.' Even her brother Charles Spencer later agreed that as a child she had a tendency to lie. Some people, including the Spencer family, tended to dismiss Diana's claims of unhappiness. 'I think in her perception it seemed like that but it wasn't the reality. It was much happier than she felt it was in retrospect,' a cousin said. Yet a man who was close to her before she began her relationship with Prince Charles was convinced that the departure of her mother 'had a very severe, dramatic effect on her'.[2]

People who witnessed the early days after Frances's departure tend to bear out Diana's view. A cook, engaged by Lady Fermoy, who arrived shortly after Frances left when Diana was six, had a very different impression of life at Park House at the time. 'It was not in my recollection a happy household. Lord Althorp was absent a lot of the time and not cheerful . . . Diana was very quiet, kept herself to herself. The children never cried [during the day] but did sob at night when they had gone to bed.' A Norfolk neighbour remembers giving a birthday party for one of her sons at the time: 'It was July and all the children were enjoying themselves in the garden except for poor Diana – she refused to join in and I said to the young nanny who was with her, "What can we do to encourage her to join the other children?" Her answer was: "Nothing, she is a very sad little girl." This was just after her mother had bolted.'[3]

Years later, in 1992, Diana would claim in tapes recorded by Peter Settelen, 'My father told me about five years ago that he would find me on the doorstep: "You didn't speak. You just sat there. You just, you know, you just never spoke."' Diana, at six, was just the age when her mother's unexplained disappearance hit hard: her sisters, aged ten and thirteen, were better equipped to cope; Charles, at only three, cried for his mother at night but was unable to understand or rationalize her departure from his life as Diana did.

But if Diana was shocked and confused by her mother's unexplained disappearance from her life, her father was equally so. When he was at home he shut himself away: 'He was really miserable after the divorce, basically shell-shocked,' Charles Spencer said. 'He used to sit in the study the whole time.' Frances's name was never mentioned. Emotions were raw on both sides: 'Frances went through agonies when she lost her children,' a contemporary recalled.[4]

Luckily for Diana, she was initially unaware of the bitter behind-the-scenes battles between Frances and Johnnie both over the terms of the divorce and the custody of the children. Frances lost all the way down the line: in two custody cases when Ruth Fermoy sided with Johnnie against her and in the divorce case in which her cause was not helped by Mrs Shand Kydd, whose own divorce petition cited Frances as the co-respondent. When Frances petitioned on the grounds of cruelty, Johnnie countersued by reason of her adultery. Frances lost and costs were awarded against her. She was publicly branded an unfit mother, a 'bolter' (after a character in Nancy Mitford's *The Pursuit of Love*, 1945) and an adulteress. The Althorp divorce caused an upheaval in Norfolk society where Frances was widely condemned for what was seen as her desertion of her children.

Diana was not, however, too young to be sensitive to people's curious stares when they attended church at Sandringham or were taken by Ruth Fermoy to Ladyman's tea rooms in King's Lynn. Although there was nothing beyond bald announcements in the London newspapers about the proceedings, all north Norfolk from top to bottom of the social scale knew about it and most of them sympathized with the deserted father and his children.

A Norfolk neighbour left a widower with a number of children around the time of the Althorp divorce used to employ house-keeper/nannies who had previously been at Park House. 'They had usually left Johnnie Althorp and were full of stories about the awful [atmosphere] . . . how Frances would ring the children up every night just as they went to bed, and always upset them. It was a very unhappy set-up.'[5]

Whatever Diana's recollections of her sadness in the first year after her mother left, as time went on that view became a distortion of the truth. Mary Clarke, whom Diana's father engaged to look after the two younger children in February 1971, remembered: 'When I look back to life at Park House, I do think to myself what a wonderful free and easy life we had. Always I remember just laughter and jokes. Diana was a real tease.'[6] Diana spent the first fourteen years of her life at Park House, a solid Victorian mansion built of the rust-coloured local carrstone with large bow windows, a servants' wing and stabling. It was no architectural gem, but the Spencer children remembered it as 'lovely'. The house was large and roomy with open fires in every main room including the nursery, while background heating was provided by huge Edwardian radiators. The entrance led into a flagged hall with huge stone slabs, from which a stone staircase with wrought-iron balustrade led to the upper floor. Off the hall there were big, light rooms with marble fireplaces, bow windows and cornices with tongue and egg moulding. A large cedar tree, planted at the time the house was built, still stands on the lawn in front of the house, cattle graze in the fields beyond and surrounding trees provide shelter from the icy winds blowing in from the Wash to the north and the North Sea to the east. The windows look out beyond the lawn to green fields and to the south over Sandringham Park.

Mary Clarke's memory of life at Park House was very different from the unhappy household of a previous employee's recollection. 'I was impressed from the start by how happy and self-contained the children were,' she wrote, 'and how they always found so much to do to amuse themselves.'7 A cousin remembers Park House as 'a great family house, everything was family about it, nothing daunting. You felt it was well used and enjoyed but predictable. Not opulent, nothing of that kind, just cosy and predictable.' Diana kept a huge collection of stuffed furry animals in her bedroom; poignantly, she referred to them as 'my family'. There were lots of live animals: Johnnie's black Labrador gun dog, Jill the springer spaniel, Diana's bad-tempered cat Marmalade, and her collection of hamsters, rabbits and guinea pigs. 'She loved animals when she was a child,' her mother said. 'I think you want something to love, and she loved everything that was small and furry or had feathers. She had rabbits, guinea pigs, hamsters; a long succession of animals to care for. She outgrew it and took on people . . . But the animals were super-comfortable and rather well catered for – well looked after, well cleaned out. She had a great consciousness they were dependent on her. She did the dirty work.' There were ponies in the fields and stables, Diana could ride by the time she was three, although after an accident in which she broke her arm her enthusiasm for horses disappeared. There were swimming and tennis parties with the children of the local gentry when Diana liked to show off her diving skills. The family owned a beach hut at Brancaster where they picnicked, and also played and paddled on the huge beach at Holkham.

Diana became used to playing to the camera at an early age. Her father was a passionate photographer, snapping away on every occasion to fill the albums which he dedicated to each of his children. His early pictures registered Diana's shy habit of looking upwards from under her fringe, a habit which never left her. But, like all stars, she never took a bad picture: the camera loved her and she instinctively responded to the lens levelled at her. She had the capacity to pose but yet make the pose look natural, a lifelong characteristic. Wherever she was, she communicated with the camera.

The Spencer children were, with the exception of Diana, all bright academically. Her failure to keep up with her siblings in this area gave Diana a secret inferiority complex which she balanced by her belief in her own instinct. 'Diana was not stupid,' a cousin said of her. 'She was intelligent with this very, very quick wit.' Sarah, six years older than she was, the elder sister whom she hero-worshipped, was named after the Spencers' formidable ancestor, Sarah Jennings, Duchess of Marlborough, and had many of her namesake's qualities. 'She is a most interesting character,' a cousin said of her. 'The most complex of them all I would have said. Very strong, very alive and alert, intelligent. Not terribly nice. An interesting woman but tough, without Diana's gentle side. She knows what she wants.' Sarah had that foxy look inherited from the red-haired Spencers and the overwhelming confidence of her mother. Jane, the least assertive of the four, managed to spend more time with her mother and Diana did not become close to her until later. Charles, another red-headed Spencer and academically the brightest, was an equally strong character but wary, controlling and complex in his relationships. When he grew up, a relation was to say that he was a control freak and that they all, even his mother, were 'terrified of him'. But during their childhood Diana mothered him and the two were very close. 'I've always seen him as the brains in the family,' Diana told Morton in 1991. 'I still see that. He's got S levels and things like that. I think that my brother being the youngest and the only boy was quite precious [to the family as the heir to Althorp] . . . I was the girl who was supposed to be a boy. Being third in line was a very good position to be in − I got away with murder. I was my father's favourite, no doubt about that.

'I longed to be as good as Charles in the schoolroom. I was never jealous of him. I so understand him. He's very like me as opposed to my two sisters. Like me he will always suffer. There's something in us that attracts that department . . .'[8]

In the absence of their parents, the children congregated in the big kitchen begging for treats from the cook. It was a pattern in Diana's behaviour: even when she grew up and married she preferred the company of her staff to that of the 'grown-ups'. The kitchen or the butler's pantry was where she felt at home. The children had a nanny who was so young and inexperienced that she was more of a childminder than a nanny; they ignored her for the company of the cook. Ruth Fermoy, living four miles away at nearby Hillington, was the distant power in the household, hiring the staff and supporting Johnnie. The staff was headed by a couple, Johnnie's former army batman, Mr Smith, and his wife, who lived over the stables and ran the house, doing most of the work, including the shopping, except the nannying and the cooking. They were devoted to Johnnie and aloof with the other staff, the nanny and the cook, whom they treated as outsiders. They all lived off the estate so venison and pheasant featured largely on the menu. 'Bought food', food from the regular shops, was rarely allowed. Vegetables came straight from the garden. The children complained – 'Can't we have lamb chops' – but to no avail.

The children reacted differently to their situation: although Sarah and Jane, being older and at boarding school when the separation happened, were less affected, Sarah at least reacted by being naughty, as indeed to some extent they all did. Sarah was the worst behaved, 'a horror' an employee recalled: she would bring her pony into the kitchen and ride it round the table despite the cook's protests. Diana remembered being extremely badly behaved towards the young and inexperienced 'nannies' who were imposed on them, sticking pins into their seat cushions and throwing their clothes out of the window. Both parents were so traumatized by feelings of guilt (on Frances's side), humiliation and despair (on Johnnie's), that they spoiled the children and exercised little parental control. Like many children of divorce, the Spencers manipulated their parents to get what they wanted. Diana became extremely adept at pushing and cajoling for what she wanted in the certainty that no one would say no to her Machiavellian behaviour, which she would indulge in with devastating effect years later.

Ostracized as a bolter, Frances never came back to Norfolk. Park House, for all its amenities, conspicuously lacked a maternal figure. Ruth Fermoy and Cynthia Spencer did their best to cheer the children, teaching them bridge and card games. Lady Margaret Douglas-Home, Jolly Jack's sister, was a stimulating presence in the children's life; known as 'Aunt Margaret', she was in fact their great-aunt. As Charles remembered, 'Aunt Margaret was a life-enhancing force, her deep and generous laugh always at the ready, a passion for gossip evidence of an enquiring, rather than a malicious mind. To visit her in her small cottage in Burnham Market . . . was to experience humour of the greatest breadth, and intelligence of a rare intensity . . . Few were not bewitched by her mischievous chuckle.'[9]

After her divorce was made final in April 1969, with Johnnie granted a divorce on the grounds of her adultery and given custody of the children, Frances had married Peter Shand Kydd in May 1969. Before that there had been agonizing weekend visits by the two younger children to their mother in London: 'I remember Mummy crying an awful lot and every Saturday when we went up for weekends, every Saturday night, standard procedure, she would start crying. On Saturday we would both see her crying. "What's the matter, Mummy?" "Oh, I don't want you to leave tomorrow . . ."' It was, as Diana said, 'devastating' for a nine-year-old. 'Holidays were always very grim because we had a four-week holiday. Two weeks Mummy and two weeks Daddy and the trauma of going from one house to another and each individual parent trying to make it up in their area with material things rather than the actual tactile stuff, which is what we both craved for but neither of us ever got. When I say neither of us my other two sisters were busy at prep school and were sort of out of the house whereas my brother and I were very much stuck together.'[10] A year before she died, Ruth Fermoy, looking back, told a cousin, 'I feel those two younger ones have been very, very damaged by the separation, divorce, which the older two hadn't.' Years later Diana told one of her mother figures how difficult it had been for her because 'her mother would buy her a dress [then] her father would buy her another one. And there were always these disputes. And for holidays, for ever. Torn between the two . . . she loved her father but I don't think she really loved her mother, she felt sorry for her mother sometimes . . . but she didn't trust her . . .'[11] The children, according to people who knew them, had an 'awful upbringing' with no rules beyond eating everything on their plates and writing thank-you letters.

Again Diana was exaggerating: the sadness of the early years after the divorce blotted out the happy times of her Norfolk childhood. As Mary Clarke wrote: 'A child who was truly, deeply traumatized, would not be able to maintain the contentment Diana continually displayed, apart from those occasional hiccups, throughout the time I knew her.' These 'hiccups' were prompted by the children's returning from their time with their mother: Charles took the situation quite naturally but Diana behaved strangely, the result perhaps of her mother's emotive farewell: 'Don't worry, you'll be all right, you'll settle, don't forget what I said, please ring me.' When Mary Clarke told them how happy their father would be to see them, Diana glanced sideways at her and said how sad her mother would be to be all on her own. Charles, used to his sister's dramatizations, said sharply, 'You know Mummy is not on her own, Diana, and you always say that about Daddy too.' When they reached Park House, Diana's bubbly self was replaced by a shy, deliberately withdrawn, little girl. She thought that if she appeared too excited to see him he might think that she was happier with him than with her mother. When Johnnie held out the prospect of a tea party at Sandringham with Princes Andrew and Edward, Diana said she didn't want to go, pleading a headache; showing a strength of will characteristic of her, she resisted all her father's attempts to persuade her.[12] Whether this was a misguided attempt to show loyalty to her mother by punishing her father, or whether she felt that the distress caused her by their split deserved to be demonstrated, is impossible to tell. Similar incidents were to occur later in life when she behaved in the same way to her husband.

According to Mary Clarke such royal invitations were rare; the two families did not often socialize. The Spencer children took their royal neighbours for granted and were not in awe of them. Among the few occasions when they did see the Royal Family was Sunday church which they attended only when the Queen was in residence; Johnnie thought that the Queen would notice their absence and think it odd. 'We were all shunted over to Sandringham for [sic] holidays. Used to go and see *Chitty Chitty Bang Bang*, the film. We hated it so much. We hated going over there. The atmosphere was always very strange when we went there and I used to kick and fight anyone who tried to make us go over there and Daddy was most insistent because it was rude,' Diana recalled.[13]

The Reverend Reginald Sweet, Latin teacher and chaplain at her second school, however, had a different story to tell: 'Diana was very keen on Prince Andrew,' he recalled. 'He was her great holiday friend. She had all these photographs on her desk and . . . she said, "Mr Sweet, when I grow up I'm going to marry Prince Andrew." I said, "Really, Diana?" "Yes, I'm going to marry him and he's my friend." The impression I got is that they knew each other very well and used to spend time together during the holidays.'[14] Diana's nanny, Janet Thompson, remembered walking into the drawing room at Sandringham to find the Queen playing hide and seek with the six-year-old Andrew and five-year-old Diana. At tea, Charles walked in, very much the elder brother. 'Everything all right? Looks like a good party to me.'[15]

In reality Diana knew that both her parents loved her and that she was her father's favourite. When the children got to know Peter Shand Kydd they liked him very much. 'Peter was humorous, generous, spontaneous and exciting,' Charles recorded. Diana and Charles's first meeting with him was in 1969 at Liverpool Street Station when they arrived off the train from Norwich. Diana remembered saying to Frances, 'Where's your new husband? "He's at the ticket barrier." And there was this very good-looking, handsome man and we were longing to love him and we accepted him and he was great to us and spoilt us rotten.'[16] It was Peter Shand Kydd who first christened Diana 'Duch', short for 'Duchess'.

The name, prompted by Diana's at times haughty behaviour, stuck: not only her family but all her Sloaney friends used it. When Peter and Frances moved to Itchenor in West Sussex, the children spent happy holidays there sailing with him and his three children. His presence made their time with their mother more relaxing and normal. When, after the second custody case, it was agreed that Johnnie and Frances should share the children's time together, Frances and Peter started looking for a proper home with plenty of space. They found an eighteenth-century farmhouse, Ardencaple, on the Isle of Seil off the west coast of Scotland, with 1000 acres of wild farmland and spectacular views. Diana and Charles loved their visits, the freedom, the beauty and the wild landscape – sailing, fishing, lobster-potting. Diana kept a Shetland pony called Soufflé there. At her boarding school, West Heath, she pinned a poster of the island above her bed. Charles Spencer recalled Ardencaple as 'a magical place which Diana and I adored'. Later the Shand Kydds bought a 2000-acre ranch at Yass in New South Wales where they spent six weeks each summer, and the children joined them there.

Diana's education was of the undemanding nature which in those days applied to girls of her age and class. She was first taught by her mother's governess, Gertrude Allen, known as 'Ally', who lived in the nearby village of Dersingham. Ally would collect Diana from Park House and take her to a neighbour's house for morning lessons with the children of the local gentry; while the children ate their packed lunches in the nursery with the owner and the children's nanny, Ally ate hers in isolated splendour in the dining room, her lunch specially prepared by the resident cook. Afterwards she would take the children for a walk accompanied by her ferocious dog.

In January 1968 Diana was enrolled at Silfield private school, a day school for girls and boys in Gayton, on the outskirts of King's Lynn. The school, housed in a large early twentieth-century suburban family house in a variety of architectural styles, was, as a notice board still proclaims, 'founded in 1955 for 5–11-year-olds'. There was a good-sized garden dominated by a large monkey puzzle tree contemporary with the house, and rambling wooden outbuildings including a 30-foot room with wooden panelling and false timbering and a fireplace which served as an assembly and games room. A small school with forty pupils, attended by the children of local farmers and gentry (including Diana's best friend, Alexandra Loyd, daughter of the Queen's estate agent at Sandringham), it was a cosy place with a family atmosphere. Diana was remembered by the headmistress, Jean Lowe, for her kindness to younger children, her love of animals and 'general helpfulness' but not for her academic potential. Later, she was shown up by her younger brother, Charles, who revenged himself for her superior strength and height in their sibling fights by calling her 'Brian' after the slow-witted snail in the children's programme *The Magic Roundabout*. It was here too, the first closed organization outside her home of which she had experience, that she found she was the only child of divorced parents. Sadly, she used to dedicate her work in art class 'To Mummy and Daddy'.

When she was nine Diana went to board at Riddlesworth Hall, some one and a half hours' drive from Sandringham. At first she had resented being made to leave her father, towards whom she had become very protective since the divorce but, despite her complaints – 'if you love me you won't leave me here' – she confessed that she 'loved being at school'. She boasted about being naughty and wanting to laugh and muck about, of taking a dare and escaping from her dormitory to run down the drive in the dark. Riddlesworth was a rectangular classical-style house, standing high with many windows and views over the surrounding gardens and fields. It had the feel of a lived-in house; elaborate light fittings, glass cases of stuffed birds and rather gloomy trophies of large animals were traces of the previous occupants. There were plaster and gilt ceilings in the larger rooms which were light and well proportioned; the general atmosphere was cheerful and friendly. Diana was not among strangers; several of the girls she knew from the surrounding families were there with her: Alexandra Loyd, her cousin Diana Wake-Walker, and Claire Pratt, daughter of her godmother, Sarah Pratt. Pupils were encouraged to bring pets, which were housed in 'Pets' Corner' in the garden within sight of the house. Diana became head of Pets' Corner and brought her treasured guinea pig Peanuts with her. She never carried off any academic prizes but she did win a prize with Peanuts for 'Best Kept Guinea Pig' and the Leggatt Cup 'for helpfulness'. She won prizes for swimming and diving: 'But in the academic department, you might as well forget about that!' she laughed. 'I ate and ate. It was always a great joke – let's get Diana to eat three kippers and six pieces of bread. I did all that,' the future bulimic said proudly. What with the pets and the Norfolk friends, school was merely an extension of her normal life and simple, restricted horizon.

Johnnie Althorp always drove Diana back to Riddlesworth, much as he had joined in the school run to Silfield, and where he was remembered for his easy manner and interest in people. At Riddlesworth, the headmistress, Patricia Wood, said that all the kitchen staff and grounds people particularly remembered him. 'When you talked to the kitchen ladies they couldn't remember much about Diana because she was just one of the little girls, but they could all remember her father. He was a very conspicuous gentleman . . . very tall and noticeable and almost the first thing he did when he brought her to the school after the holidays was to go down in the kitchens and talk to them.'[17] Johnnie was interested in everybody he met, regardless of background, a quality Diana inherited from him. 'My father,' Sarah told an interviewer, 'had an instinctive way with people . . . People would talk to him and he was gripped . . . He loved people. And Diana did too. I don't think that quality has got anything to do with upbringing. I think you've either got it or you haven't . . . it's either in you when you're born, or it's not.'[18]

Aged twelve, in September 1973, after three years at Riddlesworth, Diana followed Sarah and Jane to a new school, West Heath, near Sevenoaks in Kent. Located in another splendid country house, West Heath was the natural progression from Riddlesworth: small – there were only 120 girls – friendly, with the emphasis on happiness and good behaviour rather than academic achievement. In many ways such schools were throwbacks to the fifties, when girls of good family were not expected to do much more than prepare themselves for marriage. 'Hamsters and knitting were what they were about,' a contemporary remembered. 'Everyone came out confident and happy,' a schoolmate recorded, 'and there was very little angst . . . It was a relaxed place.' When Diana arrived, Jane, 'the good Spencer' then aged sixteen, was a prefect with an excellent academic record. Sarah was no longer there, having been expelled for drunkenness two years earlier. She had been a success both academically and in sport, winning prizes and appearing in the school plays. But, brilliant, forceful and wilful, she was bored at West Heath. Somehow, according to her own admission, she laid hands on an astonishing variety of drink. 'I used to drink because I was bored,' she said. 'I would drink anything: whisky, Cointreau, gin, sherry or, most often, vodka because the staff couldn't smell that.'[19] But one day in 1971 the staff did notice: she was drunk and instantly expelled. A few years later there were to be further signs of trouble when she was affected by serious eating disorders.

In her own way Diana was a success at West Heath, although she liked later on to emphasize her image as a rebel. The head-mistress, Ruth Rudge, a keen observer, recorded that when Diana first arrived she was 'wary of adults, often prickly with her peers . . . but was lucky enough to find herself in a group of lively, talented, caring individuals, some of whom she already knew, and soon gained confidence in her new surroundings and found her niche socially'.[20] The friends she made at West Heath, notably Carolyn Pride and Laura Greig, were to become part of her loyal inner circle, supporting her through thick and thin, through the depths of despair and beyond. The trauma of her parents' divorce never quite left her: '. . . she came and talked to me quite a lot,' the matron, Violet Allen, said. 'Of course she missed her mother and father. The other [girls] who had divorces felt the same way. Some accepted it and some had more difficulty with it. No doubt about it, Diana found it difficult to accept. She was vulnerable in some things. I can't put a finger on it, but it probably all had to do with the insecurity and break-up of [her parents'] marriage.'[21]

She learned to play the piano, took lessons in ballet, tap and ballroom dance – her greatest relaxation. She won the school dancing competition one year and cups in swimming and diving every year. She developed her strong sense of sympathy for the suffering and the needy when she visited the mentally handicapped in the local hospital: when there were dances she would manoeuvre the wheelchairs from the front, facing the patients as if she were dancing with them, instead of, as was more usual, pushing from behind. In her day-to-day life Diana was at times fierce in her emotional responses, unforgiving to people who had offended her. 'She had a very strong character,' her headmistress said. 'She went about getting what she wanted . . .' In her last year Diana was named a prefect, and carried out her role so successfully that she was awarded a special prize for service – 'for anyone who has done things that otherwise might have gone unsung,' Ruth Rudge said. 'She was dependable in her own doings, reliable, and went out of her way to help people. She was generous with her time.'[22] When she was not being dutiful and dependable, Diana immersed herself in the romantic world of Barbara Cartland's novels in which strong men wooed virgin brides and love triumphed over all. It was perhaps the worst preparation for life in general and her own life in particular that she could have had.

Just as Diana was creating her own stable world on her own terms at West Heath, life at Park House and her relationship with her father there, the hitherto immutable centre for her since childhood, was about to change forever. The one thing the children had always dreaded happened. A new, powerful woman came into their father's life – Raine Legge, then Countess of Dartmouth. The first inkling they had of Raine's existence had come in the summer of 1972 when Johnnie invited Raine to lunch at Park House. Raine Dartmouth, or Legge as she was always then known, was a formidable woman, a beauty, immaculately dressed, made-up and coiffed, with a sharp intelligence and a will as determined as any of the Spencer children. She and Johnnie had met and fallen in love although Raine was still married to her first husband and was the mother of four children. She was also the daughter of another formidable character, the immensely successful Barbara Cartland, Diana's favourite novelist.

Sarah, it seems, who now had a London life, had heard gossip about her father's friendship with Lady Dartmouth which she had passed on to Diana and her siblings. The children were determined that no one should come between them and their beloved father whom they regarded as their property. When Johnnie told them he had invited Lady Dartmouth to lunch, the children's hackles were immediately raised. Diana's reaction to this immaculate vision, so far removed from the county ladies of their experience, was suppressed giggles. Raine was charming and gracious but oblivious to the children's covert hostility or, if she was not, determined not to let it bother her. In the end Sarah, with no other outlet for her enmity, burped loudly and deliberately. Johnnie said 'Sarah!' to which she cheekily replied that in Arab countries a burp was recognized as a sign of appreciation. Her father was so appalled that he told her to leave the table, which she did. Diana attempted to defend her, only to be told, 'That's enough, Diana.' Loyally, Diana riposted that she did not feel well and asked permission to leave, a request which her father readily granted. It had not been a good beginning.

The children's antennae were quivering at the prospect of this new woman in their father's life. 'We didn't like her one bit,' Charles said. 'As a child you instinctively feel things and with her I very much instinctively felt things.' The next encounter was to be at Sarah's coming-out party for her eighteenth birthday the following year, a fabulous occasion arranged by Johnnie at Castle Rising, a Norman ruin in Norfolk. Raine was among the four hundred guests and had taken a hand in its organization, finding a costume for Johnnie as Henry VIII and for Sarah a dress worn by Geneviève Bujold as Anne Boleyn in the 1969 film *Anne of the Thousand Days*. Sarah was in her element dancing with her boyfriend, Gerald Grosvenor, heir to the Duke of Westminster, and driving off in her father's birthday present to her, a green MGB GT sports car.

Sarah may have been too happy to notice the growing relationship between her father and the Countess of Dartmouth. Raine was determined to land Johnnie as her second husband. Her first, Gerald Legge, was already on his way out as far as she was concerned: she frequently gave dinner parties without him. Raine was dogged, ambitious and devastatingly efficient: by the time she and Johnnie met again for the first time since his marriage, she had already led a successful and high-profile public life as a councillor for Westminster for eleven years, for eight as the LCC member for Lewisham West, then as a member of the newly formed Greater London Council, when she had made her name opposing the licensing of the film of James Joyce's *Ulysses*, which she described as 'disgusting and degrading'. 'I like things that present life and sex in a glamorous way,'[23] she declared, true to the theme of her mother's novels. She had been a great success as chairman of the Historic Buildings Board; in 1971 she became a member of the English Tourist Board and headed an advisory committee to the government on the environment. When she resigned from the committee in protest at the Covent Garden development scheme, she became a national figure and a surprising heroine to the liberal left. 'It is all too easy to dismiss this particular woman ... as a good-looking, immaculately dressed, effusive member of the aristocracy who somehow gets offered positions of power', the *Guardian* wrote, '[but] behind the saccharine image there stands an extremely able politician, a feminine but tough bargainer . . .' In 1972 she was asked to become Chairman of the United Kingdom Executive Committee for European Architectural Heritage Year 1975. Her mission was to preserve historic towns and buildings; she wrote a book, *What Is Our Heritage?*, and co-opted Johnnie Spencer to the Youth Panel to promote the cause in his capacity as chairman of the National Association of Boys' Clubs. She also asked him to help with photographs for her book: it was obvious to colleagues that the couple were in love.

Johnnie was attracted to strong women and, if anything, Raine was even more forceful and dynamic than Frances. He had been lonely ever since Frances left: Raine's looks, wit and physical attraction bowled him over. Being rather slow and diffident he left her to make all the running. Raine was much brighter than Johnnie but found a vulnerability in him that appealed to her. She mothered and organized him. There was also a strong physical attraction between them (*Private Eye* later reported that en route from London to Northamptonshire they had stopped off at a motel for a few hours). Diana, who had mothered her father as much as she did her younger brother, had always thought of herself as first in his affections. But Raine could give him everything he got from Diana and more. Diana was about to receive a double shock.

3. 'I'm Lady Diana'

'I remember being a fat, podgy, no make-up, unsmart lady but I made a lot of noise and he [Prince Charles] liked that' (Diana to Andrew Morton)[1]

On 9 June 1975, Jack, 7th Earl Spencer, died and Diana's cosy family life at Park House came to an end. At first she was excited by her new title, Lady Diana, so much grander than the former Hon[ourable], and ran round West Heath shouting, 'I'm Lady Diana . . .' It was when she got home for the holidays that the real impact of the change in the family's circumstances hit her. Park House was being packed up in preparation for the move to the Spencer family home, Althorp. Her father was no longer Viscount Althorp but the 8th Earl Spencer. Diana's reaction to all this was to binge on peaches with her friend Alex Loyd at the beach hut at Brancaster.

Diana recalled: 'When I was 13 [actually fourteen; Diana was born 1 July 1961] we moved to Althorp in Northampton and that was a terrible wrench, leaving Norfolk, because that's where everybody who I'd grown up with lived. We had to move because grandfather died and life took a very big turn because my step-mother, Raine, appeared on the scene, supposedly incognito. She used to sort of join us, accidentally find us in places and come and sit down and pour [sic] us with presents and we all hated her so much because we thought she was going to take Daddy away from us . . .'[2] Leaving the house in which she had been born and spent all the years of her life so far was like another abandonment, another stage in her life like the departure of her mother. They had rarely visited Althorp and their feared grandfather and they had not liked it. Charles described it as 'a difficult phase in all our lives: uprooted from our childhood haunts and friends, and marooned in a park the size of Monaco', while the 121-room house seemed to them 'such an old man's house, reflecting my grandfather's Edwardian tastes, in a chilling time warp complete with the permeating smell of Trumper's hair oil and the ubiquitous tocking of grandfather clocks – their ticking always seemed too subtle a sound, getting absorbed in the oak of the floorboards and the fabric of the tapestries'.[3]

While Althorp was never to be 'home' to Diana as Park House had been, it reconnected her to her ancestors in a way which was to make her able to stand up to and even look down on the Royal Family. Even to someone as uninterested in history as Diana, the grandeur of Althorp, and the serried ranks of five centuries of distinguished forebears looking down on her from its walls, could not fail to impart a sense of the historic importance of her bloodlines. A historian friend of Diana's put it this way: 'Diana had sort of vaguely grasped, although being historically ignorant had not completely grasped, that those old Whig families like the Cavendishes and the Russells and her lot and one or two others, they in a way felt they were older and grander than the royal house, that they had put the House of Hanover on the throne when they were just German princelings, absolutely nothing, come from nowhere, couldn't speak a word of English . . . Parliament made George I monarch under the direction of the Whig oligarchy of which her family was a very important constituent founding member. So that in some way she had not married above her by marrying Prince Charles, if anything she'd married beneath her. Now I'm not sure that she ever formulated this view precisely in her mind, but it was sort of there I felt. "Who is he [Prince Charles] to look down on me and to say 'They're praising you because you're married to me, not because they like you'. 'You know, "Who is he to say this?" '[4] Traditionally, the Spencers and their aristocratic connections like the Cavendishes (Dukes of Devonshire) were Whigs who upheld the rights of the people against the overweening power of the monarch, as opposed to the Tory tradition of loyalty to the throne. 'The Tory tradition in the aristocracy,' said the historian Ben Pimlott, 'was deeply loyal to the monarchy; the Whig tradition was basically rather contemptuous. This difference can be exaggerated but there's a grain of truth, not necessarily in their traditions but in their style, and how they related to those traditions. The Whigs were individualists.'[5]

Althorp is not a beautiful house – the warm brick of the original Tudor great mansion was covered over in the late eighteenth century with silvery white tiles which give it a cold appearance – but it is surrounded by idyllic English countryside, the rolling acres of grassland which nurtured the sheep whose wool was the source of the original Spencer fortune. Spencers had occupied Althorp for nearly five centuries since the original John Spencer, known as 'the Founder', had acquired the land in 1507 and begun to build his mansion, acquiring more land, planting trees and creating the surrounding park. The family also owned the magnificent eighteenth-century Spencer House in London overlooking Green Park, but this was rented out in Diana's day. Spencer wealth and possessions had increased over the centuries, some of the more splendid through the first Diana Spencer, daughter of Lady Anne Churchill, whose parents were John Churchill, 1st Duke of Marlborough and his wife, Sarah Jennings, one of the most remarkable and difficult women of her day. The Spencer tendency for falling out with members of the family – it is said Sarah changed her will fifty times – may well have been passed down from her. The Churchill connection was much cherished by the family who were extremely proud of being related to the 1st Duke of Marlborough, whose great victories over the French in the first decade of the eighteenth century had brought him fame and riches and the great palace of Blenheim, named after his most celebrated victory and built for him by a grateful nation. Winston Churchill was born Winston Spencer Churchill: one day Diana's grandfather, Jack Spencer, found Winston Churchill in his cherished Muniment Room, smoking a cigar while researching the life of their mutual ancestor, the 1st Duke of Marlborough. Peremptorily he ordered Churchill to douse his cigar in a glass of water. Sarah, the 1st Duchess, had left her Spencer heirs her great collections of paintings and jewellery and the Marlborough Silver, the reward for the 1st Duke's campaigns, including the lavish gold and silver pieces bestowed on him by Queen Anne after Blenheim.

Diana's ancestors included not only Sarah Jennings, whose pride led her to snub even her sovereign and former friend, Queen Anne, but also another outstanding woman, Georgiana, Duchess of Devonshire, the headstrong beauty whose reckless exploits in Whig politics and at the gaming tables made her the most famous woman of her day. The blood of these distant ancestors meant that Diana was never going to be the mousy little girl some people thought – or perhaps hoped – that she would be. 'Spencers are very difficult and complicated people,' a Spencer relation said. 'The Queen Mother once said to me, "You know the Spencer women are extremely unusual and difficult!" and that's how they are. They also have an unforgiving side to them which seems to run through the family a bit. And I think that that way she had with the inability to sustain friendships and relationships seems to be one of the characteristics of them.' She said of her own Spencer mother: 'She was incredibly like Diana. In the same things. The sort of manipulation of reality, as I call it, and the conflict and then reunion and so on.'[6]

At first life at Althorp when Diana and Charles moved there seemed like a continuation of their childhood, although on a grand scale. Although latterly there had been a butler named Betts at Park House, his services had been abruptly dispensed with when the house was closed. At Althorp, however, there was not only a butler, Ainsley Pendrey, who had served the previous Earl, but a footman as well and seven other indoor servants. 'The early days were very happy ones and jolly good fun, with no bowing and scraping,' Betty Andrews, who started work at Althorp in 1975, told Angela Levin, author of a joint biography of Johnnie and Raine. The children would rush into the kitchen to find something to eat. 'Diana even used to cook for the staff. She loved to make bread and butter pudding for us and rice or milk pudding for herself,' Betty Andrews recalled.[7] Diana, always so domesticated, did her own washing and ironing and often Charles's too. This nurturing, almost domestic slave, side of Diana repeated itself in

later life: she would do all the household chores for her sister Sarah,
iron shirts for her platonic boyfriends before her marriage and, in
the year of her death, do the ironing for Annabel Goldsmith and
Jemima Khan on their trip to Pakistan. It was never a Marie
Antoinette act, rather a response to a need in herself, to be useful,
to show her skills, and to be 'tidy', another of her favourite
words. At school people noticed her obsessive tidiness. She even
used the word 'tidy' about keeping her virginity for the right
man. The atmosphere at Althorp, according to Andrews, was
'happy-go-lucky – all three sisters got on well together'. Diana
would toboggan down the grand front staircase on a tea tray, and
dance by herself in the great Wootton Hall, designed as the
entrance to the house in the early eighteenth century, with pictures
and plasterwork reflecting the family passion for hunting.

Raine's presence radically changed the atmosphere. She had
always wanted a grand country house, which Gerald Dartmouth
had not possessed. Although not yet married to Johnnie, she was
ever-present, staying in the India Silk Bedroom across the corridor
from Johnnie's room. She began to redecorate the house, paying
the cost herself. Johnnie was cash poor, as always, and now faced
with a £2 million bill for death duties. She was desperate to marry
Johnnie and began to fear that his hostile children would eventually
frustrate her. None of them, and Sarah in particular, made any
secret of their dislike. Sarah, never averse to talking to reporters,
used their inquisitive telephone calls to drop acid into the newspapers about Raine. To one inquiry about Lord Spencer's relationship with Lady Dartmouth, she replied that her father was in bed
with Lady Dartmouth and she wasn't going to disturb them. She
told another: 'Since my grandfather died last June and we moved
from Sandringham to Althorp, Lady Dartmouth has been an all
too frequent visitor . . .'[8] When asked why Lady Dartmouth was
spending so much time at Althorp, she replied, 'She is helping my
father to open the house on a commercial basis. In my grandfather's
time he did not care for the idea of the public walking around his
house. Lady Dartmouth is writing a guide for it with my father.'
Diana's protest was characteristic: a member of the paying public

remembered seeing her 'acting the part of Cinderella' sitting beside the fire as the public walked past. The children used to chant 'Raine, Raine, go away' intending that she should hear them.

But Raine did not go away. In May 1976 Gerald Dartmouth obtained a divorce on the grounds of her adultery; two months later, on 14 July 1976, Johnnie and Raine married at Caxton Hall register office in London. He did not tell his children beforehand what he was going to do. Their fury knew no bounds, as he had anticipated. In 1992 Diana told Peter Settelen: 'Sarah rang me up, she said, "Have you seen the newspapers?" So I said, "What?" "Daddy's married Raine." I said, "My God, how do you know that?" "It's in the *Express*." We were so angry, but Sarah said, "Right, Duch" – my nickname was Duch – "you go in and sort him out."

'He said, "I want to explain to you why, um, I've got married to Raine." And I said, "Well, we don't like her." And he said, "I know that, but you'll grow to love her, as I have." And I said, "Well, we won't." I kept on saying we not I . . . I was the little crusader here . . . and I got really angry and I, if I remember rightly, I slapped him across the face, and I said, "That's from all of us, for hurting us", and walked out of the room and slammed the door. He followed me and he got me by the wrist and turned me round and said, "Don't you ever talk to me like that again." And I said, "Well, don't you ever do that to us again", and walked off.'[9]

The four Spencer children had always stood together, metaphorically and physically. 'They were always very close as young people. Always did everything together, on any family occasion they were always in a group together, quite daunting for other people – it seemed like they were protecting each other . . .' a Spencer relation said. For anyone less concentrated on her goal than Raine Dartmouth, the hostile Spencer children gathered like a praetorian guard round their father would have been deeply intimidating. There had even been moments when she feared Johnnie's devotion to his children would prevent him from marrying her. After the wedding, when Raine became undisputed mistress of Althorp, things became even worse. The children's proprietorial attitude towards their father had not changed, and now they felt excluded. They remained impervious to Raine's charms. When friends were invited to stay at Althorp by Johnnie and Raine, they noticed 'a terrible air of strain between all three girls' which was 'very, very awkward' and that the sisters avoided saying a word to Raine if they could. On one social weekend in Yorkshire where there was a ball for the young at Haddon Hall, a friend of Johnnie's and Raine's sat next to Diana at lunch. 'Suddenly her eyes glinted, and she said, "You're a friend of my stepmother's, aren't you?" He replied, "I hope I'm a friend of your father's too."' – 'It was very unpleasant,' he commented. Sarah, who was in touch with the media, was more active in her enmity – leaking disagreeable stories about Raine to a tabloid reporter.[10] Even Jane, the quietest and least unstable of the Spencer quartet, 'the best of the lot' in a family friend's opinion, could not entirely restrain her hostility. On being asked at a dinner how often she went to Althorp, she replied loudly in Raine's hearing – 'When I'm asked.'

So Diana, like the others, felt a kind of estrangement from her father. She loved him but she saw less of him. He remained a loving father but in her view he belonged to Raine and not to her. It did not help the following year when she took her O levels. She took them twice and failed them twice and as a result had to leave West Heath at the age of sixteen. Diana said, 'At the age of fourteen I just remember thinking that I wasn't very good at anything, that I was hopeless. My brother was always the one who was getting exams at school and I was the dropout . . .'[11] 'I was always told by my family that I was the thick one and that my brother was the clever one and I was always so conscious of that.' 'I used to go to the headmistress,' she added, 'crying, saying, I wish I wasn't so stupid,' she said later.[12] Ruth Rudge denies her ever having done this: 'I never remember walking around with her and feeding her aspirins the night before, which I have done a number of times with other girls, [but] I didn't see any signs of panic when she took exams.'[13] Friends of Diana's have attributed it to 'sheer laziness and the fact that she was never pushed'. She excelled in the things she liked doing but, when it came to academic work, she simply gave up even before she started. A relative explained it: 'I think she was not stupid, she was intelligent and she had this very, very quick wit, but I think it reflected on her lack of confidence, her inability to achieve at school and sometimes if you're emotionally damaged in some way you can't sustain concentration or learning, and I think a certain part of you cuts out the ability to absorb and process and construct, and I think that's what happened to her. She certainly wasn't stupid.' The same relation attributed Diana's backwardness in formal education to her status as a 're-placement baby', the girl born after the death of John: 'I have noticed in other families where there has been what's called a replacement baby, that the baby that's been born after a death has certain things imposed on it which are not really relevant and they seem to feel things which have perhaps been in other people's minds . . .' In compensation, Diana developed an almost mystical belief in the power and rightness of her own instinct which was to guide her, for better or for worse, through her entire life. She had, or so she later claimed, a sense of her own destiny, that she was apart from the rest, designed for higher things. If so, who needs exams?

Things were changing in all their lives: Raine was extremely social. There were constant house parties, balls, shooting parties: the children were banished to the nursery floor to leave room for the guests. Entertaining became more formal, and under Raine, demanding and a perfectionist, staff turnover was high. A senior employee told Angela Levin of the children's reaction to their stepmother: 'With the exception of Jane, who wasn't too bad, the children could not have been more difficult and cold to Raine. There was open hostility, not just to her as a person. They also disliked the way she dominated and became so possessive of their father which made them feel they had to compete with her for his attention.'[14] Rupert Hambro recalled his impression: 'It was as if she had put an iron fence around him. She also had a way of making people who played a part in his life before she arrived feel small. She was totally insensitive to Johnnie's family, his life and his interests. When you did see him she was his mouthpiece and if you asked him anything, she would answer. A lot of people are incredibly happy in an environment that takes any pressure away from them. I would describe Lord Spencer as being pretty close to that . . .'[15] Johnnie Spencer's aunt, Lady Margaret Douglas-Home, who knew the children well, saw to the heart of the problem: 'I don't think Raine went about it the right way,' she said. 'I don't think she is made to be a stepmother. She must be the only pebble on the beach and wasn't willing to take second place to Johnnie's children. She used to claim all of him the whole time and didn't like them interfering in her life with Johnnie. The children never liked it and they were old enough to know. I was very sorry for them. They looked miserable.'[16]

According to a friend of Raine's the great strength in the Althorp household during this time of strain was Pendrey the butler whom he described as 'droll and amusing and a great pillar'. He and his wife Maudie, the housekeeper, a Norfolk farmer's daughter, were a refuge for Diana, as Mrs Pendrey recalled:

When she came to live at Althorp, she was always shy. She used to blush ever so easily too, used to go scarlet. My husband adored Diana, we all did. She would come and see her father about every six or seven weeks. When we knew Diana was coming for the weekend my husband would get all her favourite food in and make sure she had everything up in her bedroom. She used to sleep in the nursery, in a little black iron bed . . . When she came to Althorp the first thing she did was come and find my husband, because she was a very lovely, very polite little girl – always called him Mr. Pendrey – . . . of course he used to spoil her.

After her father remarried, she used to come and talk to us quite a lot. She sometimes used to come and have lunch with us. She never had airs and graces. Diana was just an ordinary lovely girl. She was very sweet and all the staff loved her. They used to put flowers in her bedroom when she used to come to Althorp. We used to make a fuss of her and make sure she was someone important. My husband said to me, when he saw her start growing up . . . 'You wait. She's going to be someone very special'.[17]

Staying with friends in Norfolk one September weekend Diana
had a premonition about her father. By her own account she told
her friends that she felt her father was going to 'drop down' and
that 'if he dies, he'll die immediately, otherwise he'll survive'. Next
day, 19 September 1978, Johnnie collapsed as he was crossing the
courtyard at Althorp: he had suffered a massive cerebral haemorrhage. He was taken unconscious to Northampton General Hospital where he developed pneumonia. Raine, despite the danger,
insisted that he be transferred to the National Hospital for Nervous
Diseases in Queen Square, London, where the facilities would be
better. In a deep coma he was put on a life-support machine, and
subsequently underwent a four-hour brain operation. Raine was
heroic: sitting beside his bed as he lay unconscious, willing him to
live. He appeared to recover, then four weeks after the operation he
contracted pseudomonas, a rare virulent bacterium unresponsive to
normal antibiotics, and was transferred to the Brompton Hospital.
There he remained on the critical list and almost died eight times.
Raine saved his life. Desperate, she asked her friend Bill Cavendish-
Bentinck, later Duke of Portland and a director of the German
pharmaceutical company Bayer, whether the company had any
drug under testing that might help his condition. Cavendish-
Bentinck told her that there was indeed one, Azlocillin, but that
it was not yet on the market and that she needed the approval of
Johnnie's doctors before it was tried out on him. She bullied them
into agreement: 'I'd rather he died my way, doing something, than
your way, doing nothing.' Samples were flown from Germany and
given to Johnnie. Almost miraculously he recovered. Later he gave
Raine a magnificent parure of rubies from Van Cleef & Arpels for
saving his life.

Gratitude does not seem to have been among the feelings
Raine's devotion to Johnnie provoked in his children. At one
point Raine instructed nurses at Queen Square to prevent the
children from disturbing their seriously ill father while she was
with him. They waited for her to leave before sneaking in. A nurse
remembered that they would have Sarah going up in the lift as

Raine was coming down. Unsurprisingly, they were rude to her, Jane being the only one to say hello. Diana, devastated, was in tears, although by her own account she was 'frightfully calm'. 'We saw another side of Raine which we hadn't anticipated,' she recalled, 'as she basically blocked us out of the hospital, she wouldn't let us see Daddy ... Anyway he got better and he basically changed character. He was one person before and another person after. He's remained estranged but adoring since.'[13]

Meanwhile, Diana's destiny had been taking her away from school and childhood towards a new and unexpected life. Since the previous summer Prince Charles had become involved with her sister Sarah. The two had met when Sarah, as an eligible twenty-two-year-old, was invited to join the house party at Windsor Castle for the racing week at Royal Ascot, at the instigation of Henriette Abel Smith, her godmother and one of the Queen's ladies-in-waiting. Prince Andrew, whom she had known as a child, introduced her to Prince Charles. Despite asking her tactlessly, 'Do you have anorexia?' – she was obviously very thin but denied the illness – the two got on. Sarah Spencer was recovering from a traumatic two years, suffering from the eating disorders anorexia nervosa and bulimia, setting a pattern for Diana's own reaction to stress. Years later Diana told patients at the Priory, a private clinic treating addictions on the outskirts of London, that she had first had symptoms of bulimia in the mid-seventies, attributing it to Sarah's experience: 'It started because Sarah was anorexic and I idolized her so much that I wanted to be like her.' If this is so – and Diana's statements are not always the truth of a situation, but sometimes her rereading of it from a distance in time – it certainly did not affect her seriously. While Sarah, who was 5 foot 7 inches tall, went down to 5 stone 10 pounds, photographs of Diana at the time show no signs whatever of serious slimming. Sarah suffered for two years: it was so severe at first that Frances had her taken to hospital. Frances attributed the illness to Sarah's break-up with Gerald Grosvenor after returning from a three-month stay with the Shand Kydds in Australia. This may be so but

Sarah had already shown signs of addiction problems when she drank to alleviate her boredom at school: the split with Grosvenor may well, however, have precipitated it.

Prince Charles enjoyed Sarah's sparkiness and irreverent wit and they made each other laugh. By mid-July the press were following their relationship: Sarah was seen with the Prince at polo and – always a test of the seriousness of one of Prince Charles's relationships – invited by the Queen to Balmoral. Sarah was extremely attractive, vital and witty: Prince Charles was amused by her but not, it seems, physically attracted. Diana later asserted that Sarah had been surprised that he had never tried to go to bed with her. Sarah invited Charles to a shoot at Althorp in November 1977. Diana was given the weekend off from West Heath to attend, meeting the Prince for the first time in a ploughed field near Nobottle Wood when Charles, according to his official biographer, found her 'jolly' and 'bouncy', a pretty, unaffected teenager. Diana herself recorded, perhaps with the benefit of hindsight, that her first impression was 'God, what a sad man'. Sarah, she said cattily in one of her favourite phrases, was 'all over him like a bad rash'.

At the dance that night at Althorp, Charles showed that he was attracted by the sixteen-year-old's high spirits. Diana said, 'I remember being a fat, podgy, no make-up, unsmart lady but I made a lot of noise and he liked that and he came up to me after dinner and we had a big dance and he said: "Will you show me the gallery [the Picture Gallery, a notable feature of Althorp] and I was just about to show him the gallery and my sister Sarah comes up and tells me to push off and I said, "At least let me tell you where the switches are because you won't know where they are", and I disappeared. And he was charm itself and when I stood next to him next day [out shooting], a 16-year-old for someone like that to show you any attention – I was just so sort of amazed. "Why would anyone like him be interested in me?" And it *was* interest.'[19]

Even her siblings began to notice that Diana had changed. 'She suddenly became sort of magnetic and people were interested in her as a character when she hit about 16,' her brother Charles, who had gone up to Eton that year, 1977, remembered. 'Before then she was quiet – I mean always up to something . . . never dull – but quite quiet and shy. But I think as she started to become a pretty young woman as opposed to a girl, she got some confidence then. That started to open her up quite a lot and I think she realised then that she had a knack for being the life and soul of the party. People really enjoyed being around her.'[20]

Diana always gave it to be understood in her later accounts that it was Prince Charles who made the running, but her piano teacher and form mistress at West Heath, Penny Walker, gave a different version:

She was always talking about Prince Charles . . . I can remember the weekend she came back after she'd met him, because she couldn't talk about anything else. She said: 'I've met him! At last I've met him' . . . She had pictures of him up in her cubicle. It wasn't entirely unusual for a girl from that kind of background, but it was unusual because it was so consistent all the time she was at school. Her only talk was of him and meeting him. I'm not sure there was any talk about marrying, but she just seemed completely besotted, dreaming of escape, I should think, into fairytale.[21]

Early the next year, 1978, Diana was dispatched to a finishing school, the Institut Alpin Videmanette, in Switzerland, where she was homesick. Always an obsessive letter writer, she wrote 120 letters in her first month there. She learned to ski but felt out of her depth with the other girls, who were mostly Spanish or Italian. At the end of one term, it was recognized that there was no point in keeping her there and she was allowed to come home. She was back in London for her sister Jane's wedding. Jane had become engaged in 1977 to a Norfolk neighbour, Robert Fellowes, son of the Queen's Sandringham land agent Sir William 'Billy' Fellowes, and they were married in April 1978 with Diana as chief brides-maid. Jane was only twenty, Robert Fellowes thirty-six, only five years younger than Jane's mother. He too had been taught by Ally as a young boy and had moved in exactly the same Norfolk circles

as the Spencer children when they lived at Park House. He was
also, like many of their relations, a courtier and member of the
royal household as the Queen's assistant private secretary. Tall,
slim and discreet, he had the perfect Establishment credentials,
then considered a prerequisite for royal service. He was an Etonian
and had served in the Scots Guards. As Jane put it somewhat un-
romantically, 'We have known each other all our lives and have
gradually grown closer.' Sarah, typically, stated, 'We had been
trying to trap him for years.'

The wedding itself took place at the Guards Chapel, Wellington
Barracks, a few hundred yards from Buckingham Palace, the bridegroom's 'office', and the reception was held at the old royal palace
of St James's, again part of the royal enclave. The Queen Mother
arrived with Ruth Fermoy, and the Duchess of Kent and Duke
and Duchess of Gloucester were among the guests, underlining
the fact that the young couple were part of the 'magic circle' round
the Crown. Frances paid for everything but, as a friend said, 'she
was almost a guest at her own daughter's wedding'. The fact that
she and Johnnie were not on speaking terms was obvious to
everyone who knew them. Raine was very much in evidence and
one of the wedding organizers had to be deputed to keep her out
of the family photographs. At the wedding, Diana bounced up to
one of the best known of the royal press gang, James Whitaker,
then of the *Daily Mirror*, one of Sarah's chief media contacts, and
introduced herself saying, 'You're James Whitaker, aren't you? I
know all about you. I'm Sarah's baby sister.' It was the beginning
of Diana's lifelong affair with the media.

Diana's approach to James Whitaker, perhaps the best known
of the 'rat pack' of tabloid reporters, was almost certainly prompted
by his recent role in her sister's life, specifically the ending of her
close friendship with Prince Charles. Sarah, according to Diana,
had by now 'got frightfully excited about the whole thing'. Over-
excited, perhaps. She had been invited to spend a weekend at
Sandringham, and in February Charles asked her to join his skiing
party for a ten-day holiday in Klosters, Switzerland. By now the
tabloids had Sarah in the frame as Charles's girlfriend, following

her on the slopes and taking photographs. Sarah, according to
Whitaker, enjoyed flirting with the media and reading about herself
in the press. She subscribed to Durrants cutting service, not only
the English cutting service but Durrants worldwide, in order not
to miss a word, and kept albums of cuttings about herself. On her
return from Switzerland she unwisely lunched with two reporters
from the *Sun* and the *Daily Mail*, two of the most widely read
popular papers, and talked about her relationship with Charles.
One month later she made matters worse by giving Whitaker an
extended interview to be published as a long article in the magazine
Woman's Own (Whitaker wrote it under the pseudonym Jeremy
Slazenger in order not to upset his regular employer, the *Sun*). She
had told Whitaker of her drinking and expulsion from school and
her anorexia, even exaggerating it by saying that her gynaecologist
had told her she would never be able to have children (she later
had three), and that she had lost virtually all the enamel on her
teeth. She had also offered to provide photographs revealing her
painful thinness which were so upsetting that the publishers for
her sake decided not to print them. She boasted of having had
'thousands of boyfriends'. More seriously, she went on to discuss
Prince Charles, 'a romantic who falls in love easily', and denied
she was in love with him: 'I'm not in love with Prince Charles.
I'm a whirlwind sort of lady, as opposed to a person who goes in
for slow-developing courtships. I can assure you that if there was
to be any engagement between Prince Charles and myself, then it
would have happened by now. I wouldn't marry anyone I didn't
love – whether it was the dustman or the King of England. If he
asked me I would turn him down. He doesn't want to marry
anyway. He's not ready for marriage yet . . . Our whole approach
has been a brotherly-sisterly one, never anything else . . . There's
no question of me being the future Queen of England. I don't
think he's met her yet.'

Poor Sarah compounded her foolishness, as she later told
Whitaker, by then picking up the telephone and calling Prince
Charles: 'I think I've just done something very stupid, Sir.' 'What
have you done?' he asked. She replied, 'I've just given an interview

to James Whitaker for *Woman's Own*.' Charles just said, 'Yes, Sarah, you have done something extremely stupid.'[22] Talking to the tabloids was a cardinal sin in royal eyes; talking about Prince Charles to the tabloids was to prove fatal to their relationship.

Despite her own faux pas over the Prince, Sarah was not pleased when Diana came into the picture, as she recalled: 'then she [Sarah] saw something different happening which I hadn't twigged on to, i.e. when he had his 30th birthday dance [on 14 November 1978] I was asked too . . .'[23] From that dinner at Althorp Diana had fallen for Charles with all the passion of youthful love, and with a youthful conviction that she was going to get him.

Diana was completely unsophisticated: she had never moved outside her narrow social circles, never been abroad apart from the vain sojourn in Switzerland, never been to university or indeed read a book beyond Barbara Cartland. Looking after children was the only career Diana had envisaged at that time. While Jane and Sarah both had the credentials to land jobs at *Vogue*, the family considered that looking after children was indeed all Diana was capable of. Some of them, like her great-aunt Lady Margaret Douglas-Home, were concerned that Diana had no aim in life. Indeed, for Diana at that time, her dream was to go to London and share in the independent lives of her sisters and her friends there. After three months of pressure, she was allowed to share her mother Frances's Cadogan Square flat with two other girls, Laura Greig, her West Heath school friend and the most long-lasting of her school-day friendships, and Sophie Kimball, whom she had met at Videmanette. Privileged, living in her mother's flat and paid for by her parents, she did not feel the need to try for a well-paid job: a three-month cookery course in Wimbledon was followed by a stint as an apprentice teacher at Miss Vacani's ballet studio in Kensington which she left when she felt intimidated by the parents. She then took various low-paid jobs, house cleaning and child care, for employers whom she later derided as 'velvet hair bands', a reference to the prim Alice-band style in fashion among a certain class of unimaginative, rather prissy English girls since the fifties.

Looking after children remained the focus of her working life.

She went to work as a part-time assistant at the Young England kindergarten run by Kay King, a West Heath old girl, where, according to Miss King, she showed 'this incredible ability' to get down to the children's level. 'They responded so well to her, [and] she was completely at ease with them.' She also worked part-time as a nanny recruited by an agency, Occasional and Permanent Nannies, which recommended her as 'sweet-tempered, good with children, willing to do whatever she's asked'. There was only one condition: Diana would only work in the smartest, safest areas of London within easy reach of where she lived. And when she went to work for an American couple, Patrick and Mary Robertson, she indicated another: she would not work at evenings or weekends so that her social life could continue unimpeded.

Mary Robertson found her beautiful ('an English rose'), shy, polite and helpful in the extreme but even in those days very private and guarding that privacy. Mrs Robertson had no idea of Diana's aristocratic background and Diana never said anything about it. When asked if she had had a nice weekend she would simply say she had been 'in the country' or, if she had been to see her sister Jane at Kensington Palace, she would say only that she had been 'to see my sister's baby in Kensington'. When Mrs Robertson once admired her haircut and asked who the hairdresser was, she referred vaguely to 'a little hairdresser near my flat'. 'I knew I couldn't push,' Mrs Robertson commented. Diana never mentioned her mother and only rarely her family. If Charles, to whom Mrs Robertson said Diana was 'devoted', came up from Eton, she would ask permission to leave early, forbearing even to say that he was at Eton. Along with Diana's discretion about her social life, Mrs Robertson wrote, she was 'aware of a natural delicacy or refinement that guarded her innermost feelings. I considered her emotional distance as a sign of respect for her own privacy and that of others . . . I thought this aura was her most intriguing quality.' In 1980, she said, Diana was a 'happy normal teenager, enjoying her first experience of independence, busy with her two child-care jobs, and having fun with her friends'.[24]

In May 1980, Sarah married Neil McCorquodale, a Coldstream

Guards officer and gentleman farmer who happened to be a distant connection of Raine, described by a friend as 'solid, very steady, private, quiet; with a good sense of humour'. He was, in short, exactly the type of man whom Lady Diana Spencer could, and perhaps should, have married and never been heard of again. McCorquodale had need of these qualities for Sarah, mercurial as ever, had called off the wedding in February. Finally it took place in the Spencer parish church, St Mary the Virgin, Great Brington, with the reception at Althorp. Again, Frances paid for the wedding, and again Raine and her mother, Barbara Cartland, were well to the fore. Diana was a bridesmaid. She still appeared, according to one observer, 'this rather shy, really very mousy-haired creature'.

By this time, Diana had moved (in July 1979) to 60 Coleherne Court, a smart £50,000-mansion block flat on the borders of South Kensington and Chelsea, found for her by Sarah, who was working for the estate agent Savills, and given to her by her mother as a coming-of-age present. She shared it with three girlfriends: Carolyn Pride, her friend since West Heath, Anne Bolton and Virginia Pitman. Among her other jobs she used to be employed to do the chores for Sarah in her mews house in Elm Park Lane, Chelsea. According to a friend who shared the flat, 'Diana hero-worshipped her [Sarah] but Sarah treated her like a doormat'. She was paid £1 an hour and if she didn't do the job properly she had to do it again.[25] Nor was her social life any more exciting. Diana disliked parties and had turned down her parents' offer of a coming-out ball. She attended quite a few dances during country house weekends with her friends but mostly she preferred sitting at home, watching television and giggling with her friends or careering about London in her Mini Metro, playing silly tricks on their men friends. Diana's male friends were typical upper-class, rather conventional young men; several of them were officers, others undergraduates, most of them with a county background. None of them, apparently, was allowed to become more than just friends, however much they might have liked to get closer. One of her men friends, Rory Scott, who found her sexually attractive, never made the distance. 'She was always a little aloof,' he said. 'You always felt that there was a lot you would never know about her.' She had a dirty laugh and liked lavatorial jokes, said one friend. Men found her very sexy, tactile, flirtatious: she laughed at their jokes but drew the line at serious flirting. In that she was, a friend said, 'unusual at a time when her contemporaries would "go like rabbits".'. The friend thought it was 'rubbish all that stuff about saving herself for something'. Diana, she divined, was afraid of sex. Other friends, like Carolyn Pride, later Bartholomew, perhaps rationalizing after the event, took the view which Diana herself propagated when she said, 'I knew I had to keep myself tidy for what lay ahead.' Bartholomew told Andrew Morton in 1991, 'I'm not a terribly spiritual person but I do believe that she was meant to do what she is doing and she certainly believes that. She was surrounded by this golden aura which stopped men going any further; whether they would have liked to or not, it never happened.'[26]

It may be that Diana secretly thought of herself as special and destined for higher things in compensation for the ordinariness and limited horizons of her everyday life. It is a quality of icons that they have a focused vision of themselves and their future. Grace Kelly and Jackie Bouvier dreamed of being stars and of marrying special men. So did Diana. Behind the jolly English-rose façade, she nurtured extraordinary qualities, but they were not apparent yet. Nothing could have prepared her for the royal future which suddenly appeared on her horizon.

4. Enter the Prince

'I believe in a case like yours that a man should sow his wild oats before settling down. But for a wife he should choose a suitable and sweet-charactered girl before she meets anyone else she might fall for' (Earl Mountbatten to Charles[1])

At the age of thirty, Prince Charles Philip Arthur George was slim, muscled, shy, kind and deeply confused. He had been born on 14 November 1948 at Buckingham Palace, official seat of the ruling dynasty of Great Britain, as befitted the future heir to the throne. And as such he had been the focus of interest from the moment his life began.

His mother, then Princess Elizabeth, was only twenty-two when he was born, and had been married to the former Prince Philip of Greece, now Prince Philip, Duke of Edinburgh, for just a year. In 1952, when he was three and a half years old, his grandfather, King George VI, died and his young mother became Queen of Great Britain and Northern Ireland, Defender of the Faith and Head of the Commonwealth. As Queen she had the weight of her duties to cope with – in the year of her Coronation, for instance, when Charles was four, she and the Duke of Edinburgh undertook a six-month tour of the Commonwealth. In the circumstances Charles saw far less of his parents than did other children of his age. When he did see them – and both made a great deal of effort to make his life as 'normal' as possible, playing with him and trying to be there when he had his evening bath and supper – there was still no escaping the fact that his mother was the Queen, Head of State, Head of the Armed Forces and Governor of the Established Church, the apex of a large royal household dedicated to serving her every wish. She saw her duty first and foremost as her 'job', following her father's footsteps as sovereign, with all the hard work and dedication which that entailed. As Queen, she was inevitably surrounded by an aura, blocking all real intimacy: Prince Charles has remained in awe of her all his life.

He was (and still is) equally in awe of his father, Prince Philip, who, despite a difficult childhood, had emerged as a success in every field he tackled, at school, in the navy and as consort to the Queen. Extremely handsome and formidably strong-willed, the Duke of Edinburgh dominated the family: it was he who decreed the course of Charles's education which largely followed the steps he himself had taken. A preparatory day school in London, Hill House in Knightsbridge, where the shy boy came into contact with unknown children of his own age for the first time, was followed by a preparatory boarding school, Cheam in Surrey. Charles was nine years old when he was sat down in front of the television by his headmaster to watch himself declared Prince of Wales (the hereditary title of the heir to the throne) to a cheering crowd of thousands of Welshmen. It came as an unexplained shock and only served to increase the difficulty of maintaining the illusion that he was 'just another schoolboy'. He was desperately homesick and made no friends at Cheam.

Cheam was followed by a far more harrowing experience – Gordonstoun, the tough educational establishment on the northeast coast of Scotland which his father had attended, and which had been founded by the German educationalist Kurt Hahn, on the model of his original establishment in Germany. Gordonstoun was intended to produce self-reliant leaders in the mode of Charles's father, who had excelled at everything sporting and became Captain of Cricket. Charles, shy and vulnerable, was bullied all the more because he was 'different' and royal; boys lined up for the distinction of roughing up the heir to the throne at rugby. Most kept their distance from him for fear of being labelled as toadies: some went in for active physical bullying, shoving his head down the lavatory or beating him with pillows. The physical discomfort was extreme: snow drove in horizontal from the North Sea through the open windows of the unheated wooden dormi-

tories. There were obligatory cold showers, runs and stormy
sessions in open sailing boats on the North Sea. Again, he made
no friends; his parents rarely visited, often sending the Dean of
Windsor, the Right Rev. Robin Woods, in their stead. His only
glimpse of home comforts was staying with his beloved maternal
grandmother, Queen Elizabeth, at her Scottish home, Birkhall, on
the royal Balmoral estate, which he ever after referred to as 'the
most wonderful place in the world'. His refuge was music, to
which he was introduced by his grandmother, and the stage, always
a home for people who are not totally sure of their own identity.

At home in London his refuge was his nanny, Mabel Anderson.
'Mabel saved my life,' he used to say. Mabel was his guardian
angel, ever present in his young life. When he contracted infectious
diseases such as chicken pox, he would be sent away to preserve
the Queen's health, accompanied by Mabel, often to Holkham,
the Leicesters' stately home on the Norfolk coast not far from
Sandringham. And home life, much as he cherished it in comparison with his school experiences, could be tough and demanding.
His parents believed that being the heir to the throne involved
rigorous training. His sister, Anne, outgoing, determined and tom-
boyish, was always much closer in character to his father, who was
often dismayed by Charles's 'wimpishness' and made no secret of
it. He could be a bully and often was to Charles, embarrassing him
and putting him down in front of other people. His mother,
although loving him, was non-confrontational and left the over-
seeing of his education largely to his father.

With his future involvement with the Commonwealth in
mind, Charles was given a year off from Gordonstoun to attend
Timbertop; this he liked because of its location in the Australian
bush and its connection with nature, which he both enjoyed and
revered. Gordonstoun had been followed by university, Trinity
College, Cambridge, under the wise guidance of Rab Butler, a
distinguished former Conservative minister, and by a brief and
uncomfortable period at the Welsh university Aberystwyth,
designed to familiarize him with the distant country which was his
'principality'. Charles dutifully learned Welsh and showed courage

in facing up to the hostility of the Welsh nationalists who threatened to disrupt his formal installation as Prince of Wales in 1969.

Under the guidance of his father and his great-uncle, Earl Mountbatten, he was launched on a series of military training courses, piloting aircraft, parachute jumping, and Dartmouth Royal Naval School, culminating in a five-year spell in the navy. As a result of these macho heroics, the newspapers dubbed him 'Action Man'. Charles drove himself hard physically in a bid to show his father he was not the wimp he thought he was. He rode hard to hounds and at polo, pushing himself to the limit although his horsemanship was not of the highest standard. He faced physical danger as if it were a challenge to be overcome, but at heart he was not as tough as he appeared. On one occasion when he telephoned his mother to express his distress at the death of one of his sailors, the Queen was heard to remark, 'Charles really must toughen up'. He remained shy, sensitive and insecure, a good, kind person who became increasingly spoiled by the indulgence of those around him. He was loved and cosseted by his mother's household, notably Lady Susan Hussey, one of the Queen's Women of the Bedchamber and only eleven years his senior. His grandmother, the Queen Mother, adored him, as did his aunt, the vivacious and intelligent Princess Margaret. Once he was given his own household, he was spoiled by his entourage, principally by his valets, a tradition which was to continue. This cosseting and ministering to his every need had, by the time he left the navy in 1976, had its effect on his character. He began to resent the relentless demands of 'duty', of having his every day planned, of being told what to do by senior courtiers.

Squadron Leader David Checketts, who had been Charles's mentor and adviser since 1966 when he had accompanied the young prince to Timbertop, was the first victim of Charles's determination to assert his independence. Checketts, an urbane, grammar school-educated public relations man with a distinguished RAF record, had been, as Charles's biographer Anthony Holden put it, 'a pillar in the young Prince's uncertain public life, rarely more than six feet away, always ready to help him through difficulties and defuse awkward situations. Through the end of his schooldays, his time at Cambridge, his investiture and his Service career, Prince Charles owed Checketts a huge debt for the smooth progress of his day-to-day administrative needs and the grand strategy of his emergence into public life.'[2] Checketts had acted as a brake on the Prince's more headstrong impulses and public statements and had expressed occasional disapproval of his private life. Prince Charles had become increasingly unwilling to accept criticism whether direct or implied, or, indeed, opposition to his ideas. To Checketts's despair Prince Charles now seemed bent on pleasing only himself. He had developed a passion for blood sports, shooting and particularly hunting, despite warnings from the Palace that the popular tide was running against them. In summer he ardently pursued another 'elitist' sport, polo, encouraged by his father, who had been an enthusiastic player until injury forced him to retire. In 1979, now aged fifty, Checketts had resigned his post as Charles's private secretary. His departure was much regretted by Michael Colborne, a former naval petty officer who had served with the Prince on HMS *Norfolk* and whose appointment in 1974 as the Prince's personal secretary had been arranged under Mountbatten's unparalleled influence. A grammar school boy like David Checketts, Colborne's appeal to Charles had been his directness, his willingness to say what he thought. 'He desperately needed somebody who could sit in his office and speak common sense to him, and say no. We had these wonderful ten years together of lots of arguments, but he asked me not to change so I thought I'll show him the greatest respect but if I don't agree, I'm going to say so.'[3]

The truth is that the Prince had changed a great deal from the dutiful, biddable young man who left the navy in December 1976. As his official biographer, Jonathan Dimbleby, wrote:

Unable to find a suitable challenge for his ill-focused energy, the Prince had more time on his hands than he either wished or cared to admit. To his friends he seemed troubled by anxiety and discontent, which he sometimes allowed to affect his behaviour towards his staff. Easily provoked by minor irritations, he became uncharacteristically impatient and peremptory. Whereas a decade earlier his comments about the official programmes put before him had been innocent and dutiful, by the late seventies his response to yet another 'Away Day' could seem reluctant and jaundiced.[4]

Charles had inherited the capacity to blow up into sudden fierce fits of temper which his grandfather George VI had displayed to an alarming extent and which were known in the family as his 'gnashes'. 'For no apparent reason,' Dimbleby wrote, 'the Prince would suddenly give way to an alarming display of uncontrolled anger, his face suffused with intense emotion.' Invariably the anger was disproportionate to its cause, usually some minor mistake or annoyance, and vented on his closest aides, Checketts and Colborne.

Hitherto, in the absence of a strong relationship with his parents, his great mentor had been his father's uncle, Earl Mountbatten, who was in effect a surrogate father to him. Charles used to call Mountbatten 'Grandpapa' and address him as 'honorary grandfather': Mountbatten responded by referring to Charles as his 'honorary grandson'. By the time Charles was twenty-three Mountbatten had become his closest confidant and the greatest single influence on his life.

Mountbatten, who had had first-hand experience of the Abdication Crisis of 1936 when Edward VIII, Charles's great-uncle, had chosen to abdicate the throne in order to marry the American divorcee Wallis Simpson, had lately begun to worry about the Prince's wilfulness and lack of direction, comparing him with his great-uncle Edward VIII, always known in the family as David. Observing the Prince's thoughtless, often selfish and inconsiderate behaviour, Mountbatten sternly warned him: 'I thought you were beginning on the downward slope which wrecked your Uncle David's life and led to his disgraceful Abdication and his futile life ever after.'[5] Mountbatten criticized a sudden change of plan by Charles which would have entailed the cancellation of a US Coastguard crew's Easter vacation: '. . . how unkind and thoughtless – so typical of how your uncle David started,' Mountbatten wrote.

'. . . I spent the night worrying whether you would continue on your uncle David's sad course or take a pull.'[6]

Ironically, it was Mountbatten who pointed Charles down the road which led to Camilla and eventually to Diana. 'I believe in a case like yours,' Mountbatten wrote, 'that a man should sow his wild oats before settling down. But for a wife he should choose a suitable and sweet-charactered girl before she meets anyone else she might fall for.' Significantly, he added, 'I think it is disturbing for women to have experiences if they have to remain on a pedestal after marriage.'[7] Unfortunately for his recipe for a successful dynastic marriage, Charles had already met and fallen in love with a girl who did not quite fit the bill. He had met his 'ideal woman' seven years earlier when he was twenty-three: Camilla Shand, introduced to him by his university girlfriend Lucia Santa Cruz. Camilla, a pretty, witty, confident blonde, was the perfect answer to a vulnerable young man like Prince Charles, still very young and unsophisticated for his age. 'Camilla has great sexual power,' a friend affirmed. A courtier related to the family intimated that Camilla was sexually aware quite early: 'she was quite a little goer at fifteen and well organized by her mother'.[8] She was warm and uncomplicated and, importantly, shared his love of the countryside, dogs, horses and hunting. Ironically, the closest link between Camilla and Charles was a sexual one even before they began an affair. Camilla's great-grandmother on her mother's side was the notorious Alice Keppel, wife of Colonel the Hon. George Keppel and mistress of Charles's great-great-grandfather, King Edward VII. Camilla was fascinated by her powerful great-grandmother's career and the thought of emulating her must have been in the forefront of her mind when she famously remarked to him, 'My great-grandmother was your great-great-grandfather's mistress . . .'

Camilla was fifteen months older than Charles but he had always liked the company of older women, with whom he felt more at ease than he did with young girls. He was emotionally lonely and lacking in self-confidence. Camilla's parents were well-connected county people but far from being a part of the high aristocracy.

Camilla's mother, the Hon. Rosalind Cubitt, was Mrs Keppel's granddaughter; her mother, Sonia, had married into the Cubitt family, descendants of the Cubitt builders of Belgravia who had been ennobled with the title Barons Ashcombe. Her father, war hero Major Bruce Shand, became Master of the local hunt, the Cottesmore. Both, and Camilla's mother in particular, were socially ambitious, with a wide circle of upper-class friends in Sussex and London. Camilla and her brother Mark and sister Annabel were brought up in a close-knit family. Confident, good-looking and exceptionally attractive, the three children were destined for social success. Camilla rode to hounds with bravery and skill: she had had a conventional education with the emphasis on social graces rather than intellectual achievement: undistinguished school, finishing school abroad, Queen's secretarial college – almost a prerequisite for debutantes – followed by the Season. Like many girls of her background, her main aim in life was the getting, pleasing and keeping of a man, and in this she was certainly following in her great-grandmother's footsteps. 'I think she sees herself as her great-grandmother, Mrs Keppel,' one of the Queen Mother's ladies-in-waiting told the author in 1993.

Charles and Camilla first met in the summer of 1970, on the polo ground, Smith's Lawn, in Windsor Great Park, where most of his romances began. Their rapport was instantaneous. The romance was encouraged by Mountbatten who saw Camilla as ideal mistress material who could pave the way for his grand-daughter, Amanda Knatchbull, who was still in her early teens, to take over as the virgin bride. The couple spent weekends together at Mountbatten's country house, Broadlands. After a while, the sharp-eyed Mountbatten became aware that Charles was becoming very attached to Camilla and warned him not to get too fond of a girl, who, for all her attractions, he saw as insufficiently aristocratic and insufficiently virginal to be acceptable as a royal bride. There seemed no future in the relationship and, moreover, Camilla was in love with Andrew Parker Bowles with whom she had been having an on and off affair since 1967. Parker Bowles, a handsome Guards officer, was notoriously attractive to women and repeatedly unfaithful to Camilla, who, however, had never given up on him. She was fond of Charles but in love with Parker Bowles. Andrew himself was having an affair with Princess Anne: unkind friends suggested that getting her own back on Andrew by bedding the Princess's brother was a factor in Camilla's relationship with Charles. An older friend of Camilla's remembers an evening at Annabel's, the nightclub which was at the centre of London society: 'I can remember the triangle when Andrew Parker Bowles was there. Princess Anne was in love with Parker Bowles, Camilla was in love with Andrew, Charles was in love with Camilla, Camilla was having some of it but she was also potty about Andrew – and all this intrigue was going on. They were younger than me so I remember watching it all, the whole thing. It was just bad luck. And then off Charles goes to sea and I think Camilla wouldn't have been quite as sad as he was because she was mad about Andrew. But even if she hadn't been, would she have been allowed to marry Charles?'[9]

The answer was undoubtedly no. Camilla's affairs were known in society and at court. The Parker Bowles family moved in royal circles: Andrew's father Derek, charming, witty and a good gossip, was a close friend of the Queen Mother. His mother, Dame Ann, was the daughter of the rich Sir Humphrey de Trafford, twice steward of the Jockey Club, whose wife was a member of the equally rich and aristocratic Cadogan family. Everybody liked Camilla, whom a friend described as having 'laughing eyes . . . warm and full of fun', but she was not considered in those days aristocratic enough for the Prince of Wales and her reputation would certainly have prevented any thought of marriage.

Charles was powerfully attracted to Camilla but three weeks before Christmas 1972 he was posted to the frigate HMS *Minerva* and later left for the Caribbean. It has been suggested by one of Mountbatten's close circle that he arranged for Charles to be posted overseas to get him away from Camilla and to pave the way for a possible engagement to his own granddaughter, Amanda Knatch-bull.[10] Before Charles left he invited Camilla and Mountbatten to tour the ship. She returned the following weekend. Afterwards he wrote sadly to Mountbatten that it was 'the last time I shall see her for eight months'. But if Charles was not ready for marriage, Camilla and Andrew Parker Bowles were. Parker Bowles's romance with Princess Anne ended when she fell for Captain Mark Phillips. On 15 March 1973 he and Camilla were engaged and married in a huge society wedding in July. Camilla had got her man.

After Camilla, Prince Charles played the field. According to his valet, Stephen Barry, who had worked for him since 1970 and knew all the intimate details of his life, Charles's recipe for the perfect woman was that she should be tall, blonde, curvaceous and with an English rose complexion. His first serious involvement was in fact with Mountbatten's granddaughter, Amanda Knatchbull (a brunette), on and off over a period from 1974 to 1979. Mountbatten actively promoted the match: Charles proposed; Amanda, unwilling to step on to the royal treadmill and well aware of what it entailed, refused him.

During this period Charles dated a number of beautiful upper-class and not so upper-class girls. 'All his romances seemed to start at polo matches,' Stephen Barry wrote.[11] Among them were Lady Jane Wellesley, daughter of the Duke of Wellington, a family friend rather than a romance; Georgiana Russell, who got fed up with standing in cold Scottish rivers and married someone else; and Sabrina Guinness. Two of them were important to him: Davina Sheffield and Anna Wallace. Davina, a delightful, tall blonde, was rather in the Diana mode but, Barry said, 'more grown up'. They had seemed set for marriage, she had received the royal seal of approval, being invited to lunch with the Queen at Windsor, and cheerfully passed the Balmoral test, when a former boyfriend ungallantly revealed in the press that he and Davina had lived together. Rumours of an engagement died down after that. Charles could not afford to marry anyone who could create any kind of scandal. The Royal Family had been keen for him to marry the lovely and artistic Lady Leonora Grosvenor, sister of Sarah Spencer's former boyfriend, Gerald, but in 1975 she married the Queen's cousin, Patrick, Earl of Lichfield, instead.

Charles met Anna Wallace, another tall, beautiful blonde, described by Barry as 'a marvellous-looking girl with a sparkling personality and presence' on the hunting field. Like Davina Sheffield, she had had the honour of lunching with the Queen, a sure sign that the relationship was taken seriously. She ended their friendship after quarrelling publicly with the Prince at a Windsor ball in honour of the Queen Mother's eightieth birthday and again at a polo ball at Stowell Park, the home of Lord and Lady Vestey. The cause this time was the Prince's ignoring Anna to spend the entire evening with Camilla Parker Bowles. Anna, who was well aware of the importance of Camilla in Charles's life, walked out on him and shortly afterwards married the Hon. John Fermor-Hesketh. There were others less serious: the actress Susan George, US admiral's daughter Laura-Jo Watkins, and, of course, Sarah Spencer.

The 'World's Most Eligible Bachelor' had become the 'Playboy Prince'. As Sarah Spencer had said, Charles was a romantic and fell in love easily, but in fact his sexual libido was low, he was frightened of and shy with young women and unable to make a commitment. Like most weak men he was capable of behaving worse than if he had been sure of his own mind. These qualities and the fact that most of the women he pursued, like Amanda Knatchbull, Lady Jane Wellesley and Anna Wallace, who moved in the same circles as he did, were only too aware of the stultifying nature of royal life and were repelled by it, made the finding of a bride difficult. Moreover, Charles himself in the mid-seventies was happy as a bachelor: he enjoyed the freedom of being able to do as he pleased and kept his girls at a distance. He made the dates when it suited him, never collected the girls beforehand. They were expected to arrange their own transport unless they were special friends. He never gave them presents and only rarely sent flowers. It was made quite clear that he controlled the relationship so that things could not get out of hand. Only three women were truly important in Charles's life: his mother, the Queen, his grandmother, 'Grannie', and his nanny, Mabel Anderson.

He was only really at ease with confident married women

older than himself: two of them in particular, the boisterous Australian Dale Harper, later Lady Tryon, nicknamed 'Kanga', and, supremely, Camilla Parker Bowles. A friend remembers how she first met Dale at a weekend house party at Lord Tryon's house: 'There was this Australian girl, rather vulgar, great fun, to whom Anthony Tryon had lent his Volvo estate to drive down and she had crashed it – not fatally – so she was in a great state of semi-hysterics . . . "That's all right," said Anthony. "That's all right." So Dale came along and absolutely exploded on the scene and Anthony was a friend of Prince Charles so of course Dale immediately got onto Prince Charles and would often tell stories of what she had taught Prince Charles. Can you believe that? On the Queen's Flight flying to Australia. She would report what she had taught him. Mind boggling . . .'[12]

At the Cirencester Polo Ball in the summer of 1980 the physical passion of Charles for Camilla was obvious to everyone. 'Charles spent the whole evening with Camilla,' Jane Ward, a former girlfriend of the Prince, recalled. 'Charles and the Parker Bowleses shared the same table, and Charles spent the whole evening dancing with Camilla. They were kissing passionately as they danced – on and on they went, kissing each other, French kissing, dance after dance.'[13] Andrew Parker Bowles apparently could not have cared less. He had, as a friend put it, 'other fish to fry', and the fact that his wife was having a passionate sexual affair with the heir to the throne flattered him rather than otherwise.

Royal reporter James Whitaker remembers how, when Prince Charles was going through a period of two years' enthusiasm for cross-country events in 1975–6, 'virtually always there were Camilla and Dale Tryon and so was Stephen Barry. He would bring the boots out of the car and he would carry all HRH's clobber and gear . . . and helped him dress, and the two other girls fussed around and made sure he had a drink and made sure the organizers knew where he was, made sure people got out of his way when he went to the starting lines . . .'[14] Barry, who as Charles's valet since 1970 had acted as his virtual wife, had in return been outrageously indulged. 'He dressed beautifully, his shirts and ties were all from Turnbull & Asser, he was a very amusing, outrageous homosexual who was so extrovert he was absurd, and he got more and more confident as it went on.' 'He was exotic and extravagant and behaved disgracefully. He would give parties at Ascot where he would roll about the lawn fighting with other gays and serving Dom Perignon champagne.'[15] A lady-in-waiting to the Queen remembered Barry: 'He modelled himself on Prince Charles and looked just like him ... And at some intellectual party I went to, I happened to meet somebody who had found out who I worked for and said, "I wonder if you know Stephen Barry?" And I said, "Yes, of course I know him. I walk down the corridor with him every day." "Oh, he's a great friend of mine. He's shown me all the pictures at Clarence House [then the London home of the Queen Mother] and he's very interested in the Arts." So next morning I walked down the corridor with him [Barry] and I said, "I met a friend of yours last night. He said he did enjoy seeing the pictures at Clarence House." And Stephen went bright purple.' When she reported this to a senior courtier, he advised her, 'Be careful. The Queen Mother's probably given him permission to do so.' According to a lady-in-waiting, Barry gave 'very noisy parties' with 'loud music' in the room beneath the one she used at the Palace. 'But Prince Charles liked him,' she added. 'He always stood up to him and didn't make too many mistakes.'[16] According to Whitaker, Barry was on friendly terms with Camilla but when Diana, whom he perceived as a threat to his position, arrived, he left.

Charles had apparently resumed his sexual relationship with Camilla in 1979 but as she was married it was considered – in those days – unthinkable that the relationship should be legitimized. The Parker Bowleses – at least from Andrew's point of view – had an open marriage. He did not feel obliged to give up his pursuit of women despite the fact that he was now married and the father of two children. He condoned his wife's relationship with Charles and the two men were friends but, in military circles, the heir to the throne's relationship with the wife of a brother officer was considered to break the rules, so much so that the Queen's former

private secretary felt bound to inform the Queen of their disquiet.
'Ma'am,' he said, 'the Prince of Wales is having an affair with the
wife of a brother officer and the Regiment don't like it.' She
looked down and said nothing, determined to continue her policy
of non-intervention in her children's lives.

Camilla's role in the Prince's life was more than purely physical;
she was also his intimate adviser, usurping Mountbatten's role as
his mentor. The Prince had ceased to pay as much attention to his
'honorary grandfather' as he had in his younger days. He found
other mentors – he was 'an intellectual pillow', his father said
scornfully, while a courtier commented, 'Prince Charles goes
through gurus like other people do socks'. In his search for self-
fulfilment and the meaning of life he had come under the influence
of Laurens van der Post, a protagonist of Jungian ideas. In 1977 he
and van der Post had spent five days in the Aberdare Mountains
of Kenya, exploring the natural world around them in long walks,
followed by evenings of intense discussion of the 'inner world'.
He then formed a deep emotional and spiritual relationship with a
young Indian woman who had sent him a book called *The Path of
the Masters*, a guide to the spiritual wisdom of the Eastern gurus.
When her influence manifested itself in vegetarianism and above
all opposition to the killing of animals which led him to cancel
his shooting, his new private secretary, Edward Adeane, became
alarmed. 'It's got to be stopped,' he declared. In the event, this
enthusiasm was as short lived as many preceding ones, although
his interest in non-Christian faiths remained.

Then, in August 1979, Mountbatten was blown up in his fishing
boat by the IRA off the coast of Sligo. Charles was devastated. He
had been dreading the moment when Mountbatten might die:
now that it had come so suddenly and violently he was desolate.
'I have lost someone infinitely special in my life,' he wrote. '. . . In
some extraordinary way he combined grandfather, great-uncle,
father, brother and friend . . . Life will *never* be the same now
that he has gone . . .'[17] As Charles realized, no one could replace
Mountbatten in his role of friend and counsellor, and above all his
willingness to tell him things he didn't want to hear. Charles

accepted criticism from Mountbatten that he would never have taken from anyone else. Mountbatten's death occurred at a critical moment in Charles's life when, dissatisfied with himself and with the course his life was taking, he was seriously contemplating marriage. 'I must say I am becoming rather worried by all this talk about being self-centred and getting worse every year. I'm told that marriage is the only cure for me – and maybe it is!' he had written to a friend on 15 April 1979.[18]

The trouble with Charles was that he did not want to marry. He had everything he needed without a wife (including Camilla). 'He was a loner, he liked silence,' said one of his staff. 'And later when he found he had a wife to talk to and to consider, it threw him.' Charles had led an entirely self-centred life: when he went away for a weekend he did not have to lift a finger: 'Stephen would be ready with the Range Rover, loaded up with everything he needed, his painting brushes . . . everything.' The shock at the loss of his beloved mentor, and the memory of Mountbatten's strictures, were no doubt a crucial influence on Charles's increasing conviction that he must do his duty and take a wife. Camilla's influence on his life even increased with the loss of Mountbatten. She was to play a dominant role in Charles's choice.

5. 'Whatever Love Means'

'Diana was very simple, rosy cheeks, a schoolgirl. Totally sort of innocent . . .
They were all delighted' (a courtier describing Diana on her first visit to
Birkhall in 1980)

Lady Diana Spencer, tall and blonde, curvy (as she then was) with
a clear English-rose complexion, very young, impeccably born and
with no scandal attached to her name, perfectly fitted all the criteria
for a royal bride. Given that the Prince had to marry and seemed
to be attracted to Diana, Camilla, in a spectacular misreading of
Diana's true character, saw it as in her own interest that Charles
should choose such a shy young girl who would pose no threat to
her position in his heart and mind. It suited her to befriend Diana
and encourage Charles towards the girl she truly believed to be
the best choice available. She had already effectively seen off
Anna Wallace. Diana, younger, less fiery, seemed infinitely more
malleable.

Indeed, Diana must have remained at the back of Charles's
mind, since when he met her again at a house party at Petworth
in July 1980, his reaction to her took her by surprise:

. . . Charles came in. He was all over me again and it was very strange.
I thought 'Well, this isn't very cool'. I thought men were not supposed
to be so obvious, I thought this was very odd. The first night we sat
down on a bale at the barbecue at this house and he'd just finished with
Anna Wallace. I said: 'You looked so sad when you walked up the aisle
at Lord Mountbatten's funeral.' I said: 'It was the most tragic thing I've
ever seen. My heart bled for you when I watched. I thought, "It's wrong,
you're lonely – you should be with somebody to look after you."'

The next minute he leapt on me practically and I thought this was very strange too, and I wasn't quite sure how to cope with all this. Anyway we talked about lots of things and anyway that was it. Frigid wasn't the word. Big F when it comes to that. He said: 'You must come to London with me tomorrow. I've got to work at Buckingham Palace, you must come to work with me.' I thought this was too much. I said, 'No, I can't.' I thought 'How will I explain my presence at Buckingham Palace when I'm supposed to be staying [the weekend] with Philip [son of the hosts].'[1]

Diana was a lovely young girl, 'high-spirited and larky and fun' as a royal relation put it; 'she had a lot of good in her, a lot of natural good that was not a pose.' It was, above all, her extraordinary powers of empathy, her ability, as she later put it, 'to smell out suffering', which attracted the Prince. Her empathy with him over Mountbatten's death and his own deep sadness and need for consolation touched the Prince deeply. Charles, it would seem, was strangely interested in this young girl who had actually had the self-possession to turn him down. He invited her to join him on the royal yacht *Britannia*, for the annual Cowes week sailing holiday. This time he did not expect her just to turn up on her own but, significantly, asked his assistant private secretary, Oliver Everett, to look after her: '. . . he [Charles] had lots of older friends there and I was fairly intimidated but they were all over me like a bad rash. I felt very strange about the whole thing, obviously someone was talking,' Diana later recalled.[2]

That 'someone' was Charles himself. According to his official biographer, he 'surprised one of his closest confidantes [unnamed] . . . by intimating to her that he had met the girl he intended to marry'. The 'confidante' had responded that if that was the case he should keep quiet about it. Charles, however, went on to praise Diana's open and easy manner . . . her warmth . . . her enthusiasm for rural life, and her background through which she knew a little of his family and certainly enough, he presumed, to have few fears of marrying into it.[3] As an insider, Charles seems to have had little conception of what marrying into the Royal Family would actually mean, and was never properly to understand the pressures Diana underwent when she did enter the royal circle.

In *Britannia*, however, the open and easy manner which Diana had acquired from her parents when talking to strangers made her instantly popular with the crew who, according to Barry, 'fell in love with her to a man'. The royal servants liked her and the general impression was 'Isn't Lady Di lovely?' and that she might well be in line for 'the job'. Yet, whatever Charles may have confessed to his confidante, he was careful not to show anything in public. 'The Prince himself didn't seem to take too much notice of her at the beginning, but *her* eyes followed him everywhere,' Barry recorded.[4]

Unaware as yet of Camilla Parker Bowles's role in her destiny, Diana was invited to stay at Balmoral in September while her sister Jane and brother-in-law Robert Fellowes were there. 'I stayed back at the Castle because of all the press interest,' Diana remembered, '. . . Mr and Mrs Parker Bowles were there at all my visits. I was the youngest there by a long way. Charles used to ring me up and say "Would you like to come for a walk, come for a barbecue?" so I said: "Yes, please." I thought all this was wonderful.'[5] Charles's old friends warmed to her as she was so obviously happy and he seemed so attracted to her. Patty Palmer-Tomkinson, married to Hampshire farmer Charles Palmer-Tomkinson, and one of Charles's closest friends, remembered how enchanted she had been with Diana: 'We went stalking together, we got hot, we got tired, she fell into a bog, she got covered in mud, laughed her head off, got puce in the face, hair glued to her forehead because it was pouring with rain . . . she was a sort of wonderful English schoolgirl who was game for anything, naturally young but sweet and clearly determined and enthusiastic about him, very much wanted him.'[6]

One of the Queen Mother's guests at Birkhall remembered an occasion when the house party from Balmoral came over for drinks. Nicholas Soames, a friend of the Prince's since childhood who also acted as his equerry, and Camilla Parker Bowles, were among them, with Diana. 'I was somewhat surprised to see Diana in purple stockings seated on the floor in front of Queen Elizabeth – Camilla Parker Bowles was obviously there to vet this poor girl who had no idea what she was letting herself in for,' the guest commented.[7]

Diana was invited up to Scotland again in October, this time to Birkhall itself, one of Charles's favourite places from his school days. While Charles went out stalking, Diana remained at the house, doing her needlepoint. The fact that the Queen Mother had herself invited Diana to stay was significant; she was clearly in favour of Diana as a possible bride for her beloved grandson. Some authorities have it that Ruth Fermoy pressed Diana's claims on Queen Elizabeth. Others close to Queen Elizabeth deny that she played a leading role: 'Ruth wasn't against it,' said a courtier; 'to tell the truth she was rather for it, and no doubt had said something to Queen Elizabeth. [But] I think Queen Elizabeth came from a different angle and that is that Cynthia Spencer, Diana's grand-mother, had been a great friend and the Spencer family were "friends of the royal family".' 'It was so surprising,' she went on, describing Diana's Birkhall visit: 'She [Diana] was very simple, rosy cheeks [like] a schoolgirl. And charming. Totally sort of innocent . . . They were all delighted. Before she came up, one of the Queen's ladies-in-waiting had rung me up and said, "Do take care about this one, I think it's serious." And there was no doubt that the Queen Mother was anxious about it, she checked the bedroom and all that sort of thing which she wouldn't normally have done for a nineteen-year-old girl. So one sort of knew that it was being planned or being hoped for . . .' After Diana and Charles had left, she recalled, 'Ruth was at the airport on her way to go into waiting and she came running towards me and said, "How did the visit go? Was she all right? Was it all right?" '[8]

In pushing the claims of Diana, Ruth Fermoy was at the very least guilty of a cynical act. She of all people would have known of the Camilla situation and she of all people would have known what she was getting Diana into. Undoubtedly she must have found the temptation of being the grandmother of the future Queen too much to resist, despite knowing her granddaughter's character and, equally, being aware of the nature of the court. During the engagement, when a friend said to her how wonderful it was that the bride loved music, she did volunteer enigmatically 'She'll need that', but the closest she ever came to warning Diana of what lay ahead was to tell her that she would find the Royal Family's sense of humour very different from her own. In the end she collaborated with the Spencer family – and indeed Diana's own feelings – in pushing her into the marriage.

In true courtier fashion, Ruth Fermoy was swiftly to change her tune when the marriage began to reveal its fault lines. Indeed, when Jonathan Dimbleby was writing his authorized biography of the Prince, conscious of her role in history she told him that in private she had been against the marriage but (as a courtier) had 'thought it wrong to share her doubts'. According to a private source she made a deathbed statement to Dimbleby along the same lines. She also told him, ingenuously: 'If I'd said to him [Charles], "You're making a very great mistake", he probably wouldn't have paid the slightest attention because he was being driven"[9] – 'driven' not only by his family but by the counsels of Camilla, still an important part of his life, and the weight of public expectation that he should do his duty.

Barry, a close and interested observer, thought that 'things seemed to be blossoming' from the time of the Birkhall visit. Charles invited her to Highgrove, his new house in Gloucestershire, the first he had personally owned. Charles was delighted with it, but Diana, according to Barry, was unimpressed. It was a standard Cotswold manor house, small by Althorp standards, in a mess and with only three habitable bedrooms. Diana did not yet know it, but the principal appeal of Highgrove for Charles was that it was only fifteen miles' drive from Bolehyde Manor, home of Andrew and Camilla Parker Bowles. It was also within easy reach of one of his favourite hunts, the Beaufort, where Charles's relationship with Camilla was well known to members, who described her as riding 'in his pocket'. Just at that time, Prince and Princess Michael of Kent were negotiating to buy their country house, Nether Lypiatt, in the same area. They were surprised to find Charles bitterly opposed to their proposed purchase, and it was only through the intervention of another member of the Royal Family that he was persuaded to give up his opposition. Friends surmised that the only reason for his opposing the Kents' buying Nether Lypiatt was that they might become aware of his closeness to Camilla, Princess Michael herself being a keen rider to hounds.

Diana was driven down to Highgrove by Barry three times that autumn, where she would hang around the house and gardens waiting for Charles to return home from hunting, a foretaste of her life to come. After tea and a simple early dinner together, Charles drove her back to London. The mere fact of his presence seemed to him to be enough for her and to compensate for hours of dreary waiting. Perhaps Diana liked it like that: it was a very old-fashioned courtship along the lines prescribed by Barbara Cartland, now her step-grandmother.

Public interest in the possibility of Diana as Charles's future bride was reaching fever pitch. 'HE'S IN LOVE AGAIN! LADY DI IS THE NEW GIRL FOR CHARLES' blared the headline in the *Sun* on 8 September 1980. James Whitaker, stationed at Balmoral, had been the source of the tip-off. Watching from a vantage point above the River Dee, where Charles was fishing, he had spotted Diana looking back at him from behind a tree, using her make-up mirror: 'What a cunning lady, I thought,' he later wrote. 'This one was clearly going to give us a lot of trouble . . . You had to be a real professional to think of using a mirror to watch us watching her.'[10] That same month, Nigel Dempster, the gossip columnist of the *Daily Mail*, broke the story that Diana was Charles's new girlfriend and that his choice had been approved by 'the two happily married women who influence [him] most on personal matters, Lady Tryon and Camilla Parker Bowles'.[11] In London reporters laid siege to Coleherne Court, posting themselves near Mary Robertson's mews house and outside the Young England kindergarten. It was there that one day, in an effort to persuade them to go away, Diana allowed herself to be photographed against the sun in a Madonna-like pose, holding one child in her arms and another by the hand. The sun streamed through her long, flimsy skirt revealing the stunning legs which were among her principal features and inflaming male passions all over the world. The tabloid reporters besieging her flat fell in love with her: by invariably being polite, tolerant and good-tempered, she made them her friends. She flirted with them, giving them the famous 'shy Di' look with lowered eyes. 'You knew deep down it was a game she played, and a very clever one . . . not cynical, but by doing this, she won everybody over,' said tabloid reporter Harry Arnold.[12] Worse still for Diana than the relentless lenses outside the flat were the midnight telephone calls from the press; she concealed the strain it caused her, but in private she wept.

Charles took elaborate precautions so that he and Diana could meet in London without attracting press attention. Diana would ring Barry, say simply 'It's Diana' and tell him where she could be picked up – from Ruth Fermoy's Eaton Square flat or from Jane Fellowes' house at Kensington Palace. Returning home she would be dropped behind the block of flats at Coleherne Court to escape the media stationed at the front. To Barry she appeared still as a simple, giggly teenage girl with an addiction to sweets – Yorkie bars and bags of toffees. But she was already showing signs of trying to influence the Prince's appearance, buying him sweaters and ties in his favourite blue and replacing the formal shoes custom-made for him by Lobb of St James's with more modern slip-ons. 'You'll never get away with those,' Barry warned her. 'He's always had his shoes made to order.' Diana just grinned and that evening he saw the Prince walking around trying to get used to them.

Diana was invited to celebrate Charles's thirty-second birthday (14 November 1980) with an intimate Royal Family gathering at Wood Farm, the ten-bedroom house on the Sandringham estate which the family use when the Big House is closed. Saturday was spent shooting but the gathering hordes of media at the gates curtailed Diana's visit. Their attentions meant that Charles and Diana could not even take a walk together so a stratagem for her escape to London was arranged, cutting short the planned long weekend. She was safely back at Coleherne Court while the media mob remained freezing in Norfolk at the gates of Wood Farm.

Both the press and the royal staff were convinced that an engagement would be announced. In Norfolk the Duke of Edinburgh
grumbled about the 'bloody press' spoiling his shooting.

While Diana was still at Sandringham the 'Royal Love Train'
scandal broke: on 16 November the *Sunday Mirror* printed a story
that on 5 November Diana had slipped into the royal train as it
stood in a Wiltshire siding to spend the night with Charles. The
story was patently untrue as far as Diana was concerned; that night,
with Charles, she had attended a party for Princess Margaret at the
Ritz and was photographed arriving there. She had gone home to
Coleherne Court at about 1 a.m.; Charles, however, had left earlier
around ten or ten thirty and had taken the train to an official
engagement; the mystery woman was supposed to have boarded
the train at about midnight. The report created a furore: the Queen
was furious and her press secretary, Michael Shea, was deputed to
write to the editor of the *Sunday Mirror* denying the incident. 'The
Woman on the Train' was certainly not Diana, but many people
believed – and still do – that it was Camilla. The official line has
always been that there was nothing whatever in the story. James
Whitaker, however, then writing for the *Daily Star*, followed up
the story which had first come through a local press man. 'I went
down to the siding . . . I went up into the signal box and I paid
the signal man some money and I saw his log book, and they'd
logged a person getting on the train . . . down the road at the
station . . . they had an official log of somebody going on that
train, a woman.'[13] A respected media commentator found the
Palace reaction fishy. 'Diana was definitely in London at the time
with witnesses; all the Palace had to do was to simply say "Diana
was in London, she never went near the train and this is the proof."
Why didn't they do it? Because Diana herself would have been
spooked by that story. Who was on the train? So they had to deny
the train incident altogether.'[14] In the face of repeated official
denials, the editor of the *Sunday Mirror*, Bob Edwards, came to
believe that he had made a mistake over the story, certainly as far
as Diana was concerned. At Christmas 1986, however, he received
a Christmas card from Woodrow Wyatt, later Lord Wyatt of

Weeford, the Labour politician and journalist who, despite his politics, moved in royal circles. The message was: 'It was Camilla.'

The Royal Love Train incident added fuel to the Duke of Edinburgh's 'ultimatum', as Prince Charles interpreted it, that he should either propose to Lady Diana Spencer or stop seeing her as he would damage her reputation and expose her to persecution by the press if he continued to do so. To the Royal Family, and indeed to Charles, Lady Diana seemed the answer to their prayers. 'Characteristically,' Dimbleby wrote, 'the Queen refrained from tendering her opinion but Queen Elizabeth the Queen Mother, who was a significant influence, counselled strongly in favour of marriage, as did her lady-in-waiting, Ruth Fermoy . . . Diana Spencer's grandmother.'[15] The Queen Mother is said to have told Charles one day at Royal Lodge, 'There's Diana Spencer – that's the girl you should marry. But don't marry her if you don't love her. If you do, grab her because if you don't there are plenty of others who will.' Ruth Fermoy added to the general pressure for the marriage by putting it about that if Charles did not marry Diana after all this fuss, she would be ruined. One of the Queen Mother's courtiers was overheard to say over tea at Clarence House, when the question of the engagement seemed to be hanging fire, that 'Charles must make his mind up, if he discards Diana she's got no future at all . . .' One of his colleagues told him, 'You must be joking – a pretty girl of nineteen, just because the Prince of Wales doesn't want to marry her, you're living in another world.' Ruth Fermoy, she said, had been putting it about that 'she'll be finished if the Prince of Wales discards her now'. 'Arrant rubbish,'[16] the courtier commented.

After Christmas at Althorp, where, according to her stepmother, Diana spent much of her time walking in the park crying over Charles's failure to propose, she joined her flatmates for New Year's Eve before driving down to Sandringham to join the royal house party, using her grandmother's silver VW Golf instead of her own well-known Mini Metro. Once again the press mob turned up in force, disrupting the Duke of Edinburgh's shooting party and rendering him apoplectic, while Charles bitterly told the press pack that he wished their editors 'a nasty New Year'. Diana spent the time waiting for Charles to return from shooting, and slipping away to visit her old home, Park House, now standing empty and deserted. But the feelings between the couple were becoming stronger, and obvious to the court insiders watching them. At Sandringham that January a lady-in-waiting remembered that they turned back the carpet to dance and 'they danced like mad, Prince Charles and Diana – there was this electric thing between them'. Later she asked the couple, 'That was the moment you fell for each other, wasn't it?' Both of them, she said, agreed.[17] A second visit to Sandringham had to be abandoned because of press attention but instead Charles and Diana had a secret rendez-vous at Highgrove. Diana spent the night there and on the return journey to London Barry, who was as usual driving her on a 'dawn dash' to get back to her kindergarten job, recalled, 'She was a very happy young woman . . . relaxed, smiling – and not chattering.' Charles had not actually proposed, but something must have happened to make Diana think that he would. Diana later told friends that Charles had proposed to her in Camilla Parker Bowles's garden at Bolehyde.[18] Whether he actually proposed to her there, or gave her a very strong indication that he would like to marry her, is open to speculation.

Close friends of Charles's (later among Diana's foremost enemies) became alarmed at the possibility. Norton and Penny Romsey, Mountbatten's grandson and his wife, were against Diana from the beginning. They thought that she was in love with the idea of being Princess of Wales, rather than with the Prince himself. They noticed her friendly relationship with the press pack pursuing her and that she seemed to pose for their cameras. According to Dimbleby, in January 1981 both of them raised their doubts with the Prince, to no avail. Close observers such as Barry denied their allegation: 'She was most certainly in love with her Prince,' he stated. 'She was always available when he called, and she always fitted in with his plans. She obviously adored being with him, and in January the Prince wrote a memo to his office telling them to give her a copy of his weekly engagements so that she would know where he was'[19] – the first time he had ever done so for a girl. Whatever the world may have thought, Diana was deeply in love with Charles and continued to love him even after he had rejected her. 'She hero-worshipped him,' one of her staff was to say. He was the older man in whom she thought she could place her trust, who would love her and look after her as her own father never had.

Nicholas Soames, for one, dared not raise the subject with the Prince but told the Duke of Edinburgh's private secretary, Lord Rupert Nevill, what he thought about the Duke of Edinburgh's 'ultimatum', calling the proposed engagement 'a mismatch'. Soames, Winston Churchill's grandson, was the same age as Charles whom he had known in his early teens fishing in Scotland. He had first met Diana at Birkhall, when he had come away 'amazed' at the possibility that Charles might marry 'this very sweet teenager'. 'She was very sweet,' he said, '[but] it was just like talking to a teenager and not a very clever one either.' Soames and the Romseys were part of Charles's inner circle of friends and absolutely devoted to him. They were quite sincere in their views that this marriage would be a disaster: they were right in the end but not just for the reasons they gave.

Charles himself was, he confessed, in a 'confused and anxious state of mind'. 'It is just a matter of taking an unusual plunge into some rather unknown circumstances that inevitably disturbs me but I expect it will be the right thing in the end.' 'It all seems so ridiculous,' he added, 'because I do so very much want to do the right thing for this Country and for my family – but I'm terrified sometimes of making a promise and then perhaps living to regret it.'[20] And so Charles dithered on, as indeed he well might. He was in love with Camilla, who satisfied his every need. She was, as she herself said, his 'Girl Friday' as well as his lover. And he was attracted to Diana but not in love with her. Everyone, meanwhile was getting impatient for an outcome. Charles went for his annual skiing holiday in Klosters, accompanied by the Palmer-Tonkinsons, who were initially in favour of Diana and who bolstered his wavering resolve.

'The feeling was,' Diana recalled, 'I wish Prince Charles would hurry up and get on with it. The Queen was fed up. Then Charles rang me up from Klosters and said: "I've got something to ask you." Instinct in a female, you know what's coming. Anyway, I sat up all night with my girls [her three flatmates], saying "What do I say, what do I do?" bearing in mind that there was someone else around.' 'Anyway, next day I went to Windsor and I arrived about 5 o'clock and he sat down and said: "I've missed you so much." But there was never anything tactile about him. It was extraordinary, but I didn't have anything else to go by because I had never had a boyfriend. I'd always kept them away, thought they were all trouble – and I couldn't handle it emotionally, I was very screwed up, I thought. Anyway, so he said, "Will you marry me?" and I laughed. I remember thinking, "This is a joke", and I said, "Yeah, OK", and laughed. He was deadly serious. He said: "You do realize that one day you will be Queen." And a voice said to me inside: "You won't be Queen but you'll have a tough role." So I thought OK, so I said: "Yes." I said, "I love you so much, I love you so much." He said: "Whatever love means." He said it then. So I thought that was great! I thought he meant that! And so he ran upstairs and rang his mother.'[21]

To Diana, Camilla seemed to be ever present and increasingly she had begun to question Camilla's role in Charles's life. 'By that time,' Diana recalled of the period of her secret engagement, 'I'd realized that there's somebody else around. I'd been staying at Bolehyde [Manor, the Parker Bowleses' home] an awful lot and I couldn't understand why she [Camilla] kept saying to me, "Don't push him into doing this, don't do that." She knew so much about what he was doing privately . . . if we were going to stay at Broadlands, I couldn't understand it. [Broadlands was now the property of Mountbatten's grandson, Norton Knatchbull, Lord Romsey, and his wife, close friends of Charles and also of Camilla.] Eventually I worked it all out and found the proof of the pudding and people willing to talk to me.'[22]

Nevertheless, in a state of euphoria, Diana went off to Australia to spend three weeks with her mother planning the wedding.

Frances was determined that on this last holiday on their own before the wedding, Diana should have some real peace and privacy. While the press besieged the Shand Kydd ranch at Yass and Peter Shand Kydd asserted that Diana was 'on a different continent', Frances and Diana were together in a rented beach house at Mollymook, 200 kilometres south of Sydney. Diana spent peaceful days incognito, swimming and surfing on the beautiful beach, not even daring to accompany her mother shopping in case she was recognized. Her stay at Mollymook was, she recalled later, 'the last time I walked alone'. She later alleged that, during her time in Australia, Charles never once telephoned her and that when she rang him he was always out and never called back. This was another instance of her later embroidering the facts to make the picture more dramatic. In truth, according to Barry, Diana and Charles spoke 'constantly but guardedly on the telephone' when she was in Australia, and Charles himself said in a television interview that the first time he tried to call her the Shand Kydd household was so wary of the press that at first they refused to let him speak to her and he had considerable trouble establishing his identity. When she got back home, however, he was not there to welcome her: Michael Colborne sent Sergeant Lewis round with what Diana described as 'this huge, huge bunch of smelly flowers'. 'I knew they weren't from Charles,' she said bitterly, 'because there was no note. It was just somebody being very tactful in the office.'

On 24 February the engagement of the Prince of Wales and Lady Diana Spencer was publicly announced. The couple were interviewed in the garden of Buckingham Palace with the Palace looming in the background. Diana looked very young, her thick blonde hair unbecomingly cut, her figure in a mumsy blue suit looking distinctly chubby, but despite her shyness she seemed more self-possessed than Charles, who was always embarrassed when faced with personal questions and uneasy with television interviews. The occasion seemed more awkward than happy. 'Can you find the right words to sum up how you feel today?' they were asked. 'Difficult to find the right sort of words,' Charles replied, glancing at Diana as she nodded. 'Just delighted and happy. I'm amazed that she's brave enough to take me on.' 'And I suppose in love?' said the interviewer. 'Of course,' said Diana, grimacing shyly and rolling her eyes. 'Whatever in love means,' Charles famously replied. Around the world, people who watched the interview drew in their breath. It seemed to bode ill for the future. Four days later, Diana wrote in her round childish hand, in answer to a letter of congratulations: 'Reading through all the letters, it's amazing how many people have said that married life is the best – I wonder if I'll be saying that in twenty years' time!'[23]

The letter was headed 'Clarence House, February 28th' on plain notepaper in her own hand. On the evening of the day her engagement was announced, Diana moved into the Queen Mother's London home, Clarence House, to protect her from the press. Coleherne Court had become untenable. It was, as her Scotland Yard police protection officer told her: '. . . the last night of freedom ever in the rest of your life . . .'. Diana, in dramatic mode, later said that his words were 'like a sword went in my heart'. On the bed of her first-floor bedroom was a note from Camilla, congratulating her and suggesting lunch. (When, later, the lunch took place during Charles's absence in Australia and New Zealand, Camilla, Diana said, questioned her closely as to whether she intended to hunt or not, the implication being that if not, Camilla would have the hunting field – and specifically the nearby Beaufort Hunt – to herself to meet Charles.) Whatever Diana may have said later, she was in a state of euphoria on the evening of her engagement. After a dinner consisting of her elders – the Queen Mother, Ruth Fermoy and the Queen Mother's private secretary and great friend, Sir Martin Gilliatt – when everyone else had gone to bed, she ended up in the office of William Tallon, the Queen Mother's trusted page, where, spotting a folding bicycle, she seized it and spent the rest of the evening riding round the room singing, 'I'm going to marry the Prince of Wales, I'm going to marry the Prince of Wales . . .'[24]

One seasoned royal observer, Hugo Vickers, had his reservations, however:

Prince Charles is a weak man who doesn't really know what he wants. It is not unknown that he prefers the company of older married ladies. This is almost the royal disease. He was for ages in the arms of Lady Tryon . . . But Camilla Parker Bowles is the one. She has had a hold for some time.

One can only imagine the corner into which the Prince has painted himself. His father no doubt had some choice words on the subject and instructed him to pull out his finger and get hitched. But to whom. If it is known that he [prefers women] of mature years he is in a pickle. For he can't marry anyone with a past. 'Tis said that he didn't even screw [xx] which is ludicrous as surely that is the only point of [xx]. Yet it is not ludicrous if he really loves Mrs P-B . . .

. . . The Prince has got the heat on him & he must wed. Mrs P-B reckons that Lady Diana is sufficiently moronic that we can have our Princess of Wales and she can go on having our Prince . . . ages ago [x] told [x] that the delay for the engagement was due to Mrs PB's reluctance to hand him over.

As for Lady Diana, well she wanted it . . . Evidently she knows all about it & is so in love with him that she is determined to win him over. The verdict is that they have not slept together yet ('Not before the wedding, remember' this P-B perhaps). But to be fair all augurs well because she is a kind girl and I have no doubt she will make him happy . . .[25]

'In my immaturity, which was enormous,' Diana later recalled, 'I thought that he was very much in love with me, which he was, but he always had a sort of besotted look about him looking back at it, but it wasn't the genuine sort. "Who was this girl who was so different?" but he couldn't understand because his immaturity was quite big in that department too . . .'[26]

Two days after the announcement of her engagement, Diana moved into Buckingham Palace, symbolically cutting herself off from normal life for ever. Buckingham Palace, to an outsider, is not a welcoming place. A huge forecourt with railings and, at the gates, police boxes and security ramps, separate it from the public. It is the official royal headquarters in London, the office of the

'Family Firm'. Its vast grey bulk is intimidating. Inside a maze of corridors runs round a central courtyard, dark and redolent of the past, with busts on pedestals and paintings lining the walls. The Palace is quite unlike anywhere else in ordinary experience: there are courtiers, uniformed footmen and the sense that it is a great hive centring on the distant and unseen figure of the Queen. It is the physical expression of the British monarchy, formal, formidably organized, founded on dignity and deference.

Diana, 'nineteen going on fifteen' as one royal servant described her, felt swallowed up by it, its walls isolating her from her 'girls' at Coleherne Court, even her own family. She was allotted her own suite of rooms on the Chamber (former Nursery) Floor overlooking the Mall. The rooms, which had previously been occupied by the royal governess and nanny, Miss Peebles and then the famous Mabel Anderson, were smaller than the usual palace rooms. She had a sitting room, bedroom and bathroom and the use of the old nursery kitchen. She spent her days there sewing, reading and watching television, particularly her favourite soap, *Crossroads*, and waiting for Prince Charles to come home to his apartment down the corridor. She had been given her own aide in the Prince of Wales's office on the ground floor. Oliver Everett, formerly the Prince's assistant private secretary, had returned to his diplomatic career with a post in the Madrid embassy, but had been recalled at the Prince's special request in February 1981 to work with Diana. Lady Susan Hussey was assigned to keep her company and 'show her the ropes'. Diana shared the office with the Prince's people, including his principal private secretary, the Hon. Edward Adeane, who had succeeded David Checketts.

Edward Adeane was a courtier born and bred: great-grandson of the famous Lord Stamfordham who had been private secretary to Queen Victoria and George V, and son of Lord Adeane, private secretary to George VI and to the Queen. Witty and erudite, he had a sense of humour and independence of mind which made him unusual for a courtier, and he was later to resign when he felt that the Prince of Wales would not take his advice. He was kind to Diana, although somewhat baffled by her, uneducated but

Park House, where Lady Diana Spencer was born on 1 July 1961,
her family home for fourteen years.

Diana's father, Johnnie, Viscount Althorp, with his bride-to-be,
the Hon. Frances Roche, in 1954.

3

Diana's paternal grandmother, Lady Cynthia Hamilton (1892–1972). Diana inherited both her beauty and her empathy with the sick and suffering.

4

Sarah Jennings, 1st Duchess of Marlborough, one of the most formidably difficult and forceful women of her age, who bequeathed to the Spencers not only her wealth and possessions but her contrary temperament.

5

The Spencers at Park House, 1972. Edward John 'Johnnie' Althorp, later 8th Earl Spencer, with his four children, after their mother Frances left. From left: Sarah, Charles, Jane and Diana.

Diana as a child outside Park House, displaying the long legs,
alluring smile and the capacity to look natural while posing,
which were her lifelong characteristics.

Nine-year-old Diana goes to board at Riddlesworth Hall: 'If you love me, you won't leave me here,' she told her father fiercely on arrival at the school.

A pensive Lady Diana Spencer at the wedding of her eldest sister, Lady Sarah, to Neil McCorquodale in May 1980, just over a year before her own wedding to Prince Charles.

The 8th Earl Spencer and his second wife, Raine, in front of Althorp.

Lady Diana Spencer surrounded by press photographers outside her flat in Coleherne Court shortly before the announcement of her engagement to Prince Charles – the beginning of the constant attention that would bedevil her brief life.

'That dress': a buxom, newly engaged Lady Diana Spencer with Prince Charles and Princess Grace of Monaco at a gala at the London Guildhall.

'We're all delighted': Charles and Diana posing with the Queen after the Privy Council granted the couple permission to marry.

The two women in Charles's life: Camilla Parker Bowles and Lady Diana Spencer at Ludlow racecourse.

Prince Charles with another close woman friend – Lady Tryon, known as 'Kanga', at the christening of her son, Anthony.

Prince Charles and Lady Diana Spencer attending a final rehearsal at
St Paul's forty-eight hours before the ceremony. Diana later claimed
to have 'absolutely collapsed', sobbing because of the 'Camilla thing
rearing its head the whole way through our engagement', but one of
her bride-maids remembered the occasion differently. 'She and Charles
were really in love ... cuddling on the sofa ... during rehearsals they
had their arms linked and were skipping down the aisles.'

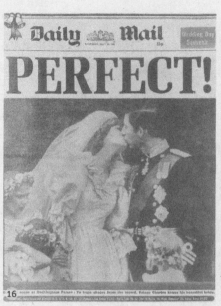

Daily Mail

Wedding Day Souvenir

PERFECT!

The balcony kiss: the beginning of the nation's obsession with the 'fairy-tale' marriage.

Wifely tenderness: Diana adjusts her husband's tie on arrival at RAF Lossiemouth, Scotland, from their honeymoon aboard *Britannia*.

Charles and Diana on their Balmoral honeymoon. Diana, tanned and newly glamorous, drapes a possessive arm round her husband's shoulders.

charming teenagers not having been part of his life hitherto. Diana
teased him and, despite her objection to his cigar-smoking, later
recorded her affection for him. 'Edward Adeane,' she said, was
wonderful – 'we got on so well. Very much the bachelor and I
was always trying to find him the ideal woman but I didn't succeed
at all. He said: "I know some nice ladies who might be ladies-in-
waiting. Will you come and see them and meet them?" So I said
"Yes" to them all, even though I didn't really know them . . .'
'What I can remember,' she added, 'is that I didn't want to do
anything at all on my own. I was too frightened. So I stuck with
whatever Charles did.'[27]

Yet despite the stated willingness of people to help her, no one
really knew what to do with her, the first Princess of Wales since
before the First World War. The root of the problem was that no
one had thought of a real role for her beyond the fact that she was
to be the wife of the Prince of Wales. People went about their
appointed business in the Palace while Diana floundered, not
knowing what to do with herself. She was frequently alone, as
Charles's official duties took him on tour to Australia and New
Zealand and all over the country. 'What amazed me was that there
was nobody in the family who was going to take her under their
wing and tell her what to do or instruct her,' said a member of the
household. The fairy tale was proving unexpectedly dreary, lonely
and intimidating.

Diana yearned for 'ordinary people' who would make her feel
at home. One such person was the Prince's personal secretary,
Michael Colborne, who was, as his title suggests, privy to the
personal side of Charles's life. Colborne did his best to provide a
simple common-sense approach in the office: his informal duty
was 'to look after Lady Diana'. That had been the refrain since the
first time Colborne had met her before the engagement on a
dramatic day at Highgrove after the Prince's favourite horse,
Allibar, had died under him while steeplechasing. The Prince,
dreadfully upset, had had to go ahead with his official duties, taking
a helicopter to Bristol for an appointment. 'Please look after her,'
Charles had said before leaving. 'She was then just nineteen and

quite chubby, nicely chubby,' Colborne recalled, '[but] I realized straight away very attractive. And the first thing she said to me was "Can I call you Michael?" And I said, "Well his Royal Highness does, yes." She said, "Will you call me Diana?" I said, "No, because you know, later on you're going to become the Princess and then we can't do it, so let's start from now. I just call you Ma'am and that's it . . . We got on very well and then from the engagement to the wedding she shared my office at the front of the Palace . . . she didn't like me going to lunch, always wanted me to stay . . . just to talk about things.'

Diana may have been 'Lady Diana' and born into the aristocracy but her haphazard upbringing and her education at cosy, undemanding schools had left her unprepared to face this upper-class manifestation of the British Establishment, with its disregard for other people's feelings. Despite the fact that her brother-in-law, Robert Fellowes, was the Queen's assistant private secretary, she was suspicious and resentful of the Palace courtiers – 'the household' as they were known – who were all older than she was and used to toeing an invisible social line. To her they were the 'grown-ups' who misunderstood her and wanted to bend her to their ways. 'Grown-up' was a word which she often used and not in a favourable sense: to be 'grown up' was to inhabit an oppressive, alien world. The 'grown-ups' unfortunately included most members of the household supporting the Royal Family and particularly those among them like Oliver Everett and Lady Susan Hussey who were deputed to guide her. Diana was classless in a way in which only people to whom class really means nothing can be. And she was rebellious, disliking being told what to do.

The innate coldness and distance of the members of the Royal Family when they were at Buckingham Palace, each with their own separate apartments, did not help to make her feel at home. 'What was amazing in the Palace,' a member of staff recalled, 'was that each household was a water-tight compartment. I couldn't understand how the Queen didn't know what the Duke [of Edinburgh] was doing and the Duke didn't know what the Queen was doing. Then they'd go somewhere and the Queen Mother would be on the other side of the street . . .'[28] The Queen, the one member of the family revered by Diana, was busy and remote. Diana would go to see her and even take her little presents of china figures: despite what many people have inferred the Queen was, according to a member of Diana's staff, 'very, very supportive'. Charles was fond but also always busy and he had little time to devote to his adoring young fiancée. Diana missed the life of giggling and spontaneous humour she had been used to in the past. 'I missed my girls so much I wanted to go back there and sit and giggle and borrow clothes and chat about silly things, just being in my safe shell again . . . I couldn't believe how cold everyone was [at Buckingham Palace].'[29]

She gave small lunches in her sitting room for her 'girls' from Coleherne Court, and for her mother and sister Jane. Mostly, however, she was alone, and for comfort she turned to the staff at Buckingham Palace, just as she had at Park House and at Althorp. Diana would spend evenings at the home of Colborne, dubbed 'Uncle Michael', and his wife Shirley. She also became friendly with several other members of the Palace staff. One of them was Mark Simpson (whose title was nursery footman although the nursery no longer existed) who had been deputed to look after her. Simpson was one of those Walter Mitty-like people, gay, fantastic and fantasizing, who are attracted to the romance of royalty like moths to a flame. Mark had started life as a nursery footman at the age of seventeen, looking after Prince Edward, taking him to school and accompanying him to the dentist. Good-looking, popular and ever helpful, he was a favourite for royal tours and holidays and on *Britannia*. Two days after her wedding, when she was on the first part of her honeymoon at Broadlands, Diana wrote a 'thank-you' letter to Simpson: 'I just wanted to thank you for all your kindness and patience you've showed towards me since I moved into B[uckingham] P[alace],' she wrote. 'My stay was made so much easier by your company as it got terribly lonely & we had so many laughs & for that I can't thank you enough.' Mark, it appears, had supplied her with secret bowls of cornflakes (later she said that the eating disorder of binging and vomiting first attacked her at this time and her yearning for bowls of cornflakes was probably a symptom of this). The letter was written in almost schoolgirl terms with an endearing fallibility as to spelling and the 'smiley face' illustration which she loved to use. 'The bad news is that I haven't eaten *any* cerial [sic] – sob. How am I going to cope without my bowls of cerial . . .'[30]

On her twentieth birthday, 1 July 1981, Diana gave a small party for six of her friends among the Palace staff with a chocolate cake specially made for her by one of the chefs. The guests included her dresser (lady's maid), Evelyn Dagley, Cyril Dickman, the fatherly Palace steward and most senior member of the staff, her policeman, the housemaid who looked after her rooms and the chef who cooked the cake. A year later she wrote to Mark Simpson: 'Of course I remembered last birthday – I drank too much Pimms and ate a mass of chocolate cake . . .'[31] 'In the afternoon,' Cyril Dickman remembered, 'she came wandering down to where my office was . . . and she gave the boys all a slice of cake. They never could get her to take it back up. But you know that was the sort of person she was.' 'In those days, that first six months before they were married, she used to go down to the kitchens an awful lot, because the Palace is a lonely place and if you're on your own . . . She didn't have anything in common really with a lot of them, the Family were all working – they had all their engagements . . .' said another member of staff. 'She did a lot of this, particularly at Sandringham and Balmoral, she just wandered around everywhere. Nowhere was safe, the pantry and the kitchen . . . I think she just wanted to talk to people . . . At Sandringham she often appeared after tea and she went through and saw the pantry boys and had a chat with them and then she had tea with Mervyn [the chef]. She'd just wander in . . .'[32]

'It seemed funny to us,' Stephen Barry commented, 'she just wasn't adjusting to being royal.' Some people disapproved of Diana's familiarity with the staff. A senior member of the Queen Mother's household disliked the way that one of the Palace staff in particular would feed her with malicious gossip about the household. On one occasion at Sandringham he put her firmly in her place: 'She was sitting in the pantry, swinging her legs. And she looked at me and said, "You don't approve of me being here, do you?" He replied, "No, Your Royal Highness, I don't. Not at all. This is servants' quarters, you should be in the saloon learning your craft." And I turned on my heel, and walked out,' he recalled.[33]

Of all Diana's family, Frances Shand Kydd was the one who gave her the fullest support. While her father, still partially estranged after the Raine row, turned up once or twice, he was still suffering the effects of his stroke and a member of staff described him as 'charming, but not always on the ball, always delightful but not going to be a forceful view because he just wasn't at that stage of his existence'. Frances, however, was 'very, very sharp, very on the ball . . . always around asking questions'. But while Johnnie Spencer was a welcome figure with the family, Frances had been *persona non grata* since her 'bolting days', and her defensive attitudes undoubtedly affected her daughter. 'From February to July she [Frances] was in and out all the time and I found her such an attractive woman – beautiful blue eyes like Diana's – then she sort of disappeared,' recalled one official. In the run-up to the wedding, Frances occupied herself with taking Diana shopping for her trousseau. She pressed royal aides to tell her how much her daughter would be given in clothes allowance, only to be gently rebuffed with the assurance that it would be what was necessary. It was Frances who recommended that Diana use her interior designer, the South African-born Dudley Poplak, for the redecoration of Highgrove where Charles had had the rooms painted white, leaving Diana a clean slate.

Part of Diana's problem lay in her basic insecurity coupled with a determination to be her own person. Insecurity made her suspicious of people like Lady Susan Hussey and Oliver Everett, who had been in the Prince's life before her arrival and whose loyalty would inevitably be to him. Susan Hussey was, as one courtier described her, 'a female Mountbatten' to the Prince: 'Sue Hussey is totally and utterly devoted to the Prince and is probably the closest person to him . . . in a way because of her proximity to the Queen and how long she'd been there, she knew him absolutely backwards and he could relax totally with her . . . she has remained one of his best friends.' Lady Susan 'had huge loyalty to him, she wanted Diana to prove to be a success so therefore she gave all her support to her . . . she couldn't have been more helpful, friendly, courteous . . .'[34] Outwardly Diana got on with Lady Susan but inwardly she was as suspicious of her as she was of anyone who had been close to the Prince. She would ask Colborne, 'What hold does that woman have on my husband?' Oliver Everett did his best to help her understand the role that was facing her, providing lists of biographies of previous consorts and, earlier that year, even suggesting she should learn some Welsh in advance of a Welsh visit. His suggestions were treated with scorn. She never read the books and her reaction to his idea about learning Welsh was 'You must be joking'. She did not like the implication that she was ignorant and she resented being told what to do. Had she taken his advice to read about the lives of previous Princesses of Wales she might have been more conscious of what was expected of her. She might also have been aware of the suffering of Queen Alexandra, wife of Edward VII, at his repeated infidelities and particularly at his long-term relationship with Alice Keppel, great-grandmother and role model to Camilla Parker Bowles.

Diana found the intense, unceasing media spotlight focused on her difficult. Every step she took beyond the Palace was watched and recorded, making her nervous and afraid of getting anything wrong. The outstanding example of this was the episode of 'the dress', when Diana wore a strapless black dress to a gala at the London Guildhall on 9 March. Unwittingly she had broken a long-standing royal rule that the family never wear black except for mourning, as Prince Charles discouragingly informed her. The décolleté showed too much soon-to-be-royal flesh. 'I remember my first [royal] engagement so well,' Diana said as she relived the memory for Andrew Morton. '*So* excited. Black dress from the Emanuels [Elizabeth and David, designers of the wedding dress] and I thought it was OK because girls my age wore this dress. I hadn't appreciated that I was now seen as a royal lady . . . Black to me was the smartest colour you could possibly have at the age of

19. It was a real grown-up dress. I was quite big-chested then and they all got frightfully excited . . . It was a horrendous occasion. I didn't know whether to go out of the door first. I didn't know whether your handbag should be in your left hand or your right. I was terrified really – at the time everything was all over the place.'[35] When Diana confessed her feelings to Princess Grace of Monaco, whom she greatly admired, Grace replied: 'Don't worry, it gets worse!' On one occasion in a car with the Queen's press secretary, Michael Shea, she broke down in tears on seeing a huge picture poster of herself. 'I can't take this any more,' she sobbed.

From that time, her weight plummeted. According to her later account this is when she began to suffer from the eating disorder bulimia, gorging herself on bowls of cereal and custard and then vomiting. Later she said that it was first prompted by a chance remark by Prince Charles at the time of the engagement, when he put his arm round her waist and joked, 'Oh, a bit chubby here, aren't we?' Diana, like all bulimia sufferers, could not live with the image of herself as 'chubby': she felt she could control her life by forcing her body to lose weight. No one seems to have noticed what she was doing except Carolyn Bartholomew, who recorded: 'She went to live at Buckingham Palace and then the tears started. This little thing got so thin. I was so worried about her. She wasn't happy, she was suddenly plunged into all this pressure and it was a nightmare for her. She was dizzy with it, bombarded from all sides. It was a whirlwind and she was ashen, she was grey . . .'[36]

The happiness of her relationship with Charles was punctuated by her increasing fears over Camilla, concerns which he failed to understand. As he saw it, he had promised himself to Diana and that was it. Where other men might have tried to dissemble their feelings, he could not. 'Prince Charles always wore his heart on his sleeve,' said a friend. He was too honest for his own good, too emotional to realize the consequence of what he was saying, as the many indiscreet outpourings in letters to friends quoted by his biographer Dimbleby showed. Diana hero-worshipped him: 'Charles is very deep,' she told Robert Runcie, Archbishop of Canterbury, when they met that spring for premarital instruction.

The more she worshipped, the more jealous and possessive she became. The rows were always about Camilla. The evening before Charles left for a prolonged tour of Australia and New Zealand, Camilla telephoned when Charles and Diana were talking in the library together. On realizing it was Camilla, Diana magnanimously left the room to let them talk. When she saw him off at the airport the next day, she was in tears, later confessing that they were prompted by Camilla's telephone call rather than Charles's imminent departure. On another occasion Diana, who was given to eavesdropping, heard Charles in his bath talking to Camilla on the telephone: 'Whatever happens I will always love you,' he said. Friends say that was typical of the way he spoke to his women friends but to Diana it was a confirmation of what she suspected. 'We had a filthy row,' she said. Ascot week in June, just two weeks before the wedding, was another difficult moment: for a nineteen-year-old girl the pressures of being treated by the public and the media as if she were a film star were taking their toll. 'Diana was going through a terribly difficult time of adjustment and was feeling very claustrophobic,' one observer said. During tea at the back of royal box at the races she was practically in tears and had to be escorted home early.[37] And during that week Charles expressed his worries to an old friend, one of his mother's ladies-in-waiting: 'She's so much younger than me, do you think that matters?' he asked. As she commented later:

It was not like talking to someone who was just about to get married and was thrilled to bits and longing for his life with her. And I – if it had been anyone else – I think I would have said, 'Look for heaven's sake' . . . I mean if it had been one of my children and they weren't quite sure – I would have said to them, 'Well, if you're not sure, don't do it.' But you couldn't say it to him really because everything was planned. Mugs being made with their faces and all these kind of things. You can't suddenly abandon something like that with ease. And I don't think he actually wanted to – I think he felt that he wanted it to be right but I could tell there were doubts and it was very sad . . .[38]

By June, Diana's distress and her jealousy of Camilla – what Charles referred to as her 'other side' – had affected him. The jolly, happy teenager who had enchanted them all at Balmoral six months earlier had metamorphosed into an emotionally demanding young woman. Coming as he did from a family not given to introspection over the effect of their behaviour on others, Charles was simply surprised, never imagining that his own behaviour or the royal surroundings to which he had become so accustomed could have had anything to do with it. Only in March, shortly after the engagement, he had written to friends, 'I do believe I am very lucky that someone as special as Diana seems to love me so much. I am already discovering how nice it is to have someone around to share things with.' Significantly, he added: 'Other people's happiness and enthusiasm at the whole thing is also a most "encouraging" element and it makes me so proud that so many people have such admiration and affection for Diana.'[39]

Neither Spencers nor Windsors had doubts about the marriage. The Duke of Edinburgh had expressed his delight to a friend three weeks before the engagement was announced: 'Isn't it wonderful that they're going to get married? We're delighted.' And they were, the friend confirmed, adding, 'It all seemed so perfect . . . They were so anxious for him to get married that they didn't look beneath the surface. They knew she came from a broken home but they thought a family atmosphere would be the answer . . .'[40] If Ruth Fermoy harboured doubts, as she later told Dimbleby, she was too much of a courtier to express them, beyond warning Diana in what must have been the understatement of the year: 'Darling, you must understand that their sense of humour and their lifestyle are different and I don't think it will suit you.' But according to Johnnie's cousin Robert Spencer, 'I remember what an amazing thrill [it was] for us that the Prince had chosen our Diana, and everybody thought at the time, with no reason not to, that she was young enough to be totally moulded into conforming as the future Queen.'[41] Only the perspicacious Princess Margaret foresaw the breakers ahead, the rock on which the marriage would founder. To a friend who said how delighted they must be with the wedding, she replied: 'We're extremely relieved but she [Camilla Parker Bowles] has no intention of giving him up.'[42]

The biggest explosion came over her discovery of a bracelet from Charles destined for Camilla with the initials GF (for 'Girl Friday') engraved on it. It was on Michael Colborne's desk among a heap of trinkets intended as farewell presents for various former girlfriends, including Susan George. Colborne was called out of the office and Diana went in, saw the parcel, opened it and rushed out. 'What have you done to Lady Diana?' the Prince's private secretary, Edward Adeane, asked Colborne as he came into the office. 'She rushed out in tears and disappeared.' Colborne saw her later 'pretty red-eyed'. When she accosted Charles about it he told her bluntly that it was indeed for Camilla and that he was going to give it to her at a farewell lunch on 27 July, two days before the wedding. At polo at Tidworth barracks, the Wiltshire headquarters of the 13/18 Hussars, on 25 July Diana was seen to be distraught, unable to bear the thought of that farewell lunch. With reason she doubted that it would really mean farewell. Sententiously, Dimbleby underlined the couple's noble acceptance of fate: 'His [Charles's] feelings for Camilla Parker Bowles had not changed but they had both accepted that their intimacy could no longer be maintained . . .'[43] If his feelings for Camilla and hers for him were unchanged, then one might justifiably wonder how he could contemplate marrying a twenty-year-old girl who adored him. The 1980s were not the 1890s: the Alice Keppel/Edward VII relationship had required a complaisant Queen Alexandra, a role which Diana would not be prepared to play.

On the day Charles presented the famous bracelet to his lover, Diana lunched with her sisters, Jane and Sarah. When she told them she couldn't go through with the marriage, their pragmatic response that it was too late to draw back – 'Don't worry, Duch, your face is on the tea towels so it's too late to chicken out now' – cheered her and made her laugh. Despite her adoration for Charles, Diana had had doubts over her ability to cope with the consequences of the marriage. Her close friend Carolyn told James Whitaker that not only was Diana worried about the age gap between her and Charles but she had realized that she had not had a single weekend away with Charles unless they were at Bolehyde Manor or Camilla was otherwise present. While Charles was away in Australia, she had gone to her father in tears, confessing her doubts about the marriage.[44] At the wedding rehearsal in St Paul's forty-eight hours before the ceremony, Diana said, she broke down, sobbing: 'Absolutely collapsed . . . because of all sorts of things. The Camilla thing rearing its head the whole way through our engagement and I was desperately trying to be mature about the situation but I didn't have the foundations to do it and I couldn't talk to anyone about it.'[45] If she did truly collapse, she did it in private. Eleven-year-old Sarah Jane Gaselee, one of her bridesmaids who was there, recalled: 'I don't think she was stressed by it or anything; it didn't appear that way. What I do remember is that she and Charles were really in love as far as I could see, at that age. I saw them cuddling on the sofa and during the rehearsals they had their arms linked and were skipping down the aisles. It was all really happy, or so I thought.'[46]

But that night, at the Queen's ball at Buckingham Palace, two guests found Diana in tears: Charles had danced only once with her and the remainder of the evening with Camilla, and gone off with her.[47] The story that Charles spent the night with Camilla at Buckingham Palace after the ball as Diana slept in Clarence House is, however, untrue. Diana was not at Clarence House on the night of the ball, but in her apartment in Buckingham Palace, and she and Charles left the ball at the same time. Camilla was at the ball with her husband and in any case it is highly unlikely that the Prince would have taken such a risk at that juncture. The two of them may have spent some time alone together earlier in the evening but the 'spending the night' story, told to James Whitaker, allegedly by Barry (who, however, denied it in his own book), was also categorically denied by Michael Colborne: 'It didn't happen, that's for certain. It couldn't have happened without a lot of people knowing . . .' Later, Andrew Parker Bowles told Nigel Dempster the story was absolutely untrue. Nor was Charles with Camilla on the eve of the wedding: with Diana he hosted a party at Mark's Club in Mayfair for his own staff who had not been invited to the wedding ball.* Afterwards Diana went back to Clarence House to sleep, while Charles returned to Buckingham Palace, where, after the fireworks in Hyde Park, he spent some time at a window watching the crowds in the Mall and chatting to Lady Susan Hussey.

At Clarence House with her sister Jane on the eve of the wedding, Diana had a fit of pre-wedding nerves and was violently sick. But that night Charles sent her a signet ring bearing the Prince of Wales feathers and a loving note which said: 'I'm so proud of you and when you come up I'll be there at the altar for you tomorrow. Just look 'em in the eye and knock them dead.' From her room at Clarence House Diana could hear the explosions of the magnificent fireworks display in Hyde Park celebrating her wedding eve. It was certainly too late to chicken out now.

---

* The party was organized by Michael Colborne and paid for by Ronnie Driver, father of the actress Minnie Driver, who invited some of his showbusiness friends, including Michael Caine.

6. The Beginning of the 'Fairy Tale'

'The essential basis of that tragedy was that she was in love with him when she married him . . .' (Victor Edelstein, couturier)

Diana became an international media star on the day of her wedding, 29 July 1981. In terms of worldwide television, it was the greatest royal event ever staged: three-quarters of a billion people watched as 'Lady Di' became 'Princess Di' and from that moment on she was never to be out of the limelight, becoming an icon of the status of Marilyn Monroe or Jackie Kennedy. The beauty she had become was almost unrecognizable from the shy, chubby girl of engagement day only five months previously. Slim, almost fragile looking, she was radiant in her dress of ivory silk with its huge train, the magnificent Spencer tiara holding her billowing tulle veil. The moment when the passionate bride kissed her not so passionate groom on the lips on the balcony of Buckingham Palace in full view of the watching millions etched itself on the public consciousness as the remembered image of the 'fairy tale' which the Archbishop of Canterbury, presiding at the wedding, had pronounced it to be. Inextricably – and dangerously – the private and public faces of monarchy were seen as intertwined. Prompted by the romance of the 'princely marriage', polls showed the popularity of the monarchy as higher than it had been even at the time of the Queen's Coronation and her Silver Jubilee. It was the apogee of the twentieth-century monarchy. Dangerously too for Diana, the world became involved in what they saw as 'Our Story', when the fairy-tale princess and her dashing prince became *their* property.

Charles and Diana were carried away by the euphoria of the cheering crowds lining the streets, frenetically waving flags and shouting 'I love you'. The sun shone and all doubts and unhappiness seemed forgotten. Despite her sickness the previous evening, Diana had been reassured by Charles's present of the ring. In the run-up to the wedding there had been one of the not infrequent outbreaks of Spencer trouble which had resulted in Barbara Cartland, who was, after all, the bride's step-grandmother, staying away, while Diana had banned both Camilla and Lady Tryon from the guest list for the wedding breakfast. At St Paul's Cathedral, Diana had to concentrate on getting her sick father up the long aisle without mishap. One of the officiating clergy (Dean Webster) told friends how touching it was to see the way she practically carried him, walking painfully slowly, up the aisle. There before the altar, Charles stood waiting for her: 'I remember being so in love with my husband that I couldn't take my eyes off him,' Diana recalled. 'I just absolutely thought I was the luckiest girl in the world.'[1] 'You look beautiful,' he whispered to her. 'Beautiful for you,' she replied.

The feelings of jealousy of Camilla which had haunted her throughout her engagement melted away. Charles was her husband, the 'other woman' just a face in the crowd. As she made her way down the aisle, she spotted Camilla in pale grey with a pillbox hat, her son Tom (Charles's godson) standing on a chair beside her. The image remained with her but at the time, she said, she thought, 'Well, there you are, that's it, let's hope that's over with . . .'[2] As if to emphasize, however, how much the Parker Bowles family was part of the royal circle and inescapably, therefore, of her own future, Camilla's husband Andrew rode beside the Queen's carriage in his role as Commander of the 1st and 2nd divisions of the Sovereign's Escort both to and from St Paul's, and then accompanied Charles and Diana as they drove away from Buckingham Palace en route to the first stage of their honeymoon at Broadlands.

Despite the delirium surrounding her, Diana was alert enough not only to keep a watchful eye on her ailing father but even to notice that one of her bridesmaids, Catherine Cameron, aged only five, who had ridden back from the ceremony in a horse-drawn carriage, had suffered an allergic reaction to the horse and arrived at Buckingham Palace with streaming eyes and swollen face. A shot taken by Patrick Lichfield shows her concern for the little girl as soon as they arrive, bending down to comfort her while the Queen extends a comforting hand. 'I noticed that she was extremely quick to comfort the child,' Lichfield remembered. 'She had a lot of other things to think about: she had to be on the balcony, do the waving, she had to go and do the group photographs again and again and again, you know, so the whole thing was ahead of her, and yet she found time to make this gesture, which was in itself touching . . .'[3] That night she took the time to telephone the people who had helped her, including make-up artist Barbara Daly. 'I thought how remarkable that was,' Daly remembered. 'I can't imagine many people doing that after a day like that. There are many beautiful people in the world, but Diana had that extra thing, which is really a very genuine warmth because she had a very loving and compassionate heart.'[4]

There was a happy family atmosphere about the whole occasion at the Palace epitomized by Lichfield's informal shot of an exhausted Diana collapsed on the floor in a heap of ivory silk and taffeta, surrounded by her giggling bridesmaids, her quizzically smiling husband and two grinning brothers-in-law. At the going away, as the open carriage trailing tin cans and balloons attached by Edward and Andrew pulled away from the portico, the Queen started running behind it waving as everyone threw confetti. 'It felt just like a family wedding,' recalled Mountbatten's granddaughter, India Hicks, one of the bridesmaids, 'until they pulled outside the gates and it changed . . .'[5]

Diana and Charles spent the first two days of their honeymoon at Mountbatten's country home, Broadlands, now the property of Norton and Penny Romsey and the scene of Charles's courtship of Camilla just under ten years earlier. They slept in the same bed the Queen had used on her honeymoon with Prince Philip in November 1947. They then (to the indignation of the Spanish, whose royal family had consequently boycotted the wedding) flew to Gibraltar to join the royal yacht *Britannia*. Honeymooning on a yacht with a crew of two hundred was not a romantic experience. As Charles's official biographer put it, 'even an intimate dinner by candlelight was hardly a private affair, accompanied as it was by the camaraderie of senior officers at the table and a band of Royal Marines playing a romantic medley in the background'.[6] Diana's hopes of romantic bliss had been dashed by the time they left Broadlands: 'Second night, out come the van der Post novels [sic] he hadn't read. Seven of them – they came on our honeymoon. We read them and we had to analyse them over lunch everyday,' she later recalled.[7] A lady-in-waiting at Balmoral discussed the horrors of honeymoons in her day with Diana, who replied, 'Well, I bet your husband didn't read a book by an old boy called Jung the whole time.'[8]

Nor was there any hint of romance in the bridegroom's correspondence: 'All I can say is that marriage is very jolly and it's extremely nice being together in *Britannia*,' he wrote on the second day of their cruise. 'Diana dashes about chatting up all the sailors and the cooks in the galley etc. While I remain hermit-like on the verandah deck, sunk with pure joy into one of Laurens van der Post's books . . .'[9] It sounded as if he drew more 'pure joy' from van der Post's books than from the company of his young bride. He might have been an indulgent father observing the antics of a newly acquired puppy. Moreover, the shadow of Camilla, whom Diana thought she had left behind, hung over the *Britannia* honeymoon. 'She was on the telephone every day,' a friend said. 'And on *Britannia*. I know that's true because the poor girl was so upset that she told lots of people afterwards when she came back . . .'[10] Diana was devastated when Charles opened his wallet one day and two photographs of Camilla fell out. A few days later, as they were about to receive the Egyptian President, Anwar Sadat, and his wife for a banquet on board, Diana noticed that Charles was wearing cufflinks engraved with entwined 'Cs', a present from Camilla. Charles himself admitted that they were and was unable to understand why he shouldn't have worn them on his honeymoon. Years later Diana told friends in crude terms that their physical relationship on board *Britannia* had not been a success.[11] Poor

Diana, for all her youth and beauty, was sexually inexperienced, unable to compete on that level with the women Charles had known before. However honestly he tried, the image of Camilla was hard to erase and the two experiences did not compare.

Not once in his authorized version of the marriage did Dimbleby indicate that Prince Charles loved Diana. In his biography of the Prince, written after the Waleses' separation, he followed the official line which was to demote Diana's importance in Charles's life and to emphasize her difficult behaviour. Yet after Diana's death, Charles was to tell several intimate friends, 'There was a time when we were very much in love.'[12] As a royal relation recalls, 'When he talks about her sometimes, he will say, "You know we did love each other very much." Suddenly out of the blue, "You know there was a time when we did love each other very much." So there was something.'[13] All her life Diana herself always maintained that Charles was in love with her when they married and, so it seems, for a relatively brief time and in a limited way, he was. An eyewitness who was at Balmoral every holiday said that for the first few years 'when they used to arrive at picnics and things hand in hand they really looked devoted'.

Dimbleby's account of the couple's honeymoon, both on *Britannia* and through September at Craigowan Lodge on the Balmoral estate, is limited to biased descriptions of her state of mind. It was, in the Dimbleby version, Diana's failure to understand her husband that cast shadows over the relationship: 'For the Prince it [their stay at Balmoral] was a blissful interlude at his favourite home, complete with his books, his fishing rod, and his friends. He assumed that Diana would share his happiness but . . . she was quite unable to surrender herself to his good humour. So far from being the focus of her husband's attention, he seemed to go out of his way to avoid the moments of intimacy that she craved. Instead − or so it appeared to her − he seemed either to prefer his own company or to have others about him as well as her.'[14] Van der Post also featured at Balmoral: Charles's idea of bliss was to read the sage's books out loud to Diana as they sat on a hilltop. The familiar surroundings brought back to her images of

Camilla who had so often been in attendance at Birkhall. She dreamed of her at night, constantly suspecting Charles of ringing her up to ask her advice about his marriage. It was an obsession: as Dimbleby put it, 'Her insecurity about his feelings for her were fed by the canker of jealousy.' Yet both sides, writing with hindsight, exaggerated the misery of that time: at an informal photo call on the banks of the River Dee, the couple looked fond and Diana radiant. She was already transformed from the mousy girl of a few months previously: her hair was coloured blonde and with bare brown legs and tanned complexion she looked for the first time not just beautiful but glamorous. Sarah McCorquodale told James Whitaker, with whom she was constantly in touch, that Diana had far preferred the time at Balmoral to the days on *Britannia*, that Charles had been sweet to her, leaving loving notes and trinkets under her pillow, 'things which she found enchanting'.[15]

Yet, again with hindsight, that Deeside photo call said it all. While Diana, gazing seductively at the press, her legs adopting a ballet position, draped a possessive arm round his shoulders, Charles looked stiff, nervous and worried, the dead salmon lying as a trophy at his feet. In fact at Balmoral as at Buckingham Palace, Diana was finding it difficult to adapt to life in the Royal Family. She felt hemmed in and isolated, incapable of reaching beyond the invisible barrier which now separated her from the rest of the world. 'All the guests at Balmoral coming to stay just stared at me the whole time, treated me like glass,' she recalled, '[but] as far as I was concerned I was Diana.'[16] She herself had none of the deference which most people felt in the presence of royalty, or even of gratitude that she had been made a member of the exclusive circle. She thought, almost certainly correctly, that her in-laws and their friends and staff were looking at her critically. She thought they were old-fashioned and stuffy, they regarded her as 'a silly girl'. She clung to her sense of herself as 'Diana' which was battered by her perennial feelings of inadequacy; her behaviour, her sulks and bouts of tears, her leaving the table early at dinner or on occasions even refusing to come down, were interpreted as rudeness. The family operated by their own rules and traditions; her refusal to follow or even to try to understand them mystified her in-laws, utterly unused to being confronted by such behaviour. Her upbringing had not taught her to behave 'properly', as her resentment at her husband for always offering a drink to the Queen and the Queen Mother before turning to her showed. Even in ordinary families mother and grandmother would come before wife in such circumstances. 'But I had to be told that that was normal because I always thought it was the wife first,' she complained.[17] A royal relation commented, 'At Balmoral on their honeymoon she started saying that she wouldn't come down to dinner and him being asked by the Queen to go upstairs and persuade her, and then coming down red-faced and saying "I can't". Can you imagine any of us with our mother-in-law, can you imagine anybody, whether they were staying with their mother-in-law in a hovel somewhere, who would actually start to not do what their mother-in-law wanted on their honeymoon?'[18] Diana's defiant behaviour might have been allowed by her indulgent father at Park House: anywhere else, however, it would have been considered unacceptable and at Balmoral in the presence of the Queen it was outrageous.

Unsurprisingly, therefore, her relations with her royal in-laws were not easy. Although she revered the Queen, the aura which surrounded her mother-in-law, coupled with her innate shyness and reserve, precluded intimacy. Diana had once said that she saw her role as building bridges between her husband and his parents. Charles was in awe of his mother and intimidated by his father: it soon became obvious to Diana that no such role was envisaged for her either by her husband or her in-laws. The Duke of Edinburgh, always sympathetic to a pretty young girl, did his best to jolly her along, whirling her into dinner when she hung back overcome with shyness. Prince Andrew she had known and liked since childhood, Prince Edward she simply ignored. Princess Anne, the strongest character of the younger royals, had little time for Diana. Of the older generation, the Queen Mother remained an enigma to Diana herself, although those who knew her well detected she did not like her; that Diana's grandmother, Ruth Fermoy, later joined the ranks of those who denigrated her could be taken as an accurate reflection of her friend and employer's views. Only Princess Margaret was to become Diana's real friend and champion within the family. In her youth she, like Diana, had been the media star of the Royal Family, glamorous, idolized and criticized: no stranger to defiant behaviour herself, she empathized with Diana, seeing in her a reflection of her own rebellious self. Yet a relation denied that the Royal Family was 'cliquey': 'When you're staying there, it's not that they're all very cliquey together, and it's not all in-jokes which you can't join in on ... they're not really touchy-feely, close-knit – it's not the in-joke that's going on from last night, it's not at all them and us. In a funny sort of way they're quite distant with each other. It doesn't make it too difficult for a stranger coming in, because you're not coming up against a family that is so strongly knit together that you are the object of attention, that you're on the outside and they've all got their in-names and their in-this and you don't know what they're talking about. But,' she added, 'if you don't like the great outdoors, if you don't like getting wet, putting on your gumboots, I can see that it's not the easiest, and I think that in the lead-up to this whole thing, she must have given the impression that she did like the great outdoors . . .'[19]

Part Scottish herself through her grandmother Ruth, Diana always denied disliking Scotland: she loved visiting her mother on the Isle of Seil. 'I was rather surprised that she took so violently against that sort of [Balmoral] life,' said a member of the court, 'because she was really quite keen when she came up for that weekend at Birkhall. They were out on the hills all the time and she appeared to be perfectly happy with it. I think it was the sort of relentlessness of it.'[20] What Diana hated was the regimented life of Balmoral, the emphasis on outdoor activities whatever the weather, the focusing on shooting and stalking and fishing (all sports which she detested) as the *raison d'être* of life there. Despite being on holiday, the Royal Family adhered rigidly to the forms of previous years: women guests would be expected to change their clothes four times a day, from something to wear down to breakfast into sporting clothes for lunch and out with the guns, back to change for tea and then into a long dress for dinner. Courtiers would be in attendance and, to a young girl like Diana, the whole place was oppressive and deadly dull.

It was becoming obvious to perceptive observers that the couple were basically incompatible. Both were psychologically needy, each seeking comfort, devotion and reassurance which the other could not provide (and, in Charles's case, had already found in Camilla). Charles was old for his age, Diana young for hers. Despite his essential kindness, Charles was too spoiled and self-centred to begin to understand Diana, while for her part she was too insecure and blinkered to understand the man he was, or to make allowances for him. The pattern of his life had been set for years and he was not about to change it for anyone. Frustrated, Diana began to play the tricks which she had played on her father to get what she wanted: sulks, tears, withdrawal, utter self-absorption. Perplexed and worried, Charles did what he could to placate her, inviting her flatmates up to stay and summoning 'Uncle Michael' from London to spend the day with her. 'I was summoned to Scotland, rung up on the Saturday night to catch the night sleeper on the Sunday and I spent probably the worst day of my life. I was having my breakfast in the kitchen and then he [Charles] came in and said he was going stalking with Lord Romsey . . . and then the Princess came in and we disappeared into the front room of Craigowan and didn't get out of there until four o'clock. There was a big white clock there and I think it went the slowest it's ever been in its life. At some stage I think it was going backwards. We had tears, we had temper, we had everything that day . . .'[21] Asked what the Prince's particular sin that day had been, the source replied that 'he'd started that attitude of his "You find your enjoyment, I've got mine" – and she didn't like the killing thing, to go stalking up a hill was about the last thing she wanted to do'.[22] Laurens van der Post, whose works had cast a shadow over her honeymoon, was recruited to analyse Diana, the result being mutual incomprehension. 'Laurens didn't understand me,' Diana later recalled. 'Everybody saw I was getting thinner and I was being sicker and sicker.

Basically they thought I could adapt to being Princess of Wales overnight . . .'23 She was sent down to London to see analysts and psychiatrists and given a Valium prescription in a vain attempt to calm her. Vain because there could be no effective cure for her unhappiness, which was caused by basic insecurity and the tortured fears of unrequited love. The shadow of Camilla had lain over the relationship from the start. According to Dimbleby, Charles's friends with whom he had 'agonized' before ending the relationship with Camilla, considered that Diana had 'already reached the point of obsession'.

Media interest in Diana remained intense to a degree which no one had foreseen. Unworthy and inadequate as she felt herself, Diana somehow managed to cope with being the focus of this huge attention from public and media. On their first public engagement, a three-day tour of Wales in October, the world's press turned up in force, Japanese and American television crews descending on Welsh villages and towns none of them had ever heard of before. Diana was feeling 'ghastly', as one of her staff described it: on the second day of the tour she received confirmation of her pregnancy. She felt sick and apprehensive of people's expectations of her. 'I cried a lot in the car, saying I couldn't get out, couldn't cope with the crowds . . . He [Charles] said, "You've just got to get out and do it" . . . He tried his hardest and he did really well in that department, got me out and once I was out, I was able to do my bit.'24 She did it superlatively, kneeling to talk to the children, bending down to speak to the elderly in their wheelchairs, exuding sympathy and compassion. 'She was just remarkable,' said a newly appointed member of her staff. 'We set off with no idea what we were really meant to be doing. She immediately saw how to deal with people. She would bend down to children, she got down on her haunches. Talking to very elderly men and holding their hand while they were sitting out in the cold. Probably completely tongue-tied, totally overwhelmed at actually meeting the Prince and Princess of Wales – but she would just talk. It was just that ability to know how to talk to people which was there from day one. She knew instinctively how to react to people, just ordinary people . . . And she had been told that she should make a speech in Welsh, standing up.' Despite her shyness, Diana, who had been coached in the language by an elderly peer. managed it, no easy task for a twenty-year-old.

'This was her first walkabout as such,' remembered Dickie Arbiter, who was, at the time, one of the royal correspondents accompanying the tour, 'and she did it as if she had done it all her life, trying to please everybody, switching from one side of the road to the other, because all people were doing was "We want D:, we want Di, we want Di". And that's something he [Charles] had to get used to . . . the trouble was that he was playing the supporting role, not the starring role. That started almost immediately with the first visit they did . . .'[25] 'People wanted to see her, not him, and he couldn't stomach it,' said an aide. 'I was with Prince Charles and nobody came to us,' said a former police protection officer on the tour; 'everybody wanted her and that was the start of it really. I think she started thinking and people started looking at her as a divine something . . .'[26] Diana was not yet the glamorous being she later became; she was not well dressed and her hair had returned to mouse, yet no one who saw her operating on that first tour could doubt the enormous rapport she had with the crowds. It was a new way of being royal although nobody realized it at the time. Nor did anyone in the Royal Family, not even Prince Charles who had been very supportive and protective of her during the Welsh tour, appreciate what an achievement it had been for the twenty-year-old girl with no training for the role. 'She was amazed,' said one of her staff, 'that after those few days in Wales nobody said anything, that the Queen didn't pick up the telephone and say "Well done". It was the lack of recognition that she got – and the same from Prince Charles – if he had come to her and said well done or a little bit more . . . But again, he had done it all his life: he didn't realize what it would have been like for a relatively shy twenty-year-old.'[27]

Pregnancy increased Diana's malaise, her sickness and her instability. When they returned to London at the end of October, they had no home of their own, just a relatively cramped apartment on an upper floor of Buckingham Palace: bedroom, sitting room, study, bathroom and two dressing rooms. Diana's dressing room was the only room which was exclusively hers. 'There was no thought,' an aide said, 'as to where she could see her girlfriends, or where she might be able to make a cup of coffee. You know, those silly little things. If she wanted to have a cup of coffee or tea or boil an egg, she had to summon a footman.'[28] Charles was used to it; he had been born and brought up in the Palace. Nonetheless, as one of Diana's aides said, 'It's extraordinary that a man of thirty-two was still living in Mummy's home and it made it very isolating for her . . . if you walk across the courtyard from the gate to the Privy Purse door, the world and his wife are looking at you. And for her friends who were aged nineteen, twenty, it's quite intimidating. And then you have to be escorted upstairs by a footman . . .'[29] 'One or two of Diana's girlfriends were quite worried about her loneliness,' another courtier recalled. 'In the early days when she was pregnant with William, I know she rang one up and said, "Can I come round? I'm so terribly lonely . . ."'[30]

The imbalance between her empty life and Charles's busy one became more marked. He had a programme of official duties, she had none. 'One thing she couldn't accept was this wonderful word called Duty,' a member of Charles's staff said. 'I sat with her one day and she was talking about it and I said, "If you get that diary for next year out, you could write it up: Trooping the Colour, Remembrance Day Service, do a couple of royal tours, you'll go to Balmoral, you'll go to Sandringham, you'll be shooting . . . you could virtually fill half of that up anyway, and you've got to keep on doing it. And unfortunately, your husband, it's his duty. He lives in awe of his mother so you'll never change him."'[31] Diana, besotted with Charles, still failed to comprehend why he could not spend more time with her. Worse still was that no one seemed to take her seriously. 'She was disregarded and that was what probably hurt more than anything else,' said one of her staff. Another recalled that she used to complain 'that there was no equality in the marriage and that the Prince of Wales never for one second considered her to be an equal which was an impossible situation for her'.[32] This royal attitude is common to all the senior members of the family, who never consider other people, their lives, their feelings or opinions. Many of the courtiers share the same view, hard for outsiders to comprehend. For Diana, determined to cling to her sense of self, it was baffling and frustrating to a degree. As one of Diana's staff remarked to Dimbleby, no one had approached her predicament with imagination: 'I don't think they had really thought about her role . . .'

It was not until September, three months after the wedding, that ladies-in-waiting were appointed to her, an indication of the strange lack of foresight and consideration where she was concerned. The ladies-in-waiting included Lavinia Baring, Hazel West and Anne Beckwith Smith. Anne Beckwith Smith was ten years older than Diana but she had been at West Heath and knew Diana's sisters, so there was common ground. Much of their time was taken up with the deluge of presents and correspondence generated by the wedding and then by the announcement of Diana's pregnancy. One 'wonderful' woman who had taken early retirement from Downing Street was there to cope. 'She was just marvellous, she wrote wonderful letters to children and grown-ups, and she kept a record. I think we had something like 28,000 letters, presents and cards, just for William. Every little old lady was knitting beautiful things, a layette and things like that. We always put the things she might like or something that was special aside.'[33]

Away from the gloom of Buckingham Palace, Christmas at Windsor was a rare period of peace and happiness for Charles and Diana. Christmas sees the Royal Family at their jolliest, with silly jokes and clowning, something which Charles greatly enjoys, and an exchange of the most commonplace and utilitarian presents which amazed Diana. Charles wrote to a friend: 'We've had such a lovely Christmas – the two of us. It has been extraordinarily happy and cosy [one of the Prince's highest accolades] being able to share it together . . . Next year will, I feel sure, be even nicer, with a small one to join in as well . . .'[34] Sandringham in January, however, was a different matter. Diana had always disliked going there, even as a child. The proximity of her beloved Park House, now deserted, upset her with its memories of freedom lost and hopes disappointed. As at Balmoral, the focus was on shooting, which she detested and Charles (despite his brief flirtation with Eastern philosophies) greatly enjoyed. Again, it was a source of conflict.

An incident took place there in January which Diana described to Andrew Morton:

I threw myself down the stairs [at Sandringham]. Charles said I was crying wolf and I said I felt so desperate and I was crying my eyes out and he said: 'I'm not going to listen. You're always doing this to me. I'm going riding now.' So I threw myself down the stairs. The Queen comes out, absolutely horrified, shaking – she was so frightened. I knew I wasn't going to lose the baby; quite bruised round the stomach. Charles went out riding and when he came back, you know, it was just dismissal, total dismissal. He just carried on out of the door.[35]

This was a fabrication, a dramatization of an incident which was purely an accident told to Andrew Morton through a desire to shock. Diana may well have had a row with Charles beforehand in an effort to prevent him going out riding but, according to eyewitnesses, she did not throw herself down two flights of stairs but tripped as she went down wide, shallow steps at the bottom, landing in front of a member of staff who was talking to the Queen Mother. Diana even rang a member of her staff at the time and told her what had happened: 'I must tell you, you will probably hear about it – I tripped and fell down the stairs. And what luck, what would happen but I had to land at the feet of the Queen Mother. Oh God, if I had to trip why did I have to do it in front of her? . . .'[36] This misrepresentation was typical of much of Diana's dramatic view of her past distorted by the reality of her position ten years later. According to newspaper reports at the time, Charles called a local doctor and sat with Diana until he arrived. When the examination proved that neither she nor the baby had suffered injury, she rested and he took her to a royal barbecue several hours later.

Next month, Charles took Diana off to the Brabournes' house, Windermere, on Eleuthera in the Bahamas, staying with their son Norton and his wife Penny for what he described as 'a second honeymoon'. This time the tabloids excelled themselves: James Whitaker of the *Star* and Harry Arnold of the *Sun* supervised intrusive photographs of Diana, five months pregnant and wearing a bikini, from a nearby beach. 'CAREFREE DI THREW ROYAL CAUTION TO THE WINDS TO WEAR HER REVEALING OUTFIT' ran the *Sun*'s headline. The Queen was outraged, denouncing the tabloids' 'unprecedented . . . breach of privacy'. Just how carefree Diana was is open to question; the Romseys intimated to Dimbleby that she objected when Charles wanted to read or paint and openly expressed her boredom with his conversation. They were also probably among the 'tiny circle of his most trusted friends' with whom Charles discussed Diana's misery and who urged him to tell her to 'pull herself together' and stop indulging in self-pity. Charles apparently insisted that he was to blame and that it was too much to expect anyone to be married to the heir to the throne. While this may well have been true, he would have to have been very obtuse not to realize that the core of his wife's despair was her suspicion that he did not really love her.

Tabloid pressure on Diana increased: media expert Roy Greenslade called the bikini photographs the great turning point in the relationship with the press: 'Here was an intense interest, sexual interest really, in this woman. The press – editors and reporters – were in love with Diana . . . she looked terrific, she sold magazine covers, no one could get enough of her.'[37] Pressure intensified until finally, on 21 June, she gave birth to William Arthur Philip Louis. 'William had to be induced,' she told Morton,[38] 'because I couldn't handle the press pressure any longer, it was becoming unbearable. It was as if everybody was monitoring every day for me . . .' For Diana, guarding her privacy had become an obsession; but courtiers regarded the birth of a son to the Prince and Princess of Wales as an important royal event to be shared with the public, as all births, deaths and marriages have traditionally been. Diana had what was known in her office as a 'foot stamp' when her officials told her that they would come to the hospital to keep the people informed. 'What's that got to do with you?' was her furious response.[39] William's birth came just over a month before their first wedding anniversary: Diana had had little time to accustom herself to being Princess of Wales and now she was a mother; and not just any mother, but the mother of the future King. Charles, who attended the birth, was ecstatic, writing to his godmother Patricia Brabourne: 'I am *so* thankful that I was beside Diana's bedside the whole time because by the end of the day I really felt as though I'd shared deeply in the process of birth and as a result was rewarded by seeing a small creature which belonged to *us* even though he seemed to belong to everyone else as well! I have never seen such scenes as there were outside the hospital when I left that night – everyone had gone berserk with excitement . . .'[40]

When Diana arrived back at their new London home, Kensington Palace, Princess Margaret had organized a welcome reception outside. Everyone waved and cheered. It was perhaps the high point of Diana's life as Princess of Wales. She had fulfilled her duty to the Crown.

7. 'Di-mania'

'In Australia . . . one was aware of little tensions. He [Charles] couldn't understand that people wanted to see her' (a member of Diana's staff on her Australian tour, March 1983)

Diana now had a new baby and a new London home: Apartments 8 and 9 in Kensington Palace, the dark, redbrick, seventeenth-century collection of buildings in Kensington Gardens which had harboured members of the Royal Family for more than three hundred years. Queen Mary (wife of William III) and Queen Anne had died there: Queen Victoria was born and brought up there before her accession as Queen. George VI, Edward VIII and his brothers used to refer to it as the 'aunt-heap', an allusion to the number of elderly royal relations who lived there. In modern terms, you could call it a royal condominium. The apartments, however, bear no relation to modern flats: they are attached houses, comprising several floors with state rooms as well as domestic offices. When Charles and Diana moved in, Princess Margaret occupied Apartment 10 where she lived in considerable splendour attended by numerous staff. Other royal neighbours were the eighty-one-year-old (born 25 December 1901) Princess Alice, Duchess of Gloucester, with her son and daughter-in-law, Prince Richard, Duke of Gloucester, and his wife, Birgitte, and Prince and Princess Michael of Kent. The Duke and Duchess of Kent lived nearby at Wren House, Palace Green, while Diana's sister Jane and brother-in-law Robert Fellowes lived down the drive in the Old Barracks. All of them were grace-and-favour tenants of the Queen. There had been a suggestion that Charles and Diana should occupy the far more splendid Spencer House overlooking Green Park, left to the younger Spencers under the terms of their father's will, but the costs of restoration had ruled that out. Perhaps, too, it had been considered unsuitable for the Prince of Wales to live in a house belonging to his wife's family.

Although living in a palace sounds very splendid, there were certain physical drawbacks to 'KP', as it was always known. Behind the splendid south-facing façade is a warren of courtyards and gardens surrounded by blocks of apartments. In fact the Waleses' apartment was far from suitable to the needs of the heir to the throne and his family. 'It was a small apartment,' said one of the staff who worked there. 'It needed to be bigger really. They had a sitting room and a study each, then a drawing room, then a dining room and that was it really as far as reception rooms went. Not a lot of corridor space . . . so it wasn't very comfortable. They needed a second reception room downstairs so that upstairs would be private, but the way it was it was all in together. They should have moved initially to somewhere bigger . . . They were far too important to be in such a small apartment. I think the apartment contributed to certain tensions . . . they were on top of one another as regards what they were supposed to be doing . . .'[1]

Patrick Jephson, who joined the Princess's staff in January 1988, serving first as equerry to the Princess and then as her private secretary, was surprised to find the apartment smaller and gloomier than he had expected. Despite the wide lawns and trees of the surrounding Kensington Gardens, the Waleses' apartment was dark and viewless, tucked away in the heart of the palace complex. There was virtually no privacy: 'Everybody could hear everybody else,' Jephson wrote. 'If you needed to get away from someone there was just not enough space.'[2] Most of the time the house was deathly quiet: the Prince and Princess were usually out and the staff retreated to their places behind the scenes. Outside the sun might be shining, the birds singing and children playing, but inside the apartment there was an historic silence and not enough light. 'If you sent the staff home, closed the curtains and forgot to turn on *all* the lights, no amount of TV channels, loud music or ringing telephones could keep the darkness at bay,' Jephson recalled.[3] For

Diana, despite its convenience in the heart of London, 'KP' was to be less a home than a prison.

She had cooperated over the decoration with Dudley Poplak, who was recommended by her mother and who had also been working with her on the redecoration of Highgrove. The decoration was a mixture of grand and contemporary: the seventeenth-century entrance hall, with its impressive staircase and baroque plaster ceiling (destroyed by a bomb during the Second World War, and subsequently restored), was carpeted in green and grey patterned with the Prince of Wales feathers, a theme emphasized throughout the house. On the first floor the reception rooms, the drawing and dining rooms were furnished either with wedding presents or furniture and paintings, and a tapestry from the Royal Collections, including a Veronese, *The Mystic Marriage of St Catherine*.

Diana and Charles had studies on the same floor. Diana's sitting room was feminine in dusty pink and grey-blue, with a pink sofa and, in a window alcove beside her desk, her school tuck box, stencilled D. Spencer, in which she kept her most private possessions. The room was a grown-up version of a teenager's room, with soft toys and cushions with slogans like 'Good girls go to heaven – bad girls go everywhere', and children's school paintings on the walls. Every surface was crammed with photographs, enamel boxes, porcelain figurines. It was cheerful, girlish and very cluttered, smelling deliciously of her favourite flowers, lilies, potpourri and scented candles.

Charles's more masculine room housed a box-kennel for his cherished yellow Labrador, Harvey, and on his desk a photograph of himself with his father, the Duke of Edinburgh, and the wry, or perhaps even defiant, inscription in Charles's handwriting: 'I was not born to follow in my father's footsteps.' In the master bedroom, the 7-foot 6-inch oak bed from his apartment at Buckingham Palace presented the poignant, even somewhat pathetic spectacle of the couple's toy animals ranged upon it: Charles's worn teddy, which he took everywhere with him and was tucked up in the bed at night by his valet, and Diana's 'family' from Park House, overflowing from the bed to shelves. It would be unkind to put too much emphasis on this attachment to childhood toys but it is hard to imagine such a collection featuring in the bedroom of, say, a Wall Street banker and his socialite wife.

Highgrove had been decorated by Diana and Poplak far more to her taste than Charles's. A royal relation described Diana and Poplak's schemes as 'terrible, like a sort of Trust House Forte idea of a modern princess's drawing room . . . three new magazines on this low table and the day's newspapers on that, I mean awful'.[4] It was to Highgrove (Kensington Palace was not yet ready) that Charles and Diana had returned after their Balmoral honeymoon. According to Stephen Barry, Charles had not seen the house since before the wedding: now the Princess, 'very excited, led him round, showing him every room. "Are you pleased?" she kept asking him. You could tell from his expression that he was. "He likes it," she said to me triumphantly. "And it's my dream house now."'[5] Yet Diana came to hate Highgrove, which became more Charles's house than hers; where he spent days hunting in the winter, playing polo in the summer and mixing with his horsey friends, while Bolehyde Manor, the Parker Bowleses' house, was in menacing proximity. Immediately after the separation, Charles, whose taste was more discriminating than Diana's, substituted his own style and that of his chosen decorator, Robert Kime, for hers. Although it had been their first shared home, Diana used to say that it was never her 'cup of tea'. For Charles it had always been his ideal house; he had chosen it himself instead of Chevening, the splendid eighteenth-century house in Kent which had been allotted as his official residence. His excuse to the then Prime Minister, Margaret Thatcher, for abandoning Chevening was that it was too far away from his properties in the Duchy of Cornwall. The real reason, however, was that Highgrove was in the heart of 'horse country' and convenient for the Prince's two favourite sporting activities, polo and hunting. It was also conveniently close to the home of Andrew and Camilla Parker Bowles. At Highgrove Charles could fulfil his cherished dream of creating a splendid garden which he had begun with the expert advice of a circle of grand gardening ladies including Molly, Marchioness of Salisbury, and Rosemary Verey.

'Horsey' people were anathema to Diana, who was spiralling into deep post-natal depression after the birth of William. She was twenty-one that July but no one – not even her family – thought to give her a twenty-first birthday party. A new friend came to lunch, Sarah Ferguson, whom Diana had met at the Cowdray Park polo two years before when Charles first made his advances and who was soon to become very much a part of Diana's life when she married Prince Andrew four years later. Charles, however, did arrange a candlelit picnic dinner at the Queen's House at Kew for their first wedding anniversary. At Balmoral that autumn, she became sicker and thinner, the scenes of screaming, crying and throwing things more frequent. Charles worried but he did not understand post-natal depression. No one in the Royal Family recognized either that or her bulimia.

Bulimia nervosa, as it is called, is an eating disorder where people have a cycle of binge eating and purging by vomiting; they can have a binge–purge cycle which occurs at least twice a week for three months or more. Its cause is not fully understood but it may develop owing to a combination of emotional, physical and social triggers. It can be caused by low self-esteem, which certainly characterized Diana, or mood problems, especially depression, from which she was suffering after the birth of William. Finally, it can be due to a specific emotionally upsetting event such as abusive family relationships. Later, the doctor who treated Diana attributed her bulimia directly to her problems with Charles and it became noticeably worse in surroundings with unhappy memories or in difficult situations, such as family gatherings at Sandringham and Balmoral. The general feeling in the royal circle was that Diana was 'an extremely tiresome girl', 'basically a bad character . . . [with] flaws in her character' and that they had 'no patience with all this about being sick'.[6] Diana in her desperate depression became, as even her own staff admitted, 'very unpredictable'. By her own account she began to mutilate herself in an attempt to focus Charles's attention on her: the 'cutting' cannot have been very severe as she was so often seen wearing low-cut, sleeveless evening dresses and no scars were ever evident. But, as a result of these episodes, in mid-October he took her down to London again for psychiatric treatment. The analysts, as is their wont, probed Diana's family background, blaming everything on her 'broken home', which was hardly helpful in the circumstances.[7] While the Prince ordered his friends to say nothing (despite writing letters in which he told of his difficulties with his wife), the public nature of some of Diana's erratic behaviour made it inevitable that the rumour machine would start up. The most glaring instance came at a major royal public occasion, the British Legion Festival of Remembrance at the Albert Hall on 13 November 1982, always attended by the senior members of the Royal Family.

That evening, before leaving, Charles and Diana had a major row which resulted in Diana's refusing to go. He left without her but she then had a change of heart and determined to go after all, despite her staff warning her that it was now too late and she would arrive at the Albert Hall after the Queen, an unpardonable breach of protocol. Diana paid no attention and turned up, causing a commotion as a seat had to be found for her, and there she sat, clearly continuing the row with Charles in public view. Anne Robinson, editing the *Sunday Mirror* that weekend, put James Whitaker on to the story – 'James, I want you to find out why Princess Diana is looking as awful as she is. She behaved awfully at the Albert Hall and she looks f------- awful. She's so thin. Go and find out.' Whitaker rang his main contact, Sarah McCorquodale, who confirmed that the family were very concerned over Diana's loss of weight. 'We think she could be anorexic . . .' Robinson ran the story, and the result was a major complaint from the Palace which cost her her job.

Among the media curiosity to know the truth of what was going on was at fever pitch. Nigel Dempster, probably the best connected of the gossip-columnist diarists to the circles in which Charles's friends moved, having at first rubbished the rival journalist's report, then appeared on US television to denounce Diana as a 'fiend' and a 'monster', claiming that she was 'very much ruling the roost' and that Charles was 'desperately unhappy'. He later asserted that he had the information 'straight from one of Prince Charles's staff'. With tongue firmly in cheek, Auberon Waugh headlined a piece 'GOSSIP COLUMNIST ATTACKS PRINCESS FAIRYTALE. NATION RISES IN ANGER'. Cracking the crystal through which an adoring public gazed at the fairy-tale couple was not welcomed. Just after the birth of Prince William, Victoria Glendinning, reviewing a selection of royal books, quoted Robert Lacey as saying, 'it is important to us that the magic does not die', adding, 'and that is why we hope the fairy story will end in the proper way and that the Princess of Wales and her Prince and their son will live happily ever after'. The trouble, however, as the acute Lacey pointed out, was that Charles got 'the woman "we" wanted'. As far as the press was concerned, however, though no one wanted to believe the reports of cracks in the marriage, the 'fairy tale', which was still the image the general public cherished, had turned into a soap opera which was more like the current American favourites *Dynasty* and *Dallas* in which skulduggery, infidelity and double-dealing were the norm.

'At the point at which there began to be more hard and fast evidence, her weeping in public, that kind of incident, cancelling going to places at the last minute, him turning up alone when she had been expected . . . the whispers became more insistent that it [the marriage] was indeed going down,' said a well-known media analyst. 'And the press loved this because it was a drama, and it was a drama in which . . . because of the nature of the Palace's press relations which is "never admit, never deny", you more or less could get away with anything . . . You could actually schedule a news story on Di which would be inevitably a story about some difficulty in the marriage – some hint at what's been happening this weekend, he's been at Highgrove or she's been at Highgrove and he hasn't or she hasn't . . . the royal rat pack began to feed off each other [as to] who could outdo the next one with a more outrageous claim . . .'[8]

Media comment only increased Diana's unhappiness and the

pressure on her. She devoured the news, almost living her life by proxy through the press. *The Times* and *Telegraph* were the papers officially delivered to her but copies of the tabloids found their way to her via the back stairs. Consciousness of growing criticism of her within royal circles and especially from Charles's friends, added to the hostile comment in some of the newspapers, drove her to despair. Ruth Fermoy, always reflecting court opinions, told Roy Strong in March 1982 that Diana 'had a lot to learn' about royal life,[9] opening herself further to Archbishop Runcie: 'Ruth was very distressed with Diana's behaviour,' the Archbishop recalled. 'She [Ruth] was totally and wholly a Charles person, because she'd seen him grow up, loved him like all the women of the court do, and regarded Diana as an actress, a schemer.'[10] Charles, while still sympathetic, remained baffled by Diana's illness. Out hunting in March 1983, he turned to two lady companions and asked them: 'Have you ever been very, very sick? I don't understand it and my mother doesn't either . . .'[11]

One might wonder why – considering Diana's family were worried about her weight loss and that Sarah and her mother had had first-hand experience of Sarah's eating disorder – none of her family came forward to help her. Frances Shand Kydd had been curiously absent from her daughter's life for two years following the wedding. Diana had been upset by Frances's disclosures about her marriage break-up to the author Gordon Honeycombe, and Frances had made some curious statements to the *Daily Mail*, putting a favourable spin on her absence from her daughter's life: 'I am a firm believer in maternal redundancy,' she said. 'When daughters marry they set up a new home and they don't want mother-in-law hanging around. They should be free to make their own decisions and maybe to make their own mistakes.' This begged the question: Frances was Diana's mother, not her mother-in-law, but her absence from her daughter's life was confirmed by one of the Waleses' officials: 'After the wedding, she sort of disappeared,' he said. Diana's sister Jane was in the awkward position of being married to the Queen's assistant private secretary, which involved having to tread carefully where the

Waleses were concerned; she was a level-headed woman who was not much moved by Diana's more dramatic performances. She went round to check on Diana and found marks on her chest. Sarah, who was closer to Diana, had her own married life on a farm in Lincolnshire and, in any case, often found it wiser to keep her distance from Diana. Her brother Charles was away most of the time, at Eton and then Oxford. Johnnie Spencer, according to an entry in the visitors' book, had been one of the first visitors to the new apartment at Kensington Palace, but the sales of Althorp treasures which had begun shortly after Johnnie's recovery from illness were a further source of controversy between Raine and his children. News of the sales had led to much criticism in the press. According to *The Times* in December 1982 the Spencers had sold £2 million worth of art which they claimed was to pay the costs of refurbishing Althorp, but in September of that year they had bought three houses in Bognor Regis, which cast some doubt on their claim.

Yet, as with all depressive illnesses, there were periods of light among the clouds: in September, Diana had been well enough to attend the funeral of Princess Grace of Monaco who had died of injuries sustained in a car crash. Diana had greatly admired Grace, feeling a sense of empathy with her as another outsider who had married into a ruling family, and whose marriage also had not turned out the fairy tale it had initially been thought to be. 'I remember meeting Princess Grace and how wonderful and serene she was,' Diana recalled of the evening she had worn *'that* dress', 'but there was troubled water under her, I saw that.'[12] Charles's initial reaction when told she had wanted to go to the funeral in Monaco had been negative: it would be the first time she officially represented the Royal Family on a solo engagement. Diana, however, had been determined to go and on her own initiative written to the Queen about it and obtained her agreement. One of Diana's staff who accompanied her to Monaco later told a television programme, 'She was absolutely brilliant. She came into her own. And on the aircraft back she burst into tears with exhaustion. She asked "Will Charles be there to meet us?" We looked at her big eyes looking out of the window in expectation. She said, "There's one police car." That meant Charles wasn't coming.' Another remembered, 'She rang up and asked me "Have you seen the papers?" I said, "You were absolutely brilliant, Ma'am." She said, "Thanks for saying that because nobody at Balmoral has mentioned it." '[13] 'It was always important to Diana to feel appreciated from an early age,' her brother Charles said in a television interview after her death; 'she was childlike, wanting approval – "Am I doing OK?"'

The couple's joint tour of Australia in March 1983, accompanied by William, and New Zealand, was a pivotal moment in the marriage. Outwardly it was a glorious success but behind the scenes people travelling on the tour noticed 'little tensions' between them. It was the beginning of worldwide 'Di-mania'. Instead of seven photographers being there, there were seventy. Before there was one from each paper and a couple of freelances. Now they were coming from France, Germany, America and Japan. One hundred thousand people turned out to see them in Brisbane. 'The police are concerned about an element of hysteria that has become evident among the huge crowds that have turned out to see the Royal couple in the New South Wales cities of Sydney, Newcastle and Maitland over the past 48 hours,' a newspaper reported. A security officer told the reporter: 'We haven't seen this in royal tours here before. It is more akin to Beatlemania.' The adulation of the crowds at first terrified and then empowered Diana. This was something she could do, and do well. It was a part she was born to play.

It was the first time a hint was seen of Prince Charles's jealousy of Diana's huge appeal to the crowds, which was to be an increasingly divisive factor in the couple's relationship. Although he concealed it nobly and even joked about it, it was nonetheless humiliating for a man who since childhood had been the centre of attention wherever he went, to be upstaged by his wife, a novice on royal occasions. It was not pleasant to hear the crowds groaning, 'Oh, we've got old Big Ears', when they saw he was going to be on their side of the walkabout, or to hear the hysterical screams for

'Lady Di'. The scale of the adulation of his wife worried him. 'How can anyone, let alone a twenty-one-year-old, be expected to come out of all this obsessed and crazed attention unscathed?' he wrote to a friend.[14] Diana, according to a letter seen by Dimbleby, wrote that her black moods had vanished and that she felt ashamed of the way she had been behaving in the past. Now, she said, she only thought of Charles and the job. Alone together with William at the sheep station where they left him with his nanny, Charles wrote to Hugh and Emilie van Cutsem, '. . . we were extremely happy there whenever we were allowed to escape. The great joy is that we were totally alone together . . .'[15] At the same time he pondered glumly on the nature of the public's reaction to them, which was unlike anything he had ever experienced before. 'Maybe the wedding, because it was so well done and because it made such a wonderful, almost Hollywood-style film, has distorted people's view of things? Whatever the case it frightens me and I know for a fact that it petrifies Diana.'[16] Petrified at times, maybe, but also excited by the scale of the public's approval of her: Diana had discovered her great gift for satisfying people's expectations, communicating with them, lifting their spirits. Her rapport with ordinary people in public and in private was to be an enormous source of strength and comfort to her. There was no doubt about her media status: a Spanish magazine covered the tour under the headline 'THE FRONT PAGE GIRL', while *Tatler* dubbed her 'Number one, indisputable brand leader'. Their subsequent seventeen-day tour of Canada was also a huge media success, particularly for Diana: one newspaper described how journalists lavished particular attention on Diana, 'gorging themselves on her fresh good looks and her fetching ways'. Another paper, the *Ottawa Citizen*, referred to Charles as an 'also-ran'.

'I think they were happy, they had William out there, a sort of family enclave,' a member of staff recalled. 'But one was aware of little tensions. He couldn't understand that people wanted to see her. He couldn't understand that they wanted to see a beautiful woman rather than a man in a suit. And that was really sad, actually. It was so unnecessary because together they were absolute dynamite. But one was just aware of a sort of petulance in him and she, I think, found it very difficult, knowing how to cope with that. And she was quite emotional at that time, there were tears . . . she didn't understand and it was all very stressful . . .'[17] Things, however, were to go from bad to worse, and Charles's resentment at his wife's popularity began to poison their relationship. His puzzlement at people's reaction to her was palpable, as he once said to a friend: 'Why do they love her so much? All she ever did was to say "yes" to me . . .'[18]

Consciousness that she was a real success boosted Diana's still fragile confidence. While she had confessed to the wife of a Nova Scotia editor that 'the wolf-pack-like British tabloid press' still upset her – 'When they write something horrible I get a horrible feeling right here,' she said, pointing to her chest, 'and I don't want to go outside' – she told the Premier of Newfoundland that she felt she was doing her job as Princess of Wales 'better now than I previously did'. Like many others before him, Premier Peckford was struck by 'her really soft spot for people who are sick and disabled,' he said. 'She almost cried when she was told that little boy who had presented her with a bouquet was blind.' Worldwide adulation for Diana continued to grow: one British magazine dubbed her 'Royal Superstar': according to a recent American poll she was 'the most popular woman in the world'. *Paris-Match* said that she was more popular in France than even Brigitte Bardot, while the editor of *Ladies Home Journal* proclaimed, 'without a doubt she is the greatest media personality of the decade. One comes along every ten years – Jackie, Liz Taylor and now Diana.' Excessive press attention was by now inevitable: pictures of Diana sold newspapers and magazines. Popular women's magazines such as *Woman* and *Woman's Own* reported sales increased by up to forty thousand in weeks when Diana featured on the cover. One editor said that his sales dropped by 15 per cent when she was not on the cover. 'She's the one that's news, the one they want to see. We often think, for heaven's sake we've had her on for the last seven months, let's try someone else. It doesn't work.'

Between the two tours the couple had travelled on 30 April via

The Prince and Princess of Wales wave from Caernarvon Castle on their first
public engagement, a three-day tour of Wales in October 1981.

Diana riding with the Queen at Sandringham and looking back at the photographer. In fact, Diana had loathed horses ever since a childhood accident.

30 May 1982: a heavily pregnant Diana with the Queen watching polo at the Guards Polo Club, Windsor. Prince William was to be born on 21 June.

4 August 1982: Diana holds the newly christened Prince William Arthur Philip Louis. Prince Charles, the Duke of Edinburgh, the Queen and the Queen Mother look on. With barely a year to become used to being the Princess of Wales, Diana is now the mother of the future King.

Diana looking gaunt less than five months after William's birth. She is at the Guildhall to raise funds for Birthright, one of her many charities.

24

Australia, March 1983: the beginning of 'Di-mania' is very much in evidence on the royal couple's official tour of Australia and New Zealand. The trip also marked the beginning of tensions between Charles and Diana.

The Prince and Princess of Wales leaving hospital with Henry Charles Albert David – Prince Harry – born on 15 September 1984. Both Diana and Charles claimed that they would like to have had a daughter but by now their relationship was such that there were to be no more children.

June 1985: an apparently spontaneous moment of affection – Charles kisses Diana after she presents him with a prize at a polo match in Cirencester.

The 'surprise' Diana prepared for Charles's thirty-seventh birthday:
performing with Wayne Sleep at Covent Garden.

June 1985: an angry row between Diana and Charles at
a Windsor polo match.

July 1986. 'Happy families': Diana
and Charles pose with William
and Harry at Highgrove.

1985: watching a polo match at Smith's
Lawn with police bodyguard Barry
Mannakee. Diana, in her loneliness,
became close to Mannakee, who was
removed from his post and sacked from
royal service a few months later.

May 1987: Charles and Diana arrive at the
Cannes Film Festival. Charles has just told her
that Barry Mannakee had been killed in
a motorcycle crash.

1987. 'The Merry Wives of Windsor':
the Duchess of York and Diana at the Derby, Epsom.

Charles and Diana at the Saudi Experience, London, 1986. The strained
relationship between the couple is all too evident.

August 1989: Diana and James Hewitt at the Inter Regimental Polo
Championship, Tidworth, Wiltshire.

private jet, lent them by Armand Hammer, from Los Angeles to the Bahamas to spend ten days at the Romseys' villa. Long-lens photographs published in a Spanish magazine showed Charles and Diana on a beach – happy and playful with each other, walking hand in hard: on one occasion the Prince hefted her over his shoulder to dump her in the water. 'The Prince, away from protocol, reveals himself as truly in love with Diana' the caption ran. Back in England for their second wedding anniversary, the couple publicly demonstrated their affection: 'They looked more like they were on honeymoon,' said a spectator.

But there was a downside to this public success and apparent happiness – the private difficulties. Prince Charles's friends lined up to denigrate Diana. While they were not aware, or did not recognize, that the marriage still had a chance, they seemed to think they should encourage the Prince to regret it. Charles's complaining letters had their effect. None of them, however, appeared to realize that, in encouraging Charles to feel that his marriage was hopeless, they were setting him on a course which might endanger the monarchy. It now seems incredible that these people, in order to curry favour or to maintain their influence with the Prince, should have actually attempted to undermine his marriage. One might ask oneself what they were trying to achieve.

Leaked stories began to appear, bolstering Dempster's claim that Diana was a 'fiend' and a 'monster'. Diana, according to the stories, was responsible for an exodus of staff and a dog. The first to go was Stephen Barry, the much indulged valet, who was intuitive enough to recognize that his reign and influence over Charles would end with the Prince's marriage. Most of the staff believed that she did 'winkle' Barry out of his position: 'he was keeping the Prince way back in the Dark Ages,' said one, 'she wanted to drift him into the present. Stephen . . . one of his great claims to fame was that he kept the Prince of Wales in the top worst dressed list for years and kept himself in the best . . .' On the honeymoon at Craigowan, Barry was completely insouciant as far as his duties were concerned. 'There's Stephen, Sunday morning, whacking great gin and tonic, radio under one arm, all the papers under the

other. "Darling, I'm just off to do a little heavy pressing . . ."
Three hours later he's snoring his head off,' one member of staff
remembered.[19] Diana was no fool where domestic staff were concerned and Barry himself recognized that his happy years of getting
away with everything with the indulgence of the Prince of Wales
would soon be over. He jumped before he was pushed.

Alan Fisher, whom Charles and Diana had met at Althorp where
he was acting as extra butler when they were staying there for a
big party, also left. It was rumoured that he did not like Diana, but
it was also said that, having worked in the past for people like the
Windsors and Bing Crosby, he did not like the way things were
done at Highgrove and Kensington Palace. The unkindest accusation concerned Harvey, the Prince's beloved yellow Labrador,
who had been bred by the Queen and accompanied Charles everywhere. The rumour ran that Diana had banished Harvey as she
had some of Charles's friends. In fact, Harvey was old and incon-
tinent, his hind legs dragged behind him and he was no longer
capable of getting up the stairs. He was given to the Prince's
comptroller, Colonel Creasy, to look after.

The saddest departure was that of Oliver Everett, who had acted
as the Princess's private secretary and aide from before her wedding.
Charming, highly educated and a skilful polo player, Everett had
given up a promising diplomatic career to answer the Prince's call
'to look after Diana'. At first they had got on well, joking and
chatting in the light-hearted manner which Diana enjoyed in her
relations with her staff. Suddenly, in a way which was, sadly, to
become characteristic of her, she turned against him for some
perceived although totally minor offence. She demanded that
Charles tell him to go, and go he did at the end of 1983. It was
evident that the Royal Family and household thought he had been
badly treated, since he was subsequently given the desirable post
of royal librarian at Windsor.

The resignations of Edward Adeane and Michael Colborne were
both unfairly attributed to Diana. Adeane, a top libel lawyer with
a first-class brain and a dry wit, managed to get on with Diana
although as personalities they were worlds apart. He was shocked

when, working on the preparations for the Australian tour, he discovered that the future Queen of England did not know the name of the capital of Australia.[20] Adeane was seriously taken aback when, after the birth of William, he was told to give up his early morning meeting with Charles because Diana insisted that William's father should spend some time in the nursery with his son. That was not at all how things had been in Adeane's father's time.

Yet it was the Prince, not the Princess, who prompted Adeane's departure. Adeane appreciated the conscientious way Diana dealt with her paperwork, in contrast to the confusion of her husband's handling of his office affairs. The Prince, said a former member of his staff, 'was a muddler and liked it like that so that he could blame other people, throw up his hands and say "Oh, the office!"' Edward Adeane, who had been brought up in the tradition of his father, the Queen's private secretary, had become increasingly annoyed with the confusion, the Prince's habit of taking the advice of the last person he had seen, of refusing to listen to Adeane's and taking private initiatives of which his private secretary was unaware until it was too late to stop him. The last straw for the private secretary was the Prince's notorious speech on 30 May 1934 given at Hampton Court Palace at a dinner in honour of the 150th anniversary of the Royal Institute of British Architects, when he compared the new design for the wing of the National Gallery in Trafalgar Square to 'a monstrous carbuncle on the face of a much-loved and elegant friend', and launched an attack on modern architecture and architects. Edward Adeane had vehemently opposed the Prince's plan for his speech: it was not only insulting to his hosts, the architectural profession, but pre-empted the judgement of the public inquiry on the development which was then in progress. While he attempted to persuade the Prince against the speech even in the car going down to Hampton Court, he did not know that Charles had already leaked the text to *The Times* and the *Guardian* for publication the next day.[21] Adeane resigned six months later after yet another row.

Michael Colborne's resignation was partly prompted, it was

rumoured, by the snobbery of the household, who could not envisage a grammar school boy with the title of Comptroller of the Prince's Household. Whatever the truth of that, a root cause of Colborne's going was the increasing difficulty he experienced in treading the tightrope between Prince and Princess. 'I couldn't look after two,' he said. 'I mean, he wanted me to do one thing and she wanted me to do another so I thought the best thing was to get out while the going was good. And I resigned in the April [1984] but didn't get out till the December because they kept asking me to change my mind, to stay on and do this and that.' The last straw for Colborne, as it had been for Adeane, was the behaviour of the increasingly edgy and jealous Prince on the April trip to Canada which followed the couple's Australian tour in 1983. Colborne had spent the afternoon with Diana at her request while Charles went about his official business. When Charles returned, he flew into one of his towering, shouting rages, accusing Colborne of neglecting him for Diana. Outside the door, hearing everything that had gone on, was a sobbing Diana. The Prince took her in his arms, but the damage had been done. Diana was aware of the resentment eating away at her husband, but there was nothing she could do about it.

For Colborne, who had borne the brunt of the Prince's tirades many times before, this was a row too far. 'I get an inner gut feeling when things are going to change,' Colborne said. 'I had ten wonderful years.' Members of the Queen's household, aware that Colborne was one of the few people whom Diana listened to and trusted, attempted to dissuade him. The effect of the resignations of both Adeane and Colborne was to diminish the numbers of people who could genuinely be called impartial in the Prince's office.

Diana's unattainable desire to have her husband all to herself, and his early willingness to do anything to please her and to avoid the constant rows, did result in the distancing of some of Charles's closest friends. Nicholas Soames, who for years had been accustomed to speak to him on the telephone at least once a week, heard nothing from the Prince for two and a half years. It goes without saying that the Parker Bowleses' and the Tryons did not receive invitations, a point which Diana had made very clear by crossing them off the list for the wedding breakfast in 1981. The Romseys, Brabournes and Palmer-Tomkinsons also found themselves blacklisted: Charles had let drop during one of their rows that Norton Romsey had advised him not to marry Diana. According to a royal relation, Diana crossed every single woman of Charles's previous acquaintance off their mutual Christmas card list.

Camilla's family and Charles's close friends were very upset when he ceased to get in touch with them. Not only were they genuinely fond of him but they also basked in the glow which surrounds royal access. 'I think they were a little put out that they didn't see him and gone were the close contacts and everything else,' a neighbour said.[22] Charles's friends – and Camilla's – were the country house set, the owners of great houses like Bowood in Wiltshire, Chatsworth in Derbyshire, families with resonant names like Shelburne and Willoughby de Broke. Diana was offending a powerful network reaching from the country to the court and she would not easily be forgiven. In social terms, despite being Princess of Wales and a Spencer, she had no comparable network of her own. Stories of her possessiveness were bandied round by the exiles, no doubt giving rise to the 'fiend' and 'monster' accusations. The mantra was that Diana was a scheming girl who had set her cap at Charles and got him, that she was 'a really nasty person', or at best an unhappy one. She was 'impossible to live with – the reason why so many staff had left'. Her treatment of Prince Charles had been cruel and domineering from the start. One friend recalled when the couple came to have a drink during their engagement period: Diana had left her engagement ring in another room and peremptorily ordered Charles to go and fetch it. The visiting couple had initially applauded her firmness with the Prince: 'at the time I thought this was good news but later it turned out not to be at all . . .' Diana, they said, 'tortured' Prince Charles, saying, 'No one wants to see you, they all want to see me', and, 'You'll never be King, no one wants you to be King.' Charles's riposte, according to Diana, would be, 'They only come to see you because you're married to me.'[23] When Diana's uncle Lord Fermoy, of whom she was very fond, shot himself in August 1984 after a long struggle against depression, the tragedy strengthened comments about 'bad Fermoy blood': Frances was a bolter, her sister Mary a recluse and Fermoy himself a depressive. Diana was, therefore, 'tainted'. Much was made of Ruth Fermoy quoting a school report on Diana describing her as 'the most scheming little girl I have ever met'.

While this last may have carried an element of truth, and it could indeed be said that Diana's desire that Charles 'should give up everything' for her was totally unrealistic, considering that he had official duties and responsibilities as Prince of Wales and was a spoilt bachelor already set in his ways to boot, the evidence is that, although she undoubtedly treated him badly when in one of her moods, she still loved him far more than he ever loved her. 'Prince Charles was so self-centred that he couldn't handle the situation with Diana when she behaved erratically [but] she was besotted with him and always put him first,' a member of their staff said. 'The Princess was very much in love with him – romantically so and at the same time rather afraid of him.'[24] The irony of the situation was that she was terrified of losing Charles and, above all, of his going back to Camilla, but her tormented behaviour only succeeded in turning him away from her. At some point, probably in 1983, Charles and Camilla began to get in touch again. Diana believed that Camilla had never gone away and that she had always kept in touch.

The allegation that Diana 'dominated' Charles was described as nonsense by Andrew Neil, then editor of the *Sunday Times*, who, with Charles Douglas-Home, editor of *The Times* and Diana's first cousin, lunched with the couple at Kensington Palace in April 1984. 'It was clear the royal couple had very little in common,' wrote Neil. 'Charles roamed far and wide on the issues of the day . . . Diana played little part in the conversation . . . Charles made no attempt to involve her.'[25] 'The Princess would consult Prince Charles on everything and he liked that,' a member of staff said. 'She was very anxious to get everything right.'[26]

At this point there was still intimacy between them. On Valentine's Day 1984 Diana's second pregnancy was announced. As Diana recalled it:

then between William and Harry being born it is total darkness. I can't remember much, I've blotted it out, it was such pain. However, Harry appeared by a miracle. We were very, very close to each other the six weeks before Harry was born, the closest we've ever, ever been and ever will be. Then suddenly as Harry was born it just went bang, our marriage, the whole thing went down the drain. I knew Harry was going to be a boy because I saw the scan. Charles always wanted a girl. I knew Harry was a boy and I didn't tell him. Harry arrived, Harry had red hair, Harry was a boy. [His] first comment was 'Oh God, it's a boy', second comment, 'and he's even got red hair'. Something inside me closed off. By then I knew he had gone back to his lady . . .[27]

At fittings with her couturier, Jasper Conran, Diana would break down in tears, pleading pathetically, 'Please make me look sexy for my husband . . .'. She was only twenty-three and the couple had been married barely three years. Prince Henry Charles Albert David, always known as Harry, was born on 15 September 1984. There were to be no more children.

8. 'The Best Double Act in the World'

'How awful incompatibility is, and how dreadfully destructive it can be for the players in this extraordinary drama. It has all the ingredients of a Greek tragedy' (Prince Charles to a friend[1])

'I think she was happiest almost when they were expecting Harry and soon after,' a close aide said. 'Again, I don't believe Prince Charles was upset that it was another boy. I think that was a complete fallacy [which took root] in her life later on . . . He was delighted with Harry.'[2] Both Charles and Diana enjoyed being parents: Charles in his Buckingham Palace days used to love going up to the nursery when Andrew and Edward were young, playing with them and talking to them while they were being bathed. With Harry, as with William, he took his fatherly duties seriously, even to changing nappies. He cut down on his engagements to the extent that it was publicly noticed, so that he could be at home more with the children. Shortly after Harry's birth, Diana wrote describing William's reaction to his new brother: 'William has totally taken over his brother and Charles and I are hardly allowed near as he covers Harry in an endless supply of hugs and kisses.' They had been deluged with baby clothes by the public: 'The reaction to our small son's arrival has been totally overwhelming – having been sent millions of pink (!) clothes for the last nine months.'[3]

Harry had been christened on 21 December 1984 in St George's Chapel, Windsor. The godparents were Lady Sarah Armstrong-Jones, the painter Bryan Organ, Gerald Ward, Prince Andrew, Lady Vestey (a friend of both Charles and Diana) and Diana's former flatmate Carolyn Bartholomew. Princess Anne was the only one of Charles's siblings not to attend the christening; it was

announced that she and her husband were unable to attend owing
to 'a long-standing private engagement that had been fixed far in
advance of the christening'. When it turned out that the long-
standing engagement was nothing more crucial than shooting with
Mark Phillips's father, the press mischievously intimated that
Princess Anne had 'snubbed' Diana who had not invited her to be
a godparent. The outstanding beauty of the three generations –
Diana, her mother and her grandmother – was evident in the
formal photographs of the occasion taken by Snowdon, but while
Diana looked radiant and Ruth Fermoy serene, poor Frances Shand
Kydd, unnerved by the presence of Raine and Johnnie, and aware
that the Royal Family neither liked nor approved of her, looked
tense, sad and isolated. Her husband, Peter Shand Kydd, was not,
apparently, present, although Diana's brother and sisters were.

In theory, Diana now had what she had always wanted: a home
and children, and a husband whom she loved. At Christmas she
would attach loving notes to her presents to him: 'to my adorable,
wonderful hubby with special love at Christmas . . .'. 'My boys' in
particular were the centre of her world and her life revolved around
them, more so as she became lonelier in her later years. She would
stick notes on a door: 'I love William and Harry'. She organized
children's parties for them when the chef, Mervyn Wycherley,
baked cakes shaped as Thomas the Tank Engine or some other
popular toy. 'Everything was done for the boys,' a member of staff
recalled. 'She took a lot of trouble. One birthday party she organized a bouncy castle in the middle of the quadrangle at Kensington
Palace and we hired bear suits and raided their birthday party . . .
William was very smart, he could recognize people by their shoes.'[4]
William was christened the Wombat and Harry was Harry Snail.
She was strict with them, rationing their chocolate allowance and
insisting that they pick things up after them.

Diana was a modern mother, absolutely devoted to her children
and dedicated to putting them first and arranging her life round
them. 'The thing that mattered most to her was her sons,' said Sam
McKnight, her friend and hairdresser, who saw a good deal of her
in the family setting at Kensington Palace. 'They were at the heart

of her life and her absolute preoccupation was to give them as normal a life as possible. She saw her whole mission as being to prepare them for their future roles but she wanted that to be based on as normal a life as possible.'⁵ Diana is often depicted as a rebel but she was committed to the monarchy and to her sons' roles in its future. It was the monarchy as she saw it, popular and communicating with the people, doing good in a heartfelt rather than distant and dutiful way. She wanted 'her boys' to know how other people lived and insisted that they should go to ordinary little schools with other children; first, Mrs Jane Mynors' nursery school and then Wetherby School. Her protection officer, Ken Wharfe, who had guarded the boys before being transferred to Diana, if asked what he would remember best about the Princess said: 'I always say that it would be my memory of her influence over the children as a mother and her care of them, because it was one arena that she felt totally confident in. I suspect, right from the day they were born she knew "this is the way I want these children to grow up". They were still in a very privileged, fortunate position, they were not going to be re-housed in any local funded programme, but given that, she did everything she could to give them a normal upbringing.'⁶

'The days were always set around taking William and Harry to school and, wherever possible, being home to pick them up. Or at least be in the house when they got back . . . She'd arrive at school in the morning in a tracksuit, no make-up, drop the kid off, say "hello" to the other children . . . One of the other parents would say, "Oh, William's coming round to us tomorrow night." "Oh, that's fine," she'd say. So they would go off to his friend's.' She would invite them back and 'they'd all come back to the nursery at some point, throw jelly at each other and have a fight behind the garden . . . So there was this natural interchange of friends that was approved in its entirety by the princess because the prince chose to be elsewhere . . . And I think that the success of that is what we see in William and Harry . . . I'm absolutely certain that that is why a lot of their friends now are the friends they met at prep school, through Eton and so forth . . .

'The reality of her life was so much more than this image of somebody performing on the royal circuit, shaking hands and taking bunches of flowers. Here was somebody with this incredibly complex life, able to find time, with all these pressures, to take her children to school and be there for them. But also educate them in a way that was going to be of value to them in later life. For example there weren't any grand teas . . . butlers laying tables . . . neatly cut fingers of tomato sandwiches. They'd sit with their mother in front of the television with a bowl of beans on toast . . . or we'd go into the kitchen and just sit there and knock up something together. So the children would have this interaction with normal people. And so it was a great education to them, frowned upon, I might add, by the prince, I think, in those early stages. I don't think he'd like what he deemed familiarity. I think it was crucial to William and Harry for where they now find themselves. [7]

Diana was obsessed with protecting them from the press, arranging things through her excellent press secretary, Vic Chapman, so that they were not overwhelmed and yet would become used to the odd photo opportunity. She was determined that they would never suffer what amounted to the press persecution she experienced.

'I do remember one day at school,' a friend said,

when William was in the school play. He was very little, probably three and a half – and he came out with his school friends, all dressed up in their little nativity outfits. And there was this huge bank of photographers all on ladders. They've even got big coats and woolly hats. They look like a rabble and they've all got these big cameras. It's terrifying, anyway, let alone if you're a little tiny boy. And, everyone was shouting out, 'William, William, William!' It must have been incredibly difficult for a child that age to understand why they were all calling for him. I asked her once, 'What do you do about that?' Because she was very, very aware of this and was very worried about this with him. And she said she had had to say to him, 'You're going to go to school today, there's going to be all of these people who want to take your picture, and if you're a good boy and you let them take your picture, then I'll take you to Thorpe Park next week.'[8]

Shortly after Harry's birth, Diana began to involve herself in charity work, replacing Princess Margaret, at the Princess's own suggestion, as president of Barnardo's, the children's charity. In 1984 with Barnardo's, Diana, still only twenty-three, embarked on the course which, after motherhood, was to give her increasingly difficult life meaning. Roger Singleton, the chief executive, was amazed that so young a woman could have such rapport with people of all ages at Barnardo's projects round the country.

Her capacity to make people feel good was really quite exceptional and I've seen her sit in a group of young mums struggling to bring up a handful of children, very often on their own, almost choking with cigarette smoke. Perhaps some of them themselves were in the care of public authorities when they were children. She would just sit and listen to what their everyday lives were like. Very often she didn't say a great deal in response although she would always answer questions about herself and her own children. But after she'd gone . . . that group of people would feel sheer exhilaration about the fact that they'd been able to talk to a senior person in public life . . . She left them with the very full impression that she understood what they were talking about and she knew what it was like . . . That was a particular skill and I would say that her biggest single contribution to Barnardo's was the difference she was able to make by dint of those visits to people's lives. I can visit those same projects five or ten years later and if some of the same people are involved they will almost invariably bring out the photographs and say 'Do you remember?'[9]

Despite her young age, Diana was a professional in her private life as well as professional duties. 'She took being mistress of the house very seriously,' a member of staff said. 'And she would do the menus for both [houses] in the menu book each week. She knew what she had to do and she did it.'[10] Each day she would see the butler and give him a list of what needed doing, who was coming to lunch or tea, or what appointments she or the Prince might have. However much she might complain that she didn't understand what being the Princess of Wales entailed, she was very domesticated and her Althorp background had taught her how the household should be run.

Similarly, she was considerably more professional than her husband when it came to dealing with her public life. While Prince Charles's secretaries might compare getting him to work on a regular basis to 'nailing jelly to a wall', Diana, even in these first years, was direct and competent in her attitude to paperwork and to her staff. Her principal aide in her early years was Anne Beckwith Smith who acted as private-secretary cum lady-in-waiting. One observer paid tribute to Anne's importance in Diana's professional life. 'Anne would be the last person to say it, but she was an excellent source of support and guidance to someone who was new to the Royal Family, very much in the public gaze and having to cope with public embarrassments especially around the patently obvious fact that she was more popular than her husband . . . in the full glare of publicity with people drawing attention to it, it couldn't have been easy.'[11]

From the beginning, only a few months after the wedding, Beckwith Smith had been impressed by how Diana handled a first meeting, and subsequently by a thoughtful note from Balmoral welcoming her to the staff on her first morning at Buckingham Palace. No one, Diana intimated, knew what precisely they were going to do, but they would muddle through together. As she developed, Diana emphasized 'her team' which she named the 'A-team', after the American TV series. In future no one would be in any doubt as to which was the 'B-team'. 'She was efficient,' said a member of the team, 'she turned things round quickly, you sent her things and she turned them round. On the whole she was extremely conscientious professionally.' As she matured and the demands of her public life multiplied, she became even more so. Patrick Jephson, who became her private secretary in 1988, described her as 'quick and decisive', and she expected him to be the same.[12] 'This,' he added waspishly, 'was at least partly to draw a distinction between herself and the Prince, whose capacity to sit on paperwork was legendary.' Diana's *modus operandi* in opening the 'Bag', which contained all correspondence, memoranda and other paperwork from the joint office at St James's Palace forwarded to Kensington Palace, was described by Jephson:

She would snap the little plastic seal [of the large red plastic envelope], pull back the heavy zip and delve inside. Balancing the inner cardboard file on her lap, she quickly sorted the papers into piles. Fashion catalogues or designers' bills were dealt with first; then loose minutes from the secretaries about things like therapists' appointments or school events for the boys; the personal mail – some of it saved for private reading later; then real work – memos that required a decision, outline programmes, draft speeches, invitations, suggested letters . . .[13]

She would leave notes for members of staff in her round girlish handwriting, sometimes even notes for herself. She had a compulsive desire to communicate, to reach out to people, even if she hardly knew them, people like the manager of the shoe shop she patronized, Charles Jourdan, to whom she wrote a sympathetic letter when she heard he had lost his job. She also wrote to staff from her past life, like Mrs Pendrey, wife of the butler at Althorp; one such letter, written three months after William's birth, read poignantly: 'William has brought us such happiness and contentment & consequently I can't wait for masses more . . .'[14]

But, according to Diana, Charles no longer shared her bed after William was born and she never had 'masses more' children or the daughter she longed for. Whether he did 'go back to his lady' in 1983/4, as Diana alleged, or, as Jonathan Dimbleby affirmed in a statement passed by Charles, only in 1986, 'after the irretrievable breakdown of the marriage', Camilla remained present in Diana's mind and no doubt in Charles's mind also. Diana's continuing jealousy and neediness made Camilla all the more attractive in contrast. A mutual friend said of Camilla and her undoubted attraction: 'It's hard to describe. She's got laughing eyes, she's full of fun and she's rather motherly and I can see what it is – what Charles must love in her. At the time I remember thinking "Oh God, she's got something Diana hasn't got" which is a sort of warmth . . . I mean my children adore her. She's warm and motherly. At the same time she must have known what she was doing then. There's no question . . . She must have been just as jealous [of Diana, as Diana of her]. How must she have felt when she saw this young girl – I know she contrived it, she obviously manipulated it a bit, but how must she have felt when this beautiful young girl married him? It must have been awful . . . knowing he had to marry. How could she possibly have lived with that?"[15]

The answer is that, as Princess Margaret had foreseen, Camilla never gave up on Prince Charles. Although Jonathan Dimbleby asserted that apart from 'a few telephone conversations during the four months of his engagement and only one after his marriage (when he rang to report that the Princess was pregnant with William) they had not talked to each other at all', Camilla was interested enough in the whole scenario form a close [telephonic] relationship with a powerful tabloid journalist which lasted from 1982 to 1992. 'I mean here was the unique example, surely unprecedented,' a well-informed observer commented, '. . . here was a woman who was as close as it is possible to be to the Prince of Wales, a man of supposed rectitude in his dealings with the press. And yet she is talking to the editor [sic] of the most popular paper in the country, and the most scurrilous, and the most intrusive and the one that's been most hostile to him . . .' Stuart Higgins told Sally Bedell Smith, an early and authoritative biographer of Diana:

I talked to her once a week for ten years . . . I talked to her about Diana and Charles. She guided me on things that were not true or things that were off the beam. Everything was behind closed doors, and I didn't write about her, although I spoke to her all the time during that period. I didn't sense that she and Charles were out of touch. I felt she was involved, but not necessarily in a romance or affair with Charles. I never sensed that she was out of contact, though I definitely believe there was a cessation in the relationship and that Charles put an effort into the marriage . . . Our relationship was two ways. We had some long conversations. She was really trying to gauge whether the press was on to her [and Charles] so it was a question of keeping her in touch, too.[16]

It was a curious relationship which illustrated the web of understanding and complicity in the circle around Charles. 'She was always trying to find out what he [Stuart Higgins] knew . . . why was she doing that? There were extraordinary things on the phone . . . he'd ring her and say "they say you're about to do this" and she'd half cup the phone, not properly cup it and say "Andrew, guess what they're saying about us now" . . . and even Stuart was utterly baffled by how incredibly open this whole thing was between her and Parker Bowles and – obviously – between her and Charles . . . He [Higgins] could run stories past her.'

While Camilla was the shadow over the marriage, another factor was driving the couple apart: the way in which Diana, through no fault of her own, outshone her husband in their public lives. It cannot be denied that Diana had a mischievous desire to annoy and an apparently endless capacity to do so. That past November she had even gone so far as to upstage the Queen in public at the State Opening of Parliament. It was typical of her to do it with a fashion statement – in this case an entirely new upswept style with a chignon – which made her look regal – and older. Her new style was widely criticized by admirers and enemies alike. *Daily Express* fashion editor Jackie Modlinger wailed, unfairly as it happened, 'They've made her into a right royal clone . . .' 'Is she still our Princess Di?' the newspaper asked. Diana's coiffure generated far greater column inches than the government's programme for the new session of Parliament: 'The entire popular press without exception abandoned the attempt to squeeze excitement out of the Government's legislative programme and devoted several columns each to the most radical and contentious item revealed there, Princess Diana's new hairstyle.' Diana had driven to the Palace of Westminster in a carriage with the Queen, who, as usual, gave no hint of her feelings, but Prince Philip was said to have been enraged that press coverage of the day both in photographs and comment had elevated the Princess's image to the detriment of the Queen's on what should have been a solemn state occasion. Once again the newspapers reflected the nation's possessive obsession with 'our Princess Di'. Not long afterwards, on 21 November, Diana chose to exhibit another new hairstyle, dubbed by the papers 'the Vera Lynn style of the 1940s', at the Remembrance Day Service to the dead of two world wars at the Cenotaph in Whitehall, when she shared a balcony with the Queen Mother, Princess Alice, the Duchess of Gloucester, Princess Anne and King Olaf of Norway.

The two important tours the couple undertook in 1985, for all their success, brought the problem into high relief. Their joint seventeen-day tour of Italy in April 1985 was one of those times, even though staff who accompanied them remembered it as a 'very happy' trip. At Milan, in a borrowed palace, one of the staff, engaged in moving round the furniture to give the huge room a more lived-in air, found the couple waltzing round him. Prince Charles had been hugely looking forward to this, his second visit to Italy, but once again he found himself taking a back seat to his wife and her wardrobe. 'They were both popular,' a member of staff recalled, 'but even then the Prince of Wales couldn't cope with his wife's popularity.'[17] The couple stayed with the renowned aesthete Sir Harold Acton at his magnificent villa, La Pietra, on the outskirts of Florence. Diana was fascinated by Sir Harold who, an observer said, 'made up to her in his mandarin way'. At the Uffizi Diana stood amazed in front of Rubens' huge masterpiece, *The Horrors of War* – 'Did one man really paint all that?' she asked Sir Harold. As Charles praised Brunelleschi's great dome standing majestically above the Duomo, the newspapers commented: 'the Church could have been in the Mile End Road for all anyone cared. What really mattered, the pictures which would be carried by virtually every TV station and newspaper in the Western world, was Princess Diana's latest outfit.' The Waleses' press secretary, Vic Chapman, briefed the four-hundred-strong press contingent each day with details of the Princess's wardrobe. In Rome, they had a private audience with Pope John Paul II, which awed Diana;

Charles had wanted to attend a private mass with the Pope but the Queen, with her customary caution, headed him off. They lunched with President Pertini and dined at the smartest club in Rome, the Circolo della Caccia.

To make things worse, the British press lectured Charles on his duty to Diana: 'Charles must – and does – look at his life long-term. And at the moment it is Diana who is important,' the *Mail on Sunday* representative in Rome declared. 'The Italian tour has seen a new phase in their relationship,' he wrote. 'Few in the Palace entourage now deny that the marriage did go through an awkward stage when the Princess was pregnant with Prince Harry . . . some reporters who follow the Princess around the world full-time believe his coolness has continued. At the start of their marriage, Prince Charles was constantly seen to be taking his wife by the hand or the elbow.

'It happens less these days but two small incidents summed up for me how Charles and Diana feel about each other now. The first happened at Florence Town Hall when the Prince gave a speech in Italian. He obviously found the moment a strain. As he finished the speech the Princess leaned over and said "Well done, darling". Her eyes shone and he smiled warmly back.

'The second came when the Prince stopped opposite a self-portrait of the artist Filippo Lippi. It obviously reminded him of someone. He put his arm around Diana's shoulder and whispered something in her ear. She burst into a fit of giggles.

'*Such intimate moments show a man and a woman deeply in love.*'

At times like these, when the Charles–Diana partnership was acclaimed as the best double act in the world, the general enthusiasm carried them through. Unfortunately, the enthusiasm was largely for Diana's beauty and the glamour of the fairy-tale romance in which everyone still wanted to believe and in which the vast majority of those who did not pick up the media's hints still did. From the Palace point of view, however, such headlines as 'PRINCE HAS SECOND BILLING TO TRIVIA' were deeply disappointing.

A new international tour was planned for the couple – their first joint visit to the United States preceded by yet another tour of

Australia. By this time rumours of the couple's marital difficulties were common currency in media circles. Tina Brown, the Oxford-educated British journalist who was then editing the American magazine *Vanity Fair*, wove them together in a piece published in advance of their US visit, which underlined their differences: 'Diana is a very young twenty-four, he is a very old thirty-six'; in taste in music (Diana was unfairly pictured as glued to her Walkman and pop music while Charles organized musical evenings with the Royal Philharmonic); their differences over friends – he bored with her Sloanes and Hooray Henrys, she with his intellectual gurus and horsey couples from Gloucestershire – which was true. Both, she claimed, had lost touch with reality but, she finished somewhat improbably, reality was still there if they looked for it. 'He's in just the kind of mood to fall in love with a nursery school teacher in flat shoes who's kind to guinea pigs and babies. If he looks hard enough, she's still there . . .' the piece ended. The fairy tale was not yet doomed; there could still be a happy ending.

Fortunately for Buckingham Palace a timely interview with the couple designed to counteract the marriage rumours was ready for transmission. With skill and considerable self-control Charles and Diana put across the image of a diverse but essentially united couple. Diana, who had been coached by Sir Richard Attenborough, displayed confidence as she spoke of her role as 'supporting my husband whenever I can . . . and, also most important, being a mother and wife'. Only the sly upwards look from under her eyelashes gave any clue that she might have been playing a part, tongue in cheek. Charles admitted to 'becoming more eccentric as I grow older', defending his interests in alternative medicine and his criticism of modern architecture on the grounds that he hoped occasionally to 'throw a rock into the pond and watch the ripples create a certain amount of discussion and hopefully to see whether something better can come out . . .' Tina Brown's views were largely condemned; even the *Sun* declared that 'Di and Charles are so very much in love'.

On tour in Australia and the United States that autumn, Charles and Diana kept up the façade of a relaxed, happy couple with consummate ease, even in the presence of Mary Robertson, Diana's old employer, who visited them at the British Embassy in Washington on 8 November after their arrival from Australia. She was immediately struck by the change in Diana, blossoming from 'a naïve, unaffected teenager into a stunning, poised, adult', and particularly by how 'chatty and outgoing she had become . . . no trace of shyness left'.[18] Charles and Diana, she recalled, 'seemed very amicable together, even joking mildly about wanting a girl "the next time"'.[19] At the banquet and ball given by President and Mrs Reagan for eighty select guests, Diana looked stunning in an eight-strand pearl choker and an off-the-shoulder black dress by Victor Edelstein, and her dance with John Travolta was the star turn of the evening. She shone in a crew-necked white lace and satin gown at the British Embassy dinner and in an off-the-shoulder silver embroidered sheath at the dinner at the National Gallery of Art. Smiling, radiant, slim but not skeletal, she looked the picture of health and happiness. Photographs of the same occasions showed a less than radiant Charles, although, as previously in Australia when he had danced with Diana who was wearing an astounding emerald necklace as a headband, he put on a good show of affection and harmony when he took to the floor with her at the White House.

He was still smarting with resentment at the treatment he had received from certain sections of the press and public in Australia where it had become all too obvious that Diana was the draw for the vast crowds. 'So infatuated was the throng at every walkabout,' Dimbleby wrote, 'that as they got out to "work" the crowd, an involuntary moan of disappointment would rise from that part of the crowd which turned out to be nearest to the Prince and furthest from the Princess. Even as they drove through the streets, the Prince could hear the cries of disappointment, "Oh no, she's on the wrong side."'[20] Worse, sections of the crowd held up placards caricaturing his sticking-out ears; it was agony for him to have to confront 'the fatuous remarks and insults made to me; rude things shouted out, gestures made, plastic masks waved about, woundingly unnecessary things written in the papers about me etc,' he told a friend.[21] Not surprisingly, it sapped his confidence and made him long to escape the ordeal.

The Prince was happier in surroundings where he was appreciated, like 'Bunny' Mellon's estate, Upperville in Virginia, where the hostess, one of America's *grandes dames*, was a renowned gardener who also owned a superb stud. He was more relaxed too when they reached Florida for a polo match, exchanging a suitably sweet kiss with Diana as she presented the trophies. The principal reason for the visit to Palm Beach was a fund-raising dinner for one of the Prince's young people's charities hosted by the social-climbing and deeply controversial octogenarian chairman of Occidental Petroleum, Armand Hammer. Hammer had been wooing the Prince since 1977 when he had opened an exhibition of Sir Winston Churchill's watercolours and Hammer gave him one of the paintings as a contribution to the Queen's Silver Jubilee Appeal, of which Charles was chairman. Since then Charles, who seemed to have no qualms about accepting largesse from millionaires like Hammer and John Latsis, the Greek shipping magnate, had frequently been the beneficiary of favours from Hammer, including use of the private jet that had flown him and Diana from Los Angeles to the Bahamas after their previous visit to Australia. To be fair to Charles, the shadowy rumours surrounding Hammer – of his being a KGB stooge helping money-laundering to finance Soviet espionage activities, of bribing middlemen to arrange his oil concession in Libya, and misappropriating Occidental funds for his own use – had not yet been brought into the open. In pursuit of funds for his favourite charities Charles was prepared to overlook their source. Since the money was not for him, it never seemed to occur to him that renting out himself – and his wife – was undignified and unworthy of his royal position. One Palm Beach resident had written to the Prince's new private secretary, Sir John Riddell: 'We would like His Royal Highness to know that many loyal Americans would be offended if they looked upon a scenario in which one saw the Heir to the British Throne in any way to be in the pocket of a man they regard as a friend and ally of the Soviet Union and who seems to betray the best interests of the United

States, and therefore, of Britain.' Another anti-Communist described Hammer as 'a Soviet-sympathising slicker of dubious character and integrity . . . [who] has used guile, gold and gall to rope in a lot of good, well-meaning people, including British royalty, to help him organise a testimonial to himself'.[22] Ignoring all advice, the Prince went ahead, flying down to Palm Beach with Diana in Hammer's jet and making a well-received speech at the dinner where he had the much-appreciated pleasure of dancing with Joan Collins whose wit did not distract him from her eye-catching cleavage.

Diana, it seems, had sharper antennae where people were concerned. According to Charles's biographer, Anthony Holden, she had vetoed his suggestion that Hammer should be invited to be a godfather to William, describing him as this 'rather reptilian old man'. On the occasion of the Florida dinner, apparently, she made her distaste for Hammer apparent, as she towered over him on the dance floor. 'The Princess's instinct for people was spot on until the later years when it deserted her,' a member of her staff said. 'She used to say to Charles "Why are we having these people to dinner?", i.e. she knew they had ulterior motives for sucking up like being invited to shoot at Sandringham. He never seemed to realize that if he wasn't the Prince of Wales, they wouldn't give him the time of day . . .'[23]

Diana's success on these tours, instead of gratifying her husband, had only resulted in increasing his jealousy of her. 'He didn't understand her appeal and resented it,' a member of the Waleses' staff said. 'He didn't understand that people don't get excited by a man in a suit.' 'There was no way anyone could compete with that, the beautiful clothes, and then she was tall, slim and getting educated about dress sense and it worked beautifully. It's a perfect recipe, isn't it? It's a young woman becoming a woman, maturing, learning how to wear things, but always that freshness. I think that was her secret. She could be dressed in the most fantastic thing but she could walk up to someone, smile at them – no shyness – no one's going to resist that.' 'She had a great gift for people, perhaps too much so, she could go into a room and go directly to someone – people fell in love with her – men and women too.'[24]

One important person did appreciate Diana's public success – the Queen, to whom the prestige of the monarchy was always all-important. 'The Queen liked her success – the glamour she brought to the monarchy,' a member of staff said. 'Diana always said she had immediate access to the Queen and it helped.' Although the Queen took no positive action as far as the Waleses' marriage was concerned, whenever the subject was raised Diana described her as looking worried and twiddling her glasses in her hands. She was, of course, anxious that the marriage should work and indulged Diana. 'Diana could do what she liked,' a member of the Royal Family said. 'Absolutely what she liked. She realized quite early on that there was nobody, not even the Queen, who would stand in her way. Because they were worried about her. Mustn't upset Diana . . .'[25]

As *Time* magazine put it in its cover story for the US visit of Charles and Diana, their storybook marriage had become a night-time soap opera, 'Palace Dallas', behind the imperturbable Windsor front. 'The Princess, once known as Shy Di, has been transformed as "Dynasty Di"; and Prince Charles, once dubbed Action Man for his intrepid sky- and skin-diving, has become a hermetic, mystical crank.' But, the magazine concluded, 'if "The Windsors" is like a primetime serial, it is one that, before Lady Diana Spencer joined the cast, was having ratings problems . . . Then, like an inspired casting director, Charles picked an unlikely *ingénue* for the role of Princess: the girl next door. *Voilà!* She became the biggest star of all and made "The Windsors" the most watched show of all time.'[26] But if the Queen was alleged to have appreciated what Diana's success contributed to the monarchy (and it is hard to believe that anyone could have known the Queen's feelings on that subject), a powerful section of her courtiers took the view that Diana was upstaging not only Charles but their illustrious employer and took umbrage on her behalf.

'To be perfectly honest,' said a member of staff, 'you wouldn't know what the Queen felt. And I think anybody who says they do know is absolutely wrong because she would never say. What I think is the case is that a lot of her household were very jealous of Diana – and I'm talking about earlier rather than later. And they saw that as threatening their Queen. There is terrible rivalry between all the different [royal] households. It's very difficult to get it across to anybody who has never worked there that it's not like a company, you are not working for the monarchy or the Royal Family. You are working for your individual and that is the difference.' Between Charles's friends and some of the Queen's people, a venomous attitude towards Diana was developing. '[One of Diana's friends] happened to be at a dinner party with a member of the Queen's household and they were slating Diana and this person said, "I don't think you should be doing that", and reported it back to Diana and Diana reported it to the Queen. The Queen remonstrated with them.'[27]

Increasingly, however, the couple's different approach to their royal duties was becoming a debate as to the nature of a modern monarchy. Charles, heir to the throne from the age of three, regarded the attention of the populace as a God-given right to which he was by birth entitled, which he could ennoble by his humane interest and his genuine attempts to communicate with people, while inwardly bemoaning his lot. He worried about issues, was concerned about people and did his best, usually successfully, to communicate that concern. In his own view he was the human face of the monarchy whose ceremonial aspects his mother represented. Hitherto, the monarchy had been supposed to be popular without doing much about it, certainly not descending to crowd level. Diana changed all that. Her glamour, her ability to communicate, her genuine rapport with the elderly, the sick and the young, her empathy which enabled her to guide the hand of an old blind man to touch her face when he was in tears because he could not see her, the witty repartee which lightened her dialogue with officials, combined to present a vision of the role of a member of the Royal Family which was utterly new and, to royal officialdom, confusing and in some way challenging to royal dignity. Charles felt unfairly outshone; Diana, with some reason, felt that her efforts to enhance the couple's public image were unappreciated. She enjoyed being regarded as a superstar but behind the walls of Kensington Palace and Highgrove she wanted the Barbara Cartland cliché of loving wife and husband, with adorable children. Increasingly the public success made private harmony more difficult. Caught between the radiant public image of herself and her own insecurities and longing for love and appreciation, she made demands on Charles to which he could not and would not respond.

Diana still hoped for Charles's love and approbation. Much as she loved him, she showed little real understanding of the kind of man he was: bred into him was a horror of public exhibitionism or displays of emotion. Secretly she prepared a surprise for Charles; whether she thought it was something he would appreciate or whether she wanted to show him what a desirable woman she was, underlining what he was missing, is impossible to guess. Charles's thirty-seventh birthday was to be celebrated at a gala evening at the Royal Opera House, Covent Garden. At the end of the performance Diana slipped out of the royal box to change into a slinky, body-hugging, silver dress, to perform something she had been secretly rehearsing with the Royal Ballet star Wayne Sleep, a dance routine to Billy Joel's 'Uptown Girl'. To see the Princess of Wales cavorting in a sexy number on a public stage was a severe shock to Charles's sense of royal propriety: how Diana could ever have thought otherwise is a measure of the distance between them and between her way of thinking and the inbred royal mind. She received eight curtain calls and a standing ovation, then dropped a curtsey to her husband in the royal box. 'Look what you're missing' did indeed seem to be her message: it fell on deaf ears. Charles was horrified. He saw the episode not as a gesture of love towards him but as yet another example of Diana courting the public eye.

The stage was set for another downturn in their private relationship.

9. 'Charles has gone back to his Lady'

'You know about Camilla, don't you? . . . I don't know how to deal with it. It's there and I can't do anything about it . . .' (Diana to Ken Wharfe, 1986[1])

The couple's sex life was virtually non-existent by then. Diana was only twenty-four: the contrast between the adulation she received in public and the total lack of appreciation she found when she returned home was hard to take. When asked by Peter Settelen, her voice coach, who taped their sessions, 'There's virtually no sexual relations between the two of you? . . .' she replied, 'Well, there was. There was, there was. But it was odd, very odd. But it was there, it was there and then it fizzled out about seven years ago . . . Well, seven was Harry. It was eight . . .' Asked how she knew it was odd, she replied, 'Instinct told me. It was just so odd. I just don't know. There was never a requirement for it from [sic] his case. Sort of once every three weeks, and I kept thinking, and then I followed a pattern; he used to see his lady once every three weeks before we got married . . .'[2] It seems that sex never mattered very much to Diana, certainly not as much as expressions of love and appreciation. Her careful preservation of her virginity – 'keeping myself tidy' – hardly indicated a passionately sexual temperament. With the consciousness of Camilla in the background and her husband's infrequent sexual advances, she was probably, like many beautiful and inexperienced women, insecure about her own sexual attraction. She liked to flirt and was immensely successful at it: men of all ages would go weak at the knees when she fluttered her eyelashes at them, focusing on them with her amazing blue eyes. Her lavatorial sense of humour, fondness for coarse jokes and fascination with other people's sexual behaviour indicated a vicarious rather than a practical interest in sex.

The role of the Royalty and Diplomatic Protection Department officers in the life of the 'principal' they are entrusted to protect is a curious one. The men are SAS-trained in threat avoidance while driving, the use of a gun, fitness and awareness, regularly tested and expected to keep up with the latest intelligence. 'From '72 until recently the IRA was the biggest threat,' one said. 'You get the nutters, you always got the nutters, but your main intelligence was that the IRA said that members of the Royal Family, while working and representing the Royal Family, were a legitimate target.' From the moment Diana symbolically entered the Royal Family on the night she went to stay at Clarence House, she became used to the presence of policemen dedicated to her protection.

Her private protection officer became part of her life: with her when she walked in the park, with her when she went shopping; wearing black tie he shadowed her at evening events, played informally with the children at home. One of Diana's first protection officers, Graham Smith, who was on *Britannia* for the honeymoon, became a father figure to her; she visited him in hospital just before he died of cancer. Diana was absolutely open with her protection officers, almost to the point of embarrassing them. It was Graham Smith who warned one of his successors of the frankness he could expect. 'He said, "Look, Ken, whatever I say it's going to be confirmed by her because you'll be a part of it."' 'In a way,' Wharfe said, 'this was probably one of Diana's strengths but it was also a weakness. I'm not so certain it's a good idea to keep telling people everything.'[3] Naturally the 'principal' and the policeman would become close. In 1985 Diana, in her loneliness and longing for love, comfort and appreciation, became close, perhaps too close, to her protection officer Barry Mannakee. When asked about Mannakee, a member of staff recalled him as 'Really a very nice man, very down to earth . . . genuine . . . a nice person to have around. He came across as being someone you thought "if there was a crisis, I'd be glad to have him standing next to me".'⁴ There has been much gossip and rumour about Diana's relations with Barry Mannakee. Diana, in the tapes she made with Peter Settelen, recorded in 1992 but broadcast on NBC, one of the major US networks, after her death, in the autumn of 2004, admitted to a crush on him: 'I fell deeply in love with someone who worked in this environment. And he was the greatest fella I've ever had.' 'I was always walking around trying to see him . . . I just wore my heart on my sleeve and was only happy when he was around . . . I was like a little girl in front of him the whole time. Desperate for praise. Desperate.' She even half-joked about running away with him (although he had a wife and children). When asked by Settelen, 'What you're saying is that there had been sexual . . . ?' Diana replied 'No'.⁵ A later lover, James Hewitt, claimed that she told him that a teddy bear on her bed had been given her by Mannakee, and that he had been her lover. Hewitt's testimony, given in his second book about his affair with Diana, cannot be corroborated but any sexual affair was denied to Mannakee's successor, Ken Wharfe, by the house staff who would have known of it had it happened. This may have been out of a loyal desire to protect Diana: the rumour in the Kensington Palace village alleged that Mannakee used to go and see Diana when Charles was not there, and that he really cared for her, comforting her and fulfilling her needs.

What had happened, or was witnessed on one occasion, was Mannakee in Diana's sitting room, jacket off, having a cup of tea, laughing and joking and giving her a cuddle before he left. That was his downfall. As Diana told Settelen, '. . . it all got so difficult. And people got so jealous. Bitchy in this house [Kensington Palace]. And eventually he had to go . . . it was all found out and he was chucked out.'⁶ Word from the staff got to the chief protection officer, Colin Trimming, who worked principally for the Prince of Wales. Mannakee was removed from his post overnight and sacked from royal service a few months later. Not one of Diana's staff believed Mannakee had slept with the Princess: 'He was just stupid . . . familiar and arrogant' was the general opinion. Did Charles know of it? Trimming was very much the Prince's creature and recipient of his favours; it seems likely that, if asked why Mannakee had left so suddenly, he would have given 'overfamiliarity' as the reason. Certainly Charles knew enough about Mannakee to inform Diana when he was killed in a motorcycle accident two years later. He told her when they were travelling together in the back of a limousine en route to RAF Northolt to catch a plane to the Cannes Film Festival. Diana thought he had done it with deliberate cruelty. She fantasized about Mannakee, consulting clairvoyants in an attempt to contact him, having disturbing dreams about him, that 'he was very unhappy wherever he's gone to'. She found out where he had been buried (he had been cremated and his ashes scattered), and laid flowers for him. The dreams stopped.

The death of Mannakee has been resurrected as part of the investigation into Diana's own death. Mannakee believed that he was in danger: 'He thought that if ever anything happened [between him and Diana], something would happen [to him] and he was terrified.'[7] Diana, always a fan of conspiracy theories, believed it too. She asked Andrew Morton to find out the truth. In fact, it had been a simple, tragic road accident: Mannakee had been riding pillion on a friend's motorcycle, when an inexperienced woman driver pulled out of a side road, turning right across their path. Mannakee was thrown off, went through the car's rear window and was killed instantly. It was not the type of 'accident' which could have been set up beforehand.

If Charles had indeed known of his wife's affection for her detective, there is little reason to suppose that he cared. In court circles, where it was known, it would have been regarded as yet another instance of Diana's 'not knowing how to behave'.

Into Diana's life at this critical point, eager to be her new best friend, came 'Fergie' – Sarah Ferguson, the bouncing, cheerful and loud daughter of Prince Charles's polo manager, Ronald Ferguson, always known by Sarah as 'Dads'. Fergie muscled her way into Diana's life: 'I met Fergie when Charles was getting near me,' Diana told Morton, 'and she kept rearing her head for some reason, and she seemed to know all about the royal set-up, things like that.

She just sort of encouraged it. I don't know, she just suddenly appeared and she sat in the front pew of our wedding – and everything like that. She came to lunch at Buckingham Palace and didn't seem daunted by it all. I wasn't quite sure how to take it . . .'[8] In royal life, as P G. Wodehouse put it, 'nothing propinks like propinquity'. Contrary to perceived opinion, the Royal Family do not have a wide group of friends and tend to marry within the closed circle of people they actually meet who have been provided for them. The Queen herself met Prince Philip through his uncle, Lord Mountbatten; Diana was in essence 'the girl next door'; Fergie's passport to the royal circle was her father and, once again, polo was the entrée, as it had been for a succession of Prince Charles's girlfriends, including Camilla Parker Bowles.

Fergie and Diana had indeed first met in polo surroundings – at the Cowdray Park tournament on the weekend when Diana, staying with the de Passes, had shared a hay bale with Prince Charles with such momentous results. Fergie, although with aristocratic connections, had not been born into a 'great family' like Diana and there was no stately home in the background, simply an agreeable Hampshire farm, Dummer Down. Like Diana, she was no intellectual and, as with Diana, her parents had separated, although later and under less painful circumstances than Diana's. Fergie had had a more down-to-earth upbringing than Diana, ponies, gymkhanas and all the usual middle-class country pursuits. She had attended Queen's secretarial college in South Kensington – the same institution attended by Camilla – graduating in 1977 with the perceptive report: 'Bright, bouncy redhead. She's a bit slapdash. But she has initiative and personality which she will use to her advantage when she gets older.'

Sarah Ferguson was a Sloane, living south of the Thames where she, like many other impecunious daughters of the middle class, shared a flat and commuted to a job north of the river. She had been doing a variety of jobs to make ends meet, although her finances were always precarious, her most recent job being acquisitions director for the Richard Burton gallery. She had been having a relationship with a racing driver, Paddy McNally, based in Verbier, and had longed to marry him while secretly realizing he had no real intention of marrying her. She had been hurt that, after being invited to Diana's wedding, she was not on the more select list for the wedding breakfast but nonetheless, in her own words, she 'stayed close to Diana, kept having lunch with her each week'.

It was Diana who provided her entrée into the royal circle. Ronald Ferguson's credentials as the Prince's polo manager would not have been enough in the snobbish ambiance of the court to qualify his daughter for official admittance into the inner circle. 'A polo manager is not considered a gentleman in the household,' said an observer; 'it's not the same level as the courtier.' 'Fergie's a good girl. She's got no harm in her. She's just vulgar. It's not her fault, that's the way she was born and brought up. That's the milieu. She was a chalet girl having an affair with her boss. She wanted to marry him, she was older than his children, he kicked her out. She cried on Diana's shoulder.' When Diana put in a request that Sarah should become one of her ladies-in-waiting, it was firmly turned down as 'most unsuitable'. 'Diana was furious,' a witness said. 'I think it was the first time she had been turned down . . . she told me the courtiers, the Men in Grey – not the Queen – "they dared to turn down my request", that sort of attitude. And I said, "She's not exactly suitable, is she?" But that wasn't the point . . . Diana decided she was going to show them. Diana promoted Fergie's marriage to Andrew from Day One.'[9] She invited Fergie to dinner at Kensington Palace to meet Andrew when they hit it off straight away, given as they both were to boisterous behaviour and 'idiot jokes'.

Andrew was Diana's favourite among her younger in-laws; they had almost grown up together, and she was sorry for him after the failure of his romance with the American Koo Stark. (Koo had been popular with everyone, Diana included, and had seemed set to become engaged to Andrew when a newspaper turned up some hazy stills of a lesbian shower scene in a film made by Henry Herbert, and Koo went the way of many of Charles's hopefuls.)

The friendship quietly developed: Andrew invited Sarah to a New Year's house party at Sandringham and confessed his love. In February, after Fergie returned from a skiing holiday with Charles and Diana, Andrew proposed to her at Floors Castle, home of the Duke of Roxburghe. On 15 March the Queen gave her consent, four days later the engagement was announced and Fergie left 40 Lavender Terrace, Clapham, for ever. Press and public were ecstatic at this new royal romance – Fergie, it was agreed, was to be the 'breath of fresh air' the Royal Family needed.

Fergie was to refer to herself in her autobiography, *My Story*, as Diana's best friend. This was a distortion of the truth. Fergie had hauled herself into the royal circle through Diana and from then on the two girls were in competition for royal and public favour. It had begun that February at Verbier, where Diana was not at her best, feeling sick and longing to stay inside, while Fergie, an expert skier, shone on the slopes and made everybody laugh with her antics. According to Fergie it was on this occasion that Charles, provoked by Diana's moping, prodded her with the unkind question, 'Why can't you be more like Fergie', a phrase which was to become a refrain. But Fergie did inspire Diana to be happier, to enjoy her lot and have fun.

On the day of the wedding, 23 July 1986, *The Times* leader greeted Fergie as 'a level-headed and attractive young woman', which was somewhat wide of the mark. Attractive yes, level-headed never, as a prank on the evening of Andrew's stag night demonstrated. On 15 July, a week before the wedding, Andrew held his stag night attended by show-business celebrities like Elton John and David Frost. 'I desperately wanted to gate-crash,' Fergie wrote, but the house was impregnable with high walls and a squadron of guards. With Diana and a few friends they staged a hen night which involved wearing grey wigs, dressing up as policewomen and pretending to arrest a 'prostitute' at the gates of Buckingham Palace. They were put in a police van and driven down the Mall until one of the policemen recognized Diana: 'Oh my heavens, it's the Princess of Wales in drag!' he exclaimed. The girls went on to Annabel's, the fashionable nightclub in Berkeley Square, hoping to surprise Andrew there but, having inveigled themselves in, they found him gone. After stopping the traffic in Berkeley Square, they succeeded in tricking the policeman on the Palace gates and shut them in Andrew's face as his car approached. Fearing an ambush, he screeched into reverse. 'It was about then,' said Fergie, 'that I wondered if we had gone a bit too far.' Technically the impersonation of police officers is a criminal offence, as some Members of Parliament pointed out.

'The Princess was rather in awe of her [Fergie],' one of her staff said. 'Fergie had her own agenda and used to get Diana into trouble and then disappear.'[10] The idea of going to Annabel's dressed up as a policewoman would never have occurred to Diana. Nor would the equally silly incident of the two royal ladies poking the bottoms of friends at Ascot in 1987. 'If you see where the photograph was taken – where the press stand when they take photographs at Ascot, the Royal Enclosure, well it was right there, so it was done as a photo op.,' said Dickie Arbiter. 'The Princess used to say wistfully that Fergie's friends were much nicer – i.e. more fun – than hers were,' said a member of her staff. 'But when Diana cut her off, Fergie was desperate to get back in with her.'[11]

The advent of bouncing, jolly, sporty Fergie with her mane of red hair and Rubenesque charms, made Diana's life more difficult. At Sarah's wedding, which was so obviously a marriage of love, observers noted that Charles and Diana did not exchange a word during the ceremony. 'FABULOUS FERGIE' trumpeted one headline, while the 'First Lady of Fleet Street', Jean Rook, was less complimentary, calling her 'an unbrushed red setter struggling to get out of a hand-knitted potato sack'. 'They were always made out to be so close,' Arbiter said, 'but they weren't close at all. Diana always wanted to be number one. She felt she was number one in their [the Waleses'] joint office and she was going to be number one when it came to the in-laws.' As far as Diana was concerned, almost all Fergie's initiatives were detrimental to her.

'I wasn't quite sure how to take it,' Diana told Morton.

Suddenly everybody said: 'Oh, isn't she marvellous, a breath of fresh air, thank God she's more fun than Diana.' So Diana was listening and reading every line. I felt terribly insecure. I thought maybe I ought to be like Fergie and my husband said: 'I wish you would be like Fergie – all jolly. Why are you always so miserable? Why can't you be like Grannie [the Queen Mother] . . .' I made so many balls-ups trying to be like Fergie. I went to a pop concert, Spider concert, David Bowie, with David Waterhouse and David Linley [Princess Margaret's son by Lord Snowdon] . . . I went in leather trousers which I thought was the right thing to do, completely putting out of mind that I was the future Queen and future Queens don't wear leather like that in public. So I thought that was frightfully 'with it', frightfully pleased to act my own age. Slapped hands. The same summer at Ascot I put a brolly up somebody's backside. In my astrological chart Penny Thornton always said to me: 'Everything you will do this summer you will pay for.' I did, definitely. I learnt a lot.[12]

It was Fergie who introduced Diana to an array of therapists, astrologers, psychics and healers who were to feed the more unstable side of her personality over the following years.

Two months before the Yorks' wedding Charles and Diana had undertaken an official trip to Canada for Expo '86, followed by Japan. In March that year, perhaps after comparing the un-complicated happiness of his brother and fiancée with the tortured state of his own marriage, Charles had written to a friend: 'It's agony to know that someone is hating it all so much . . . It is like being trapped in a rather desperate cul-de-sac with no apparent means of exit . . . It seems so unfair on her . . .'[13] In Vancouver, Diana, once again prey to her eating disorder, fainted by his side, only to receive minimum sympathy. Diana, it appeared, thought that he was convinced she had done it on purpose to gain sym-pathy and to distract attention from himself. When Charles spoke from the heart of 'the soul of mankind' and 'the beauty and harmony' that lay deep therein like the reflection in a 'mirror-calm lake', the British press jeered, advising him to look at his own bald spot in a mirror. But when Charles had said, '. . . so

often the beauty and harmony is obscured and ruffled by un-
accountable storms', he was undoubtedly referring to his own
private life. [4] Yet to their staff, the couple kept up appearances.
Diana wrote a warm note after the tours to the butler who had
looked after them, thanking him for his care. Referring to the
Canada and Tokyo tours she said: 'Both . . . were particularly
demanding and your day started and finished long after ours and
along with the jetlag and endless time changes must have left you
feeling totally exhausted. Your support and endurance are vital to
us and somehow you managed to appear calm and always there
with a smile on our return. Both of us wanted you to know how
enormously we appreciated everything you did for us while we
were in Canada and Japan . . .' Whatever her troubles, Diana
endeavoured to keep a calm face in front of her household. The
same could not be said for Prince Charles whose complaining
letters to his friends left no doubt of his feelings. By November he
was openly appealing to his friends for help: 'Frequently I feel
nowadays that I'm in a kind of cage, pacing up and down in it
and longing to be free. How awful incompatibility is, and how
dreadfully destructive it can be for the players in this extraordinary
drama. It has all the ingredients of a Greek tragedy . . . I fear I'm
going to need every bit of help every now and then for which I
feel rather ashamed . . .'[15]

Help was, of course, forthcoming. Charles's friends rallied to his
side against 'that tiresome girl' who had tried to banish them. The
Brabournes, the Romseys, the Palmer-Tomkinsons and Nicholas
Soames reappeared in his life. Conveniently, the Parker Bowleses
had moved from Bolehyde Manor to Middlewich House, which
was even nearer to Highgrove. Now, even according to his official
biographer, Charles once again began to talk to Camilla on the
telephone, and they started to see each other at Highgrove. Conveniently also, Andrew Parker Bowles had a new appointment
which kept him in London during the week. It would be true, as
Dimbleby wrote, that Camilla Parker Bowles helped Charles out
of the depression and sense of hopelessness he felt in the face of
what had by now become the tabloids' persecution of him: 'In

Camilla Parker Bowles, the Prince found the warmth, the understanding and the steadiness for which he had always longed and
had never been able to find with any other person . . .'[16] Unfortunately it would also be true that, while indulging in his affair, the
Prince did not treat Diana with any more consideration than he
had before, his nagging guilt turning him even more against her.

Diana, who had long suspected that her husband had 'gone back
to his Lady' if not physically but in his heart, had somehow received
definite knowledge of his rapprochement with Camilla. At the
Marivent Palace on Majorca, where she and Charles were guests
of the King and Queen of Spain, Don Juan Carlos and Doña Sofia,
Diana called in her new protection officer, Detective Ken Wharfe.
She was alone. 'Everyone's gone out, the Prince has gone out
painting. I don't want to go out,' she told Wharfe. 'I just thought
you ought to know one or two things.' 'Golly, such as?' Wharfe
asked. 'And she said, "Well, you know about Camilla, don't you?"
Which I did,' Wharfe commented, 'because my colleagues had
said . . . and I said, "Well, you know, Ma'am, I don't really want
to get involved with this, it's not really my remit." And she said,
"Well, it may not be, Ken, but I'm telling you because I might go
into, really, mood swings and then you'll know why. It's not
because of anybody else, it's because of her and I don't know how
to deal with it." So I said, "What do you mean, deal with it?"
And she said, "Well, I don't know how to deal with it. It's there
and I can't do anything about it. It's not as if it's just re-emerged,
Ken, this has actually been here ever since I've been married and
I accepted that it was a long-term friend and thought that it would
just fade away." I said, "Well, have you spoken to your husband
about it?" and she said, "Oh, he wouldn't listen, he doesn't listen,
it's just a waste of time . . ."'[17] Diana sulked and Charles flew off
early to Balmoral, the only place where he felt at peace and
protected from the press.

Later that year, in a tit-for-tat gesture, she began an affair with
James Hewitt, a cavalry officer whom she had first met that summer. Hewitt, in Wharfe's opinion, was 'a huge protest vote'
directed at Charles. Unfortunately for her, by the time Charles got

to know of it – and one can be sure that the police rumour mill would have made sure that he did – it was a source of relief rather than anger.

Born into a services family in Londonderry, Northern Ireland, in 1958, James Hewitt was educated at Millfield School and Sandhurst and then joined the Life Guards and attained the rank of major. Tall, with thick, reddish blond wavy hair and an athletic figure, Hewitt had good manners, a boyish charm and was attractive and attentive to women. He was also a good polo player and it was when playing for the army against Prince Charles, representing the navy, at the polo ground at Tidworth, Wiltshire, home of the 13/18 Hussars, in 1981 that he had first set eyes on Diana. She was in tears, crying, she later told Hewitt, because of her fear that Charles did not love her as she loved him. He had seen her again at Buckingham Palace on the day of the Yorks' wedding, when he was in charge of security. She was sitting on the stairs, barefoot, animated and natural, chatting to some members of staff, her knees scrunched up under her chin, her fingers playing with her bare toes. Hewitt was struck by her loveliness: he was soon to see her again and be introduced to her at a drinks party given by her lady-in-waiting, Hazel West, and her husband, Buckingham Palace comptroller Lieutenant Colonel George West, at their St James's Palace apartment. Hewitt had become known to the courtiers through his acquaintance with Sir Martin Gilliatt, the Queen Mother's private secretary, who occasionally invited him to drinks in his room at St James's Palace. He was surprised at the invitation as it was a small party and he would not normally have expected to have been invited. Asked whether Diana might have had a hand in it, he replied, 'Hazel more or less let that slip, I think. I got on quite well with Hazel and George but only in passing. They wouldn't normally have asked me to one of their cocktail parties.'[18]

In conversation at the Wests', Diana told him of her fear of horses since a childhood accident and that she would like to conquer her fear and take up riding again. Hewitt, as she must have known, was a staff captain in the Household Division with responsibilities for running the Household Division stables. A few days later she telephoned him and the lessons began from Knightsbridge Barracks, conveniently close to Kensington Palace: Diana was chaperoned by Hazel West, the only one of her ladies-in-waiting who could ride and also with whom she was on friendly, relaxed terms. Later, apparently, Diana told Hewitt that she had only started the riding lessons so that she could see him: there had been an immediate attraction between them from the start. Again, asked about this, Hewitt demurred: 'I can't see that anyone would find me attractive [but] if you analyse it she was very keen and she had a busy schedule and she managed to squeeze in seeing me and she remained frightened of horses and she didn't really enjoy it . . .'[19]

Hewitt was very much Diana's type – she had a weakness for men in uniform – and not being in any way intellectual was definitely unthreatening. According to his biographer, Anna Pasternak, Hewitt 'had learned to respect and cherish women physically' and had become an expert lover, beginning with a woman eight years his senior, a pupil at his mother's riding school. Perhaps Diana sensed this and, suffering from her sexual rejection by her husband, felt that Hewitt, kind and unthreatening, was what she needed. Within a few weeks she had fallen in love with Hewitt (as she was to admit in her 1995 *Panorama* interview – 'Yes, I adored him . . . Yes, I was in love with him') and he with her. It became a risky physical affair, beginning with meetings at Kensington Palace, and going on to snatched weekends at Highgrove and visits to his mother's house in Devon.

Diana was sexually inexperienced. Before her marriage, she told Hewitt, there had been a moment or moments of the 'quick fumble' nature, but, as he put it, she had been 'more of a virgin' than her contemporaries. There could have been no real sexual passion in her encounters with Charles, spoiled as he was by experienced older women like Kanga Tryon and in any case already deeply committed to Camilla Parker Bowles. According to Hewitt, after many conversations on the subject with Diana, he thought that Charles 'held a torch for Camilla and he fancied her and he wanted to sleep with her . . . he obviously didn't want to sleep with Diana and she needed that. You know the chemistry is not there and you fall out of love, you don't fancy the person and you probably feel a bit hemmed in. I think you just sort of reject them.' At one stage she suggested to Hewitt – and to other friends of hers – that Charles said he might be gay. 'That was his excuse to her.'

Hewitt was subsequently ostracized by senior army people for his temerity in having an affair with the wife of the heir to the throne but, in fact, it is difficult to blame him for that. 'She was utterly charming and natural and fresh and vivacious and rather lovely,' he recalled. 'There was a certain chemistry straight away. Unfortunate, but there we are.'[20] At first Diana managed to hide her vulnerability. 'She hid that very well, actually, but I became more and more a shoulder to lean on, and she then learned to open up to me and express her concerns and her fears and her worries and the fact that she was feeling worthless, and that sort of thing,' Hewitt said. 'I mean very early on in the [officers' mess] places where we met she would try and be happy, try and be positive but there was an underlying unhappiness which one had to address . . . and then you talk it through and make it better.'[21]

Eventually the subject of bulimia came up. Hewitt had never heard of it and when Diana confessed she had this problem – 'I'd have liked to have seen the look on my face at the time . . . I think I was pretty revolted by it,' he said. 'But I didn't really discuss it in depth with her and she said, "Actually, when I'm with you I don't have it", so there was no need. I mean, she explained the whole thing and I learned to cope with it. It was a shock and she explained that when she was unhappy she would go to the fridge and gorge herself and then be sick and then do it again . . .' During the periods they spent together, it did not happen – 'I spent twenty-four/forty-eight hours with her actually side by side so I would have known, I believe that. But then in the intervening days it would happen again when she was back in Kensington Palace, so it was horrid. And you could feel it in her body. You could feel the effects of it . . . the flesh wasn't firm, the skin didn't fit the flesh . . .'²² As the bulimia became less frequent her body shape improved, as did her breath, which had held the telltale symptoms.

Subsequently, although the affair became known to inner circles via the Royal Protection Squad officers, no attempt whatsoever was made to stop it. Early in the relationship, Charles and Diana had come to some accommodation, comparing diaries to avoid the risk of one being caught by the other, or, at the very least, to avoid meeting each other. Diana 'told me that they had a diary conference every week so she knew where he was and he knew where she was'.²³ According to Hewitt, it was Diana who initiated the physical affair. 'Strange as it may seem,' he wrote, 'I had no real option.' Diana was emotionally and physically fragile, racked by bulimia and painfully thin. 'She was a woman deeply damaged by rejection,' he said. 'Whether it was true or not, she saw herself as being wholly alone in a hostile world . . .'²⁴ At the Palace, she told Hewitt, the only person who could really help her was the Queen. 'Things were so bad at one stage that she did summon up courage to make an appointment to explain the whole situation. Diana said she met with a very concerned response. The Queen promised she would do what she could to take some pressure off her and later newspaper editors were asked not to subject her to too much scrutiny. But when it came to the issue of her marriage to Charles, the Queen said there was nothing she could do. It would be wrong to intervene.'²⁵ As Diana was to put it later, when she asked the Queen what to do, the Queen replied, 'I don't know what you should do. Charles is hopeless.'²⁶

The misery caused by her failing marriage continued to gnaw at her self-esteem. There were moments of happiness when she was with Hewitt. 'She'd come down and stay [at Hewitt's mother's house in Devon] and she'd arrive with laughter and smiles and love and then on a Sunday evening she would be a bit gloomy but very little other than fun and laughter and enjoyment in the intervening time,' Hewitt recalled of their weekends together.²⁷ Over the period from the summer of 1986 until just before Hewitt left for a tour of duty with the army in Germany, their relationship restored Diana to a measure of health and happiness. 'He was good for her,' a close aide of Diana's at the time said; 'he made her happy.'[28]

10. A Dying Marriage

'What have the newspapers ever done for me?' (Diana resents press persecution, 1987)

'By 1987 it [Kensington Palace] was the backdrop to a dying marriage and its walls had heard many angry words . . .' Diana's new equerry, Patrick Jephson, recalled in his memoirs. He had been recruited to replace Richard Aylard, who from then on was seconded to work for Charles. For the moment Diana's contingent – the 'A-team' – worked in an office at St James's Palace with Charles's in relative amity, having moved that spring from Buckingham Palace. In insider shorthand this was 'BP' (Buckingham Palace), 'SJP' (St James's Palace), and, of course, the base, 'KP' (Kensington Palace). The move was, in effect, a signal that Charles intended to secure his independence from his mother's establishment, a move which was to result in increasingly crossed signals between the two.

Jephson soon realized that the princely marriage was in freefall and that the chief preoccupation of the couple's staff was to conceal this from the public, for the sake both of the monarchy and of the young princes. The most dangerous moments from their point of view were the joint overseas tours – when British and foreign press assembled to probe the state of the royal marriage. Diana had commissioned a portrait by the photographer Terence Donovan which presented a new, more resolute image: with short, glossy hair, bare-necked above an off-the-shoulder evening dress, her expression sad and wary but with a determined set to her mouth. The picture was taken on the eve of the first joint tour of the new year, a visit by Charles and Diana to Portugal in February 1987, to commemorate the Valentine's Day wedding six hundred years before, of an English girl, Philippa of Lancaster, daughter of John of Gaunt, to the King of Portugal, João I. While the press focused on the fact that the couple occupied separate bedroom suites in the beautiful eighteenth-century palace of Queluz just outside Lisbon, the serious purpose of the visit, to concentrate on Anglo-Portuguese trade, seemed to be forgotten. Diana, in playful mood and almost certainly inspired by a desire to upstage and annoy Prince Charles, ostentatiously flirted with the President of Portugal: 'Are you cold?' President Soares asked her, looking at her off-the-shoulder evening dress. 'No, but if I were, would you take off your jacket to keep me warm?' Diana riposted. As they sat down she spotted his white braces beneath his dinner jacket, reached out, put her hand inside his jacket and twanged them. 'You're a socialist,' she said, 'shouldn't you be wearing red braces?' At the ballet on another evening, Diana playfully asked Soares, 'What colour are you wearing tonight?' Soares opened his jacket and Diana tweaked his braces again. The Prince, touring Lisbon in stormy, sunless spring weather, was reported as looking 'somewhat dour'.

Public playfulness was Diana's way of teasing Charles. It was one of the few weapons left to her, something she could get away with without arousing an explosive fit of anger. Various people have testified to her fear of Charles, Jephson among them: 'I learned that, among other feelings he stirred in her, many of them still warm and affectionate, the Princess also felt fear. Except when she was roused with her own formidable brand of indignation, she would go to great lengths to avoid needlessly provoking the Prince. When she felt herself to be on the receiving end of his anger, before her characteristic defiance set in, I often saw a look of trepidation cross her face, as if she were once again a small girl in trouble with the grown-ups . . .'[1]

On a joint skiing trip to Klosters later, Diana was inspired by the presence of Fergie to clown around for the photographers. While the press clicked away, the royal brothers, according to reports, 'looked faintly disapproving' and Prince Charles snapped, 'Come on, come on'. Even the *Daily Mail* thought Diana's behaviour 'undignified'. Without Charles, Diana enjoyed the après-ski life, with a party of young men, most of whom she had met with Fergie, including Philip Dunne and David Waterhouse. At home, Waterhouse became one of Diana's bridge set (a game Charles did not play). She had begun to replace her old school friends with a more sophisticated circle: Julia Samuel, Catherine Soames (at the time still married to Nicholas Soames; they were divorced in 1990) and Kate Menzies. Diana was now compart-mentalizing her life in a way which was to become characteristic of her. Asked whether she kept his existence from her friends, Hewitt replied, 'They must have known a wee bit because we went to the opera together, but that was only once. But she did keep me separate from them . . .'[2] Hewitt was not part of Diana's London group although still very much on the scene: they spent weekends in Devon with his family, escorted by Ken Wharfe, and, on some occasions, at Highgrove 'chaperoned' by Diana's most faithful friend, Carolyn Bartholomew, and her husband William. Diana was by now aware that when her husband was alone at Highgrove, Camilla came over, often acting as hostess. According to Hewitt, this was one aspect of her new life which upset her dreadfully – that Camilla would come and 'be the lady of the house when she was not there'.

Charles's rejection of her both personally and sexually in favour of Camilla made it inevitable that Diana should seek consolation and companionship with other men. She played safe, keeping friendships within her own class. The men were, to quote Ken Wharfe, 'invariably good-looking, public school-educated, and from landed families . . . They played bridge tolerably and enjoyed going with her to the cinema or to dine . . . at the trendiest restaurants, but small talk, the ability to chat endlessly for hours about almost nothing at all, seemed to be their speciality. They also had to know how to please the Princess which meant sharing her liking for risqué jokes and playing adult games like Twister.'[3] Diana's flirtations with men like Philip Dunne, nicknamed Super-man for his resemblance to Clark Kent, and David Waterhouse excited the tabloids to the extent that the notorious paparazzo Jason Fraser stationed himself outside the South Kensington mews house belonging to Kate Menzies, one of Diana's 'safe' houses, where she had been spending the evening with Waterhouse, and succeeded in photographing Diana coming out. (Ken Wharfe grabbed him and forced him to hand over the film.) The fact that Waterhouse was mentioned by Dimbleby as 'a frequent visitor to Kensington Palace, arriving to spend long hours with his dog' indicates that he was the closest of the men friends. With these men and girlfriends like Julia Samuel, Catherine Soames and Kate Menzies, Diana had a group to sustain her in her new, more separate life. And then for sex, romance and the satisfaction of her need for adoration, there was Hewitt. His presence and unselfish support were still important in bolstering her self-confidence.

Meanwhile, Fergie and Diana were no longer the close friends they once had appeared to be. Diana was not amused when the American press pointed to Fergie as her rival not only for the affections of the Royal Family but in the fashion stakes as well. That summer *Vanity Fair* had stated that Fergie had lost 28 pounds and ordered twenty Yves Saint Laurent outfits, outshining Diana, who remained loyal to British designers. At Ascot in June, sections of the press declared, 'Sarah wins by a head in the fashion stakes'. As if to rub it in, the cover of the *Sunday Times Magazine* of 19 July featured Fergie with the caption 'Move over Diana' and inside an article contrasting the two women distinctly to Sarah's advantage, with Diana labelled 'Beauty and Duty' and Fergie 'Freedom and Fun'. That year the papers had been full of Fabulous Fergie, learning to fly, appearing with twenty-three model aeroplanes pinned to her hair, clowning around boisterously at the televised *It's a Royal Knockout* programme. Charles, perspicaciously, had forbidden Diana to take part in this undignified affair. On the visit to Portugal, apparently, Diana had taxed the press with being more interested in Fergie than in her. On tour with Andrew in Canada in July, Fergie had been a roaring success, particularly when pictured in a Davy Crockett hat and paddling a canoe. Recently, too, the newspapers had taken to criticizing Diana for her disco excursions, her pop concerts, her dancing all night with Philip Dunne at the Worcester wedding ball and her choice of companions such as nightclub owner Peter Stringfellow and pop stars like Elton John and Boy George. Diana can hardly be criticized for preferring fun to serious dinners with her husband's friends and mentors.

On a more serious side, Fergie was more popular with the Royal Family than Diana was, particularly with the 'Top Lady' as Diana sometimes called her – the Queen. 'The Queen loved Fergie,' said a courtier, 'who took part in everything – maybe wearing bright pink pants but loving it.'[4] Fergie fitted in perfectly with the family's cherished outdoor life. Unlike Diana she was an expert rider and loved horses. She learned to carriage drive, Prince Philip's favourite sport now he could no longer play polo. At Buckingham Palace, while Andrew was away five nights a week on naval duty, Fergie would be invited to dinner by the Queen. However, where the Palace servants had loved and cherished Diana, Fergie shocked their higher echelons with her very unroyal ways: drinking in the pub behind the Royal Mews, and holding indecorous parties with the Palace footmen where she and her father would pass round extremely risqué presents. She would burst into dinner parties, shouting 'Curtsey, curtsey, curtsey' to the other women, as a triumphant joke. When warned by her godmother that she would have to change her ways to fit in with the court, she shrugged her shoulders and replied, 'Oh, I'll just be myself'. Unfortunately for both Sarah and the family this would turn out to be only too true, but for the moment Sarah's vivacity carried all before her.

'I got terribly jealous and she got jealous of me,' Diana confided. 'She kept saying to me, "You mustn't worry, Duch, everything is going to be fine, let me do this, let me do that." I couldn't understand it, she was actually enjoying being where she was [at Balmoral and Sandringham] whereas I was fighting to survive. I couldn't understand how she could find it so easy. I thought she would be like me and put her head down and be shy. No, a different kettle of fish altogether and she wooed everybody in this family and did it so well. She left me looking like dirt . . . up in Scotland she used to do everything that I never did. So I thought,

"This can't last, the energy of this creature is unbelievable." Meanwhile everybody [was] looking at me – "It's a pity Diana has gone so introverted and quiet, she was so busy and trying to sort herself out . . ."[5]

By now Charles had mentally and physically withdrawn himself from Diana. It had become increasingly difficult for him to bear her presence. Always a loner, he sought solitude as a relief from marital disharmony – a four-day visit to the Kalahari Desert with Laurens van der Post in March was followed by three days living the life of a crofter in the Outer Hebrides, earning himself cruel jibes in the popular press: 'A Loon Again – the potty Prince's strange quest for inner satisfaction'. An outburst of renewed speculation on the state of the royal marriage came in October that year when it dawned on media commentators how many days the couple had spent apart. After their joint visit to Spain/Majorca earlier in the year, Charles had gone to Italy on a painting holiday while Diana had returned to England. It was noted that they had spent their sixth wedding anniversary apart – he in Cornwall, she in Tidworth. After the usual Balmoral holiday, they had been in London together on 16 September to accompany Harry to his first school, after which Charles had returned to Scotland, allegedly to oversee the Balmoral estate. They were not seen together again until 21 October when they made a brief – six-hour – visit to Wales to offer condolence to flood victims in the Carmarthen area. They hardly exchanged a word then Charles flew back to Scotland, leaving Diana to return home alone. For anyone used to the Prince's habits, this preference for the peace and quiet of Birkhall was nothing very surprising. Always set in his ways, he was not about to change them for his son's schooldays or to accommodate his wife. 'The Prince had always spent that period of the year in Scotland and didn't see why he shouldn't go on doing so,' said an aide. 'For example, when Diana insisted that they return to London for the beginning of the school term, Charles's reaction was to ask why they could not join the local school for the time being.'[6]

Earlier that year, in January 1987, William's much-loved nanny of four and a half years, Barbara Barnes, left 'by mutual agreement'.

Observers thought that Diana was jealous of her son's affection for Barbara. The final split seems to have come when Barnes was invited over to Mustique by her former employers, Lord and Lady Glenconner. No objection was raised at the time but when Barbara returned she was given the cold shoulder by Diana – rumour had it that Diana thought her nanny 'shouldn't go to a place like that with people like that', in other words it was 'above her station'. Receiving no answer when she asked, 'What have I done wrong?', Barnes left, finding herself no longer able to stand the atmosphere. William, however, remained loyal, asking her to his eighteenth and twenty-first birthday parties.

The contrast between pictures of Charles painting and relaxing on his own on Deeside, while Diana did the school run in London, was enough to precipitate a wave of hostile headlines with the tabloids showing a savagery they had not displayed before: '33 days apart', 'Charles and Diana are not speaking', 'Patch up your marriage, Di'. Reports that Charles had been seen with Kanga Tryon (which turned out to be the work of a notorious Fleet Street hoaxer, Rocky Ryan) caused frenzy. It was the end of the press honeymoon. The *Sun*, enraged by a reported remark of Diana's, 'What have the newspapers ever done for me?', turned viciously on their former darling: 'The *Sun* can answer Her Loveliness in one word – EVERYTHING! The newspapers have made her one of the most famous women in the world. They have given her an aura of glamour and romance. Without them the entire Windsor family would soon become as dull and commonplace as the rulers of Denmark and Sweden. Were that to happen, people might begin to ask what is the point in having royals at all. Including lovely Princess Di.'

The rumours brought newspapermen to track Charles down in his retreat; they had, in his words, 'unleashed a positive hurricane of self-righteous, pontificating, censorious claptrap in the newspapers . . . and . . . led to car loads of beastly photographers etc., careering about Balmoral and following me up the track to Loch Muick . . .'[7] In the same letter he expressed a fellow feeling for

Diana who, back at Kensington Palace, was pursued by paparazzi on motorbikes.

One well-known psychologist diagnosed the popular press as suffering from a double delusion: first that it saw itself as the creator of the royal couple and found it difficult when its creation began to behave in a way which the press had not planned or envisaged; second that it could destroy them if it wished. 'It seems to be done out of spite,' he commented. Alan Rusbridger, in 'A nasty twist to the fairytale', gave an account of the press pack trying to prime members of the public to ask awkward questions on royal visits, a technique which apparently failed. The Waleses' marriage difficulties even featured on chat shows in Britain and the US. Meanwhile, the general public went on hoping that the apparent rift was not terminal and were not prepared to believe the rumours, while, in the face of the deluge, Buckingham Palace stonewalled, knowing the truth but wishing to conceal it for as long as possible.

As her marriage unravelled, Diana continued her charitable activities, particularly those supporting the young, the elderly and the suffering with whom she had a unique rapport, specifically the children's charity Barnardo's, of which she had become President in 1984, Help the Aged and the AIDS Foundation.

'She was completely brilliant in the way she related to everybody,' a Chair of Barnardo's recalled of the period of the charity's relaunch four years later in 1988. 'She created so much happiness. People forget, you know. The magic of her was tangible . . . I've never experienced it before . . . quite late on when she was quite experienced we had a huge conference in Birmingham – a huge meeting for all the Barnardo's volunteers, you know all the ladies in print dresses who work in the shops and raise money. It was an enormous occasion and she came. People wouldn't come through to lunch because she was coming in the afternoon and they'd got themselves an aisle seat and they literally wanted to touch the hem of her dress. And when she did come I was walking beside her as we went into this room and she was really very experienced by then but as we came in the atmosphere was so extraordinary that even she stopped and said, "Oh, my goodness!" She was reeling. And then afterwards she walked around talking to the people who were there and as I was behind her I saw their reaction. She would chat to them for a bit and then she would move on and as she moved on they were literally weak at the knees. They sort of crumpled and clutched each other. There was that thing about her magic . . . it was a phenomenon, a real phenomenon. And everybody she met just fell under that spell, women as well as men. Men were just floored by her when she said goodbye, got into her car and gave them that look underneath her eyelashes with those wonderful eyes – and most of the top-flight Barnardo's were men and I was there to sort of catch them as their knees buckled.'

Her appeal ranged from rebellious teenagers to Hollywood stars. 'Her relating to children was not just the cuddly ones who were crawling over her as she was getting down to eye level and talking to them and they said things like "Are you a real princess?" Also the hairy ones with the Mohican hairdos and the rest of it, she was brilliant to them too. We had a big AIDS conference and after she had done her thing about AIDS which was phenomenal really, she spent some time walking around the people who were there. And there were some really grumpy, bolshie teenagers sitting around the floor, they never moved when she came by. She just looked down and said, "Are you all right down there?" And it was perfect. It made them feel slightly idiotic but didn't put them down really.'

At a Barnardo's event, the Champion Children lunch for those who had won prizes for being brave or doing exceptional things, Sylvester Stallone had put pressure on Barnardo's to be allowed to come and to sit next to the Princess. 'In the end, he didn't sit next to her; they had a child, a very ill child, sitting between Diana and Stallone, and never for one moment did she make that child feel left out. She flirted brilliantly with Stallone with the child. I remember her saying to him, "Tracy and I have decided we would like to ask you whether you are married at this moment?" It was so clever. Then at one moment Sylvester Stallone got up and started to walk out and she said, "Oh, got a better invitation then?"

'I never realized until after she died that she went on with those relationships with quite a lot of people who were suffering some kind of hardship, and she went on and wrote to them and things like that. I never knew that. Clearly it was a very, very important thing for her emotionally to have that relationship with people as she was giving them happiness . . . I mean it actually made her feel a good person, which she needed to feel, I think. And you knew when she got into her car and was whisked away that her fun for the day was over really. You felt that . . . Going back to Kensington Palace where there was nobody to talk to her, ask her if she had had a nice time . . .'[8]

Most of the charities noticed the change from shy young woman to confident individual overcoming her inhibitions about public speaking and taking on some surprisingly radical causes. They saw a connection with the public that bypassed the Establishment and, to some extent, the media. Diana, alone of the Royal Family, seemed to understand that this rapport with the public was something to which a modern monarchy should aspire. It was no longer enough just to turn up and smile; people needed to feel that she really cared about them.

Despite her personal problems Diana had now become established in the public mind as 'caring Di'. Her most high-profile moment had come in 1987 at the opening of the first UK AIDS ward. Professor Mike Adler, the doctor in charge of the ward, had written to Buckingham Palace asking if a member of the Royal Family would open the ward, apparently expressing a preference for Prince Charles. This was at a time when AIDS was regarded as 'the Gay Plague' exclusively connected to homosexuality in men: the Palace, clearly nervous about unfortunate connotations, preferred to send Diana rather than the heir to the throne. 'On the day she was very nervous and we were very nervous. We had been crawled over for weeks by the media and the Palace. But the moment she started meeting the patients she did relax and then there was that very famous photo of her shaking hands with a patient who had AIDS and that was wired all over the world. It made a tremendous impact.'[9] Baroness Jay, a founder director of

the National AIDS Trust, recalled, 'There was the huge fuss about
her not wearing gloves, and the fact that she didn't and that the
world's media took it up was the moment we realized the power
she had to influence public perceptions and she wasn't even at the
height of her power then . . .'[10]

'The following day the pictures were all over every paper,'
said the photographer Arthur Edwards. 'Diana with these AIDS
patients. She chatted to them, joked with them . . . made them
feel good. This was her magic. People were amazed to realize this
wasn't a disease you ran away from; it was perfectly safe. And she
was going against all the old guard at Buckingham Palace. I believe
she single-handedly took the stigma out of AIDS.'[11] 'There was a
lot of negative sniping in the background from the traditional
courtier class,' said Dickie Arbiter, former Palace press spokesman
then press secretary to the Prince and Princess of Wales, 'who just
thought this was not what royals do.'[12] Princess Anne, the Princess
Royal, made a speech a year later (26 January 1988) describing
AIDS as 'an own goal by the human race' which implicitly raised
questions of guilt. Establishment disapproval only spurred Diana
on, an additional factor in the empathy she felt towards the
sufferers. She was drawn to the vulnerable, the weak and the
unrecognized. It touched a personal chord with her, linking with
the rejection and marginalization which she felt she was suffering.
And as a result of the impact she had made with the AIDS
photograph, people started to be interested in what she was doing,
rather than what she was wearing.

Perhaps Diana's biggest public contribution in the AIDS field
was her visit to the Harlem Hospital Center in New York in
February 1989. In the view of the head of the paediatric unit at
the hospital dealing with children with AIDS, Diana's involvement
in the issue transformed the perception of AIDS in the United
States. 'She had this very magical way with the kids and they were
immediately attracted to her. Then she did what I realized only in
retrospect was so important: she had her picture taken with a child
with AIDS. And of course that picture went around the world
. . . the really extraordinary thing that happened is that people

began calling, saying: "I didn't realise about these kids with AIDS until Princess Diana visited Harlem Hospital . . ." Suddenly we had a whole group of willing foster parents who wanted kids with AIDS . . . and at the end of two years for all of New York City, there was a surplus of foster parents wanting kids with AIDS . . . I know in my heart that Princess Diana is the one who made this possible.'[13] She was accused by her enemies of using these sick children as a photo opportunity. Photographer Tim Graham defended her: 'She definitely understood the power of images, but it wasn't just for the camera. The photographers would be in the room for two minutes to do the picture, and then we would all leave, but I know she would stay and talk to the other patients and pick up the other kids.'[14] Her friend Marguerite Littman said: 'She was somebody that people admired – and that's an understatement – who embraced and helped people who had AIDS. She made it OK, just as simple as that . . . she didn't need the publicity, not like a movie star doing it. There was no reason for her taking up something that the royal family wouldn't embrace . . . they certainly didn't encourage her. So it seems to me that she did it out of compassion . . .'[15] What is more, Diana made sure that she kept in touch with some of the children later. One particular child, Shamir, was known throughout the AIDS centre for his foul language, most of it sex-related. 'Shamir comes out of his room and runs up to Princess Diana and jumps up into her arms and begins to whisper into her ear . . . We will never know what he said, but she began to chuckle and sat him down and chatted with him. He went into a foster home in Brooklyn and she wrote to him a couple of times until he died.'[16]

People were beginning to see her as more than just a clothes horse but Diana herself was certainly aware of the power of the image. As she realized the power she could wield in aid of the causes she believed in, she was becoming aware of the aura she projected which gave her that power. She had begun to fight back against her rejection by Charles, besotted as he was by an older and far less physically attractive woman. 'She first started to become glamorous when her marriage began to go wrong,' said Victor

Edelstein.[17] She jogged, exercised, swam fierce lengths in the Palace
pool, and played tennis at the smart Vanderbilt Club in Shepherd's
Bush. In July she played doubles against a pair which included
Steffi Graf. Tim Graham published a volume of photographs he
had taken of Diana over the past eight years, comparing her shyness
in 1980 to the confident smiling Princess of 1988. 'Princess Diana
can make the act of strapping a child into a car seat seem glamorous,' he wrote. 'Whatever she does, she has total charm. That did
not happen eight years ago when I first photographed her. Then
she modestly looked at her feet all the time. Now the moment she
steps out of a car the eyes come up and the smile is already starting.'
She was photographed, wildly popular at Wembley, presenting the
FA Cup to the winners. Dressed in khaki cover alls and pink
trainers, she attended a day's training with the 13/18 Royal Hussars
on Salisbury Plain. She fired a 76mm gun and drove a tracked
armoured reconnaissance vehicle before eating a field lunch of
steak and kidney pie.

Meanwhile, Charles pursued his own causes with passion: he
turned green with a vengeance, surrounding himself with environmental advisers including Jonathon Porritt and his new aide,
Richard Aylard, formerly Diana's equerry, who had studied
zoology at university before becoming a naval officer. Unfortunately for the Prince he was ahead of his time on green issues and
received little sympathy, not least from government ministers in
the business of retaining jobs in the mining industries, or global
companies to whom environmental concerns clashed with the
demands for profit. Mrs Thatcher was enraged by his interest in
housing and the inner cities and particularly by his Disraelian
depiction of Britain as divided between the haves and have-nots.
Undeterred by the unwillingness of ministers to listen to him,
Charles launched his own crusades. In a powerful speech at Mansion House in December 1987 he accused property developers and
their consultants of being more destructive of Britain's cities than
the Luftwaffe, with particular reference to plans for the redevelop-
ment of Paternoster Square round St Paul's Cathedral. He compared the sensitive post-war reconstruction of European cities with

the 'Rape of Britain' which had occurred in Bristol, Birmingham, Newcastle and other cities. Addressing an audience largely composed of architects and planners, he said: 'In the space of a mere 15 years, in the 60's and 70's, and in spite of elaborate rules supposedly designed to protect that great view [St Paul's], your predecessors as architects and developers of the City of London wrecked the London skyline and desecrated the dome of St Paul's . . . Can you imagine the French building those same towers round Notre Dame? The Italians walling in St Mark's in Venice?'

The *Sunday Times* rightly praised Prince Charles for his serious-ness and the effort he made to carve out a role for himself in his country's life from which he was virtually excluded as long as his mother remained on the throne, in other words, for as long as she lived. Unfortunately for him, he did not enjoy the ceremonial role his position demanded and the public expected. While carrying out engagements with grace and charm, he inwardly seethed, confiding to his diary and to his friends a picture of a being eternally put-upon, self-pitying and resentful. His innate pessimism undermined enjoyment of everything, even the birth of his chil-dren. After visiting Prince Harry in hospital he recalled: 'I looked down on him and I thought, "Poor little thing, what have I brought this poor child into the world for?"'[18]

There was a disconnection between Charles's concern for the environment and the private pleasures he enjoyed – as shown, for instance, in his passion for his gas-guzzling Aston Martin. 'One day a new, rich, racing-green Bentley was delivered to Highgrove; en route it had been given a silver coach line down the side. Charles walked out of the door to inspect it: "Mmm . . . that was meant to be my racing colours . . . Take it away." £10,000 later the car returns as the Prince wanted it. One day, after a day's hunting with the Belvoir, the Prince and his policeman were returning home; driving down the lane after heavy rain they found a large pool of water and on the far side cars which had been following the hunt and two men on a tractor. Halfway across, water came pouring in and they realized that the other cars hadn't driven through the water – they had been stuck in the water and been towed out by the tractor.' The tractor men approached in delighted anticipation. ' "Hello, look who we've got here . . ." The Bentley was towed out in a sodden state, all its electrics blown, and sent back to the manufacturers with instructions to provide another one the next day because the Prince had an engagement. There were only two similar models available – one in Scotland and one in Germany. The one in Scotland was duly driven down to the Bentley plant where it was refitted to the Prince's specifications. People worked all hours and drove through the night to get it to Highgrove on time. At eight o'clock the next morning, it was there ready and waiting. The Prince walked out of the door and took one look at it: "It's black. I hate black." Turns round and walks back inside. "Oh well, we'll take the Vauxhall . . ." [19]

Charles's failure to realize or to accept that his private behaviour impinged on his public duty was becoming more serious by the day. If Diana could be accused of failing to understand the concept of duty – which was in fact no longer true of her since, despite her personal unhappiness, her duties as Princess of Wales still came first – how much more was it true of Prince Charles who simply failed to make the connection between his desire for Camilla and his increasing aversion to his wife, the mother of the future King, and his public duty as heir to the throne. He was becoming ever more like his great-uncle David, whose example Mountbatten had held up as a warning to him never to follow. Charles may have looked more like his father and his 'honorary grandfather' but in character – even in some of his physical mannerisms – he was more like his great-uncle, even in his habit of fiddling with his cufflinks and adjusting his tie, famously characteristic of Edward VIII. He was like him, too, in his self-pity and apparent resentment of the 'stunts' which being Prince of Wales demanded; like him in regarding his father as an ogre; like him, above all, in putting his desire for 'the woman I love' beyond considerations of the future of the monarchy and people's expectations of it.

Yet it is hard not to feel some sympathy for the Prince, cast from that year on as the villain in the royal soap opera. Penny Junor, author of a biography of Charles published in June 1987, for which she had been granted an interview with the Prince, claimed on BBC Radio 4 that Charles 'had lost confidence' and despaired at being 'outshone by his wife', that he was 'a sad character' with 'the loneliest position on earth' who 'did not have the support he should have from a wife', concluding that 'he married the wrong person'. Under the caption headline 'She's a winner of a wife, so why do they keep on trying to wound her?', columnist Lynda Lee-Potter riposted that Charles was lucky to get her, and so was the nation. Critics derided Diana's lack of intellect, Lee-Potter observed, but she certainly had the qualities her role required: an abundance of charm, intuition, a sense of duty, humour and common sense. To those who criticized Diana's glamour she claimed that 'to watch her crouch down next to anybody old, sick or young is not to see somebody with no more thought than the latest hemline . . .' Diana, in her charity role, was interpreting royalty as the people wanted it, connecting the Royal Family to the people in a personal way which hitherto had been the Queen Mother's secret of success. While Diana's charity activities such as Barnardo's and Help the Aged received the widest publicity, Charles's causes – the environment, public housing, modern architecture among others – were not the type to engage the interest of the tabloid press who labelled him 'loony' or 'the potty prince'. Unfortunately for Diana, on every public occasion they shared she did indeed outshine him. When the couple visited Enniskillen in Northern Ireland in the wake of the IRA bombing outrage in November, it was Diana who drew the photographers, not Charles.

In 1987 the monarchy took a sharp downturn in popularity, for which observers blamed the erosion of previous respect resulting from the antics of the younger royals: specifically the rumbustious *It's a Royal Knockout*, in which Andrew, Fergie, Edward and even Anne took part. Edward did not help the image of the monarchy by storming out of a post-show press conference, offended by the reporters' lack of enthusiasm. Fergie's and Diana's pranks with their umbrellas at Royal Ascot had also made a poor impression. Cracks began to show in the smoothly functioning edifice which the Queen had maintained with such devotion since her Coronation in 1953 as the media became increasingly confident of their licence to probe, knowing that, however outrageous their allegations, the reaction at the Palace would be 'No comment'. And it was, above all, the state of the royal marriage which was to shake that edifice to its foundations, as Palace officials were only too aware. They knew that the rumours were true but had no alternative but to maintain their silence.

The *Sunday Times* editorialized:

The Royal Family has become so used to being treated like a soap opera by large sections of the media that some of its members are beginning to act as if they are in one. This past week alone saw Prince Edward play the touchy, misunderstood youth, ready to rage against cynical journalists who did not share his passions. Prince Charles had a walk-on part as the bad-tempered husband who scolds his wife for sitting on the bonnet of his precious sports car . . . the carefree Princess Diana was meanwhile wandering round Royal Ascot playfully jabbing anybody in sight with her brolly; and the Duchess of York was at her jolly-hockey-sticks best (or worst) cheering on her team against other royal sports in a television charity fundraiser [*It's a Royal Knockout*].

While praising Prince Charles for his seriousness, the newspaper warned:

. . . there is something deeply unhealthy about the public's currently grotesque public appetite for all things royal, the lengths to which sections of the media will go to feed it and the extent to which the younger royals will go to accommodate it. If the Royal Family increasingly feels obliged to go down this road, then it is choosing a path which will eventually undermine our monarchy to its foundations. The present intense public fascination with the Royal Family cannot be sustained without doing it great harm . . .

Praising the Queen for providing the ideal role model, the *Sunday Times* pointed out that, as a result, the monarchy had enjoyed unprecedented popularity in post-war Britain and that 'unlike the 19th century there is no republican movement to worry about . . .'[20] But a poll later that year was to show a 10 per cent drop in the public popularity of the monarchy during 1987.

Given the particular qualities of both Charles and Diana and what they had to offer the people, it was a tragedy that they were increasingly driven apart. The strains in the relationship were clearly taking a physical toll on Diana: attending a Memorial Service alone for the victims of the King's Cross Underground Station fire, on 5 December 1987, she appeared rake-thin in her black coat. Four days later with Prince Charles at an awards ceremony held at the Victoria & Albert Museum, the director Roy Strong recorded her appearance in his diary: 'She is very, very thin and was in a little navy-blue suit, very tall, with all freshness sunk beneath an abundance of unnecessary make-up and hair lacquered to bounce.'[21]

Within the shell of their marriage Charles and Diana had almost no shared interests beyond their children. Music could have been one of them: despite the popular conception of 'Disco Di' bopping along to pop music on her Walkman, Diana loved classical music – particularly Verdi's Requiem which she would listen to over and over again. Although not as gifted as her grandmother Ruth, she had learned piano at school and was a fluent player even without music. She adored ballet and had once cherished an ambition to be a dancer; she loved opera – Verdi and Rossini – but not Wagner, which Charles loved. 'If she was criticized for not going to the opera with the Prince of Wales then she could be forgiven because it was invariably rather heavy stuff. All this business about the Pop Princess is not strictly true . . . I mean, yes, she loved pop music but she loved classical music too. She was perceived as a pop princess, she was perceived as a fashion icon but she would wear British designer dresses because it was good for British fashion, she had to be dressed as one would expect a royal princess and a beautiful one at that to be dressed.'[22]

When it came to the children, this was an area in which Charles, with his responsibilities, could not compete with Diana. William had entered Wetherby School that year, and at his first school sports day both parents had competed in their respective parents' races. Diana, toned by jogging and swimming, won the mothers' race and the publicity photographs, while Charles, despite his morning exercises and zeal for physical fitness, trailed unsuccessfully in the fathers' event and, perhaps fortunately, was not pictured in the press. Diana was not remotely interested in his great causes, nor in his private passion for his Highgrove garden. On his side Charles, increasingly resentful of her popularity, never now praised her for her efforts on public engagements and was more likely to direct snide remarks such as 'Not that dress again', which undermined her confidence.

Diana's disillusionment with the sham in which she was forced to take part nearly caused her to refuse to participate in the next joint tour – to Berlin on 1 November for the city's 750th anniversary celebrations – designed by the Palace to put on a good show and stifle the rumours. 'The world's most glamorous couple' act was at its superlative best. 'The Prince and Princess of Wales arrived in West Berlin . . . smiling and apparently at ease,' *The Times* reported. However, the popular German tabloid *Bild am Sonntag* warned, 'everybody will be watching how their marriage stands . . .' Charles and Diana were on their best behaviour; he referred to her as 'one of the most glamorous colonels in the British Army' (she was Colonel-in-Chief of the Royal Hampshire Regiment) and whispered to his wife during the speech of welcome, causing her to giggle. 'Happiness in Berlin' the *Daily Mail* cheered, noting that at one point, after they had got into their limousine to leave an event, Prince Charles slid an arm round Diana's waist. 'Triumph of the Tender Tour' headed one report from Hanover: 'Germany bade farewell to the Prince and Princess of Wales yesterday, after a week during which the Royal couple showed their tenderness and affection for one another . . . Unostentatiously, but with obvious sincerity, the Prince showed devotion to his wife; he presented her with a piece of chocolate as soon as he was out of sight of the press, murmuring: "For you."' Only Diana was aware that, far from being a demonstration of affection, it was yet another cruel put-down, a reference to her bulimia which only she would have understood.

Charles's jealousy of Diana's success with the public, and the lack of recognition he extended to her, was one of the principal causes of the failure of the marriage, fuelling a resentment in Diana which was to manifest itself in the most spectacular and destructive way possible within a few years.

11. Diana Fights Back

'He [Charles] makes my life real torture . . . but the distancing will be because . . . I go out and do my bit in the way I know and leave him behind' (Diana to James Gilbey[1])

In January 1988 Charles and Diana flew to Australia to take part in Australia's bicentennial celebrations in Sydney: on the surface it was happy and successful but, as before, Charles felt upstaged by Diana. In Sydney on the first day Diana surprised everyone by singing the words of Australia's national anthem 'Advance, Australia Fair'; Charles did not know the words. Almost two million onlookers 'were captivated by Diana', chanting 'We love Di!': as she and Prince Charles walked through a Guard of Honour at the Sydney Opera House, one man yelled, 'Three cheers for Diana!' and a thunderous roar erupted. Yet at a ball in Melbourne the following day, the couple jived energetically to Glenn Miller's 'In the Mood'. 'THEY'RE IN THE MOOD FOR LOVE . . . AND JIVING TOO' ran one headline. 'Seldom has so much happiness radiated from the couple so recently at the centre of hurtful marriage rumours,' the report went. Seeing the photographs back in London, a jealous James Hewitt was surprised that Diana could act so happily and affectionately with Charles, about whom at times she had expressed herself in vitriolic terms. But in Melbourne Diana once again eclipsed Charles, putting on a polished performance of Rachmaninov at the piano without sheet music, following Charles's reluctant attempt to play the cello, and effortlessly stealing his photo opportunity.

In March of that year they were in Charles's favourite skiing resort, Klosters, with Fergie, Patty Palmer-Tomkinson, her husband Charles, and a friend, former equerry to the Queen, Major

Hugh Lindsay. Lindsay was a favourite of all the members of the Royal Family, not least because he had the courage and frankness to tell the younger ones off if he felt it necessary. 'Why are you all so bloody rude to the servants?' he was heard to explode one day at Balmoral.[2] Perhaps because of this outspokenness, he was, Diana claimed, closer to her and to Fergie than he was to Charles. On the afternoon of 10 March, at the chalet they were sharing, Diana was in bed with a severe cold when Fergie returned, pale and shaken. She was four months pregnant and had had a skiing accident, ending up upside down in a ditch. That afternoon an avalanche swept down on Charles and his party as they were skiing off piste with their guide, Bruno Sprecher. Charles, Charles Palmer-Tomkinson and Sprecher escaped but Patty Palmer-Tomkinson was buried by the snow and Hugh Lindsay was killed. He had been married eight months earlier and his wife Sarah was six months pregnant. Diana proudly told Andrew Morton that she had taken charge: packing Lindsay's belongings, retrieving his body from hospital and consoling Sarah at Highgrove on their return. What she did not tell Morton, however, is that when she first heard of the accident, she was convinced it was Charles who had been killed, having been told by one of her therapists that he would 'die of suffocation in a foreign country'. 'She went to see all sorts of weird and wonderful people who tell fortunes,' Hewitt said, 'and one of them said an accident would befall Charles and that very nearly came true when Hugh Lindsay died in that skiing accident. She rang me from there and said, "It nearly happened" . . .'[3]

The accident was a body blow to Charles who felt it deeply. He was not helped by the British tabloid press which chose to blame him: 'ACCUSED. Official: Charles did cause the killer avalanche' the *Sun* headline blared a week later. The official report, however, blamed no one: as no one member of the party had a specific leadership role, it said, 'it was the task of each single member to assess the dangers and carry the responsibility for himself'.

That summer, Diana, her marriage in disarray, could no longer turn to her mother for comfort. Frances Shand Kydd had made several attempts to help the couple the previous year at Highgrove, without success, but now her own marriage was over. Peter Shand Kydd left her for another woman and in June they were divorced. She was devastated by a second failure and humiliated at being abandoned by the husband for whom she had given up so much. Asked why the marriage failed, a relation said laconically, 'They were both drinking a lot.' For four years Frances sank into depression, unable to help Diana any more than she was able to help herself. They had had an up-and-down, volatile relationship and frequently quarrelled over the telephone. Now, besieged by the press on the Isle of Seil, longing for her husband to return to her, she refused Diana's invitations to come to Kensington Palace.

Diana's bulimia had grown worse as the strains in her marriage intensified. Under pressure from Carolyn Bartholomew, she had begun treatment for it with Dr Maurice Lipsedge, who had treated her sister Sarah. The affair with Hewitt had helped restore her confidence but at every turn something connected with Charles would upset her, causing a fresh outbreak.

Diana's twenty-seventh birthday had been greeted with united praise from the press for her 'star quality', as 'the feminine ideal' and 'the best thing to happen to the royals'. She had realized, as she told Morton, that her antics at Ascot the previous year, her appearing in tight leather trousers and dancing till the small hours with men who were not her husband was not how the public wanted their princess to appear, and that such behaviour only gave ammunition to her enemies in her husband's camp. This frivolous image had been replaced in the public mind by her charitable activities and her virtues as a mother. The existence of James Hewitt was, amazingly, still a tightly kept secret. Yet, whatever she may have said to James Hewitt in private – and by his account it was vituperative – she was still anxious to win Charles's approbation. As Hewitt said, 'She still tried to make him love her and she cared.' For their seventh wedding anniversary that July she had made a video of herself dancing to a song from her favourite musical, *Phantom of the Opera*, 'All I Ask of You'. It was both a tease and a plea. The tragedy was that she was still in love with Charles, and secretly longed to win him back.

The Queen celebrated Charles's fortieth birthday on 14 November 1988 with a ball at Buckingham Palace. 'Although by then they were living virtually separate lives in private, Charles encouraged Diana to invite some friends of her own so that she would be more at ease,' Hewitt wrote. 'I had never met Diana on a formal occasion like this before and for the first time I experienced the incredible aura that just radiated from her, overpowering and almost eclipsing the presence of Charles and his parents. She had told me that one of her "crimes" was that she got more attention than he did, most notably when they were on a visit to Australia . . .'[4] As always in conspicuously royal surroundings, worshipped as a public figure but inwardly devastated by the presence of her husband's lover and his accommodating friends, and faced by the utter sham of her marriage, Diana was emotionally paralysed. Clive James had been introduced to her the previous year at Cannes, when she had shone: 'She came up like the sun,' he said, 'came up giggling.' Now, at Buckingham Palace, he noticed the difference in her: 'the lights in her face were dimmed down to about three-quarter strength . . . She was still there physically, but her soul had gone AWOL . . .'[5]

Only just over a week earlier, with Charles on an official visit to Paris, the couple had staged their most recent triumphant joint tour. Diana had arrived in a red and black Chanel outfit by Lagerfeld which she had chosen herself from a video sent to her at Kensington Palace. But on this occasion Charles had been allowed to shine, delivering speeches on the political future of Europe in fluent French, which, Diana admitted, she understood but couldn't speak. His Savile Row tailoring was much admired. *France-Soir* stated, 'They have conquered Paris – he with his charm and politics, she with her smile and Chanel suit.' Diana had specially requested in advance a visit to the Institut Pasteur to meet Professor Luc Montagnier, one of the pioneers who had isolated the AIDS virus in 1983. 'She was generally well informed on the topic,' he said, adding, 'It is very important that those in the public eye are seen to be involving themselves in supporting the campaign against AIDS and efforts on behalf of AIDS patients.' Diana, he said, would be seeing 'some very sick people' at the Institut. At a banquet given by the Minister of Culture, Jack Lang, at the Château de Chambord, Charles sat next to Princess Caroline of Monaco, once touted as his bride (they had been famously bored with each other and the press photograph of them sitting next to each other at Chambord suggested that things had not changed). After the cabaret and fan dance by the French star Zizi Jeanmaire, Diana chose to put on another of her dance exhibitions, shimmying provocatively in front of her husband. What he thought of this display was not recorded; it was yet another example of Diana's misjudging a situation where Charles was concerned. At the Arc de Triomphe ceremony to remember the dead of two world wars, Charles, wearing the uniform of the colonel of the Welsh Guards, with ribbons, sash and sword, eclipsed a demure Diana in veiled hat and long black coat. 'Prince Charles set the seal on his triumphant debut as the royal Statesman of Europe . . . yesterday,' an English newspaper reported. 'It was the final honour for a Prince, whose trip had been accorded virtual State Visit priority, and who enhanced his growing reputation as a statesman with speeches on architecture and European unity. In many ways Charles outshone his wife . . .'

The visit had to some extent been overshadowed by the serialization in the *Sunday Times* of Anthony Holden's biography of the Prince, its publication timed to coincide with Charles's fortieth birthday. Phrases such as 'Their marriage has reached a stage of mutual and cold indifference' and '[Diana] has a husband who no longer understands her – nor even, it seems, much likes her'[6] had stunned the nation, triggering ferocious denunciations from people who still did not wish to believe the fairty tale had really ended, and from others who feared the effect such a failure would have on the standing of the monarchy. In Paris, observers noted that, at one event at the Musée d'Orsay, Diana, visibly irritated, repeatedly jabbed at Charles with her knee, and at the Arc de Triomphe parade spoke to him continually without receiving an answer. Nevertheless, the magazine added, on numerous occasions the couple exchanged complicit glances and Charles never failed to translate for Diana when people addressed her. Although Holden was absolutely correct, only a relatively small circle knew the truth.

Dr Lipsedge's treatment of Diana for her bulimia had helped her enormously. Within six months, he predicted, she would be a different person if only she could manage to keep her food down. He also attributed her bulimia to her problems with her husband. Charles, instead of understanding her illness, was revolted by it. At times, according to Morton, he would watch her eat and then say sarcastically, 'Is that going to reappear later? What a waste.' Lipsedge's treatment calmed her; from vomiting regularly four times a day, it was reduced to once every three weeks, usually triggered by visits to Balmoral and Sandringham, or to Highgrove which she now regarded as hostile territory. Regaining her courage, she decided to confront Camilla, whom she regarded, perhaps even more than she did Charles, as the cause of her misery. The occasion was to be the fortieth birthday party for Camilla's sister, Annabel Elliot, hosted by their mutual friend Lady Annabel Goldsmith at her beautiful house on Ham Common, Richmond. It represented a gathering of the Highgrove Set – all the people whom Diana despised and dreaded – and originally the plan had been to invite only Charles and not Diana. When Lady Annabel heard of this she vetoed it; if they were going to use her house, she insisted, Diana must be invited. Incredibly, none of Camilla's and Annabel's friends appears to have expected Diana to go – including Charles. A party which included Camilla was his territory and, undoubtedly in his view, Diana should have had the sense to realize it. In the car on the way down he needled her, repeatedly asking her why she wanted to go.

After dinner Diana noticed that Charles was absent – as was Camilla. Determined to confront them, she called on her detective, Ken Wharfe, who was sitting in the kitchen, for support. She found them in the children's play area in the basement, deep in conversation. Despite Diana's pleas, Wharfe, determined not to be a party to any scene between the three, made his excuses and left. We only have Diana's account of what happened next. According to her there was another man present and she sat down and joined in the conversation, whereupon he said, 'I think we should go upstairs now.' As they stood up Diana said, 'Camilla, I'd love to have a word with you if it's possible . . .' After the men had left, Camilla and Diana sat down again, Diana saying to Camilla: 'I would just like you to know that I know exactly what is going on between you and Charles; I wasn't born yesterday.' Someone came down to see what was going on and Diana, before leaving, said: 'I'm sorry I'm in the way, I obviously am in the way and it must be hell for both of you but I do know what is going on. Don't treat me like an idiot.' In another version Diana told Camilla to 'leave my husband alone'. According to Ken Wharfe, who was accompanying the couple back to Kensington Palace, the return journey was 'chilly and tense' with Diana repeating to her silent husband, over and over again, 'How could you have done this to me? It was so humiliating. How could you?'[7] Apology or explanation came there none. Crying alone that night at Kensington Palace, Diana considered her marriage was over. That would not deter her from trying to win her husband back. Over frequent lunches in the following year with two friends Diana, 'half-joking, half-serious', would plan how to bring him back to her and, above all, into her bed: 'she wanted to have another baby, she was desperate to have another baby . . . she continued to love him.'[8]

Whatever she felt in private, Diana remained meticulous in her public duties. She was fanatically punctual. 'She was very good at her homework,' Patrick Jephson recalled, 'and usually swotted up the main points of the programme before she left the Palace . . . Once on duty she hardly ever coasted. She took a professional pride in giving her public full value, which was one reason why they were ready to wait for her in vast numbers in any weather for even a fleeting glimpse of her.'[9] As the helicopter's rotor blades wound slowly to a stop, she would undo her seat belt, stooping by the door, waiting for it to be slid open, poised like an athlete before the starting gun. Sometimes, between engagements, she would ease her tension by comfort-eating sweets, devouring a whole fruit and nut chocolate bar at a sitting. Otherwise she would escape the solemn atmosphere of official functions by making coarse jokes to her entourage and shrieking with laughter. 'The theme of sex was a standard feature of her joke repertoire,' Jephson reported. 'She seemed immune to the embarrassment it might cause others. Careful never to exceed the bounds of good taste while in the public eye, her reticence was thrown to the winds as soon as she felt she was in relatively safe surroundings ... The desire to shock outweighed any possible pleasure she might have gained from the humour of what she said.' Occasionally she would refer to her in-laws with nicknames. Charles was 'The Boy Wonder' or 'The Great White Hope', Prince Philip 'Stavros' and her in-laws generally 'The Germans'.[10]

Jephson, before he accompanied the Princess on his first 'away day' with her, had been expecting 'an essentially shallow person . . . a sort of royal super-Sloane'. Instead what he found was a polished and confident performance from a professional celebrity: 'Every gesture, every glance and every word – at least in public – had been consciously planned. Sometimes the planning had taken only a split second, but that simply showed how quickly she thought and how sharp were her public-pleasing instincts ... Behind the good looks and expensive grooming there was much more than the bimbo caricature to which her critics ... would have liked to limit her. That first day I saw, from her effect on the people she met, that she had a powerful, even hypnotic, charisma.' Her 'quicksilver one-liners', he said, played a key part in the impression she left. Her spontaneity cut through the self-conscious small talk of British social nervousness. She reacted instinctively against pomposity. With an audience of drug addicts, mental patients or battered wives, she would listen to a 'turgid briefing' from an earnest therapist before leaning forward with a smile and perfect timing to whisper loudly, 'Does he always go on like this?' She had made contact and everybody laughed. It was a technique which gave her public that feeling of intimate knowledge which is the secret ingredient of devotion. Yet even her wittiest remark contained a nugget of sympathy, understanding or concern. 'She may have been short of O levels, but she never dropped a public clanger, never mocked disability or disfiguration.'[11]

From first-hand experience gained by accompanying Diana on hundreds of her engagements, Jephson concluded that 'much of the Princess's compassion was very definitely the genuine article':

As I watched her at a dying child's bedside, holding the girl's newly cold hand and comforting the stricken parents, she seemed to share their grief. Not self-consciously like a stranger, not distantly like a counsellor . . . Instead it just seemed that a tranquillity gathered round her. Into this stillness the weeping mother and heartbroken father poured out their sorrow and there, somehow, it was safe. The young woman with the smart suit and soulful eyes had no answers for them, but they were left feeling that somewhere inside she knew at least part of what they were feeling.[12]

Diana, Jephson said, did indeed share some of what they were feeling; yet it had none of the clear grief and suffering of bereavement but came from something dark and complex within her, the product of years of stunted emotional growth. 'The compassion she showed others was not drawn from some deep supply within her. Rather it was a reflection of the attention she herself craved. Once we had returned her to the lonely privacy of her palace, I sensed she had little left over for herself . . . As for the cumulative, corrosive effect of all this on her own sense of self-worth, I was to discover that it could be severe,' he added. 'Even at the outset I could see that receiving credit for virtues she did not possess could not satisfy the hunger for recognition that burned within the Princess of Wales.'[13]

Diana's lack of self-esteem born of a feeling of rejection since the day her mother left was at the root of her complex personality. The golden girl, shining, witty, affectionate, had a dark, self-destructive side which caused the self-mutilation, the bulimia, the mood swings, the difficulty in sustaining relationships. Diana found it hard to believe people loved her for herself and therefore easily came to distrust their motives, turning against them and cutting them out of her life. There may have been a hint of manic depression to the mood swings and she was taking Prozac for her bulimia. 'She had terrible mood swings, for instance when she had the binge of eat eat eat and then she would throw up and after that she was on a high. Laughing and a bit too much for her normal self,' said a close friend.[14] The friend, accustomed to seeing the symptoms in another member of her family, suggested they consult a doctor who she knew would be discreet. After talking to Diana, however, his verdict was that she seemed all right. The only cure for her suffering would have been the love and approbation of the Prince of Wales which she so passionately desired, something which would always be denied her. His was the final rejection: the way in which he consistently denigrated her reduced her to despair: 'My husband made me feel so inadequate in every possible way that each time I came up for air he pushed me down again . . .'[15] 'She was not a mad woman, she was a wounded woman,' a friend of hers said.[16] Another friend, Rosa Monckton, called her 'a wounded animal': increasingly her dark, wounded side would drive her to acts of self-destruction, paranoia and apparent cruelty. Deep within her, her always fragile psyche splintered under the pressure, divided between her instinct for the good and her reactive, cruel side.

'Diana had such a conflict of personalities within one character,' Rosa Monckton wrote. 'She was complicated on the one hand and simple and naïve on the other. These two coexisted, sometimes awkwardly, and made her life more difficult than it should have been. Her dark side was that of a wounded, trapped animal, and her bright side was that of a luminous being . . . But as a wounded animal she could be terrifying . . . it was born of some basic desire to hurt those whom she felt had betrayed her . . .'[17]

Yet she was very far from the whining, self-pitying individual she has been portrayed as being in tapes and books which she, in her worst victim mode, inspired. (In this she compared favourably with her husband who in reality had so little about which to complain.) 'The truth is,' Jephson said, 'that what amazed me every day was how gutsy she was, how positive she was. And the proof of that always for me was no matter how dark things were – and we had some dreadful days – if you were able to give her a humorous lead she was far happier and far more ready to see the lighter side in the darkest situation. The pity was that Diana, out of a sense of low self-esteem and an irresistible wish to be a victim, instead of being what she actually was – rather stoical – when there was an option for victimhood, she would select it. And she would select friends and advisers who fed that wish . . . This rather tragic picture that was presented was not the whole person at all. The tragedy was that the whole person wasn't given the chance to flower.'[18]

Faced with the reality of her unfaithful and unloving husband, Diana tried to solve her problems, mental, psychological and physical, by consulting a series of astrologers, therapists, masseurs, psychics and tarot card readers, some of them at the suggestion of Mara Berni, a close friend and owner of the San Lorenzo restaurant in Knightsbridge, introduced to her by Fergie. While many of the people round her scoffed and disapproved, Diana was embarking on a spiritual journey which calmed her and gave her strength to face her daily life. She believed in astrology in so far as she sought the answers from them that she wanted to hear. The first astrologer was Penny Thornton, referred to her by Fergie, whom she initially consulted in 1986. In February 1989, possibly after the Goldsmith party episode, she went to another, Debbie Frank. She was pathetically credulous as she thrashed about for a solution to her problems.

From December 1988 she also consulted Stephen Twigg, a 'mind–body' therapist who specialized in deep massage, diet consultation and new age advice. At his suggestion she tried vitamin supplements, detoxifying processes and the Hay Diet. She used aromatherapy, hypnotherapy and acupuncture in her search for physical relaxation and inner calm. Diana was, as her biographer Sally Bedell Smith, wrote, 'vulnerable and gullible . . . she leaned on her therapists as she did [on] her friends and lovers',[19] calling them at all hours of the day or night. Oonagh Shanley-Toffolo, who first visited her in September 1989, encouraged her to a more spiritual outlook with meditation and prayer. Oonagh Toffolo's first impression was of a shy and retiring person. who emanated sadness and vulnerability.

Meanwhile, changes were taking place in Diana's principal private relationship – with James Hewitt. Poor Hewitt, who had given of his best in support of a needy Diana, sometimes. as Anna Pasternak recounted, to the bounds of his physical capabilities, was, as far as Diana was concerned, expendable. She lavished presents on him – one of her foibles was to dress the men she liked, and therefore Hewitt, whom, she later said, she had 'dressed from head to toe'. Her loyalty to him, however, was finite, as he was soon to find out. In May he and Diana – but not Prince Charles – attended a ball at Althorp in honour of Raine's sixtieth birthday (which actually fell in September). Diana led him to the pool pavilion that night and they made love there. Hewitt, however, committed the cardinal sin in her eyes of leaving her to follow his career. He was posted to Germany with his regiment that autumn and, despite all Diana's tearful protests and accusations of desertion, determined to go.

On 16 September 1989 her beloved brother Charles married Victoria Lockwood. Diana attended the wedding at St Mary's, Great Brington, and the subsequent reception at Althorp. Relations between the Spencer children and their stepmother had gone from bad to worse since their father had recovered from his illness, grateful for his life to Raine and now entirely in her hands. The sales of silver, furniture, archives and manuscript music, drawings and paintings which then took place – to avoid publicity – to dealers at below market-value prices, had attracted increasing criticism. In April 1987 *Harpers & Queen* launched a devastating attack on the Spencer sales, with a detailed listing of the objects which had disappeared. Many items were sold via a London dealer against his charges for the 'restoration' of Althorp's interior, 'restoration' which incurred the withering scorn of arbiters of taste. Bright gilding abounded; the beautiful wooden floor of the great Long Gallery was close carpeted, the set of chairs from the Spencer House Great Room was broken up, six going to the dealer in payment for his restoration work which involved the remaining white and gold eighteenth-century chairs with green brocade seats being transformed with glittering gilt and upholstering in mango-coloured stamped velvet. Two solid gold ice pails made for the 1st Duke of Marlborough were sold, again via a dealer, for £1 million. The money, it was argued by Lord and Lady Spencer, was to be spent on the restoration of Althorp, and indeed some of it was: in many of the rooms double-glazing was installed to keep out the Northamptonshire draughts, while close carpeting made the bedrooms more comfortable if less authentic. The handsome stable block, restored by Johnnie's father Jack and intended to house a family museum, now housed The Shop, a 'place of unmatched tawdriness' according to the critics. Some people surmised that the sales were subconscious revenge by Johnnie on his fierce, unloving father, Jack Spencer, who had expended all passion and love on the preservation of Althorp and its treasures. Raine simply had a strong, unsentimental business drive: the house was to be profitable and made over in her own image (a garish portrait of herself hung in pride of place at the head of the main staircase). Three villas were bought at Bognor – 'Tradewinds', 'Hacienda' and 'Water's Edge House' – and a five-storey house in Mayfair.

Diana expressed the children's fury when she attacked Raine at Charles's wedding: 'I took it upon myself to air everyone's grievances in my family. I stuck up for Mummy and my mother said that was the first time in 22 years anyone had ever stuck up for her. I said everything I possibly could . . . I was so angry. I said: I hate you so much, if only you knew how much we all hated you for what you've done, you've ruined the house, you spend Daddy's money and what for?'[20] According to one account she also physically attacked Raine, giving her a sharp shove in the back so that she fell down some stairs on to a landing.

That summer, at Julia Samuel's thirtieth birthday party, she had met a man whom she had known in her first days in London, when they had had a long talk about their unsatisfactory love lives – he with a failed romance, she with her failing marriage. James Gilbey, charming and popular, who worked as a dealer in expensive cars, was the son of a family who had founded their fortunes on Gilbey's gin. He was the nephew of England's most distinguished Catholic cleric, Monsignor Alfred Gilbey, a highly sophisticated and social man whose home was the Travellers' Club on Pall Mall. They began to meet in London, at Mara Berni's or at Gilbey's flat nearby in Lennox Gardens, Knightsbridge. Once they spent a secret weekend at a rented farmhouse near Blakenham in Norfolk.

From the famous 'Squidgygate' tapes recorded on New Year's Eve 1989 and released two years later, it seems that the relationship had become serious in the autumn of 1989 after the departure of Hewitt for Germany. Gilbey was clearly besotted with Diana who, although six years younger than he was, was clearly calling the tune. The passion seemed to have been all on his side – 'Squidgy . . . love you, love you, love you . . .' he moaned at one point, and there were strong erotic undertones to their conversation. The two of them were planning a brief, secret rendezvous in London the next night, Diana on the excuse of needing acupuncture and back treatment. The tapes were, above all, revealing of Diana's state of mind at the time and of her relationships then both with her husband and the royal in-laws.

Christmas at Sandringham that year seems to have been unusually frigid. Diana's unhappiness over the family Christmas was manifest. In answer to Gilbey's query, 'And so, darling, what other lows today?' she replied, 'So that was it, I was very bad at lunch. And I nearly started blubbing. I just felt really sad and empty, and I thought, Bloody hell, after all I've done for this fucking family . . .' The Queen Mother puzzled her: 'His grand-mother is always looking at me with a strange look in her eyes. It's not hatred. It's sort of interest and pity mixed in one. I am not quite sure. I don't understand it. Every time I look up she's looking at me and then looks away and smiles . . . It's affection, affection – it's definitely affection . . . It's not hostile anyway . . .' In this Diana's instinct, in which she placed so much faith, had led her astray. Charles's beloved grandmother had no affection for Diana, whom she had been heard to declare a 'liar'. Not only did Queen Elizabeth have the high standards of behaviour befitting the granddaughter of a clergyman, which she was, but her loyalty to Prince Charles was absolute. She was capable of 'ostriching', closing her eyes to his behaviour in terms of his adultery with Camilla; indeed, she continued to invite the Parker Bowleses to stay when Charles was there just as if nothing had happened. Her eldest grandson's happiness had always been one of her priorities since he was a lonely little boy. He was suffering because of his marriage to Diana, therefore it was Diana's fault. The state of the marriage was taboo in Queen Elizabeth's presence; privately she would have attributed the difficulties to Diana's 'unreasonable behaviour'. The Queen Mother was cool and clever in a way which Diana could never hope to emulate. Diana very much wanted to believe Queen Elizabeth, the matriarch of the Royal Family and revered by everyone, felt 'affection' towards her. It was indicative of her comprehensive failure to understand how the Royal Family worked which caused her so much pain.

Increasingly Diana saw herself as a 'victim' and a rebel. Talking about her relationship with Charles she said: 'It's just so difficult, so complicated. He makes my life real, real torture, I've decided. But the distancing will be because I go out and – I hate the word – conquer the world. I don't mean that. I mean I'll go out and do my bit in the way I know how and I leave him behind. That's what I see happening.' By now, on the eve of 1990, after just under ten years of marriage to the Prince of Wales, Diana already saw her role; how she could 'leave him behind'. She reported a conversation she had with the Bishop of Norwich which illustrated both her resentment of and rebelliousness towards what she saw as 'the Establishment'. The unfortunate bishop tried a line which he thought would be an easy introduction but which Diana saw as patronizing. This is the conversation as recorded on the Squidgygate tapes, with Diana as the main character, the conqueror, the Bishop as the vanquished and James Gilbey the supporting chorus:

DIANA . . . He said: 'I want you to tell me how you talk to people who are ill and dying. How do you cope?'

JG He wanted to learn. He was so hopeless at it himself.

DIANA . . . I said: 'I'm just myself.'

JG They can't get to grips that, underneath there is such a beautiful person in you . . . They can't think that it isn't cluttered up by this idea of untold riches.

DIANA I know. He kept wittering on about how one must never think how good one is at one's job. There's always something you can learn round the next corner. I said: 'Well, if people know me, they know I'm not like that.'

JG Yes. Absolutely right. So did you give him a hard time?

DIANA I did, actually, in the end. I said: 'I know this sounds crazy, but I've lived before.' He said: 'How do you know?' I said: 'Because I'm a wise old thing.'

JG Oh, darling Squidge, did you? Very brave thing to say, actually . . .

DIANA It was, wasn't it?

JG Very. Full marks. Ninety-nine out of 100.

DIANA I said 'Also I'm aware that people I have loved and have died and are in the spirit world look after me.' He looked horrified. I thought, ' f he's the bishop HE should say that sort of thing' . . .

DIANA . . . with that bishop. I said: 'I understand people's suffering, people's pain, more than you will ever know', and he said: 'That's obvious by what you're doing for the AIDS.' I said: 'It's not only people with AIDS, it's anyone who suffers. I can smell them a mile away.'

After this exchange, the flummoxed bishop turned the conversation to children's toys. Triumphant Diana, she told Gilbey, thought, 'Ah! Defeated you.'

Diana was not being unfair when she described Charles as making her life 'absolute torture'. His jealousy and resentment of her had led him to treat her with what amounted to emotional cruelty. Aware as he was of her vulnerability, he could not refrain from constant pinpricks to her already low self-esteem, putting her down in public in the most humiliating way. Patrick Jephson witnessed an incident on the royal couple's tour of the Gulf States earlier that year, in March 1989. The royal host was offering his visitors coffee:

The royal host and his senior guest [the Prince of Wales] were sticking manfully to their scripts . . . Plainly uncomfortable, the Princess was not joining in either, nor was she invited to by the Prince or her host.

She seemed to have created an invisible barrier round herself, as if to say that she was apart from the polite charade going on around her. To me she looked excluded and vulnerable. To the host as well, presumably, because eventually he leaned across the Prince to ask her politely what she was going to do during her visit. Under the unexpected attention she visibly brightened, perhaps thinking – as I was – of the serious programme we had arranged: visits to a day centre for mentally handicapped children, a clinic for immigrant women and a girls' business studies class.

The Prince also turned towards her, looking as if he were seeing her for the first time, ruefully indulgent, patronising. There was an expectant hush. Before she could reply, he said with studied innocence, 'Shopping, isn't it, darling?'

The words dropped into the marble stillness like bricks into plate glass. The Princess coloured, mumbled something inaudible and lapsed into silence. There was an awkward pause, broken by the Prince pointedly resuming his conversation with a host whose aquiline features now registered a politer version of the disbelief I felt.

When we were outside again I cornered John Riddell [former private secretary to the Prince and Princess of Wales]. 'Did I see what I thought I saw in there?' I asked him.

He looked at me pityingly. 'Oh yes, Patrick. Indeed you did. That is the world we have to live in.'[21]

It was a world in which Diana would find it increasingly hard to live.

12. The War of the Waleses

'Diana was obsessed with Charles. And I think that all the wrong steps she took in life were because of him . . . either to hurt him or show off to him'
(a close friend of Diana[1])

In June 1990 Prince Charles broke his right arm falling from a horse during a polo match at Cirencester. The accident marked a distinct stage in the downward spiral of his marriage. To Diana's anguish and humiliation he made it quite clear that her attention was unwanted, and that the only person he required in charge of his convalescence was Camilla. While Diana visited him publicly during the two hospital stays needed for operations on his arm, in private Camilla was by his side at Highgrove where he now spent most of his time.

By now, editors were aware of Camilla's role in Charles's life. Max Hastings, then editor of the *Daily Telegraph*, recalled being told by 'a friend of the Prince's': 'You have got to get your mind round the fact that there is only one woman in the Prince's life, and that is Camilla.' 'This,' he told Diana's biographer, Sally Bedell Smith, 'was in 1990, when everyone knew there was trouble, but there was still no idea of a divorce.'[2] The closeness of the relationship, however, only became public knowledge with the publication just over three years later of the infamous Camillagate tapes, originally recorded in December 1989 shortly before Diana's New Year's Eve conversations with James Gilbey.

These revealed a couple totally in love, emotionally and sexually, consumed with longing for each other. Charles's puerile dirty talk about being reincarnated as a Tampax inside Camilla's trousers and her eager responses – '. . . Just what I need at the moment . . . I can't bear a Sunday night without you . . .' – demonstrated their

physical need for each other. Camilla's role in Charles's life as
principal comforter and soul mate was clearly revealed: 'You're a
clever old thing. An awfully good brain lurking there, isn't there,'
she told him. 'Your great achievement is to love me,' Charles said.
'Oh darling, easier than falling off a chair,' Camilla replied. 'You
suffer all those indignities and tortures and calumnies,' he
responded. 'I'd suffer anything for you. That's love. It's the strength
of love,' she told him. Fortunately for Diana's peace of mind, the
contents of the tape were not revealed until January 1993 when
the full extent of the conspiracy of Charles's friends to provide
rendezvous for the lovers came to light. A web of deception
surrounded the affair, from people whom she had thought of as
mutual friends, who provided safe houses where Charles and
Camilla could spend the night, to loyal Highgrove staff who had
no alternative but to cover up for the Prince both to ingratiate
themselves with their principal employer and to spare her pain.
Long before the eventual separation, the Waleses' staff had divided
into two camps. Most of them did not enjoy being used in the
deception of Diana, even to the extent of the butler being asked
to wrap a sapphire and diamond brooch as a present to Camilla
from Charles, while the Prince's gift to Diana was a paltry souvenir
straw hat decorated with fruit, acquired during a trip to Cornwall.

Unlike many unfaithful husbands who are kinder to their wives
as a result of their adultery, Charles by now seemed almost to hate
his wife. And despite her declarations of love for Charles, Diana's
screaming scenes only succeeded in alienating him further. While
their disharmony was concealed from outsiders, the unhappy relationship created tensions within the family. At Balmoral
later that summer, with problems in both the Wales and the York
marriages, the atmosphere was noticeably difficult. The Queen,
unusually, expressed her frustration at Prince Charles, his arm in a
sling, who had chosen to take the van Cutsems' choice of doctor
rather than hers. It was a celebration of Princess Margaret's sixtieth
birthday but the atmosphere was far from cordial – there were
endless evening picnics at which Prince Charles appeared 'in a
very cross mood'. Colin Glenconner 'did some silly things with

napkins to amuse Fergie and Di, when they all did a number and everybody laughed except Prince Charles'. Asked if he found it amusing he said icily, clearly referring to his wife and sister-in-law, 'Little things please little minds.'[3]

At Balmoral, Fergie and Diana appeared as allies once again but, as Diana's secretary Patrick Jephson pointed out, 'running through it all was her mistrust of Fergie'.[4] In her Squidgygate conversation with James Gilbey on New Year's Eve 1989, Diana had referred cautiously to Fergie: 'The redhead is being actually quite supportive . . .' Gilbey had warned her that Sarah was not to be trusted, that she had her own agenda and was trying to hang on to Diana's coat-tails. Her former popularity with the public had disappeared, after the Australia visit when she had been severely criticized for leaving the baby Beatrice behind for six weeks. She was slated for her weight, her dress, her penchant for free holidays, and she was becoming increasingly unpopular at court. 'I just worry that she's desperately trying to get back in. She's trying to tag on . . . She knows that your PR is so good, she's trying to tag on to that.' Charles, Diana told Gilbey, had been trying to help Fergie, calling on a Royal Family favourite, the broadcaster Sir Jimmy Savile, to advise her on improving her image. Diana, more cautious and instinctive than Sarah, watched 'the redhead's' head-long rush towards destruction with more than a little Schaden-freude. Always sensitive of her public image, she was well aware that Fergie's infatuation with an American, which she made little effort to conceal, and her open defiance of the Queen's senior courtiers, including her cousin and particular *bête noire*, Sir Robert Fellowes, was not the way to proceed. Fergie, as has often been said, was indeed the 'yellow canary' used by miners to test for dangerous gases underground.

There is little evidence that Sarah listened to Savile's advice any more than she did to anyone else's. By August 1990 her marriage was in trouble. Sarah was evidently bored with her husband whose frequent absences on naval duty left her at a loose end. Sarah told a friend that in 1988 Andrew had spent only forty-two nights at home out of a year. Once the Yorks' controversial home,

Sunninghill Park, dubbed Southyork for its *Dallas*-like ostentation, was finished in the summer of 1990, she was not prepared to live as a naval wife in married quarters or even in a rented house near Andrew's base, and when he was at home she found his preferred way of relaxation boring. Andrew liked to watch videos and play golf and, when the couple entertained, Sarah found his behaviour embarrassingly boorish. At dinner parties he was served first and gobbled down his food regardless of the other guests, and he had a fondness for telling loud and unfunny naval jokes. To the Queen's household it appeared that he had no control over his wife's behaviour, while to Sarah it seemed that he was not prepared to stand up for her when she was lectured by his mother's courtiers. Andrew, sadly, still loved his wife but, as Sarah's father had told his mistress, she had been in love with the Royal Family rather than her husband. Now both 'love affairs' were cooling from Sarah's point of view.

The man with whom Sarah had fallen in love was the handsome Texan Steve Wyatt, whom she had met in Houston at the home of his mother, the glamorous Saks heiress, Lynn Sakowitz Wyatt. Wyatt's stepfather, Oscar, one of the richest and toughest men in Texas, could offer Sarah all the luxury that a huge ranch and a fleet of private planes could provide. Sarah had flown to New York in the Wyatts' plane and stayed at their expense at the Plaza Athénée. Her affair with Wyatt continued when he was transferred to London; she was photographed with him and her daughters at the Wyatts' villa on Cap Ferrat (formerly the home of Somerset Maugham) and again, according to Sarah, at a weekend house party in Gloucestershire. Later that summer the extent to which Sarah had become involved with Wyatt was blatantly revealed. Declining an invitation to dinner with Lord McAlpine and his wife, she instead, at Wyatt's instigation, gave a dinner in her second-floor Buckingham Palace apartment to Ramzi Sultan, an Iraqi oil dealer, whose country was about to invade Kuwait and who was therefore very much *persona non grata* to the British government. Blithely unaware of the faux pas she had committed, Sarah took both Ramzi and Wyatt, uninvited, to join the

McAlpines later that night, making no secret of her attraction to Wyatt. With a complete lack of propriety, she obtained an invitation for Wyatt to the Christmas ball held that year by the Queen to celebrate the ninetieth, sixtieth and thirtieth birthdays respectively of the Queen Mother, Princess Margaret and Prince Andrew. Just over a year later Wyatt, warned off by his socially astute mother, returned to the United States, leaving behind on the top of a wardrobe in his former flat holiday snaps of himself with Fergie and her children to be found by a window cleaner and passed to the newspapers. (Sarah herself claimed that the flat had been searched and found to be 'clean', implying that the photographs had been placed there at the instigation of the *Daily Mail*.) By then Fergie had linked up with another Texan, John Bryan, in a liaison which was to prove her downfall.

Yet Diana, lacking in self-confidence and always aware that her affair with James Hewitt, even though temporarily in abeyance, could destroy her reputation, still kept up her competition with Fergie for public esteem. 'No matter what misfortunes publicly befell her sister-in-law,' Jephson wrote, 'the Princess would still torture herself with the thought that she might yet become a real rival rather than just a useful counterpart to her own good fortune.'[5] Sometimes she appeared to be in direct competition with her sister-in-law, as when she reacted to a newspaper report of 'caring Fergie'; she would complain to Jephson, 'Patrick! We seem to be reading rather a lot about the red-haired lady . . .'[6], whereupon a charitable counterstrike would be arranged. But if some of these charity duties were thus cynically motivated, Diana's actual performances were undertaken in a genuine spirit. Often her charitable forays took place when she was bored, cooped up in Balmoral, longing for an outlet and not totally unaware of the good publicity to be earned by being seen to visit a hospice while her in-laws were known to be slaughtering game. The less the Royal Family seemed to appreciate her, the more Diana felt the need to be wanted by the public, to receive from their response the unconditional love and understanding which she so badly needed. Yet Diana's responses, according to Jephson, who accompanied her on numberless public occasions and charitable duties, were not feigned. 'The impression I had formed on that first outing . . . − that she genuinely cared − was not untrue. It was the instinctive reaction of any sensitive adult, heightened by a strong maternal instinct and a personal acquaintance with pain . . . Not even the best actress could sustain such a convincing show of compassion for so long; nor would those on the receiving end be so easily fooled.'[7]

The Queen's courtiers, although wary of the future, still, unlike the principals themselves, hoped that somehow the Waleses' marriage would survive in some form. Sir William Heseltine, the Queen's private secretary, who retired that year, was relieved by Diana's assurance: 'Don't worry, I'll stick it out.'[8] Two tours that year, to the Far East and to Hungary, sent the spurious message to the world that all was well. Jephson described them as 'the last grand gestures of togetherness' which produced some misleadingly optimistic comments about how well they seemed to be getting on. Photo opportunities featured the couple gazing romantically across the River Danube, and enjoying themselves on the upper deck of a river boat, looking for all the world as if they were on holiday together. You had to be very close to the action, said Jephson, who accompanied them, to perceive the guerrilla warfare being waged below the surface. Point scoring against Charles was a game which Diana played with consummate skill: she was photographed holding hands with the Hungarian President's wife during the arrival ceremony (it was the story with all the papers at home, she later told Morton) and posing with romantic Magyar horsemen. Patrick Jephson, who was to leave her five years later in a mood of some disillusionment, described the delicate balance between sincerity and ulterior motive in her actions. There was no doubt, he wrote, that her underlying intention was 'to attract attention, to signal an independence from her marriage, and to exert by guile and gamesmanship the strength she felt unable to express openly. Foreign tours, no less than home engagements, were vehicles for a subliminal message: I am not a dumb clothes-horse, a junior player in a marriage that frustrates me: I am a figure in my own right, and none too scrupulous.'⁹

In private, Diana was playing a dangerous game. Hewitt returned from Germany before Christmas before being ordered to the Gulf War in January and they resumed their passionate affair. Prince Charles was aware of it, as he was also of the relationship with James Gilbey, probably through Superintendent Colin Trimming, head of the Waleses' protection squad, who reported everything back to his boss. Sometime around the end of the year Diana – possibly from Gilbey, who had been confronted with the tape by the *Sun* – learned that that newspaper had a copy of the recording. The owner, Rupert Murdoch, and Andrew Knight, chairman of News International, proprietors of the *Sun* and the *News of the World*, decided that the material was too controversial to publish and the tape was put into a safe where it would remain for two and a half years. The *News of the World* also had a story alleging Diana's affair with James Hewitt from Hewitt's batman, Lance Corporal Malcolm Leete, which they proposed to publish. Knight also sat on this story; the fact that he didn't believe it showed how skilful – or lucky – Diana had been in covering up the affair.

Diana was still in love with Hewitt after he flew out to serve with his regiment in the Gulf, where war had been going on since the previous August. She was obsessed with war news and wrote Hewitt a series of passionate letters, often as frequently as four times a day, expressing her longing and loneliness, putting her every thought down on paper. She said that she was 'finally trying to understand herself'. She told him that she could not stand the deception in her marriage any longer and that she had given Charles an ultimatum that 'something had to be done' about it. Moreover – an indication of the direction her thoughts were tending towards – she wrote that she felt frantic that 'the truth about Charles and Camilla . . . had not become public knowledge'.¹⁰ Some people, like Max Hastings, did know, but out of loyalty to the monarch and perhaps for fear of finding themselves in court (like Penny Junor, who was sued by Andrew and Camilla

Parker Bowles for misidentifying Camilla) kept their knowledge
to themselves. Diana determined to find a way to get the story
into the public domain, just as she was determined that Hewitt
should remain in the shadows.

But on that front, things were becoming difficult. The *Daily
Mail* now not only had a copy of the Squidgygate tapes, but their
chief royal reporter, Richard Kay, had made friends with the naïve
Hewitt in the Gulf, even to the extent of lending him his satellite
telephone to make calls – which he did, to his mother and to
Diana, their numbers registering on the telephone.[11] The previous
year Diana had made friends with the paper's editor, David English,
who was later to become her chief media mentor. Yet it was Nigel
Dempster who in February 1991 first publicly named Hewitt as a
friend of Diana's. 'Nigel Dempster outed him,' said a fellow
reporter. 'And I believe that Andrew Parker Bowles was the source,
and it was designed, I think, to take the heat off the Parker Bowleses
at that time.' Then, in the following month, Hewitt was exposed
in the *News of the World* by his estranged girlfriend, Emma Stewardson, who revealed that Diana had been sending letters and
expensive presents to the Gulf (where Richard Kay had noted the
quality of the hampers of food which Hewitt enjoyed). No one,
however, went so far as actually to claim they were lovers. For
Diana, however, the hints were enough; as so often in her relationships, she became suspicious that he was using her, that he was
becoming 'too serious', that he was more in love with her position
than he was with her. This was unfair: James Hewitt was genuinely
in love with her and the relationship was almost as dangerous for
him and his career as it was for her. She had given him hope for
the future in her letters, talking of her belief that in July 'her life
would change'. 'Her determination to be free was so strong,'
Hewitt later recalled, 'that I had formed a real hope that some time
in the future we could be together.'[12] In fact the *News of the World*
revelations had sealed his fate. After a couple of meetings on his
return from the Gulf, Diana told him on the telephone that it
would be better if they 'cooled it'. The cut-off came in the usual
manner: when he telephoned the Palace, his call was not put

through. He was sent to Germany: when he returned to England, despite his being conveniently stationed at Knightsbridge Barracks, less than a mile from Kensington Palace, his dream was over. According to Ken Wharfe, with whom Diana discussed her relations with Hewitt, she had explained to him that she had to resolve the many problems in her life and could not do so while conducting an adulterous affair. Typically, when Hewitt accepted his dismissal with good grace, she was slightly irritated, having expected at the very least protestations of undying love.

With Hewitt out of the way, Diana concentrated on her war with Charles. Yet another joint trip, this time to Brazil that spring when, once again, the couple put up a good show in public, inspired optimism in the press. The *Sunday Mirror* described them as presenting 'a united front to the world . . . their closeness sent a shiver of excitement around the massed ranks of media men and women'. Yet only the previous December, Diana had told James Hewitt that there were times when she could not bear to be in the same room as Charles. And on the trip to Brazil, despite attempts to put on a show, Charles's jealousy of Diana manifested itself in dismissive comments, not just in private but in front of the British Ambassador to Brazil and the recently appointed Brazilian Ambassador in London, Paulo Tarso Flecha de Lima and his wife Lucia, soon to become one of Diana's greatest and most trusted friends. Onlookers observed that there was great tension: 'They were on speaking terms, but it was very tense. It was not a normal conversation between husband and wife. He would talk to her, she would answer. But he was already very dismissive of her. On the plane she was reading some papers, remarking to the Ambassadress, "This is my homework about Brazil." Charles chipped in, "Oh, she doesn't know a thing about Brazil." [13] Public put-downs by the heir to the throne in front of high-ranking officials fuelled Diana's desire to escape from the sham her marriage had become.

According to Hewitt, Diana had planned an 'escape' in July, as her thirtieth birthday and the tenth anniversary of her marriage came up, determined that this period would be a watershed in her

life. What kind of watershed it was to be he did not specify, but it
seems probable that Diana envisaged a dramatic breakaway (with
the inevitable exposure of Camilla), not divorce, but a separate
court and acknowledgement of her position as mother of the future
King. Again according to Hewitt, the timing she had worked out
had been thwarted by the fact that the Yorks' marriage was also
on the rocks. Sarah had been on the telephone to Diana wondering
what to do. Lesley Player, Ronald Ferguson's mistress (whom at
one time he had shared with Steve Wyatt), said that Sarah and
Diana had a pact to leave their husbands at the same time. If such
a pact existed, Diana was too canny to go ahead with it. Hewitt
implied that pressure had been put on her by Buckingham Palace:
'There was no way the Palace was going to let both royal couples
announce they were splitting up at the same time,' he wrote.
'Diana had been informed in no uncertain terms that the effect on
the Royal Family would be disastrous.'[14]

Nevertheless, Diana forged ahead with her pledge made to
Gilbey in the Squidgygate tapes when she had boasted: 'I'm going
to go out and conquer the world, I'm going to leave him [Charles]
behind . . .' 'Diana was obsessed with Charles,' a close friend said.
'And I think all the wrong steps she took in life were because of
him . . . either to hurt him or to show off to him.' 'She was a very,
very special person. She had a wonderful side to her – bright,
courageous and unique. But she also had a very dark side to her
personality, a very destructive side.'[15] This friend saw Diana's
collaboration in Andrew Morton's *Diana: Her True Story* as 'the
first move in her self-destruction'. Diana herself explained her
decision as being a psychological necessity: 'It's because my life
being as complicated as it is the only way for me to survive is to
let people know what I have been going through.'[16] Her confidante
thought there might be an element of vengeance on Charles and
Camilla in her motivation. Morton himself was puzzled by her
willingness to open her heart to a virtual stranger. 'If it was a way
of getting at her husband, it's a remarkably reckless and foolhardy
exercise,' he said. 'If it's a way of changing her life then the simplest
way would be to speak to the Queen and Prince Charles.'[17] There

was, he said, no deliberate decision to do a book with him; it just happened gradually. Diana knew Morton as a prominent member of the royal media pack. He was tall, good-looking, genial and university educated. They had met and chatted together on occasion, and he was also in contact with Dr James Colthurst, an old friend of Diana's who was to act as go-between for Morton and Diana. Morton, through Colthurst, had done Diana some favours, including advising her on the safest way to dispense with her hairdresser, Richard Dalton, without his going to the newspapers to sell his story. Morton advised her to write him an honest letter, buy him a good present and send him on his way. The strategy worked. Morton also kept her happy by writing sympathetic pieces about her in the papers.

'I think she wanted people to know what life was really like for her. I used the phrase "the prisoner in the Palace" and all that kind of thing. She felt constrained by the environment in which she worked. She felt there was no out, she felt disempowered both as a woman and as a human being. She felt trapped, not just in her marriage but by the system. And she felt, essentially, that when somebody comes along and is able to do something for her and make her look good – I mean I was writing pretty pro pieces and there was the Dalton episode, little things like that meant a lot because when you don't have any control over your life, then to have control through another agent – i.e. myself – was tremendously liberating.'[18]

Colthurst arrived at Kensington Palace armed with a tape recorder and a list of prompt questions one morning in May 1991. Neither he nor Morton was prepared for the deluge of words, which Diana delivered – thirty thousand in that one session. 'The first tape was just like – I can't emphasise it strongly enough – just like the desperate confessional, wanting to get everything out, it was ten years of her betrayal and unhappiness, depression and ridicule . . . And it just came flowing out in a huge torrent . . .' 'Did she really think it through? The answer is No. Because I and Mike [Michael O'Mara, Morton's publisher] and James had to do a lot of thinking it through for her. So, for example, the idea of bringing friends in, keeping her in the background, wasn't her idea, it was our idea.'[19] Added to that was a strain of aristocratic recklessness inherited from her Spencer forebears and, perhaps even more, from her mother, Frances, 'the bolter', which impelled her to go ahead regardless of the consequences. Morton also thought there might be an element of getting her retaliation in first, of putting Charles's adultery with Camilla in the public domain before her affair with James Hewitt was exposed. Diana wanted to expose the sham of her marriage and her role in the Royal Family, to expose the behaviour of Charles and Camilla and her own helplessness in the face of their betrayal.

Another reason for the involvement of Diana's friends was the dawning realization that Diana's version of events was not always strictly the truth. In *Diana: Her True Story*, Diana was recounting the reality of her life as she saw it in 1991–2 (towards the end of her life, Diana would frequently say that what she thought in 1991 was not how she saw things in 1996), a reality dominated by Charles and Camilla, her illness, the predictions of her astrologers and the constriction of the royal circle. Perhaps the most poignant testimony of all was that of Carolyn Bartholomew, who had known Diana since her school days and watched anxiously from the sidelines the deterioration in her health and happiness. 'She's not happy now, but once she was . . .' Carolyn told Morton. Diana's friends felt duty bound to help her by exposing the living lie she was enduring.

But if Diana felt threatened and constricted by 'the system', royal officials, even before the bombshell of the Morton book burst in June 1992, were wary of Diana as an unknown quantity. Buckingham Palace tended to regard the chaotic office of the Prince of Wales at St James's Palace as something of a joke. 'One of the reasons Buckingham Palace runs on smooth lines by and large is that people decades ago learned what the Queen wanted and how to do it and a way to get on with it,' one of Diana's aides said. 'I think from Buckingham Palace, St James's seemed a bit of a madhouse, and the maddest component was this strange, very tall, very blonde, very articulate, very charming, very powerful, very regal person' – Diana.[20] Until 1990 the charming Sir John Riddell had been private secretary and treasurer to the Prince and Princess of Wales. Aristocratic, with the required background of Eton, the Rifle Brigade and the City, Riddell's presence had ensured that relations with Buckingham Palace, where Diana's brother-in-law, Robert Fellowes, had now become principal private secretary, with the Marlborough-educated, Foreign Office-trained Robin Janvrin as his deputy, ran on an even keel. Even he, however, would treat the Princess's representatives, Anne Beckwith Smith and Patrick Jephson, as very much the junior branch of the operation, summing up a meeting with kindly condescension: 'And meantime Her Royal Highness will continue to do very little, but do it very well . . .' 'The Prince had had an organization before Diana came along and it was never really expected that she would make much of an impression on it, and when, rather irritatingly, she became more and more of a figure in her own right, the machinery didn't really exist to accommodate her in anything other than a purely decorative role. And as she became more productive in carrying out royal engagements, this was viewed with amused tolerance,' an aide to the Princess recalled.[21]

Riddell withdrew gladly from the Waleses' fray to the City, replaced briefly by Sir Christopher Airey and then, in what amounted to a palace coup, by Airey's deputy, Commander Richard Aylard, the grammar school-educated former naval officer who had read zoology at Reading University and acted as Diana's equerry from 1985 to 1988. Diana had regarded him as a turncoat when he left her to become assistant private secretary and comptroller to the Waleses' joint office. Later, she began to regard him as an enemy when in 1991 he became private secretary and treasurer to the Prince. In the background, the Prince's party at court regarded Diana as 'a mystery and a threat and somebody to be demeaned, mocked or briefed against, or constrained and restrained in some way. They used to talk very patronisingly about "putting her in a box where she couldn't do too much harm" . . .'[22] While the Queen's principal aides, Robert Fellowes and Robin

Janvrin, 'tried very hard to remain even-handed, to keep the Queen above the fray . . . people in the Prince's camp – and they were outside St James's as much as inside . . . liked to think they could invoke the authority of the Crown against Diana, which I thought was the height of arrogance and double standards, especially since the Crown herself chose to remain pretty much aloof.'[23]

The British Establishment, from courtiers down to aristocrats and their hangers-on in the country, can be a formidable and isolating force; small wonder, therefore, that Diana felt trapped and alone in what she felt to be her fight for survival. Beyond that she could not rely on her family: she had argued too much with her mother and grandmother. Frances, far away in the west of Scotland, had made her own life there where she ran a newsagent's and gift shop and was popular with the villagers as a crusader for local good causes. In the evenings, however, she could be incoherent. 'I can't speak to my mother after 5.30,' Diana complained, as she sought advice and comfort from mother figures Lady Annabel Goldsmith and Ambassadress Flecha de Lima. Frances Shand Kydd was still a remarkably attractive woman and loved by her grandchildren, who nicknamed her 'Supergran', but, as far as Diana was concerned, the relationship was volatile rather than supportive. 'I would say that, like the rest of her [Diana's] family, when the chips were really down, I'm afraid they weren't able, or perhaps willing, to give Diana the support she needed. She and her mother fought too much, there was far too much water under the bridge going way back . . .'[24] According to Andrew Morton, Diana felt 'constantly disappointed by her father'. 'She would say, "He arrives at six'o'clock", pointing to the entry in the visitors' book, "departs at 6.08." She adored him, loved him desperately . . . I remember he once rang from Japan saying, "I'm going to buy you a really lavish present." And she said to him, "I don't want that, I just want for you to be here with me." '[25] He was by now infirm and totally dependent on the devotion of Raine; moreover in September 1991 another Spencer family row broke out over the extent of Johnnie and Raine's sales of Althorp's contents. Nor was there support from her brother and sisters.

Charles, whom she adored, was involved in his own life and had problems in his marriage: Jane, mindful of her husband's career at Buckingham Palace, was in a very difficult position, while Sarah, in the words of a mutual friend, 'found it better to keep a safe distance between herself and Diana'.

So Diana was obliged to rely on the support of her friends and of her allies in the media. It was there that the war against Charles was publicly fought out. Sadly, the theme emphasized by Diana and the press was of Charles's failings as a father compared with her maternal devotion. A trip with the children to Thorpe Park brought headlines critical of Charles from her favourite *Daily Mail*. Under the headline 'CHARLES THE ABSENT ROYAL FATHER' the newspaper asked, 'Why do we not see from him the demonstrations of warmth, affection or closeness Diana frequently displays towards her sons in public?' Later Diana took William and Harry on a skiing holiday to Lech in Austria. Once again, Charles did not accompany them; once again his absence was noted by the press. In June media outrage stormed round Charles when William was hit on the head by a golf ball at his private preparatory boarding school, Ludgrove, sustaining a depressed fracture of his forehead. Both Charles and Diana accompanied William from Ludgrove to the Great Ormond Street Hospital for Sick Children in London for surgery. It was in no way to be a risky operation: Charles therefore decided to carry out a long-standing engagement to entertain British and European officials to a performance of *Tosca* and to travel to Yorkshire overnight to fulfil another official engagement. Diana spent the night in a bedside vigil at the hospital. Over the following days the press was in full cry, contrasting Charles's lack of caring with Diana's maternal devotion. 'WHAT KIND OF DAD ARE YOU?' the *Sun* shouted, while the *Daily Express* branded the Prince 'A PHANTOM FATHER', and another newspaper featured 'THE EXHAUSTED FACE OF A LOVING MOTHER'. Charles very much resented the mileage Diana extracted from the incident, accusing her of exaggerating the seriousness of William's injury for her own ends. Yet Diana did indeed feel bitter at the lack of support from Charles, expressing her feelings privately to friends.

The truth was that neither could bear the presence of the other and it must be asked whether it was not really better for the children for their parents to be apart. They were naturally aware of the fierce rows that took place: William used to listen at the door, taking in every word. Later, in her *Panorama* interview, Diana recalled her elder son pushing Kleenex tissues under the bathroom door as she sat sobbing on the other side. On one occasion Harry attacked his father, beating on his legs with his fists and shouting, 'I hate you, I hate you, you make Mummy cry . . .'

Diana continued her campaign in the press. The large-circulation popular press headed by the *Daily Mail*, the middle/upper-class tabloid, was on her side, thanks principally to its editor, David English, and royal reporter Richard Kay, deputed by English to be their contact with the Princess. Other well-known journalists were sympathetic: Anthony Holden, distinguished journalist and biographer; Andrew Morton, then a freelance who, while working with Diana on her life story, published favourable articles in the influential *Sunday Times*. In the tabloid press, James Whitaker and Harry Arnold tended to take the Princess's side, while Nigel Dempster of the *Mail* and Ross Benson of the *Express*, both of whom had contacts within Charles's circle, often stood out for the Prince.

Diana's thirtieth birthday on 1 July 1991 and her tenth wedding anniversary on the 29th, the two occasions which she had originally intended to use to make some sort of statement about her marriage, represented the next round. Now that she was engaged on the Morton book, Diana had shelved any plans for dramatic statements, but she did not intend to let the occasion pass without a demonstration. On 28 June a story, probably inspired by David English, was headlined in the *Mail* to the effect that Diana planned to spend her birthday apart from her husband.[26] She would be in London, lunching at the Savoy and hosting a party for her close friends, while Charles remained at Highgrove. 'That was PR straight from Diana,' Nigel Dempster told Sally Bedell Smith. Two days later he received a telephone call from one of Charles's friends, 'a well-bred lady's voice' putting the case for Charles: 'Charles has offered her anything for her birthday – lunch, dinner, a ball, but she has refused because she wants to be a martyr.' Dempster produced a front-page story for the *Mail*: under the headline 'CHARLES AND DIANA: CAUSE FOR CONCERN' he revealed that Diana had thwarted Charles's plans for her birthday and that there was 'a growing coolness in the marriage'.[27] After this furore, the couple spent their tenth wedding anniversary dining quietly at Highgrove; an article in the *Sunday Times* apparently celebrating this rapprochement, written by Morton, was headed 'Truce'. Far from representing any real reconciliation, however, the article, Morton admitted, was written specifically to prevent any momentum building up in the press over the unhappy marriage, to maintain his own reputation for inside knowledge of the royal scene but not so much as to allow his colleagues to 'cotton on so much that they would then start to follow the trail'. 'I wrote it quite deliberately to put them off the scent,' he said; 'the pieces I was writing were designed for her. You've got to bear in mind that for her, that the whole object for me was to get that book out unscathed . . . The game plan was that kind of balancing act, to show sophisticated observers . . . that I knew what I was talking about but at the same time not to let them get in on it.'[28] Morton, anxious for verification of the main story, indicated to Diana that he needed evidence of the Charles/Camilla relationship: in August she found notes from Camilla to Charles (how she did so has not been disclosed), which she found deeply upsetting, and showed them to Morton.

Meanwhile, according to Sarah Ferguson's account, 1991 was the year that she and Diana first put words to the unspeakable idea that they had been discussing for some time: that one or both of them might leave the Royal Family. They burned the phone wires into the night trading secrets and jokes that no one else would understand. Sarah even sent Diana a tape of the film *The Great Escape*. Sarah had been marked down as out of control for some time by the Queen's courtiers and her officials, dubbed by Sarah and Diana 'the grey men', principally 'Mr Z' (by whom she almost certainly meant Robert Fellowes, who also happened to be a cousin). The Ramzi Sultan affair had alerted them to Sarah's relationship with Steve Wyatt. These 'new American friends', she was told, 'were not the right sort of people' she should be mixing with. Sarah was in debt, her extravagance funded by unlimited credit at 'the Queen's bank', Coutts & Co. The miles she travelled on freebie holidays far exceeded those expended on official duties. In 1990 she had dropped to last in the royal engagements list, with ten fewer than the ninety-year-old Queen Mother. Sarah Ferguson was likeable, jolly and amusing but, in the famous words of one of the Queen's senior courtiers, she 'was never cut out to be a royal princess'.[29] 'Diana wasn't as bad,' said a royal official. 'But [for] Fergie who already had a life, it's like catching a wild animal and caging them up – they want to get out.'[30]

At Balmoral late that summer both girls behaved like rebellious teenagers. In her book, Sarah recalled how one night after dinner, she and Diana slipped out of the back door, commandeered a quad bike and drove it at speed down the golf course, damaging the greens. And to compound their bad behaviour they were foolish enough to stop at the lodge occupied by Robert Fellowes and his family and ring the bell, although it was almost midnight. They then 'liberated' the Queen Mother's stately Daimler limousine and, with Diana at the wheel wearing the chauffeur's cap and Sarah in the back imitating the Queen Mother's royal wave, did wheel spins on the gravel drive surrounding the castle. Diana, Princess of Wales, was thirty years old, Sarah, Duchess of York, thirty-two – two spoiled princesses who had absorbed the adulation and cosseting to their every whim which membership of the Royal Family involved, but failed to understand the true implications of their position. 'The thing that was hard on Diana – and Sarah Ferguson,' one of the Queen Mother's ladies said, 'was that they were both totally uneducated. They had no idea of what the constitutional monarchy was, either of them. They thought it was a mixture of Hollywood and William Hickey, they really did, they thought it was endless freebies and romantic princes riding about and everybody cheering. I don't think they had a clue.'[31]

Typical of the 'me' generation, they were neither prepared to

35

Diana and William photographed with Dodi (left) and Mohamed Al Fayed at a polo match in 1988.

36

June 1989: Charles and Diana with William and Harry prepare for a cycling trip in Tresco during their holiday in the Scilly Isles.

Diana returns to her old school, Riddlesworth Hall, and walks in the grounds with pupils and her former headmistress. Ken Wharfe, her protection officer, can be glimpsed at the far left.

38

Diana and Charles at an Arab feast
on their tour of the Gulf States in
March 1989.

The notorious AIDS handshake
that made headlines.

39

Will Carling (left) and Diana at Twickenham.

James Gilbey pictured post–
'Squidgygate' revelations.

Charles and
Diana walking at
Highgrove, 1989.

1 July 1990: Diana collects Charles from Cirencester Hospital, his arm in a sling after a polo accident. She drove straight to Kensington Palace after he made it clear that Camilla would nurse him.

Diana and William share a tender moment.

São Paulo, Brazil, April 1991: Diana visits a hostel for abandoned children, many of whom are HIV positive or suffering from AIDS.

Hyderabad, India, February 1992: Diana visits Mianpur Old Age Welfare Centre and has her feet touched as a sign of respect.

47

Lech, Austria, 30 March 1992: Diana and Charles leave their skiing holiday after news of Earl Spencer's death. Diana could not bear the thought of yet another 'happy families' act for the media and it took a telephone call from the Queen to persuade her to make a joint journey back to England.

48

49

Public sympathy causes Diana to break down on a visit to Ashworth Hospice, Liverpool, in 1992, just as Andrew Morton's book, *Diana: Her True Story*, is serialized.

Oliver Hoare, 1994, pictured as the news breaks that Diana has been making anonymous telephone calls to his house.

Diana and her sisters, Sarah (left) and Jane (right), after a night out.

South Korea, November 1992. 'The Glums': Charles and Diana on their last official trip together, attending a presidential banquet in Seoul. Their separation would be announced one month later.

compromise on what they saw as personal fulfilment nor to consider fully the implications of what they were about to do. Between them they would be responsible for the greatest crisis of the British monarchy since Edward VIII had abdicated to marry 'the woman I love'.

13. The Volcano Erupts

'. . . you got this flavour of intense unhappiness, real movement, almost as if the people at the Palace could see this volcano about to explode and just being petrified what to do about it. And in fact Diana wrote to someone before the book came out, "I can feel this volcano is going to explode but I can cope . . ."' (Andrew Morton[1])

While the royal household struggled to keep the lid on the swirling currents surrounding the Wales and York marriages, no one dared warn the Queen of what might happen. The year 1992 would mark the fortieth anniversary of her accession to the throne: the Queen in her Christmas broadcast message to her people, unaware that her family was crumbling around her, chose to emphasize the family theme as she affirmed her determination to serve as their monarch in the years to come: 'With your prayers and your help, and the love and support of my family, I shall try and help you in the years to come . . .'

The first shock to the family came in the first month of the year. On 15 January the *Mail* published the photographs of Steve Wyatt and Sarah on holiday with the children which a window cleaner and odd-job man had found on top of the wardrobe in Wyatt's vacant flat. This time the naïve, long-suffering Prince Andrew, in his father-in-law's words, 'hit the roof'. 'They were only holiday snaps,' Ronald Ferguson told Lesley Player, 'but they show that Texan fellow in a basket chair with his arm around her [Sarah] — and the one that really annoyed Andrew was little Beatrice with no clothes on being cuddled by him . . .'[2] Six days after the publication, Andrew and Sarah agreed to separate and travelled down to Sandringham to tell the Queen of their decision. According to Sarah, the Queen asked them to reconsider and no announcement was made for the time being. According to Sarah's autobiography she was determined to divorce Andrew in order to escape 'the Firm' in which 'grey man Z' (Robert Fellowes) had been joined by a new press secretary, 'grey man X' (Charles Anson). Without mentioning the developments in her private life which had led her to the decision, she blamed the grey men and their bully-boy tactics. They were determined to oust her and to protect Diana, she said. She did not mention Wyatt, who had left for the United States that month, apparently vowing eternal love, nor did she mention his replacement, another Texan, John Bryan.

Sarah was apparently expecting Diana to follow suit in bolting from the family but it soon became evident that she had no intention of doing so – yet. Perhaps in order to distance herself from the rumours surrounding Sarah, she appears to have been behind the lead in the *Daily Mail* on 18 March when a front-page 'exclusive' by Richard Kay and Andrew Morton declared that 'the Palace is preparing to announce the separation of the Duke and Duchess of York'. The story precipitated the Palace into action: the following day they did indeed issue a statement that lawyers acting for the Duchess of York had initiated discussions about a formal separation, accompanied by the pious hope that the media would spare the Duke and Duchess and their children 'any intrusion'. Their hope that the story could be kept quiet until after the General Election campaign then in progress had vanished. Sarah immediately suspected Diana since both Richard Kay and Andrew Morton were close to her and therefore the story must have been prompted by her, possibly to deflect any speculation about her own situation in the run-up to the publication in June of Andrew Morton's book. A representative of a public relations firm was summoned to Sunninghill Park. He arrived to find only Andrew there: Sarah was upstairs with John Bryan who had now taken over her affairs. They later appeared downstairs together in a state of high excitement. Sarah attacked the man for the bad publicity she had had to endure and indicated that John Bryan would be a more effective adviser. Tempers flared and the Yorks, with another guest, left the room (although it later transpired that they had been listening at the door). There was a scene during which champagne flutes were smashed. Witnesses commented that Andrew seemed to be frightened of Sarah and now hated Diana, his former friend, on his brother's account.

Diana was intent on her own survival and had no intention of becoming embroiled in her sister-in-law's self-induced troubles. She distanced herself from Sarah and carried on her own public relations campaign. In February she travelled with Charles on a visit to India which was to feature the famous 'Princess alone' photograph of a pensive Diana seated in front of the Taj Mahal, romantic monument to the enduring love of the Mogul Emperor Shah Jehan for his dead wife, Mumtaz Mahal. The impact of the picture showed Diana's phenomenal public relations skills. In itself, the location of the shot was absolutely normal; it was taken from the only spot to which the authorities would allow media access. Charles himself had sat on the same bench on his visit twelve years before, when he had given a hostage to fortune by saying, 'One day I would like to bring my wife here.' At the time, Charles himself was at a meeting for business leaders in Bangalore – the separation of itineraries was normal practice on intercontinental visits such as this. 'The trouble with these visits,' said Dickie Arbiter, the couple's press secretary who accompanied them, '[is that] they only last for four days, five at the most, and everybody wants a piece of the action. They are only two people and they can only do so much so they have to split and do what was required of them.'³ The media, aware of Charles's previous pledge, put their own interpretation on the picture, following the precise line Diana intended. Famously, she followed it up with the cruel 'kiss that never was' at a polo match when, as Charles bent towards her to kiss her for a much awaited photo opportunity, she swiftly averted her head at the last moment, so that he was pictured pecking ineptly at her neck. 'Oh, Come On You Can Do Better Than That, Charles!' the *Mirror* admonished.

Such well-publicized images of a marriage in trouble caused consternation at the Palace, where the top officials had already picked up rumours of the Morton book and were desperate to shore up the marriage of the heir to the throne. It was only to get worse. On 29 March, Johnnie Spencer died suddenly of a heart attack in the Humana Hospital Wellington in north London where he had been recovering from mild pneumonia. His death was quite unexpected: Diana, who had visited him with William on 25 March, had left the following day for a family skiing holiday with Charles in Lech. None of the family was with Johnnie when he died, not even Raine who had felt able to go down to Althorp to supervise funding events. Diana, distraught in Lech, prepared to fly home without Charles. On this occasion of her private grief she could not bear the thought of yet another 'happy families' act for the media. Charles, his private secretary Richard Aylard and Dickie Arbiter tried to persuade her to go with her husband for the sake of the public image of the Prince and of their marriage. It took a telephone call from the Queen to persuade her to make a joint journey back to England. Even then the couple's private estrangement was such that, on arrival at Kensington Palace, Charles departed immediately for Highgrove, leaving Diana alone to grieve for her adored father. On 1 April she drove down to Althorp for the funeral at the family church of St Mary the Virgin, Great Brington. Charles flew over by helicopter to join her in the car for the church, maintaining the fiction of a supportive husband. Immediately after lunch, he flew back to London. Following her father's coffin out of the church with Raine, Diana's instinctive sympathy caused her to take the first step towards ending the feud with her stepmother. 'She did a very moving thing at Johnnie's funeral, Diana,' a relation who attended said. 'Raine was on that side and Diana was on this side, and when they left their seats she went over to Raine and held her hand and walked down the church with her. I was very impressed with that because I thought it showed a desire to reconcile everything, and in front of the whole congregation doing that . . . so that it was evident to every-body what she had done. And I thought that was very tender . . . bringing Raine in and not isolating her.'[4] Frances Shand Kydd did not attend, although she was present – making herself as inconspicuous as possible – at the London memorial service on 19 May.

By then Diana was standing on the edge of the abyss – the pre-publication serialization of the Morton book which would precipitate her isolation from the Royal Family. For some time she had hugged the secret triumphantly as she looked forward to putting her case to her public, exposing Charles and Camilla and revealing the sham of her 'fairy-tale' marriage. But, with less than a month to go, she began to be apprehensive of the consequences of what she had done. 'I was with them going to Expo '92 in Seville,' said one of her close aides. 'She said, "You don't know what I've done." She was scared, really scared.[5] I think she was just beginning to realize . . .' To David Puttnam, former film producer and future Labour peer, she confided, 'I've done something which I may really live to regret . . .' Sitting next to Puttnam at a dinner meeting of powerful media executives called the Thirty Club at Claridge's in March, she confessed that she was terrified of the consequences. Puttnam was then governor of the National AIDS Trust of which she became President. 'Before, she was talking about wanting to do something unusual, big,' Puttnam recalled, 'so I arranged for her to address all the media owners, Rupert Murdoch, Conrad Black . . . at the Thirty Club . . . she was absolutely terrified, so I coached her through it, we worked out what she would do, we even set it up so that there were some interviews by very, very young interviewers. And she was brilliant, and she knew she was brilliant. The speech about the incidence of AIDS in women was a really "grown up" thing to do.' It may be that seeing the media power ranked in front of her brought home to her for the first time what she was getting herself into. At dinner, to Puttnam's surprise, she 'suddenly started confiding in me how unhappy things were in her marriage. She said "Neither of us has been perfect, but I've done a really stupid thing. I have allowed a book to be written. I felt it was a good idea, a way of clearing the air, but now I think it was a very stupid thing that will cause all kinds of terrible trouble", adding, "I would like to reel the movie back. It is the daftest thing I have ever done.'⁶ On the day the serialization of the Morton book came out, she rang the Waleses' press secretary Dickie Arbiter in a panic: 'What do I do?' 'You don't do anything,' Arbiter replied. 'Why didn't you tell me when I first asked you four months ago what help you had given the Morton book? You swore you hadn't given any.' And on that day, Diana still repeated, 'I haven't given any help.'⁷

By now thoroughly apprehensive, Diana was given an opportunity to demonstrate both her courage in the face of private anxiety and her value as an ambassador of the Royal Family and the British nation with an official visit to Egypt on 10 May. Ironically, as her private secretary Patrick Jephson noted, while the Princess flew out on her official tour in an aircraft paid for by the British taxpayer, the plane was diverted to land the Prince (on his eighth holiday of the year) and a party of friends in Turkey. In yet another example of the Prince's poor PR, when Diana flew back to London the same plane was forced to double back to Turkey again since the Prince's plans had not dovetailed with the Princess's official schedule. Despite a sobbing fit on the plane, possibly induced by apprehension over the Morton book but also perhaps because of the presence of the Prince and his friends off on their holiday, underlining the separateness of their ways, she heroically pulled herself together before the arrival at Cairo. 'No matter how close she came to the edge of bottling out,' Jephson wrote, 'she always produced the last-minute effort of will that could turn imminent disaster into serene triumph.' Immaculately groomed, she played her part in the arrival ceremony with 'consummate professionalism, poise and devotion to duty'. 'I wondered,' Jephson added, 'if her opponents really understood the bloody-minded determination of the woman they were seeking to banish into the backwaters of royal life.'⁸ Not only was Diana a huge success with her hosts, President Hosni Mubarak and his wife, but she won the admiration of the travelling press pack, alert for any sign of weakness. A report in the *Sunday Times* congratulated Diana on her courage. 'It is a mark of her confidence that even after the recent publicity about her marriage she is prepared to walk into a room of tabloid hacks. The transformation in Diana is quite incredible. Diana will never be a great intellectual but she is a very shrewd sharp woman with amazing strength of character.'⁹

Yet even she had underestimated the bombshell effect of the public revelations of the reality of a marriage – which the majority had firmly believed, or wished to believe, was still the fairy tale of that July day in 1981 – when they were published in the *Sunday Times* beginning on 7 June 1992. The book told of Diana's psychological problems, the bulimia, self-mutilation and depression – including the Sandringham suicide attempt that never was. Charles's infidelity with Camilla and his unkindness to Diana were similarly revealed. The nation as a whole was shocked and angry. There was disillusionment with the Royal Family, and hence the monarchy, which had been building over the antics of Sarah and Diana; with *It's a Royal Knockout*; with the Yorks selling pictures of themselves with their babies to *Hello!*; with Princess Anne's divorce from Mark Phillips in 1992, accompanied by the rumours of her affair with one of her policemen. Middle England, brought up to regard the Royal Family as role models, 'ourselves behaving better', was shaken to the core. The heir to the throne came out worst of all: a cynical adulterer who mistreated his virgin bride and selfishly ignored his children. This last was a recent theme of Diana's which she had been putting across in the press: James Gilbey quoted her as saying. 'She thinks he is a bad father, a selfish father; the children have to tie in with whatever he's doing.'

The representation of Diana as a victim struggling to free herself from the crushing weight of an ultra-traditional family and an adulterous, uncaring husband won her widespread sympathy from the public at large, as she had intended. The trouble about the book from the Royal Family's point of view was that its essential presentation of Diana as a virgin sacrifice offered up on the altar of the dynasty was near enough to the truth to be believable. At first, however, it was dismissed as a journalistic fabrication. Diana's repeated denials of collaboration to her brother-in-law, Robert Fellowes, who assured the chairman of the Press Complaints Commission, Lord McGregor, that she had not been involved, led to his statement condemning the press for 'dabbling their fingers in the stuff of other people's souls'. Her friends who had collaborated in the Morton book were accused of betraying Diana by revealing her secrets. A photo opportunity was arranged at the request of Carolyn's husband, William Bartholomew, who was determined that Diana should be seen publicly supporting his wife.[10] A cousin of the Queen remembered being told by a photographer that Diana herself had telephoned him telling him to be at the Bartholomews' Fulham house at a precise time.[11] Diana's evident approval of what Carolyn had done and the use of photographs from the Spencer family album gave Morton's revelations authenticity. One of the contributors, Angela Serota, a friend of Andrew Knight, executive director of News International, told Knight that Diana had indeed authorized her friends to cooperate with Morton.[12] When the Bartholomew photographs appeared, McGregor, who had received Robert Fellowes' assurances, rang him in Paris, where he was with the Queen, to berate him for deceiving him. Fellowes, who had asked Diana several times if she had been involved and received direct denials from her, had believed her. He was fond of his sister-in-law, whom he had known since childhood, and, being an upright man of Christian principles, had thought it inconceivable that she could have lied to him. He apologized to Lord McGregor and the Press Complaints Commission for misleading them and offered his resignation to the Queen who refused it. The affair greatly damaged Diana's future relations with her sister and brother-in-law, whom she had lied to and betrayed, making him look ridiculous to his own official circle. She continued to deny that she herself had been responsible for the book or that she had spoken to the author. No one believed her on the first count, although her undoubted responsibility for the second was not to be publicly revealed until Morton published extracts from the tapes after her death.

While Diana had succeeded in her aim of revealing the sham of her marriage and gaining the sympathy of the wider public, the British Establishment and the upper echelons of British society were outraged at what they saw as a betrayal of the Queen and the monarchy on her part. It was the first self-destructive step towards the final parting of the ways. Diana never wanted a divorce; in her heart she still loved Charles to the point of obsession and saw him as her husband. She still hoped that she could have it all: remaining in the Royal Family, keeping her children and her title as Princess of Wales, while keeping a separate court. 'Diana would never have got out,' Dickie Arbiter affirmed. But, although at a private meeting with Charles the day after the serialization began they agreed to separate on the grounds of incompatibility, Diana continued to feel a passionate resentment over her treatment, refusing to play an accommodating Queen Alexandra to Charles and Camilla's Edward VII and Mrs Keppel. Like Sarah Ferguson, she was a child of a modern generation which was not prepared to accept the upper-class conventional marriage in which fidelity and romance did not play a part. But, unlike Sarah Ferguson, who for selfish reasons turned her back on a husband who loved and supported her through all her infidelities and antics, Diana had every reason to complain as the loving, inexperienced bride who had been used and abused by an uncaring, selfish husband incapable of giving her the love she craved, nor even the normal married life she had dreamed of. Moreover, as she saw it – and who is to say she was wrong? – he was backed up by a powerful social set and ultimately by the Palace, who had tried to silence and sideline her.

Jonathan Dimbleby wrote of the aftermath of the serialization:

After the publication of the first instalment of the Morton book, a handful of the Prince's closest friends, including the Romseys and van Cutsems, felt compelled to tell both the Queen and Prince Philip how stoical they thought the Prince had been through the long trauma of the marriage. Perhaps nudged by this intervention but certainly shocked by the media blitzkrieg surrounding the publication of the book, both the Queen and the Duke, who had been at pains not to take sides, rallied to the Prince; in particular, the Duke wrote a long and sympathetic letter to him in which he praised what he saw as his son's saint-like fortitude. It was in this atmosphere that the Queen and Prince discussed for the first time whether he should seek a separation from the Princess.[13]

The Prince went on to consult Lord Goodman, lawyer and adviser to the powerful, as to his position, but took no further steps.

As Charles's authorized biographer, Dimbleby is well informed and reliable on the Prince's side of the story, although no official biographer can be entirely impartial. What he did not say, however, is that despite their initial shock at the effect of the book in battering down the wall of confidentiality traditionally surrounding the family, and at Diana's deviousness in first encouraging it and then concealing its progress, the Queen and Prince Philip were not at heart totally unsympathetic to Diana. The Prince's first reaction was anger at his daughter-in-law for bringing the situation and its accompanying scandal into the open. With the Morton book, she had 'destroyed everything', he wrote to her. Yet the Queen and Prince Philip disapproved of Charles's adultery with Camilla which, far more than any unreasonable behaviour of Diana's, had brought scandal on the monarchy. Indeed, at Easter the following year, a courtier was amazed when Charles, who was sitting beside her, exploded in fury at his father: 'You should have seen the letter he wrote me . . . !'[14] 'What Charles has done is very wrong,' Prince Philip wrote in a compassionate letter to his daughter-in-law. Both the Queen and Prince Philip were – and are – strong in their religious feelings and convictions; divorce was abhorrent to them and they hoped above all that it need not come to that, both for the sake of the young princes and the monarchy – 'the image of a family on the throne', as Walter Bagehot had put it. It was the Prince's party at the Palace and in society who undermined Diana by implying or saying publicly, as one certainly did, that Diana was mad – 'that bad Fermoy blood'. The general Palace view – but not in the Queen's office – was detestation of Diana for her revelation of family secrets and sympathy for 'the poor Prince'. The fact that the basis of her story was the truth counted for nothing in the face of her breach of the rules.

Yet, despite everything, the royal show rumbled on: the traditional celebration of the Queen's official birthday, Trooping the Colour, went ahead with Diana as part of the family party standing on Buckingham Palace balcony for the RAF fly-past as if nothing

had happened. Fergie, however, was nowhere to be seen. As the
second instalment of the Morton serialization hit the news-stands
on 14 June, the family were at Windsor for the racing at Ascot.
The following day the Queen and Prince Philip had a meeting
with Charles and Diana, during which the subject of divorce was
mentioned but rejected. The Queen was led to believe that Diana
would stand by Charles and suggested a six-month cooling-off
period. Once again Diana was asked if she had collaborated on the
book and once again she denied it, in tears. Prince Philip, by
her later account, was 'angry, raging and unpleasant'[15] and later
cold-shouldered her in the royal box.[16] On the opening day, as
the Queen and the rest of her family drove in open carriages down
the course, the disgraced Sarah took her two daughters to wave at
their grandmother from the rails. The Queen waved back but
inwardly she no doubt despaired at yet another manifestation of
what the press now liked to call her 'dysfunctional' family. Guests
at lunch at the Castle noted that the Queen seemed to be 'in a
pretty bad temper' and when she did talk to her guests she was less
than her usual gracious self. In the royal box after lunch, again, no
one dared speak to her.

At the end of June Diana gave yet another demonstration of the
crowd-pleasing qualities which made her such a valuable royal
asset. On a visit to Belfast (security had been breached by the
leaking of her visit the night before), she paid a spectacularly
successful visit to the Republican heartland, the Falls Road, the
dominion of the IRA. An estimated twenty thousand people came
to 'shout for Diana'. The Morton revelations had evidently made
their impact and there was no doubting where the popular sympa-
thies lay. As the *Daily Mirror* front page put it under a banner
headline 'WE WANT DI!', frontline Belfast had 'a message for the
Royals'. Even the normally anti-monarchist Dublin press reported
sympathetically on the Princess. It was a timely reminder of her
popular appeal, and her enemies responded accordingly. On the
same day as the papers published ecstatic reports of her success in
Northern Ireland, others carried stories that could only have been

planted by her enemies, clearly suggesting that the Princess suffered from mental instability.[17]

At the end of July both Charles and Diana attended a dinner to celebrate the Queen's fortieth anniversary on the throne and in August, after a brief, unsatisfactory 'family holiday' on millionaire John Latsis's yacht, they flew up to Balmoral for the annual family holiday. They were all there when, on 20 August, the *Daily Mirror* published the notorious 'toe-sucking' pictures featuring Sarah and her 'financial adviser' John Bryan on holiday in the South of France with the two little princesses. Nothing was said when Andrew, forewarned by Sarah, went down to face the younger members of the family at the breakfast table littered with newspapers blaring headlines and explicit photographs. Sarah herself went to face a furious Queen at 9.30. One can only imagine the conversation. While the scandal raged in the press, at Balmoral it was as if nothing had happened. Sarah remained for a further three days, sitting in her usual place beside Andrew. A young member of the family said to a relation, 'You won't believe it – nobody said a word. There was Fergie sitting next to Andrew and the topless pictures all over the papers . . .'[18]

Four days after the publication of the 'toe-sucking' pictures of Sarah and John Bryan, it was Diana's turn for embarrassment. The *Sun* published the Squidgygate tapes of the conversations between Diana and James Gilbey on New Year's Eve 1989 under the heading 'MY LIFE IS TORTURE', which not only underlined the deep rift between herself and Charles but her difficulties with the Royal Family in general and, more damagingly, her close relationship with Gilbey. The terms in which she had spoken of the family's ingratitude and lack of appreciation of her dutiful public efforts – 'after all I've done for this f . . . family' – were difficult for the Palace to come to terms with. The *Sun* then alleged that Diana and Hewitt had had a 'physical relationship' with no evidence beyond analysis of their 'body language' in photographs of them together. Diana suspected a conspiracy to destroy her but there was none beyond the destructive effect of the relentless tabloid circulation war. In these circumstances and after the publication of the Morton book which, however much she may have regretted it, still represented her 'manifesto', her protest against the sham of her marriage, it was hardly surprising that she dug in her heels over the projected joint tour of South Korea.

'As the Prince's staff contemplated the nightmarish task of explaining to the Korean authorities that the Princess would not after all be accompanying her husband on the first royal visit to their country,' Dimbleby's official account ran,

Peter Westmacott, the deputy private secretary to the royal couple, was obliged to do the Korean 'recce' as if he were organising a joint visit – which, from his conversation with the Princess, he was convinced would not in fact take place. At Balmoral, the Prince tried to persuade the Princess to change her mind. Even the Queen intervened to advise her daughter-in-law that she ought to go. Finally the Prince told her bluntly that she would have to come up with an explanation of her own for staying behind. At this, the Princess finally relented, saying meekly that as the Queen had asked her to go she would after all accompany him.[19]

The resulting tour, as Diana knew it would be, was a public relations disaster. The glum faces of the couple only served to indicate the depths to which the marriage had sunk. There could no longer be any pretence that the situation was salvageable. On the aeroplane returning from Korea, the Prince wrote one of his gloomy, self-pitying letters, recounting his despair that Diana could not be 'a friend' to him and how he had been battling the temptation to cancel his engagements: 'I feel so unsuited to the ghastly business of human intrigue and general nastiness . . . I don't know what will happen from *now* on but I *dread* it.'[20]

In contrast, Diana's subsequent solo visit to Paris on 13 November represented in Jephson's eyes her 'apogee'. Greeted with the welcoming message 'COURAGE PRINCESSE!', Diana went through the perfectly orchestrated schedule at the peak of her beauty and professionalism, charming President Mitterrand, the French public and the press alike. For Jephson that moment represented Diana at her best. Strengthened by her stand over the Morton book, she had not yet encountered the pitfalls which awaited her bid for independence. 'To my eyes,' Morton wrote, 'knowing what she had already endured and what lay ahead in the immediate future, there was something heroic in her.'

For Diana the endgame of the first phase was near. The final confrontation of the year came in a quarrel over one of Charles's annual November shooting weekends at Sandringham, planned for the 20th and timed to coincide with an exeat from Ludgrove so that William and Harry could join them. In a last act of defiance, Diana decided not to go and, moreover, to inform Charles that she would be taking the children to see their grandmother, the Queen, at Windsor, or, if she could not stay there, to Highgrove. The Prince metaphorically stamped his foot and threatened her with his authority – he could not be defied in the eyes of his friends. Diana held her ground. His intemperate attitude gave her the excuse she needed to write a defiant letter which, paraphrased, said, more or less: 'Given the way things are between us I'm not sure I want to subject myself to the company of your friends and I certainly don't want to subject the boys to the company of your friends given that we both know who might be there . . .'[21]

According to Dimbleby, it had 'become the custom for the royal couple to invite some sixteen friends to stay for three days of relaxation, shooting, and walking'.[22] In practice, the 'friends' were all Charles's, not Diana's, and by now they had almost no friends in common. Charles's friends, Diana well knew, would include the inner circle who provided safe houses for his rendezvous with Camilla. As Diana complained to Jephson, 'They're all *his* friends. I'm going to be completely outnumbered.'[23] And as a friend said 'She'd been put through this Sandringham ordeal over and over again . . . it was a real little love-in for the Prince's buddies and his whole household was mobilized to make it an extraordinary expression of his regal position. It was a [Michael] Fawcett production in overdrive, playing King in the Queen's house . . .'[24] Diana's position, while absolutely understandable as regards her own presence in the house, was less tenable when it came to preventing the boys from seeing their father. Unfortunately, they were her principal weapon and in her rage and distress she was not above using them as pawns in the war with her husband.

Charles's patience finally snapped. He would not be defied like this in front of his friends, or, as Dimbleby judiciously put it: 'Unable to see any future in a relationship conducted on these terms, he decided he had no choice but to ask his wife for a legal separation.'[25] On 25 November he and Diana met privately at Kensington Palace and agreed to put the matter in the hands of their lawyers. Discussions continued for some weeks over the matters to be agreed, principally arrangements over the children, secondly a financial settlement for her upkeep, and lastly and most controversially, Diana's future role as a working member of the Royal Family, described, according to Jephson who took part in the negotiations as 'a semi-detached member of the Royal Family'.

'It was at about this time,' Jephson commented with distaste, 'that the phrase "loose cannon" became popular.'[26] The Queen herself, he said, was taking great trouble to remain neutral, but the Prince's advisers (he did not name them but hinted that they were not his legal ones) seemed determined to thwart Diana's ambitions to become an independent royal operator, attempting to restrict her use of the Queen's Flight and the royal train, and downgrading the protocol accorded to her when on official visits. In the end, since the Queen declined to come down on the Prince's side, Diana got almost everything she wanted in the final negotiations except for the financial settlement which was not agreed until the divorce was finalized in 1996. The only stipulation made by the Queen was that Diana should not represent her abroad. Significantly, in an attempt to promote fairness and bipartisanship between the households and staff of all the Palaces, the Lord Chamberlain circulated a letter impressing on everybody the necessity of understanding for both sides. Whether it actually made any difference to the attitudes in the opposing camps is doubtful but it was useful in emphasizing the neutrality of the Crown (that is, the Queen) in the disputes between the Waleses.

On 9 December in the House of Commons, the Prime Minister, John Major, read out the prepared statement issued by Buckingham Palace:

It is announced from Buckingham Palace that, with regret, the Prince and Princess of Wales have decided to separate. Their Royal Highnesses have no plans to divorce and their constitutional positions are unaffected. This decision has been reached amicably and they will both continue to participate fully in the upbringing of their children.

Their Royal Highnesses will continue to carry out full and separate programmes of public engagements and will, from time to time, attend family occasions and national events together.

While the first statement was received by Members of Parliament in respectful silence, the Prime Minister's following words to the effect that 'there was no reason why the Princess of Wales should not be crowned Queen Consort in due course . . .' produced a collective gasp. The idea that the Princess of Wales, living apart from her husband and at daggers drawn with him, could still be crowned Queen Consort struck most people as absurd. The idea that the Prince of Wales's succession was assured as Head of the Church of England, even if constitutionally correct, also required some swallowing. The Archbishop of Canterbury, when officially consulted before the statement, said that for the separation to be widely accepted two important provisos should be met: 'both parents would have to be seen to maintain close bonds with their children; and extra-marital love affairs that might be brought to public attention would need to be avoided'.[27] It would soon become obvious that the Archbishop's second proviso was very far from being met.

Symbolically, on Friday 20 November, the start of the fateful Sandringham weekend, Windsor Castle caught fire. The images of flames shooting from the great castle on the hill, home of the British monarchy for almost a thousand years, seized the imagination of people around the world. Not only did it represent the bonfire which had finally consumed the Waleses' marriage, but with it perished the 'family' image which had been so carefully cultivated.

14. The First Step Towards the Abyss

'She was lost without him' (a friend's comment on Diana after the separation)

At Kensington Palace after the separation was agreed there was a lightening of the atmosphere and a sense of solidarity between the house and office staff which had not been there before. They were all on the Princess's team now: a party was held, Diana played the piano and everyone sang and danced: '. . . we glowed with the sudden feeling that the grown-ups had gone out for the evening and would not be back for hours . . . if they were going to come back at all,'[1] Jephson recalled. Yet, when James Hewitt telephoned to congratulate her on having successfully made 'the Great Escape', she sounded 'very flat and down'. At both their residences, the separation was symbolized by the removal of the Prince's personal possessions (including his lavatory) from Kensington Palace and Diana's from Highgrove: the couple's respective interior designers, Robert Kime and Dudley Poplak, were instructed to wipe out all traces of their common life together.

An immediate consequence of the separation of the two households was the division of the staff. Some were offered the choice of which household they chose to remain with, some were not. At Kensington Palace the charming, loyal and discreet head butler, Harold Brown, remained with the Princess; the Highgrove butler, Paul Burrell, was assigned to Kensington Palace against his wishes. With his wife, Maria, and two sons, Burrell was happy in his cottage on the Highgrove estate and was extremely unwilling to be transferred to the Princess's service. 'He was blubbing and bad-mouthing her,' said a fellow member of staff. In fact, Diana hardly needed two butlers at Kensington Palace but Burrell had been a favoured footman to the Queen at Buckingham Palace while his wife had worked for the Duke of Edinburgh and they were therefore entitled to consideration. The Prince, it was alleged, did not want to keep Burrell on at Highgrove since he (Burrell) was only too aware of what was going on in the Prince's private life. Burrell became devoted to, even obsessed with, Diana and later succeeded in manoeuvring Harold Brown out of her good graces. At the Prince of Wales's side, his valet, Michael Fawcett, now became the most powerful figure on his domestic staff. Both Burrell and Fawcett were to become notorious in the years up to and following Diana's death. Mervyn Wycherley, the Waleses' chef, who had been transferred from the royal household on their marriage, remained with her. 'Muscular, flamboyant and extremely witty,' Wharfe wrote, 'Mervyn was devoted to the Princess and she was fond of him in return. Much more than the man who prepared her food . . . he became a close friend whose loyalty to her was unquestioned. There were some, however,' he added mysteriously, 'who wanted to break their intimacy, seeing it as a threat to their own positions.'[2] Both Burrell with Diana and Fawcett with Charles were jealous of their respective closeness to their employers and undermined anybody who posed any kind of threat to their positions.

At first it seemed as if Diana had won hands down. She had got all she wanted – access to the children and a subsidized, independent life of her own. *Vanity Fair* called it 'DI'S PALACE COUP' in a headline of February 1993. On 13 January the publication of the Camillagate tapes had cut what remained of the moral high ground from beneath Charles's feet. The mutual passion of the couple (and Charles's silly language) served to underline the fact that the Morton representation of Diana as the betrayed wife was the truth. Tabloid newspapers speculated that the tapes could cost the adulterous Prince the throne. Much sanctimonious nonsense was written but the central fact that the Prince of Wales had betrayed his wife, the mother of his children, over a long period of time and, with the connivance of a circle of aristocratic friends, had deceived Diana, brought his popularity to an all-time low. In contrast Diana, the innocent victim of the deception, was resoundingly vindicated. Times – and the press – had changed since Charles's great-grandfather, Edward VII, enjoyed with impunity regular winter holidays with Camilla's great-grandmother, Mrs Keppel, at Biarritz or on luxurious shooting weekends at the country estates of his aristocratic or plutocratic friends.

Yet Diana felt bereft without Charles, the focus of her life over the past eleven years. However hostile, however undermining he might have been to her at times, she was unused to living alone without a male prop in her life. The future seemed very uncertain even if materially luxurious, and her life was in limbo without the predictable form she had enjoyed (or, rather, resented) within the unchanging pattern of the Royal Family. From now on she would have to operate exclusively at the dictate of her own instincts (not always a wise motive for action) with the guiding hand of Patrick Jephson. She began to gather round her a band of loyal friends and advisers. Carolyn Bartholomew was still a friend, as was Laura Greig (now Lonsdale). Sadly, some of her circle – Julia Samuel, Kate Menzies and Catherine Soames – would not survive the nature of Diana's friendships, when she would abruptly and definitively cut off contact for some perceived disloyalty or misdemeanour. The most long-lasting of these younger friends was Rosa Monckton, born the Hon. Rosamond Monckton, daughter of Viscount Monckton of Brenchley, and wife of journalist the Hon. Dominic Lawson, the son of a former Chancellor of the Exchequer and at that time editor of the prestigious *Spectator* magazine. Rosa Monckton, a clever, ambitious woman, became head of Tiffany & Co. She had her ups and downs with Diana, who sometimes suspected her of using her to further her own purposes, but the two women always made up. At Diana's instigation, Rosa's stillborn child was buried in the garden at Kensington Palace, and she became godmother to the Lawsons' daughter, Domenica. A major row took place when Diana attended the christening party for Domenica only to find herself photographed at the event by *Hello!* magazine. Diana took her role as godmother seriously and would look after Domenica herself when needed.

With Rosa, the two women close to Diana for the remainder
of her life were glamorous mother figures, Lady Annabel Goldsmith and the Brazilian Ambassadress, Lucia Flecha de Lima.
Another older woman, Elsa, Lady Bowker, was the recipient of
many confidences about her love life. Lady Annabel, a daughter
of the 8th Marquess of Londonderry, had formerly been married
to Mark Birley, founder of the smartest of London nightclubs
which he named after her. Glamorous, popular and sociable, Lady
Annabel had two sons and a daughter by Birley, and subsequently
two more sons and a daughter by the fabulously rich Sir James
Goldsmith, international financier and celebrated gambler. Annabel Elliot, Camilla Parker Bowles's sister, was a particular friend of
Annabel's and it was at her birthday party at the Goldsmith house,
Ormeley Lodge, on Ham Common, that Diana's face-to-face
interview with Camilla had taken place. The Camilla connection
was, in a perverse way, an attraction for Diana, as was later the
marriage of Annabel's beautiful daughter Jemima to Imran Khan,
when the Pakistani connection became important to her.

Annabel was a contemporary of Diana's mother, Frances, and
had known her well. Her own children ranged from Rupert Birley,
born in 1955, to the youngest, Zac Goldsmith, born in 1980,
and with nephews, nieces and stepchildren the Goldsmith house
supplied a wonderful family atmosphere which attracted Diana.
Ben Goldsmith was only just over two years older than William,
and Diana would bring the children with her to marathon Sunday
lunches at Ormeley. Or she would come alone to relax and be
herself – witty, funny and charming. 'Oh, she could be funny,' an
observer said. 'She'd walk in on Sunday lunch, sweep in, rush in,
kiss all the staff, come running in and sit down, and she'd have us
all in stitches, and sometimes she would bring the boys and they
would go off and play tennis, and sometimes she'd send William
down because she said William was like a caged lion [at Kensington
Palace].'3

The Brazilian Ambassadress, Lucia Flecha de Lima, was even
closer to Diana: the embassy on Mount Street was a refuge for her
and she often spent weekends there. The Ambassador, Paulo Tarso,

and his wife and children were almost a second family to her. Beautiful, chic, forthright and outgoing, Lucia was a loyal and candid friend. Only once did they fall out when Lucia told Diana off over something she had done and Diana got on her royal high horse. With Lucia, Annabel and the other older women she liked and trusted, such as Marguerite Littman and Pamela Harlech, Diana never showed her darker side; she was always funny, charming, light-hearted, although there were times when she did reveal to Lucia her misery over her marriage and her anger about what she saw as Charles's unkindness. Diana confided copies of Prince Philip's letters to Lucia for safe keeping; Rosa Monckton, apparently, helped draft her replies.

The letters were written over the months following the publication of the Morton book, with which, Prince Philip had told Diana, she had destroyed everything. Diana was furious at his criticism but in fact Prince Philip's letters were a heartfelt attempt to put things right. Appealing to her sense of duty, he told her how, when he (referring to himself as 'Pa' and the Queen as 'Ma') and the Queen had married, they had thought that they would have a few years ahead of them to live their own life but then, when the Queen's father died, the Queen had had to renounce her own family life and he had to give up his own career for the sake of the family. He wanted Charles and Diana to stay together but living separate lives while continuing with their duties. He said that Charles's behaviour with Camilla was really wrong – he even, apparently, expressed surprise that Charles could prefer someone of Camilla's looks and age to Diana. Touchingly, he wrote how 'Ma and I' were very worried about the situation.[4] 'Contrary to what people say, she [Diana] got on very well with Prince Philip,' a friend said. 'She really did. He was nice to her. He said to her once – she thought he was going to tell her off – he tapped her on the shoulder one day and he said, "Now look here, young lady, if you ever think of having an affair for God's sake keep it in the family, where you can keep it quiet." And she was rather taken aback!!' 'And the other thing he said to her when she was in trouble and had started [the divorce proceedings], he

said, "Now if you're a bad girl, you are going to lose your title."
And she said "No, Pa, no I can't, because I've already got one",
which was quite funny and he laughed.'⁵ 'The Queen and Prince
Philip were never at loggerheads with Diana as people made out,'
a courtier said. Diana continued to take the boys to tea with their
grandmother, although it was a cause of sadness to her that the
two of them were not on the same wavelength when it came to
conversation. Indeed, one courtier described the Queen as 'frigid'
when Diana and the boys came to tea, but it was not so much
frigidity as shyness and a certain awkwardness. It was also partly
generational: the Queen's view of bringing up children and Diana's
could hardly have been more different. Once at Balmoral, when
William was small, his nanny was on holiday and Diana naturally
looked after him, the Queen's reaction was one of surprise: 'I
don't understand why Diana has to do this; there are millions of
housemaids around.' Princess Margaret, who had liked Diana from
the beginning and tried to help her with the details of her public
role, sympathized with her in her marital troubles which she herself
had experienced, remaining friendly with Diana even after the
Morton affair, telling Prince Charles, whom she adored, 'I'm not
going to give her up. I like her and she's my friend.' And when
Diana sent her a Hermès scarf as a birthday present in August 1993,
Princess Margaret's letter of thanks began 'Darling Diana'. The
Snowdon children, David Linley and Sarah Armstrong-Jones, both
adored Diana.

By this time, Diana had become involved in another affair: with
Oliver Hoare, a handsome Old Etonian dealer in Islamic art,
married to a French heiress, Diane de Waldner. Hoare was charming and universally popular. He and his wife were friends of Prince
Charles and, ironically, Hoare had come into Diana's life as a result
of his efforts to mediate between her and the Prince in 1991. 'He
is the most charming man,' a friend said. 'He is really fascinating
. . . I think Diana picked him because he was one of Charles's
good friends. His interests are Charles's interests. He loves art, he
loves literature, very much like Charles, you know.'⁶ 'Oliver Hoare
was divine, and charming,' a friend said, 'but what was appalling

was that he was a great friend of Prince Charles's, they used to go on holiday together with Derek Hill, the painter and Charles's friend and artistic mentor, going to Italy and looking at Islamic stuff. I'm very fond of Oliver but he's always been badly behaved. His behaviour was absolutely atrocious. And poor old Prince Charles didn't know it was going on until afterwards.'[7]

Diana had first met Oliver Hoare with his wife during Ascot week at Windsor in the mid-eighties. Diane Hoare's parents, Baron Geoffroi de Waldner and his wife Louise, were friends of the Queen Mother. Rich, Anglophile and, like Queen Elizabeth, racing enthusiasts, they fitted perfectly into the Ascot racing scene. Louise de Waldner owned a chateau in the South of France where Charles often went to paint and, later, to rendezvous with Camilla. Oliver, glamorous though penniless, had a cosmopolitan background. He was only distantly related to the rich English banking family of the same name. His mother, Irina, was a Czech émigrée, his father, Reginald, an English civil servant who had managed to send their son to Eton and then to the Sorbonne. Beyond his Etonian charm and manners, Hoare had an exotic, bohemian background: at one point in his life he had become a part of Rudolph Nureyev's uninhibited circle before rejoining the Establishment as head of the Islamic department at Christie's London auction house. He had a wide circle of friends, including David Sulzberger of the *New York Times* dynasty who became his business partner, and whom he had met in Tehran where he had learned Arabic and Persian and begun to collect Middle Eastern art and antiquities. He had in fact begun his career there as a protégé of a beautiful, influential older woman, Harmoush Bowler, a princess of the Hajar dynasty. 'She was a very rich Iranian lady of great style and elegance,' said a friend, 'and Oliver was somebody she discovered. She taught him all about the Orient and the arts and everything like that. He went on with it but she was the first to interest him in it. I remember him sitting at her feet playing the guitar . . .' 'She was very generous. And so Oliver really made himself. Oliver was self-made and very beautiful.'[8]

Hoare married the striking and intelligent Diane de Waldner in

1976, but subsequently had a four-year affair with Ayesha Gul, a fascinating Turkish woman, married to the controversial tycoon Asil Nadir. Oliver Hoare, with his thick dark hair, mobile, attractively lined features and articulate charm, appealed to both sexes. Although quite unlike the men Diana had previously been attracted to, she was drawn to Hoare from the first, while his interest in ballet gave them a bond in common. Oliver and Diane became friends of the couple, as they also were of Andrew and Camilla Parker Bowles. Diana found him fascinating not only for his physical attractions but his status as a friend of Charles's which would give their relationship added piquancy, as did the fact that the Hoares were friends of Camilla. On the other side of the coin, Hoare's Turkish contacts provided him with safe houses, and even a yacht, where he could carry on his romance with Diana.[9]

As with James Hewitt, secretive Diana managed to keep knowledge of her relationship with Oliver Hoare from the newspapers. Even the frequency with which she called Hoare – as often as twenty times a day, beginning in September 1992 – remained a secret for another two years.[10] She called him in his car, and apparently made a string of anonymous calls to his home as many as twenty times a week, some as late as midnight. She would wait until Hoare answered and then hang up. The couple met at the homes of Diana's friends the Flecha de Limas and another of her mother figures, Elsa, Lady Bowker. On other occasions, Diana would smuggle him into Kensington Palace – either in the boot of her green Rover with blacked-out windows or driven in by Paul Burrell under a blanket. These cloak-and-dagger operations were a waste of time: Kensington Palace being the heavily guarded small village that it is, there was no question of keeping his visits secret. According to one of Princess Margaret's staff: 'this business where Burrell kept saying he used to sneak people into the Palace was an absolute joke, because one, the policeman on the gate knew exactly what he was doing bringing people in under the blanket and then he [Burrell] would drive into Princess Margaret's courtyard which hasn't got security cameras but everyone knows what's going on because as you go into the courtyard there's an old drain and every time a car hits it it goes, clonk, clonk, clonk. So sometimes Princess Margaret would go and see who it was for herself . . . And she [Diana] would park outside Princess Margaret's offices and then this chap would run in and of course all the staff upstairs would see him. It was no secret at all . . .'[11] 'She'd drive in sometimes and Princess Margaret would say, "Whose is that car?" knowing full well whose it was. "Go and find out who it is." And I'd have to go over and tap the window and she'd open it very gingerly and I'd say, "Why don't you go away?" . . . And then I'd have to tell a downright lie to Princess Margaret. I'd say the driver doesn't know where he's going but I've told him to go off round the corner . . . but she knew I was telling lies . . .' 'And then the next time I saw her [Diana] I'd say, "Look, you're far better off bringing people right to your front door . . . because nobody would bat an eyelid . . ."'[12] Ken Wharfe, Diana's protection officer, told the same story. 'An old uniformed police sergeant said to me, "Got a bit of a security problem, sir . . . The Princess came in the other night, sir . . . a man got out of the boot, sir." I said, "Who was that?" "Well, I think it was Mr Hoare, sir." The cloak-and-dagger act, both witnesses said, was Burrell's idea: 'Burrell actually said, "The best way to get him in is in the boot of a car." And stupidly she did it. I said, "Look, Ma'am, this is not a good idea. If you think you're going to get away with it, you're not."'[13] Wharfe and Hoare, according to the former, heartily disliked each other, so Wharfe greatly enjoyed an incident in 1993 when the smoke alarm shrilled through the apartments at Kensington Palace at 3.30 a.m. In the hallway of Diana's apartment he found a 'dishevelled' Hoare puffing on a cigar. Diana, who hated the smell of smoke, had obviously told him to smoke in the hallway, forgetting that this would set the alarms off.[14]

'Next morning,' Wharfe wrote, 'I tried to make a joke of the incident. Diana, however, clearly did not want to talk about it. So when I suggested that she had been playing cards, perhaps strip poker, she flushed scarlet and went back to her room.' 'No doubt,' he went on, 'I had overstepped the mark, but by this time she was already in danger of losing all sense of perspective. She knew this, yet she was not prepared to admit it, and I realized that, where I was concerned, it could only be a matter of time before there was a parting of the ways . . .'[15]

According to Ken Wharfe, who was in a position to monitor the comings and goings of Diana's men, Diana, as she confessed to him, 'absolutely adored' Oliver Hoare to the point of obsession. Her love for him – which was reciprocated ('He loved her very much,' a close friend said), her romantic hopes for a future together which could never be realized, and the difficulties she always experienced in sustaining a relationship – formed the background to her life over the next three years. 'I think Hoare was instrumental in a lot that changed the course of the Princess's life,' said Wharfe.[16]

In the year after the separation, Diana came to realize clearly that, rather than the freedom she had hoped for, she was more constrained than she had ever been. The Palace, in the form of Robert Fellowes, his deputy Robin Janvrin and press secretary Charles Anson, were not inimical to her and were always willing to help if possible. Her 'team', comprising her private secretary Patrick Jephson and the popular Australian Geoff Crawford, seconded to be her press secretary, were utterly loyal. John Major and the members of his government were sympathetic. But beyond them were 'the friends of Charles' looking for every false step she might make and resentful of her popularity. To combat them, and to maintain her all-important position in the heart of the British people, Diana had recourse to the weapon which she wielded with consummate skill – the press. And as allies in the continuing war against Charles, Diana enlisted powerful individuals, media figures, editors, pundits and opinion makers, who fell easy victim to her beauty, wit and alluring charm.

Complementing the stream of therapists, psychics and their like whom Diana continued to favour in her unending quest to understand herself and find peace of mind, a number of influential men from the media came to lunch at Kensington Palace to dispense their wisdom and guide her in her public career. David

Puttnam, Jacob Rothschild, Peter Palumbo, Paul Johnson, Clive
James, Gordon Reece, Max Hastings, Piers Morgan and Auberon
Waugh were among the figures whose advice she sought and
usually, characteristically, ignored.

One recalled: 'The two things I particularly stressed to her were,
one, have absolutely nothing to do with the media under any
circumstances – and she was very shocked at this – and I said,
"You think that you can manipulate them but in fact that is not
how it works. They will end by manipulating you and by distress-
ing you and by destroying you as they always do. And there is no
absolute defence against them because we live in a country where
the media are on top now . . . The best possible defence against
them for somebody in your position is to have nothing to do with
them. Never speak to them under any circumstances. That will
minimize the danger and damage they can do to you. She agreed
. . . but of course she didn't because she thought she could
[manipulate them], so they got her.

'The second thing I said was "No sex". I said, "That is absolutely
fatal. You'll have to do without it and be very virginal and so on,
and, if you don't like it – hard cheese." That made her laugh and
she said, "Oh, you're so right, absolutely", and the next thing you
knew she was in bed with x . . .'[17]

The *Telegraph* editor, Max Hastings, not known for his suscepti-
bility to women, found himself unable to resist invitations to
Kensington Palace, his low opinion of the Prince of Wales making
him more open to the Princess. Diana had wangled an introduction
to him through her friends Peter and Hayat Palumbo and had
charmed him as thoroughly as she did most men, as he wrote in
his diary: 'I was obliged to acknowledge . . . that like others of my
kind, I found myself unable to keep my distance . . . Diana . . .
had become a masterly media lobbyist. Selected journalists and
editors were regularly invited to see her. Most of us deluded
ourselves that we were offering her advice. I am not aware of any
instance in which she acted upon any of the sage words that were
offered. But of course, she charmed us brilliantly.'[18]

Anthony Holden, writing in *Vanity Fair*, detected a master plan to establish Diana in her own right: 'Diana's staff is discreetly orchestrating a rapid move to centre stage, an upgrading from minor to major player in a drama whose plot gets thicker every time',[19] citing as an example Diana's stunningly successful solo visit to Paris the previous November when she had been feted by President Mitterrand as if she were a Head of State and not a mere 'semi-detached member of the Royal Family'. Diana wanted a role as ambassador-at-large, and courted John Major and sympathetic ministers like the Foreign Secretary, Douglas Hurd (and subsequently his successor, Malcolm Rifkind). As Foreign Secretary and therefore in a position to authorize and assist her foreign excursions, Hurd was a particular target. At a European summit in Edinburgh just two days after the announcement of her separation, Hurd described Diana in his memoirs as 'bestowing that special mixture of beauty and charm which melted men's bones. Presidents, prime ministers and foreign ministers as they dined could make no sense of what was happening in our Royal Family,' he wrote, 'but were content to bask for an hour or two in an extraordinary radiance.'[20] Hurd wrote that there was never any question of her having a formal appointment as a roving ambassador but that the good causes with which she was associated wanted her help overseas and she was keen to provide it. 'She looked to me for support in just one matter important to her . . . her overseas work. I was glad, or more accurately, enchanted, to give it.'[21]

In March, Diana toured Nepal to view British aid projects in the official company of the minister concerned, Lynda Chalker. While Prince Charles, attended by a much reduced press pack, was pictured glumly trying his hand at peasant farming in Mexico, the Princess, against the more colourful background of Kathmandu, attracted a good deal of media attention, much of which focused on the non-playing of the national anthem when she arrived, interpreted as a Palace downgrading of Diana, which it was not. This was a simple working visit, not a state occasion, and the absence of the anthem had passed without notice on similar visits to Egypt, Pakistan and Hungary before the separation. While Douglas Hurd was at pains to stress that at no time did the Palace seek to downgrade Diana or cut her contact with the Foreign Office, St James's Palace, the Prince's office, was a different matter altogether. At a party held in St James's around the time of Diana's Nepal visit, ostensibly concerning historic buildings in Prague, a guest was 'absolutely appalled that all that had happened at this party was people trashing Diana; they never talked about historic buildings in Prague at all'.[22]

As with Nepal, Diana's tour of Zimbabwe in July was a resounding success. Diana had taken care not only to keep the Queen informed of her plans but also Princess Anne, who had made charitable visits to Africa her particular territory. Nor did she seek to meet Heads of State as of right; she had no need to. A beaming Robert Mugabe told the press: 'She brings a little light into your life . . . naturally you feel elated, you feel good!'[23] The presence and cooperation of the top management of Diana's three charities relevant to her tour – the Red Cross, Help the Aged and the Leprosy Mission – gave the visit a serious, humanitarian aspect. On a visit to a hospice for children orphaned by AIDS, Diana wept: none of the children was over five years old and none was expected to reach the age of six.[24] Comments by the more respected correspondents on the tour emphasized the need for Diana's work to be taken seriously. Robert Hardman, then court correspondent for the *Daily Telegraph*, a newspaper usually expected to take the 'traditional', sceptical, view of Diana wrote approvingly: 'The latest tour has been a public relations triumph not just for her favourite charities but for the Princess herself. Africa, until now the undisputed realm of the Princess Royal [Anne], has a new champion . . .' He also delivered a warning on behalf of his more sophisticated and cynical readers: 'Visits are vital if the Princess is to maintain her world profile and thus continue the work she sees as her mission. But she will need to use them sparingly and vary the diet. Too much of what cynics call the Mother Teresa routine could lead to compassion indigestion by the media . . .'[25]

Yet Diana was sincere in her compassion, despite the 'Mother Teresa' moments. From Harare she flew out to the Red Cross

Mazerera feeding centre in the bush. Diana stood by a huge iron cooking pot doling out food to tiny children who had trekked seven miles on foot for their only meal of the day. It made a great photo opportunity – one British newspaper ran the headline 'DINNER LADY' – DIANA SERVES UP ROYAL TREAT FOR HUNGRY CHILDREN' – but, Ken Wharfe recalled, she was close to tears as she recounted her experiences of the day, knowing that she was going back to her comfortable life while the children were returning to poverty, drought and hunger. 'Those who believe that Diana's work was nothing more than a series of photo-opportunities in glamorous locations around the world,' he wrote, 'should have seen this drained, exhausted woman sitting in the back of the helicopter that day and heard her speak of the heart-breaking scenes she had just witnessed.'[26]

At home, Diana concentrated on women's issues to which she could relate. Determined to be seen as a professional, she employed a voice coach, Peter Settelen, to teach her voice techniques to improve her public speaking. She visited the Chiswick Family Refuge for women victims of domestic violence in April 1993, following it up with several visits and attendance at a high-profile conference on domestic violence at the Queen Elizabeth II Conference Centre. A visit to Great Ormond Street Hospital, where she learned more about a subject close to her – eating disorders in young women – led to her speech in Kensington Town Hall in April 1993 which was widely publicized and brought eating disorders to the top of the public agenda. Diana was delighted with the speech, not only because Settelen had taught her how to express emotion in public speaking (too much so in the view of Diana's aides) but because she had come close to expressing her personal experience and suffering. As patron of the charity Turning Point, she spoke at a conference in June 1993 about the need for support of mentally ill women. The conference was chaired by Libby Purves who said, 'The [Princess] is one of us, a wife, a mother, a daughter who has known problems in her own life and who has courageously used these experiences to comfort other people.' It did not escape the general public that no other member cf the Royal Family would have addressed personal issues in such a way.

On the world, or rather the European, stage, Diana's march towards acceptance as a major figure continued. In company with the Crown Prince of Luxembourg she attended a British trade fair; in Brussels as patron of Help the Aged she attended events and discussed provision for the elderly with the EU Commissioner for Social Affairs, took tea with Queen Fabiola and attended a reception at the British Ambassador's residence. In London, at the invitation of Conrad Black, she was a guest at the Hollingsworth dinner at Spencer House, which her family still owned, among a crowd of all the top people in the British and American media, and in Cambridge she laid the foundation stone of the new Queen's Building at Emmanuel College at the invitation of Lord St John of Fawsley. 'All over the system which operated the interfaces between royalty and government,' Jephson summed up her achievements for the year, 'the simple reality was dawning that the Princess of Wales remained a major player, certainly in media terms.'

One of her last public engagements of 1993 served as a reminder of the quasi-royal status she had maintained through her own efforts that year. With the Queen's approval she headed the Remembrance Day service in Enniskillen, Northern Ireland. The ceremony was given additional poignancy by the memory of the same service in the same place six years before when eleven people had been blown up by an IRA bomb. The square still bore the scars of that terrible day, as did many of the people standing there. Diana, slim, elegant and solemn, stood at the head of the mourners and soldiers, prime target of a terrorist attack had there been another one. During the two minutes' silence, a pair of swans flew directly overhead, silhouetted against the clear winter sky. 'Did you see the birds?' she asked Jephson. 'It was so moving. I couldn't help feeling they meant something.' 'You mean the spirit of the dead?' he asked. 'Yes. Something like that. Or peace.'[27]

But underneath the smoothly regal exterior, the conflicting currents of her private life were pushing her towards yet another

self-destructive, contradictory decision. Another door closed on
her former life with the death that summer of Ruth Fermoy. Lady
Fermoy had been deeply upset by the Morton book and the
separation, ashamed in front of her fellow courtiers that her own
granddaughter should have been responsible for going public with
the details of her unhappy marriage. Even before the Morton
bombshell, Diana had regarded her grandmother as siding with her
enemies, telling Morton that on the Queen Mother's ninetieth
birthday (4 August 1990) the atmosphere had been 'grim and
stilted'. 'They are all anti-me,' she added. 'My grandmother has
done a good hatchet job on me.'[28] There had been several angry
exchanges between them in the past, and at one point, after Ruth
had been particularly critical of her behaviour, Diana threw her
grandmother out of the house. As Lady Fermoy was dying, Diana
made two visits to her, so at least she was on terms with her
when she did die. She flew to Lady Fermoy's funeral with her
grandmother's old friend and employer, the Queen Mother, who
undoubtedly shared her lady-in-waiting's view of Diana's behaviour. The previous month she had closed another old feud,
with Raine, Countess Spencer, inviting her to lunch at Kensington
Palace with her new husband, the Comte de Chambrun. The two
women now got on famously and frequently lunched together
over the following years. The reconciliation was part of Diana's
campaign to clear her life of past unpleasantness wherever she
could. An element in the reconciliation may also have been Diana's
urge to spite her brother Charles after a recent row.

As part of her new life Diana had envisaged a country house as
a bolt hole from the fortress of Kensington Palace, somewhere she
could take the boys during holiday times and the weekends which
they spent with her. In June her brother Charles had offered her
the Garden House on the Althorp estate at a rent of £12,000 a
year. Diana rushed down with Dudley Poplak to make plans for
the house, highly excited at the prospect of a new home of her
own. A fortnight later her hopes were dashed when her brother
wrote withdrawing his offer on the grounds that the police and
press interference caused by her presence on the estate would make

family life impossible at Althorp, and suggesting she should rent a farmhouse outside the park if she wanted to. 'Diana used to say "At least my family never let me down",' said one of her staff. 'And then they did.' When the letter arrived she called the member of staff (it was not, as Paul Burrell later alleged, himself) upstairs and showed him the letter, dreadfully upset. She was devastated, then angry, writing her brother a letter in which she no doubt expressed her feelings as strongly as she could. When he telephoned she slammed down the receiver, and when Charles Spencer received her letter he returned it unopened, with the comment that he doubted whether reading it 'would help our relationship'.[29] Communication between them ceased for a few months, and it seems their relationship was never quite the same as it had been before the Garden House row. In the opinion of Ken Wharfe, who, as the Princess's protection officer, was in a position to know: 'Spencer couldn't have been more helpful. He offered her the house on the estate which was actually too small and I actually said it was too near the perimeter fence. He even offered her his house, the Pheasantry, within the grounds of his estate . . . [but] the local police were having heart attacks by the day and when they did present their security plans I said, "Well, maybe they have a case" . . .'[30] Significantly, in view of future developments, the episode strengthened her determination to get rid of her police protection. 'He [Spencer] has a point,' she told Ken Wharfe despondently. 'Why would anyone want the fuss that goes with me?'[31]

Another disagreement took place between Diana and two of her closest friends that spring. Known as 'the Leap of Lech' it was a reckless move even by Diana's impetuous standards. At the end of March 1993, Diana took her boys skiing in a party which included her friends Catherine Soames and Kate Menzies and their children. The reaction of the international paparazzi was a foretaste of the problem which was to dog Diana until the end. Diana was a cash cow to the photographers who competed fiercely with each other to get the best, that is, the closest and most dramatic, shot. Not content with a photo opportunity on the slopes, they crowded round the Princess and her sons as they entered the Hotel Arlberg where they were staying. Diana, unusually for her, began to panic, screaming 'Go Away' at the paparazzi. Ken Wharfe stepped in and pushed one particularly persistent man to the ground; there followed a mêlée during which Wharfe was able to shepherd Diana and the boys inside. Diana, Wharfe said, was on an emotional see-saw throughout the holiday. 'Her feelings about Hoare had unsettled her. She was falling out with everybody right, left and centre, seemingly unable to help herself . . . She had always been erratic but in the past she had invariably pulled herself back from the brink.'[32] Not this time. In the small hours of the morning, when all the hotel's outside doors were firmly locked, Diana jumped from her first-floor balcony, a twenty-foot drop, into deep snow and took off without informing any of her protection squad.

She returned at 5.30 in the morning. Immediate speculation was that she had gone to meet Oliver Hoare, who was staying at Zurs, but had she done that she would have had to take a taxi, and the whole adventure would have been too risky even for risk-taking Diana. A more likely hypothesis was that she was escaping from her party in order to meet a journalist with whom she was on close terms. Kate Menzies and Catherine Soames were in Diana's confidence. They knew about James Hewitt and no doubt about Oliver Hoare and they would have understood a romantic escapade; but contact with a journalist, however honourable he might be, was another matter altogether. Apparently they told Diana exactly what they thought, which did not please her. Diana, like her separated husband, did not take criticism well.

Underlying Diana's actions at this period was her media war with her husband. Even holidays with the boys could be turned to her advantage. Pictures showing her at Disneyland, Florida, or on the beach with William and Harry would serve to underline in the public mind what a good mother she was, the subtext being comparison with her selfish, uncaring husband. Arriving at Disneyland in August 1993, Ken Wharfe noted that Diana's chief channel to the media, Richard Kay, was booked to arrive the same day as Diana, at the same hotel, and that the booking had been made on the very day Diana had told Wharfe she would like to go to Florida. Unfortunately for the British press, although they had been mysteriously alerted to her movements, the Disney system of VIP security frustrated them: not one photograph appeared in the press. Moving on to the Menzies' house on the smart development of Lyford Cay in the Bahamas, Diana still appeared angry and upset by a telephone call from her lawyer which reminded her of the problems with her husband awaiting her back home. She made attempts to be photographed which, for security reasons, Wharfe frustrated. 'I'll do what I want,' she told him. 'I think it's so unfair that I can't do what I want. I just want to be normal . . .'[33]

On their return to England, Diana began to give Wharfe the cold shoulder, the inevitable preamble to dismissal. The atmosphere between them became so frosty that Wharfe decided to jump before he was pushed. It had been building up for some time: Wharfe's attempts to prevent her doing what she wanted, however unwise, and his readiness to criticize her when she was going wrong, had angered the Princess. Others speculated that the parting had come because Wharfe knew too much about her, having seen her in some very unroyal situations. Wharfe himself speculated that Oliver Hoare had had a hand in it, as the two men disliked each other and Wharfe had first-hand knowledge of their affair. Another member of the Waleses' staff, her chauffeur, Simon Solari, left at around the same time as Wharfe. Like Wharfe, he had become the subject of her suspicions since, as her driver, he knew a great deal about her movements and she began to wonder whether he could be trusted not to betray her. He therefore elected to change to working for the Prince as one of his valets. As such he too was to fall foul of Michael Fawcett.

Perhaps the last straw was Wharfe's attitude to the 'gym photos' affair when photographs of Diana working out at a gym – LA Fitness in west London – originally taken in May 1993, were published in the *Sunday Mirror* in November. The 'Peeping Tom' pictures caused an outcry against the *Mirror* for invading Diana's privacy and she took legal action against the newspaper. Wharfe suspected – and he was not alone – that Diana had colluded with

Bryce Taylor, the owner of the gym, to have the pictures taken to use against the *Mirror*. 'I remain convinced,' he wrote, 'that she had invented an elaborate sting to ensnare a newspaper and then milk the publicity – and the public's sympathy – for all they were worth.'[34] Wharfe knew Diana well enough by then to understand that such a devious plan was not beyond her. Yet, despite everything that had passed between them, the loyal detective appreciated Diana's unique qualities: 'She was a truly inspirational woman who had the ability to change things for the better. She knew how to lift people from the greyness of normality and make them feel truly special. She did the same with me.'[35]

Despite colluding in these invasions of privacy – as she undoubtedly did in manipulating the media to ensure the maximum publicity for herself – Diana was becoming increasingly resentful over her lack of a private life and the demands made on her by her public role. She felt that she could no longer bear the restrictions of having a protection officer always with her, aware of her every move, in power over her to the extent that either the media or her husband could reveal her private life and its secrets. In November, in the wake of the gym photos furore, she decided on a second headstrong, reckless step on the path to self-destruction. In a single speech on 3 December, delivered at the Dorchester at a meeting in aid of the Headway Foundation, she threw overboard all the good work she had done that year in establishing a role for herself. She intended, she said, to withdraw to a considerable extent from public life: 'I hope you can find it in your hearts to understand and to give me the time and space that has been lacking in recent years . . .' she said. 'When I started my public life twelve years ago, I understood that the media might be interested in what I did. I realized that their attention would inevitably focus on . . . our private lives. But I was not aware of how overwhelming that attention would become; nor the extent to which it would affect both my public duties and my personal life in a manner that's been hard to bear . . .'

While she emphasized that her decision had the backing of the Queen and Prince Philip (who had in fact, without success, attempted to prevent her from injecting so much drama into her decision) she conspicuously omitted mentioning Prince Charles, whose publicity campaign against her, she implied, had had much to do with her decision.

When she sat down, obviously upset, with her head down, biting her lip, tears sprang to her eyes. The main beneficiaries of Diana's high profile – the media and charity organizations – were bewildered. One pressman expressed their feelings when he asked rhetorically, 'Have we killed the goose that lays the golden eggs?' It did not take long for the tabloids to find the villain of the piece: 'CHARLES FORCED DIANA TO GO: SAD PRINCESS QUITS PUBLIC LIFE' was the *Sun*'s headline, its theme being that 'the campaign to downgrade' Diana and Charles's 'sophisticated propaganda machine' had driven her out. But, as usual with Diana, the motives for her dramatic decision were not quite so simple.

15. The Inconsequential Years

'If I can't believe what I've been told about her . . . then I can't believe any of it' (Jonathan Dimbleby[1])

As always with Diana there were many motives that had persuaded her to announce her withdrawal from public life. One was that she truly felt she needed 'time and space' for herself. Since the separation, she had carried on alone, trying to keep up with the public work so necessary for maintaining her profile, making an effort for her public, fighting her media war with her husband and seeking to manipulate her own publicity. In the white glare of the media spotlight she had become anxious that people close to her should remain loyal, should not reveal the darker corners of her life. She had become, to some extent, paranoid. It is easy to blame her for her publicity seeking; her determination to make a public drama of her withdrawal with the Headway speech had caused consternation to her aides and Buckingham Palace and there had been anxious conferences over the drafting of her speech in an effort to tone down its effect.

There is no doubt that Diana was under extreme pressure. The separation had left her lonely, abandoned, bitter, sad and uncertain of the future. 'I think she always had this issue within herself,' said the daughter of one of her closest friends, 'which was "I want to be the Princess of Wales, I want to be Charles's wife and I want to have a normal family life". Finally she didn't have any of that. She was no longer Charles's wife. It's very hard to find a role for yourself and she wanted to be loved, she was constantly seeking approval, constantly, there was not a minute off. And I think she felt she was rejected by her mother; her mother left, her husband left her and I don't think it's easy for a woman in her position to have so much pressure, to have so many eyes on you that analyse everything you do every single day. I would have gone bonkers myself.'[2]

In her quest for personal freedom, Diana took the step which was ultimately to have fatal implications: she dispensed with her right to police protection. If it momentarily gave her a feeling of liberation, it also left her open to persecution by the paparazzi who became increasingly merciless. Only a few months later, in May 1994, flying out to Malaga on a private holiday with friends, she found herself totally unprotected on arrival at the airport and things did not improve over the rest of the holiday when she was stalked with long-range lenses. One photographer succeeded in getting a 'topless' photograph of Diana sunbathing when she adjusted a strap. Eduardo Junco, proprietor of *Hola!*, the original model of *Hello!*, picked up news of the photographs and bought them to prevent their publication. In London photographs were taken of her panic-stricken dodging round parked cars outside the house of her therapist, Susie Orbach, and in other places where she could be expected to be found. All of this was a direct consequence of her dismissal of her protection officers, and the situation was to become worse.

And there was a personal reason. Asked why Diana had taken the decision when she did, a close friend said: 'Because at that moment she thought she'd be able to have a normal life with someone else . . . That was her explanation at the time.'[3] The 'someone else' was Oliver Hoare. The 'anonymous' telephone calls to Hoare's house had resumed in 1993. Naturally, Diane Hoare became angry and suspicious, as his chauffeur later told the newspapers. Around the time of Diana's speech, she threw her husband out and he retreated to a friend's flat in Pimlico. The move no doubt raised Diana's hopes of a happy ending. Her confidante Elsa Bowker, to whom Hoare had introduced her, told Diana's biographer that Diana wanted to marry Hoare and buy a house in Italy with him. Hoare had told Elsa Bowker that he thought Diana 'was radiant inside and he loved that'; he had, Bowker said, 'done a lot for her. He helped give her confidence but it was never enough. Diana had wonderful qualities of heart but she was terribly possessive. If she loved someone, he had to leave everything, including children. Her possessiveness frightened men. Everything became a drama.'⁴ As Sally Bedell Smith told it, Oliver Hoare was confronted with the magnitude of Diana's insecurities one evening when his wife was away and he had to be with his sick daughter. Diana refused to believe that this was not an excuse to go and see his wife and, as he was driving her home, she jumped out of the car in a traffic jam in Sloane Square and disappeared. Hoare was so worried that he never got to see his daughter, instead spending three hours driving round London looking for Diana. He finally found her weeping in Kensington Gardens near the Palace.⁵

In January 1994, after a two-month separation. Hoare returned to his wife. Diana can no longer have been under the illusion that he would leave his wife and children. 'He is a very good father, a good person,' a mutual friend said. 'He always said he could never leave his family.'⁶ The relationship continued nonetheless and was noted by the media: In December 1993 they had been seen sitting together in his car for an hour, Diana's head on his shoulder. They breakfasted together at 7 a.m. at the Chelsea Harbour Club where Diana was currently working out, and in March 1994 they were caught by a photographer driving into Kensington Palace after dinner with a friend. The theme was still favourable, rather than prurient. Diana, one newspaper reported, was tearfully pouring out her heart to her loyal friend.⁷ More dangerously still, after Hoare returned to his wife in January the silent calls to his house had resumed. By now, after complaints from the Hoares the previous October, the police had equipped their telephone with a computerized code that could activate tracers. Over the next six days the police had tracked a dozen silent calls made between 8 a.m. and midnight originating from Kensington Palace and Diana's mobile telephone.⁸ When, on police advice, Hoare challenged Diana by name, the calls stopped for a while but then started up again, traced to public telephone booths in Kensington and Notting Hill. Scotland Yard alerted the head of the Royalty and Diplomatic Protection Department; a message was conveyed from the Palace to Kensington Palace, intimating that a prosecution under nuisance call laws might be considered. The calls stopped but Diana's relationship with Oliver Hoare had continued.

Andrew Morton, who was preparing a follow-up book on Diana post-separation (*Diana: Her New Life*) for publication in 1994, asserted that the influence of Diana's astrologers could not be ruled out in the motivation of her decision and its timing. Diana believed that she would never be Queen but, equally, that Charles would never be King, his exit being either voluntary, abdication in favour of William, or involuntary, by accidental death. Recently, apparently, one of them had predicted that, owing to his unpopularity, Charles would have to resign as heir to the throne, leaving that position to William.[9] Another version of this continuing theme was that he would retreat to Italy with Camilla and fulfil himself by painting. Diana saw her eventual role in relation to the monarchy as Queen Mother, guiding the destinies of William, the future King.

'My boys' – or, as Gilbey had put it in the Squidgygate conversation of 1989, the 'lovebugs' – remained the unchanging focus of her life. Both were now boarding at their preparatory school, Ludgrove. When they were away, Diana was lonely at home by herself at Kensington Palace. She deeply missed her greatest friend, Lucia Flecha de Lima, and her family with whom she had been used to spend the weekends, when they left for a new post in Washington in November 1993. When the boys were at home for the prescribed weekends or part holidays, her life revolved around them. Diana has been pictured as an empty-headed woman with no idea beyond her personal benefit, but, perhaps because of her own experience of a hereditary position, and the importance of 'the heir', she understood very well the meaning of the hereditary monarchy and William's place in the scheme of things. Despite her own difficulties with her husband and his family, she was not about to deflect those problems on to her children. She was determined that they should be brought up in as 'normal' (one of her favourite words) a way as possible both at home and in the

world outside. This went beyond expeditions to Thorpe Park
and Disneyland, or shopping expeditions when they, unlike other
members of the Royal Family, paid with their own money; she
took them to share her own experiences of people much less
fortunate than themselves. While some of the Royal Family –
including the boys' father – disapproved of the ultra-democratic
way in which they were brought up, Diana believed it was essential
for them to see life beyond the royal enclave in a way which it
had not been thought important for their father to experience.

William in particular learned to be at ease with the homeless;
later, when Harry was old enough, she involved him too. Diana
had already visited The Passage on her own in June 1989. On
two subsequent occasions, inspired by her friend the Catholic
Archbishop of Westminster, Cardinal Basil Hume, she took first
William and then both boys to The Passage Day Centre and Night
Centre attached to Westminster Cathedral. Diana and William
arrived on 20 December 1993 unannounced; there were no press
with her, nor did the people in The Passage know that she was
coming. Sister Bridie Dowd, director of The Passage at the time,
recalled how, when they walked into The Passage, a long area
with people sitting at tables along the wall, the atmosphere was
electric: 'They just moved to their feet right away. They were so
taken with the fact that she was there.' Diana, shadowed by Sister
Bridie, had difficulty moving among the people and talking to
them because 'they wanted to hold on to her, because she had
that great ability to listen to people and really to make you feel
that she heard every word that you were saying and even what
you weren't saying . . . She made you feel that she was listening
with her eyes as well as her ears. Her eye contact was very very
special . . .'[10]

Diana told Sister Bridie that she 'wanted William to be aware
of the other side of life. She didn't want him to grow up cosseted.
And she had talked to him about it and he had seen photographs
and said he would like to visit. So that was his first visit to any
centre for homeless people. It was before he went to Centrepoint.
And that was a huge thing for him to do because going into The

Passage was very intimidating. There could be a hundred people in The Passage at any one time. People from all walks of life who for one reason or another had experienced difficulties, who had dropped out of society for whatever reason. Some who had been to university . . . two university lecturers, ex-priests, a very broad mix of people . . . Many of them were street homeless, others were homeless living in hostels . . . people who were insecurely housed, people who were lonely or people who had drink problems . . .'[11] 'There were people who have been in the army and when they left just weren't able to cope, two nurses who were not well enough in themselves to keep a job, people whose marriages haven't worked out, people who have been made redundant.' They would be made welcome, given a cup of tea, breakfast, lunch; there were washing facilities, showers and clothing stores, education classes and counselling. And William? 'He was very shy initially and stayed close to Mum for a while,' Sister Bridie said. 'But the people were very good and very sensitive to his needs and talked to him about football. Once he got talking to them he was absolutely fine. He was reserved. He was a child, but you could see the potential there.'[12] Later both William and Harry accompanied their mother to the Night Centre and played chess with the people there. Diana's vision of a popular monarchy was a potent one which was to survive her death, even in an attenuated form.

Diana was concerned for William who was sensitive and to some extent, like his father, a worrier. It was, after all, William on whom she leaned in her unhappy periods, who had listened at doors and heard things it would have been better for him not to have heard. Despite that, theirs was a very normal, not a neurotic relationship. Anybody who has listened to the Settelen tapes broadcast on NBC will have heard the boys jeering their mother good-humouredly when they thought she had gone too far — 'Isn't she *awful*!!' She was less concerned about Harry, a cheeky, cheerful boy who had inherited her optimistic temperament but none of her problems. Sensitive to the fact that the boys' future positions would be so very unequal, she was intent on involving them both in their future role. William would be King but it was important to them both that Harry should be there to support him.

In the background over the two years since the separation were the long drawn-out divorce negotiations, pressed by Charles, fended off at a meeting in October 1993 by Diana, who repeatedly told friends that she did not want to divorce. Both sides manoeuvred to win over public opinion. Since the summer of 1992, Charles's camp had planned a riposte to Andrew Morton's book that would win back the high ground for the Prince. 'Prince Charles wanted it as a justification after the Morton book,' one of his close circle recalled.[13] This was to be a biography by the broadcaster Jonathan Dimbleby, already seen by the Prince as a sympathetic figure for his green views and the fact that he had once worked at Windsor Home Farm. It was to be an authorized book based on interviews with the Prince's friends and staff and use of the Prince's correspondence and diaries. Officially, it was to mark the twenty-fifth anniversary of Charles's investiture as Prince of Wales. It had initially been intended as a television documentary: 'Well, the original concept when I was involved was a celebratory documentary to mark his twenty-fifth anniversary,' recalled Dickie Arbiter. 'Harmless sort of thing, jolly fine fellow, the organizations, bland but big plug for the organizations rather than for the man, because the organizations are the key . . . so we use that vehicle. Then Aylard moved the goalposts. "The Prince has decided that [it should include personal matters]" and I said, "I'm sure the Prince hasn't decided that, I'm sure you've decided, but you do realize it's going to be warts and all?" He said, "Oh, we'll do that." And I said, "Richard, I really do mean WARTS AND ALL." And he said, "Yes, go ahead." So I said, "Well, I'll do your bidding because that's my job to lay on the facilities for the crew, but I don't agree with it."'

The project was given a cautious welcome by the Palace who may have hoped to monitor it – 'fact-checking' – but refused cooperation by Diana's staff who, rightly as it turned out, foresaw that a panegyric to the Prince could hardly fail to be unfavourable to the Princess. The Prince and his camp cannot be blamed for aiming to raise his public profile and to emphasize the good work he did, which was still often derided or ignored. The effect of the Morton book on his reputation had been devastating, and the efforts of his friends through the media had been largely unsuccessful. A tabloid editor said, 'Charles's friends, Romseys, van Cutsems, etc, were at it all the time, ringing me up, giving me stuff . . .'[14] Charles, it seems, could not win. Diana worked her magic even on Jonathan Dimbleby. Although she had refused an interview, exposure to her personality over lunch had its intended effect.

'The Princess,' Jephson wrote, 'put on a great performance in which regality and informality were mixed in proportions that would frustrate the most determined critic. She ate her lunch with obvious enthusiasm and laughingly sympathised with Dimbleby's Herculean task on the Prince's behalf. After she had departed in a cloud of fond farewells, I caught on Jonathan's face the dazed look familiar to me from so many others who had just received her dazzling best . . .'

Asked how the impression he had received compared with what he had been told, he seemed 'momentarily uncomfortable', replying: 'if I can't believe what I've been told about her . . , then I can't believe any of it'.[15]

The programme went out on 29 June 1994. Given the personal content, it seems unlikely that the Palace would have had any input beyond providing facilities. There was apprehension among the Queen's circle, and rightly so, as it turned out. 'He's on a hiding to nothing' was the general opinion, hoping that it might not be even worse. They were as yet unaware of just how personal the programme would turn out to be; those who were begged the Prince not to do it. One of his aides resigned. The main thrust of the programme, the public man, his charities and his views of the causes he believed in, came across as a sympathetic portrait of a good man with serious intentions. The programme was aimed at the young, the future King's constituency, showing the Prince, normally an indifferent television performer, at his best as an environmental crusader, speaking articulately, passionately and without notes. With pop star Phil Collins at a holiday camp organized by his successful inner-city youth help foundation, the Prince's Trust, he appeared at ease and in his element.

Unfortunately, the 'hook' of the programme for which it would always be remembered was his answer to Jonathan Dimbleby's direct question as to whether he had been faithful in his marriage. Charles replied that he had – until his marriage 'had irretrievably broken down'. He went further to describe Camilla Parker Bowles as a 'very dear friend' whom he would continue to see. Nothing could have been calculated to infuriate Diana more. It invited a response and, in due course, one would be forthcoming.

While the general public applauded the Prince for his honesty, people close to the Royal Family, and indeed the Waleses and Camilla, were unanimous in their condemnation. Charles had complained of the media's insensitivity to the feelings of his sons with their 'Charles v Di' stories but here he was on television watched by millions, first pictured relaxing with his sons and then confessing that he had been unfaithful to their mother. The royal establishment from top to bottom was shocked. Chief among Diana's crimes had been 'speaking to the media' but here was the heir to the throne publicly proclaiming his adultery and, not only that, his devotion to his mistress and his intention to carry on exactly as he had been doing in the past. The most charitable view was that he and Diana 'had been driven mad by the media'. 'That's what brought the house down . . . the advice had been "Look, don't talk about your marriage at all, let Jonathan ask you as many questions as he likes but you just say 'Look, my marriage, just like anybody else's, is entirely private'." [He should have said] "It's not your business and it's not the audience's business" and the whole of England would have stood up and said, "Good on you. Absolutely right." So what mileage was there in talking about it? It was a red rag to a bull . . .'[16] At Balmoral Charles asked a close friend, the Duchess of Westminster, what she thought about the interview. 'She was very outspoken and she said, "Well, actually, Sir, I didn't think it was very good" and he got into a frightful rage, didn't speak to her the whole weekend – he's very petty, Charles. He went straight to the private secretary [Aylard], blamed him, just flew at him, he screamed and shouted and yelled at him. I mean Charles is terribly spoiled . . .'17

Whatever the public approval rating may have been, in the words of the Palace aide the interview 'brought the house down' as far as the loyal household staff was concerned. It was indeed 'a red rag to a bull'. Several bulls, to be precise. Talking to the media had been the ultimate sin, inconceivable for a member of the Royal Family to do, and yet here was the heir to the throne admitting his adultery on television and pledging his loyalty to his mistress. Loyal servants were outraged. Charles's valet, Ken Stronach, 'the most loyal and discreet of all' according to colleagues, beside himself, went to a newspaper with damaging stories about Charles and Camilla. He repented and tried to withdraw; the newspaper went ahead anyway. The experience destroyed him. 'The general feeling was,' said his colleague, 'that having been made to sign things and lying down the line for their master, this has been [for them] the ultimate betrayal.'18 Loyal staff, trained to absolute discretion following the example of the Queen and the Duke of Edinburgh, were dismayed, fearing that the monarchy was disintegrating. The reaction of a royal aide who went with a colleague to view the interview was: 'God Save the Queen, long may she reign over us.'

The other consequence of the programme, which in the end was to be more far-reaching in its effect, was Andrew Parker Bowles's decision to divorce Camilla. While he had been perfectly willing to countenance his wife's relationship with Prince Charles as long as it remained discreet – or, at least, not public knowledge – Charles's admission, coming as it did only just a year after the Camillagate tapes, had put their relationship beyond question, placing Parker Bowles in an impossible position. The day after the programme was broadcast, the Prince's private secretary, Richard Aylard, admitted in a press conference that the woman in question was Camilla. In January 1995 Andrew and Camilla Parker Bowles divorced.

Diana feigned indifference. On the evening the programme was shown, she fulfilled a long-standing engagement at the Serpentine

Gallery, photographed wearing a sexy, clinging black dress which showed off her tanned, toned legs. Her whole manner radiated confidence. 'She bounded out of the car in that wonderfully athletic way she had,' Peter Palumbo, who, as chairman of the gallery, was on hand to greet her, recalled.[19] The underlying message was, 'Look at me . . . look what you've thrown away and see how much I care.' The photograph appeared on all the front pages. The *Sun*'s take on it was: 'The Thrilla he left to woo Camilla', accompanied by an unflattering photograph of Camilla. While Diana was angry under the surface, she had a certain admiration for Charles's courage and honesty in revealing what he did, as, it appeared, did the general public. Her own riposte would have to wait until the notorious *Panorama* interview eighteen months later.

Beneath the radiance, Diana was concerned that her media image was slipping: the press knew that Diana manipulated her own publicity, tipping off favoured newspapers as to her whereabouts when she wanted them to be known. She had been hoist with her own petard in early June 1994 when she was photographed having a clandestine rendezvous with Richard Kay of the *Daily Mail* in his parked car. At the instance of his editor, David English, Kay had been assigned to Diana 'as a sympathetic ear' and had been working closely with her since 1993. Tall, lean, good-looking and transparently trustworthy, Kay had become genuinely friendly both with Diana and the Spencer family and had been acting as her media mouthpiece for some time. Jealous rival newspapers now had photographic evidence of her closeness to Kay, and a hypocritical howl of rage went up.

More trouble lay ahead. In March James Hewitt, at Diana's instigation, gave an interview to Anna Pasternak which was published in the *Daily Express*, giving an anodyne account of the relationship. Diana had asked him to talk to Andrew Morton but he had refused, finding in Pasternak what he thought to be a more sympathetic ear. As far as Diana was concerned, Hewitt said, 'It was a pre-emptive strike, but the rumours grew stronger than they were before.' Diana's strategy failed: where she had intended the public to swallow the story of an innocent friendship, Hewitt was roundly condemned for cashing in on their relationship. 'Diana was happy for it to go out,' Hewitt told Bedell Smith. 'But once it backfired, the support I got from her was non-existent . . .' Hewitt had already been ostracized in high-level quarters when knowledge of the affair became widespread. As an officer and a gentleman, it was thought, he should not have contemplated a physical affair with the wife of the heir to the throne. In March he had had to leave the army and his future seemed uncertain. Now Diana had cut him off for doing her bidding. He felt bitter and abandoned; the result would be Pasternak's Mills and Boon-ish version of the affair to be published in October 1994 as *Princess in Love*.

In mid-August 1994 Diana was holidaying with the Flecha de Limas on the fashionable island of Martha's Vineyard off the Massachusetts coast. Sally Bedell Smith, invited to join the party for lunch on the beach, noticed that Diana 'seemed strikingly subdued . . . preoccupied', moving her chair apart from the group to talk intently with her confidante and mentor, Lucia. Later she cut short her holiday and returned home. The reason was that she had learned that the Pasternak book about her affair with James Hewitt, based on the passionate letters she had written him in the Gulf, was to be published in the autumn. She was deeply upset at what she saw as this betrayal, although, had she been shrewd enough not to cut Hewitt, it might have been avoided.

August was not to be a good month in the media for Diana. Quite apart from the Hewitt rumours, the newspapers had picked up on the nuisance calls story with regard to Oliver Hoare: the public were amazed to read of Diana as a 'phone pest' which suggested that she was psychologically unstable. Diana asked Hoare to make a public statement; understandably, in consideration of his family, he refused. Women were understanding, considering that Diana, lonely and in need of reassurance, had wanted to hear Hoare's voice. Yet the fact that Hoare was married with children did show her in an unfavourable light. The scandal subsided but the negative publicity she had attracted and the revelation of her two affairs, which it implied, unnerved her.

Anna Pasternak's account of the Hewitt affair, which confirmed their physical relationship, was published on 3 October. However, Diana escaped lightly: after all, she had been abandoned by Charles for his lover and Hewitt was unmarried, so there was no 'marriage wrecker' shadow hanging over it. The ceiling fell in on Hewitt, who from then on became a tabloid hate figure. 'Love Rat and Cad' declared the *Sun* and it is by these epithets that he is apparently to be forever known. It was, after all, Diana who dumped Hewitt when it no longer suited her and she had found a new interest in Oliver Hoare. Hewitt had fallen genuinely in love with her and, if her later television confession is to be believed, she with him. He had given her confidence through some of her darkest days and she had emerged stronger with her confidence revived. Hewitt was naïve, gullible, the reverse of streetwise. He should have kept his mouth shut and never have allowed himself to be lured into cooperation with Pasternak but he did and paid for it. After that he was dead in the water while Diana sailed radiantly on.

At the time, however, she felt the betrayal deeply. In a letter dated 11 October 1994 to Chryssie Fitzgerald, the reflexologist who also carried out her colonic irrigation treatment, she described what had happened as 'THE toughest week yet I have had to face'; when she had come for her appointment she had been 'in a total state of shock and very distressed about Hewitt's so-called revelations'. She had been equally hurt, she wrote, on hearing what Sarah, Duchess of York, had said about her. The two women shared most of their therapists and psychics – Sarah to an almost excessive degree. Despite their rapprochement over the past two years, when they had made common ground over their troubles with the Royal Family, there was no real depth to their relationship and a considerable tinge of jealousy. Sarah, not infrequently and always unwisely, made her feelings about Diana known, sometimes to whoever answered the telephone at Kensington Palace. In this case she had obviously unburdened herself to Chryssie Fitzgerald. 'I never expected to hear on top of all that [the Hewitt revelations] about someone else's hatred for me & what accompanies those feelings,' Diana wrote. 'It hurt so [double underlined] much to hear from you, Chryssie, that Sarah found me a problem . . .' Chryssie and Diana appear to have parted company around that time, a frequent occurrence where Diana was concerned.

The great publishing event of the autumn was to be Jonathan Dimbleby's biography of the Prince, something to which Diana, with reason, had been looking forward with some apprehension. Dimbleby had done his estimable best to be fair; his remark to Jephson after his lunch with Diana was indicative of the kind of information he had been receiving about her from Charles's circle. It was, of course, the case for Charles, as opposed to Morton's case for Diana. Since Diana herself had first brought her depression, lack of self-confidence, bulimia and attempts at self-harm into the public domain with the Morton book, she could hardly complain about finding them reported in Dimbleby's biography. A quick glance at the index to the book would be enough to reinforce her fears: 'weight loss', volatile behaviour', 'jealousy of Camilla Parker Bowles', 'attempts to control the Prince's life', 'resentment of the Prince's interests', 'self-absorption', 'marriage breaks down irretrievably' . . .[20] This last, Dimbleby, forced to give a date by the Prince's television confession, attributed to 1986, illustrating this particularly with the Prince's failure to sympathize with Diana when she fainted in Canada on their official visit for Expo '86. 'The truth was that he had started to withdraw the support which for so long had drained his reserves of sympathy and compassion.' The truth was, rather, that Charles's failure to respond to her need for affection and his lack of understanding for her predicament (unlike his sympathetic reaction to her sister Sarah's anorexia) had been evident far earlier than the summer of 1986. Basically, the cause of Diana's affliction was not only post-natal depression after the birth of William but her early realization that Charles did not truly love her and that this marriage in which she had invested so much hope could never approximate to her romantic dreams. Charles's true love for Camilla Parker Bowles and his powerful sexual attraction to her above all other women had made those dreams impossible. Charles had abandoned Diana, not she him.

From the point of view of the monarchy, something which
Dimbleby glossed over, the failure of the Waleses' marriage was a
tragedy of missed opportunities.

16. Towards a New World

'A friend . . . once asked her if she gambled. "Not with cards but with life . . ."'[1]

Increasingly, as problems at home mounted, Diana had begun to see a new life for herself in the United States prompted, perhaps, by the refuge which the Flecha de Limas' embassy in Washington represented for her, as a home from home, just as the Mount Street embassy had been for her before they left. Jacqueline Kennedy Onassis's death from non-Hodgkin's lymphoma at the early age of sixty-four on 19 May 1994 had made worldwide news, her iconic status as American royalty confirmed by the solemn public manner of her passing. Mourning spectators and television cameras focused on her Fifth Avenue apartment, retailing pictures round the world. After JFK's assassination in 1963, Jackie, then as pressured by publicity and semi-royal status as Diana now was, had made her escape into the protection of Aristotle Onassis, whose vast wealth, private island and ocean-going yacht could provide her with the privacy she craved. When Jackie had returned to America permanently after Onassis's death, her friends had formed a praetorian guard around her and her quasi-royal status had won her respect and consideration from the paparazzi (with the notable exception of Ron Galella). If Jackie could do it, why couldn't she? Diana thought. Jackie still had her beauty, trailing clouds of glamour when she left America to marry Onassis in 1968 aged thirty-nine; when she returned for good in 1975 she was still beautiful but in her late forties and, to her fans, distant and mysterious. Diana was in her thirties, at the height of her radiant beauty and glamour. It was a delusion to think that she would ever have been left alone.

And there was even an Onassis figure on the horizon: billionaire

Teddy Forstmann, partner of Forstmann Little and chairman at the time of Gulfstream Aerospace, whom she had met through one of her particular mentors, Jacob Rothschild. Lord Rothschild, who was on the advisory board of Forstmann's company, had introduced her to Forstmann at an Independence Day dinner which he had given at Spencer House. Forstmann was charming with dark good looks and they had quickly become firm friends: later that summer they had met again and played tennis together when she was on holiday with Lucia Flecha de Lima and her family on Martha's Vineyard. 'He came over two or three times to see her,' a friend said. 'Friendly visits, I don't think they even held hands.' 'They didn't have an affair,' she went on, '[although] he was besotted by her . . . when she flicked those eyes [at him] . . . in a way Teddy would have been the ideal man for her, [but] Teddy is a very selfish man.' But, although Diana's thoughts were definitely tending in that direction, Forstmann's were not. He was level-headed enough not to want the disruption marriage to Diana would have caused in his life. 'She thought that way [i.e. marriage],' the friend said, 'but he didn't. There was a moment when she thought it would be a good idea for her because he had a private plane; she could come and go across the Atlantic to see her children. It was a problem for her to see her children but not to live in England. [But] I think in a way she knew that the only way out would be a non-Englishman with money.'[2] Patrick Jephson, who was with Diana on her second tour, was impressed with Forstmann: 'I think it was his common sense, delivered straight and with the confidence that only experience and pots of self-made money can bring, that was his greatest service to the Princess,' he wrote; '. . . what's more, he was kind to her.'[3]

In October she made a five-day visit to the United States which was an unqualified success. As opposed to the implacable hostility of the British Establishment and the hot and cold treatment given her by the British media, she was met with enthusiastic and uncritical appreciation. In New York the artist Nelson Shanks, who had painted what was generally considered to be the best portrait of Diana, gave a dinner for her at the National Arts Club in New

York where she was welcomed with a bear hug by one of her greatest admirers, Luciano Pavarotti. She stayed at the Carlyle Hotel (from then on her favourite hotel), where the manager, James Sherwin, made it a home from home for her, before flying by private jet, a Gulfstream IV provided by Forstmann, to Washington the next day to stay with the Flecha de Limas. Forstmann was her escort at a dinner given in her honour by the most influential woman in Washington, Katharine 'Kay' Graham, owner of the *Washington Post*.

Kay Graham had first met Diana when the Flecha de Limas brought her over to Graham's private beach on Martha's Vineyard. Later, Kay Graham recalled being immediately struck by Diana's 'natural, low-key charm'. 'We seemed to enjoy each other,' she wrote. 'From that point on we were able to have easy and candid conversations during long walks on the beach.' Diana came over to play tennis at Kay Graham's house. On the drive back to the Flecha de Limas, Diana talked 'lovingly' to Kay about her sons: 'I want them to grow up knowing there are poor people as well as palaces,' she said. 'If you spent time with her,' Kay Graham wrote, 'you felt Diana's extraordinary strength, as well as vulnerability and her somewhat mocking and ever-present sense of humour.' 'I asked her if she had ever thought of going to college now that she was alone,' she recalled. 'She found my question hard to believe, and commented with irony, "I've already had an education".' A friend of Graham's who met Diana on 'the Vineyard' once asked her if she gambled. 'Not with cards,' she answered, 'but with life.'[4]

On the Vineyard in August, Diana, just after she arrived, had heard that Elizabeth Glaser, with whom she had corresponded and who was a well-known AIDS patient, was on the island. Diana dropped everything to pay her a long private visit. In Washington that October, Diana was still searching for the right way to focus her energies. She had, she said, heaps of requests but she had to decide in which area she could do most good. 'Make sure it matters to you,' a fellow guest told her. 'Because if it doesn't you can't make it matter to others.'[5] Later she told Kay Graham that if she had to talk about a cause she would make sure that she went to see the problem and learned about it first, saying that she was only going to work in areas where she thought her presence could make a difference.[6]

At a lunch given the next day in her honour by the British Ambassador, Sir Robin Renwick, and his wife, Diana sat at a table which included two major figures in American public life, the President's wife, Hillary Clinton, and the hero of the Gulf War, General Colin Powell, only recently retired as Chairman of the Joint Chiefs of Staff. Diana and Colin Powell hit it off immediately: then, after lunch, she retired for a private talk with Hillary Clinton whom she had first met at the D-Day celebrations in June. The two women had much in common: 'We talked of the challenges of public life and the struggle to protect our children from the scrutiny of the world,' Hillary recalled. 'She told me of her new hopes and plans for using her position to focus attention on the needs of suffering people. Although she seemed vulnerable and unsure about the direction her life was taking, I sensed in her a reservoir of resilience and determination that would help her take charge of her own life and help others, despite great obstacles.' Later in their relationship, Diana spoke with heartfelt feeling of the 'disease' of not being loved.[7]

On her return to London Diana, still exhilarated by her experiences, wrote a note to Patrick Jephson, thanking him for his 'strength and support' and saying how 'thrilled' she was 'by the new path we are treading'.[8] Jephson called it a delusion to think that anything positive could come out of what had been not much more than a happy social trip but at least, he added, it was a positive delusion. After a year of more or less minor activity which had included backing out of a suggested presence on the International Committee of the Red Cross, Diana took up her charity work again with enthusiasm. She visited two special hospitals for mental patients, Carstairs in central Scotland and Broadmoor in southern England, visiting Carstairs in the company of Jayne Zito, whose fiancé had been killed by a schizophrenic mistakenly released into the community. At Broadmoor, Diana attended – alone – a meeting of the patients' council which consisted of the patients themselves. 'I watched her take her seat in what was to be a private session of the council, surrounded by men who were thought to be a serious threat to the public,' Jephson wrote. 'As the door closed, I heard her voice and whatever she said raised an immediate warm laugh of greeting.'[9] She ended the year visiting Paris in her role as President of Barnardo's, touring the community projects in the poorer parts of the city but ending on a regal note with a banquet in the Hall of Mirrors at the Palace of Versailles given in her honour where she charmed President Mitterrand. As she 'made a majestic exit', she was applauded by nine hundred guests: it was Diana 'going out to conquer the world'.

Meanwhile, Jonathan Dimbleby had published his biography of the Prince, serialized in the *Sunday Times* that autumn: Diana returned to find her husband and not herself the focus of publicity, very little of it favourable. Well written and authoritative though the book was, it was also, unsurprisingly, one-sided. Everything that had gone wrong in Charles's life was somebody else's fault, particularly inadequate parenting by a remote mother and a bullying father who had been 'unable or unwilling to proffer . . . the affection and appreciation' Charles had craved. Diana's neuroses were to blame for the failure of the marriage. Only Camilla emerged with any credit from the Prince's self-pitying account. As one reviewer put it, she was portrayed as a kind of virginal Mills and Boon heroine: 'Her warmth, her lack of ambition or guile, her good humour and her gentleness endeared her to the household . . .' Dimbleby wrote.

In mid-September, pre-publication, there had been 'a terrific explosion from the Queen' when it was discovered that the Prince had handed over to Dimbleby a drawerful of papers which included not just his childhood diaries but also State Papers, without bothering to check what was there. He was forced to take them back and go through them. Recently he had been staying with his grandmother at Birkhall. 'He'll only be coming here for one day,' the Queen said grimly. 'And he chose the day of the Ghillies' Ball when there wouldn't be time to talk,' a courtier recalled.[10] The general opinion among the Royal Family and the household was

that 'it was a great error to do this book at all. In fact washing your
dirty linen in public for somebody in that position is a very stupid
thing to do,' said a courtier. 'There's no doubt that their policy of
never talking or giving interviews in the past has been a very good
one.' 'Things have been rather difficult here,' a courtier told a
member of the family from Buckingham Palace, 'but they've
calmed down a bit, thank God.'[11] 'I remember having long conversations with him [Charles] about his children and how he mustn't
do anything to hurt them. So what does he do? He does this book,
the most hurting thing in the world.'[12] Whatever else he may have
been trying to achieve by the book, publicly blaming his father
and mother for his own shortcomings was unkind and hurtful, to
say the least. Princess Anne and her brothers telephoned Charles
objecting to his depiction of his parents: 'they rang and told him
off and he sulked against them for weeks,' an aide recalled.[13]
Publicly everyone blamed Richard Aylard, who was to be the
scapegoat for the affair.

Monarchists who had condemned Diana over the Morton
book were outraged by the Prince and the Dimbleby book. Even
Charles Moore, a prominent media figure and stalwart monarchist, was prompted to say: 'When the Royal couple separated I
wrote a column in this space [the *Spectator*] which criticised the
Princess for indulging her "craving for private happiness" and
ended "how do you know some will object that the Prince does
not suffer from this same debilitating craving? I do not know but
since he is the next King I do not think we should discuss the
matter." Now he is forcing us all to discuss it, wrenching the
conversation back, just when we hoped it might stop, to him and
his woes.'[14]

Tensions were aroused by the Dimbleby episode between Buckingham Palace and St James's Palace. The Waleses' media war was
irksome and embarrassing for Buckingham Palace. That Charles
should let Diana take command of the press and in fact provoke
her to it and then lose the moral high ground was a source of
discomfort. 'I think that sense of frustration and anger and disappointment which undoubtedly radiated from the centre of the

royal establishment is directed on the Prince,' said one of Charles's aides, 'and it's hard to argue against it sometimes.'[15] There was a distinct feeling that, as far as St James's Palace was concerned, things were out of control.

And it was true that Diana commanded the media heights. Margaret Thatcher's public relations guru, Gordon Reece, had introduced Diana to David English, editor of the *Daily Mail*. The parent company, Associated Press, then took what English described, apologetically, to representatives of the Prince as 'a commercial decision' to support Diana, who sold newspapers, as opposed to the Prince, who did not. The powerful Murdoch press, proprietors of *The Times*, *Sunday Times*, *Sun* and *News of the World*, was, for much the same reasons, inclined to favour Diana. 'Diana was quite friendly with Murdoch himself,' said an expert in the media field. 'They had a correspondence. They would see each other occasionally and they would write to each other. She wrote to him . . .'[16] Relations between Charles and Murdoch, who was not naturally a monarchist and hated inherited privilege, were non-existent. A meeting between them in the late eighties organized by ex-King Constantine of Greece had had the opposite effect to that intended. '. . . Murdoch went away thinking that the Prince was this sort of pinko commie leftie sort of weirdo – and I think those kind of words were used – and the Prince went away thinking he [Murdoch] was a kind of crypto-fascist megalomaniac, so that didn't work. So I think that News Corporation generally had an agenda and Diana was very, for them, commercially she was very powerful . . .'[17] The Telegraph Group, the most conservative and naturally pro-monarchist media organization, was then owned by the Canadian-born tycoon Conrad Black. 'Conrad Black and the Prince of Wales didn't get on,' said the aide. 'Max Hastings, when he was editor [of the *Daily Telegraph*] couldn't stand the Prince of Wales – it's all in his book – thought the Prince was unfit to be King, should stand aside for William . . . Express Newspapers were the only real group which were friendly with him [the Prince of Wales]. She [Diana] commanded the media, there's no doubt about it. Because a picture of Diana sold papers . . .'[18] And, while the Prince dealt with the press through his aides, Diana had deliberately set out personally to charm the editors, from the broadsheets to the tabloids, influential columnists like Auberon Waugh and Paul Johnson, and media celebrities like Clive James.

Diana's seduction of one of the more ruthless tabloid editors, brash thirty-year-old Piers Morgan of the *Daily Mirror*, which he recorded after her death in his memoirs, provides an interesting illustration of her methods. Meeting at a reception for the charity Childline at the Savoy in January 1996, Diana asked Morgan jokingly how all these editors claimed to know everything about her when they hadn't even met her. ' "Now's your chance to enlighten me, your royal highness," I replied. She eyed me up. "Hmm . . . I don't have the time, I'm afraid . . ." Then she giggled. "Or the inclination, come to that!" ' She moved on, leaving Morgan agape. 'It was fascinating just watching her work the room,' he wrote. 'Everyone, and I include myself in this, just melted in her presence. She is radiant, sexy, and very direct – so you get the feeling you're the only one she cares about for the few seconds she's talking to you. It's a class act.'[19] On 8 May she invited him to lunch at Kensington Palace. Morgan was as excited as a schoolboy. 'Diana's the biggest star in the world and I am getting a private audience . . . *Wow!*'[20] Morgan was even more excited when William joined them for lunch. It was a frank conversation and Morgan was allowed to ask Diana anything he liked, despite, surprisingly, the presence of William, who, he noted in his memoirs, 'is clearly in the loop on most of her bizarre world, and in particular, the men who come into it from time to time'.[21] But Morgan, despite the temporary intimacy, knew that Diana was calling the shots. 'She knows she's got me over a barrel,' he wrote later. 'If I want any more from her, I am going to have to play the game by her rules.'[22]

At the opposite end of the press spectrum was Peter Stothard, then editor of *The Times*. Their meeting had come in May 1994 when Diana had concerns about leaks on the subject of her expenditure, put at more than £3,000 a week, via her husband and his friends. 'My husband said it at a dinner party last week,' she told him, 'where it got to Ross Benson and to Nigel Dempster . . .'[23] Diana's approach to the intellectual Stothard was not quite the same as her dealings with Piers Morgan. He found her extremely sophisticated 'about the media, her use of it and its use of her'. The interview was conducted on her terms, within strict but surprising lines. Flatteringly, inside those lines were 'the very aspects of her life which most people keep outside in discussion with media editors – her husband, his mistress, her in-laws, her own fragile sense of herself. Within minutes I felt I was talking to someone I knew. By the time she had toyed herself through her foie gras and lamb, I knew things about her that I did not know about my closest friends . . . The speed with which she ran through her list of subjects would not have disgraced a bank chairman anxious to catch the Ascot train.'[24] Lacking Diana's sophistication, it seems, Stothard quite failed to catch the story Diana had meant him to take in – how she had saved a tramp from drowning in the Serpentine. Although she dragged him to University College Hospital where she was to visit the rescued tramp, Stothard still failed to see the light until the story appeared in all the newspapers the next day, including his own – but without a briefing from him. Diana the Good Samaritan had been designed to counter Diana the Spendthrift.

As an estranged member of the Royal Family, Diana was in limbo. She relied ever more on her close friends, particularly Lucia Flecha de Lima, even though she was in Washington. Lucia was, according to Diana's butler, Paul Burrell, best friend, mother figure and counsellor rolled into one. Even now that the time difference between England and America made communication more difficult, their relationship continued to grow, becoming stronger as the years went by. In Washington, Lucia would set her alarm clock for 3 a.m. so that she could speak to Diana at the start of her day. 'If the princess needed advice or consolation, she rang Lucia,' Burrell wrote,[25] and Lucia was ready to answer whenever Diana needed her. 'I faxed an endless stream of messages across the Atlantic to her,' Burrell continued. Diana repeatedly told him how 'marvellous' Lucia was, that she could not cope without her, and that Lucia was 'like a mother to her'.[26] According to Burrell, who was best placed to know, Diana's 'surrogate family' now included first of all Lucia, then Lady Annabel Goldsmith, Rosa Monckton, Susie Kassem and Diana's doctor, Dr Mary Loveday. Richard Kay had by now transcended the role of media mouthpiece: he was a confidant – at least for what she needed him to hear – and helped her with her speech writing and correspondence. Sarah Ferguson was also close to Diana at that time. She was living apart from Andrew, although not yet divorced, with her daughters Beatrice and Eugenie at Romenda Lodge, Virginia Water. Diana frequently went down there to lunch, particularly at weekends, taking William and Harry, if they were at home, to see their cousins. Diana adored the York children and kept their childish paintings on her walls. At this time, the two women were constantly on the telephone to each other, gossiping, complaining about the treatment they were receiving from royal circles and the press, or discussing the latest words of wisdom from one of their gurus.

Outside this inner circle, Diana had a wider network of advisers – such as Clive James – who would lunch with her at Kensington Palace to offer her their expert wisdom when she asked for it. As with all her friendships, she compartmentalized these relationships. They came to Kensington Palace or lunched with her in restaurants *à deux*; only Diana knew what she had told each of them, and Diana was absolutely in control of the friendship. Apart from Raine de Chambrun, these counsellors were all men, intelligent, successful, who were nonetheless besotted with the Princess and protective towards her. Clive James, indeed, was an admirer of Charles yet he could not resist the lure of Diana. 'Even before I met her I had guessed she was a handful . . . Clearly on a hair trigger, she was unstable at best, and when the squeeze was on she was a fruitcake on the rampage,' he recalled. 'But even while reaching this conclusion I was already smitten, and from then on everything I found out about her at first hand, even – especially, her failings and her follies, only made me love her more . . .'[27] James forgave her even when she lied to him, as when she denied having anything to do with the Morton book: '"I really had nothing to do with that Andrew Morton book," she said. "But after my friends talked to him, I had to stand by them." She looked me straight in the eye when she said this, so I could see how plausible she was when she was telling a whopper.'[28]

Another confidant and friend was David Puttnam. It was he who had arranged the Thirty Club dinner for her in 1994 to address and impress the media magnates, he who had – with Patrick Jephson – urged her to form a Princess of Wales Trust to fund her charitable giving. (She later rejected the idea – apparently on the advice of Colin Powell – since it would be seen as setting herself up in opposition to Charles's cherished Prince's Trust.) 'She drew you into her life in quite a definite way,' said one of her friends, 'the drawing-in involved deep confidences which she knew the person in question would never betray, as if it were a secret compact.'[29] She would talk about her personal life in what one friend described as 'sometimes . . . excruciating detail'. Diana was fascinated by the cinema, identifying with some of the stars, particularly Marilyn Monroe. 'She loved Marilyn Monroe, she really did,' said a friend. 'And I got hold of a fantastic biography, a documentary from America, and I don't know what made me do it, but before sending it to her I thought I'd have a look at it. And I looked at it and never sent it. And I never sent it because I thought this is not good stuff for Diana to be looking at. So the point here is that I was dealing with a sufficiently vulnerable person, that this ostensibly fascinating piece of material about someone she admired could actually have a different context . . . I think without doubt she [Diana] had suicidal tendencies. But people with whom I've had that conversation have said that in a sense she was too selfish for that, that's not the way she would have done anything – and then there were the children . . .'[30]

Extraordinarily, Diana would be the same age as Monroe when she died. (Charles, who of all people would have been aware of her recklessness and her bravery, is alleged to have said that she would either get herself killed or end up in a wheelchair.) Perhaps with hindsight (these conversations took place some eight years after Diana died) the theme of death ran through several such conversations. Clive James wrote: 'I was even convinced . . . that she would get herself killed . . .'[31]

17. Fall from Grace

'Events of the last few weeks . . . have enforced the perception of the Princess as a predatory figure preying on other women's men'[1]

Early in 1995, Diana drew up what her secretary called 'her own, very private manifesto'. She wanted her 'true worth to be recognised', the chance to use her 'healing interests and abilities', to 'address increasing world problems', 'to make a contribution on a world platform . . . and to deal with many countries'.[2] In essence she saw her priority as being 'survival against the forces who had so nearly suffocated her'. That year she was to make no fewer than ten overseas trips. Sadly, as Jephson revealed, these brilliantly successful trips, which did more good for the British image abroad than months of trade visits and business initiatives, were regarded with suspicion at Buckingham Palace and the Foreign Office. 'I think they're all scared of the Princess of Wales,' a member of the Royal Family said at the time.[3] Diana had cultivated a relationship with the Foreign Secretary, Douglas Hurd, who had regarded her with 'a kind of paternally concerned interest' but he left office that year to be replaced by Malcolm Rifkind. If not to the bureaucrats, 'the grey men' whom Diana so resented, Diana's beauty, charisma and fame made her welcome wherever she went in the world. 'While I fenced tensely with officials in Buckingham Palace and the Foreign Office about the precise definition of the Queen's stricture that the Princess should not represent her abroad,' Jephson wrote, 'Presidents, Kings and even – in the case of Japan – an Emperor let it be known that they expected the Princess of Wales to come to tea when she was in town.'[4]

Typically of Diana, she had called in the best advice before the Japanese tour – her friend Clive James, the Australian writer, wit, poet and broadcaster who had been among her legion of platonic admirers for the past few years. James presented a television show which featured Japanese wannabes doing the most outrageous stunts. He was also a serious student of the Japanese language and Japanese literature. Diana asked him what would be the best thing she could do there, apart from her hospital visits. James advised her to learn some Japanese phrases and sent her his Japanese teacher. Diana, in his words, 'flew to Japan, addressed a hundred and twenty-five million people in their own language, and made the most stunning impact'.[5] The published purpose of the visit was to enable Diana to acquaint herself with the work of various charitable centres for the old, the young and the disabled, and to formalize the link between Great Ormond Street Hospital for Sick Children, of which she was president, and Tokyo's National Children's Hospital. As Jephson put it, 'such innocent objectives nevertheless attracted scrutiny from those now convinced that the Princess of Wales was a dangerous guided missile, ready at a moment's notice to explode with devastating effects for British diplomacy and the prestige abroad of the British royal family'.[6] Diana was invited to tea at the Imperial Palace, the ultimate accolade for a visitor to Japan. She mischievously made the most of it. Already towering over the diminutive imperial couple, she chose the highest heels she could find. 'It's very important to wear really high heels,' she joked with Jephson. 'I'm already taller than the Emperor, but it won't do any harm to look just that bit taller!' Next day the eye-catching photographs of the meeting featured Diana, curtseying respectfully low, the main feature of the picture being the consequent exposure of 'a generous expanse of athletic royal thigh'.[7]

Diana followed this up with a highly successful fund-raising trip to Hong Kong under the auspices of entrepreneur David Tang and with the blessing of the Governor, Chris Patten. In one evening she raised a quarter of a million pounds for medical and youth charities in Hong Kong and China, notably for the work of the Leprosy Mission, a cause to which she was especially attached. She made fund-raising charity trips to Venice, Paris and New York and two more official visits – to Russia and Argentina. She carried out 127 public engagements as compared with only ten in 1994 following her 'time and space speech'. On one such trip, Diana's companions witnessed one of the odder manifestations of her compassionate impulses. While they were eating their dinner in first class, Diana was sitting apart listening to her Walkman. Suddenly she scratched off the Walkman, leapt to her feet and dashed into the compartment behind, to return with a yelling baby in her arms. Despite all her efforts to calm it, the baby continued to scream and there soon appeared its anxious and somewhat alarmed mother to whom Diana had no alternative but to relinquish the child.

But at the same time as her public exploits were winning her praise, the old, reckless, self-destructive Diana was at work. In February Oliver Hoare's chauffeur went to the *News of the World* with damning details of their affair. By now even Diana recognized there was no future in their relationship and, after the *News of the World* revelations, that it was positively dangerous for her to continue. She dumped Hoare, who wrote her a characteristically charming letter thanking her for all the happiness she had given him and returning her present of a pair of her father's cufflinks. Despite her resolutions as to her public career, in private she could not find happiness. The year 1995 was to be a particularly difficult and unstable year for her. She was lonely at Kensington Palace with both the boys away at boarding school. During one of her visits to the Chelsea Harbour gym in Fulham, she met England rugby hero Will Carling, whose dark, rugged good looks and sporting celebrity appealed to her. They met at the Harbour Club and at Kensington Palace; Carling confessed that his marriage was in trouble, Diana sympathized.

Diana led him on, while at the same time mocking him to the staff at Kensington Palace as 'my puppy dog'[8] (he always visited accompanied by his black Labrador). The same 'puppy' simile was used by Carling's former personal assistant, Hilary Ryan, in a *News of the World* report in August that Diana had been having 'secret trysts' with Carling at Kensington Palace. She told of furtive meetings, long, secretive phone calls, and the pet names they used for each other. No evidence was produced of any physical relationship, although it was rumoured that Carling had made some indiscreet – indeed ungentlemanly – remarks about Diana to fellow rugby players. Will Carling gave a newspaper interview confessing that his meetings with Diana had been a mistake, and that he regretted the distress he had caused his wife Julia. Julia Carling herself was no shrinking violet and experienced at dealing with the media. She told the same newspaper that she did not want her husband seeing Diana again, saying, 'She picked the wrong couple this time.' (Ever supportive, Prince William told Diana in front of Piers Morgan that at school he used a photograph of Julia Carling as a dart board.) The effect of Julia Carling's stand on Diana's public reputation was to tarnish her in a way that had not happened before. Following on the Hoare affair, and now this, the tabloids described her as a home wrecker. She became the butt of snide jokes. On the BBC's sports quiz *They Think It's All Over*, the England cricketer David Gower and the footballer Gary Lineker laughed heartily at jokes about Diana and men made by comedienne Jo Brand. It was no secret that Diana had asked Lineker to lunch and that his wife had absolutely forbidden it. Asked by presenter Nick Hancock if he had lunched with her, Lineker replied ungallantly, 'That woman's too much trouble.'[9] But Carling, it seems, could not keep away from Diana. The stories were repeated at the end of September when the Carlings split. In Diana's circle it was alleged that Diana had turned her back on her old friends Kate Menzies and Catherine Soames when they had criticized her over the Carling affair.[10]

On 20 August 1995, a vicious attack on Diana appeared in the *Mail on Sunday* under Nigel Dempster's byline: 'Is Diana the Mistress of Manipulation?' the headline asked. The subhead was even more damaging: 'Mental anguish behind fall of Diana the "saint"'. 'Events of the last few weeks, concerning Diana's so-called relationship with Will Carling, the recently married captain of the England rugby football team, have enforced the perception of the Princess as a predatory figure preying on other women's men,' the article announced. She was known as 'Zuleika' (after the *femme fatale* of Max Beerbohm's novel *Zuleika Dobson*) 'among those who wish to see her marginalized from mainstream British life'. She was like her mother, who was a bolter, and had failed to sustain a marriage, the newspaper asserted, adding a comment by 'an observer': 'The apple does not fall far from the tree.' Worst of all, the article asserted that Diana was suffering from a mental illness.

Rumours of mental instability had been circulated by Diana's enemies within St James's Palace. It was alleged at the time the Dimbleby book was being written that Diana had a psychological profile which was found to fit a well-recognized if controversial condition called Borderline Personality Disorder, or BPD for short. Eight symptoms characterizing BPD had been put forward at the time, most of which neatly fitted Diana's behaviour, all of which were quoted in the *Mail on Sunday* piece. This theory was allegedly considered unsuitable for inclusion in the Dimbleby biography; it was, to put it mildly, diagnosis from a distance and extremely damaging. Put otherwise, it was another manifestation of the continuing argument between partisans of the Prince and those of the Princess: was Diana disturbed before she married or did his behaviour with Camilla and the circumstances surrounding the couple drive her to bulimia and irrational behaviour? Diana was not unaware of the whispers in Charles's circle and from his defenders in Buckingham Palace that she was 'mentally unstable' as a result of 'bad blood' (a favourite in aristocratic circles, in which bloodlines were so important) deriving from the Fermoys – dating particularly from the suicide of her uncle Edmund in August 1984. In 1994, however, the BPD allegation had been considered too scandalous to make public. But for Diana's enemies it was too good to waste, hence its publication in Dempster's column. The allegations were repeated later that year on a television programme, but their first formal manifestation did not come out until the publication of the book by pro-Charles author Penny Junor, entitled *Charles: Victim or Villain?*, published in 1998, after Diana's death. According to Junor, it was several years before the Prince realized that Diana had a problem.

In fact, the theme of Junor's book went further: Diana had always been mad, bad and dangerous to know and this had been the case long before she knew the Prince. The father of one of Diana's Norfolk schoolfriends had gone so far as to make specific inquiries about where Diana would next be going to school. He was concerned about the effect his daughter's friendship with Diana would have on her. Junor's book also included what is rumoured to have been Ruth Fermoy's deathbed statement to Dimbleby, that she could have kicked herself for not having the courage to warn the Prince about Diana before they married, a statement that hardly fitted the facts as they were in 1980. The argument that the unfortunate Prince was dealing with what amounted to a madwoman was too basic to the case of Charles v Diana and it was never going to go unsubstantiated for long.

At the time the *Mail* article was published, Diana was suffering feelings of continuing insecurity and increasing paranoia. Alone in the claustrophobic atmosphere of Kensington Palace, she would imagine all sorts of things; among them was her conviction that she was being bugged: 'She had a wild and vivid imagination,' a former aide said. 'You know, talk of bugs – I have to say this was absolute nonsense because besides the private lines, the other lines there came through Buckingham Palace switchboard and if they wanted to listen in they could listen in without putting bugs on and she knew as well as anybody else that the majority of her calls went through Buckingham Palace because it was a safety valve. Because all sorts of peculiar people would telephone. So to avoid that, she would give the switchboard number and they would filter. They wouldn't put anybody through without talking to the principal first, saying I have so and so on the line . . .'[11] A senior ex-police officer also dismissed the idea that Diana was being bugged: 'Some people are very ready to believe that there is this undue interest, that their house is being bugged or their letters being opened or their phone is being tapped . . . but the reality is that it's terribly difficult to get permission to do any of those . . .

There are not the facilities to do instant tap at the drop of a hat. The permissions one has to get, the difficulty in getting it, the difficulty in actually technically doing it is quite considerable. That doesn't stop people believing that they are being tapped or followed or whatever. And it's usually the sign of someone who's quite paranoid . . .'[12]

But beyond actual bugging, Diana did have grounds for her suspicions in another way. 'It must have been very difficult for her,' a close friend said. 'She was spied on, I've no doubt about it. I think that after she withdrew her police bodyguards, I think the police continued to maintain an interest in her, they say because they needed to be sure she was safe but one wonders . . . there's a lot of prurient stuff went on, a lot of people took a great deal of pleasure in finding out who she was seeing and making sure it was leaked to the papers . . .'[13]

One day the well-informed *Daily Mail* told Jephson that the Princess did not trust the loyalty of even those close to her. 'I knew my employer well enough to recognise a career prospects review when I saw it,' Jephson wrote. That year others who had served Diana long and loyally were made redundant, namely head butler Harold Brown and the head chef, Mervyn Wycherley, surplus to requirements now that Diana's divorce was approaching. Brown's loyalty and discretion were recognized by Princess Margaret who hired him herself, ensuring he kept his apartment.

The beneficiary of all these redundancies was Paul Burrell, the former Palace footman, who had not wanted to leave his comfortable family cottage at Highgrove when the division of the Waleses' staff had taken place in 1992. 'He was on to a good thing down there,' said a former aide of Diana's. 'He liked the country, was used to the country, and it wasn't a case that Diana had asked for him, it was a case that the Prince didn't want him because he had shown whose camp he was in. And so you could hardly fire someone because they happened to be in someone else's camp; you find him another job and that's what he did.'

By 1995, however, Burrell had become to some extent Diana's

confidant, or at least confidential servant. Despite having a wife and two children, Burrell was besotted with his employer, even to the extent of adopting her mannerisms; nothing was too much in order to please her. He spent long hours at Kensington Palace with her, to the annoyance of his wife, who might have said, as Diana was subsequently to say, that there were 'three of us' in the marriage. It was an emotional attachment: Diana became the centre of his world. 'She got rid of all her dressers and staff and people like that,' said David Griffin, Princess Margaret's chauffeur, who had frequent conversations with Diana while waiting outside the Palace for his employer. 'And then he [Burrell] started to take on a role, like we used to call him Mrs Danvers [the sinister housekeeper in Daphne du Maurier's *Rebecca*] and everywhere she used to go he'd appear, and that sort of thing. Stupid things, like she used to ask me "Can you give my car a going-over", which I did. He came out one morning and said, "I'll do this from now on . . . he thought it was a great honour for me to do it . . ."[14] Diana was as popular with the Kensington Palace staff as her butler was not: no doubt jealousy may have played a part but, used as they were to serving the Royal Family, the relationship between the Princess and her butler was a source of comment: 'We used to call them "the Odd Couple" sometimes,' Griffin said. 'It wasn't done in a detrimental way, but it seemed sort of strange . . .'[15] Even Burrell was not exempt from Diana's suspicion and, in some cases, understandably. On one occasion Griffin was passing her front door when Diana came out. 'She slammed the door with such ferocity that I thought "Oh!!" and I said, "Good morning, we're not in a very happy mood today, are we?" "No, we're not," she said. "Oh," I said, "what's happened?" And she said, "He'll have to go." And I said, "Who's got to go?" She said, "He [Burrell] will", and I said, "Who?" "I caught him going through my letters," she says.' Later, Diana seriously intended to sack him when she discovered that he was running up huge telephone bills on her account.

One piece of evidence illustrating Diana's state of mind in the autumn of 1995, the famous 'letter' stating that her husband planned to have her killed, was published by Paul Burrell and dated, he said, October 1996. The letter ran:

> I am sitting here at my desk today in October, longing for someone to hug me and encourage me to keep strong and hold my head high. This particular phase in my life is the most dangerous. My husband [not in the book but published later] is planning 'an accident' in my car, brake failure and serious head injury in order to make the path clear for Charles to marry.
>
> I have been battered, bruised and abused mentally by a system for 15 years now, but I feel no resentment, I carry no hatred. I am weary of the battles, but I will never surrender. I am strong inside and maybe that is a problem for my enemies.
>
> Thank you Charles, for putting me through such hell and for giving me the opportunity to learn from the cruel things you have done to me. I have gone forward fast and have cried more than anyone will ever know. The anguish nearly killed me, but my inner strength has never let me down, and my guides have taken such good care of me up there. Aren't I fortunate to have their wings to protect me . . .[16]

Friends of Diana say that the mood in which this statement was written was more indicative of her state of mind in the autumn of 1995 than 1996. It could also be pointed out that in October 1996, after their divorce had come through, there would have been no necessity – even if he had had the inclination – for Charles to have her killed so that he could remarry which, by October 1996, he was legally free to do. Colin Tebbutt, ex-Royalty and Diplomatic Protection Department, now running his own security firm, was asked by Diana in 1995 to drive for her and provide protection with a two-man back-up when she needed him. Tebbutt had concerns about the letter: '. . . because being in charge of transport and still being a great friend of the private secretary, Michael Gibbins . . . why wasn't it pointed out to me? Why didn't somebody say to the team who were driving the car . . . and I knew the man who supplied it and the car was always under lock and key and always in a garage with an electrical lock. Could nobody say to me, "Colin, the brakes are dodgy" or "Somebody's going to make an attempt on her life"? Why didn't Burrell tell the private secretary to tell the chauffeur or the security team?'[17]

Other people who worked closely with the Princess did not believe that, although the text was undoubtedly in Diana's hand, it was addressed to Burrell in particular. 'Now, if she'd written that to Paul, it would have been "Dearest Paul" and in that case it would have been very much in his [Burrell's] interest to show that letter, but the very fact we didn't see it [the superscription] and the very fact that it wasn't even on the letter with not even a signing off [signature]. I know for a fact that it was a memo to herself and she would not bullet point it, she would just get it down.'[18] Another aide confirmed, 'this alleged letter to Burrell, yes she wrote it, the paper was genuine, the writing was genuine, but she did write notes to herself'. Often the theme of these memoranda would be the result of a conversation she had had recently and wanted to jot down as a memo to herself. They might, equally, be the result of some consultation with one of her therapists or clairvoyants. The point is that the memo was an expression of Diana's state of mind at the time and an illustration of the forces driving her towards what would turn out to be the greatest mistake of her life, the notorious *Panorama* interview. A year later, the idea of writing a memo such as this would never have crossed her mind. Yet, such had been the impact when Burrell's book was serialized, and so seriously was it taken when Burrell reproduced the text in his book, that Lord Stevens, the retired head of the Metropolitan Police, went so far as to interview Prince Charles about it for the purposes of his inquiry in 2005 into the death of Diana.

The idea of giving a spectacular television interview had been taking shape in Diana's mind throughout 1995, sparked by her meetings with two media giants of American television, Oprah Winfrey and Barbara Walters, both of whom she had invited to lunch with her at Kensington Palace, while her friends Clive James and David Frost had tried to lure her on to their shows as the ultimate celebrity guest.[19] In the end it was a rank outsider, Martin Bashir, who persuaded her to give what was to become perhaps the most notorious television interview of all time. Bashir, then a junior journalist on the BBC's *Panorama*, succeeded where the other luminaries failed and he did so by preying on Diana's fears for her security and safety. His original idea had been to do an investigative programme on the current fears about the activities of the Security Services in monitoring the lives of celebrities and the Royal Family which had been prevalent since the publication of the Squidgygate and Camillagate tapes in 1992 and 1993 respectively.[20] Andrew Morton, in his last book on Diana, published in 2004, was convinced that there would have been no interview had Bashir not tapped in to Diana's secret fears. According to Morton, Bashir first met Diana's brother, Charles, at Althorp in the summer of 1995 in order to discuss his suspicions of being bugged. Charles was suing the *Daily Express* for a series of articles alleging that he had helped to launder the proceeds of a multimillion-pound fraud carried out in New York by his close friend and best man at his first wedding, Darius Guppy. Spencer won £50,000 damages and an apology. At the same time he had taken out an injunction against his former head of security, James Waller, forbidding him from disclosing information about his private life and that of members of the Royal Family; this had followed the publication in March 1994 of a letter Charles had written to Diana in December 1993 warning her that her public appearances were damaging her popularity.

Allegedly through Spencer, Bashir secretly met Diana, whose insecurities he fed by convincing her that her apartment was being bugged. In order to advance his cause with Charles Spencer and Diana, according to Morton and, later, the *Mail on Sunday* (April 1996), Bashir had a set of forged bank statements made up by a graphic designer showing payments made to James Waller and a former business partner of Waller's, Robert Harper, from *Today*, the newspaper which had published Spencer's letter to Diana, and a Jersey-based company for unspecified services. Whatever the truth of the matter, something happened to persuade Diana to give the interview. The prime motive, according to this reading of the affair and the sentence of her October memo, written at the time of the negotiations with Bashir about the interview, about Prince Charles arranging her 'accidental death' and her references to 'my enemies', was fear for her own safety and a determination to make herself so popular as to be invulnerable. The interview was to be a pre-emptive strike. Diana's biographer, Sally Bedell Smith, attributes this paranoia to Bashir's warnings and it was at about the time of their meetings that Diana had insisted on having her apartment and her car swept for bugs. Bashir also apparently warned her not to trust Catherine Soames and Kate Menzies, although she had in fact already parted company with them, and, significantly, Julia Samuel, one of the most intelligent of her friends, whom she then dropped.[21]

Diana had previously consulted three of her media mentors, David Puttnam, Clive James and David Attenborough, about doing the Bashir interview. 'Because we had told her not to do it,' said one, 'in all three cases she gave us the impression that she'd listened to us and had decided not to do it and all three of us got quite a shock when she did.'[22] 'I mean, my argument was very simple, rather cynical in a way . . . whenever she used to bang on about the possibility of doing something like these interviews, was – you'd be mad to do it because once you've done it the weapon that it is ceases to exist, so you're handing over the one serious weapon that you have, and in a sense you're then just a victim of events, you have no control over events; whilst you haven't done it you are actually in control of events. So that was my position . . . and when I said that she always said, "You're absolutely right, of course you're right, I absolutely understand that." '[23] Clive James wrote in his remembrance of Diana after her death: 'I counselled her against it. I said if that happened the two camps thing would go nuclear, and continue until there was nothing left. She would be on the run forever and there would be nowhere to go . . . She seemed convinced, but of course she was pretending. She had already decided.'[24]

Several things moved Diana to take the fatal step of the *Panorama* interview: her longing to put her case to the people over the heads of her 'enemies' in the Establishment; her love of publicity on her own terms; her intrinsic belief in the rightness of her own instinct even over all the wise opinions she had been given by people who had only her interests at heart; her determination to counter allegations of Borderline Personality Disorder; and lastly, and, least attractively if understandably, the desire for vengeance. This was evident in her instructions to the BBC over when to release the news of the broadcast. On Diana's specific instruction[25] the BBC released their press announcement on 14 November, an unwelcome forty-seventh birthday surprise for Charles, on an official visit to Tokyo. Photographs taken at the time show him cutting a celebratory cake, his face expressing total dismay.[26] That morning Diana called the Palace to inform them of the interview which was to take place in six days' time. The Royal Family were, with justification as it turned out, appalled at what they regarded as the second betrayal after the Morton book. It was by now too late to do anything but wait and see.

The fifty-five-minute programme went out on 20 November. Dressed in black, wearing little jewellery, her eyes heavily ringed with kohl, Diana was in victim mode but nonetheless defiant, and seemingly oblivious to the significance of what she said in the context of the monarchy. Her words echoed the October 1995 letter as she spoke of her sufferings, her betrayal by her husband, the efforts of people to destroy her by painting her as mad, her bulimia; she admitted to her love affair with Hewitt, but with no one else. ('Yes, I adored him, yes, I was in love with him. But I was very let down.') Above all, the attack was directed at her husband, his mistress and their friends. They – 'her enemies' – had said she was 'unstable, sick and should be in a home of some sort in order to get better', and, when asked if Charles agreed with them, she said, quoting (without attribution) from a book by the former hostage Brian Keenan, 'there's no better way to dismantle a personality than to isolate it'. Asked what part Camilla Parker Bowles had played in the break-up of her marriage, she replied in

the most memorable phrase of the evening, 'Well, there were three
of us in this marriage, so it was a bit crowded.' She admitted to
helping with the Morton book because she had wanted the true
story of her unhappy marriage to be made public: 'I was at the end
of my tether. I was desperate. I think I was so fed up with being
seen as someone who was a basket-case, because I am a very strong
person and I know that causes complications in the system that I
live in.' The word 'strong' came in no fewer than four times. Some
people 'in the Establishment that I married into, have decided that
I'm a non-starter. Because I do things differently, because I don't
go by a rule book, because I lead from the heart, not the head.'
She, however, wanted to reign not officially but as a Queen of
Hearts (a phrase borrowed from the works of her step-
grandmother, Barbara Cartland) and to be an ambassador for
Britain, giving affection and helping 'other people in distress'.

The key moment of the programme – the point at which Diana
cut herself off from the monarchy and the Royal Family – came
when she cast doubt on Charles's fitness to rule, and raised a further
doubt as to whether he would succeed to the throne. 'It's a very
demanding role, being Prince of Wales', she said, 'but it's an
equally more demanding role being King. And because I know
the character, I would think that the top job, as I call it, would
bring enormous limitations to him, and I don't know whether he
could adapt to that.' 'My wish,' she added with a sly dig, 'is that
my husband finds peace of mind.' Speaking of herself in the third
person, always a bad sign, she declared with an undertone of
menace as well as defiance: 'She won't go quietly.'

It was a stunning – and to some a shocking – performance,
watched by fifteen million people in Britain and millions more
round the world. Diana's friends were horrified: 'Diana at her
worst,' Rosa Monckton wrote. 'A brilliant suicide note,' said
another. Camilla, watching with her family, apparently laughed at
the theatricality of the 'Mad Cow', as she sometimes referred to
Diana (possibly in reference to BSE) but its effect on her standing
with the public would be even more drastic than the Morton book
had been. Nicholas Soames loyally rushed on to the BBC's serious

news programme *Newsnight* to declare that the interview showed 'the advanced stages of paranoia'.

The week before the broadcast, when it was too late for him to derail her plans, Diana finally told Patrick Jephson she had done the interview. He immediately rang the Queen's press secretary. Over the car phone Charles Anson was his usual laid-back self but there is no doubt that the news of what Diana intended to do caused consternation to the Queen and her staff. Diana refused to reveal the content of what she intended to say to anyone and the fact that it was to go out on *Panorama*, the BBC's flagship current affairs programme, only served to increase nervous suspicion. As it happened, even the chairman of the BBC, Sir Marmaduke Hussey, had been kept in the dark for the simple reason that he was married to one of the Queen's and Charles's favourite Women of the Bedchamber, Lady Susan Hussey. Had he been told of the project he would undoubtedly have moved heaven and earth to stop it. The director-general, John Birt, Hussey's chief executive, was in on the plan but did not inform his chairman, nor did he make any effort to stop it or even to tone down the content. The result was a serious rift between the Palace and the BBC. Nothing the Palace, Jephson or even Diana's lawyer, Lord Mishcon, could put forward succeeded in getting Diana either to reconsider or to reveal what she was going to say. After watching *Panorama*, the Palace, Jephson and the Princess's press secretary, Geoff Crawford, were in a state of shock. Crawford resigned immediately, although he accompanied the Princess on her tour of Argentina two days later. Jephson, his plans for Diana's rehabilitation and reintegration into the royal circle in ruins, determined to resign as soon as he decently could.

Diana remained resolutely convinced she had done the right thing. The night before, she had telephoned one of her mother figures: 'She rang me and said to me, "I've done the most wonderful interview, I've put everything right." I was slightly worried about it. She said, "You will watch it, won't you, and tell me in the morning?" I watched it, and it was so frightful I – literally – was thinking I'm never going to be able to stand up for her again because it's so frightful, the *Panorama* thing. She rang me. The telephone rang at eight o'clock in the morning – she was an early riser, like me – and I couldn't . . . I had to pretend to be on the other line because what was I going to say to her? Well, it was so frightful that I did, I told her that I wasn't mad about it and she was furious . . . I said it was a frightful mistake, and she didn't like that at all, she hated being criticized. But it was appalling, it was a total error of judgement.'[27] Diana's friend, who knew both Charles and Camilla well and was much liked in court circles, encapsulated the reaction of everyone who wished her well. In terms of a royal future, she had thrown herself off the edge of the cliff. The interview finished her friendship with Princess Margaret who was outraged by Diana's remarks about Charles and the succession and wrote her a stinging letter to tell her so, and Margaret's children, previously so friendly, avoided her. The interview was devastating for her sons; in her lack of consideration for their feelings and her public admission of adultery she had behaved no better than Charles. It was rumoured that William would not speak to her for several days.

In public relations terms, however, the interview was a popular success. Diana had appealed to her own followers, the converted: favourable results of newspaper polls helped convince her that she had done the right thing. Two days after the interview, buoyed up with confidence, she left for a pre-arranged charities trip to the Argentine, Britain's erstwhile enemy in the Falklands War. The democratic President, Carlos Menem, took Diana's visit as a signal that 'Argentina has gradually regained a position in the world which it had lost'. Faced with her return to London and normality – at least her form of it – realization of the possible consequences of what she had done had begun to dawn on Diana. Patrick Jephson commented sharply, 'she had taken the biggest possible injection of her favourite drug, and now she felt even worse'.[28]

While St James's Palace may have been happy to see Diana publicly imploding, Buckingham Palace was not. Jephson was still trying to put together the broken pieces of Diana's relationship with the Palace, presenting a blueprint for their future dealings.

He suggested that Diana's secretarial staff should move to offices in Buckingham Palace, and that the Queen's press office should deal with her public relations. He proposed removing her from dependence on Charles for her financial support, and that Buckingham Palace should provide domestic back-up for her apartment at Kensington Palace. Finally, her areas of work both abroad and at home, charitable and public, should be clearly defined and agreed. Both he and Diana attended a meeting at the Palace, when it became obvious that, while Jephson might have hoped to lure his thoroughbred into the safety of the Palace stable, the Queen's staff were not entirely willing to receive her, having been bruised once too often by Diana's initiatives, of which the *Panorama* interview had been just one too many. On 29 November, Jephson and Diana attended a meeting with the Queen's principal officials at the Palace, headed by her brother-in-law, Robert (Sir Robert since 1991) Fellowes. Given the guarded response his proposals received, Jephson soon realized they were doomed. 'Whatever goodwill there might have been at Buckingham Palace towards her as a person,' he recalled, '– and I had no doubt there was plenty, not least from Robert himself – the offence she had caused was too great. It was a classic case of "love the sinner hate the sin".'[29] Furthermore, the Prince's team were not willing to see the Princess transferred to the shelter of Buckingham Palace, as Jephson proposed. 'A move under the wing of the senior household, and hence to the centre of royal power, was hardly going to have the marginalising [of Diana] effect they undoubtedly hoped for,' Jephson commented.

Still unaware that events were moving on without her, Diana flew with Jephson by Concorde to New York to receive a humanitarian award from her old admirer Henry Kissinger on 12 December. It was an American occasion of the kind which always stimulated and empowered her in distinct contrast to the difficult atmosphere reigning at home. 'There were motorcades, Secret Service agents, adoring crowds and rooms full of rich, powerful and beautiful people to be charmed,' Jephson wrote of his last foreign trip with his employer. As a gesture of appreciation,

Diana appointed her old friend and supporter Liz Tilberis, formerly editor of *Vogue* in London, now New York editor of *Harper's* and suffering from what was to be terminal cancer, as her honorary lady-in-waiting. She returned to the Harlem Children's Hospital, scene of her moving visit six years earlier. As always, the welcome she received in America had its effect on her: Diana in New York, Jephson recalled, was a different person from his temperamental London employer.

She returned to the gloomy confines of Kensington Palace full of confidence to take on 'her enemies', the first of whom was to be Alexandra 'Tiggy' Legge-Bourke, employed by Charles to be his Girl Friday and to look after William and Harry. Diana had been jealous of Tiggy's closeness to her sons since her appointment, when a photograph of Charles kissing her on a skiing holiday had convinced her, quite groundlessly, that Charles and Tiggy were having an affair. Tiggy's visits to her private gynaecologist that year prompted Diana, disastrously, to conclude that she had had a termination and that the baby had been fathered by Charles. At the Christmas staff lunch on 14 December, she confronted the unfortunate young woman. '*So sorry* to hear about the baby,' she smiled. Tiggy was horror-struck, almost fainted, and had to be helped from the room by Charles's valet Michael Fawcett. Diana was triumphant but at St James's and Buckingham Palace, where Tiggy was universally liked, there was consternation and disgust. Tiggy instructed her lawyers; Sir Robert Fellowes telephoned Diana to find out precisely what her allegation implied when Diana gleefully repeated the allegation to him. Sir Robert investigated and found the whole affair groundless, as he informed Diana in a stern official letter rebutting what she had said. Her allegations were completely without foundation, he told her; Tiggy's relationship with the Prince had never been anything other than a professional one: 'on the date of the supposed abortion, she was at Highgrove with William and Harry. It is in your own best interests that you withdraw these allegations . . .' Attached was a private note to Diana: 'This letter is sent from one who really believes that you've got this whole thing dreadfully wrong, and that you *must* realise it – please.'[30] Later that month, lunching with friends at a favourite Italian restaurant in Chelsea, La Famiglia, before going down to Eton to meet Charles for the Christmas carol service, she was 'very pensive' and 'very nervous': 'she was very brittle and her mouth was much tighter, she was doing that whole lowering the head thing,' an observer said.[31] Diana, the goddess of New York, had metamorphosed into Diana, the Naughty Little Girl, about to meet the Grown-ups.

Diana had become obsessed with the unfortunate Tiggy. In the notorious 'Burrell letter' of October 1995 Diana had indicated that Charles was planning a car accident to remove her from the scene and enable him to marry not Camilla, but Tiggy. Diana's extreme possessiveness over her 'boys' had fuelled her anger, triggering her unreasonable and inexcusable behaviour.

The blow fell a week before she was due to take William and Harry to Sandringham for Christmas. A letter arrived from the Queen, addressed in her handwriting to 'Dearest Diana' and ending 'With love from Mama'. Its content, however, was stark: having consulted both the Prime Minister and the Archbishop of Canterbury, the Queen had come to the conclusion that it would be in the best interests of the country to end the uncertainty and for Charles and Diana to take steps to divorce. Diana, according to her butler Burrell, to whom, he said, she showed the Queen's letter, sat down to reply, saying to her mother-in-law that she needed time to reflect. Time, however, was exactly what she was not going to be given; a letter from Charles arrived. Their marriage was beyond repair, he wrote, representing a 'national and personal tragedy'; since divorce was inevitable, it should be done quickly in order to resolve the 'sad and complicated situation'.[32] The 'fairy tale' was definitively over.

As a gesture of goodwill, the Queen still extended her invitation to Diana to spend Christmas at Sandringham. A royal invitation amounts to a royal command but Diana had gone too far to care. Discussing the Queen's letter with her butler, she had shown no interest in the constitutional issues of divorce. Enraged that the government and the Church had been consulted over her marriage, she had 'yelled', 'This is my marriage and it is no one else's business.' As for the Queen's reference to 'the interests of the country', her reaction was 'In the country's interests, is it? What about the interests of me? What about the interests of my boys?' To show her displeasure, she refused the Queen's invitation to Sandringham and spent Christmas instead at Althorp. It can hardly have been a very happy one: the marriages of both the younger Spencers were in trouble and both would end in divorce.

18. Out on a Limb

'She knew she had nowhere to go' (a member of Diana's circle)

By the end of 1995 Diana was in limbo. The past year had been the most confused and difficult of her life so far. Now, with the *Panorama* interview, she had cut herself off from the Royal Family, the real source of her power and celebrity. She may have been the prime architect of her own downfall, but she was not the only one. St James's Palace had long regarded her as the principal obstacle to the heir to the throne's popularity; his friends had queued up to denigrate her, the newspapers tracked her every movement and every public word. There were ample reasons for the paranoia which had haunted her through 1995 and would continue to do so as negotiations for her divorce progressed.

In January 1996 Patrick Jephson resigned. *Panorama*, which she had kept secret from him until it was too late to do anything about it, was the trigger which had convinced him that, after eight years' service, he must escape from his relationship with Diana. He had been fascinated, almost besotted, by her, as was every man close to her. Diana had joked and laughed with him, given him expensive presents – Hermès ties were a favourite for all her men friends – paid for expensive lunches. In return he had served her with utter devotion to the detriment of his private life. The secrecy with which the *Panorama* affair had been conducted had finally caused the scales to fall from his eyes. He determined to jump before he was pushed. Perhaps Diana, with her acute instincts, had sensed this; she initiated the process by cutting him out of her official confidence, replacing him as her speech writer with Richard Kay and, more recently, Martin Bashir, who acted in some cases almost as her private secretary. According to Jephson, she had begun to

send him venomous anonymous messages on his pager, as she had
to other members of her staff who had fallen into disfavour.[1] Diana
regarded his departure, which formally took effect on 22 January,
as a personal act of treachery. She had prepared a riposte with a
story in the *Mail* to be run the following day stating that he
had been sacked for professional incompetence. Jephson had been
tipped off about it and timed his resignation to forestall it.

Like almost all the people – men and women – who had been
cut out of Diana's life, after the initial bitterness Jephson remained
loyal to her: his subsequent memoir, *Shadows of a Princess*, published
four years later, although frank about her failings paid tribute to
her outstanding courage and charisma. 'You cannot just walk away
from the Princess of Wales,' he wrote.[2] There was bitterness on
Diana's side, too, at what she saw as a personal betrayal. She
telephoned friends who might have been prepared to employ him
and even fell out for a time with one of her mentors, David
Puttnam, whom she suspected of luring Jephson away from her.
Other people who had been sacked or driven out by her retained
a liking, loyalty and sympathy for her, understanding the impossibility of her life and not blaming her for it. Everyone denied that
she was mad, or had ever been so, blaming rather the people who
had failed to help her or understand her and, indeed, had driven
her to her present predicament.

Her butler, Paul Burrell, who now, since the departure of
Jephson, had become Diana's gatekeeper and the repository of her
secrets, had described Diana as 'heartbroken' in the week before
Christmas 1995.[3] She still loved Charles and did not want a divorce.
Now, with that interview, she had played into his hands. While
she might refuse the Queen's invitation to Christmas at Sandringham, she could not refuse her mother-in-law's demand that the
couple divorce for the sake of the country. In any case, the matter
was no longer in her hands: someone leaked the news of the
Queen's letter to the press. For once it was not Diana: it would
not have been in her interest to do so. The Palace resolutely denied
any responsibility; one can only surmise that it might have come
from St James's Palace or the Prince's circle, to pre-empt any

stalling on the issue on Diana's part. Diana had no alternative but to acquiesce, although digging in her heels all the way to get what she wanted in return for the sacrifice of her dream. On 14 February she sent Charles a Valentine's card, 'with love, Diana'.

The next day, 15 February 1996, she had a meeting with the Queen at Buckingham Palace, with notes taken by the Queen's deputy private secretary, Robin Janvrin. The only account of the interview which we have is that given by Paul Burrell, now privy to all the Princess's secrets and, indeed, her correspondence (whether authorized or not). At any rate, his account would have been Diana-inspired: this would have been how she recounted it to him. Diana made her position clear to the Queen: 'I do not want a divorce. I still love Charles. None of what happened is my fault,' she said.[4] She then unburdened herself: 'She unbottled years of suspicion and emotion before the Queen, and not for the first time,' Burrell wrote. She spoke of her enemies who were jealous of her popularity with the public. 'She knew she could talk to the Queen. Answers and solutions were rarely forthcoming, but Her Majesty always provided a sympathetic ear.'[5] The one subject on which the Princess and the Queen were in total agreement was the welfare of Princes William and Harry. The Queen assured Diana that she should not worry about the custody of her sons, always Diana's primary concern. 'Whatever may transpire in the future, nothing will change the fact that you are the mother of both William and Harry. My concern is only that those children have been the battleground of a marriage that has broken down,' the Queen said.[6] Diana expressed her hurt that she had received letters from both Her Majesty and the Prince of Wales at the same time urging divorce. The Queen said that although the exchange of letters had led nowhere, she remained of the opinion she had expressed at the time: 'The present situation is not doing anybody any good, either country, family or children.' The underlying message was that there could be no going back, and that the sooner the divorce was agreed, the better.[7]

Then came the question of Diana's future which would involve how she would be viewed by the Royal Family and the public.

This turned on the question of whether she would be entitled to keep the title 'Her Royal Highness' after the divorce. The Palace later insisted that dropping the title was Diana's idea, a statement she hotly contested but one that was probably true at the time. The Queen made her views clear when she said that she thought the title of Diana, Princess of Wales, would be more appropriate, and said it was a matter for discussion with Charles. Diana may have acted hastily in offering to give it up and then regretted it, not realizing, perhaps, the significance of the title to the Queen as implying membership of the Royal Family. Historically, the refusal of King George VI to grant Wallis Simpson the title of HRH on her marriage to his brother, the former Edward VIII, now Duke of Windsor, had caused an irreparable rift between them. The King's decision, made on the grounds that it was for him and him alone to decide who should and who should not be considered as a member of the Royal Family, overriding the common-law principle that a wife should take her husband's style or title, was controversial then and remains so today. At the time it was also privately considered undesirable that a twice-divorced woman of questionable reputation, who might divorce again, should go about the world as a member of the Royal Family calling herself 'Her Royal Highness'. (Who knows whether such thoughts had not lingered on into the 1990s?) The Queen had been eleven years old when her uncle had married Wallis, certainly old enough to remember the huge upset the abdication and its aftermath had caused her family. As she did in so much, she would have been conscious of precedent and of following her father's example. In her mind, a divorced wife of a Prince of Wales could no longer claim membership by marriage of the Royal Family, hence her statement, 'Speaking personally, I think that the title "Diana, Princess of Wales" would be more appropriate.'

Diana soon realized that she did not want to give up her title, telling her friends how 'hurt' she was by the proposal, and how humiliating it would be for her to curtsey to lesser royals. The public did not understand the royal way of thinking: to them, it appeared a petty and vindictive move against Diana which was to resonate with disastrous consequences at the time of her death. Diana was still the mother of the future King and it would probably have been more politic to have made her an exception, leaving her the HRH at least until she remarried.

On 28 February Charles and Diana had a private meeting at St James's Palace, during which, according to friends, she told him, 'Whatever happens, I will always love you.' Prince Charles's response is not recorded. No one else was present and subsequently, to the fury of both St James's and Buckingham Palaces, Diana jumped the gun with her own version of the meeting. Since Jephson's departure, Diana had appointed Jane Atkinson as her press adviser, and Michael Gibbins as her private secretary. Jane Atkinson was waiting in Diana's office with her lawyer, Anthony Julius of Mishcon de Reya, when Diana returned, determined to pre-empt the Prince with a press statement. She indicated that she had consented to a divorce, and that they both had agreed that she would continue to be consulted about all decisions concerning the children, that she would live at Kensington Palace but continue to keep her office at St James's Palace. Outraged at what they saw as a blatant breach of confidentiality (and a pre-emptive strike in the legal war) the Queen's officials issued their own statement pointing out that what Diana had represented as 'decisions' were merely 'requests' and that details about the divorce remained to be discussed before being settled. Further, Diana used Richard Kay to leak the accusation that the Queen and Prince Charles had pressured her into giving up the title HRH.

Once again, Diana's use of the media, 'going public' on private affairs, infuriated the Palace, and even the Queen. Charles Anson, the Queen's press secretary, came forward to make a statement denying Diana's claim that the Queen and Prince Charles had pressed her to give up her title. 'The decision to drop the title is the Princess's and the Princess's alone,' Anson said. 'It is wrong that the Queen or the Prince asked her. I am saying categorically that is not true. The Palace does not say something specific on a point like this unless we are absolutely sure of the facts.' Instead of keeping the Queen on side, Diana had, as she had with her defiant

refusal of the Sandringham invitation, thrown down the gauntlet
to her royal in-laws. Ill-tempered divorce discussions dragged on
into July until Charles presented her with his final settlement offer.
(Before this, at the end of June, Diana had made one last-ditch
attempt to keep the HRH, leaking the story via Richard Kay that
the Palace now insisted she keep the title as mother of the future
King – which was quite untrue.)

Diana's resistance, and, no doubt, the unarguable fact that she
had moral right on her side, paid off. Compared with the meagre
settlement given to the Duchess of York for her divorce in May,
Charles's offer – underwritten by the Queen, since he was forbidden by law to sell off Duchy of Cornwall assets to pay for it –
was a generous one. Diana would receive a lump sum of £15
million, plus some £400,000 a year to run her office. Diana's title
would be 'Diana, Princess of Wales' and she would be 'regarded
as a member of the Royal Family', which made the withdrawal of
the title HRH even more peculiar. She would be invited to state
and national occasions when she would be treated as if she still had
the title. Her public role would be 'for her to decide' although
any working trips overseas – as distinct from private holidays –
would require consultation with the Foreign Office and permission
from the Queen (standard practice for members of the Royal
Family). She would have access to royal flights and to the state
apartments in St James's Palace for entertaining. She would also
have the use of all the royal jewellery, eventually to be passed on
to the wives of her sons. The couple would sign a confidentiality
agreement, prohibiting them from discussing the terms of the
divorce or any details of their lives together. On 15 July Diana and
Charles filed their decree nisi, the document declaring that their
marriage would be dissolved six weeks later, on 28 August. Two
days after that, on 30 August 1996, an entry appeared in the *London
Gazette* (the traditional place for such royal pronouncements): 'The
Queen has been pleased by Letters Patent under the Great Seal of
the Realm dated 21 August 1996 to declare that a former wife . . .
of a son of a Sovereign of these Realms, of a son of a son of a
Sovereign and of the eldest living son of the eldest son of the

Prince of Wales shall not be entitled to hold and enjoy the style, title or attribute of Royal Highness.' The language may have been archaic, but the meaning was stark: Diana was to be stripped of her title.

Yet nothing could compensate for the final end of the marriage by which Diana had set such store, the final end to her romantic dreams of a loving marriage with husband and children. Diana had fought, but ultimately she had lost, as much through her own impetuous misjudgement as through any Machiavellian manoeuvres by the Palace. Both the Queen and the Duke of Edinburgh had counselled her to live apart but in harmony with her husband. Recklessly, and against all advice, she had determined to follow her instinct down unwary paths, refusing to compromise. Perhaps she should have read about the life of Edward VII and Queen Alexandra sooner, but if she had it is unlikely that it would have made any difference. Alexandra had compromised and made her own life, increasingly isolated at Sandringham, but with the respect of her husband and the love of the public. As the daughter of the King of Denmark, she knew the royal rules and played by them. She was also fortunate in having a loving and close family to support her and to whom she could retreat in times of trouble. Diana had none of those advantages and paid the price of resistance to the rules; she was now alone, divorced, and had left the field clear for her rival, Camilla.

Three friends stood by her through thick and thin – Lucia Flecha de Lima, Annabel Goldsmith and Rosa Monckton. Only Rosa saw what Lucia called Diana's 'dark side'. At Ormeley Lodge, the Goldsmiths' house, where she was one of the family, observers saw only her charming and witty personality. 'She was so funny,' one said. 'She used to have us on the floor with laughter, some of the remarks she made . . .'[8] When she heard that Lucia's husband, Paulo Tarso, had had a stroke and was in hospital in Washington, Diana, without telling anyone, flew straight there to visit him. 'She couldn't see herself as other people saw her, how people were totally in awe of her. She would come into a room and people would stop,' said Flecha de Lima's daughter, Beatriz. 'When my father was in hospital and she flew to America . . . Again this is why we loved her so much, she had this kind of thing that was unbelievable, which was, my father is in the hospital, he had a stroke and she flew without anybody saying "Please come" . . . The next day she flew and she came to the hospital and the floor where my father was there was the Coca-Cola machine, with a slow queue of people just to take a glimpse of her, people would not leave the floor, they wanted to see her . . . and my father had to be woken up from time to time, people saying "Paulo, Paulo" and [he] would not respond. Then Princess Diana whispered "Paulo" and he woke up. Then there was this man screaming for the doctor, saying, "I'm hallucinating . . . I thought I saw Princess Diana." [9]

Diana's social friends received the same compassionate treatment in crises. When the husband of Pamela Harlech, whom Diana knew through her work for the English National Ballet, died, Diana went out of her way to ensure that his widow did not feel lonely, telephoning her, asking her to lunch. 'That was the nursing side of her,' Lady Harlech said. 'Diana was wonderful to me after Terence died,' said Diana Donovan, widow of the celebrated photographer who had been a great friend of Diana's. 'He died in late 1996 so in all that time she was quite a presence in my life, really an incredibly supportive presence for a young girl to be supporting an older woman. The first call I got on that Christmas Day of 1996 was from her. She was in the Caribbean . . .' [10]

'What people don't understand about Diana was the incredible pressure she was under. All the time,' said a friend. 'Incredible pressure from when she was nineteen . . .' [11] That pressure led her to seek release in 'fun' urban social circles which she now regarded as 'normal life'. These circles included the people whose names were to be found in the 'High Life' column written by Taki Theodoracopulos in the *Spectator*, people who on the whole were never going to give her the support or even respect she required. Diana desperately needed sympathy and understanding. She found both in a new friend who was part of the Goldsmith circle, Lady Cosima Somerset.

Cosima Somerset, then thought to be the daughter of Annabel Goldsmith's brother, Alastair, 9th Marquess of Londonderry, met Diana at lunch at Ormeley Lodge in January 1996. Cosima's mother, the beautiful and much loved Nicolette, had killed herself in August 1993 at the age of fifty-two. Cosima herself had separated that month from her second husband, Lord John Somerset, a younger son of the 11th Duke of Beaufort, and had recently left their children, aged five and three, with their father at Badminton, the stately home of the Somerset Dukes of Beaufort, in Gloucestershire. Cosima herself had been brought up as Lady Cosima Vane-Tempest-Stewart at Wynyard, the English estate of the Marquesses of Londonderry until it was sold by Alastair. Meeting Diana at a lunch for only the three of them – Annabel, Diana and Cosima – she had seen in Diana's eyes 'true empathy'. 'The parallel of our experience was exact,' she recalled. In tears, Cosima told Diana that she felt as if 'the umbilical cord between myself and my children had been cut again . . . I was beginning to mourn what had for decades been a great part of my life. I had formed a deep bond with Badminton and everybody who belonged there. Badminton had healed the pain of losing Wynyard, my father's estate near Durham, where I spent my childhood . . . In Diana's eyes I saw that she understood. All she said was, "Cosi, you will get used to it." '12 'At a moment of great pain,' Cosima wrote, 'I fell in love with this girl.'13

The two women became inseparable, constantly on the telephone to each other, sending each other videos. After a trip to Lahore with Diana and Annabel Goldsmith in February, Cosima wrote: 'What we had experienced was real intimacy and companionship, and from that moment I felt that she was my sister and that we had both been adopted into Annabel's ever-growing family.'14 The day after they returned home to London, Diana sent Cosima a scented candle in a clay pot with the note, 'I hope this candle lights some of your darkest moments.' Cosima found the gesture 'almost telepathic'; she lit Diana's candle every day for six months. They met once a week for lunch at Kensington Palace – 'almost like a mutual therapy session, full of silences and outpourings'. 'We shared the experience of being separated from our husbands and uncertain about what the future held. We had both broken away from large, powerful families and therefore we had lost our protection. Both of us were considered "hysterical, unbalanced, paranoid, foolish".'[15] Both of them sought explanations for their painful, chaotic lives in the spiritual and the psychic, for some reason finding comfort in the idea that life is predestined.

In May that year the two of them spent a weekend at La Residencia in Majorca, gossiping, talking about everything – childhoods, children, marriages. On the drive down the mountains to the airport, Cosima gained an insight into the nightmare aspects of Diana's life. As they left the gates of La Residencia, driven by the hotel manager, they were immediately pursued by paparazzi in cars and on motorbikes. They careered down the winding road with the convoy in hot pursuit; as they hit a dual carriageway at speed, a motorbike drew alongside. The paparazzo on the pillion pointed his lens right up against the car window. 'I felt as if Diana had almost been assaulted,' Cosima said, 'but she remained ice cool. Her coolness was shocking to me, for I had been sure the car would crash.' All Diana said was, 'Welcome to my world . . .'[16] It was an eerie foretaste of things to come.

Although ostensibly in aid of Annabel's son-in-law Imran Khan's cancer hospital in Lahore, where the former Pakistan cricket star, now a politician, lived with his young wife, Annabel's daughter Jemima, there was another, more personal reason for Diana's visit to Pakistan. Diana had been in love since the previous autumn with a handsome Pakistani heart surgeon, Hasnat Khan, whom she had met while visiting the sick husband of her therapist friend and counsellor, Oonagh Shanley-Toffolo, at the Royal Brompton Hospital in west London. Diana had been treated by Oonagh, perhaps the most trusted of the long list of psychic helpers, since 1989, when they had met through Mara Berni, of San Lorenzo. Diana was at the hospital with Oonagh when her husband Joseph suffered a relapse after his triple bypass operation on 31 August. Hasnat Khan, assistant to the celebrated Professor Sir Magdi

Yacoub who had performed Joseph Toffolo's operation, came into the room and was introduced to Diana. While preoccupied with Toffolo's condition, he barely noticed Diana; she, however, was immediately struck by him. After he had left the room she apparently said to Oonagh, 'Isn't he drop-dead gorgeous?' She later told another of her therapists, Simone Simmons, that she was sure her meeting with him was 'karmic'.[17] For the remaining years of her life, her passion for Hasnat underlay various initiatives she would take, the visit to Pakistan with Annabel and Cosi being one of them.

The answer to her prayers was thirty-six years old, born into a rich middle-class family living in Jhelum, in the province of Lahore in Pakistan. He had studied medicine at the King Edward Hospital in Lahore, then moved to Sydney where his uncle, a distinguished heart surgeon, arranged a position for him at St Vincent's Hospital. In 1992, after the murder of his mentor, cardiac specialist Dr Victor Chang, Khan left Australia for England. Kind, honourable and compassionate, as well as being a dedicated professional, Hasnat seemed to personify to Diana everything she had ever looked for in a man and never found. She had become interested in Islam and Islamic philosophy – Sufism in particular – through Oliver Hoare but as early as the autumn of 1990, at the time of the Gulf War, she had attended at her own request a lecture on Islam given by the Cambridge professor Akbar Ahmed at the Royal Anthropological Institute. In the lecture Professor Ahmed had emphasized the importance of the family in Islam and afterwards Diana had asked him in private what she could do to help: 'How can I improve the understanding between Islam and the West? What role can I play?' The professor later thought that he had raised 'a tiny spark' of interest in Islam in Diana, that she might have been seeing it as a civilization where not only is there a position for women but where women are loved and respected and given the attention and care they deserve. In fact Diana had been planning an official visit to Pakistan that year which had had to be postponed. It finally took place in September 1991, when Diana had arranged to have a prior briefing by Professor Ahmed. Anxious to make a good

impression, Diana had asked his advice as to how she should dress
and what she should say if asked to speak. Ahmed advised her to
quote from the work of Sir Allama Mohammad Iqbal, Pakistan's
national poet, giving her a passage which would become relevant
to her own life later when she met Hasnat Khan: 'There are so
many people who wander about in jungles searching for something, but I will become the servant of that person who has got
love for humanity.'[18]

Diana arrived in Pakistan for her first visit on 22 September. She
was assigned a woman member of the new Cabinet to accompany
and guide her through her tour of healthcare and educational
institutions. Syeda Abida Hussain, a successful woman in her own
right, was unimpressed by Diana's romantic perception of Muslim
men. Diana, she said, appeared to be fascinated by the Pakistani
male image, the strong Muslim man whom she saw as being
protective towards women. It seemed to be all she wanted to talk
about.

Imran Khan, who was based in London where he enjoyed
considerable social and sexual success but whom she had not yet
met, seemed to Diana to combine the ideal qualities of East and
West: sophisticated but with the strong background of Muslim
culture. By the autumn of 1995, when Diana first encountered
Hasnat, she had met Imran at the centre of her social life, the
Goldsmith household. Imran had married the beautiful twenty-
one-year-old Goldsmith heiress Jemima in June and taken her to
live in Lahore with his family in the time-honoured Muslim tradition. Jemima (whose father was Jewish) had converted to Islam
and wore the shalwar kameez. Diana very much admired Jemima,
although she was university-educated and more than ten years
younger. Her family thought that Diana empathized with Jemima
Khan and visualized herself leading the same life.[19] In February
1996 Diana, Annabel and Cosima Somerset flew out to Lahore
in the Goldsmith private jet for a fund-raising dinner in aid of
Imran's cancer hospital. That was, at least, the ostensible motive.
Privately, Diana was determined to meet, and if possible win over,
Hasnat's family in Pakistan. In the event, fear of press publicity

prevented the meeting but Diana conscientiously fulfilled her
charity obligations to Imran. A friend touring the hospital with
her was worn out by Diana's determination not to disappoint: 'I
thought we were never going to get out of that . . . hospital. She
went into every room, she practically picked up every child. She
went from room to room; now you don't have to do that to make
your impression but she got herself right into the whole thing,
sometimes with humour, sometimes with compassion, she was
utterly, utterly dedicated . . . I was absolutely exhausted but she
kept on going. I think we started at eight or nine in the morning
and we didn't sit down to lunch until something like 3.30 . . .'[20]
'She made more for that hospital than anyone, the fund-raising
dinner that night was amazing . . .'[21] Back in London, on 4 July,
the day on which details of the proposed divorce settlement were
published in the press, Diana attended a fund-raising dinner for
Imran's hospital at the Dorchester Hotel. In a gesture which, to
herself at least, symbolized her breakaway from the Royal Family,
she wore the shalwar kameez designed for her by Rizwan Beyg
in Lahore for her February visit. She was thinking, of course, of
Hasnat: over the next thirteen months thoughts of him would
dominate her actions. Immediately after the dinner, she drove
herself up to Stratford-upon-Avon to visit his relations.

It was a secret affair, shared, apparently, with therapists Shanley-
Toffolo and Simmons, but kept for some time even from Burrell.
Diana made nightly visits to Khan at the Royal Brompton and
nearly got herself into trouble when she was spotted by a camera-
man in the car park, only escaping detection by spinning a story
to Clive Goodman, the accompanying reporter from the *News of
the World*. In a brunette wig and casual clothes – leggings and
trainers – she and Khan would make nightly expeditions to Ronnie
Scott's jazz club. Diana, in true Marie Antoinette fashion, thrilled
to the unfamiliar experience of joining a queue to get in. Later,
Burrell would pick Khan up at the KFC near the hospital and
drive him into Kensington Palace, as they thought *incccnnu* and
under a blanket. They did not, however, escape the notice of
Princess Margaret's eagle-eyed staff. 'Here comes Khan in MOA

[the registration number of Diana's car]', the cry went up. Once inside, Khan would turn on the television and often watch a football match. Hasnat Khan broke every rule in Diana's book: he was overweight, smoked and ate junk food; nevertheless she was besotted with him. His medical skills fascinated her; she read Gray's *Anatomy of the Human Body* and watched surgical operations. Caught on camera by Sky News she was accused of phony ghoulishness. But despite tabloid sniffing, the affair remained secret for some time.

Shortly after the announcement of her filing for divorce on 15 July 1996, Diana let it be known that she was drastically curtailing her charity patronages, retaining only six: the homeless charity Centrepoint, the Leprosy Mission, the National AIDS Trust, the English National Ballet, Great Ormond Street Hospital for Sick Children and the Royal Marsden Hospital. Unfortunately she could not avoid injecting a sour note into the announcement which she ordered Jane Atkinson to put out: 'The move is entirely because of her loss of royal status . . . The loss in her standing will not be beneficial to those charities and her pulling power must be diminished. She can no longer give them the strong position they are entitled to.' Diana got a bad press over both her decision and her statement, which indeed could have been interpreted as a dig at her soon to be ex-in-laws. Nonetheless, since she was in theory retiring into private life, it was only natural that she should want to cut down on her public commitments and keep the causes which were particularly important to her – AIDS, lepers, the sick, the dying and the dispossessed. The English National Ballet she kept because of her love of ballet and belief in the company, something which she emphasized on the day her divorce was finalized by visiting the ballet school.

'On the day her marriage ended,' her driver-cum-security man Colin Tebbutt recalled, 'we were at the Ballet School round the back of the Albert Hall. I always remember at 10.26 we had the official Jaguar and at 10.28 we didn't have it any more (well, at least we had it to drive away). And there was an enormous amount of interest when we came out of that Ballet School . . . the Princess looked great, she was wearing her engagement ring and she flashed her engagement ring, and I thought she had great, great strength that day . . .'[22] 'She asked if she could come to rehearsal,' Pamela Harlech said. 'I think she just wanted to get out and I think she also wanted to be seen to be fine and having a good time, and she came to a rehearsal and that mews [Jay Mews] was absolutely stacked with press.'[23]

But for all her emotional intelligence and talk of wanting a 'normal' life, Diana was conservative enough at heart to resent no longer being the member of the Royal Family which the title Her Royal Highness had declared her to be. Always lacking in self-esteem, she seemed not to realize that her worldwide celebrity was such that she would always be 'Princess Diana' or 'Princess Di' to the public, that she had reached a different plane from merely being royal. In June she had made a three-day trip to Chicago to raise money for cancer charities where, according to her American biographer, she had attracted large, enthusiastic crowds that recalled the early days of 'Di-mania'.

And now Diana was reaching beyond her old circle to celebrities – Elton John, Gianni Versace among them – and in particular to those who were as vulnerable to the price of fame as she was. She saw herself as a therapist, and she had certainly had plenty of experience on the receiving end. In May 1996 she introduced herself to Michael Barrymore, the popular British television star who was being treated for alcohol and drug addiction and who had recently come out as gay after twenty years of marriage. While he was in a clinic, Diana's office forwarded a note. 'She so understands what he and Cheryl [Barrymore's wife and manager] are going through. She hopes that people will let them have their own space and time. She also hopes they will be able to meet with her a little bit later. She sends lots of love.' Martin Bashir telephoned to make an appointment with Barrymore, then, when Diana was about to arrive, telephoned twice to ensure that Cheryl Barrymore would not be present at the interview.

Diana and Barrymore spent several hours in this first private meeting from which Cheryl Barrymore had been specifically excluded. Despite the prohibition, Cheryl checked up on them, to find them sprawled together on adjoining sofas, chatting away like old friends. 'It was very cosy for a first visit,' she noted. Neither of them looked up or noticed her entry: she went away leaving them together for a couple of hours until she heard Diana leave. The next morning Burrell arrived with a handwritten note to Barrymore saying how much Diana had enjoyed the visit, how much they had in common, and that they should meet again soon. 'It quickly became a regular thing,' Cheryl recalled. 'Martin Bashir would phone to make arrangements, a meeting would take place, and the following day Paul Burrell would deliver another gushing note saying how enjoyable it had been.'[24] It was somehow poignantly illustrative of Diana's estrangement from Establishment circles, that the Princess of Wales should make use of a television journalist and a butler for her confidential missions.

The theme of their conversations was their own problems in the context of celebrity. Significantly, Diana would say that only three people in England counted as far as the media was concerned: herself, Barrymore and 'Gazza' – Paul Gascoigne, a superbly talented but troubled England footballer, who had set off down the road to self-destruction. 'She seemed to think that there was a front-page rotation for stars with a problem, and saw Barrymore and Gazza as stand-ins to give her a break,' Cheryl wrote. Slowly it became clear that Diana was drawing Barrymore further and further into her world. She talked to him about her own problems and insecurities. 'She seemed to feel that, by opening up herself, she would help him unload his troubles,' Cheryl wrote, but to her the confidences seemed to be more than a cry for help. 'Diana seemed to believe they could achieve something truly great . . . together because they had the key weapon: massive public affection . . . [Diana was] telling Michael how they were really going to teach a few people some lessons . . .' Quite who she meant she did not say, at least not in front of Cheryl, but it could be surmised that the targets would be Charles and Camilla and their friends. Finally, to Barrymore's fury, Cheryl suggested Diana should leave and from then on their meetings took place at Kensington Palace.

Cheryl was kept in the dark about their conversations but, she alleged, Diana's influence caused him increasingly to lose any sense of reality. 'Over the year or so that Diana and Michael entertained each other, things got steadily worse,' she wrote. 'She encouraged a way of thinking that was hardly normal, and he was starting to lose the ability to see when something was nonsense . . . He would often have a distant look in his eyes, almost like a religious conversion . . .'[25] The words 'my public' were becoming all too frequent. Dangerously, both were beginning to believe too much in the huge power of celebrity legitimized by public affection.

In her role as international celebrity fund-raiser, Diana made two more trips to the United States that year: once to Washington to raise money for Katharine Graham's charity, the Nina Hyde Center for Breast Cancer Research, at a high-powered gala for eight hundred people from the worlds of society and fashion. Kay Graham gave a lunch in her honour, and Hillary Clinton a White House breakfast for 110, where Diana received a standing ovation. America increasingly became the focus of Diana's dreams of a new life of her own, deluding herself that in a country so rich in celebrities she might escape the constant press persecution which dogged her closer to home.

Over the years leading up to their final divorces in 1996 – Sarah's on 30 May and Diana's on 28 August – Diana and her sister-in-law had been close, in cahoots against 'the grey men' of the Queen's and the Prince of Wales's households. The unfortunate Sir Robert Fellowes happened to be related to both of them, being not only Diana's brother-in-law but also Sarah's cousin. But while he remained fond of Diana, whom he called by her nickname Duch, he and the other courtiers now detested Sarah on Andrew's behalf. The Duke of York remained obsessed with his wife and on the best of terms with her, despite her sexual relationship with the louche John Bryan, her 'financial adviser', he of the toe-sucking pictures which had caused such scandal. Unlike Diana, who maintained her star status and popularity with the public, Sarah was an object of ridicule for her relationship with Bryan, who was declared

bankrupt in August 1996 (by which time his relationship with
Sarah was over), for her debts and her frantic attempts to redeem
herself by writing books – *Budgie the Helicopter* and a book on
Queen Victoria's travels, actually written by the scholarly Benita
Stoney, niece of the royal librarian, Oliver Everett. Her announcement on a charity visit to Portugal that she had twice taken AIDS
tests – once before her marriage to Prince Andrew in 1986 – had
not helped.

On one occasion the Palace had blocked Sarah's hopes of
becoming a goodwill ambassador for refugees and the UNHCR,
in the footsteps of Audrey Hepburn and Sophia Loren. Sarah had
been thrilled at the prospect, which would have seen her upstaging
'the Blonde', as she called Diana. Beneath their friendship as 'the
Wicked Wives of Windsor', as they called themselves, the old
rivalry, however, survived. Both of them were therapy junkies,
swapping the latest exciting forecast from their psychic mediums
and fortune-tellers – Rita Rogers and astrologer Penny Thornton
among them. A persistent shared delusion was that Charles would
never become King, that he would die, or be forced to abdicate,
leaving Prince Andrew as Regent until Prince William came of
age. After one consultation, Sarah was reported as 'bursting with
excitement': she had received a prediction that Charles was about
to die – having survived one avalanche, he would not survive a
second. She telephoned Diana to inform her she was about to
become a widow. In Sarah's version of the Charles death scenario,
the boys would be killed with him, leaving Andrew to become
King, when she would definitely outrank 'the Blonde'. The
Queen Mother, regarded by both Diana and Sarah as 'the Chief
Leper in the Leper Colony', was another royal candidate predicted
to succumb.[26] Both women happily shared this belief which would
remove the chief obstacles to their royal futures.

It was basically an unequal relationship: Diana outranked Sarah
in almost every way that mattered, in beauty and in status. Diana
had always been rich in her own right, with an impeccable pedigree
stretching back over the centuries. Sarah, although well connected,
had always been relatively poor and was now desperately in debt.

There were old rivalries, notably the Queen's undoubted preference for Sarah in the early years of the York marriage: an identity
of interests which Diana would never achieve despite the Queen's
even-handed treatment of her daughters-in-law. The bottom line
now was that Sarah's misbehaviour had far eclipsed Diana's. Somehow, a letter from Princess Margaret to Sarah informing her in no
uncertain terms that she had let down the Royal Family came into
the public domain. John Bryan's former business partner and friend
Allan Starkie quoted Sarah as saying, 'One of the overriding reasons
I should go back to Andrew is simply to say "Fuck you" to all
those people who said it couldn't be done, and all those people
who have been backstabbing me. But it would mean returning to
a joyless life, living as a nun, and giving up JB [John Bryan].'[27]
Starkie, it must be said, had many reasons for wanting to get his
own back on both Sarah and Bryan.

One theme above all others illustrates the underlying rivalry
between Sarah and Diana and their obsession with celebrity – this
time with John F. Kennedy Jr, son of the assassinated President,
dubbed 'the Sexiest Man Alive', 'Hunk of the Year' and 'the
Handsomest Man in the World' by *People* magazine in 1988. Sarah
apparently had a dream that she would marry John Kennedy and
become First Lady of America. In pursuit of this dream, she had
obtained his telephone number on one of her visits to New York
and asked him if he would like to come round for drinks or dinner
at the Carlyle Hotel where she was staying. Two hours later,
however, a member of Kennedy's staff called back to say he would
be unavoidably detained and would have to cancel their date.
Sarah's mortification can only be imagined when she heard that
Diana and JFK Jr had had a meeting at the Carlyle when Diana
was in New York in December 1995. Kennedy had requested the
meeting, hoping to persuade Diana to appear on the cover of the
first issue of his magazine *George*. Diana turned him down. Rumour
later spread that they had had a brief but passionate encounter.
Unfortunately for rumour, Patrick Jephson had been present when
the meeting took place, a witness to its disappointingly platonic
nature. An absurd coda to the JFK Jr obsession came after Allan

Starkie attempted suicide in 1995. Sarah telephoned Rita Rogers with the news, to be told that he would try it again and this time would succeed. If Starkie is to be believed, and the story appears too bizarre to be invented, Sarah then asked him to do her a favour: 'When you're dead, would you find JFK and explain to him that I am destined to marry John-John and become the First Lady of the United States? But I would like him to help me with this and approach John-John in his dreams and try to explain it to him and convince him . . .'[28]

In 1996 three books about Sarah were published: one by Allan Starkie, one by the 'Pyramid Lady', Vasso Kortesis, the repository of many of Sarah's confidences over the years, and a self-justifying ghost-written autobiography by Sarah herself, *My Story*. The book and Sarah's tour of the United States to publicize it led to what was to be the final rift between her and Diana. The book contained various references to Diana which seemed to her to be breaches of confidence: that she was weepy and reclusive at Balmoral in 1986 where Sarah's radiance compared favourably with Diana's gloom. Annoying, too, was Sarah's stress on what she saw as her close and caring relationship with the Queen. Even more offensive to Diana was Sarah's reference to catching verrucas from Diana's borrowed shoes.[29] Petty though it may have been, in Diana's eyes it was disloyalty and in 'Duch's' world once you were gone you were gone. They never spoke again, nor were William and Harry allowed to visit their cousins, Beatrice and Eugenie. Despite Sarah's attempts at reconciliation, there was to be no way back. They would still be estranged when Diana died.

19. Stirring Beneath the Surface

'The divorce was more or less done and dusted – but she had very strong views on Charles's household . . . she used to tell me she was more concerned about Charles and the people around him'[1]

'It's the 28th August 1996 – 15 years of marriage have now been signed off,' Diana wrote on the day her divorce was finalized. 'I never wanted a divorce and always dreamed of a happy marriage with loving support from Charles. Although that was never meant to be, we do have two wonderful boys who are deeply loved by their parents. A part of me will always love Charles, but how I wish he'd looked after me and been proud of my work.

'It has been a turbulent 15 years, having to face the envy, jealousy and hatred from Charles's friends and family – they have so misunderstood me and that has been painful and brought enormous heartache.

'I want so much to be Charles's best friend as I understand more than anyone what he is about and what makes him tick . . .'[2]

'There was a big change after the divorce had come through, I somehow felt she was very much happier. She was on a much more even keel,' a former lady-in-waiting said.[3] Anthony Holden, who lunched with Diana in October, recalled her mood as she considered the possibility that Charles and Camilla might now get married.

'She said to me, "Oh, I don't care, they can get married, they probably ought to get married, it doesn't bother me now." She was in what I would call a fairly serene mood and I think genuinely wanted [it] for the children's sake. She would never have liked Camilla because she blamed Camilla, to my mind justifiably, for the break-up of her marriage with Charles. But she was in the sort of "Oh, what the hell, shrug shoulders, let them do what they want" mode but slightly more generous than that, actually. "Well, I hope they'll be very happy", she'd say, but she'd very much have the children in mind, I think.'[4]

'Diana was blooming after her divorce,' a friend said. The reason was directly linked to her passion for Hasnat Khan, which, although it was still secret, she pursued in her public as well as her private life. The doctor's absorption in his work and his hatred for the publicity which surrounded Diana only made him more attractive to her. Despite his comfortable background in Pakistan, Khan was not rich and Diana did everything she could to advance his career. Her idea appears to have been that he should find work outside England where they could marry and live together in peace. On 13 October 1996 she flew to Rimini to receive a humanitarian award at a conference on health, the annual congress of the Pio Manzù Centre, an international think tank presided over by the ex-President of the Soviet Union, Mikhail Gorbachev. Diana made a speech on the opening day of the congress on her chosen topic: 'The challenge of an ageing population'. Dr Christiaan Barnard, the famous South African surgeon who had carried out the first human heart transplant in 1967, also attended the congress to receive an award.

Sitting next to Barnard at dinner, Diana spoke to him about Hasnat and asked him to help get him a position in South Africa. Later, after her death, Barnard revealed that Diana had told him she wanted to marry Hasnat and have two daughters; she was, he said, obviously very much in love with him and would have married him if he had agreed.[5] On her return to London, she wrote to Barnard and telephoned him about job possibilities for Hasnat, and subsequently asked him to dinner twice at Kensington Palace to discuss it. The problem for her was that Hasnat was determined to finish the Ph.D. he was studying for under Dr Magdi Yacoub and was not remotely interested in leaving England until he had done so. He was quite unaware of Diana's campaign on his behalf and was furious when he later found out. Having, at Diana's suggestion, met Barnard on one of his London visits,

Hasnat had, at Barnard's request, sent him his CV under the impression that this might be for a position after he had taken his Ph.D. He only found out what Diana had been plotting when he received a job offer from an American hospital.

His anger did not deter Diana. She also considered Australia a possibility and later that month flew to Sydney for fund-raising events connected with the Victor Chang Institute, set up in memory of Hasnat's late mentor. Diana raised one million Australian dollars for the cardiac centre during her visit, a demonstration to Khan of how much her fame and her abilities could help him in his chosen career, and while she was there she arranged to meet old friends of Hasnat. She had even hoped Hasnat might fly out to Sydney, but the huge publicity surrounding her visit made this impossible. In terms of publicity Diana was reaping the consequences not only of her worldwide celebrity but of her previous visits to Australia where Di-mania had been born. Without the Royalty and Diplomatic Protection Department and with inadequate security provided by her hosts, Diana was hounded: women crowded round her table to stare and often to touch her; when she got up to dance, she was quickly surrounded by gawping couples, some of whom made sure they brushed against her. She was mobbed when she tried to go to the lavatory and forced to flee. In the hotel chosen for her she had to lie low with the curtains drawn even in daytime. If she had ever thought that her divorce from the Royal Family would bring her freedom and a normal life, this experience should have disabused her.

The Australian visit was a disaster in other ways. Her romance with Hasnat was outed by the *Sunday Mirror* (3 November 1996) which claimed to have made the connection between her midnight hospital visits, her interest in medicine expressed by her attendance at heart operations and the object of her current visit. The reason behind all this focused attention, the newspaper declared, was her love for Dr Hasnat Khan. Terrified of the effect this unwanted publicity might have on Hasnat, Diana tried to deflect it by her old method, leaking a counterstory to the press through Richard Kay, in Australia with the press pack. Her denial appeared in the

Daily Mail the following day in which she was described as upset at the effect these untrue allegations might have on William and Harry and as 'laughing herself silly' over them. Hasnat was deeply offended by the story and temporarily cut off relations with Diana. The incident underlined further what his life with Diana might be like. To woo him back Diana deployed her two confidants, Martin Bashir and Paul Burrell, to socialize with him and keep him on side.

Her relationship with Hasnat and the finality of the divorce had helped her distance herself from thoughts of Charles and Camilla. She no longer felt resentful of Camilla, even sympathizing with the bad publicity her relationship with Charles generated. Nevertheless, Charles and his household still featured large in her thoughts. Richard Aylard, whom she had regarded as the arch-enemy, was to depart at the end of the year, replaced by the assistant private secretary, Stephen Lamport. Of great interest to Diana was the arrival there in 1996 of Mark Bolland as deputy private secretary. Bolland, formerly of the Press Complaints Commission, was a man whose skill with the media was well known, and who had been recommended by friends of Camilla. Camilla's position in the life of the heir to the throne was the principal – but unspoken – cause of resentment between the households of the Queen and her heir. Bolland did little to diminish this; his chief preoccupation was to improve the Prince of Wales's image by subtly gaining public acceptance of the role of Camilla in his life. 'We were all trying to manoeuvre the Prince back into public life in a more respectable way, and trying to find a path for Camilla through it all,' Bolland said. 'At the time before Diana died, it was our view that the Prince was in such a bad position in terms of public reputation and esteem, he went through that ridicule stage . . . it was our view that one of the levers which would bring him up was Camilla, people starting to think better of Camilla would help him . . .' Bolland was clever enough to see that being perceived as trying to do down Diana, public idol number one, would be self-defeating. 'One of the things I went there at the beginning to do,' he recalled, 'was to end this War of the Waleses, the media war fought on their behalf by various people around them, which was also influenced directly by them, more so by her than by him but he was quite capable of nodding and winking to people when it suited, although he's not going to ring up a newspaper and do it himself like she did . . . One of the things that had to be done at that time was to try and disengage from all of that and having to reassure her [Diana] that I wasn't going to be souping up the campaign again but actually the reverse.'[6]

From his days with the PCC, Bolland had had experience of dealing behind the scenes with the various royal offices: 'One had a sense of what a mess the situation was . . . it was far more a mess on his side than on her side . . . at the time [when he was at the PCC] I was actually very friendly with Robert Fellowes and Charles Anson . . . and you know, St James's Palace was very much a poor relation, it was all a bit of a muddle . . . And when I went to work for the Prince of Wales those relationships broke up, particularly it seemed over the Camilla situation where they took a view and the Prince had a view and I had to choose but it was a shame . . . because if anything when we were at the PCC the relationships with Buckingham Palace were very important, then the Spencers and Kensington Palace to a lesser extent, and then St James's Palace way down the list . . . When William went to Eton [September 1995] the whole putting together of a contract with the press that kept the media away from William was actually a Buckingham Palace initiative, that Charles Anson started off . . . Diana, who must have been talked to by David English about it, played ball . . . was happy with the thing, and St James's Palace were very, very reluctant to participate and actually at Buckingham Palace, Charles and Robert very much made it in terms of the internal dynamic of the Palace, their initiative. You know the Queen wanted to stand up and look after her grandchildren, we know those two other offices hate each other and are dysfunctional but we are going to make sure that the right thing happens for the grandchildren.'

David English had great influence with Diana, and in Bolland's case helped reassure her that Bolland was not there to put her down. 'He had said to her, "You know who the enemy is, you know who are the people Mark needs to deal with and who you need to deal with as well . . ."; he said to her, "Mark is not there to run things against you and if he did I'd stop it anyway."' Reassured, Diana invited Bolland to Kensington Palace, which caused near panic at St James's Palace: 'There was a big, kind of, is this the right thing to do? Is Diana going to convert Mark into her way of thinking? They all had a view, even the Prince had a view. Anyway, they decided it was safe, I wasn't going to succumb to charm . . .'7 Diana did indeed try to exercise her charm: 'She was always very kind, she was always incredibly polite – she'd send me notes, she'd send my mother notes, send my mother signed photographs, all those tricks she employed and every time anything [like that] happened, I was always told by the [St James's] staff, "You see, this is what she does." But my mother liked it – it was a sweet thing for her to do – [but] it wasn't going to change the world for me. She'd ring up – she was clearly sensitive about the outing of Camilla process and understood that had to happen but she didn't want it to happen in a way which overdid things.'8

Diana, he said, had very strong opinions about the children, 'how they should be portrayed, how much they should be portrayed with their father and all that'. Poignantly, Bolland recalled how she didn't want the children to end up in the situation she was in 'in terms of just being consumed every day'.

Lord Wakeham, as chairman of the Press Complaints Commission, dealt directly with Buckingham Palace and with Diana, always her own media expert. Treading a delicate tightrope between the palaces and the press, it was his concern to use the monarchy to establish an informal code of conduct which would avoid the necessity for draconian and unworkable privacy laws. In this context it had often been his unenviable job to deal with both Diana and Sarah, who would ring up with some complaint and then, a few hours later, withdraw it. 'We used to get telephone calls either from her or from some friend of hers or from Fergie who she was very close to at one time,' Wakeham recalled, 'and they would ring up and complain about something, and we would say, "You must get someone to write in so that we can deal with it; we can't deal with complaints just over the telephone like that", and there was all hell let loose while we rushed around . . . and then they'd just drop it, just forget about it. You'd hear nothing, they wouldn't give you any details – so there was this scatterbrained approach to it.'[9] Of Diana's fabled skills in dealing with the press, Wakeham said, '. . . there was a certain schoolgirl idealism about her and a certain lack of practicality but, because she moved in high places with high things, she maybe gave her own thoughts more weight and value than perhaps they really had. And perhaps it's understandable, when you're living in that world – no ma'am, yes ma'am, what a wonderful thought ma'am and everything else type of business – the most trite remark can be thought wise . . . I think that was the problem she had . . .'[10] At one point in 1995, when Diana was getting rough treatment from certain sections of the press, her private secretary came to see Wakeham: 'There was a lot going on,' Bolland, then at the PCC, recalled. 'She was working on too many fronts and his line was "You've got to do something, John, to calm everything down and Wakeham did then go off and talk to the chairman of News International, the chairman of this, the chairman of that. It did trigger a process . . .'[11]

Bolland confirmed that Buckingham Palace had been sympathetic towards Diana. 'I don't think Buckingham Palace ever did brief against her,' Bolland said. 'Certainly when I knew Robert and Charles during my time at the PCC, we never heard anything that came from them other than a sort of care, no matter how exasperating she was. *Panorama* was around then and they were very disappointed about that. They would never be drawn on her. What St James's Palace did, what Richard Aylard did, I don't know.'[12] At the launch of the new policy to raise the profiles of Charles and Camilla without antagonizing Diana, Aylard had to go since he was seen by all the main media as architect of the campaign against Diana from St James's Palace. Also against Aylard was Camilla, a powerful force with the Prince. 'Camilla blamed him entirely for the Dimbleby thing, for the adultery [admission],' an aide said. 'She thinks it couldn't possibly be the Prince's fault and that he was manipulated into doing it and she wasn't treated properly about it or told about it properly. And the statement that was put out later about the Prince having no intention of remarrying, that was the final straw, but the Dimbleby thing really made her marriage situation completely untenable. She, and the people round her, never forgave him [Aylard]. And she will never forgive him for that.'[13]

Diana still kept up her connection with Charles. 'Occasionally, if she got in a fix with the media, which did happen from time to time, she would ring him up. It was quite interesting; whenever she really got into trouble she would ring him and he would always be there, also he would ring her up and speak his mind – "I don't want to be involved, I can't cope any more, I've had enough of it" etc, etc, "do anything you can to deal with it, use my name, spend my money, sort it out. I don't want to know but just deal with it".'[14] Charles would still send her flowers on her birthday with a card to 'Dearest Diana'.

Despite the divorce, there was no diminution in Diana's pre-occupation with her ex-husband. This was best demonstrated by a curious incident which was to have repercussions long after her death. It concerned Prince Charles's personal staff. Valets and dressers have traditionally had access to and influence with their employers far exceeding that of principal officers of the household, including private secretaries. Margaret MacDonald, always known as 'Bobo', the Queen's childhood nursery maid and subsequently her principal dresser, had been, until her death, the only person to whom the Queen told 'everything'. Bobo's influence over the Queen had been widely feared among the Palace staff and the household; even the Queen's couturiers were bullied by her. 'Miss MacDonald was the Queen's eyes and ears at the Palace and it didn't do you any good to fall foul of Miss MacDonald,' said a member of the Queen's domestic staff. 'If things went wrong Miss MacDonald would make more fuss than the Queen would. If you upset Miss MacDonald, it was for life . . .'[15] Staff on the royal yacht who had to serve Bobo with champagne on a tray, or bring in her breakfast, used to call her 'the QE III'.

The story of the Prince of Wales's valets was rather different from the dominion of Bobo. James 'Jem' MacDonald, who had found the Prince's grandfather, King George VI. dead and who had 'coddled' the young Prince as he grew up, had been succeeded by the flamboyant Stephen Barry and Barry in turn by Ken Stronach, loyal until, shocked and appalled by the Prince's Dimbleby interview, he had talked to the newspapers. He had been replaced by the assistant valet, Michael Fawcett, who had entered royal service as one of the Queen's footmen in 1981. Fawcett, a far more dominant figure, had begun to assert himself as early as 1985. Protective, indeed exploitative, of the Prince and reputed to bully the other staff, Fawcett used his royal connection to obtain goods and favours. He became a director of the Prince's shirtmakers, Turnbull & Asser, and later was given permanent access to a suite at the Ritz. Suppliers who fell out with him were given short shrift. Staff who criticized him or his activities got the sack. 'He was quite ruthless and would get rid of anybody who stood in his way.'[16] 'He's very dangerous,' said a fellow member of staff. 'And the Princess could see that, she knew that . . . people like him butter the Prince up all the time. They created the Prince and they were expert at creating division between the two [Charles and Diana] and one wonders how much they were responsible for it.'[17] 'He's a big man who finds it easy to impose himself.'[18] 'That's how he got on really. It was his size that he was able to use to be so forceful.'[19] At one point Camilla, Fawcett and Mark Bolland formed a powerful trio at St James's Palace – 'Because between the three of them . . . nobody could put up a challenge . . .'[20]

Diana's chance, as she saw it, to make trouble at St James's Palace came through a conversation with the Prince's orderly, George Smith: 'George Smith was a veteran of the Falklands War, a corporal in the Welsh Guards, a loyal man, a squaddie who had put his life at risk to fight for his country . . .' said a member of Diana's staff.[21] 'He was a good man, a decent man that worked his butt off as a soldier and was recommended by his colonel to work as an orderly for the Prince of Wales. Now you don't get that recommendation if you're an absolute idiot, and you don't get it if you're a drunk . . .'[22] George Smith became caught up in a Palace web which was to destroy him mentally and physically. Diana was in the habit, which the Prince rightly regarded as dangerous, of picking up members of her staff for a chat in the kitchen. 'You could be walking in the corridor or the grounds of Kensington Palace and the Princess would say, "Oh, what are you doing, x?" And I'd say, "Nothing much." And she'd say, "I'm going to the kitchen, why don't you come and have a cup of tea?" And you don't turn it down. Similarly George Smith would be there and she'd say, "George." – "Oh, hello, Ma'am." "What are you doing, George? Are you going to see Mervyn [the chef]?" "I'll see you up there then." Of course, poor old George gets up there and it doesn't take long before he's cornered, locked in but feeling safe to talk . . .'[23]

Poor George Smith was simply not equipped to deal with the intricacy of life in the Waleses' household. 'George Smith arrived there in his uniform and was whisked off to Jermyn Street by Michael Fawcett and togged up with a three-piece suit, a Turnbull & Asser shirt and tie, and a pair of shoes from Trickers,' said a staff member. 'So suddenly you have this robot that's no longer George Smith . . . And then you have the open door to the drinks cupboard, you have the open door to the kitchen, so there's plenty of food, there's plenty of drink and plenty of travel, there's a car, there's Highgrove, and you get lost in all of this.'[24] In conversation with Smith, Diana picked up his claim that he had been the victim of homosexual rape by a member of the Prince's staff. In August 1996, armed with Richard Kay's tape recorder, Diana made two visits to Smith (accompanied on one occasion by her personal secretary, Victoria Mendham) to record his allegations.

Friends of Diana doubt that the contents of the tape were intended as ammunition against her husband. 'The divorce was more or less done and dusted – but she still had very strong views on Charles's household . . . she loved causing trouble for St James's Palace, and it did cause a lot of trouble . . .'[25] If, however, she had wanted to do real damage, then she would have handed the tape to the police; instead she told Charles about it. News of its existence did not surface until after the collapse of the Burrell trial in November 2002, when it became evident that the stone Diana had thrown into St James's complacent pool had had ever-widening consequences.

On 11 November 2002, Prince Charles requested his recently appointed private secretary Sir Michael Peat, together with Edmund Lawson QC, to investigate – among other matters – whether there had been 'an improper cover-up of the rape allegation made by Mr George Smith in 1996'. The Peat Report was made public on 13 March 2003. The inquiry was not directed at discovering the truth or otherwise of George Smith's allegations but only as to whether there had been a deliberate cover-up of the affair. Smith had been working for the Prince as a 'Travelling Orderly' after joining the household on secondment from the Welsh Guards in 1987, and was later promoted to 'Assistant Valet' in 1993.[26] In October 1995 Smith was described as 'chronically depressed', his wife having left him, and suffering from post-traumatic problems as a result of his service in the Falklands, where he had been on HMS *Galahad* when the ship was attacked and caught fire with horrific results. He apparently told an assistant personnel officer that he had been raped by 'AA' (the 'alleged assailant', whose identity was known to the Prince of Wales's office and to the press). According to Smith he made his first report of the rape allegation to the Princess of Wales and her personal secretary, Victoria Mendham, at Kensington Palace. He was quoted as describing his visit to Diana later to the police: 'I went to see her and she was just asking me about all different stuff about AA.'[27] He said that he had repeated his allegations to the Princess sometime in 1996 when she had visited him during his third stay at the Priory. He also said that the Princess had visited him at his home in Twickenham, when 'we definitely talked about both rapes'.[28] The first rape is said to have occurred in 1988 when he had only recently joined the household. The second rape of Smith by AA is alleged to have taken place in 1995 but this only emerged later in an interview with Smith by the *Daily Mail* in 2002, by which time Smith could have been said to have become unreliable due to his problems.

Diana telephoned Mrs Yaxley, head of personnel in the Prince of Wales's household, in the autumn of 1996 and told her of a 'horrendous' allegation made by George Smith about another member of staff. Having made sure that someone else knew of the allegation, Diana then telephoned her husband. Charles reacted fiercely and called his solicitor, Fiona Shackleton, from the royal lawyers Farrer & Co., who made a note of their telephone conversation, reporting Charles's words: 'Diana has been interfering & visiting George Smith, a valet who was suffering from post-traumatic stress syndrome from Falklands – George was now alleging that AA had raped him years ago.' Charles told her he knew this to be untrue and wanted the matter cleared up. George, he said, must go: he was sorry for him because he was an alcoholic but he could not have him causing trouble in the household 'by spreading untruths about AA', adding that 'AA was in a terrible state.' Fiona Shackleton was to telephone Diana's lawyer, Anthony Julius, 'to tell him to stop Diana interfering & to sort out George making sure he was properly looked after'.[29] Smith apparently went to his local police at Hounslow and on '13th–15th' of October (1996) told them of his background and personal problems including the alleged rape in 1988 and identified the alleged rapist by name. The police note read: 'Victim states that one night they got very drunk and AA raped him.' In view of Smith's earlier – apparently unfounded – allegations about an armed stalker who had approached him at his home and in the street – and his unwillingness to proceed with the rape allegation, the police did not investigate further.

On 17 October Fiona Shackleton interviewed Mrs Yaxley who told her that Smith had been 'reissuing' his rape allegations; Mrs Yaxley also apparently told her that the Princess of Wales 'hates' AA. Mrs Yaxley wrote that day to the Princess of Wales asking her for a copy of the 'notes made in the summer' which Smith told her had been given to her. Diana replied on 21 October: 'I am afraid that I am unable to accede to your request because I have made a commitment of confidentiality to George', adding enigmatically, 'the purpose of my drawing this to your attention is so that you, with all your resources, might be able to deal with the matter.'

Fiona Shackleton noted to Anthony Julius that they wanted to find out the truth of the allegation 'without press involvement', adding 'we want minimal involvement between the two Households'. Somehow someone in the press had picked up on the story. Diana denied through her solicitor that she had been involved; as the story was well known – 'black rumours, very dangerous' – as one member of staff described it, the leak could have come from anybody. Colin Trimming, the Prince's eyes and ears at Kensington Palace, affirmed that Smith had 'a fairly close social or "drinking" relationship' with two members of Diana's staff. She also said she had not visited Smith since August.

Notes from Fiona Shackleton's meeting with George Smith state: 'Mr Smith did not convey that he "withdrew" his allegation. Rather he said that he did not wish to "press charges"; and he volunteered what was, apparently, his reason, namely that AA was "too powerful". AA's alleged "power" within the Household has been referred to by many of those interviewed by us and Mr Smith's view of this was clearly shared by others.'[50]

From early on Diana had taken what Michael Gibbins, her private secretary, described as 'a close personal interest' in what was happening. She and Gibbins had hired a solicitor for Smith, whose previous solicitor had backed out on the grounds that the matter was 'too big'. It had been decided that, as Charles had said from the beginning, 'George must go'. Gibbins told the solicitor, Chris Benson, that his understanding of the formal reason for the termination of his employment was his dependency on alcohol . . . but that Diana had told him that the substantive reason was the rape allegation. Gibbins advised Benson that, although he could not directly divulge his awareness of that allegation to the Prince's lawyers, he should use that knowledge to gain advantage in obtaining a favourable settlement.

The Peat Report admitted that, although Fiona Shackleton had suggested at the beginning that there should be a wider investigation of the truth of the allegations, there had been none for various reasons, which did not reflect well on St James's Palace. This started from the top, according to Fiona Shackleton, in a meeting on 30 April 2001 with the police and Lady Sarah McCorquodale during the investigations concerning the Burrell trial. Shackleton is recorded in notes by the investigating officer, Mrs De Brunner, as saying: 'I had written instructions from the boss, to make the whole business go away, which I did, but it was one of the lowest points of my professional career.'[31] Fiona Shackleton later denied that she had said this, specifically that she had had written instructions from the Prince 'to make the whole business go away'. She also denied saying that it had been one of the lowest points of her professional career. 'I may well have said "pretty sad about it generally" because of George and his predicament'; further, she said by way of clarification, 'by investigating the allegation I was exceeding the precise instructions I had been given and I was under pressure for a solution to be reached more speedily than I was able to achieve. To that extent it was a very difficult situation for me personally.'[32]

According to the Peat Report, interestingly, 'the fact that the allegation came to be reported initially via The Princess of Wales served to devalue it; the acrimony then existing between St James's and Kensington Palaces was such that this was suspected to be just another "shot" in the battle'. It was put to those charged with drawing up the report that: 'All we had was one poor, sad individual making an allegation of assault some years before to The Princess, who, at that time, quite frankly wanted to find ways of hurting/embarrassing her husband.'

On 18 October, Fiona Shackleton had advised that an investigation should be conducted. On 21 October at a 'Household' meeting with Sir Stephen Lamport, the incoming private secretary, and other senior officers, Mrs Shackleton noted, 'S[tephen] L[amport] wondered if some form of agreement could be reached with George to settle this matter which would avoid an investigation'. Lamport's explanation for this was that he was 'anxious to avoid unnecessary publicity in respect of an allegation believed to be untrue and "withdrawn"'. In fact, there was confusion as to whether or not George Smith had 'withdrawn' the allegation, rather than deciding not to proceed with it because of his 'terror' of AA. Again, it was stressed that no one at that level believed the rape allegation. Colin Trimming, as 'a high-ranking Police Officer and as a long-term associate of the Household', although apparently unaware that George Smith had made his allegation to anyone other than the Princess of Wales, or the Hounslow Police, did not advise any investigation either internally or by the police because 'he also disbelieved the allegation'.³³ Other explanations for the failure to investigate illuminated the general muddle and confusion in the Prince of Wales's household. Unsurprisingly, the report found that there had been no deliberate attempt at a cover-up: 'There was plainly an acute anxiety to prevent, insofar as was possible, the repetition and publication of what was believed to be a false allegation. There was not, however, as we conclude, a desire to suppress the truth.'³⁴

The public remained unaware of this potentially sensational material until the Burrell trial when the existence of Diana's tape of Smith's allegations came out. According to police notes of a meeting on 12 June 2001 during the investigation of alleged theft of Diana's property, Lady Sarah McCorquodale said: 'Found box in Diana's apartment. PB [Paul Burrell] asked to look after it because I was going on a train and it was too cumbersome. PB's got the box. In the box: letters, tape. Tape about a rape.' Someone unnamed then said: 'Tape of GS balling [sic] about being raped by AA . . .' Shackleton then said, 'I know all about that. I was asked to make it go away.' She 'became muted' and said, 'It was a terrible business. He was paid. I had to go to Twickenham to see him. He was a pathetic figure. It was the low point of my 22-year legal career.' Later, the Crown Prosecution Service notes did not refer to 'making it go away' or to the 'low point' of Fiona Shackleton's career, giving as explanation that they were 'off the record', but they do mention Lady Sarah's reference to the tape. the box and its contents: 'There is a recording of a male, George Smith, raped by AA and his description of it, Patrick Jefferson's [sic] letter of resignation, James Hewitt's signet ring and documents relating to the divorce.'

In the end, George Smith got a settlement which was worth more than twice the amount he would have got in normal compensation for dismissal. Expelled from the existence he had enjoyed in the royal household, he split up with his wife and went to live with his father in Wales. Still suffering from post-traumatic stress when interviewed by a journalist in 2002 (*Daily Mail*, 9 November 2002), he renewed his rape allegations and added that the man who had attacked him had stolen the tape from Diana's apartment. The mystery concerning the tape and the box continued when Lady Sarah McCorquodale eventually recovered the box from the police – she said she had given it to Burrell but it was not found in the police raid on his Cheshire house looking for 'the Crown Jewels', as the mahogany box was known. George Smith died, aged only forty-five, in 2005.

Meanwhile, following complaints of bullying by other staff in 1998, Prince Charles's favourite servant, Michael Fawcett, resigned. Charles was extremely reluctant to see him go and, allegedly after the intervention of Mark Bolland and Camilla Parker Bowles, he was reinstated as 'Personal Consultant' to the Prince of Wales, with a retainer and the use of a £450,000 house, a grace-and-favour property of the Duchy of Cornwall. As the organizer of stylish events – 'he is a genius at organizing events,' a guest said [35] – for the Prince he became even more indispensable.

George Smith's story had also been material for Diana's teasing of Charles – something which she was always unable to resist. An aide to Charles remembers how, when 'all this was going on in the background, Diana said to the Prince: "Poor George . . . what ghastly people you employ . . . Poor darling . . . Such a shame for you", all that sort of thing, she was such a wonderful carer, she knew exactly which buttons to press . . . I always remember when she rang up, when we heard that Blair might become Prime Minister: "Oh I had dinner with Mr Blair and his wife last night

– they're so concerned about you, darling, they so much want to help . . . It's so kind of them but they don't want to upset me and I said to them 'I don't mind'." You can imagine it. Wonderful!'[36] Diana had certainly succeeded in stirring up the mud for St James's Palace; the details of the unsavoury affair were only to come to light more than five years after her death.

20. Diana the Hunted

*'For photographers, Diana became the pot of gold at the end of the
rainbow . . .'*[1]

'The "third stage" of her life was the one between her divorce
and her death,' a friend wrote. Diana was engaged in making a
new life for herself. As a single woman she was enjoying a much
freer social life; as a public figure she was making her compassion
practically useful; she was continuing to be an excellent mother.
Everything was beginning to fall into place . . .'[2]

As the new year of 1997 opened, Diana seemed to be standing on
a pinnacle of celebrity which she herself had created, a remarkable
achievement for the shy teenager who had captured the Prince of
Wales just over fifteen years before. 'Diana was globally transformed in my view in that last year of her life,' her friend Richard
Kay said. 'That's when she became the big figure that she was.'[3]
At lunch with her in Kensington Palace, Anthony Holden was
astounded by the people she knew or had met: 'She'd just come
back from seeing Hillary Clinton in Washington; we talked about
that. She'd been to see the Pope; we talked about that. Talked
about the Queen Mother. We talked about, you know, the six
most famous people in the world, all of whom she had seen in the
last month or so.' They discussed the possibility of her setting up
a charitable trust, the idea of which had cropped up at various
times in recent years. Then she said: 'What if I gave you a name?
I was speaking the other day to Colin Powell and he strongly
advised me not to form a foundation. There are complicated this,
you lose control of that, there are tax implications . . .' 'I was very
much struck by the way she said, "If I gave you a name" – we'd
already discussed everybody you'd ever heard of –'[4] Beyond the

celebrities, she had a worldwide public not only for her beauty and charm, but for her compassion for the poor and sick which communicated itself to anyone who saw her. And, as she frequently said, she was determined to use this power to help people.

She had already taken a step which symbolized the sloughing off of her old life, deciding to auction her old wardrobe for charity. The idea had been William's. He had said, 'Mummy, you're running out of cupboard space and you're not going to wear any of those again, and I really think something should be done with them, and what will you do with them, send them to a charity shop?' Diana said, 'No, I can't do that. They're too well known, they're too well photographed, why don't we make some money for charity out of it?' When Meredith Etherington-Smith asked William if it had been his idea, 'He said, "Yes, it was my idea – we don't want Mummy wearing any of those again" – and he said it rather firmly.'[5] Some of the clothes were more than ten years old, dating from her earlier, frillier period, before Victor Edelstein had given her a more sophisticated look.

The vehicle was to be a Christie's sale of the clothes for the benefit of the National AIDS Trust, which included two of her friends, Marguerite Littman and Christopher Balfour, chairman of Christie's, with whom she had first discussed the project at lunch in July 1996. Meredith Etherington-Smith, then marketing director of Christie's Worldwide, was to be their representative for the sale, handling all aspects of it, including the cataloguing of each item.

'Christopher Balfour summoned me one morning and said, "Interesting project for you. The Princess of Wales wants to sell her clothes." I said, "Don't be stupid, what are you talking about?" And he said, "She wants to sell her clothes because she's not going to be wearing kind of big ball dresses any more, she's got a new life, she wants to sell them in aid of Marguerite's AIDS Crisis Trust and the Royal Marsden . . . You leg it down to Kensington Palace and meet her . . ."'[6] Wearing her good luck black jacket with starfish buttons, Meredith arrived at the Palace to be met by Burrell, 'smiling but looking slightly nervy'. He took her coat, asking her to wait. 'He nips upstairs and I subsequently learned from her that he'd actually gone to say, "She looks all right . . ." because she was actually rather nervous, she was as nervous as I was about meeting me for some reason. Apparently I passed muster – I was filtered through by the butler and went up this very grand staircase which was obviously part of the original baroque KP, to see this amazing human being dressed in a white T-shirt and sneakers and a navy blue cardigan, also looking rather nervous . . .'

'It's very curious,' Meredith recalled. 'I've met a lot of very famous people but no one as famous as Diana, visually famous anyway. But there's a difference between visual fame and people who are famous for who they really are. In the months after September 1996 when we first met, I formed a very different opinion of her from the one I had read about. What I'd thought she was like was totally unlike the side of her she presented to me.'[7]

Meredith surmised that Diana was very comfortable in the company of older women. 'I think possibly, without being too psychotherapeutic about it, because of the lack of a mother . . . most of her confidantes apart from Rosa Monckton, were actually older women – Annabel Goldsmith, Elsa, Marguerite – and I think she felt very comfortable, they weren't competition, they were fun and she could become slightly girly with them without the baggage of "I'm the most beautiful person in the world" . . .' It was decided that Diana should be involved all the time. '"It's going to be partners",' Meredith said. '"I'll never do anything and make any decision without referring to you."' 'There wasn't one decision that wasn't discussed with her, faxed to her, okayed by her . . . And as a result of that, I worked with her for nine months, pretty much, and we didn't have one what I call eyelash moment.' Asked what she meant, Meredith explained: 'That sort of look, when she kind of retreated into herself and that hair came over the forehead and the head went down and she looked up [through her lashes] . . . it was a very nice and fun working partnership.'[8]

Meredith bought a green leather book which Diana filled with the catalogue entries in her big loopy writing. 'That writing reminds me so much of so many people who were at West Heath . . . She was not a stupid Sloane, she was much more perceptive about herself than you would ever think from just looking at the image or reading the press or seeing her on television. I think she was one of the smartest people I've ever met. Because West Heath was basically knitting for Sloanes when she was there. In my generation we used to laugh at them, we used to say they did O levels in Hamster Husbandry, and I think it was a shame because she had great natural common sense . . .'9

Meredith realized that it would be wise to keep a certain distance between them. 'She was a tremendous charmer in the fact that she wanted to draw people into her web and then, having drawn them into the web, when they were totally enslaved by her, then she got bored . . . I felt my job was to always be slightly removed . . . At the second or third meeting, she said, "You must call me Diana." I said, "Actually no, I'd be happier with Ma'am, because as far as I'm concerned that's what you have been and you are . . ." Which went down really well. She said, "Come on, call me Diana", and I said "No", and a slight distance was maintained. Because she talked about other people, "so and so is getting kind of boring, she's ringing up the whole time", I said to her, "Your problem is you are too damn charming and they get completely enthralled by you and have to have the fix", and she laughed and said, "I suppose you're right." And I said, "It's a weapon isn't it, charm? You can convert people." And she said, "You're quite right, but I haven't had that many weapons in my life. What you've got you use." '10

Among other things, they discussed Diana's campaign against the use of landmines. Diana told Meredith that she had written to the Foreign Office asking them if she could become a roving ambassador – 'Of course they turned me down . . I've decided to do it on my own and I'm going to do it for a cause and the cause is going to be landmines. It's appalling the damage they do, and no one cares and they just spray them all over the place like ghastly bulbs. At least I can do something good with this kind of presence, you know, the opportunities I have, well, they're not opportunities, they're huge open gateways . . .'[11]

'Discouraged from becoming a roving unofficial ambassador,' William Deedes, who accompanied her to both Angola and Bosnia on landmine research trips, wrote,

she sought to address herself to various issues in the world which were being neglected. There were millions of them [landmines] scattered round the world. They lurked wherever there had been conflict. A few charitable organisations were engaged in locating and lifting them, but it was discouraging as well as dangerous work because more mines were being constantly laid in the wars bedevilling Africa. The manufacturers of these mines represented a huge vested interest, which reduced the chances . . . of an international ban . . . defence forces in Britain, America and much of Europe saw the mines, properly laid and charted, as legitimate means of defence . . .[12]

Diana had been in discussion with Mike Whitlam, head of the British Red Cross, about renewing her work for the organization. The result was a visit in January 1997 to Angola, the scene of prolonged civil war, under the auspices of the Red Cross and with a BBC television crew in attendance to film a documentary to raise money for the British Red Cross Landmines Appeal. Lord Deedes, who had been an advocate of a landmines ban since 1992, travelled with her for the *Daily Telegraph*, accompanied by mostly unenthusiastic and cynical members of the press corps. Deedes, who had been briefing Diana about landmines on visits to Kensington Palace, paid tribute to the drawing power of Diana's presence: 'Nobody took a blind bit of interest in landmines until she came along,' he said. The journalists, accustomed to accompanying royal visits in daintier surroundings than Angola, were, Deedes said, 'dismayed' by the state of the capital, Luanda, with stinking rubbish piled high in the hot streets. *Sunday Times* reporter Christina Lamb, young but nonetheless a veteran war reporter, had certainly been cynical about Diana in Angola. She was impressed: despite the heat and the smells Diana had come to work and work she did. Angola, said Lamb, was one of the few remaining places in the world where most people had no idea who she was, and therefore it was all the more remarkable to see the effect she had on the amputees she went among. 'The Red Cross whisked us from one hospital to the next,' Lamb wrote,

each with ever more horrific scenes of skeletal figures with missing arms, missing legs, and blown off heads – victims of some of the 16m land-mines scattered round the country. Many of the injuries were so grue-some I could not bear to look, despite years of Third World reporting. But Diana never turned her head away. Instead, she had something I'd only ever seen before in Nelson Mandela – a kind of aura that made people want to be with her, and a completely natural, straight-from-the-heart sense of how to bring hope to those who seemed to us to have little to live for.[13]

Diana insisted on going to Huambo and Cuito where the war had left the countryside infested with mines. The television reporter Sandy Gall described Diana's action as extremely cour-ageous: he had encountered mines in Afghanistan and knew how dangerous it could be to walk through 'cleared' minefields. Just before it was reluctantly agreed to allow her to visit these 'hell-holes', as Deedes described them, in London two journalists from *The Times* and the *Daily Telegraph* had entertained a junior minister, Lord Howe, to lunch. Expressing the usual Establishment view of Diana, he had been critical of her visit and called it political interference – the usual cliché 'loose cannon' came up. The minis-ter's remark caused heightened interest in Diana's trip: as Deedes put it, 'if it was causing offence to the Tory Government, that doubled its news value'.[14] Diana's comment to Deedes when he approached her in private next morning was 'idiot minister': to the cameras she insisted more diplomatically that the purpose of her visit was humanitarian and in no way political.

By now, Christina Lamb admitted, the visit had 'wiped out' all her past cynicism about Diana. 'That Lady-with-the-Lamp performance wasn't just for the cameras,' she wrote.[15]

Once, at a hospital in Huambo when the photographers had all flown back to their air-conditioned hotels to wire their pictures, I watched Diana, unaware that any journalists were still present, sit and hold the hand of Helena Ussova, a seven-year-old who'd had her intestines blown to pieces by a mine. For what seemed an age the pair just sat, no words needed. When Diana finally left, the young girl struggled through her pain to ask me if the beautiful lady was an angel . . . At the end of the Angola trip Diana said that the lasting image she'd take away was of that terribly ill young girl.[16]

The Angola visit was not the end of Diana's involvement with landmines that year. In mid-June she spoke at a conference in London on landmines under the auspices of the Mines Advisory Group held at the Royal Geographical Society, chaired by Deedes, who helped her draft her speech. With Mike Whitlam's advice she had drawn up a chart of landmine sites across the world, marked with red pins, which she kept in a corner of her sitting room at Kensington Palace. She told Deedes they should make another landmines expedition that summer, and, with the cooperation of Norwegian People's Aid and Landmine Survivors Network (LSN) from Washington, a three-day visit to Bosnia was arranged from 8 to 10 August. The party, which included Bill Deedes and Paul Burrell, by now Diana's inseparable shadow, flew out on a private jet owned by multimillionaire philanthropist George Soros. On the drive to Sarajevo they were joined by two Americans, Jerry White and Ken Rutherford, who had formed LSN after being maimed by landmines. White had lost one leg, Rutherford both. As the two Americans climbed awkwardly into the back of the Landcruiser, Diana turned round from her front seat to say, 'You can take your legs off, boys!' That broke the ice, Burrell recorded; the men had felt that they should keep their artificial limbs on in the presence of royalty.[17] Burrell, the Boswell of the landmines visits, recorded one very significant remark. Landmine victims can recall exactly where and when their accident happened: as they were discussing this, Diana remarked, 'My accident was on 29 July 1981 . . .'[18]

Deedes recalled with amusement his memory of Burrell, the protector. 'We stayed in a brand new hotel in Bosnia, and our rooms were opposite – she was one side of the corridor and I was the other side and I came out of my room in the morning and met Burrell coming out having delivered her breakfast, so I said to him, "Are you going downstairs? Let's have breakfast together." He said, "Yes, sure." I went downstairs, had my breakfast, went up to my room and found Burrell with a chair against her door looking very determined. And I said, "Hi, I thought you were coming to breakfast?" And Burrell said in tones of outrage, "The manager of this hotel burst into her room to ask her whether she approved of it because it's new." I said, "That's very continental, in Paris managers do." Anyway, he was not pleased, he sat there and said, "I'm staying here until she's dressed and ready to go out." That was an indication of the relationship – he was her protector.'[19]

On the last day of the visit they toured the ruins of Sarajevo. 'It had suffered cruelly during the Bosnian war, with mortar bombs falling constantly on the city, and much of the open space had been given over to burial grounds. Diana saw a woman tending her son's grave in one of the huge cemeteries there, walked up to her and embraced her silently, the two touching each other's faces with complete empathy.'[20] The same scene had taken place previously with a young widow whose husband had been killed by a mine while fishing. 'There being no interpreter present there could be very little said. What passed between them is beyond reckoning. When we parted, the widow seemed restored to life.' Diana had the unique gift of silent empathy. Deedes saw the two sides of Diana – 'All this,' he said, 'in the middle of a fling with Dodi Fayed.'[21] The same Diana who stood quietly embracing the bereaved mother in the Sarajevo cemetery would, within hours, be on the jet giggling with Burrell at the tabloid frenzy over her new affair. Aboard the plane she discussed with Deedes the prospect of attending an Oslo conference on landmines with a view to calling for a ban. 'Be careful,' Deedes told her. 'It's political.' 'I was going to write the speech with her . . . saying exactly how to keep out of politics for her but to get the landmine ban.'[22] On the plane, Diana made a toast: 'Here's to our next country . . .' Cambodia and Vietnam were on the list for October. She never got to Oslo or to Cambodia or Vietnam. It was 10 August 1997 and she had only twenty-one days of life to live. 'She was only involved with landmines from January 1997 until her death in August,' Bill Deedes said. 'And there's no doubt at all that while she was on the job she woke the world up as nobody else has done.' In December 1997, in the wake of a surge of opinion after Diana's death in favour of a ban on landmines, the Ottawa Landmine Accord banning landmines was drawn up, to be signed by forty countries. Mike Whitlam said: 'They would not have been talking at the Canadian meeting, where they ratified the Convention later that year, had she not gone to Angola. I would stake my life on that. They actually acknowledged what she'd done – at that meeting.'[23]

The landmines campaign had given her a new purpose in life; she publicly announced in a speech in May, about eating disorders, that she had finally beaten bulimia. She looked radiantly healthy. Even her physical appearance had changed 'from a puppy to a gorgeous lady', as one of her designers, Jacques Azagury, put it. Catherine Walker, who had dressed Diana for much of her adult life, said, 'the demure phase was over and so was her marriage but what I hadn't anticipated was how quickly she would change and begin wearing my sexier evening wear . . . her looks had changed dramatically since she had first come to see me as a pale, slightly plump, fragile-looking girl. Now she was tanned, fitter, more muscular. She had become a perfectionist, working hard on her body because of the scrutiny it was under and to help keep her sane through her marital upheaval . . .'[24] In keeping with this free, independent image, her skirts became shorter, her heels higher, the lines of her dresses simpler and sexier. Now outside the royal circle she could wear black for the first time since the disastrous outing in 'that dress' at the Guildhall.

'She was growing up in front of my eyes,' said Meredith Etherington-Smith, who saw her from September 1996 through to July 1997. 'It was the most amazing year seeing this person growing up and making choices, really important kind of choices, about landmines, taking that on, being serious about it, being really serious about this [Christie's] sale. She was professional, she was serious, she was grown up.' Even Diana's posture had changed, from the shy upward glance and hunched shoulders, to sitting erect and standing up straight. She was even stopping chewing her nails. Her fingernails, Meredith observed, 'got better as we went on'. 'She was generally more confident, she became a different sort of person, less the Princess of Wales and more Diana.'[25]

One thing she did take seriously was her role first as mother to the boys and second, as Meredith put it, as the Queen Mother of the twenty-first century. 'Her relationship with the boys was patently a wonderful one . . . She was a very good mother.[26] I expected them to be more protective of her than they were, and they weren't, they weren't mewling and puking and clustering round her. They didn't have a neurotic relationship. It seemed to me to be perfectly healthy and normal and nice and a great tribute first of all to Diana and secondly to Charles.'[27] 'Constitutional plans – well, she felt her long-distance role was to be the Queen Mother of the twenty-first century, that the influence the Queen Mother had had on her grandchildren in a way, she felt that was the kind of role which in a curious way she had been chosen for and one did feel that there was a bit of divine right entering into this, a little bit of fate. And she felt that William should be a democratic King, that the boys needed to have friends, that they needed to know their generation, they needed to know politicians, not just Tory ones, that they needed to know the Blair children. They needed to be part of contemporary English life, not an English life that was really out of date by the end of the war – and I'm paraphrasing some quite long conversations about this. And her job was to make sure they were released from the glass cage, and that when he did come to the throne, a lot of people would know him, and he wouldn't be a mystery, wouldn't be a royal freak, that he would be a person.[28] I think that she very much thought she would be a power behind the throne . . .'[29] Diana emphasized her desire that William should be 'a very English King': she felt that her Spencer blood had a lot to contribute. 'She felt that because of the spider's web of marital alliances and blood they [the Royal Family] weren't English. "I come from an English family," she had said proudly, and "we [the Spencers] are a lot older than they are." She was very proud of the Duke of Marlborough, for instance.'[30]

Diana was very anxious that her boys should not become isolated as the previous royal generation had been, as indeed their father had been. That was why she had wanted the boys, and William in particular, to go to Eton because they would have proper friends there and not sycophants. 'Diana said, "There's no messing around at Eton about someone being the heir to the throne. If you're not popular, charming, intelligent, or good at games, you're not going to rate, are you?" And so William knows a lot of people. And the interesting thing about that she said, "I think they'll be protection, those friends too. They've grown up together and they'll be protective."[31] And they are. You don't see grab shots of William that often, and why? Because his friends don't utter. She'd thought all this through. That's what I mean by being smart.'[32] 'They had money which they carried and spent and they went shopping. In other words she was trying to provide as normal a life as possible – they could come out from behind the glass window, and that was her great legacy.'

Meredith helped her shape her new modern image, with photographs by Mario Testino. One day she had commented to Diana how much better she looked in real life – without make-up, in jeans and a T-shirt and natural hair. 'You know you look so much better like that rather than with all the lacquered hair and the make-up. You've got wonderful skin, you don't need to slap all that stuff on. It's not modern. Jewellery isn't modern except for one of those little Tiffany diamond crosses – those chokers – for God's sake!' A set of photographs in the grand manner had been taken by Snowdon for the sale. 'They were fine but I wanted much more the girl who walked through the minefields. I wanted the woman I saw who looked amazing and modern. Discussing who should do them, Diana asked Meredith to choose someone she hadn't worked with before: 'I want someone new and I want to look how I feel inside. I feel like I belong to the twentieth century now, I really do. I'm doing modern things and I'm trying to lead a modern life, and I'm a single woman and that's how I want to look.'[33]

At the shoot with Testino in a Battersea studio, Diana had enjoyed herself immensely. Afterwards, as they were packing up, with music booming in the background, she started playing around, arm in arm with Mario Testino, imitating Naomi Campbell doing catwalk and Kate Moss doing catwalk. 'Everyone was screaming with laughter, including her, and she went that amazing rose pink colour [Diana always had blushed easily] and she looked fantastic, so full of energy and life. It was so sweet and so sad when I took the work prints [of the photographs] back and she said, "It was one of the happiest days of my life – and I really mean it." Looking at them she said, musing, "But these are me. Really, really me." She also said, "God, I think I look like Marilyn Monroe in those pictures . . ."' She was quite obsessed with Marilyn Monroe, Meredith said, and in one of the pictures she did look like the young Marilyn. She often talked about her, and how she had fought the studio system in Hollywood on her own and won, because they had dumped her and then had to take her back. 'I think perhaps she felt there was another woman against the world,' Meredith said. 'I remember having a conversation about it with her once and her saying that she [Monroe] wasn't just a blonde fluffy thing, she was smart, and I think she identified with that.'[34]

Diana still felt beleaguered by court circles. She told Meredith she had 'a lot of enemies'. 'That sounds a bit paranoid,' Meredith replied. 'No, you know how it works. It's justification – I'm the baddie.' 'Well, all you have to do is to be a goodie, and you are a goodie by the example you set. That's why landmines – patently you have an enormous sympathy with people less fortunate than you are.' 'You call me fortunate?' 'I do, actually. I call you fortunate because you have the rest of your life in front of you and you have amazing opportunities to do amazing things . . .' 'Yes,' she said, repeating that she had enemies and felt very much on her own sometimes. 'But you have good friends.' She replied, 'Yes. But you try fighting them [the Establishment enemies].' She was right, of course. It took a great deal of courage to face down her powerful enemies who saw the Establishment threatened by her very existence. Despite her supportive friends in all walks of life, the hostile pressure was very much alive and relentless and ready to pounce when 'goodie' Diana fell back into the ways of 'baddie Diana'. Diana believed that there was an agenda among Camilla and her circle and certain jealous courtiers to paint her as mad and sideline her in public life. 'They would have preferred her to disappear,' a friend said; 'she was deeply inconvenient – and enjoyed being deeply inconvenient.'[35]

Unfortunately, Diana could not remain 'goodie' Diana for long, without tripping up on her needier, more foolish and self-indulgent instincts. She quarrelled with her staff, helpers and 'star' friends. She quarrelled with her personal assistant Victoria Mendham, presenting her with her bill at the K Club which represented an astronomical sum for the woman to pay (Prince Charles later settled it). She quarrelled with Martin Bashir, backing out of a book she had contemplated doing with him. Under the terms of her divorce agreement, with its confidentiality clause which did not allow her to discuss her life in royal circles, the huge sums quoted by her potential publisher did not seem realistic. Moreover, it was alleged that Paul Burrell had repeated to her some disobliging comments Bashir had made to him about her. She quarrelled with Gianni Versace and Elton John when she backed out of contributing a foreword she had written to a book of photographs to raise money for John's AIDS Foundation, because, just after her divorce came through, she became nervous of what the Queen would think when she saw the book's suggestive images next to pictures of the Royal Family. (She was reconciled with Elton John at Versace's funeral in Milan on 22 July after the designer's murder in Miami.)

She did not abandon hopes of Hasnat Khan, nor of her dream of marrying him. In May she flew to Pakistan again on the pretext of helping Imran Khan and his hospital. She intended to meet

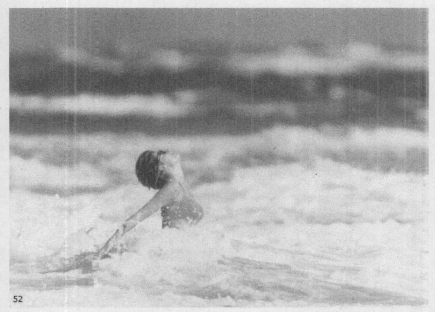

52

Diana enjoys the freedom of Nevis – her first holiday after her separation.

53

Diana is painted by Nelson Shanks as she sits for her first portrait as a
separated woman.

In 1994 Diana gave up police protection, which made her increasingly vulnerable to the ever-merciless paparazzi.

57

Post-*Panorama*, December 1995: Diana accepts an award from Henry Kissinger at the 'Humanitarian of the Year' awards ceremony, New York.

1996: Diana watching heart surgery at Harefield Hospital, Middlesex.

58

Diana with Imran and Jemima Khan and Lady Annabel Goldsmith at a fundraising gala for Imran's hospital charity in Lahore.

59

28 August 1996: Diana on the day of her
divorce from Charles, accompanied by
Lucia Flecha de Lima.

Hasnat Khan.

New York, June 1997: Diana at a gala party to launch the Christie's
auction of her dresses held in order to raise money for her charities.
She is wearing a dress by Catherine Walker.

63

Diana visiting the Lord Gage
Centre for old people, a Guinness
Trust home in Newham, East
London. Despite her global success,
Diana was always dedicated to
home-grown charities.

London, June 1997: Diana at the
Christie's pre-auction party.

64

1997: Diana comforts a grieving mother during her final campaign to ban the use of landmines in Bosnia.

65

Angola, January 1997: Diana at Neves Bendinha, an orthopaedic workshop in Luanda.

66

67

August 1997: Diana and Dodi on the yacht *Jonikal* in St Tropez.

68

Diana and Dodi leave the Ritz moments before their fatal accident.

6 September 1997: the funeral of Diana, Princess of Wales. Her coffin is followed by her ex-husband, her ex-father-in-law, her brother and her two sons.

Tribute to the 'People's Princess': flowers and wreaths outside Kensington Palace after the death of Diana – an expression of the extraordinary popularity of a princess who touched the lives of many.

Hasnat's parents, his mother in particular, and if possible to convince them that she would be a suitable wife for their son. She persuaded Jemima Khan to go with her and Jimmy Goldsmith to lend them his jet. This was Diana at her most selfish and inconsiderate; Jimmy Goldsmith, as all his close circle knew, was dying, in fact was soon to die, and the last thing a member of his family wanted to do was to leave him and fly to Pakistan. Jimmy apparently told Jemima to go but to have the jet in readiness to leave Pakistan at any moment if necessary. This time Cosima Somerset did not go with her; she had been the victim of one of Diana's cruelly abrupt breaks, the reason apparently relating to something within the Goldsmith circle.

Diana had done everything she could to get close to Hasnat Khan's family, visiting his uncle Omar and his English wife Jane at their home in Stratford, and inviting Jane to stay at Kensington Palace. Through them she had made friends with Hasnat's grandmother, Nanny Appa, and she hoped to follow Jane's example and win acceptance into the aristocratic Pathan clan. Above all she needed to win acceptance from Hasnat's mother, the formidable, university-educated Naheed, who had bitter memories of the British when, after Partition, her family had been uprooted from their home in India. In Muslim society the mother is given great respect in the close extended family where arranged marriages are the rule, and each member of the family supports the other, often sharing the same house. Naheed did not approve of Western cultural images and her son, for all his Western ways, at heart shared her cultural beliefs. Although Diana hoped to follow the example of her friend Jemima, who in marrying Imran had converted to Islam and lived in the family complex in Lahore, that marriage was eventually to fail. It was a complicated situation both for Diana and for Hasnat's parents, anxious to see their son married (two arranged engagements had not led to marriage) but nervous of the consequences where Diana was concerned. Diana was staying with Imran and Jemima in Lahore when she was invited to visit Khan's family at their Model Town home in Jhelum, some one hundred miles to the north of Lahore, to meet not only

Hasnat's mother and father but also eleven members of his family. She dressed in a blue shalwar kameez which Jemima had had made for her in Lahore, and travelled incognito with two of Hasnat's sisters in an old black Toyota Corolla to avoid press attention. Nothing was said about marriage during Diana's visit and Diana appeared sombre as she left, but in the car with one of Hasnat's sisters she seemed confident that she could continue with her modern life and her campaigns at the same time as being married to Hasnat. On her return she confessed to Imran Khan how much she wanted to marry Hasnat.

The Hasnat Khan relationship continued on and off through the summer. Although he loved her, he continued to be undecided about the prospect of marriage and Diana's needy behaviour – constant telephone calls, sitting in a car in the street outside his house – following the pattern of her previous affair with Oliver Hoare, unnerved him. When Diana tried the old tactic of jealousy, being seen and photographed with Sikh businessman Gulu Lalvani, he was so angry that he broke off relations with her, not for the first or the last time.

With her private life in turmoil, Diana had her public life to distract her. In late May she had taken William to lunch with the newly elected Prime Minister Tony Blair and his family at his official country residence, Chequers, when they had discussed a possible future role for her. Blair, who displayed a unique ability to gauge popular feeling, saw the promotional potential of Diana as other more conventional politicians had not. June was a busy month: on 19 June she was in Washington for a meeting with Hillary Clinton; she then flew to New York to see her idol, Mother Teresa. (She had met her in Rome in February 1992 after visiting her hospice and orphanage in Calcutta on her India trip with Charles. This had greatly inspired her.) They walked hand in hand through the Bronx. Two days later, back in England, she drove herself up to Stratford to see the Omar Khans and eleven members of the family over from Pakistan, including her particular friend, Hasnat's grandmother, Nanny Appa. Two days after that, on 23 June, she was back in New York for the pre-sale party at

Christie's, flying back before the auction took place on 25 June to avoid the media circus. The sale was a great success: all the dresses sold, for a total of $3,258,750; the catalogue sales alone accounted for $2.5 million. The top price of $222,500 was paid for the 'White House dress' by Victor Edelstein which she had worn dancing with John Travolta.

While in New York before the sale on 23 June, Diana had continued her campaign to win over – and perhaps to learn from – powerful women. After seeing Katharine Graham and Hillary Clinton in Washington, she lunched at the fashionable Four Seasons in New York on 23 June with Anna Wintour, editor of American *Vogue*, and the British journalist Tina Brown, then editor of the *New Yorker*. The lunch had been arranged by Anna Wintour, with whom she had worked on a breast cancer fashion benefit the previous September. Despite her brave talk of her 'strength', the joy of giving help to people who needed it and her purpose in life – speaking of the landmines campaign, apparently, with an 'eerie' expression in her eyes – Tina Brown perceptively diagnosed 'the frantic Diana' lurking beneath the shining surface, so soon to be revealed in her summer antics with Dodi Fayed.

Beneath the glitter of her public life, her worldwide celebrity, the beauty which bewitched everyone she met, she was still insecure and a prey to the sense of rejection which never left her, encapsulated in the failure of her marriage. Out of the limelight, she was lonely, shut up in the gloom of Kensington Palace with the butler and addicted to soaps (*Brookside* was a favourite). The loneliness struck hardest at weekends when the boys were with their father: 'I stay in town. If I go out, I keep my eyes down or straight ahead. Wherever I go the press find ways to spy. Often I visit a hospice.'[36] Evenings, again, were hard; sometimes accompanied, first by Patrick Jephson, then driven by Burrell, she toured the seedier parts of London, spotting drug dealers or prostitutes to whom she often gave money in an effort to make them go home. The media siege served further to isolate her; to escape them she sometimes went out sitting on the floor of a taxi; from the time she dispensed with her protection in 1994 the hunt was on. Often the paparazzi waiting outside places like her therapist Susie Orbach's house would shout obscenities at her, 'spraying her down', hoping to catch shots of her distress and tears. Her fame and her royalty made it worse; 'that three-foot royal aura' around her, which Meredith Etherington-Smith had observed, made her almost unapproachable in an intimate way. At times on private social occasions, such as a dinner party at Taki Theodoracopulos's house, she seemed almost desperate to make friends, zeroing in on people, reaching out and drawing them in. Then, in order to seem 'one of the girls', she would rivet, and sometimes repel, people with her indiscreet talk, 'inappropriate', sexual conversation, venomous remarks about former friends, and raucous 'common' laugh. She was sadly aware that the baggage of her past would make it difficult to find the Barbara Cartland married life she still yearned for. 'Who would take me on?' she said. Yet at times she concluded that she would be better off single, the mother of the future King and the promoter of great causes.

Again, she was alone, even as far as her family was concerned. Sarah McCorquodale was the closest to her and sometimes acted as her lady-in-waiting, but she lived with her family on a large farm in Lincolnshire and therefore was physically distant. Relations with Jane, who lived close by, were awkward: despite Robert Fellowes' friendly attitude to Diana, he was still the Queen's principal private secretary and could not afford to take sides. For almost all the past four years, relations with her brother Charles had been tense, first in the misunderstanding over the house and then as a result of an unkind letter written by him in April 1996 referring to Diana's 'mental problems' quoted by a ferociously loyal Paul Burrell.[37] In private conversations Charles had made no secret of his opinion that his sister was dangerous to know. The terms of Spencer's letter were bitter: 'After years of neglect on both sides, our relationship is the weakest I have with any of my sisters . . . perhaps you have more time to notice that we seldom speak . . . I will always be there for you . . . as a loving brother: albeit one that has, through fifteen years' absence, rather lost touch – to the extent I have to read Richard Kay to learn that you are coming to Althorp

. . . I long ago accepted that I was a peripheral part of your life, and that no longer saddens me. Indeed, it's easier for me and my family to be in that position as I view the consternation and hurt your fickle friendship has caused so many.' Worst of all, from Diana's point of view, went on to refer to her 'illness' (presumably bulimia) and 'mental problems': 'I fear for you. I know how manipulation and deceit are parts of the illness . . . I pray that you are getting appropriate and sympathetic treatment for your mental problems.'[38] Recently, however, they had had a rapprochement when Diana had flown to South Africa in March, ostensibly to see her brother but actually in pursuance of her campaign for Hasnat Khan, and to check out the possibilities of South Africa as a place where they could eventually live.

Saddest of all, Diana had not been on speaking terms with her mother since Frances had given an interview to *Hello!* (for charity) in which she had claimed that the withdrawal of the HRH title did not matter and made other observations to which Diana objected. Diana had not been consulted over the article but in any case their relationship had been difficult after a series of telephone calls in which Frances had criticized Diana's behaviour with men. Frances had been convicted of drink-driving the previous year and was in a fragile emotional state. She was so anguished by the breakdown of relations with Diana that she even telephoned William Tallon, the Queen Mother's page, imploring him to get Diana to speak to her. Diana, as always when she felt she had been betrayed or let down, was implacable and sadly they never spoke again.

21. Fatal Summer

'Whom the gods love, die young' (Lord Byron, *Don Juan*, Canto IV, xii, from the Greek)

At the lunch in New York in June with Tina Brown and Anna Wintour, Diana had displayed 'unease' when asked how she was going to spend the summer holidays. The truth was that at that moment she had nowhere to go. July and August are difficult months for fashionable people without an invitation to a villa or a yacht for the sun, or a country house estate in Ireland or Scotland for the fresh air and the shooting. In any case, country house life was no longer an option for Diana who had cut herself off from that set long ago. Diana and 'the boys', with their concomitant detectives and paparazzi, were not normal guests. For Diana, it was the Jackie Kennedy Onassis dilemma: how to combine great celebrity with a need for privacy and family life. Later that month, she thought she had found the answer.

Mohamed Fayed, or, as he preferred to be called, 'Al' Fayed, had been born in 1929 in a village near Alexandria, Egypt, into a modest background which he preferred to forget.[1] Fayed had risen from his lowly beginnings through his connection with the Kashoggi family, Saudis of Turkish descent, who owed their position to their connection with the rulers of Saudi Arabia. In 1954 he had married Samira, the sixteen-year-old sister of Adnan Kashoggi, his contemporary, son of the head of the family Dr Mohamed Kashoggi. Their son, Emad, always known as 'Dodi', had been born in 1955; after Fayed's divorce from Samira shortly afterwards, Dodi had been brought up in straitened circumstances by his uncle, Salah, his father's younger brother, and his Italian wife, and strictly forbidden to associate with his mother. While his father travelled the world in search of a fortune through a series of dubious enterprises, the wretched Dodi had been left at home in Alexandria. Fayed's biographer wrote that Dodi was the casualty of his father's unsuccessful ambitions. 'Barely literate, speaking poor Arabic . . . Dodi endured an isolated and loveless childhood. Frequently he cried, and he even screamed during the night. Anguished by the suffering, the father would comfort his son in a shared bed, and, the following morning, would spend over-generously on toys. Torn between earning his fortune and caring for his son, Fayed . . . did little to alleviate the boy's misery.'[2]

By 1969, through his connections with Dubai, Fayed had amassed a fortune of £2 million, a considerable sum for those days. Within two years he had acquired a Rolls-Royce with chauffeur, a chalet in Gstaad, apartments at 60 Park Lane and the honorific 'Al' before his name. By 1972 he was the proud owner of a Scottish castle, Balnagown, a villa in St Tropez, and a yacht named *Dodi*. Dodi himself had been enrolled at Sandhurst, the British military training college, attended not only by British officer candidates but also by the sons of Arab princes like King Hussein of Jordan. After only four weeks, uneducated, materially spoiled, hopelessly indolent and unathletic, the boy had begged to be withdrawn. Mohamed Fayed, meanwhile, had added Barrow Green Court, Oxted, Surrey, to his property portfolio, qualifying him to be considered as the owner of a country estate. In 1975 he bought shares in Lonrho, the company set up by 'Tiny' Rowland, a capitalist adventurer whose wealth surpassed even Fayed's. Alarmed by the Department of Trade and Industry inspectors' adverse report into Lonrho's dealings, Fayed sold out, having made £8 million on the transaction. In 1979, still in search of the social position and prestige which eluded him, he bought the Paris Ritz.

Dodi, meanwhile, was pursuing a playboy life of girls and nightclubs: his aimlessness both irritated and alarmed his father. Dodi dreamed of a career in films and, as a reward for introducing his father to a Finnish beauty queen, Heini Wathen, whom he later married, Fayed set up a film production company for Dodi. Interested only in girls and drugs, Dodi had little to contribute to the enterprise. Financial success came when Fayed's company, Allied Stars, invested 25 per cent in the Oscar-winning film *Chariots of Fire*. Dodi was billed as executive producer – in fact he had done nothing but spend money on friends, girls and cocaine, even succeeding in getting himself thrown off the set of *Chariots*. Mohamed, furious at his son's decadent lifestyle, cut off his financial support. It was not for lack of love: 'Mohamed only wanted the best for him but the way in which he went about achieving the best for him, didn't help,' said a friend. 'But he loved him, worshipped him, adored him and if anybody tells you differently, they're wrong.'[3] In 1984, Mohamed Fayed had found a new source of wealth, becoming financial adviser to the Sultan of Brunei. In 1985, after a protracted war with his old partner, Tiny Rowland, Fayed bought the House of Fraser and became the owner of what was then a British national treasure, Harrods.

By then, Mohamed and Dodi had become reconciled; when Dodi's mother Samira died in March 1986, his father forbade him from attending her funeral, definitively cutting him off from his Kashoggi relations. He gave Dodi a £150,000 monthly allowance, free accommodation in Park Lane, Paris, St Tropez and his suite at the Pierre in New York and use of his fleet of cars, including a Mercedes, a Lagonda and two Aston Martins.[4] Meanwhile, a vengeful Rowland had asked that Fayed's purchase of Harrods should be referred to the Monopolies Commission, alleging dishonesty in its financing. Questions were asked by MPs friendly to Rowland in the House of Commons and another investigation, once again by the Department of Trade and Industry, loomed. Fayed gave donations to the ruling Conservative Party and, in tandem with a parliamentary lobbyist, Ian Greer, payments for questions to MPs. This, however, did not prevent the DTI from launching an investigation into the Harrods purchase. The investigation branded the Fayed brothers, Mohamed and Ali, 'liars' but the behaviour of Rowland in pursuing his vendetta led Lord Young at the DTI to decide neither to refer the case to the Monopolies Commission nor to release the inspectors' hostile report. The report was eventually released but Fayed's devious behaviour and that of Rowland had tarnished both of them. As a result of the DTI report, when the Fayed brothers applied for British passports in 1993 their application was rejected. Fayed had been deeply offended and, as a result, turned against what he liked to imagine was the corrupt British Establishment. Despite his wealth, he was a deeply controversial figure.

And the wealth was, to say the least, ostentatious. Fayed's Gulfstream jet was decorated in deep pink with Egyptian motifs and hieroglyphics woven into the fabrics covering the walls and floors. A penthouse in the style of a Roman villa adorned the new eighth floor of 60 Park Lane, with solid gold fittings on his double bath. In Harrods, the escalator was decorated with gilded Egyptian statues cast with Mohamed Fayed's features. He had nine houses to commute to with his Gulfstream, a Sikorski helicopter and a fleet of red armoured Mercedes limousines. Yet the British Establishment, shocked by his vendetta against the Conservative government which had refused him his passport, began to turn their backs on Fayed. By 1996 he needed Diana to add to Harrods, the Villa Windsor in Paris which he had acquired in 1986, Turnbull & Asser, the Prince's shirtmakers, and *Punch* magazine.

Fayed was determined to rise to the top in British society after his acquisition of Harrods. He relished his annual meeting with the Queen at the Royal Windsor Horse Show, contriving to be photographed with the monarch even if he had to retreat to the stands as a mere spectator afterwards. Cleverly, he had diagnosed that the route into the British Royal Family lay through polo: sponsorship of a Harrods polo match in July 1986 would, he knew, lead to an introduction to the Prince and Princess of Wales (a photograph shows Diana at the event with Dodi in the background). In September 1996 he had offered Diana a directorship of Harrods; when she refused it, he offered it to Raine, who accepted.

Diana was the ultimate prize and the honey trap was his wealth. Diana had persuaded him to sponsor *The Nutcracker* for the English National Ballet. 'It was at a gala,' Pamela Harlech remembered, 'and she just said to him, "Come on, you can afford it, come on, just give it!" It was something like £400,000 – and she said, "You can afford it. It'll be good for you." And of course it was, it was terrific for Harrods because it was Christmas.'⁵ At another ballet gala dinner in early June, Fayed was sitting between Pamela Harlech and Diana when he saw his chance. 'He said, "What are you doing this summer?" And she said, "I don't know, I haven't decided what to do with the boys." He said, "Why don't you come and stay with us?" Pamela and Derek Deane, who was sitting on her other side, winced. "Don't do it. Really bad idea." But she said something like, "Well, how lovely . . .".'⁶ Dismissing her friends' warning about Fayed's reputation, she later sent a message that she would be delighted to accept.

As always with Diana, there were several reasons for her decision to take her children to stay at St Tropez with Fayed. Much as she might talk about not worrying about Camilla any more, she could not restrain her natural reaction to her old rival. Camilla's success raised the old nightmare feelings of helplessness, jealousy and despair, always potent triggers for some of her most misguided actions. July 1997 was to be Camilla month in the Prince of Wales's household. ITV were to screen a documentary about her. 'When I got to know Diana,' Richard Kay said, 'Camilla as far as she was concerned was a fading influence on her life. She was obviously always going to be there and she would always blame her [for the failure of her marriage] but she developed almost a sense of pity towards her . . . She felt that Camilla was now having a pretty hellish life in the mid-1990s because she was now undergoing the same level of interest that she herself had had many years earlier, and yet she wasn't getting anything back from it. She was getting a very bad press which I'm sure Diana was delighted about. But there were certain things that did freak her out. She was very unhappy when Channel 5 decided to do the first television biography of Camilla which ran in July 1997 and that upset her a lot. She wanted to know why television would be interested in her.'⁷ Worse, on 18 July Charles was giving a fiftieth birthday ball for Camilla at Highgrove, staged, of course, by Michael Fawcett. Two days before, on 16 July, Diana with William and Harry took

Fayed's helicopter from Kensington Palace to lunch at Barrow Green Court, then went on to Stansted for the flight to Nice on Fayed's jet, and from there via his yacht, the *Jonikal*, to the Castel Sainte Hélène, a ten-acre estate on a cliff overlooking St Tropez.

Having secured his prize, Fayed had pulled out all the stops. He even invested something in the region of £15 million buying the *Jonikal*, a 195-foot yacht built in 1991 and requiring a crew of sixteen, from a Milanese textile tycoon, just to entertain Diana.[8] More, he now saw Dodi as the ideal companion for his prized princess. Despite failure in almost all the other areas of his life, notably the business positions his father had procured for him, Dodi had had success with women. He was charming, kind and generous, reputedly good in bed, and had the ability to focus his entire attention on a woman who interested him. He had had affairs with several beautiful and well-known women and indeed would find women for his father and uncle. His principal drawback was a well-known cocaine habit. Now aged forty-two, he had one failed marriage behind him and, as Fayed well knew, a fiancée, the American model Kelly Fisher; he was due to marry her three weeks later in Los Angeles where Fayed had just paid $7.3 million for Paradise Cove, a six-bedroom seaside house in Malibu, formerly the property of Julie Andrews and her husband Blake Edwards. Determined to bring Dodi to entertain Diana, Fayed telephoned him in Paris, ordering him to dump Kelly Fisher, and sent his Gulfstream to bring him to St Tropez on 14 July. In fact, Fisher was brought down by Dodi two days later and installed to alternate between his father's lesser yachts, moored near the *Jonikal*, the 'love boat' destined to woo Diana. In London society the rumour ran that Fayed had promised Dodi $30 million if he could land Diana – but not for himself, for his father.[9]

On the morning of 18 July, the day of the Highgrove party, the tabloids were full of pictures of Diana, as she had intended they should be. She had taken particular care to make herself known to the accompanying press party, moored offshore from the Fayed villa. Wearing a sexy leopard-print bathing suit, she posed beside the swimming pool, occasionally breaking off to execute a gracefully athletic dive, in the 'look-at-me' fashion of her childhood. She rode behind Harry on a jet ski, showing a handsome cleavage. The press, assembled in boats off Fayed's beach, had no idea what was going on. They had not yet picked up on Dodi who, when he was seen with Diana and the boys in St Tropez, they assumed to be a sailor off the Fayed yacht. 'Why the press was so excited about it all,' Richard Kay recalled, 'was because they just didn't know what the hell was happening. They never knew where the story was going. In fact James Whitaker admitted that he was on the verge of a nervous breakdown and if it had carried on he would probably have cracked up. He said he just couldn't cope with the sheer stress.' Diana was not about to enlighten them but to mystify them further. Commandeering one of Fayed's speedboats, she dashed up to the press boat to announce that they should wait for something great: 'I'm going to surprise the world . . .' Questioned later by Richard Kay, she more or less admitted that it had been a meaningless stunt and a tease. Asked what this 'great' thing was, she shrugged, 'Oh, it's nothing . . . I've just had enough of everything . . .'[10] That same day, photographs flashed round the world of Fayed on the deck of the *Jonikal* with his arm round Diana, she – several inches taller than her host – with her hand resting on his shoulder. Fayed then gave an interview with a journalist in which he claimed that Diana saw him as a father figure, that her attitude to all the criticism of her stay was that these people 'can go to hell if they don't like it'. He boasted of his superb security for her to keep the press away, that he was on good terms with the Royal Family, yet was unable to resist a dig at Camilla. Diana, he said, 'doesn't think or care about Camilla Parker Bowles. She is something out of a Dracula film . . .'[11]

What, indeed, was Diana doing accepting Fayed's hospitality for herself and even more for her son, the future King of England, and his brother? When advised by friends not to go, she had replied, 'Oh, he's very naughty . . .' Fayed's speech was normally littered with his version of the English expletive 'fuggin', and he was happy to retail lurid details of his sexual exploits even to other women who didn't want to hear them. But he was expansive, a cheerful figure on holiday surrounded by his wife, Heini, and their four children, with the kind of family atmosphere that appealed to Diana. Moreover, it was a Muslim family, even if not quite on the lines of her still beloved Khans. The fact that the Establishment might look askance at Fayed made no difference whatsoever to her. Diana had never thought along Establishment lines; indeed, their disapproval may indeed have enhanced his appeal. 'Fayed has always been very nice and courteous to her and she had nowhere to go and he offered his house and she accepted,' said an old friend.[12] 'But she had a very good sense of the ridiculous and she knew how ridiculous Al Fayed is with his plane and his house and his bad taste. He gave her a watch with pearls, the kind of watch that had a pearl bracelet. And she hated it.'[13]

Diana returned to London on 20 July to face what appeared to be the final showdown with Hasnat Khan. Despite their previous troubles she had by no means given up on him and had telephoned his London flat to tell him the date of her return. Sometime during the few days she spent in London in late July – she flew to Milan on 22 July for Gianni Versace's funeral – they parted, seemingly for ever, Hasnat having told her that their marriage was impossible. Diana had told close friends that she wanted to marry Hasnat. 'He was a wonderful person and he was in love with her, he was completely besotted with her but he did not want to marry her,' said one.[14] 'Hasnat Khan has only one interest in life,' Richard Kay said. 'He was very fond of Diana but he wanted to be a very good doctor and his ultimate aim is to take the skills he's learned here back to Pakistan. And the idea that he could become Mr Diana of Wales and still be a practising doctor was just absurd, it was never going to happen. And I think she knew that too. I mean, who do you marry if you've once been married to the future King? She went almost from the sublime to the ridiculous. The idea that she could marry an impoverished hospital doctor was a wonderful Mills and Boonish sort of story line.'[15] Diana persisted, despite having told two of her mother figures that, on her Pakistan mission to meet his parents, they had been horrified at the thought of the marriage and had told her it was impossible.[16]

But now, in late July, with London emptying as people went off on their summer holidays and the boys departed with their father, romance with Dodi offered an escape. On 26 July she flew to Paris for twenty-four hours to be met by Dodi and enveloped in the Fayeds' world – private helicopter to the centre of Paris, then on to the Ritz Hotel where she was given the Imperial Suite. After dinner at Lucas Carton, the couple returned briefly to Dodi's flat in his father's apartment block on rue Arsène Houssaye, its windows overlooking the Champs-Elysées, then took a romantic walk along the Seine, hand in hand, and for once alone (the trip had been kept secret). Diana spent the night by herself in the Ritz, breakfasted with Dodi and then flew back to London. Diana was exhilarated, touched by Dodi, the first man ever to cherish her with so much thought and attention.

On 31 July she was back on the *Jonikal* for a cruise alone with Dodi (if you except numerous crew and bodyguards, butler, chef and masseuses), cruising off the coasts of Corsica and Sardinia. Dodi Fayed was simple, gentle and considerate of her every need. On this, and subsequent trips, the two of them talked unceasingly of loveless childhoods, the cinema and gossip. Importantly for Diana, Dodi was intellectually unchallenging and never made her feel inferior; at the same time he looked after her in the way she had always dreamed of and never hitherto found. It was a stress-free experience where Diana could behave in a relaxed, almost childlike way. Significantly, numbers of furry stuffed animals figured prominently in both their bedrooms: in Dodi's Paris apartment three Harrods bears sat on a table in the bedroom, three more on chairs in the dining room. He also had a collection of model aeroplanes on display in his bedroom. They played the soundtrack from the film *The English Patient* over and over again, watched DVDs and television; sometimes Diana played the piano: 'All my family play,' she told the astonished butler, René Delorm. When Dodi was busy, Diana read. She was reading, Delorm noted, a book entitled *On Being Jewish*, a curious choice for Muslim company.

Unwittingly, however, she had become caught up in a Fayed-controlled environment from which she would not escape.

Mohamed Fayed monitored the romance from afar: Dodi was in high favour owing to his obvious success with the Princess. Father and son spoke daily on the telephone, sometimes more often. Fayed was determined to extract the maximum good publicity for his son's coup. He employed the publicist Max Clifford as his adviser to supplement the skilful efforts of his spokesman, former BBC royal reporter Michael Cole. The results of his campaign were to dog the remainder of Diana and Dodi's days. On 4 August, a noted photographer, Mario Brenna, arrived in Sardinia from Monaco following a tip-off. Fayed's biographer, Tom Bower, suspected a Fayed employee was responsible; another well-informed author, Kate Snell, however, claims that Brenna was acting on a tip-off from another notorious paparazzo, Jason Fraser, who had obtained the information from a different source. Brenna had spotted the *Jonikal* moored off the bay of Cala di Volpe on the Costa Smeralda, but subsequently lost her. Later, however, he spotted the yacht travelling between Corsica and Sardinia. Using a tender, Dodi and Diana left the *Jonikal* to swim in various places, snapped and tracked by Brenna. Later, from the shore, he obtained the famous photographs of Dodi and Diana embracing on the yacht, later entitled 'the Kiss'. Back in London, Jason Fraser sold the set of pictures for huge sums – a quarter of a million pounds was paid for the first rights by the *Sunday Mirror* which published them on 10 August. The *Sun* and the *Daily Mail* paid one hundred thousand pounds each for second rights. Diana seemed no less willing than Mohamed Fayed to publicize her new affair: Richard Kay, no doubt acting on information passed to him by Diana, confirmed that it was 'her first serious romance' since the divorce.[17] It was obvious that she wanted the world to know, her specific targets probably being Hasnat Khan and her ex-husband. On 7 August, when Diana dined with Dodi at 60 Park Lane on their return to London, a horde of photographers, doubtless acting on a tip-off, were there to record her arrival. Dodi at least was innocent of having given the information: when snapped boarding a boat to take them to the *Jonikal*, he looked genuinely surprised. Diana calmly looked the other way.

Diana left for Bosnia on 8 August for the landmines campaign with Bill Deedes, returning on the 11th when, still in the Fayed embrace, she and Dodi spent a romantic night at Oxted. Ten paparazzi were waiting outside the gates as they left guarded by Trevor Rees-Jones, an ex-soldier who had become Dodi's favourite bodyguard. Giving them the slip, they drove to 60 Park Lane for dinner. 60 Park Lane was the Fayed London headquarters, the complex in which Fayed occupied the lavish seventh floor with various other relations, including Dodi, dispersed around the other floors. It was like a hotel, with centralized service from one kitchen for all the apartments. It was also the headquarters of Fayed's security operations, a private army of some thirty armed ex-soldiers from the Military Police, the SAS and the Parachute Regiment. Unlike the highly trained Royalty and Diplomatic Protection Department, which had been taught specifically how to protect its principals and had a strict code of conduct, Fayed's bodyguards were under the direct control of whichever of the Fayeds, Mohamed or Dodi, they happened to be accompanying. It was well known among Fayed's employees that disobeying Fayed meant instant dismissal, an unspoken rule that was to have fatal results. When asked to do things of which they disapproved, the saying among the men was 'It's paying the mortgage'. 'You never challenged the Boss, even if you thought professional procedures were being compromised,' Trevor Rees-Jones said.[18]

That evening Diana and Dodi went to a private screening of *Air Force One*; as Trevor Rees-Jones drove out of the underground garage of the apartment, the car was besieged by cameramen. Dodi and Diana escaped being photographed by practically lying, giggling, on the floor. A few days later, on 15 August, when Diana left for a short holiday on a boat in Greece with Rosa Monckton, Fayed saw to it that they flew out and returned on his Gulfstream. For five days they managed to escape the notice of the paparazzi, with the sole exception of a tourist who snapped them. Next day his photograph was on the front page of the *Sun*. 'It's a hunt, Rosa, it's a hunt,' Diana told her friend.

The hunt was now on in earnest, partly orchestrated by the

distant Fayed but more closely, it would appear, by Diana herself. On 21 August, the day Diana returned on the Fayed jet to Stansted, Fayed had alerted not only Nigel Dempster but also the *Sun*. That same evening Diana flew to Nice to join Dodi for a second holiday on the *Jonikal*. At the jetty in the small port of St Laurent-du-Var, where they were to join the yacht, Jason Fraser and two French showbusiness photographers were waiting. Later they were joined by more. At Monte Carlo on 25 August Dodi and Diana decided to walk in the town, accompanied by Delorm and the two body-guards, Rees-Jones and 'Kez' Wingfield. They lost their way but remained unbothered by the media. It was on this expedition that Fayed would claim that Diana and Dodi picked out a special ring from the 'Tell Me Yes' range at the jewellers Repossi, which was later, according to him, to be presented to Diana as an engagement ring. Rees-Jones emphatically denied that they visited Repossi. (They had done so, however, on the earlier *Jonikal* trip on 5 August.) A fleet of paparazzi boats dogged the *Jonikal* from then on. After Monte Carlo Dodi was beginning to panic about the paparazzi, suspecting the crew of tipping them off. The two British bodyguards, Kez and Trevor, were telephoning requests for reinforcements, only to be turned down. Later, when the couple were trying to have a quiet romantic walk on the beach at Porto Venere, they were surprised by a single paparazzo; by now even Diana seemed upset and was seen in tears by the crew. On 27 August helicopters made three sorties to hover over the *Jonikal*, driving Diana below. Dodi began to fantasize about night-vision laser devices to disrupt the cameras or blind their operators. There was a sense that Diana was beginning to be bothered about his overreaction to things like mosquitoes, asking their stewardess, 'What are these Arab men like?'[19] Later, it was to be suggested by Diana's friends that, fiercely opposed as she was to drug use, she was beginning to be suspicious about Dodi's disappearances to the bathroom. On Friday 29 August they were at Cala di Volpe, on Sardinia, again when news filtered through that they would be leaving for Paris the following day.

Arriving at Le Bourget on a stifling hot August day, the party found the paparazzi waiting and this time in their most aggressive form – on motorbikes. Diana's face was set as she got into the Mercedes to drive to the city centre. They set off in two cars, Dodi and Diana in the Mercedes guarded by Rees-Jones and driven by the usual chauffeur, Philippe Dorneau. The back-up Range Rover with the luggage, valet, maid and masseuse, guarded by Wingfield, was driven by Henri Paul, assistant head of security at the Ritz, who had been personally greeted by Dodi. Outside the airport they were buzzed by paparazzi on motorbikes darting round them, oblivious to safety. An agitated Dodi told Dorneau to accelerate and lose them and at one stage Diana screamed at the driver to 'slow down' as she was worried there might be a collision with the bikes.[20] She tried to soothe Dodi. Outdistancing their pursuers, the couple stopped to visit the Villa Windsor, the home of Diana's ex-husband's great-uncle, the Duke of Windsor, and his wife for the last thirty and more years of their lives. Diana jumped out of the car without waiting for the door to be opened for her. According to the villa's security chief, Ben Murrell, 'Diana looked flustered and her face was red. She didn't look happy. Dodi was still sitting in the car by the time Diana walked into the house. It was obvious something had occurred during the journey ... Diana looked shaken.'[21] The villa now stood empty of the furniture, which had been sent for auction. They spent precisely twenty-eight minutes there: Diana found it creepy, as she was to tell Richard Kay. Later Fayed was to claim that they spent two hours touring what he said was to be their future home together, accompanied at one stage by an interior decorator. Security cameras later proved this to be untrue. They then drove to the Ritz where Diana once again had use of the Imperial Suite. She had her hair done while Dodi visited the nearby Repossi jewellery shop, apparently to complete arrangements for the ring he had ordered for her and to inspect designs for more jewellery. The ring was then taken to the Ritz and given to Dodi who put it in his pocket.

Later, they left for Dodi's apartment on rue Arsène Houssaye to dress for dinner. There they were met by a noisy and aggressive troop of paparazzi shouting and pushing. 'This really upset the

Princess even though she was used to it,' one of the bodyguards recalled. 'The paparazzi were shouting which made them even more threatening. Dodi was particularly annoyed by their behaviour. He wasn't used to it and he asked me what could be done to get rid of them. I told him it was impossible to escape from them just like that.'[22] Similar scenes occurred when they left the apartment, as a witness testified. 'Despite the agreement made with the paparazzi, they didn't respect anything we had asked them to do . . . as soon as the couple's car moved off they behaved like real devils. They called their bikes and sped off like fools, trying to stick to the car. They could have knocked over pedestrians. People flattened themselves against walls as the paparazzi's bikes mounted the pavements and sped past.'[23] Dodi, by now thoroughly unnerved, made a change of plan. Instead of dining at the Left Bank restaurant Chez Benoît, where they were booked, he decided to switch to the Ritz to avoid the photographers. The atmosphere was becoming strained and chaotic: Dodi would not reveal his plans to the bodyguards until the last minute. Despite their best efforts there was an ugly scene on arrival at the hotel. As the mob closed in, Diana and Dodi hesitated. Cameras surrounded the car: 'The couple were engulfed. Dodi's hand went up to shield his face, the Princess looked anguished as she took a running stride towards the door. The results of Dodi's hesitation had enormously bothered the couple,' Rees-Jones recalled.[24] Inside the hotel, it was hardly any better. This was August, a deeply unfashionable time when smart people would not be seen in Paris, let alone at the Ritz. In the restaurant people stared at the couple, forcing them to break off to dine upstairs. Diana, one of the bodyguards noted, was in tears.

Yet, earlier that evening she had been on the telephone to her friends. According to Richard Kay, 'that evening Diana was as happy as I have ever known her'. She did not mention marriage; indeed, to Annabel Goldsmith she said that she needed another marriage like she needed a rash, and to Rosa Monckton in Greece she had said, 'Whatever happens in this relationship, I will continue to do my work, and to help where I am needed.' She would need the connection with reality – something lacking in Dodi's world. Speaking to Rosa on her mobile on 27 August, she had described her holiday as 'bliss'. Later Rosa Monckton wrote of Diana's holiday romance with Dodi: 'She was happy, enjoying herself, and liked the feeling of having someone who not only so obviously cared for her, but was not afraid to be seen to be doing so.'[25] But she was looking forward to being home and seeing her boys. 'I'm coming home tomorrow and the boys will be back from Scotland in the evening,' she told Kay. 'I will have a few days with them before they're back at school.' She was, he said, 'a bit troubled' because William had called her that Saturday to say that Buckingham Palace had told him he must 'perform', and present a photo call at the beginning of his third year at Eton. Both Diana and William disliked having the spotlight shone directly on him to the exclusion of Harry. Diana had once said how hard it was for Harry being overshadowed as a second son and how she and Charles had tried to ensure that everything was shared.[26] At some point she had also arranged to meet Hasnat on the Tuesday of the following week, perhaps hoping to sort out their future. Michael Gibbins had called the office of her driver/security guard, Colin Tebbutt, formerly of the protection squad, to tell him to be at Stansted on Sunday morning as she would be coming in around 10 a.m. 'She'll come back with you', he was told. 'She doesn't want to come back with the circus . . . two cars roaring through London and drawing attention to herself.'[27]

While Dodi and Diana were having dinner in the Imperial Suite at the Ritz, Dodi made a decision that would cost them their lives. To escape the paparazzi outside the front of the hotel, he decided that they would leave the hotel by the rear entrance on the rue Cambon while the limousine and the Range Rover should be seen waiting outside the front exit to give the impression they would be leaving that way. They would then go to the rue Arsène Houssaye apartment. Dodi specifically required that Henri Paul should be their driver and had confirmed his plan in a telephone call to his father, or so he said. The limousine at the back exit, a Mercedes S-280, had been hired from the nearby Etoile Limousine;

it had originally been bought second hand and did not have tinted windows which would have protected the passengers from being photographed by the paparazzi. The driver Henri Paul had been claimed by Murrell to have acted strangely, his breath smelling 'of wine and onions'. The two trained bodyguards, however, had noticed nothing when Paul sat with them as they ate in the Bar Vendôme and he drank two Pastis. Paul, it appears, had been taunting the paparazzi outside the front door which had led them to believe something would happen at the back. It later emerged that he was not a qualified chauffeur and did not have the licence required by law to drive a car registered as a limousine.

Kez Wingfield, the bodyguard who went in the other Mercedes, recalled that Diana and Dodi seemed happy when they left the Imperial Suite. 'It was obvious they'd had a glass of wine or two.'[28] But according to Colin Tebbutt and an ex-Special Branch colleague, when they later examined the CCTV tape covering the Ritz exit, Diana's manner showed that she was not happy with what was going on. As a protection squad policeman he had always taught his trainees to look at their principal's 'hands and eyes and face'. Examining the tape carefully, despite Dodi's protective arm round Diana, he said, 'she was p . . . off. You look at the face and she was taut, "Why all this fuss" . . . She'd been living with this for twenty years, she knew protection, she knew how to do things . . .' Poignantly, he added: 'I never went fast with her. She always used to scream, "Don't run over anybody, don't hit anybody" . . . always used to worry.'[29]

The bodyguard Trevor Rees-Jones, who was to accompany them, preceded Diana out of the door, followed by Dodi. Henri Paul was in the driving seat. Rees-Jones ushered Diana into the right rear seat, with Dodi on her left. Rees-Jones got into the front passenger seat. None of them fastened seat belts. Just before 12.20 a.m., Paul drove off down the rue Cambon. A small crowd of photographers observed the departure: hunting as a pack, they alerted their colleagues waiting outside the hotel's front entrance on the Place Vendôme. Paul turned into the rue de Rivoli; by the time he had reached the Place de la Concorde, both sets of paparazzi had joined the chase. Here he came to the fateful decision not to turn right on to the Champs-Elysées, the most direct route to the apartment, as he would have had to stop at several traffic lights en route, giving the pursuing paparazzi time to catch up and grab photographs of the couple through the untinted windows. Instead he decided to take the back route down the Cours La Reine/Cours Albert 1er, a stretch of dual carriageway leading to the tunnel beneath the Place d'Alma, which would enable him to pick up speed and shake off the paparazzi. In the approach to the tunnel there is a hump followed by a dip before the road bends sharply to the left at the tunnel entrance. Paul had by now shaken off the photographers. As he approached the tunnel travelling at between 118 kmh (74 mph) and 155 kmh (97 mph) he overtook a much slower white Fiat Uno in the right-hand lane, brushing its left-hand rear with his right wing just as they passed over the notorious hump. Oversteering to the left he then understeered to the right as the car reached the dip at the mouth of the tunnel. At 12.23 a.m., three minutes after leaving the Ritz, the Mercedes, out of control, slammed into the thirteenth concrete pillar dividing the roadway in the tunnel. Henri Paul and Dodi died instantly from their injuries; the inflated airbag saved Rees-Jones from death, if not disfigurement; Diana was left semi-conscious. Within seconds the paparazzi had surrounded the stricken Mercedes, now in clouds of smoke, its horn blaring, and zoomed in on their prey.

22. Death in Paris

'This is going to unleash grief like no one has ever seen anywhere in the world'
(Tony Blair to Alastair Campbell)

It took almost an hour to free Diana from the wrecked car. She appeared to her rescuers to be the least injured of the four: only a slight trickle of blood from mouth and nose indicated that anything was wrong. Yet her internal injuries were life-threatening. After the initial impact the Mercedes had spun away, rotating at high speed before crashing into the tunnel wall on the right. At the first impact Dodi and Diana had been thrown violently forward against the backs of the front seats, then the rotation of the car had flung them around against the interior. When the Mercedes finally stopped, pointing back towards the mouth of the tunnel, Diana was slumped on the floor, against the back of Rees-Jones's seat, facing down the tunnel. Her legs were twisted, one under her, the other on the seat. With her eyes closed and her face undamaged apart from a cut on her forehead, she looked beautiful and as if she were asleep. But the shock of the impact and deceleration on her body had displaced her heart from the left to the right side, severing the pulmonary vein and rupturing the pericardium (the protective sac round the heart), flooding her chest cavity with blood. She was dying, suffocating in a foreign country just as one of her psychics had predicted would be the fate of Charles.

Yet to the first doctor on the scene, Frédéric Mailliez, who had been driving through the tunnel in the opposite direction, she 'looked pretty fine . . . I thought this woman had a chance.' He put an oxygen mask over her face while attempting to clear her air passages. When the ambulance arrived, Dr Jan-Marc Martino, a surgical anaesthetist and resuscitation specialist, worked on Diana.

Before they could transfer her to the ambulance, she suffered a heart attack. She was given cardiac massage and a respiratory tube was inserted into her mouth. Then she was lifted on to a stretcher and placed in the ambulance which crawled its way with a police escort to La Pitié-Salpêtrière Hospital, stopping once on the way as Diana's blood pressure dropped to a dangerous level. She was put on a ventilator. 'She was unconscious and under artificial respiration. Her arterial blood pressure was very low but her heart was still beating.[1] X-rays revealed the horrific state of her internal injuries and afterwards she suffered a second heart attack. An incision in her chest revealed that bleeding was coming through a hole in the membrane round her heart and later that her superior left pulmonary vein was torn. Adrenalin was administered and cardiac massage kept her heart going but only just; there was no independent rhythm. Diana was to all intents and purposes already beyond help. Electric-shock therapy was administered, to no effect. At 4 a.m. (3 a.m. British time) on the morning of 31 August, she was pronounced dead.[2]

Even before the doctor had begun his treatment of Diana in the wrecked car, the paparazzi, headed by the oddly named Romuald Rat, who arrived first, began snapping the scene. In total some ten or fifteen photographers gathered, their flashes going off like machine guns. Only two of them had thought to call for assistance and even they turned immediately to photograph the grisly scene. Members of the public were appalled by their greed and insensitivity – two of their victims were, after all, dead. Shocked onlookers attacked the paparazzi; when the police arrived, it was assumed that the photographers had directly caused the accident by their pursuit of the car and seven were arrested, to be charged with involuntary manslaughter and non-assistance. The police confiscated the cameras, but when the rolls of film were developed it became obvious that no photographs had been taken before the arrival of the paparazzi on the scene, when the accident had already happened. Nonetheless, people were already trying to profit from Diana's death. Two internet websites revealed that the asking price for photographs of Diana in the car was over £600,000. In London,

Piers Morgan of the *Daily Mirror* viewed a collection of agency pictures and realized the impossibility of running them. He knew, as did every other editor, that the press was going to be accused of killing Diana.

At the hospital, the British Ambassador in Paris, Sir Michael Jay, had been waiting with the French Interior Minister, Jean-Pierre Chevènement, outside the operating theatre and had reported the accident to the Queen's deputy private secretary, Sir Robin Janvrin. At Balmoral Diana had dropped so far from the Royal Family's mental radar that Janvrin was not even aware she was in Paris. When told of her death he informed the Queen and Prince Charles, who decided that 'the boys' should not be told immediately until the situation was absolutely clear. Diana's death was officially announced at 5.45 a.m. Paris time, and flashed to an incredulous world.

Meanwhile, Colin Tebbutt and Paul Burrell had flown in with Prince Charles's security man, Ian von Tanz. At the British Embassy they were met by Sir Michael and Lady Jay and the Military Attaché, Brigadier Charles Ritchie. It was Lady Jay who produced a black cocktail frock to dress Diana's body Burrell, contrary to the calm, controlled figure featured in his somewhat self-serving book, was shaken and sobbing. At the embassy Tebbutt and Brigadier Ritchie took charge, arranging an interpreter and a car to take Tebbutt and Burrell to the Ritz to pick up Diana's things. At the Ritz, where they were apparently treated with total disdain, they discovered that Fayed had already had Diana's possessions packed up and sent to London. At La Pitié-Salpêtrière Hospital they were shown into the room where Diana lay. 'She looked calm,' Tebbutt recalled.[3] The press had got on to a nearby roof and were trying to shoot into the room, so Tebbutt found some blankets and pinned them over the windows. The room was very hot and the air stifling; Tebbutt switched on additional air conditioning and 'Diana's hair moved and so did her eyelashes – I actually thought she was alive,' Tebbutt recalled, 'and so did Paul.'[4] '[She] just looked like she was asleep . . . her face just had little scratches and her hair was hiding the injuries on her head. I didn't see the injuries although I was close, right next to her.'[5] Two undertakers stood like statues in the corner: they were to prepare the body before the arrival of the royal undertakers from London. Leadington's, as the London undertakers were called, were to arrive later, marching down the corridor ready equipped with a lead-lined coffin and the royal standard to drape over it.

Confusion at La Pitié-Salpêtrière was echoed by similar confusion at the Palace, Balmoral and Downing Street. At first it was thought that Diana had survived, then that there was a possibility of brain damage; at last it was confirmed that she had died. There was no precedent for the sudden death of a divorced Princess of Wales. At Balmoral a devastated Prince Charles braced himself to tell William and Harry the terrible news. William, apparently, said that he thought something dreadful had happened as he had kept waking up during the night. Charles, no doubt racked with guilt over his wife's fate, kept saying – presciently as it turned out – 'They're all going to blame me, aren't they?'[6] With equal prescience, Tony Blair, at home in his Sedgefield constituency, told Alastair Campbell, 'This is going to unleash grief like no one has ever seen anywhere in the world.' Again, Blair showed the sureness of his popular touch in his statement issued that morning on what Diana had meant to the nation: 'They liked her, they loved her, they regarded her as one of the people. She was the People's Princess and that is how she will stay, how she will remain in all our hearts and memories for ever.'[7]

'There were rows almost immediately Diana died,' said a royal aide. At Balmoral there was confusion as to whether Charles should stay with his sons or go to Paris to collect Diana's body and whether a Queen's Flight would be arranged to take him. Charles's aides, Stephen Lamport and Mark Bolland, convinced that the right thing to do was for him to go to Paris and bring Diana back, urged him to follow his instincts and go, even threatening to book the Prince on to a scheduled flight from Aberdeen if the Queen's Flight would not be made available.[8] There was doubt, too, whether Diana should be treated as one of the Royal Family and the mother of the future King, or whether she should be returned to the care of the Spencers. The Queen's instinct was for a private family funeral at Windsor and interment at Frogmore (in the same plot as that other royal embarrassment, the Duchess of Windsor). The Spencers would have preferred a quiet family funeral at Althorp. Somehow a consensus was reached that only a state funeral would satisfy public feeling. At Balmoral, as usual, the Royal Family carried on as if nothing had happened. They attended the customary Sunday service in Crathie Church, where Diana's name was not mentioned and had not been since the royal ruling that, with the loss of her HRH, her name should be dropped from the prayers for the Royal Family. Even the minister went ahead with the sermon he had planned to deliver before the accident, which included unsuitably jokey references to Billy Connelly. The absence of any reference to Diana apparently prompted Prince Harry to ask, 'Are you sure Mummy's really dead?' The press was equally taken aback: 'No mention of Accident' *The Times* remarked on Monday morning. The *Sun* would follow this up, asking 'DO THEY CARE?' It was the beginning of a mounting wave of criticism directed at the Queen and her family which was to reach dangerous levels of hostility by the end of the week.

On Sunday afternoon, Charles, joined at Aberdeen by Diana's sisters, flew to Paris in a BAe 146 of the Queen's Flight. Her brother Charles had been at his house in Cape Town when he heard the news. 'The telephone went in the middle of the night,' Spencer recalled:

It was the manager who runs this place [Althorp] and he said, 'We've heard there's been a car crash in Paris and Dodi Fayed's dead but your sister's just injured. We thought you should know straight away.' I went downstairs and flicked between the various satellite news stations. They were saying much the same actually. They were saying she'd been seen walking away and I thought, well, I'd better stay up and see just how bad it is and then my sister Sarah rang me and she said 'Look, I'm afraid it's really bad news. It looks like she's got brain damage.' I was totally shaken. I couldn't believe it. And then I rang my sister Jane, whose husband worked for the Queen. He [Robert Fellowes] was on another line in the background and he went 'Oh, no' and then my sister Jane said, 'I'm afraid that's it, she's died.'[9]

Before flying home, he issued a statement praising his 'unique sister', adding ominously that he always believed the press would kill her in the end. He declared that 'every proprietor and every editor of every publication' that had paid for intrusive and exploitative photographs of her 'has blood on his hands today'. His charges set the scene for the mood of public anger against the press. Diana's mother was isolated on the Isle of Seil, in a desperate state over the fate of her daughter with whom she had not been on speaking terms for the past three months. Neither Prince Charles nor the Queen telephoned her to express their condolences.

When Prince Charles and Diana's sisters arrived in Paris, they found Diana looking serene and composed in death, wearing Lady Jay's black cocktail dress and shoes, her hair freshly blow-dried, the rosary which Mother Teresa had given her in her hand. After Charles and the sisters had spent time alone with her, she was placed in a coffin for the return journey. Colin Tebbutt and Burrell accompanied the hearse on its journey through Paris: 'It was just fantastic,' Tebbutt recalled. 'They do it differently in Paris – they applaud. With the coffin, Prince Charles, the President, millions of police by now, me, Paul and the vicar [the Rev. Martin Draper], the whole of Paris was applauding . . .'[10] Prince Charles flew back to Balmoral from Northolt, apparently preferring not to accompany the family on into London. On the drive from Northolt airport to Fulham where Diana was to be deposited at the mortuary, the road was lined with thousands of people. 'I couldn't believe what we were seeing,' Tebbutt recalled. 'Lady Sarah [McCorquodale] said, "We'll have a little private funeral at Althorp", and we turned on to the A40 and Paris was moving but I just couldn't believe what we were seeing, there were thousands upon thousands of people, no traffic.' Tebbutt sent one of his drivers to take Sarah home again via the A40. This time she exclaimed, 'We're not going to get a quiet funeral!'[11] Leaving Diana's body to undergo the obligatory autopsy in Fulham (there had already been one in Paris to conform with French law), Charles flew back to Balmoral. Isolated up on Deeside, the Royal Family remained unaware of the gathering hysteria in the capital. The crowds of people of all conditions, black, white, old and young queuing for up to seven hours to sign the condolence book at St James's Palace, the mountains of flowers outside Kensington Palace, the sorrowing notes and poems pinned to the railings, represented above all Diana's constituency, the ordinary people of Britain.

Diana's body was taken from Fulham to lie in the Chapel Royal at St James's Palace. Lucia Flecha de Lima, who had set off for London as soon as she heard of Diana's death, found her coffin lying there in lonely state, without flowers: 'The first day when I arrived at the chapel there was not one single flower on her coffin. Then I said to the chaplain that if he didn't allow flowers in, I would throw open the doors of the chapel so everyone could see her there without a single flower and all the flowers outside that people had brought. I said, "Tomorrow I'll come back with my flowers for her." And I came every day. And from then on I brought flowers, not only mine but from friends and people who knew her. And I went to a flower van outside the Michelin restaurant [Bibendum in the Fulham Road] and he said: "What are they for?" And I told him, and every day after that he insisted I take flowers to her for nothing . . .'[12] 'And they [the flowers] were around her, over her coffin representing the flowers of the world, and I said to Prince Charles, "These flowers represent the people, thousands and millions of flowers all around the world that people want to give to Princess Diana." I've never felt like that in my life. I have experienced personal loss . . . but the public's reaction was extraordinary . . .'[13]

Diana was taken home to Kensington Palace for the last night before the funeral. Earlier, Lucia had been with Paul Burrell when a devastating reminder was delivered: a forensics bag containing the clothes Diana had been wearing at the time of the accident, a black top and white trousers. The black blazer was missing. Paul Burrell had spent the day arranging flowers left by the public outside the Palace and flowers sent by friends – her favourite white lilies, tulips and roses – on the floor of the hallway where the coffin would rest. The Catholic priest, Father Tony Parsons from the Carmelite Church in Kensington where Diana used to go and pray, arrived with two large church candles. That evening Frances visited with Sarah and Jane and the grandchildren to spend some time beside the coffin. Charles Spencer did not appear. Burrell had asked Sarah McCorquodale, at Lucia's request, if she could spend the vigil at Diana's coffin. The request was refused. '. . . when I told Lady Sarah how important Lucia was to the Princess, and how much she needed to be there that night, Lucia's request was denied. Lady Sarah felt it appropriate for only family to attend. The one woman,' Burrell wrote, 'who was more family than any of them was refused her final, most personal farewell.'[14]

'WHERE IS THE QUEEN WHEN THE COUNTRY NEEDS HER?' the *Sun*'s front page asked on 4 September (Thursday) after four emotional days of unofficial grief for Diana. The Queen was on holiday 550 miles away from the capital and, the newspaper said, only intended to fly in for the day on Saturday for the funeral and fly back afterwards. The Queen had overruled her senior courtiers who believed that there should be a flag flying half-mast over the Palace. The empty flagpole at the end of the Mall was 'a stark insult to Diana's memory'. Why hadn't the Queen broadcast a personal statement of sympathy to the nation? the *Sun* asked. 'The people want the Monarchy to join publicly in their mourning for Diana . . . Every hour the Palace remains empty adds to the public anger at what they perceive to be a snub to the People's Princess . . .'

'It was sometimes difficult to get across to the people up there [Balmoral] that there actually was a sort of head of feeling building on that [the flag issue] or there was a real sort of crisis brewing on such and such,' said a former aide. 'If they had all been down here, they would have sensed just driving down the Mall that there was a very ugly feeling around and they actually needed to be a bit careful.'[15] The inevitable search for a scapegoat was on: how could such a terrible tragedy have happened? Someone must be to blame.

The first target was the paparazzi and by implication the press who had paid them, then it was the drunk driver Henri Paul, and then the Royal Family who had cast Diana out. If they had not done so, the argument went, she would not have been in the Alma Tunnel with a playboy boyfriend at the end of August. And what was more, the thinking (newspaper-led, it might be pointed out) was that the Royal Family, by remaining on holiday at Balmoral rather than returning to the capital to share the nation's grief, had shown themselves to be uncaring of the People's Princess. An early focus was the empty flagpole over Buckingham Palace, head-quarters of the Royal Family, where in popular opinion a flag should have been drooping half-mast in the traditional expression of mourning.

'The Queen is a traditionalist on things like that,' the aide said. 'If it's been a precedent in the monarchy it's quite hard to change. It's nothing to do with insensitivity, it's just there is a logic to a personal Standard or flag. I mean if you [the Queen] are there it's up and if you're not, it's not.'[16] After considerable pressure, the Palace, or rather the Queen, reluctantly yielded. The Union Jack was to be flown half-mast until she was in residence. The deputy private secretary Sir Robin Janvrin emerged from a meeting to tell a member of the 'haul-up-the-Union-Jack party': 'I'm covered in blood, but you've got your flag . . .'[17] A compromise was reached whereby when the Queen came down from Balmoral, her standard went up; it came down on the Saturday, the day of the funeral, and was substituted by the Union flag at half-mast which stayed there until midnight on Sunday.[18] 'I think there was a conscious decision that on the day of the funeral there had to be a symbolic move and that was it,' said Dickie Arbiter, the most experienced royal press officer, who had also worked for the Waleses before the split. Contrary to public perception, the Queen was, Arbiter said, 'very grief-stricken' by Diana's death. 'On the day of the funeral when the Royal Family came out of Buckingham Palace as the gun carriage carrying Diana's coffin passed, the Queen bowed. And the only other time that the Queen bows is at the Cenotaph.'[19]

Finally the Royal Family seemed to have perceived that tectonic plates of emotion and grief were shifting beneath their feet. The Queen and her family flew down to London on Friday 5 September: only then did they get first-hand experience of what Diana's death meant to the people at large. Walking out of the Palace gates to mingle with the crowds they could sense the strange atmosphere, the open grief and, for the first time, an undercurrent of hostility.

That week, television journalist Jon Snow taking the public temperature among the crowds on the Mall had found a high level of anger that the Queen was not there to share their grief. The state of public feeling was such, it is alleged, that the Metropolitan Police panicked under the weight of media hype. Fearing attacks on the funeral procession and other disorder, senior police officers went so far as to telephone the army to ask if they were bringing troops into London. The army refused to contemplate any such action, but the police brought in large vans loaded with riot squads which were concealed in side streets on the day of the funeral.[20]

On the Friday evening before the funeral the Queen gave a televised broadcast about Diana and the meaning of her life. The first paragraph amounted almost to an apology: 'We have all been trying in our different ways to cope,' she said. 'It is not easy to express a sense of loss, since the initial shock is often succeeded by a mixture of other feelings – disbelief, incomprehension, anger and concern for those who remain.

'We have all felt those emotions in these last few days. So what I say to you now, as your Queen and as a grandmother, I say from my heart.'

Then she paid tribute to Diana as 'an exceptional and gifted human being', concluding that there were 'lessons to be drawn from her life and from the extraordinary and moving reaction to her death . . .'

Dressed in black, the Queen sat at a window through which the grieving crowds could be seen outside the Palace. Her delivery was firm, solemn and moving, perhaps the most personal statement she had ever publicly uttered. Her speech had been written for her by Sir Robert Fellowes, Diana's brother-in-law. Downing Street, which had been in active communication with the Palace over the week, was involved in only one phrase of the broadcast draft, 'speaking as a grandmother . . .'. 'That was their only input,' Dickie Arbiter recalled. 'That was the only real input of the funeral arrangements. They said "two minutes" silence at the Abbey – one minute was done – but they came up with nothing else. They did say to Hayden Phillips who was Permanent Secretary at what was still the Department of National Heritage – "Money is no object" – because they [the government] had to pick up the bill for the stands for the media and everything else. So they were very much on board but at the same time realized probably within half an hour of the meeting starting at Buckingham Palace on the Monday morning that these guys at Buckingham Palace knew what they were talking about.'[21]

In the event, Diana's funeral, organized at relatively short notice, showed British royal ceremonial at its best. Diana's family had been wrong to suggest a quiet family interment at Althorp. The world demanded that Diana be properly recognized and she was – with a perfectly organized spectacular but dignified ceremonial orchestrated by Palace officials from start to finish. The original blueprint for the funeral was one designed for the state funeral of the Queen Mother along a route from the Chapel Royal in St James's Palace to Westminster Abbey, down the Mall, Horse Guards Approach Road, through the Horse Guards archway into Whitehall and then down to the Abbey. On advice from the police about the huge numbers of watching people who would be involved, the route was lengthened. Diana would be brought back from her temporary resting place in the Chapel Royal, St James's Palace, to spend her last night in Kensington Palace, and the procession would start instead from there before following the usual route. Screens with speakers following her progress were set up in Hyde Park, allowing the public to witness Diana's funeral until the very end. An estimated one million people or more had travelled to London to be present on the day.

At 9.08 a.m., as the bells of Westminster Abbey began to toll,

Diana's coffin emerged from the gates of Kensington Palace on a horse-drawn gun carriage. It was draped in the royal standard and there were three bouquets laid on it: a sheaf of white tulips from William, of white longiflorum lilies from Charles Spencer and, most moving of all, a bunch of Diana's favourite white roses with the simple card inscribed 'Mummy' in Harry's twelve-year-old hand. Slowly the procession advanced down the Kensington Road to Hyde Park Corner and down Constitution Hill to Buckingham Palace where the Queen stood with other members of the family, including Princess Margaret, to honour Diana as she passed. Then it went down the Mall to be joined by Charles, Prince Philip, Charles Spencer and the two boys. Apparently, the evening before, Prince Philip had said to William that if he wanted to walk behind his mother's coffin, he would walk with him. It was a terrible ordeal for William, aged fifteen, and Harry, only twelve. As they walked they could hear people shouting 'God bless you' to them and others wailing and throwing flowers into the road.

At Westminster Abbey, a two-thousand-strong congregation waited, an extraordinary mixture of people representing the range of Diana's life, charities and friendships. The Royal Family was out in strength, Bill and Hillary Clinton were there, and Bernadette Chirac representing her husband, the President of France. There was a clutch of celebrities – Sting, Valentino, Shirley Bassey, George Michael and Elton John – and Hollywood – Tom Hanks, Steven Spielberg, Tom Cruise and Nicole Kidman. There were friends who were also celebrities like David Frost and Clive James. There were old friends like Carolyn Bartholomew and Laura Lonsdale. There were the Flecha de Limas, Annabel Goldsmith, Imran Khan and Jemima. Ruth Rudge, headmistress of West Heath, was there. The largest single contingent was made up from her charities. 'It's interesting how Diana's life became extremely compartmentalized,' said Richard Kay, 'so much so that at her funeral they put all her friends in one area of Westminster Abbey and most of them had never met each other. A lot of them didn't even know who the others were, it was quite extraordinary.' Among the congregation was Hasnat Khan who, returning home from Pakistan, had found a birthday card from Diana on his doormat and at the same time the invitation to her funeral.

'What I remember about it,' said Meredith Etherington-Smith, who was in the Abbey, 'was the utter pin-dropping silence when the coffin came in. It was obviously very, very heavy, it was lead-lined, and all you could hear was the squeaking of the soldiers' boots as they carried it. They were shaking and I thought, Christ, they're going to drop it.' Diana's favourite music was played, the hymn 'I Vow to Thee, My Country' which had been played at her wedding, the 'Libera me Domine', from Verdi's Requiem. Perhaps most moving of all was Elton John's rendition of his requiem for Marilyn Monroe, 'Candle in the Wind', rewritten for Diana, 'Goodbye England's rose . . .'. 'God knows how he pulled that off,' Etherington-Smith recalled, 'the man was shaking like a jelly . . .' Nothing could have been more appropriate for Diana who had empathized with Monroe and now had died at exactly the same age. (Her other idol, Princess Grace, whose funeral she had attended, poignantly had also died as a result of a car crash in September 1982, just fifteen years before.) The most dramatic moment was provided by Charles Spencer, whose eloquent speech electrified everyone who heard it.

It was addressed to Diana, whose name had signified the huntress but who had become 'the most hunted woman in the world'. His eulogy to his sister could hardly have been bettered: 'Diana was the very essence of compassion, of duty, of style, of beauty. All over the world she was a symbol of selfless humanity: a standard-bearer for the truly downtrodden: a very British girl whose concerns transcended nationality: someone with a natural nobility who was classless and' – here he could not resist a hit at the Royal Family who had divested her of her HRH – 'who proved in the last year that she needed no royal title to continue to generate her particular brand of magic.' He praised her for her 'wonderfully mischievous sense of humour', her energy and her 'joy for life, transmitted wherever you took your smile and the sparkle in those unforgettable eyes . . .' 'Without your God-given sensitivity,' he declared, 'we would be immersed in greater ignorance at the anguish of AIDS and HIV sufferers, the plight of the homeless, the isolation of lepers, the random destruction of landmines.' Perhaps most movingly of all was when he emphasized how, beneath the glitter of the international celebrity, Diana was still an insecure little girl at heart. 'Diana explained to me once that it was her innermost feelings of suffering that made it possible for her to connect with her constituency of the rejected. And here we come to another truth about her – for all the status, the glamour, the applause, Diana remained throughout a very insecure person at heart, almost childlike in her desire to do good for others so she could release herself from deep feelings of unworthiness . . .'

Passages in the speech were undoubtedly not just directed at the media who had hounded Diana but implicitly criticized the Royal Family and its traditions. 'On behalf of your mother and sisters we pledge that we, your blood family, will do all we can to continue the imaginative and loving way in which you were steering these two exceptional young men, so that their souls are not simply immersed by duty and tradition, but can sing openly, as you planned . . .' Many people thought that the underlying bitterness and the implied attack on the Royal Family were inappropriate for a funeral which should be a time for mutual grief and forgiveness. Others, knowing the family background at the time, considered the 'blood family' pledge to be hypocritical. But at the time, Spencer's words touched a chord with the public.

There was dead silence in the Abbey when Spencer finished his speech. 'All you could hear was far, far down beyond the door this sound like raindrops, and then that it was actually people clapping,' said one of those present.[22] A distinguished journalist also used the raindrops simile:

A sound like a distant shower of rain penetrated the walls of Westminster Abbey . . . it rolled towards us. Then it was inside the church. It rolled up the nave like a great wave. It was people clapping, first the crowds outside and then the two thousand inside . . . People don't clap at funerals; and they don't clap because people outside are clapping. But they did. It was desire, serious applause, and it marked the moment at which the meaning of what was happening on this incredible day was made plain . . . the masses listening outside, who had been claiming their own place . . . broke into the abbey. The people wanted to make their feelings felt. It wasn't enough to be one of the millions on the streets of London. It certainly wasn't enough to be one of the billion watching on television. They wanted to be in the abbey and the applause was their way of getting in.[23]

Diana had transcended celebrity, she had touched people's hearts and not only in Britain but across the world.

As the coffin began its journey to Althorp at midday, the clapping continued. So many flowers were thrown at the hearse on its way out of London that the driver had to use his windscreen wipers to clear them. At the gates of Althorp the hearse broke down, a contretemps which would certainly have appealed to Diana's sense of humour. Meanwhile, the royal train with its smart burgundy carriages pulled by two locomotives named *Prince William* and *Prince Henry* left London for Northamptonshire. On board were Prince Charles, William and Harry. Paul Burrell and Colin Tebbutt were also on the train and were invited to the subsequent family lunch at Althorp. At some point during the journey, a member of the royal household apparently offered to restore Diana's title, Her Royal Highness. It was by now a meaningless gesture. Charles Spencer refused it. (Charles Spencer had deposited his South African girlfriend with the Burrells to avoid embarrassment but she, with Burrell and Tebbutt, was the only non-family member to be present at Diana's interment on the island.)

As they were finishing lunch, Spencer announced, 'Diana is home'. The royal standard was replaced by the white, red, black and gold of the Spencer flag. In death the Spencers were reclaiming Diana just as the Royal Family had rejected her. In truth, neither side had given her the support she deserved. The small party crossed the park for the interment on the island in the centre of the small, tree-lined lake. The eight Welsh guardsmen, accompanied by their officer, carried the coffin gingerly over the temporary pontoon crossing the water to the island where a grave had been prepared and the ground consecrated. After a thirty-minute burial service, the mourners left Diana, alone on the isolated island as she had been alone in life.

Diana: The Legacy

On the eve of Diana's funeral, the Queen herself, broadcasting on television from Buckingham Palace, acknowledged her legacy. Describing her as 'an exceptional and gifted human being', she concluded that there were 'lessons to be drawn from her life and from the extraordinary and moving reaction to her death'.

It has now been twenty years since Diana died but her legacy remains: her enduring popularity – and relevance to the Royal Family – demonstrated by their continuing exhibitions in her memory – the latest, an exhibition of her iconic wardrobe, opened in February 2017 (preceded by a television programme on her dresses and their designers, and the relevance of her clothes to her personal and public life), while a memorial statue of her is to be erected outside her London home, Kensington Palace, commissioned by her sons, Princes William and Harry.

The monarchy has survived the trauma surrounding her death and the wave of anti-monarchical feeling in London in the days leading up to her funeral on 6 September 1997, when press and public turned angrily on the Queen for remaining at Balmoral while the nation grieved for 'the People's Princess'. 'Where is the Queen when her country needs her?' raged the *Sun*'s front page after four days of unofficial grief for Diana. It was alleged that the Metropolitan Police, fearing violence on the day of the funeral, asked the army if they were contemplating bringing troops into London. The answer was in the negative, but the police nonetheless brought in large vans loaded with riot squads to be concealed in the side streets on the day of the funeral. Conspiracy theories fomented by the Fayed circle even implicated the Royal Family in her death: the Duke of Edinburgh, it was alleged, had conspired with British and foreign secret services to have Diana murdered because her lover, Dodi Fayed, was a Muslim and she was expecting a baby by him. It was untrue; tests on her blood found in the Mercedes after the crash definitively proved that she was not pregnant, and nor was there any proof of a murder plot – but the fact that such theories could even have been put forward indicated the extraordinary feeling aroused by her death.

After Diana's death the monarchy survived the upheavals of the nineties: the controversy of the Queen's payment, or rather non-payment, of income tax, the divorces of Princess Anne and Captain Mark Phillips and of Sarah Ferguson and Prince Andrew. In April 2005 the Prince of Wales married Camilla Parker Bowles, a happy ending to the long-running scandal that had shadowed Diana's life but which, by the end, she had accepted. Camilla thus became Duchess of Cornwall but doubts remain as to whether she should become Queen Consort on Charles's eventual accession to the throne. Out of respect for the commemorations planned for Diana in the summer of 2017, Camilla decided to underplay her own seventieth birthday in July.

At ninety, the Queen is Britain's longest-living monarch; her husband, Prince Philip, Duke of Edinburgh, aged ninety-five, is now regarded as a national treasure, his once-reviled gaffes eagerly gobbled up by journalists who retail them as pearls. He still drives a carriage and indeed a car. In the summer of 2016 when President Obama and his First Lady, Michelle, visited Windsor Castle, the Duke drove them on a tour of the Great Park, no doubt to the impotent horror of their security men. Theirs has been a notably happy marriage. Although in public Philip pays tribute to his wife's superior royal status, in private there is equality: as one of the Queen's longest-serving Private Secretaries has said, Prince Philip is the only man in the world who treats the Queen as simply another human being and she for her part can tell him to shut up. Despite their age the royal couple still travel the country mingling with the crowds, but long-distance tours of the Queen's cherished

Commonwealth are out, devolved on to the younger members of the Royal Family, notably Prince William and his wife, Kate, now Duke and Duchess of Cambridge (lately on her own), and popular Prince Harry, ever ready to dance and play games when opportunity offers. Diana's sons get on well with their father and cherish their grandparents while regarding them with a suitable respect. 'You don't mess with Gran,' Harry is quoted as saying. The monarchy's reputation has finally steadied, and the Queen is as admired as ever she was.

Diana's legacy has been not only the family's new approachability and its commitment to communication with the public but, above all, its future through her two sons, Princes William and Harry. The marriage in April 2011 of Prince William to Kate Middleton, the only royal bride to have genuine working-class ancestry, epitomized the democratic and close family feeling which Diana had inculcated in her children. The wedding attracted worldwide interest – some 750 million watched the event on television and tourists streamed into London. Inevitably there were memories of Diana's wedding to Charles in July 1981: the balcony kiss, the bride beautiful in her voluminous wedding dress and billowing veil. In William and Kate's case the closeness of the new royal couple was apparent, holding hands both in church and on the balcony; physically they stood together, and the balcony kiss was mutual. Diana's wedding however was more formal and it was she who had to lean over to kiss her new husband on the balcony. William deliberately emphasized his mother's memory; he presented Kate with his mother's sapphire and diamond ring at their engagement, which was conspicuous on her ring finger for their photographs for the occasion. Significantly the couple were to name their second child Charlotte Elizabeth Diana, her birth underlining the future stability of the House of Windsor, emphasized by photographs of the children with their royal grandparents. To quote a recent royal writer, 'They have an heir, an heir to the heir, and now an heir to the spare for the generation to come.'[1]

Diana's careful, loving, but informal upbringing of her children has been a vital component in the family's future. Like his mother, William is very involved in his children's lives; a hands-on parent, he and Kate are trying to give their children as low-key an upbringing as possible. As William was quoted recently about his own childhood: 'You don't just live in a palace, it's very important you get out and see what goes on in the ordinary world.' In an age of instant transmission of images, the young princes' relaxed manners, inherited from their mother, have been all-important. They have shown themselves capable of coping with the relentless, sometimes intolerable, pressure on their privacy in the interest of The Family and its future, just as Diana did. William, the most vulnerable of the two princes, who had to endure much of the misery of his parents' marriage, has been protected and on occasion substituted for, by his wife in a way of which Diana would have understood and approved. Nonetheless, his absences from certain public occasions, such as the recent celebration of Commonwealth Day, attended by the rest of his family (William went skiing and clubbing with his closest male friends) have led to accusations that he does not pull his weight and unfavourable comparisons as to the number of working hours he puts in relative even to his nonagenarian grandparents.

Harry, an outgoing partygoer since childhood, when his exuberant behaviour at celebrations at the Ritz was approvingly noted by the management, has been an obvious target for journalists' reports. In recent years Harry has worked hard to focus the press and media attention on his work and his charities rather than on his love life and lifestyle. However the harassment by journalists, photographers and on social media about his relationship with Canadian actress Meghan Markle has evoked an unwonted semi-official plea from Kensington Palace to stop the distress this is causing to his new girlfriend and her family before any further damage is done. Although protected from much of the media frenzy surrounding his mother before her death, it may not be so surprising that Harry has stated that he is worried about his girlfriend's safety.

Diana herself was a media phenomenon at a time when publicity was ground-based rather than interstellar. Photographs of her cradling orphans of the landmines in Angola or holding hands with AIDS patients in New York hospitals circled the world. Then, reactions to her were reported on film and in newspapers, now, the web has left celebrities open to constant and immediate scrutiny: a new and demanding world with which the Royal Family has had to cope.

Perhaps Diana's most important legacy lies in her sons' public commitment to charity, which plays much the same part in their lives as it did in hers, including the homeless of Centrepoint, which she and William visited together in his childhood. In 2009 Princes William and Harry set up a charitable foundation together which, following the marriage of the Duke and Duchess of Cambridge in 2011, became known as The Royal Foundation of The Duke and Duchess of Cambridge and Prince Harry. The main aims of the foundation have been to work with the armed forces to give financial support to injured or psychologically damaged veterans; it will also give money to needy young people and provide financial support to poverty-stricken villages in Africa for future generations. Recent projects have included the Invictus Games, MPact Plus on prevention of addiction and working with the True Colours Trust, which helps families of children with life-threatening illnesses. Prince Harry's Sentebale charity, which helps orphans of AIDS in Lesotho, operates independently of the joint foundation. The three young royals can be seen running in marathons to raise funds for mental health and child bereavement and supporting many of the causes which were Diana's. A wide range of events is planned to mark the twentieth anniversary of her death: The Diana Award, a charity established to promote the Princess's belief in the positive power of young people, will commemorate her life by presenting a special legacy award to twenty exceptional young people from across the globe who have honoured Diana's values of service to others, and a National Kindness Day. She would have been proud of them.

★

'She won't go quietly,' Diana warned in the famous television interview she gave eighteen months before her death. Nor has she. Twenty years on her memory is still very much alive.

Source Notes

Chapter 1. The Country Girl (pp. 1–11)

1 Interview with the author 3/4/01.
2 Charles Spencer, *The Spencer Family*, p. 315.
3 Ibid., p. 321.
4 Ibid., p. 314.
5 Interview with the author 3/4/01.
6 Interview with the author 16/11/05.
7 Interview with the author 16/11/05.

Chapter 2. A Norfolk Childhood (pp. 12–28)

1 William Deedes interview with the author.
2 Interview with the author.
3 Private information.
4 Interview with the author 5/5/04.
5 Interview with the author 16/11/04.
6 Mary Clarke, *Little Girl Lost: The Troubled Childhood of Princess Diana by the Woman who Raised Her*, p. 25.
7 Ibid., p. 19.
8 Andrew Morton, *Diana: Her True Story – In Her Own Words*, p. 30.
9 Charles Spencer, *The Spencer Family*, p. 310.
10 Andrew Morton, *Diana: Her True Story – In Her Own Words*, p. 26.
11 Interview with the author 16/11/05.
12 Mary Clarke, *Little Girl Lost: The Troubled Childhood of Princess Diana by the Woman who Raised Her*, p. 178.
13 Andrew Morton, *Diana: Her True Story – In Her Own Words*, p. 26.
14 Rosalind Coward, *Diana: The Portrait*, p. 56.

15 Sarah Bradford, *Elizabeth: A Biography of Her Majesty The Queen*, p. 424.

16 Andrew Morton, *Diana: Her True Story – In Her Own Words*, p. 25.

17 Rosalind Coward, *Diana: The Portrait*, p. 47.

18 Ibid., p. 49.

19 Sally Bedell Smith, *Diana: The Life of a Troubled Princess*, p. 46.

20 Ibid., p. 47.

21 Ibid., p. 48.

22 Ibid.

23 Angela Levin, *Raine and Johnnie: The Spencers and the Scandal of Althorp*, p. 115.

Chapter 3. 'I'm Lady Diana' (pp. 29–47)

1 Andrew Morton, *Diana: Her True Story – In Her Own Words*, p. 31.

2 Ibid, p. 28.

3 Charles Spencer, *Althorp: The Story of an English House*, p. 2.

4 Interview with the author 2/1/05.

5 Rosalind Coward, *Diana: The Portrait*, p. 36.

6 Interview with the author 2/1/05.

7 Angela Levin, *Raine and Johnnie: The Spencers and the Scandal of Althorp*, p. 138.

8 Ibid., p. 140.

9 Settelen tapes.

10 Interview with the author 11/4/01.

11 Andrew Morton, *Diana: Her True Story – In Her Own Words*, p. 24.

12 Settelen tapes.

13 Letter to author 25/2/05.

14 Angela Levin, *Raine and Johnnie: The Spencers and the Scandal of Althorp*, p. 149.

15 Ibid., p. 143.

16 Ibid., p. 150.

17 Rosalind Coward, *Diana: The Portrait*, p. 70.

18 Andrew Morton, *Diana: Her True Story – In Her Own Words*, p. 29.

19 Ibid., p. 31.

20 Rosalind Coward, *Diana: The Portrait*, p. 72.

21 Ibid., p. 69.

22 James Whitaker interview with the author June 2001.

23 Andrew Morton, *Diana: Her True Story – In Her Own Words*, p. 31.

24 Mary Robertson, *The Diana I Knew*, p. 33.

25 Private information.

26 Andrew Morton, *Diana: Her True Story – In Her Own Words*, p. 105.

Chapter 4. Enter the Prince (pp. 48–62)

1 Philip Ziegler, *Mountbatten*, p. 687.

2 Anthony Holden, *Charles, Prince of Wales*, p. 22.

3 Interview with the author 5/4/05.

4 Jonathan Dimbleby, *The Prince of Wales: A Biography*, p. 243.

5 Philip Ziegler, *Mountbatten*, p. 686.

6 Ibid., p. 687.

7 Ibid.

8 Interview with the author 16/11/05.

9 Interview with the author 5/5/04.

10 Interview with the author 7/3/05.

11 Stephen Barry, *Royal Service: My Twelve Years as Valet to Prince Charles*, p. 180.

12 Interview with the author 7/3/06.

13 Christopher Wilson, *The Windsor Knot: Charles, Camilla and the Legacy of Diana*, pp. 90–91.

14 James Whitaker interview with the author June 2001.

15 James Whitaker interview with the author June 2001.

16 Interview with the author 9/3/94.

17 Jonathan Dimbleby, *The Prince of Wales: A Biography*, p. 267.

18 Ibid., p. 261.

Chapter 5. 'Whatever Love Means' (pp. 63–90)

1 Andrew Morton, *Diana: Her True Story – In Her Own Words*, p. 32.
2 Ibid.
3 Jonathan Dimbleby, *The Prince of Wales: A Biography*, pp. 279–80.
4 Stephen Barry, *Royal Service: My Twelve Years as Valet to Prince Charles*, p. 216.
5 Andrew Morton, *Diana: Her True Story – In Her Own Words*, p. 33.
6 Jonathan Dimbleby, *The Prince of Wales: A Biography*, p. 280.
7 Interview with the author.
8 Interview with the author.
9 Jonathan Dimbleby, *The Prince of Wales: A Biography*, p. 282.
10 Sally Bedell Smith, *Diana: The Life of a Troubled Princess*, p. 83.
11 Ibid., p. 87.
12 Ibid., p. 85.
13 James Whitaker interview with the author June 2001.
14 Roy Greenslade interview with the author 20/9/05.
15 Jonathan Dimbleby, *The Prince of Wales: A Biography*, p. 282.
16 Interview with the author 16/11/05.
17 Interview with the author 29/12/93.
18 Private information.
19 Stephen Barry, *Royal Service: My Twelve Years as Valet to Prince Charles*, p. 225.
20 Jonathan Dimbleby, *The Prince of Wales: A Biography*, p. 283.
21 Andrew Morton, *Diana: Her True Story – In Her Own Words*, p. 34.
22 Ibid., p. 33.
23 Letter from private collection.
24 Interview with William Tallon 24/2/04.
25 Hugo Vickers, unpublished diary, Toronto, 2 June 1981 © Hugo Vickers.
26 Andrew Morton, *Diana: Her True Story – In Her Own Words*, p. 34.
27 Ibid., p. 47.
28 Interview with the author 5/4/05.
29 Andrew Morton, *Diana: Her True Story – In Her Own Words*, p. 37.
30 Letter from private collection.

31 Ibid.

32 Interview with the author 6/4/05.

33 William Tallon interview with the author 24/2/04.

34 Interview with the author 9/3/04.

35 Andrew Morton, *Diana: Her True Story – In Her Own Words*, pp. 36, 37.

36 Andrew Morton, *Diana: Her True Story – In Her Own Words*, p. 119.

37 Sarah Bradford, *Elizabeth: A Biography of Her Majesty The Queen*, p. 431.

38 Ibid., pp. 431–2.

39 Jonathan Dimbleby, *The Prince of Wales: A Biography*, p. 234.

40 Sarah Bradford, *Elizabeth: A Biography of Her Majesty The Queen*, p. 429.

41 Robert Spencer interview with the author, 26 June 2001.

42 Hugo Vickers, unpublished diary, 26 November 2004.

43 Jonathan Dimbleby, *The Prince of Wales: A Biography*, p. 287.

44 Robert Spencer interview with the author 26/6/01.

45 Andrew Morton, *Diana: Her True Story – In Her Own Words*, pp. 40, 41.

46 Rosalind Coward, *Diana: The Portrait*, p. 84.

47 Private information.

Chapter 6. The Beginning of the 'Fairy Tale' (pp. 91–106)

1 Andrew Morton, *Diana: Her True Story – In Her Own Words*, p. 41.

2 Ibid., p. 42.

3 Rosalind Coward, *Diana: The Portrait*, pp. 98–9.

4 Ibid., p. 99.

5 Ibid., p. 91.

6 Jonathan Dimbleby, *The Prince of Wales: A Biography*, p. 293.

7 Andrew Morton, *Diana: Her True Story – In Her Own Words*, p. 42.

8 Interview with the author 16/11/05.

9 Jonathan Dimbleby, *The Prince of Wales: A Biography*, p. 294.

10 Interview with the author 7/3/06.

11 Private information.

12 Interview with the author 9/5/01.

13 Interview with the author 9/5/01.

14 Jonathan Dimbleby, *The Prince of Wales: A Biography*, p. 294.

15 James Whitaker interview with the author June 2001.

16 Andrew Morton, *Diana: Her True Story – In Her Own Words*, p. 43.

17 Ibid., p. 43.

18 Interview with the author 9/5/01.

19 Interview with the author 9/5/01.

20 Interview with the author 16/11/05.

21 Private information.

22 Private information.

23 Andrew Morton, *Diana: Her True Story – In Her Own Words*, p. 43.

24 Ibid., p. 43.

25 Interview with the author 23/2/04.

26 Colin Tebbutt interview with the author 3/3/04.

27 Private information.

28 Interview with the author 16/11/05.

29 Interview with the author 16/11/05.

30 Interview with the author 16/11/05.

31 Interview with the author 16/11/05.

32 Interview with the author.

33 Interview with the author 25/10/05.

34 Jonathan Dimbleby, *The Prince of Wales: A Biography*, p. 298.

35 Andrew Morton, *Diana: Her True Story – In Her Own Words*, p. 45.

36 Private information.

37 Roy Greenslade interview with the author 20/9/05.

38 Andrew Morton, *Diana: Her True Story – In Her Own Words*, p. 45.

39 Private information.

40 Jonathan Dimbleby, *The Prince of Wales: A Biography*, p. 304.

Chapter 7. 'Di-mania' (pp. 107–25)

1 Interview with the author 25/10/05.
2 Patrick Jephson, *Shadows of a Princess. Diana, Princess of Wales 1987–1996*, p. 7.
3 Ibid.
4 David Hicks interview with author 2/6/93.
5 Stephen Barry, *Royal Service: My Twelve Years as Valet to Prince Charles*, p. 219.
6 Interview with the author 16/11/05.
7 Jonathan Dimbleby, *The Prince of Wales: A Biography*, p. 331.
8 Roy Greenslade interview with the author September 2005.
9 Sally Bedell Smith, *Diana: The Life of a Troubled Princess*, p 140.
10 Ibid.
11 Private information.
12 Andrew Morton, *Diana, Her True Story – In Her Own Words*, p. 37.
13 Tim Clayton and Phil Craig, *Diana: Story of a Princess*, p. 15.
14 Jonathan Dimbleby, *The Prince of Wales: A Biography*, p 332.
15 Ibid.
16 Ibid., p. 333.
17 Interview with the author 25/10/05.
18 Interview with the author 25/10/05.
19 Interview with the author 6/4/05.
20 Interview with the author 6/4/05.
21 Anthony Holden, *Charles, Prince of Wales*, pp. 204–5.
22 Private information.
23 Interview with the author 16/11/05.
24 Interview with the author 25/10/05.
25 Sally Bedell Smith, *Diana: The Life of a Troubled Princess*. p. 151.
26 Interview with the author 25/10/05.
27 Andrew Morton, *Diana: Her True Story – In Her Own Words*, p. 51.

Chapter 8. 'The Best Double Act in the World'
(pp. 126–43)

1 Jonathan Dimbleby, *The Prince of Wales: A Biography*, letter from Charles to friends p. 395.

2 Interview with the author 25/10/05.

3 Letter from private collection.

4 Interview with the author 6/4/05.

5 Rosalind Coward, *Diana: The Portrait*, pp. 141–2.

6 Ibid., pp. 144–5.

7 Ibid.

8 Ibid., p. 142.

9 Ibid., p. 132.

10 Interview with the author 25/10/05.

11 Rosalind Coward, *Diana: The Portrait*, p. 156.

12 Patrick Jephson, *Shadows of a Princess*, p. 18.

13 Ibid.

14 Letter from private collection.

15 Interview with the author 15/5/04.

16 Sally Bedell Smith, *Diana: The Life of a Troubled Princess*, p. 134.

17 Interview with the author 25/10/05.

18 Mary Roberston, *The Diana I Knew*, p. 111.

19 Ibid., p. 108.

20 Jonathan Dimbleby, *The Prince of Wales: A Biography*, p. 381.

21 Ibid., p. 382.

22 Ibid., pp. 386–7.

23 Interview with the author September 2004.

24 Interview with the author September 2004.

25 Interview with the author 20/2/06.

26 *Time* magazine, 11 November 1985.

27 Interview with the author 25/10/05.

Chapter 9. 'Charles has gone back to his Lady' (pp. 144–59)

1 Ken Wharfe interview with the author 11/4/05.
2 Settelen tapes.
3 Ken Wharfe interview with the author 11/4/05.
4 Ken Wharfe interview with the author 11/4/05.
5 Settelen tapes.
6 Ibid.
7 Interview with the author 14/4/05.
8 Andrew Morton, *Diana: Her True Story – In Her Own Words*, p. 58.
9 Interview with the author 10/4/06.
10 Interview with the author 7/12/05.
11 Interview with the author 7/9/05.
12 Andrew Morton, *Diana: Her True Story – In Her Own Words*, p. 58.
13 Jonathan Dimbleby, *The Prince of Wales: A Biography*, p. 393.
14 Ibid., p. 394.
15 Ibid., p. 395.
16 Ibid.
17 Ken Wharfe interview with the author 11/4/05.
18 James Hewitt interview with the author 11/1/06.
19 James Hewitt interview with the author 11/1/06.
20 James Hewitt interview with the author 11/1/06.
21 James Hewitt interview with the author 11/1/06.
22 James Hewitt interview with the author 11/1/06.
23 James Hewitt, *Love and War*, p. 23.
24 Ibid., p. 20.
25 Ibid., p. 27.
26 Settelen tapes.
27 Interview with the author 11/1/06.
28 Interview with the author 25/10/05.

Chapter 10. A Dying Marriage (pp. 160–79)

1 Patrick Jephson, *Shadows of a Princess*, p. 63.
2 James Hewitt interview with the author 11/1/06.
3 Ken Wharfe, with Robert Jobson, *Diana: Closely Guarded Secret*, p. 77.
4 Interview with the author.
5 Andrew Morton, *Diana: Her True Story – In Her Own Words*, pp. 59, 59.
6 Interview with the author 16/11/05.
7 Jonathan Dimbleby, *The Prince of Wales: A Biography*, p. 397.
8 Interview with the author 9/11/05.
9 Mike Adler quoted in Rosalind Coward, *Diana: The Portrait*, p. 178.
10 Baroness Jay quoted in Rosalind Coward, *Diana: The Portrait*, p. 178.
11 Rosalind Coward, *Diana: The Portrait*, p. 179.
12 Interview with the author 23/2/04.
13 Rosalind Coward, *Diana: The Portrait*, pp. 183–4.
14 Ibid., p. 184.
15 Ibid.
16 Marguerite Littman interview with the author 8/12/04.
17 Victor Edelstein interview with author 22/5/01.
18 Private information.
19 Interview with the author 14/4/05.
20 *Sunday Times*.
21 Roy Strong, *The Roy Strong Diaries 1967–1997*, 10 December 1987, p. 431.
22 Dickie Arbiter interview with author 23/2/04.

Chapter 11. Diana Fights Back (pp. 180–96)

1 Squidgygate tapes 1989.
2 Sarah Bradford, *Elizabeth: A Biography of Her Majesty The Queen*, p. 444.
3 James Hewitt interview with the author 11/1/06.

4 James Hewitt, *Love and War*, p. 48.

5 Sally Bedell Smith, *Diana: The Life of a Troubled Princess*, p. 197.

6 Anthony Holden, *Charles, Prince of Wales*, p. 260.

7 Ken Wharfe, with Robert Jobson. *Diana: Closely Guarded Secret*, pp. 96–7.

8 Interview with the author 5/5/04.

9 Patrick Jephson, *Shadows of a Princess*, pp. 34–5.

10 Ibid., p. 37.

11 Ibid., pp. 38–9.

12 Ibid., p. 40.

13 Ibid.

14 Interview with the author 16/11/05.

15 Andrew Morton, *Diana: Her True Story – In Her Own Words*, p. 60.

16 Interview with the author 21/6/05.

17 Rosa Monckton, in Brian MacArthur (ed.), *Requiem: Diana, Princess of Wales 1961–1997*, pp. 64–5.

18 Patrick Jephson interview with author March 2004.

19 Sally Bedell Smith, *Diana: The Life of a Troubled Princess*, p. 189.

20 Andrew Morton, *Diana: Her True Story – In Her Own Words*, p. 29.

21 Patrick Jephson, *Shadows of a Princess*, p. 67.

Chapter 12. The War of the Waleses (pp. 197–215)

1 Close friend of Diana's in an interview with the author 16/11/05.

2 Sally Bedell Smith, *Diana: The Life of a Troubled Princess*, p. 203.

3 Interview with the author 30/10/04.

4 Patrick Jephson, *Shadows of a Princess*, p. 137.

5 Ibid., p. 147.

6 Ibid., p. 138.

7 Ibid., p. 141.

8 Sir William Heseltine interview with the author 15/7/96.

9 Patrick Jephson, *Shadows of a Princess*, pp. 131–2.

10 Sally Bedell Smith, *Diana: The Life of a Troubled Princess*, p. 205.

11 Richard Kay interview with the author 16/3/04.

12 James Hewitt, *Love and War*, p. 151.

13　Interview with the author 16/11/05.

14　James Hewitt, *Love and War*, p. 151.

15　Interview with the author 16/11/05.

16　Interview with the author 16/11/05.

17　Andrew Morton interview with the author 20/3/01.

18　Andrew Morton interview with the author 20/3/01.

19　Andrew Morton interview with the author 20/3/01.

20　Patrick Jephson interview with the author March 2004.

21　Patrick Jephson interview with the author March 2004.

22　Patrick Jephson interview with the author March 2004.

23　Patrick Jephson interview with the author March 2004.

24　Patrick Jephson interview with the author March 2004.

25　Andrew Morton interview with the author 20/3/01.

26　James Whitaker interview with the author June 2001.

27　Sally Bedell Smith, *Diana: The Life of a Troubled Princess*, p. 210.

28　Andrew Morton interview with the author 20/3/01.

29　Interview with the author 7/3/06.

30　Dickie Arbiter interview with the author 23/2/04.

31　Interview with the author 16/11/05.

Chapter 13. The Volcano Erupts (pp. 216–32)

1　Andrew Morton interview with the author 20/3/01.

2　Sarah Bradford, *Elizabeth: A Biography of Her Majesty the Queen*, p. 360.

3　Dickie Arbiter interview with the author 23/2/04.

4　Interview with the author 3/4/01.

5　Interview with the author February 2005.

6　Sally Bedell Smith, *Diana: The Life of a Troubled Princess*, p. 222.

7　Interview with the author 23/2/04.

8　Patrick Jephson, *Shadows of a Princess*, p. 235.

9　Ibid.

10　Interview with the author.

11　Jean Willis interview with the author.

12　Patrick Jephson interview with the author March 2004.

13 Jonathan Dimbleby, *The Prince of Wales: A Biography*, p. 484.

14 Interview with the author 29/12/93.

15 Sally Bedell Smith, *Diana: The Life of a Troubled Princess*, p. 228.

16 Sarah Bradford, *Elizabeth: A Biography of Her Majesty The Queen*, p. 467.

17 Patrick Jephson, *Shadows of a Princess*, p. 248.

18 Interview with the author 8/9/93.

19 Jonathan Dimbleby, *The Prince of Wales: A Biography*, p. 487.

20 Ibid., p. 488.

21 Patrick Jephson interview with the author March 2004.

22 Jonathan Dimbleby, *The Prince of Wales: A Biography*, p. 488.

23 Patrick Jephson, *Shadows of a Princess*, p. 267.

24 Patrick Jephson interview with the author March 2004.

25 Jonathan Dimbleby, *The Prince of Wales: A Biography*, p. 489.

26 Patrick Jephson, *Shadows of a Princess*, p. 272.

27 Jonathan Dimbleby, *The Prince of Wales: A Biography*, p. 491.

Chapter 14. The First Step Towards the Abyss
(pp. 233–53)

1 Patrick Jephson, *Shadows of a Princess*, p. 278.

2 Ken Wharfe, with Robert Jobson, *Closely Guarded Secret*, p. 265.

3 Interview with the author 5/5/04.

4 Interview with the author 16/11/05.

5 Interview with the author 5/5/04.

6 Interview with the author 16/11/05.

7 Interview with the author March 2005.

8 Interview with the author 30/10/04.

9 Interview with the author 30/10/04.

10 Sally Bedell Smith, *Diana: The Life of a Troubled Princess*, p. 258.

11 Interview with the author 4/11/04.

12 Interview with the author 4/11/04.

13 Ken Wharfe interview with the author 11/4/05.

14 Ken Wharfe, with Robert Jobson, *Closely Guarded Secret*, p. 186.

15 Ibid.

16 Ken Wharfe interview with the author 11/4/05.

17 Interview with the author.

18 Max Hastings, *Editor: An Inside Story of Newspapers*, pp. 336–7.

19 Patrick Jephson, *Shadows of a Princess*, p. 412.

20 Douglas Hurd, *Memoirs*, p. 474.

21 Ibid., p. 556.

22 Interview with the author February 2005.

23 Patrick Jephson, *Shadows of a Princess*, p. 297.

24 Ibid., p. 297.

25 Ibid., pp. 297–8.

26 Ken Wharfe, with Robert Jobson, *Closely Guarded Secret*, p. 231.

27 Patrick Jephson, *Shadows of a Princess*, p. 307.

28 Andrew Morton, *Diana: Her True Story – In Her Own Words*, p. 57.

29 Paul Burrell, *A Royal Duty*, p. 183.

30 Ken Wharfe interview with the author 11/4/05.

31 Ken Wharfe, with Robert Jobson, *Closely Guarded Secret*, p. 218.

32 Ibid., p. 221.

33 Ibid., p. 241.

34 Ibid., p. 229.

35 Ibid., p. 248.

Chapter 15. The Inconsequential Years (pp. 254–68)

1 Patrick Jephson, *Shadows of a Princess*, p. 293.

2 Interview with the author 27/6/05.

3 Interview with the author 16/11/05.

4 Sally Bedell Smith, *Diana: The Life of a Troubled Princess*, p. 258.

5 Ibid.

6 Interview with the author 16/11/05.

7 Sally Bedell Smith, *Diana: The Life of a Troubled Princess*, p. 260.

8 Ibid., p. 259.

9 Andrew Morton interview with the author 20/3/01.

10 Sister Bridie Dowd interview with the author 20/1/06.

11 Sister Bridie Dowd interview with the author 20/1/06.

12 Sister Bridie Dowd interview with the author 20/1/06.

13 Interview with the author.

14 Interview with the author.

15 Patrick Jephson, *Shadows of a Princess*, p. 293.

16 Interview with the author February 2004.

17 Interview with the author 5/5/04.

18 Interview with the author 23/2/95.

19 Sally Bedell Smith, *Diana: The Life of a Troubled Princess*, p. 265.

20 Jonathan Dimbleby, *The Prince of Wales: A Biography*, p. 608.

Chapter 16. Towards a New World (pp. 269–80)

1 Brian MacArthur (ed.), *Requiem: Diana, Princess of Wales 1961–1997*, p. 102.

2 Interview with the author 16/11/05.

3 Patrick Jephson. *Shadows of a Princess*, p. 343.

4 Brian MacArthur (ed.), *Requiem: Diana, Princess of Wales 1961–1997*, p. 102.

5 Ibid., p. 101.

6 Ibid., p. 102.

7 Ibid., pp. 99–100.

8 Patrick Jephson, *Shadows of a Princess*, p. 345.

9 Ibid., p. 346.

10 Interview with the author 28/9/94.

11 Interview with the author 15/11/94.

12 Interview with the author 20/7/05.

13 Michael Shea interview with the author 1/2/95.

14 Patrick Jephson, *Shadows of a Princess*, p. 345.

15 Interview with the author 2/2/04.

16 Interview with the author 2/2/04.

17 Interview with the author 2/2/04.

18 Interview with the author 2/2/04.

19 Piers Morgan, *The Insider*, p. 106.

20 Ibid., p. 115.

21 Ibid., p. 118.

22 Ibid., p. 157.

23 Brian MacArthur (ed.), *Requiem: Diana, Princess of Wales 1961–1997*, p. 123.

24 Ibid., p. 124.

25 Paul Burrell, *A Royal Duty*, p. 203.

26 Ibid., p. 203.

27 Brian MacArthur (ed.), *Requiem: Diana, Princess of Wales 1961–1997*, p. 89.

28 Ibid., p. 96.

29 Interview with the author February 2005.

30 Interview with the author February 2005.

31 Brian MacArthur (ed.), *Requiem: Diana, Princess of Wales 1961–1997*, p. 89.

Chapter 17. Fall from Grace (pp. 281–300)

1 *Mail on Sunday*, 20 August 1995.

2 Patrick Jephson, *Shadows of a Princess*, p. 351.

3 Interview with the author November 1994.

4 Patrick Jephson, *Shadows of a Princess*, p. 356.

5 Brian MacArthur (ed.), *Requiem: Diana, Princess of Wales 1961–1997*, p. 97.

6 Patrick Jephson, *Shadows of a Princess*, p. 354.

7 Ibid., p. 356.

8 Interview with the author 4/11/04.

9 Judy Wade, *The Truth: The Friends of Diana, Princess of Wales, Tell Their Stories*, p. 87.

10 Sally Bedell Smith, *Diana: The Life of a Troubled Princess*, p. 283.

11 Interview with the author 23/2/04.

12 Interview with the author March 2005.

13 Richard Kay interview with the author 16/3/04.

14 Interview with the author 4/11/04.

15 Interview with the author 4/11/04.

16 Paul Burrell, *A Royal Duty*, p. 322.

17 Colin Tebbutt interview with the author 3/4/04.

18 Ken Wharfe interview with the author 11/4/05.

19 Andrew Morton, *Diana: In Pursuit of Love*, p. 179
20 Ibid., p. 178.
21 Sally Bedell Smith, *Diana: The Life of a Troubled Princess*, p. 282.
22 Interview with the author February 2005.
23 Interview with the author February 2005.
24 Brian MacArthur (ed.), *Requiem: Diana, Princess of Wales 1961–1997*, p. 96.
25 Sally Bedell Smith, *Diana: The Life of a Troubled Princess*, p. 284.
26 Sarah Bradford, *Elizabeth: A Biography of Her Majesty The Queen*, p. 481.
27 Interview with the author 5/5/04.
28 Patrick Jephson, *Shadows of a Princess*, p. 367.
29 Ibid., p. 369.
30 Paul Burrell, *A Royal Duty*, p. 219.
31 Interview with the author 6/1/05.
32 Paul Burrell, *A Royal Duty*, pp. 221–2.

Chapter 18. Out on a Limb (pp. 301–20)

1 Patrick Jephson, *Shadows of a Princess*, p. 552.
2 Ibid., p. 560.
3 Paul Burrell, *A Royal Duty*, p. 222.
4 Ibid., pp. 225–6.
5 Ibid., p. 226.
6 Ibid.
7 Ibid., pp. 226–7.
8 Interview with the author 5/5/04.
9 Interview with the author 27/6/05.
10 Interview with the author 6/1/06.
11 Interview with the author June 2005.
12 Brian MacArthur (ed.), *Requiem: Diana, Princess of Wales 1961–1997*, p. 80.
13 Ibid., p. 80.
14 Ibid., p. 81.
15 Ibid., pp. 81–2.

16 Ibid., p. 83.

17 Kate Snell, *Diana: Her Last Love*, p. 86.

18 Ibid., p. 67.

19 Interview with the author 5/5/04.

20 Interview with the author 5/5/04.

21 Interview with the author 5/5/04.

22 Colin Tebbutt interview with the author 3/3/04.

23 Pamela Harlech interview with the author October 2004.

24 Cheryl Barrymore interview in the *Daily Mail* (21 October 2002).

25 Ibid.

26 Allan Starkie, *Fergie: Her Secret Life*, p. 76.

27 Ibid., p. 117.

28 Ibid., p. 206.

29 Sarah, The Duchess of York, *My Story*, p. 72.

Chapter 19. Stirring Beneath the Surface (pp. 321–37)

1 Richard Kay interview with the author 16/3/04.

2 Cited in Paul Burrell, *A Royal Duty*, p. 242.

3 Interview with the author 25/10/05.

4 Interview with the author February 2005.

5 Kate Snell, *Diana: Her Last Love*, p. 135.

6 Interview with the author February 2004.

7 Interview with the author February 2004.

8 Interview with the author February 2004.

9 Interview with the author January 2004.

10 Interview with the author January 2004.

11 Interview with the author February 2004.

12 Interview with the author February 2004.

13 Interview with the author 23/2/05.

14 Private information.

15 Sarah Bradford, *Elizabeth: A Biography of Her Majesty The Queen*,
     pp. 244–5.

16 Interview with the author February 2004.

17 Interview with the author September 2004.

18 Interview with the author September 2004.

19 Interview with the author September 2004.

20 Interview with the author 14/4/05.

21 Interview with the author 11/4/05.

22 Interview with the author 11/4/05.

23 Interview with the author 11/4/05.

24 Interview with the author 11/4/05.

25 Interview with Richard Kay 16/3/04.

26 *Report to His Royal Highness The Prince of Wales by Sir Michael Peat and Edmund Lawson QC*, 13 March 2003, p. 10.

27 Ibid., p. 11.

28 Ibid., p. 12.

29 Ibid., p. 13.

30 Ibid., p. 25.

31 Ibid., p. 36.

32 Ibid., p. 39.

33 Ibid., p. 43.

34 Ibid., p. 49.

35 Interview with author 6/2/04.

36 Interview with author 7/2/04.

Chapter 20. Diana the Hunted (pp. 338–55)

1 William Deedes.

2 William Rees-Mogg, in Rosalind Coward, *Diana: The Portrait*, p. 260.

3 Richard Kay interview with the author 16/3/04.

4 Interview with the author February 2006.

5 Meredith Etherington-Smith interview with the author 25/1/03.

6 Meredith Etherington-Smith interview with the author 25/1/03.

7 Meredith Etherington-Smith interview with the author 25/1/03.

8 Meredith Etherington-Smith interview with the author 25/1/03.

9 Meredith Etherington-Smith interview with the author 25/1/03.

10 Meredith Etherington-Smith interview with the author 25/1/03.

11 Meredith Etherington-Smith interview with the author 25/1/03.

12 William Deedes interview with the author 19/1/04.

13 Brian MacArthur (ed.), *Requiem: Diana, Princess of Wales 1961–1997*, p. 135.

14 William Deedes interview with the author 19/1/04.

15 Brian MacArthur (ed.), *Requiem: Diana, Princess of Wales 1961–1997*, p. 136.

16 Ibid.

17 Paul Burrell, *A Royal Duty*, p. 281.

18 Ibid.

19 William Deedes interview with the author 19/1/04.

20 Interview with the author March 2004.

21 Interview with the author March 2004.

22 William Deedes interview with the author 19/1/04.

23 Rosalind Coward, *Diana: The Portrait*, p. 294.

24 Ibid., p. 266.

25 Meredith Etherington-Smith interview with the author 25/1/03.

26 Meredith Etherington-Smith interview with the author 25/1/03.

27 Meredith Etherington-Smith interview with the author 25/1/03.

28 Meredith Etherington-Smith interview with the author 25/1/03.

29 Meredith Etherington-Smith interview with the author 25/1/03.

30 Meredith Etherington-Smith interview with the author 25/1/03.

31 Meredith Etherington-Smith interview with the author 25/1/03.

32 Meredith Etherington-Smith interview with the author 25/1/03.

33 Meredith Etherington-Smith interview with the author 25/1/03.

34 Meredith Etherington-Smith interview with the author 25/1/03.

35 Meredith Etherington-Smith interview with the author 25/1/03.

36 Brian MacArthur (ed.), *Requiem: Diana, Princess of Wales 1961–1997*, p. 113.

37 Paul Burrell, *A Royal Duty*, p. 300.

38 Ibid.

Chapter 21. Fatal Summer (pp. 356–72)

1 Tom Bower, *Fayed: The Unauthorized Biography*, pp. 6–7.
2 Ibid., p. 25.
3 Interview with the author February 2005.
4 Tom Bower, *Fayed: The Unauthorized Biography*, p. 159.
5 Pamela Harlech interview with the author October 2004.
6 Pamela Harlech interview with the author October 2004.
7 Richard Kay interview with the author 16/3/04.
8 Tom Bower, *Fayed: The Unauthorized Biography*, p. 413.
9 Interview with the author 18/2/04.
10 Richard Kay interview with the author 16/3/04.
11 Tom Bower, *Fayed: The Unauthorized Biography*, pp. 416–17.
12 Interview with the author 16/11/05.
13 Interview with the author 16/11/05.
14 Interview with the author 16/11/05.
15 Richard Kay interview with the author 16/3/04.
16 Interview with the author 16/11/05.
17 Interview with the author.
18 Trevor Rees-Jones, *The Bodyguard's Story: Diana, the Crash and the Sole Survivor*, p. 15.
19 Ibid., p. 72.
20 Martyn Gregory, *Diana: The Last Days*, p. 50.
21 Ibid., p. 49.
22 Ibid., p. 56.
23 Ibid., p. 57.
24 Trevor Rees-Jones, *The Bodyguard's Story: Diana, the Crash and the Sole Survivor*, p. 79.
25 Brian MacArthur (ed.), *Requiem: Diana, Princess of Wales 1961–1997*, p. 63.
26 Ibid., p. 55.
27 Colin Tebbut interview with the author 3/3/04.
28 Trevor Rees-Jones, *The Bodyguard's Story: Diana, the Crash and the Sole Survivor*, p. 86.
29 Colin Tebbutt interview with the author 3/3/04.

Chapter 22. Death in Paris (pp. 373–88)

1 Daniel Eyraud, vascular surgery team, cited in Martyn Gregory, *Diana: The Last Days*, p. 74.

2 Martyn Gregory, *Diana: The Last Days*, pp. 74–5.

3 Colin Tebbutt interview with the author 3/3/04.

4 Colin Tebbutt interview with the author 3/3/04.

5 Colin Tebbutt interview with the author 3/3/04.

6 Andrew Morton, *Diana: In Pursuit of Love*, p. 250.

7 Ibid., p. 251.

8 Interview with the author February 2004.

9 Rosalind Coward, *Diana: The Portrait*, p. 302.

10 Colin Tebbutt interview with the author 3/3/04.

11 Colin Tebbutt interview with the author 3/3/04.

12 Rosalind Coward, *Diana: The Portrait*, p. 304.

13 Ibid.

14 Paul Burrell, *A Royal Duty*, p. 297.

15 Interview with the author 20/7/05.

16 Interview with the author 20/7/05.

17 Interview with the author 23/2/04.

18 Dickie Arbiter interview with the author 23/2/04.

19 Dickie Arbiter interview with the author 23/2/04.

20 Private information.

21 Dickie Arbiter interview with the author 23/2/04.

22 Meredith Etherington-Smith interview with the author 25/1/03.

23 Brian MacArthur (ed.), *Requiem: Diana, Princess of Wales 1961–1997*, p. 6.

Diana: The Legacy (pp. 389–94)

1 Stephen Bates, *Royalty Inc.: Britain's Best-Known Brand*, p. 318.

Select Bibliography

Barry, Stephen P., *Royal Service: My Twelve Years as Valet to Prince Charles*, Avon Books, New York, 1984

Bates, Stephen, *Royalty Inc.: Britain's Best-Known Brand*, Aurum Press, London, 2015

Bedell Smith, Sally, *Diana: The Life of a Troubled Princess*, Aurum Press, 1999

Berry, Wendy, *The Housekeeper's Diary: Charles and Diana Before the Breakup*, Barricade Books, Inc., New York, 1995

Bower, Tom, *Fayed: The Unauthorized Biography*, Pan Books, 2001

Bradford, Sarah, *Elizabeth: A Biography of Her Majesty The Queen*, rev. edn, Penguin Books, 2002

Burchill, Julie, *Diana*, Weidenfeld & Nicolson, 1998

Burrell, Paul, *A Royal Duty*, Michael Joseph, 2003

Campbell, Lady Colin, *Diana in Private: The Princess Nobody Knows*, Smith Gryphon, 1992

Clarke, Mary, *Little Girl Lost: The Troubled Childhood of Princess Diana by the Woman who Raised Her*, Birch Lane Press, New York, 1996

Clayton, Tim, and Phil Craig, *Diana: Story of a Princess*, Hodder & Stoughton, 2001

Courtney, Nicholas, *Diana: Princess of Wales*, Park Lane Press, 1982

Coward, Rosalind, *Diana: The Portrait*, HarperCollins, n.d.

Deedes, William, *Brief Lives*, Macmillan, 2004

Delorm, René, with Barry Fox and Nadine Taylor, *Diana & Dodi: A Love Story*, Tallfellow Press, Los Angeles, 1998

Dimbleby, Jonathan, *The Prince of Wales: A Biography*, Little, Brown, 1994

Ferguson, Ronald, *The Galloping Major: My Life and Singular Times*, Macmillan, 1994

Goldsmith, Lady Annabel, *Annabel: An Unconventional Life*, Phoenix, 2004

Graham, Caroline, *Camilla – The King's Mistress: A Love Story*, Blake Publishing, 1994

Graham, Tim, with text by Tom Corby, *Diana, Princess of Wales: A Tribute*, Weidenfeld & Nicolson, n.d.

Greenslade, Roy, *Press Gang: The True Story of How Papers Make Profits from Propaganda*, Macmillan, 2003

Gregory, Martyn, *Diana: The Last Days*, Virgin Publishing, 1999, revised and updated by Virgin Books, 2004

Hastings, Max, *Editor: An Inside Story of Newspapers*, Pan Books, 2003

Hewitt, James, *Love and War*, Blake Publishing, 1999

——, *Moving On*, Blake Publishing, 2005

Holden, Anthony, *Charles, Prince of Wales*, Weidenfeld & Nicolson, 1979

——, *Charles: A Biography*, Fontana Paperbacks, 1989

——, *Charles: A Biography*, Corgi Books, 1999

Hurd, Douglas, *Memoirs*, Abacus Books, 2004

Jephson, Patrick, *Shadows of a Princess. Diana, Princess of Wales 1987–1996*, HarperCollins, 2000

——, photographs by Kent Gavin, *Portraits of a Princess: Travels with Diana*, Sidgwick & Jackson, 2004

Junor, Penny, *Diana, Princess of Wales*, Sidgwick & Jackson, 1982

——, *Charles, Victim or Villain?*, HarperCollins, 1998

Kortesis, Vasso, *The Duchess of York*, Blake Publishing, 1996

Levin, Angela, *Raine and Johnnie: The Spencers and the Scandal of Althorp*, Weidenfeld & Nicolson, 1993

MacArthur, Brian, ed., *Requiem: Diana, Princess of Wales 1961–1997 – Memories and Tributes*, Arcade Publishing, 1997

Morgan, Piers, *The Insider*, Ebury Press, 2005

Morton, Andrew, *Inside Kensington Palace*, Michael O'Mara Books, 1987

——, *Diana: Her True Story – In Her Own Words*, revised edn, Michael O'Mara Books, 1997

——, *Diana: Her New Life*, Michael O'Mara Books, 1994

——, *Diana: In Pursuit of Love*, Michael O'Mara Books, 2004

Pasternak, Anna, *Princess in Love*, Bloomsbury, 1994

Pontaut, Jean-Marie, and Jerome Dupuis, *Enquête sur la mort de Diana*, Editions Stock, Paris, 1998

Rees-Jones, Trevor, with Moira Johnston, *The Bodyguard's Story: Diana, the Crash and the Sole Survivor*, Little, Brown, 2000

Select Bibliography 419

Report to His Royal Highness The Prince of Wales by Sir Michael Peat and
Edmund Lawson QC, 13 March 2003

Riddington, Max, and Gavan Naden, Frances: The Remarkable Story of
Diana's Mother, Michael O'Mara Books, 2003

Robertson, Mary, The Diana I Knew, Judy Piatkus, 1998

Rogers, Rita, From One World to Another . . ., Pan Books, 1998

Sancton, Thomas, and Scott MacLeod, Death of a Princess: An Investigation, Weidenfeld & Nicolson, 1998

Sarah, The Duchess of York, with Jeff Coplon, My Story, Simon &
Schuster, 1996

Seward, Ingrid, The Queen and Di, HarperCollins, 2000

Shanley-Toffolo, Oonagh, The Voice of Silence: A Life of Love, Healing
and Inspiration, Rider, 2002

Simmons, Simone, with Susan Hill, Diana: The Secret Years, Michael
O'Mara Books, 1998

Snell, Kate, Diana: Her Last Love, Granada Media, 2000

Scuhami, Diana, Mrs Keppel and Her Daughter, HarperCollins, 1996

Spencer, Charles, Althorp: The Story of an English House, Viking, 1998

——, The Spencer Family, Viking, 1999

Starkie, Allan, Fergie: Her Secret Life, Michael O'Mara Books, 1996

Strong, Roy, The Roy Strong Diaries 1967–1997, Weidenfeld & Nicolson,
1997

Wade, Judy, The Truth: The Friends of Diana, Princess of Wales, Tell Their
Stories, Blake Publishing, 2001

Wharfe, Ken, with Robert Jobson, Diana: Closely Guarded Secret, revised
and expanded paperback edn, Michael O'Mara Books, 2003

Whitaker, James, Diana v. Charles, Signet, 1993

Wilson, Christopher, The Windsor Knot: Charles, Camilla and the Legacy
of Diana, Citadel Press, New York, 2002

Ziegler, Philip, Mountbatten, HarperCollins, 1985

Permissions

The author and publisher are grateful for permission to reproduce the following copyright material:

From *Diana: The Portrait* edited by Rosalind Coward. Reprinted by permission of HarperCollins*Publishers* Ltd. Copyright Rosalind Coward 2004

From *The Prince of Wales: A Biography* by Jonathan Dimbleby. Reprinted by permission of David Higham Associates. Copyright Jonathan Dimbleby, Little, Brown 1996

From *Diana: The Last Days* by Martyn Gregory. Reprinted by permission of Virgin Books. Copyright Martyn Gregory 1999, 2000, 2004, Virgin Books Ltd.

From *Shadows of a Princess: Diana, Princess of Wales 1987–1996* by Patrick Jephson. Reprinted by permission of HarperCollins*Publishers* Ltd. Copyright Patrick Jephson 2001

From *Diana: Her True Story – In Her Own Words* by Andrew Morton. Reprinted by permission of Michael O'Mara Books Ltd. Copyright Andrew Morton 2003

From *Diana: Closely Guarded Secret* by Ken Wharfe. Reprinted by permission of Michael O'Mara Books Ltd. Copyright Ken Wharfe 2002

From *The Insider* by Piers Morgan, published by Ebury Press. Reprinted by permission of The Random House Group Ltd. Copyright Piers Morgan 2005

From *Raine and Johnnie: The Spencers and the Scandal of Althorp* by Angela Levin. Reprinted by permission of Weidenfeld & Nicolson, an imprint of The Orion Publishing Group. Copyright Angela Levin 1993

Acknowledgements

I owe a great debt of gratitude to all those people who have been kind enough to help me with this book, those named below and those who have preferred not to be named. I have also been fortunate to have the taped memories of members of the royal circle recorded over a decade ago when the events described in this book and people's reactions to them were still fresh. If I have omitted anyone who should have been included, I ask their forgiveness.

A&H Associates; Dickie Arbiter LVO; Sally Bedell Smith; Michael Bentley; Mark Bolland; Tom Bower; Lord Carlile of Berriew QC; Phil Craig; Sir Geoffrey Dear QPM, DL; The Rt Hon. Lord Deedes; Sister Bridie Dowd DC, OBE; Victor Edelstein; Meredith Etherington-Smith; Tess Gilder; Robert Golden; Roy Greenslade; Geordie Greig; David Griffin RVM; Linda Hall; Pamela, Lady Harlech; Nicholas Haslam; James Hewitt; Stuart Higgins; Anthony Holden; Patrick Jephson; Richard Kay; Timothy Leese; Brian Lapping; Marguerite Littman; Christopher Loyd CVO; Robert Low; Colin and Annabel Mackay; Andrew Morton; M.J. Rockall for his kindness in making available to me his collection of Diana letters; the Reverend Michael Seed SA; Ian Shapiro of Argyll Etkin Ltd, London for giving me access to Diana documents and letters; James Sherwin; Robert Spencer; Dr Will Swift; William Tallon RVM★ Gold; Colin Tebbutt MVO; Hugo Vickers for kindly making available to me his unpublished diary and extensive collection of royal newspaper cuttings covering the Diana years; Judy Wade; Lord Wakeham PC, JP, DL, FCA; Christopher Warwick; Nigel West; Kenneth A. Wharfe MVO; James Whitaker.

I am grateful to Martin Morse Wooster for his help with American sources, Lucy Pullan for her research in newspaper archives, to Camilla Eadie and Lizzie Grant for their skilful transcriptions and general help, to Lynda Marshall for her help in picture research, and to Douglas Matthews for compiling the index.

My agent, Gillon Aitken, has been a great support, assisted by Ayesha Karim and Sally Riley. At my publishers, Viking in London, I should like to express my gratitude to Helen Fraser, Tom Weldon and Keith Taylor. Above all, Carly Cook has accompanied me almost every step of the way, going far beyond the call of duty in collecting and designing the pictures illustrating Diana's life, editing the book and seeing its completion down to the most minute and often tedious detail. Richard Collins has once again proved the most intelligent and skilful of editors. In the early stages of the book no one could have done more to encourage me than Antonia Till. Above all my husband, William Bangor, has provided me with moral support throughout and practical expertise on proof checking.

Index

Aberystwyth University, 50
Acton, Sir Harold, 135
Adeane, Hon. Edward, 61, 78–9, 88, 120–22
Adler, Mike, 169
Ahmed, Akbar, 311
AIDS: Diana's work for victims, 167–71, 183–4, 195, 220, 245, 314, 339
Airey, Sir Christopher, 209
Alexandra, Queen of Edward VII, 84, 88, 307
Allen, Gertrude, 21
Allen, Violet, 24
Althorp (estate), Northamptonshire: as Spencer home, 2, 6; Diana moves to, 29–30, 32–3, 37; character, 31; social life under Raine, 36; Charles visits, 40; art treasures sold, 115, 191–2, 210; interior restoration, 191–2; Raine's sixtieth birthday ball at, 191; Garden House, 248–9; Diana spends Christmas 1995 at, 300; Diana buried at, 387
Anderson, Mabel, 50, 58, 78
Andrew, Prince see York, Prince Andrew, Duke of
Andrews, Betty, 32
Andrews, Julie, 361
Angola, 342–4, 346
Anne, Princess Royal: character, 50; relations with Parker Bowles, 56; marriage to Mark Phillips, 57;

attitude to Diana, 97; absent from Harry's christening, 126–7; on AIDS, 170; in It's a Royal Knockout, 175; divorce from Mark Phillips, 222; charitable visits to Africa, 245; objects to Charles's depiction of parents in Dimbleby biography, 274
Anne, Queen, 32
Anson, Charles, 217, 242, 295, 305, 325
Appa, Nanny, 351–3
Arbiter, Dickie: on Diana's first walkabout, 101; on Diana's envy of Fergie's friends, 151; and Palace reaction to Diana's photographs with AIDS patients, 170; on overseas visits, 218; and death of Diana's father, 219; and serialization of Morton's book, 221; and Diana's reluctance to divorce, 224; and Dimbleby's biography of Charles, 260; and flying half-mast flag at Diana's death, 381; on Queen's tribute to Diana, 383
Ardencaple, Isle of Seil, 21
Argentina: Diana visits, 283, 295–6
Armstrong-Jones, Lady Sarah, 126, 238
Arnold, Harry, 105, 212
Atkinson, Jane, 305, 314
Attenborough, Sir David, 292
Attenborough, Sir Richard (later Baron), 137

Australia: Charles in, 50, 79, 86; Diana visits with mother, 75; Diana tours with Charles: (1983), 116; (1985), 137–8; (1988), 180; Diana's solo visit to, 323

Aylard, Richard: leaves Diana to serve Charles, 160, 209; as green adviser to Charles, 172; Diana sees as enemy, 209, 324, 328; and death of Diana's father, 219; and Dimbleby's biography of Charles, 260, 274, 328; Charles blames for TV interview, 263; leaves Charles's service, 324; and Palace treatment of Diana, 327

Azagury, Jacques, 346

Bahamas, 105, 119

Balfour, Christopher, 339

Balmoral: Diana visits, 65–6; Charles and Diana honeymoon at, 95–7; life at, 98–9; and tensions between Charles and Diana, 198–9; Fergie and Diana's behaviour at, 214

Baring, Lavinia, 103

Barnard, Dr Christiaan, 322–3

Barnardo's (children's charity), 130, 167–8, 175, 273

Barnes, Barbara, 165–6

Barry, Stephen: on Charles's romances, 57–9; imitates Charles, 59–60; serves Charles as valet, 62, 329; on Diana–Charles relationship and courtship, 65, 67; drives Diana, 72; on Diana's relations with staff, 82; on Charles at Highgrove, 110; leaves Charles's service, 119–20

Barrymore, Cheryl, 315–17

Barrymore, Michael, 315–17

Bartholomew, Carolyn (*née* Pride): at West Heath school with Diana, 24; shares London flat with Diana, 46; on Diana's sexual abstinence, 47; on Diana's eating disorder, 85, 182; on Diana's doubts about marrying Charles, 89; stands godmother to Prince Harry, 126; confides in Morton, 208, 223; Diana maintains friendship with, 235; at Diana's funeral service, 384

Bartholomew, William, 162, 223

Bashir, Martin, 291–2, 301, 315–16, 324, 350

Beatrice, Princess, 216, 320

Beckwith Smith, Anne, 103, 131, 209

Bedell Smith, Sally, 133, 190, 197, 212, 256, 265, 292

Belfast: Diana visits, 226

Benson, Ross, 212, 277

Berlin, 178

Berni, Mara, 190, 193, 310

Berry, Anthony, 4

Berry, Mary (*née* Roche; Diana's aunt), 3–4

Betts (butler), 32

Beyg, Rizwan, 313

Birkhall, Balmoral, 65–6, 165, 273

Birley, Mark, 236

Birley, Rupert, 236

Birt, John, Baron, 295

Black, Conrad, Baron, 220, 275

Blair, Tony: Diana dines with, 336–7; Diana introduces William to, 352; on Diana's death, 373, 376

Bolehyde Manor, Gloucestershire, 67, 72, 74, 110, 153

Bolland, Mark, 324–8, 336, 376

Bolton, Anne, 46

Bosnia, 342, 344, 366

Bower, Tom, 365

Bowker, Elsa, Lady, 236, 240, 255, 340

Bowler, Harmoush, 239

Brabourne, Lady Patricia *see* Mountbatten, Patricia, Countess

Brazil: Diana and Charles visit, 205

Brenna, Mario, 365

Britannia (royal yacht), 64–5, 93–4, 96, 145

British Legion Festival of Remembrance, Albert Hall (1982), 112

Broadlands (house), Hampshire, 55, 74, 93–4

Broadmoor, 272–3

Brown, Harold, 233–4, 287

Brown, Tina, 137, 353, 356

Brunei, Sultan of, 360

Bryan, John, 201, 217, 227, 317, 319

Buckingham Palace: Diana moves into, 78; life in, 80–82, 102; Queen's ball at, 89; half-mast flag at Diana's death, 380–81

Burrell, Maria, 233, 288

Burrell, Paul: moves from Highgrove to Kensington Palace, 233–4, 287; drives Hoare to see Diana, 240–41; and Diana's failure to rent Garden House, Althorp, 249; on Lucia Flecha de Lima's friendship with Diana, 277; as Diana's confidant, 287–8, 302; and Diana's letter accusing Charles of intending to have her killed, 289–90; and Queen's advice to Diana to divorce, 299; on Diana's interview with Queen over divorce, 303; and Diana's relations with Hasnat Khan, 312–14, 324; and Diana's

meeting with Michael Barrymore, 315–16; trial, 331, 334, 335; and George Smith rape allegation, 335–6; meets Meredith Etherington-Smith, 339; accompanies Diana to Bosnia, 344–5; reports Bashir's remarks to Diana, 350; tours London with Diana, 353; flies to Paris at Diana's death, 375; accompanies Diana's hearse in Paris, 378; collects Diana's belongings, 379; and Lucia Flecha de Lima's request to keep vigil over Diana, 380; at Althorp for Diana's funeral, 387

Butler, Richard Austen, Baron ('Rab'), 50

Caine, (Sir) Michael, 9cn

Cameron, Catherine, 92

'Camillagate' tapes, 234, 291

Campbell, Alastair, 376

Canada: Diana tours with Charles, 117–18, 122, 152–3; Fergie tours with Andrew, 163

Carey, George, Archbishop of Canterbury, 231

Carling, Julia, 284

Carling, Will, 283–4

Caroline, Princess of Monaco, 184

Cartland, Dame Barbara: Diana reads, 25, 44; as Raine's mother, 26; at Sarah–Neil McCorquodale wedding, 46; and Charles–Diana courtship, 68; absent from Diana's wedding, 92; romantic idealism, 143, 354; and Diana as 'Queen of Hearts', 294

Chalker, Lynda, 244

Chambrun, Comte Jean-François de, 248

Chang, Dr Victor, 311, 324

Chapman, Vic, 129, 135

Charles, Prince of Wales: at Sandringham, 20; interest in Sarah Spencer, 39–40, 42–4; first meets Diana, 40–41; birth and background, 48–9; character and qualities, 48, 51–4; relations with parents, 48–9, 50, 58, 97; education, 49–50; military/naval training, 51; blood and field sports, 52, 104, 110, 229; polo playing, 52, 55, 110; temper outbursts, 53, 122; meets and falls for Camilla, 54–5, 58–60, 73, 77, 88; naval postings, 56; romances and affairs, 57–8; and Mountbatten's death, 61–2, 63–4; spiritual interests, 61, 152, 165; and need to marry, 62; courtship of Diana, 64–73; and 'Royal Love Train' story, 70; relations with press, 72, 166, 275–6; Diana's love for, 73–4, 86, 91–2, 124, 182, 186, 197, 224, 302, 305, 321; dithers over commitment to Diana, 73–4; proposes to Diana, 74; engagement announced, 75–7; official visits abroad, 79, 86, 116, 118–19, 122, 137–41, 152, 160–61, 183–5, 195–6, 205, 244; relations with Lady Susan Hussey, 84; on Diana's chubbiness, 85; openness, 85–6; rows with Diana over Camilla, 86–7; gives presents to Camilla, 88; neglects Diana before marriage, 89; eve-of-wedding party for staff, 90; wedding and honeymoon with Diana, 91–7; feelings for Diana, 95–6; incompatibility with Diana, 99, 126, 137, 143, 153; and Diana's falling down stairs, 104; and birth

of sons, 106, 126; in Kensington Palace, 107–9; marriage difficulties and failure, 112–13, 119, 123–5, 132, 153, 160, 165–7, 177–9, 180, 186, 202, 205, 211–12, 218, 267–8; jealousy of Diana's popular appeal, 116–18, 140–43, 175, 179, 180, 195; and staff resignations and departures, 120–22; criticizes modern architecture, 121; loses old friends, 122–3; resumes relations with Camilla (1983), 124; disorganized office, 131–2, 208; Camilla maintains relations with, 133–4; visit to Italy, 135–6; mocked by crowds in Australia, 138–9; and role of monarchy, 142; and Diana's dance routine at Covent Garden, 143; discontinues sexual relations with Diana, 144; praises Fergie to Diana, 152; and Camilla's move to Middlewich House, 153; depression at tabloid persecution, 153; moves office to St James's Palace, 160; painting in Italy, 165; withdraws from Diana, 165; supports ecological and green issues, 172; view on architecture and town planning, 172–3; motor cars, 173–4; self-pity and pessimism, 173–5; press criticisms of, 176, 211; and children's upbringing, 177–8; visits Berlin, 178; tours Australia with Diana, (1883), 116; (1985), 137–8; (1988), 180; escapes avalanche in Alps, 181; fortieth birthday, 183; Holden's biography serialized, 184; and Diana's bulimia, 185, 267; breaks arm in polo match, 197; devotion to Camilla, 197–8;

antipathy to Diana, 198; knows of Diana's affairs, 203; relations with children, 211; and Diana's thirtieth birthday, 212–13; in India, 218; and death of Diana's father, 219; diverts for holiday in Turkey, 221; unpopularity after Diana's revelations, 222, 234–5; agrees separation from Diana, 224–5; on South Korea tour, 228; legal separation from Diana, 230–31; household staff after separation, 233; and 'Camillagate' tapes, 234; friendship with Oliver Hoare, 239–40; Diana's media war with, 250–51; Diana doubts prospective accession, 257, 294, 318; authorizes Dimbleby's biography, 260, 267, 273–4; divorce negotiations, 260, 299; television interview (June 1994), 261–3; and Diana's alleged mental instability, 285–6; and Diana's letter on planning fatal accident, 288–9, 292; learns of Diana's *Panorama* interview, 293; divorce settlement, 306; Bolland works for, 324–5, 327; Diana maintains contact with after divorce, 328; valets and orderlies, 329–31; and George Smith's homosexual rape allegations, 332–6; settles Diana's bill at K Club, 350; told of Diana's death, 375; informs William and Harry of Diana's death, 376; flies to Paris at Diana's death, 377–8; and public reaction to Diana's death, 379; at Diana's funeral, 384; visits Althorp for Diana's interment, 387
Cheam School, Surrey, 49

Checketts, Squadron Leader David, 51–3, 78
Chevénement, Jean-Pierre, 375
Chevening (house), Kent, 110
Chicago, 315
Chirac, Bernadette, 387
Christie's (auctioneers): sell Diana's clothes, 339, 347, 353
Churchill, (Sir) Winston Spencer, 31
Clarence House: Diana moves into, 76
Clarke, Mary, 14–15, 19
Clifford, Max, 365
Clinton, Bill, 384
Clinton, Hillary, 272, 317, 338, 353, 384
Coke, Lady Anne, 5, 8
Colborne, Michael, 52–3, 75, 79–81, 84, 88, 89, 120–22
Colborne, Shirley, 81
Cole, Michael, 365
Coleherne Court, London, 46, 68
Collins, Joan, 140
Collins, Phil, 261
Colthurst, Dr James, 207
Conran, Jasper, 125
Constantine XIII, King of the Hellenes, 275
Cornwall, Camilla, Duchess of (*formerly* Parker Bowles): family and background, 54–5; relations with Charles, 54–6, 58–62, 73, 77, 88, 133–4, 153, 197–8; relations with and marriage to Parker Bowles, 55–7; encourages Charles's marriage to Diana, 63, 67–8; at Balmoral, 65–6; house at Bolehyde Manor, 67–8; and 'Royal Love Train' story, 70–71; Diana's awareness of relations with Charles, 74, 85–6, 96, 132–4, 144;

Cornwall, Camilla, Duchess of – *cont.*
lunch with Diana following
engagement, 76; at Diana–Charles
wedding, 82; Diana and Charles
row over, 86–7; Charles gives
presents to, 88; supposedly spends
night with Charles after Queen's
ball, 89–90; Diana bans from
wedding breakfast, 92, 123;
telephones Charles on
honeymoon, 94; Charles resumes
relations with (1983), 124; contacts
with press, 133; moves to
Middlewich House, 153; supports
Charles in depression, 153–4; acts
as hostess at Highgrove, 162;
Diana confronts at party, 185–6,
236; visits Charles after breaking
arm, 197; sues Penny Junor, 203;
and Morton's *Diana: Her True
Story*, 208; Diana shows Morton
notes to Charles, 213; Charles
confesses to liaison in 1994 TV
interview, 262–3; divorced from
Andrew, 263; in Dimbleby
biography of Charles, 273; Diana
describes in *Panorama* interview,
293–4; reaction to *Panorama*
interview, 294; and Bolland's
campaign to improve Charles's
image, 324, 327; blames Aylard,
328; influence at St James's Palace,
329; and reinstatement of Michael
Fawcett, 336; Diana's jealousy of,
360; TV documentary on, 360;
Charles gives fiftieth birthday ball
for, 360
Craigowan Lodge, Balmoral, 95
Crawford, Geoffrey, 242, 295
Creasy, Colonel (Charles's
comptroller), 120

Daily Express, 211, 264, 291
Daily Mail, 201, 204, 211–13,
216–17, 275, 287, 324, 365
Daily Mirror, 218, 226–7, 276
Daily Telegraph, 245
Daly, Barbara, 93
Dartmouth, Gerald Legge, 9th Earl
of, 33–4
Deane, Derek, 360
De Brunner, Mrs (investigating
officer), 334
Deedes, William, Baron, 12, 342–5
Delorm, René, 364, 367
Dempster, Nigel, 68, 89, 112, 119,
204, 212, 277, 284–5, 367
Devonshire, Georgiana, Duchess of,
32
Diana, Princess of Wales (*née*
Spencer): birth, 1, 8; parents'
marriage breakdown and
separation from mother, 9–14, 18;
upbringing, 9, 14–17, 19; lying
and embroidery of facts, 12, 75,
223, 278–9; unhappiness as child,
12–13; photogenic nature, 15–16;
relations with parents, 19, 22–3,
35, 210; nickname ('Duch'), 20;
schooling, 21–5, 35–6; swimming
and diving, 23–4; dancing, 24,
138, 177, 184; and father's relations
with Raine, 28; moves to Althorp,
29–30, 32–3, 37; ancestry, 30–32,
348; domestic duties, 32–3,
130–31; hostility to Raine, 34;
shyness, 37; eating disorder
(bulimia), 39, 82, 85, 111, 113–14,
152, 157, 179, 182, 185, 189; first
meets Charles, 40–41; at Swiss
finishing school, 41; letter-writing,
41; moves to London, 45–6;
London boyfriends, 46–7;

appearance and style, 63, 91, 96,
134–5, 138, 140–41, 160, 177,
346–9; Charles courts, 63–73;
empathy and compassion, 64, 188,
307–8; invited to Balmoral and
Birkhall, 65–6; relations with
press, 68–9, 72, 166–7, 242–3,
326–7; and 'Royal Love Train'
story, 70–71; and Charles's
dithering over engagement, 73–4;
love for Charles, 73–4, 86, 91–2,
124, 182, 186, 197, 224, 302, 305,
321; awareness of Charles's
relations with Camilla, 74–5,
85–6, 96, 124, 132–4, 144; Charles
proposes to, 74; engagement
announced, 75–6; visits Australia
with mother, 74–5; moves into
Clarence House, 76; life at
Buckingham Palace, 78–83; lacks
role, 79, 102–3; wariness of
courtiers, 83–4; criticized for
wearing black dress, 84–5; rows
with Charles over Camilla, 86–7;
pre-marriage doubts, 88–90;
wedding and honeymoon, 91–7;
Charles's feelings for, 95–6;
uncomfortable relations with
Royal Family, 96–8; relations with
Fergie, 97, 147–52, 163–4, 199,
201, 266–7, 278, 317–19; dislikes
Balmoral, 98; incompatibility with
Charles, 99, 126, 137, 143, 153;
sulks and self-absorbed behaviour,
99; crowd appeal and common
touch, 100–101, 116–18, 134–5,
140–41, 175, 187, 226; media
interest in, 100, 105–6, 113–14,
134–5, 250, 310, 353–4, 366–9;
pregnancies and children,
100–101, 105–6, 125–6;

psychiatric analysis and treatment,
100, 112; falls down stairs at
Sandringham, 104; photographed
in Bahamas, 105; apartments in
Kensington Palace, 107–9;
depressions, 111; dislikes horsey
people, 111; tantrums, 111, 198;
marriage difficulties and failure,
112–13, 119, 123–4, 132, 158,
160, 165–7, 177–9, 186, 198, 202,
205, 211–12, 218, 267–8; attends
Princess Grace's funeral, 115; need
for approval and appreciation, 116;
visits Australia and New Zealand
with Charles, 116, 137–8, 180;
tours Canada with Charles,
117–18, 122, 152–3; and staff
resignations and departures,
119–20, 122; excludes Charles's
friends, 123; accused of scheming,
124; devotion and commitment to
sons, 127–9, 211, 238, 257, 271,
347–9; charity work, 130, 167–9,
175, 201–2, 245–7, 272–3, 317;
professional and organizational
competence, 131; visits Italy with
Charles, 135–6; tours United
States with Charles, 136–9, 141;
relations with Buckingham Palace
courtiers, 142, 209–10; and role of
monarchy, 142; performs dance
routine at Covent Garden, 143;
sexual relations with Charles cool,
144; relations with police
protection officers, 145–7; prank
with Fergie impersonating police
officers, 150–51; interest in
psychics and healers, 152, 190, 243,
318; affair with Hewitt, 154–9,
162–3, 182, 191, 201, 203–4, 208,
227, 264–6, 293; and Charles's

Diana, Princess of Wales – *cont.*
return to Camilla, 154; *Panorama*
TV interview, 156, 212, 264,
290–97, 301; sexual inexperience,
156; tour of Portugal, 160–61; fear
of Charles, 161; teasing behaviour,
161; bridge-playing, 162; men
friends, 162–3; resents Camilla's
hostess function at Highgrove,
162; social life compartmentalized,
162, 384; criticized in press for
unsuitable companions, 163–4;
Charles withdraws from, 165;
effect on others, 167–9, 180, 183;
work for AIDS patients, 168–71,
183–4, 195, 245, 314, 339; exercises,
172; behaviour criticized in press,
176, 182; musical interests, 177,
180; and children's upbringing,
177–8, 326; visits Berlin, 178;
official visit to Paris with Charles,
183–5; confronts Camilla, 185–6,
236; punctiliousness in public
duties, 186–7; bawdy jokes, 187;
wit, 187–8, 236, 307; complexity
of character, 189–90, 206; mood
swings, 189; belief in astrology,
190, 257; attacks Raine Spencer,
192; relations with James Gilbey,
192–4, 199, 203; sense of being
victim and rebel, 194, 222, 234–5;
in Gulf States, 195–6; tours of Far
East and Hungary, 202; ends
relationship with Hewitt, 204–5;
visit to Brazil, 205; collaborates
with Morton on biography,
206–8, 212, 220–23, 226, 267,
294; plans separation from Charles,
206; exploits and manipulates
relations with press, 212, 242–4,
250–52, 264, 274–7, 305; thirtieth
birthday, 212–13; shows Morton
notes from Camilla to Charles,
213; misbehaviour at Balmoral
with Fergie, 214; and Fergie's
separation from Andrew, 217–18;
in India, 218; and father's death,
219; in Egypt, 221; agrees to
separate from Charles, 224; in
Belfast, 226; and *Sun*'s publication
of 'Squidgygate' tapes, 227; solo
visits to Paris, 228, 244, 273; tour
of South Korea, 228; refuses to
join Charles for shooting weekend,
229; legal separation and
settlement, 230–31; as prospective
Queen Consort, 231; household
staff after separation, 233–4; friends
and confidants after separation,
235–7, 243, 276–9, 308–9, 340;
misses Charles after separation,
235; good relations with Prince
Philip, 237–8; affair with Oliver
Hoare, 238–42, 250, 255–7, 265,
283; foreign excursions and
goodwill visits, 244–8, 281–3, 296;
and 'Leap of Lech' incident on
skiing holiday, 249–50; gym
photographs in *Sunday Mirror*,
251–2; announces withdrawal
from public life, 252, 254;
dispenses with police protection,
255, 287, 354; on hereditary
monarchy, 257; takes sons to visit
homeless centre, 258–9; divorce
negotiations and settlement, 260,
305–6; and Charles's 1994 TV
interview, 262, 263–4; colonic
irrigations, 266; and Jonathan
Dimbleby's biography of Charles,
267; Shanks portrait of, 270; solo
visits to USA, 270–72, 315, 317,

319, 352–3, 356; prospects of death, 279–80; draws up private manifesto (1995), 281; relations with Will Carling, 283–4; press turns against (1995), 284–5; alleged mental instability, 285–6, 293; paranoia, 286–7, 295, 301, 349–50; confides in Burrell, 287–8; letter on Charles's supposed planning of fatal accident, 288–90, 292; receives humanitarian award from Kissinger, 297; Queen advises to divorce, 299, 302–3; refuses Queen invitation to spend Christmas at Sandringham, 299–300; Jephson resigns from post with, 301–2; status and title after divorce, 303–7, 315; negotiates divorce settlement, 305–6; compassion, 307–8; visits Pakistan, 309–13, 350; infatuation with Hasnat Khan, 310–14, 322–4, 350–52, 355, 370; interest in Islam, 311–12; reduces charity patronages, 314; supports Michael Barrymore, 315–17; ends relationship with Fergie, 320; accepts Charles's prospective marriage to Camilla, 321–2; solo visit to Australia, 323; maintains relations with Charles after divorce, 328; confides in staff, 330; and George Smith's homosexual rape allegations, 330, 332–7; life as single woman, 338–9; auctions clothes, 339–41, 347, 353; campaign against landmines, 341–6, 349, 366; romance with Dodi Fayed, 345, 364–70; defeats bulimia, 346; visualizes future role, 347; quarrels with staff and friends,

350–51; loneliness and insecurity, 353–4; Mohamed Fayed and, 359–63; holiday with Fayeds in St Tropez, 361–3; parts from Hasnat Khan, 363; on final fatal car journey in Paris, 370–74; death announced, 375; body in London awaiting funeral, 379; public reaction to death, 379–81; funeral, 381–8

Dimbleby, Jonathan: and lack of recognition for Diana, 13; on Charles's anxieties and discontent, 52–3; and Ruth Fermoy's disapproval of Diana–Charles marriage, 67; on Queen Mother's advising marriage for Diana and Charles, 71; on Diana's doubts about marriage, 72; on Charles's emotional openness, 85; and Diana's anxieties over Camilla, 88, 96, 100; and Charles's feelings for Diana, 95; on Diana–Charles relations, 105; and Charles's return to Camilla, 132; on Charles–Diana 1985 tour of Australia, 138; on Camilla's support for Charles in depression, 153; on Waterhouse's visits to Diana, 163; on publication of Morton's book, 224–5; on Charles's shooting weekends, 229; on Charles's decision to seek legal separation, 230; on disbelieving Diana, 254; authorized biography of Charles, 260–61, 267; TV interview with Charles (June 1994), 261–2; Charles biography serialized, 273; *The Prince of Wales*, 273–4

Disneyland, Florida 250–51
Donovan, Diana, 308

Donovan, Terence, 160, 308

Dorneau, Philippe, 368

Douglas-Home, Charles, 124

Douglas-Home, Lady Margaret, 4, 18, 37, 45

Dowd, Sister Bridie, 258–9

Draper, Rev. Martin, 378

Driver, Ronnie, 90n

Dunne, Philip, 162–3

Edelstein, Victor, 91, 171–2, 339, 357

Edward VII, King, 54, 84, 88, 235, 307

Edward VIII, King *see* Windsor, Duke of

Edward, Prince (*later* Earl of Wessex): at Sandringham, 19; and Diana–Charles wedding, 93; relations with Diana, 97; Charles plays with as child, 126; in *It's a Royal Knockout*, 175; criticized in press, 176

Edwards, Arthur, 170

Edwards, Blake, 361

Edwards, Bob, 70

Egypt, 221

Elizabeth II, Queen: at Sandringham, 20; and Charles's birth, 48; role as sovereign, 48–9; relations with Charles, 50, 58, 97; and Charles's affair with Camilla, 61; and Charles–Diana betrothal, 71; and Diana at Buckingham Palace, 81; and Diana–Charles wedding, 93; Diana's respect for, 97; and Diana's falling down stairs at Sandringham, 104; appreciates Diana's popular appeal, 141; enigmatic view of Diana, 141–2; meets Philip through Mountbatten, 148; gives consent to Andrew–Sarah Ferguson marriage, 150; Diana confides in, 158; fondness for Fergie, 164; as role model, 177; celebrates Charles's fortieth birthday, 183; exasperation with Charles, 198; and household opposition to Diana, 210; and family crises, 216, 226; and Charles–Diana separation, 224–6; fortieth anniversary of accession, 227; maintains neutrality in Charles–Diana dispute, 230–31; maintains good relations with Diana, 238; and Diana's withdrawal from public life, 252–3; anger at Charles's showing papers to Dimbleby, 273; advises Diana to divorce, 299, 302–3; and Diana's status after divorce, 304–6; counsels Diana to live apart in harmony with Charles, 307; Margaret MacDonald's influence on, 328–9; informed of Diana's death, 375; and Diana's obsequies, 377; criticized for behaviour following Diana's death, 379–82; consents to half-mast flag at Buckingham Palace, 381; broadcasts tribute to Diana, 382–3; at Diana's funeral, 384

Elizabeth the Queen Mother: entertains 7th Earl Spencer, 6; on Spencer women, 32; attends Jane–Robert Fellowes' wedding, 42; Charles's relations with, 50–51, 58, 194; Diana visits at Birkhall, Balmoral, 65–6; favours Charles–Diana marriage, 71; engagement dinner with Diana, 76; attitude to Diana, 97, 193–4;

and Diana's falling down stairs at Sandringham, 104; ninetieth birthday, 201, 248; Diana and Fergie predict death, 318

Eliot, Annabel (Camilla's sister), 185, 236

Emanuel, Elizabeth and David, 84

English, Sir David, 202, 212, 264, 275, 325

English National Ballet (ENB), 314–15, 359

Enniskillen, Northern Ireland, 175, 247

Etherington-Smith, Meredith, 339–41, 346–9, 354, 385

Eton College, 325, 348

Eugenie, Princess, 320

Everett, Oliver, 64, 78, 80, 83–4, 120, 318

Fabiola, Queen of the Belgians, 247

Far East, 202

Farrer & Co. (lawyers), 332

Fawcett, Michael, 229, 234, 251, 298, 329–30, 336, 360

Fayed, Dodi (Emad): Diana's romance with, 345, 353, 361, 364–70; birth and upbringing, 356–8; and fatal car trip in Paris, 370–72

Fayed, Heini (*née* Wathen), 357, 363

Fayed, Mohamed (Al), 356–63, 364–6, 375

Fayed, Samira (*née* Kashoggi), 356, 358

Fellowes, Jane, Lady (*née* Spencer; Diana's sister): birth, 8; qualities and character, 16; and parents' divorce, 17; hostility to Raine, 35; marriage, 41–2; stays at Balmoral, 65; and Charles's courtship of Diana, 69; Diana entertains at Buckingham Palace, 81; encourages Diana to go through with marriage, 88; home in Old Barracks, London, 107; and Diana's disturbed state, 114–15; differences with Fergie, 199; relations with Diana, 211, 354; flies to Paris at Diana's death, 377

Fellowes, Sir Robert: marries Jane, 41–2; background and career, 42; stays at Balmoral, 65, 214; as Queen's assistant private secretary, 80; London home, 107; as principal private secretary to Queen, 209; on Fergie's behaviour, 213; Fergie's wariness of, 217; Diana denies collaboration with Morton to, 222–3; helps Diana after separation, 242; and Buckingham Palace's reaction to *Panorama* interview, 297; and Diana's dispute with Tiggy Legge-Bourke, 298; hostility to Fergie, 317; relations with Mark Bolland, 325, 327; benign relations with Diana, 354; and Diana's death, 377; writes Queen's tribute speech to Diana, 383

Fellowes, Sir William ('Billy'), 41

Ferguson, Ronald, 147–9, 206, 216

Ferguson, Sarah ('Fergie'), *see* York, Sarah, Duchess of ·

Fermor-Hesketh, Anna (*née* Wallace), 57–8, 63

Fermoy, Edmund Burke Roche, 1st Baron, 3

Fermoy, Edmund James Burke Roche, 5th Baron (Diana's uncle), 3, 124

Fermoy, Frances, Lady (*née* Work; 'Fanny'), 3

Fermoy, James Boothby Burke Roche, 3rd Baron, 3

Fermoy, Maurice Roche, 4th Baron (Diana's maternal grandfather), 2–4, 7–8

Fermoy, Ruth, Lady (*née* Gill; Diana's maternal grandmother): family background, 3–4; character and qualities, 4–5; relations with Diana, 4; offers lease of Park House to Diana's parents, 8; and daughter's marriage breakdown, 10, 12–13; and Diana's childhood, 14; and upbringing of Spencer children, 17–18; attends Jane–Robert Fellowes' wedding, 42; encourages Diana's claims to Charles, 66–7, 71; and Charles's courtship of Diana, 69; engagement dinner with Diana, 76; doubts over Diana–Charles marriage, 87; denigrates Diana, 97–8, 124, 248, 286; on Diana's ignorance of royal life, 114; at Prince Harry's christening, 127; musical talents, 177; death, 248

Fisher, Kelly, 361

Fitzgerald, Chryssie, 266–7

Flecha de Lima, Beatriz, 307

Flecha de Lima, Lucia: and Charles's jealousy, 205; as Diana's friend and confidante, 210, 236–7, 240, 277–8, 307; leaves London for Washington, 257; Diana visits in USA, 265, 269–71, 277; and Diana's death, 379–80; at Diana's funeral service, 384

Flecha de Lima, Paolo Tarso, 205, 236, 240, 265, 269, 271, 307–8, 384

Forstmann, Teddy, 270

Frank, Debbie, 190

Fraser, Fiona, 8

Fraser, Jason, 162, 365, 367

Frost (Sir) David, 150, 287, 291

Galahad, HMS, 331

Galella, Ron, 269

Gall, Sandy, 344

Gaselee, Sarah Jane, 89

George VI, King: death, 48; temper, 53; refuses Royal Highness title to Wallis Simpson, 304

George, Boy, 164

George, Susan, 58, 88

George (US magazine), 319

Germany: Charles and Diana visit, 178

Gibbins, Michael, 289, 333, 370

Gilbey, Monsignor Alfred, 193

Gilbey, James, 180, 192–5, 197, 199, 203, 206, 222, 227, 257

Gilliatt, Sir Martin, 76, 155

Glaser, Elizabeth, 271

Glenconner, Anne, Lady, 166

Glenconner, Colin Tennant, 3rd Baron, 166, 198

Glendinning, Victoria, 113

Goldsmith, Lady Annabel: accompanies Diana to Pakistan, 33, 312; Diana irons for, 33; hosts Camilla's fortieth birthday party, 185, 190; as Diana's confidante, 210, 236, 278, 307, 340; and Diana's prospective remarriage, 369; at Diana's funeral service, 384

Goldsmith, Ben, 236

Goldsmith, Sir James, 236, 351

Goldsmith, Zac, 236

Goodman, Arnold, Baron, 225

Goodman, Clive, 314

Gorbachev, Mikhail, 322

Gordonstoun School, Scotland, 49

Grace, Princess of Monaco (*née* Kelly), 47, 85, 115, 385

Graf, Steffi, 172

Graham, Katharine ('Kay'), 271, 317, 357

Graham, Tim, 171–2

Great Ormond Steet Hospital for Sick Children, London, 282, 314

Greenslade, Roy, 105

Greig, Laura (*later* Lonsdale), 24, 45, 235, 384

Griffin, David, 288

Guinness, Sabrina, 57

Gul, Ayesha, 240

Gulf States: Charles and Diana tour, 195–6

Guppy, Darius, 291

Hahn, Kurt, 49

Hambro, Rupert, 36

Hammer, Armand, 119, 139–40

Hardman, Robert, 245

Harlech, Pamela, Lady, 237, 308, 315, 360

Harlem Hospital Center, New York, 170–71, 298

Harper, Robert, 291

Harrods (London store): Mohamed Fayed owns, 358–9

Harry, Prince (Henry Charles Albert David): birth and christening, 125–7, 173; Diana's devotion to, 127–9, 211, 257; schooling and upbringing, 128, 165, 257–8; holidays with Diana, 149–50; attacks father, 212; invited to join Charles on shooting weekend, 229; and parents' legal separation,

230; character and qualities, 259; visits homeless centre with mother, 259; and Tiggy Legge-Bourke, 298; and parents' divorce, 303; forbidden to visit cousins Beatrice and Eugenie, 320; holiday with Fayeds in France 360–62; position as second son, 370; informed of mother's death, 376–7; bouquet on Diana's coffin, 384; walks behind coffin at Diana's funeral, 384; at Althorp for Diana's interment, 386

Hastings, Sir Max, 197, 203, 243–4, 275

Headway Foundation, 252, 254

Help the Aged (charity), 167, 175, 245, 247

Herbert, Henry, 149

Heseltine, Sir William, 202

Hewitt, James: affair with Diana, 154–9, 162–3, 180–83, 191, 201, 203–6, 208, 240; *Sun* reports Diana's relations with, 227; friends know of affair, 250; gives interview to Anna Pasternak, 264–6; denounced by *Sun*, 266; Diana admits to affair on *Panorama* interview, 293; signet ring, 336

Hicks, India, 93

Higgins, Stuart, 133–4

Highgrove, Gloucestershire: Charles invites Diana to, 67–8, 72; Diana's redecoration, 83, 109–10; Camilla visits Charles at, 97–8, 1162; Charles's garden at, 110–11; household after Diana–Charles separation, 233; Charles gives fiftieth birthday ball for Camilla at, 360

Hill, Derek, 239
Hoare, Diane (*née* de Waldner), 238, 255–6
Hoare, Oliver: affair with Diana, 238–42, 250, 255–7, 265, 283, 352; and Wharfe's leaving Diana's service, 251
Holden, Anthony, 51, 140, 184–5, 212, 243–4, 322, 340
Holkham, Norfolk, 50
Honeycombe, Gordon, 114
Hong Kong, 282
Howe, Frederick Curzon, 7th Earl, 343
Hume, Cardinal Basil, Archbishop of Westminster, 258
Hungary, 202
Hurd, Douglas (*later* Baron), 244–5, 281
Hussey, Sir Marmaduke, 295
Hussey, Lady Susan, 51, 78, 80, 83–4, 90, 295

Imran Khan *see* Khan, Imran
India, 218
Iqbal, Sir Allama Mohammad, 312
Italy: Diana and Charles visit, 135–6; Charles's painting holiday in, 165
It's a Royal Knockout (TV programme), 163, 175–6, 222

James, Clive, 183, 243, 276, 278, 280–82, 291–2, 384
Janvrin, Sir Robin, 209, 242, 303, 375
Japan: Charles and Diana visit, 152–3; Diana visits, 281–2
Jay, Margaret, Baroness, 169
Jay, Sir Michael, 375
Jay, Sylvia, Lady, 375, 378
Jephson, Patrick: joins Diana's staff, 108; on Kensington Palace apartments, 108; on Diana's decisiveness and professionalism, 131–2, 186–7; on breakdown of Diana's marriage, 160, 230; on Diana's fear of Charles, 161; on Diana's compassion, 185; on Diana's bawdy jokes, 187; on Diana's positive nature, 189, 221; on Charles's treatment of Diana on Gulf States visit, 195–6; on Diana's relations with Fergie, 199, 201; on Diana's attracting attention, 202; Janvrin's treatment of, 209; on Diana's solo visit to Paris, 228; on Diana's resentment at Charles's house parties, 229; supports Diana in single state, 235, 242; on Diana's public achievements, 247; on Diana in Enniskillen, 248; and Dimbleby biography on Diana, 267; praises Forstmann, 270; and Diana's 1994 trip to USA, 272; on Diana's visit to Broadmoor, 273; on Diana's overseas trips, 281–2; and Diana's lack of trust, 287; accompanies Diana to New York and Argentina, 295, 297–8; and Diana's *Panorama* interview, 295–6, 301; resignation, 295, 301, 336; attempts to mend relations between Diana and Buckingham Palace, 296–7; and Diana's meeting with John F. Kennedy, Jr, 319; and George Smith rape allegation, 336; tours London with Diana, 353; *Shadows of a Princess*, 302
John, (Sir) Elton, 150, 164, 315, 350, 384–5
John Paul II, Pope, 135

Johnson, Paul, 243, 276

Jcnikal (yacht), 361–2, 364–5, 368

Jourdan, Charles, 132

Juan Carlos, King of Spain, 154

Julius, Anthony, 305, 332–3

Junco, Eduardo, 255

Junor, Penny, 174–5, 203; *Charles: Victim or Villain?*, 285–6

Kalahari Desert: Charles visits, 165

Kashoggi, Adnan, 356

Kassem, Susie, 278

Kay, Richard: makes friends with Hewitt, 204; and Diana's HRH title, 205–6; as newspaper contact with Diana, 212, 217, 250, 264, 323; and Yorks' separation, 217; as Diana's confidant, 278; appointed Diana's speech writer, 301; on Diana as global figure, 338; Charles Spencer on, 354; on Diana's relations with Dodi Fayed, 362, 370; on Hasnat Khan, 363; on Diana in Paris, 368, 369; on compartmentalization of Diana's life, 384

Keenan, Brian, 293

Kennedy, John F., 269

Kennedy, John F., Jr, 319–20

Kensington Palace: Diana and Charles's apartments in, 107–10; household after Diana–Charles separation, 233

Kent, Princess Michael of: negotiates for house at Nether Lypiatt, 67–8

Keppel, Alice, 54–5, 84, 88, 235

Khan, Hasnat, 310–14, 322–4, 350–52, 355, 363, 370, 385

Khan, Imran, 236, 310, 312, 350, 352, 384

Khan, Jemima (*née* Goldsmith), 33, 236, 310, 312, 351, 384

Khan, Naheed (Hasnat's mother), 351–2

Khan, Omar and Jane, 351–2

Kimball, Sophie, 45

Kime, Robert, 110, 233

King, Kay, 45

Kissinger, Henry, 297

Klosters, Switzerland, 73, 161, 180–81

Knatchbull, Amanda, 56–8

Knight, Andrew, 203, 223

Kortesis, Vasso, 320

Lacey, Robert, 113

Lahore, 309–11, 351

Lalvani, Gulu, 352

Lamb, Christina, 342–3

Lamport, Sir Stephen, 324, 344–5, 376

landmines: Diana campaigns against, 341–6, 349, 366

Lang, Jack, 184

Latsis, John, 139, 227

Lawson, Domenica, 235

Lawson, Dominic, 235

Lawson, Edmund, QC, 331

Lee-Potter, Lynda, 175

Leete, Lance Corporal Malcolm, 203

Legge-Bourke, Alexandra ('Tiggy'), 298–9

Leprosy Mission, 245, 314

Levin, Angela, 32, 36

Lichfield, Leonora, Countess of (*née* Lady Leonora Grosvenor), 57

Lichfield, Patrick, Earl of, 57, 93

Lindsay, Major Hugh, 181

Lindsay, Sarah, 181

Lineker, Gary, 284

Linley, David Armstrong-Jones, Viscount, 238

Lipsedge, Dr Maurice, 182, 185
Littman, Marguerite, 171, 237, 339, 340
Londonderry, Alastair Vane-Tempest-Stewart, 9th Marquess of, 309
Lonsdale, Laura *see* Greig, Laura
Loveday, Dr Mary, 278
Lowe, Jean, 22
Loyd, Alexandra, 22

McAlpine, Robert, Baron, 200–21
McCorquodale, Neil: marriage to Sarah, 45–6
McCorquodale, Lady Sarah (*née* Spencer; Diana's sister): birth, 8; qualities and character, 16; and parents' divorce, 17; drinking, 24, 40; expelled from school, 24; dislike of Raine, 26, 33–5; coming-out party, 26; eating disorders, 39, 114, 182; relations with Prince Charles, 39–40, 42–3, 58; Whitaker interviews for press article, 43–4; marriage, 45–6; Diana cleans for, 46; encourages Diana to go through with marriage, 88; admits concern over Diana's weight loss to Whitaker, 112; keeps distance from Diana, 115, 211; and George Smith homosexual rape allegations, 334, 335–6; acts as Diana's lady-in-waiting, 354; flies to Paris at Diana's death, 377; on Diana's funeral, 378, 380
MacDonald, James ('Jem'), 329
MacDonald, Margaret ('Bobo'), 328–9
McGregor, Oliver Ross McGregor, Baron, 222, 223
McKnight, Sam, 127

McNally, Paddy, 149
Mail on Sunday, 284, 291
Mailliez, Dr Frédéric, 373
Major (Sir) John, 231, 242
Majorca, 154, 165, 310
Mannakee, Barry, 145–7
Margaret, Princess: fondness for Charles, 51, 238; Diana attends party, 70; predicts marriage difficulties for Diana, 87–8; friendship with Diana, 98, 238; welcomes Diana on return from birth of William, 106; in Kensington Palace, 107; and Charles's attachment to Camilla, 133; sixtieth birthday celebrations, 198, 201; on Paul Burrell, 241; engages Harold Brown, 287; ends friendship after Diana's *Panorama* interview, 296; writes rebuking Fergie, 319; at Diana's funeral, 384
Mark's Club, Mayfair, 90
Marlborough, John Churchill, 1st Duke of, 31
Marlborough, Sarah, Duchess of (*née* Jennings), 31–2
Martha's Vineyard, Massachusetts, 265, 270–71
Martino, Dr Jan-Marc, 373
Mary, Queen of George V, 4
Mellon, 'Bunny', 139
Mendham, Victoria, 330–31, 350
Menem, Carlos, 296
Menzies, Kate, 162–3, 235, 249–50, 284, 292
Mexico, 244
Middlewich House, Gloucestershire, 153
Minerva, HMS, 56
Mishcon, Victor, Baron, 295

Mitterrand, François, 228, 244, 273
monarchy: decline in popularity,
175–7; effect of Morton's *Diana*
book on, 222, 224; Diana's view
of, 257
Monckton, Hon Rosa, 189, 235–7,
278, 294, 307, 340, 366, 369–72
Monroe, Marilyn, 279, 349, 385
Montagnier, Professor Luc, 183
Modlinger, Jackie, 134
Moore, Charles, 274
Morgan, Piers, 243, 276–7, 284, 375
Morton, Andrew: and Diana's view
of brother Charles, 16; and Diana's
innocence, 47; and Diana's black
dress, 85; and Diana's fall down
stairs at Sandringham, 104; and
Manakee's death, 147; and skiing
tragedy at Klosters, 181; and
Diana's public behaviour, 182; and
Diana in Hungary, 202; Diana
collaborates on biography with,
206–8, 217, 219–21, 278, 294; on
Diana's relations with father, 210;
newspaper reports on Diana and
Charles, 212–13; on impending
crisis for Diana, 216; on separation
of Fergie and Andrew, 217; book
serialized, 220–21, 226; effect of
Diana book, 222–5; on Diana's
heroic nature, 229; Hewitt declines
to talk to, 264; on Diana's
Panorama interview, 291; *Diana:
Her New Life*, 257; *Diana: Her True
Story*, 10, 206, 208, 222, 228, 234,
260, 267
Mountbatten, Admiral of the Fleet
Louis, 1st Earl: advice to Charles
on girlfriends and marriage, 48,
54–5; as mentor to Charles, 51,
53–4, 61–2; and Charles's

attachment to Camilla, 56–7;
death and funeral, 61–2, 63;
introduces Elizabeth and Philip,
148; warns Charles about imitating
Duke of Windsor, 174
Mountbatten, Patricia, Countess
(*formerly* Lady Patricia Brabourne),
106, 153
Mubarak, Hosni, 221
Mugabe, Robert, 245
Murdoch, Rupert, 203, 220, 275
Murrell, Ben, 368, 371
Mynors, Jane, 128

Nadir, Asil, 240
National AIDS Trust, 220, 314, 339
National Association of Boys' Clubs:
Diana's father's chairmanship, 8, 27
Neil, Andrew, 124
Nepal: Diana tours, 244–5
Nevill, Lord Rupert, 73
New York: Diana visits, 297–8, 353,
356; *see also* Harlem Hospital
Center; United States of America
New Zealand, 79, 86, 116
News of the World, 203–4, 233
Norfolk, HMS, 52
Norwich, Peter John Nott, Bishop
of, 194–5

O'Mara, Michael, 207
Onassis, Aristotle, 269
Onassis, Jacqueline (*née* Bouvier), 47,
269
Orbach, Susie, 255, 354
Organ, Bryan, 126
Ottawa Landmines Accord, 346

Pakistan: Diana visits, 309–13, 350
Palmer-Tomkinson, Charles and
Patty, 65, 73, 123, 153, 180–81

Palumbo, Hayat, 243

Palumbo, (Baron) Peter, 243, 264

Panorama (TV programme): Diana's 1995 interview on, 156, 212, 264, 290–97, 301

Paris: Charles and Diana visit, 183–5; Diana's solo visits to, 228, 244, 273; Diana with Dodi in, 364, 367–70; Diana's final car journey and death in, 370–74

Park House, Sandringham, 2–4, 10–11, 14–15, 17–19, 25, 29, 72, 103

Parker Bowles, Andrew: Camilla in love with, 55–6; affair with Princess Anne, 56–7; marriage to Camilla, 57; and Charles's involvement with Camilla, 59–60; at Balmoral, 65; denies Charles's spending night with Camilla, 89; in Sovereign's escort, 92; takes up appointment in London, 153; sues Penny Junor, 203–4; outs Hewitt, 204; divorces Camilla, 263

Parker Bowles, Dame Ann (*née* de Trafford), 56

Parker Bowles, Camilla *see* Cornwall, Camilla, Duchess of

Parker Bowles, Derek, 56

Parker Bowles, Tom, 92

Parsons, Father Tony, 380

Passage, The (homeless centre), 258–9

Pasternak, Anna, 156, 191, 264–6; *Princess in Love*, 265

Paul, Henri, 368, 370–72, 381

Pavarotti, Luciano, 271

Peat, Sir Michael, Report (2002), 331, 334

Peckford, B., 118

Peebles, Catherine, 78

Peel, Lady Delia, 2

Pendrey, Ainsley, 32, 37

Pendrey, Maudie, 37, 132

Pertini, Alessandro, 136

Petworth, Sussex, 63

Philip, Prince, Duke of Edinburgh: marriage, 48; Charles's relations with, 49–51; complains of press spoiling shooting, 70, 72; ultimatum to Charles to propose to Diana, 71, 73; welcomes Diana–Charles marriage, 87; relations with Diana, 97; anger at press's reporting Diana above Queen, 134–5; meets Elizabeth through Mountbatten, 148; carriage-driving, 164; and Charles–Diana separation, 224–6; letters to Diana, 237–8; and Diana's withdrawal from public life, 252–3; counsels Diana to live apart from Charles, 307; at Diana's funeral, 384

Phillips, Hayden, 386

Phillips, Captain Mark, 57, 222

Pimlott, Ben, 30

Pitman, Virginia, 46

Player, Lesley, 206, 216

Poplak, Dudley, 83, 109–10, 233, 248

Porritt, Jonathon, 172

Portugal: Charles and Diana visit (1987), 160–61

Powell, General Colin, 272, 279, 338

Pratt, Claire, 22

Press Complaints Commission, 326–7

Prince's Trust, 262, 279

Princess of Wales Trust: proposed, 279

Purves, Libby, 246

Puttnam, David, Baron, 220, 243, 279, 292, 302

Ramzi Sultan, 200, 214
Rat, Romuald, 374
Reagan, Ronald, 138
Red Cross: Diana supports, 245, 342–3
Reece, Gordon, 243, 275
Rees-Jones, Trevor, 366–8, 369, 371–3
Renwick, Sir Robin, 272
Riddell, Sir John, 139, 196, 209
Riddlesworth Hall (school), Norfolk, 22
Rifkind (Sir) Malcolm, 244, 281
Rimini: Pio Manzù Centre, 322
Ritchie, Brigadier Charles, 375
Roberison, Mary, 46, 68, 138
Roberison, Patrick, 46, 68
Robinson, Anne, 112
Roche, Frances, 3
Rogers, Rita, 318, 320
Romsey, Norton Knatchbull, Lord, and Penelope, Lady, (now Brabourne), 72–4, 93, 105, 119, 123, 153
Rook, Jean, 151
Rothschild, Jacob, 4th Baron, 243, 270
Rowland, 'Tiny', 357–9
Royal Institute of British Architects: Charles 150th anniversary speech, 121
Royal Marsden Hospital, 314
Royal Opera House, Covent Garden: Diana dances at, 143
Rudge, Ruth, 24–5, 35, 384
Runcie, Robert, Archbishop of Canterbury, 85, 91, 114
Rusbridger, Alan, 167

Russell, Georgiana, 57
Russia: Diana visits, 283
Rutherford, Ken, 344
Ryan, Hilary, 283
Ryan, Rocky, 166

Sadat, Anwar, 94
St James's Palace, 160
St John of Fawsley, Norman St John-Stevas, Baron, 247
St Tropez, 360–63
Salisbury, Molly, Marchioness of, 111
Samuel, Julia, 162–3, 192, 235, 292
Sandringham estate, Norfolk, 2, 19–20, 69–72, 82, 103, 193, 299
Santa Cruz, Lucia, 54
Savile, Sir Jimmy, 199
Scott, Rory, 46
Seil, Isle of (Scotland), 21, 182, 210
Serota, Angela, 223
Settelen, Peter, 13, 34, 144, 146, 246, 259
Shackleton, Fiona, 332–5
Shand, Annabel, see Elliot, Annabel
Shand, Major Bruce, 55
Shand, Mark, 55
Shand, Rosalind (née Cubitt), 55
Shand Kydd, Frances (earlier Viscountess Althorp; then Countess Spencer; née Roche; Diana's mother): and Diana's birth, 1; birth and family background, 3–4; character and qualities, 4–5, 208; marriage and children with Spencer, 4–5, 7–8; marriage breakdown, divorce and separation from children, 8–14, 17; falls for Peter Shand Kydd, 9; divorce from Peter, 13, 181–2; marries Peter, 18, 20; Diana's relations with, 19; moves to Itchenor, 21; and

Shand Kydd, Frances – *cont.*
daughter Sarah's eating disorder,
39; pays for and attends daughters'
weddings, 42, 46; visits Australia
with Diana, 75; relations with
Diana, 83, 210; absence from
Diana's life, 114; denounced, 124;
at Prince Harry's christening, 127;
on Isle of Seil (Scotland), 182, 210;
at John Spencer's memorial
service, 219–20; friendship with
Lady Annabel Goldsmith, 236;
Diana's estrangement from, 355;
and Diana's death, 378, 380
Shand Kydd, Peter: Frances falls for,
9; divorce from Frances, 13, 182;
marries Frances, 18, 20; Spencer
children's relations with, 20; at
Ardencaple, Isle of Seil, 21; and
Diana in Australia, 75; absent from
Prince Harry's christening, 127
Shanks, Nelson, 270
Shanley-Toffolo, Oonagh, 190, 310,
313
Shea, Michael, 70, 85
Sheffield, Davina, 57–8
Sherwin, James, 271
Silfield School, Gayton, King's Lynn,
21
Simmons, Simone, 311, 313
Simpson, Mark, 81–2
Simpson, Wallis *see* Windsor, Wallis,
Duchess of
Singleton, Roger, 130
Sleep, Wayne, 143
Smith, George, 329–36
Smith, Graham, 145
Smith (John Spencer's former
batman), 17
Snettisham, Norfolk, 8
Snow, Jon, 382

Snowdon, Antony Armstrong-Jones,
1st Earl of: photographs
christening of Prince Harry,
127
Soames, Catherine, 162–3, 235,
249–50, 292
Soames, Nicholas, 65, 73, 122, 153,
294
Soares, Mario Alberto Nobre Lopes,
161
Sofia, Queen of Spain, 154
Solari, Simon, 251
Somerset, Lady Cosima, 308–11,
312, 351
Somerset, Lord John, 309
Soros, George, 344
South Africa: Diana visits, 355
South Korea, 228
Spencer family, 1, 30–31
Spencer House, London, 31, 107,
247
Spencer, Charles, 9th Earl (Diana's
brother): on grandfather Jack, 6;
birth, 8; upbringing and education,
9–10, 22; and parents' marriage
breakdown, 10–11, 13, 19;
qualities and character, 16; dislikes
Raine Spencer, 26; on Diana's
growing up as adolescent, 40–41;
at Eton, 115; on Diana's need for
approval, 116; marriage, 191–2,
211; and Diana's wish to rent
Garden House, Althorp, 248–9;
and Diana's *Panorama* interview,
291–2; sues *Daily Express*, 291;
divorce, 300; deteriorating
relations with Diana, 354–5; learns
of Diana's death, 377; absent from
Diana's pre-funeral obsequies, 380;
bouquet on Diana's coffin, 384;
address at Diana's funeral service,

385–6; and Diana's interment at Althorp, 387

Spencer, Cynthia, Countess (*née* Hamilton): marriage, 2; qualities, 6–7; and upbringing of Spencer children, 18; and Diana's visit to Birkhall, 66

Spencer, Lady Jane (Diana's sister) *see* Fellowes, Jane, Lady

Spencer, John, 7th Earl (Diana's grandfather): relations with son John, 2, 6–7, 192; character and qualities, 6; death, 29

Spencer, John, 8th Earl (*earlier* Viscount Althorp; Diana's father): and Diana's birth, 1; relations with father, 2, 5–7; marriage to Frances, 4–5, 7; character and career, 7–8; marriage breakdown and divorce, 8–11, 13–14; photography, 15; Diana's relations with, 19, 22–3, 35, 210; visits Diana's school at Riddlesworth Hall, 23; meets and courts Raine Legge, 25–9; succeeds to earldom, 29; financial difficulties, 33; marriage to Raine, 34, 36–7; collapses and recovers from cerebral haemorrhage, 38–9; visits Diana at Buckingham Palace, 83; at Diana's wedding, 92; and sale of Althorp treasures, 115; visits Diana at Kensington Palace, 115; at Prince Harry's christening, 127; and sale of Althorp art treasures, 191–2; death and funeral, 219–20

Spencer, Raine, Countess (*earlier* Countess of Dartmouth; Diana's stepmother): courtship with John Spencer, 25–9; background and career, 27; Spencer children's hostility to, 33–6, 38–9, 115;

191–2; stays at Althorp, 33; marriage to John Spencer, 34; character and style, 36–7; social life, 36; and John Spencer's collapse, 38–9; at Sarah–Neil wedding, 46; at Prince Harry's christening, 127; and sale of Althorp art treasures, 191–2, 210; sixtieth birthday ball, 191; and husband's death and funeral, 219; Diana invites to Kensington Palace, 248; marries Comte de Chambrun, 248; visits and advises Diana, 278; *What Is Our Heritage?*, 27

Spencer, Robert, 87

Spencer, Lady Sarah (Diana's sister) *see* McCorquodale, Lady Sarah

Spencer, Victoria, Countess (*née* Lockwood), 191, 300

Sprecher, Bruno, 181

'Squidgygate' tapes, 193–5, 199, 203–4, 206, 227, 257, 292

Stallone, Sylvester, 168

Stark, Koo, 149

Starkie, Allan, 319–20

Stevens, John Arthur, Baron, 290

Stewardson, Emma, 204

Stoney, Benita, 318

Stotthard, Sir Peter, 276–7

Stringfellow, Peter, 164

Stronach, Ken, 263, 329

Strong, Sir Roy, 114, 177

Sulzberger, David, 239

Sun (newspaper): turns against Diana, 166; blames Charles for skiing accident, 181; and Squidgygate tapes, 203, 227; criticizes Charles for neglecting children, 221; on Diana's withdrawal from public life, 253; mocks Charles's

Sun (newspaper) – *cont.*
    preference for Camilla over Diana,
    264; denounces Hewitt, 266; prints
    photographs of Diana and Dodi
    Fayed, 365–6
Sunday Mirror, 251–2, 323, 365
Sunday Times, 173, 176–7, 184, 213,
    221–2, 273
Sunninghill Park, 200, 217
Sweet, Rev. Reginald, 20
Sydney, Australia, 323

Taj Mahal, 218
Tallon, William, 76, 355
Tang, David, 282
Taylor, Bryce, 252
Tebbutt, Colin, 289–90, 314,
    370–71, 375, 378, 387
Teresa, Mother, 352
Testino, Mario, 348–9
Thatcher, Margaret (*later* Baroness),
    110, 172
Theodoracopulos, Taki, 308,
    354
They Think It's All Over (TV
    programme), 284
Thirty Club, 220, 279
Thompson, Janet, 20
Thornton, Penny, 152, 190, 318
Tilberis, Liz, 298
Timbertop, Australia, 50–51
Time magazine, 141
Times, The, 276
Toffolo, Joseph, 310–11
Toffolo, Oonagh *see* Shanley-
    Toffolo, Oonagh
Tokyo, 153
Travolta, John, 138, 353
Trimming, Superintendent Colin,
    203, 333, 335
Trinity College, Cambridge, 50

Tryon, Dale, Lady (*née* Harper;
    'Kanga'), 59, 68, 77, 92, 123, 156,
    166
Twigg, Stephen, 190

United States of America: Charles
    and Diana visit, 136–41; Diana's
    solo visits to, 270–72, 315, 317,
    319, 352–3, 356; Diana receives
    humanitarian award in, 297
Ussova, Helena, 344

Vacani, Miss (ballet studio), 45
Van Cutsem, Hugh and Emilie, 117,
    198
van der Post, Sir Laurens, 61, 94–5,
    99, 165
Vanity Fair, 234, 243
van Tanz, Ian, 375
Verey, Rosemary, 111
Versace, Gianni, 315, 350, 363
Vestey, Celia Elizabeth, Lady, 126
Vickers, Hugo, 76–7
Videmanette: Institut Alpin,
    Switzerland, 41

Wake-Walker, Diana, 22
Wakeham, John, Baron, 326–7
Waldner, Baron Geoffroi and
    Baroness Louise de, 239–40
Waldner, Diane de *see* Hoare, Diane
Wales: Charles in, 50–51
Walker, Catherine, 346
Walker, Penny, 41
Wallace, Anna *see* Fermor-Hesketh,
    Anna
Waller, James, 291
Walters, Barbara, 290
Ward, Gerald, 126
Ward, Jane, 59
Waterhouse, David, 162–3

Wathen, Heini *see* Fayed, Heini

Watkins, Laura-Jo, 58

Waugh, Auberon, 113, 243, 276

Webster, Alan Brunskill, Dean of St Paul's, 92

Wellesley, Lady Jane, 57–8

West, Lieut. Colonel George, 155

West, Hazel, 103, 155–6

West Heath (school), near Sevenoaks, Kent, 21, 23–5, 35, 341

Westmacott, Peter, 228

Westminster Abbey: Diana's funeral service at, 384–5

Westminster, Gerald Grosvenor, 6th Duke of (*earlier* Earl Grosvenor), 26, 39

Westminster, Natalia, Duchess of, 262

Wetherby School, 128, 178

Wharfe, Ken: on Diana's devotion to sons, 128; as Diana's protection officer, 128, 145, 250; disturbed by Charles's relations with Camilla, 144, 154; Diana confides in, 145, 154; and Diana's relations with Hewitt, 162, 205; and Diana's confronting Camilla, 185–6; on Mervyn Wycherley, 234; and Diana's meetings with Hoare at Kensington Palace, 241–2; on Diana in Zimbabwe, 246; and Charles Spencer's offer of house on Althorp estate to Diana, 249; and Diana's 'Leap of Lech', 250; and Diana at Disneyland, 251; leaves Diana's service, 251–2; and Diana's gym photographs, 252

Whitaker, James: Diana approaches at sister Jane's wedding, 42; Diana's sister Sarah gives interview to, 43–4; on Stephen Barry and

Camilla, 59–60; on Charles's courtship of Diana, 68; and 'Royal Love Train' story, 70; and Diana's pre-marriage doubts, 88–9; misinformed of Camilla's spending night with Charles after Queen's ball, 89; told of Diana's honeymoon time at Balmoral, 96; follows Diana in Bahamas, 105; and Diana's behaviour at Albert Hall Remembrance (1982), 112; supports Diana against Charles, 212; troubled by Diana's holiday in St Tropez, 362

White, Jerry, 344

White, Lady Lavinia, 2

Whitlam, Mike, 46, 342, 346

William, Prince: birth, 105–6; accompanies parents on tour of Australia and New Zealand, 116–17; relations with Harry, 126; Diana's devotion to, 127–9, 211, 238, 257, 259–60; schooling and upbringing, 128, 178, 257–8; fondness for Barbara Barnes, 165–6; injured by golf ball, 211; and parents' quarrels, 212; invited to join Charles on shooting weekend, 229; and parents' legal separation, 230; at Kensington Palace, 236; holidays with Diana, 249–50; as prospective successor to Queen, 257, 318; visits homeless centre with mother, 258–9; Piers Morgan meets, 276; disparages Julia Carling, 284; cuts Diana after *Panorama* interview, 296; and Tiggy Legge-Bourke, 298; and parents' divorce, 303; forbidden to visit cousins Beatrice and Eugenie, 320; attends Eton, 325, 348, 370;

William, Prince – *cont.*
suggests sale of Diana's clothes,
339; mother's plans for as king,
347–9; meets Tony Blair, 352;
holiday with Fayed in France,
360–61, 362; photo-call, 370;
informed of mother's death, 376;
and Diana's funeral, 384; at
Althorp for Diana's interment,
387
Windermere (house), Eleuthera,
Bahamas, 105
Windsor Castle: life at, 103; fire
(1992), 231–2
Windsor, Edward, Duke of (*earlier*
King Edward VIII), 53, 174, 215,
304
Windsor, Wallis, Duchess of (*formerly*
Simpson), 53, 304, 377
Winfrey, Oprah, 290
Wingfield, 'Kez', 367–8, 371
Wintour, Anna, 355
Wood Farm, Sandringham, 69–70
Wood, Patricia, 23
Woods, Robin, Dean of Windsor,
50
Work, Frank, 3
Wyatt, Lynn Sakowitz, 200
Wyatt, Steve, 200–201, 214, 216–17
Wyatt of Weeford, Woodrow,
Baron, 70–71
Wycherley, Mervyn, 127, 234, 287

Yacoub, Sir Magdi, 310–11, 322
Yass, New South Wales, 21
Yaxley, Mrs (Charles's head of
personnel), 332
York, Prince Andrew, Duke of: at
Sandringham, 19–20; introduces
Sarah Spencer to Charles, 39; and
Diana–Charles wedding, 93;
relations with Diana, 97; courtship
and marriage to Sarah Ferguson,
111, 149–51; Charles plays with as
child, 126; stands godfather to
Prince Harry, 126; in *It's a Royal
Knockout*, 175; marriage
breakdown, 199–200, 206;
thirtieth birthday, 201; and Fergie's
affair with Wyatt, 216; separates
from Fergie, 216–18; turns against
Diana, 218; and Fergie's 'toe-
sucking' pictures, 227; remains on
friendly terms with Sarah, 317;
Sarah believes will accede to
throne, 318
York, Sarah, Duchess of (*née*
Ferguson): courtship and marriage
to Andrew, 111, 149–51; visits
Diana, 111; relations with Diana,
147–52, 163, 199, 201, 266–7,
278, 317–19; background and
career, 148–9; impersonates police
officer in prank, 150–51;
introduces Diana to psychics and
healers, 152, 190; at Klosters, 161,
180–81; as popular rival to Diana,
163–4; behaviour, 164, 175–6,
214, 224, 319; Queen's fondness
for, 164; in *It's a Royal Knockout*,
175; at Balmoral, 199; marriage
breakdown, 199–200, 206; press
criticisms of, 199; affair with
Wyatt, 200–201, 214, 216–17;
relations with John Bryan, 207,
217, 227, 317, 319; discusses
leaving Royal Family with Diana,
213; extravagance and debts, 214,
318–19; separates from Andrew,
216–18, 224; absent from
Trooping the Colour celebration,
226; shares therapists with Diana,

266, 318; divorce settlement, 306, 317; ostracized, 317; predicts royal deaths, 318; infatuation with John F. Kennedy, Jr, 319–20; books on, 320; Diana ends relationship with, 320; tours USA, 320; and Press Complaints Commission, 326;

Budgie the Helicopter, 318; *My Story*, 150, 320
Young of Graffham, David Young, Baron, 358

Zimbabwe: Diana tours, 245–6
Zito, Jayne, 272